Library of America, a nonprofit organization, champions our nation's cultural heritage by publishing America's greatest writing in authoritative new editions and providing resources for readers to explore this rich, living legacy.

JANE BOWLES

Jane Bowles

COLLECTED WRITINGS

Two Serious Ladies
In the Summer House
Stories & Other Writings
Letters

Millicent Dillon, *editor*

THE LIBRARY OF AMERICA

Visit our website at www.loa.org.

This paper meets the requirements of
ANSI/NISO Z39.48–1992 (Permanence of Paper).

Distributed to the trade in the United States
by Penguin Random House Inc.
and in Canada by Penguin Random House Canada Ltd.

Library of Congress Control Number: 2016946085
ISBN 978–1–59853–513–6

First Printing
The Library of America—288

Manufactured in the United States of America

Contents

Two Serious Ladies 1

In the Summer House 175

Stories and Other Writings

A Guatemalan Idyll 239
A Day in the Open 272
Song of an Old Woman 282
Two Skies 283
A Quarreling Pair 284
Plain Pleasures 288
Camp Cataract 300
A Stick of Green Candy 337
East Side: North Africa 347

Scenes and Fragments

Señorita Córdoba 359
Looking for Lane 376
Laura and Sally 382
Going to Massachusetts 407
The Children's Party 418
Andrew 420
Emmy Moore's Journal 426
Friday 432
"Curls and a quiet country face" 435
Lila and Frank 437
The Iron Table 440
At the Jumping Bean 443

Letters

1. To George McMillan, New York City, 1935 453
2. To Miriam Fligelman Levy, New York City, 1936 455
3. To "Spivy" LeVoe, Deal Beach, NJ, January 29, 1937 456

4. To Miriam Levy, New York City, February 1937 458
5. To Miriam Levy, New York City, June 1937 459
6. To Virgil Thomson, Asbury Park, NJ, August 31, 1937 459
7. To Virgil Thomson, San Jose, Costa Rica, March 23, 1938 460
8. To Virgil Thomson, Guatemala, April 21, 1938 460
9. To Virgil Thomson, Èze-Village, France, 1938 461
10. To Mary Oliver, Staten Island, Summer 1939 461
11. To Charles Henri Ford, Staten Island, Fall 1939 463
12. To Virgil Thomson, Taxco, Mexico, Late December 1941 464
13. To Virgil Thomson, Mexico City, January 1942 465
14. To Virgil Thomson, Taxco, Mexico, Early March 1942 467
15. To Virgil Thomson, Savannah, GA, April 1942 467
16. To Virgil Thomson, New York City, 1946 468
17. To Libby Holman, Florida, March 27, 1947 468
18. To Paul Bowles, Stamford, CT, Early August 1947 470
19. To Paul Bowles, Stamford, CT, Late August 1947 476
20. To Paul Bowles, Stamford, CT, September 1947 480
21. To Paul Bowles, Stamford, CT, Late September 1947 490
22. To Paul Bowles, Stamford, CT, October 1947 498
23. To Paul Bowles, East Montpelier, VT, December 1947 504

24. To Libby Holman, Tangier, Morocco, March 24, 1948 512
25. To Libby Holman, Tangier, Morocco, May 10, 1948 513
26. To Paul Bowles, Tangier, Morocco, July 1948 516
27. To Paul Bowles, Tangier, Morocco, c. July/August 1948 521
28. To Paul Bowles, Tangier, Morocco, c. July/August 1948 526
29. To Natasha von Hoershelman, Tangier, Morocco, August 1948 529
30. To Paul Bowles, Tangier, Morocco, August 1948 530
31. To Katharine Hamill and Natasha von Hoershelman, Tangier, Morocco, August 1948 534
32. To Paul Bowles and Oliver Smith, Tangier, Morocco, September 1948 535
33. To Paul Bowles, Tangier, Morocco, October 1, 1948 540
34. To Libby Holman and Scotty, Tangier, Morocco, October 1948 544
35. To Paul Bowles, Tangier, Morocco, October 1948 546
36. To Paul Bowles, Tangier, Morocco, October 1948 549
37. To Paul Bowles and Oliver Smith, Tangier, Morocco, October 1948 552
38. To Paul Bowles, Tangier, Morocco, November 1948 555
39. To Paul Bowles, Tangier, Morocco, November 1948 558
40. To Paul Bowles, Tangier, Morocco, December 1948 564
41. To Libby Holman, Tangier, Morocco, December 1948 567
42. To Katharine Hamill and Natasha von Hoershelman, Taghit, Algeria, March 1949 573

43. To Katharine Hamill, Tangier, Morocco, Late Spring 1949 576
44. To Libby Holman, Tangier, Morocco, August 29, 1949 579
45. To Katharine Hamill, Tangier, Morocco, Late Summer 1949 579
46. To Libby Holman, North Wales, November 1949 581
47. To Libby Holman, Paris, January 11, 1950 583
48. To Paul Bowles, Paris, January 17, 1950 585
49. To Paul Bowles, Paris, Late January 1950 590
50. To Paul Bowles, Paris, February 13, 1950 593
51. To Paul Bowles, Paris, February 13, 1950 595
52. To Libby Holman, L'Étape, Pacy-sur-Eure, France, June 17, 1950 598
53. To Libby Holman, L'Étape, Pacy-sur-Eure, France, June 26, 1950 603
54. To Mike Kahn, New York City, January 1951 . . . 606
55. To Carl Van Vechten, New York City, February 8, 1951 606
To Carl Van Vechten, New York City, February 12, 1951 607
56. To Libby Holman, New York City, February 12, 1951 607
57. To Libby Holman, New York City, February 18, 1951 608
58. To Natasha von Hoershelman and Katharine Hamill, Tangier, Morocco, June 1954 611
59. To Paul Bowles, Tangier, Morocco, c. April/May 1955 623
60. To Libby Holman, Tangier, Morocco, January 16, 1957 628
61. To Paul Bowles, Tangier, Morocco, February 1, 1957 630
62. To Paul Bowles, Tangier, Morocco, February 24, 1957 633
63. To Libby Holman, Tangier, Morocco, April 10, 1957 635
64. To Paul Bowles, Tangier, Morocco, Mid-April 1957 638

65. To Libby Holman, Tangier, Morocco, Summer 1957 640
66. To Libby Holman, Tangier, Morocco, Summer 1957 642
67. To Libby Holman, Tangier, Morocco, Summer 1957 646
68. To Libby Holman, Aboard the *S.S. Orion*, November 1957 649
69. To Paul Bowles, New York City, Early May 1958 650
70. To Paul Bowles, New York City, Late May/Early June 1958 653
71. To Libby Holman, Tangier, Morocco, 1960 . . . 656
72. To Libby Holman, Tangier, Morocco, November 15, 1960 659
73. To Libby Holman, Tangier, Morocco, April 16, 1961 661
74. To Lilla Von Saher, Tangier, Morocco, 1961 . . . 663
75. To Libby Holman, Tangier, Morocco, April 26, 1962 664
76. To Libby Holman, Tangier, Morocco, August 1962 665
77. To Libby Holman, Tangier, Morocco, August 13, 1962 666
78. To Libby Holman, Tangier, Morocco, c. November/December 1962 667
79. To Rena Bowles, Tangier, Morocco, c. December 1962 668
80. To Ruth Fainlight, Tangier, Morocco, c. March/April 1963 669
81. To Ruth Fainlight, Tangier, Morocco, c. May 1963 671
82. To Libby Holman, Tangier, Morocco, May 27, 1963 673
83. To Ruth Fainlight, Tangier, Morocco, Summer 1963 675
84. To Libby Holman, Tangier, Morocco, Summer 1963 677
85. To Isabelle Gerofi, Tangier, Morocco, September 1963 678

86. To Libby Holman, Arcila, Morocco, October 4, 1963 679
87. To Audrey Wood, Tangier, Morocco, March 1964 682
88. To Libby Holman, Tangier, Morocco, Spring 1964 683
89. To Libby Holman, Tangier, Morocco, June 18, 1964 685
90. To Libby Holman, Tangier, Morocco, June 23, 1964 686
91. To Libby Holman, Tangier, Morocco, June 30, 1964 688
92. To Libby Holman, Tangier, Morocco, August 8, 1964 691
93. To Ruth Fainlight, Tangier, Morocco, September 1964 693
94. To Libby Holman, Tangier, Morocco, November 26, 1964 695
95. To Libby Holman, Tangier, Morocco, Late January/Early February 1965 698
96. To Lawrence Stewart, Tangier, Morocco, February 1965 700
97. To Libby Holman, Tangier, Morocco, February 1965 701
98. To Libby Holman, Tangier, Morocco, February 1965 704
99. To "Frances," New York City, Early April 1965 706
100. To "Frances," Florida, c. May 1965 707
101. To Libby Holman, Florida, May 3, 1965 708
102. To Libby Holman, New York City, May 14, 1965 710
103. To Cherifa, New York City, May 20, 1965 712
104. To Libby Holman, Tangier, Morocco, August 26, 1965 713
105. To Libby Holman, Tangier, Morocco, December 1965 715
106. To Libby Holman and Louis Schanker, Tangier, Morocco, December 1965 717
107. To Libby Holman, Tangier, Morocco, April 1, 1966 717

108. To Libby Holman, Tangier, Morocco, May 10, 1966 . . . 719
109. To Hal Vursell, Miami, FL, c. July/August 1966 . . . 722
110. To Gordon Sager, Miami, FL, c. July/August 1966 . . . 723
111. To Libby Holman, Miami, FL, August 1966 . . . 724
112. To Paul Bowles, Miami, FL, August 9, 1966 . . . 725
113. To Gordon Sager, Miami, FL, August 1966 . . . 727
114. To Paul Bowles, Tangier, Morocco, September 1966 . . . 728
115. To Paul Bowles, Tangier, Morocco, September 28, 1966 . . . 729
116. To Hal Vursell, Tangier, Morocco, September 28, 1966 . . . 731
117. To Paul Bowles, Tangier, Morocco, c. September/October? 1966 . . . 732
118. To Claire Fuhs, Tangier, Morocco, September 30, 1966 . . . 734
119. To Paul Bowles, Tangier, Morocco, October 11, 1966 . . . 735
120. To Libby Holman, Tangier, Morocco, October 1966 . . . 736
121. To Carson McCullers, Tangier, Morocco, October 31, 1966 . . . 737
122. To Libby Holman, Tangier, Morocco, 1966 . . . 738
123. To "Frances," Tangier, Morocco, November 1966 . . . 738
124. To Paul Bowles, Tangier, Morocco, December 1966 . . . 739
125. To Libby Holman, Tangier, Morocco, February 1967 . . . 740
126. To Libby Holman, Málaga, Spain, 1967 . . . 740
127. To Paul Bowles, Tangier, Morocco, January 11, 1968 . . . 741
128. To Paul Bowles, Málaga, Spain, Spring 1968 . . . 741
129. To Paul Bowles, Málaga, Spain, Spring 1968 . . . 742
130. To Paul Bowles, Málaga, Spain, Spring 1968 . . . 742
131. To Paul Bowles, Málaga, Spain, c. 1968/1969 . . . 743

132. To Paul Bowles, Málaga, Spain, c. 1968/1969 743
133. To Paul Bowles, Málaga, Spain, c. 1970 744

Appendix

Everything Is Nice 747

Chronology 757
Note on the Texts 769
Notes 784
Index 807

TWO SERIOUS LADIES

To

Paul, Mother & Helvetia

Part One

CHRISTINA GOERING'S father was an American industrialist of German parentage and her mother was a New York lady of a very distinguished family. Christina spent the first half of her life in a very beautiful house (not more than an hour from the city) which she had inherited from her mother. It was in this house that she had been brought up as a child with her sister Sophie.

As a child Christina had been very much disliked by other children. She had never suffered particularly because of this, having led, even at a very early age, an active inner life that curtailed her observation of whatever went on around her, to such a degree that she never picked up the mannerisms then in vogue, and at the age of ten was called old-fashioned by other little girls. Even then she wore the look of certain fanatics who think of themselves as leaders without once having gained the respect of a single human being.

Christina was troubled horribly by ideas which never would have occurred to her companions, and at the same time took for granted a position in society which any other child would have found unbearable. Every now and then a schoolmate would take pity on her and try to spend some time with her, but far from being grateful for this, Christina would instead try her best to convert her new friend to the cult of whatever she believed in at the time.

Her sister Sophie, on the other hand, was very much admired by everyone in the school. She showed a marked talent for writing poetry and spent all her time with a quiet little girl called Mary, who was two years younger.

When Christina was thirteen years old her hair was very red (when she grew up it remained almost as red), her cheeks were sloppy and pink, and her nose showed traces of nobility.

That year Sophie brought Mary home with her nearly every day for luncheon. After they had finished eating she would take Mary for a walk through the woods, having provided a basket for each of them in which to carry back flowers. Christina was not permitted by Sophie to come along on these walks.

"You must find something of your own to do," Sophie would say to her. But it was hard for Christina to think of anything to do by herself that she enjoyed. She was in the habit of going through many mental struggles—generally of a religious nature—and she preferred to be with other people and organize games. These games, as a rule, were very moral, and often involved God. However, no one else enjoyed them and she was obliged to spend a great part of the day alone. She tried going to the woods once or twice by herself and bringing back flowers, in imitation of Mary and Sophie, but each time, fearing that she would not return with enough flowers to make a beautiful bouquet, she so encumbered herself with baskets that the walk seemed more of a hardship than a pleasure.

It was Christina's desire to have Mary to herself of an afternoon. One very sunny afternoon Sophie went inside for her piano lesson, and Mary remained seated on the grass. Christina, who had seen this from not far away, ran into the house, her heart beating with excitement. She took off her shoes and stockings and remained in a short white underslip. This was not a very pleasant sight to behold, because Christina at this time was very heavy and her legs were quite fat. (It was impossible to foresee that she would turn out to be a tall and elegant lady.) She ran out on the lawn and told Mary to watch her dance.

"Now don't take your eyes off me," she said. "I'm going to do a dance of worship to the sun. Then I'm going to show that I'd rather have God and no sun than the sun and no God. Do you understand?"

"Yes," said Mary. "Are you going to do it now?"

"Yes, I'm going to do it right here." She began the dance abruptly. It was a clumsy dance and her gestures were all undecided. When Sophie came out of the house, Christina was in the act of running backwards and forwards with her hands joined in prayer.

"What is she doing?" Sophie asked Mary.

"A dance to the sun, I think," Mary said. "She told me to sit here and watch her."

Sophie walked over to where Christina was now twirling around and around and shaking her hands weakly in the air.

"Sneak!" she said and suddenly she pushed Christina down on the grass.

For a long time after that, Christina kept away from Sophie, and consequently from Mary. She had one more occasion to be with Mary, however, and this happened because Sophie developed a terrible toothache one morning, and her governess was obliged to take her to the dentist immediately. Mary, not having heard of this, came over in the afternoon, expecting to find Sophie at home. Christina was in the tower, in which the children often gathered, and saw her coming up the walk.

"Mary," she screamed, "come on up here." When Mary arrived in the tower, Christina asked her if she would not like to play a very special game with her. "It's called 'I forgive you for all your sins,'" said Christina. "You'll have to take your dress off."

"Is it fun?" Mary asked.

"It's not for fun that we play it, but because it's necessary to play it."

"All right," said Mary, "I'll play with you." She took her dress off and Christina pulled an old burlap sack over Mary's head. She cut two holes in the burlap for Mary to see through and then she tied a cord around her waist.

"Come," said Christina, "and you will be absolved for your sins. Keep repeating to yourself: 'May the Lord forgive me for my sins.'"

She hurried down the stairs with Mary and then out across the lawn towards the woods. Christina wasn't yet sure what she was going to do, but she was very much excited. They came to a stream that skirted the woods. The banks of the stream were soft and muddy.

"Come to the water," said Christina; "I think that's how we'll wash away your sins. You'll have to stand in the mud."

"Near the mud?"

"*In* the mud. Does your sin taste bitter in your mouth? It must."

"Yes," said Mary hesitantly.

"Then you want to be clean and pure as a flower is, don't you?"

Mary did not answer.

"If you don't lie down in the mud and let me pack the mud over you and then wash you in the stream, you'll be forever condemned. Do you want to be forever condemned? This is your moment to decide."

Mary stood beneath her black hood without saying a word. Christina pushed her down on the ground and started to pack the burlap with mud.

"The mud's cold," said Mary.

"The hell fires are hot," said Christina. "If you let me do this, you won't go to hell."

"Don't take too long," said Mary.

Christina was very much agitated. Her eyes were shining. She packed more and more mud on Mary and then she said to her:

"Now you're ready to be purified in the stream."

"Oh, please no, not the water—I hate to go into the water. I'm afraid of the water."

"Forget what you are afraid of. God's watching you now and He has no sympathy for you yet."

She lifted Mary from the ground and walked into the stream, carrying her. She had forgotten to take off her own shoes and stockings. Her dress was completely covered with mud. Then she submerged Mary's body in the water. Mary was looking at her through the holes in the burlap. It did not occur to her to struggle.

"Three minutes will be enough," said Christina. "I'm going to say a little prayer for you."

"Oh, don't do that," Mary pleaded.

"Of course," said Christina, lifting her eyes to the sky.

"Dear God," she said, "make this girl Mary pure as Jesus Your Son. Wash her sins away as the water is now washing the mud away. This black burlap proves to you that she thinks she is a sinner."

"Oh, stop," whispered Mary. "He can hear you even if you just say it to yourself. You're shouting so."

"The three minutes are over, I believe," said Christina. "Come darling, now you can stand up."

"Let's run to the house," said Mary. "I'm freezing to death."

They ran to the house and up the back stairway that led to the tower. It was hot in the tower room because all the windows had been shut. Christina suddenly felt very ill.

"Go," she said to Mary, "go into the bath and clean yourself off. I'm going to draw." She was deeply troubled. "It's over," she said to herself, "the game is over. I'll tell Mary to go home after she's dried herself off. I'll give her some colored pencils to take home with her."

Mary returned from the bath wrapped in a towel. She was still shivering. Her hair was wet and straight. Her face looked smaller than it did ordinarily.

Christina looked away from her. "The game is over," she said, "it took only a few minutes—you should be dried off—I'm going out." She walked out of the room leaving Mary behind, pulling the towel closer around her shoulders.

As a grown woman Miss Goering was no better liked than she had been as a child. She was now living in her home outside New York, with her companion, Miss Gamelon.

Three months ago Miss Goering had been sitting in the parlor, looking out at the leafless trees, when her maid announced a caller.

"Is it a gentleman or a lady?" Miss Goering asked.

"A lady."

"Show her in immediately," said Miss Goering.

The maid returned followed by the caller. Miss Goering rose from her seat. "How do you do?" she said. "I don't believe I've ever laid eyes on you before this moment, but please sit down."

The lady visitor was small and stocky and appeared to be in her late thirties or early forties. She wore dark, unfashionable clothing and, but for her large gray eyes, her face might on all occasions have passed unnoticed.

"I'm your governess's cousin," she said to Miss Goering. "She was with you for many years. Do you remember her?"

"I do," said Miss Goering.

"Well, my name is Lucie Gamelon. My cousin used to talk about you and about your sister Sophie all the time. I've been meaning to call on you for years now, but one thing and another always got in the way. But then, we never know it to fail."

Miss Gamelon reddened. She had not yet been relieved of her hat and coat.

"You have a lovely home," she said. "I guess you know it and appreciate it a lot."

By this time Miss Goering was filled with curiosity concerning Miss Gamelon. "What's your business in life?" she asked her.

"Not very much, I'm afraid. I've been typing manuscripts for famous authors all my life, but there doesn't seem to be much demand for authors any more unless maybe they are doing their own typing."

Miss Goering, who was busy thinking, said nothing.

Miss Gamelon looked around helplessly.

"Do you stay here the greater portion of the time or do you travel mostly?" she asked Miss Goering unexpectedly.

"I never thought of traveling," said Miss Goering. "I don't require travel."

"Coming from the family you come from," said Miss Gamelon, "I guess you were born full of knowledge about everything. You wouldn't need to travel. I had opportunity to travel two or three times with my authors. They were willing to pay all my expenses and my full salary besides, but I never did go except once, and that was to Canada."

"You don't like to travel," said Miss Goering, staring at her.

"It doesn't agree with me. I tried it that once. My stomach was upset and I had nervous headaches all the time. That was enough. I had my warning."

"I understand perfectly," said Miss Goering.

"I always believe," continued Miss Gamelon, "that you get your warning. Some people don't heed their warnings. That's when they come into conflict. I think that anything you feel strange or nervous about, you weren't cut out to do."

"Go on," said Miss Goering.

"Well, I know, for instance, that I wasn't cut out to be an aviator. I've always had dreams of crashing down to the earth. There are quite a few things that I won't do, even if I am thought of as a stubborn mule. I won't cross a big body of water, for instance. I could have everything I wanted if I would just cross the ocean and go over to England, but I never will."

"Well," said Miss Goering, "let's have some tea and some sandwiches."

Miss Gamelon ate voraciously and complimented Miss Goering on her good food.

"I like good things to eat," she said; "I don't have so much good food any more. I did when I was working for the authors."

When they had finished tea, Miss Gamelon took leave of her hostess.

"I've had a very sociable time," she said. "I would like to stay longer, but tonight I have promised a niece of mine that I would watch over her children for her. She is going to attend a ball."

"You must be very depressed with the idea," said Miss Goering.

"Yes, you're right," Miss Gamelon replied.

"Do return soon," said Miss Goering.

The following afternoon the maid announced to Miss Goering that she had a caller. "It's the same lady that called here yesterday," said the maid.

"Well, well," thought Miss Goering, "that's good."

"How are you feeling today?" Miss Gamelon asked her, coming into the room. She spoke very naturally, not appearing to find it strange that she was returning so soon after her first visit. "I was thinking about you all last night," she said, "It's a funny thing. I always thought I should meet you. My cousin used to tell me how queer you were. I think, though, that you can make friends more quickly with queer people. Or else you don't make friends with them at all—one way or the other. Many of my authors were very queer. In that way I've had an advantage of association that most people don't have. I know something about what I call real honest-to-God maniacs, too."

Miss Goering invited Miss Gamelon to dine with her. She found her soothing and agreeable to be with. Miss Gamelon was very much impressed with the fact that Miss Goering was so nervous. Just as they were about to sit down, Miss Goering said that she couldn't face eating in the dining-room and she asked the servant to lay the table in the parlor instead. She spent a great deal of time switching the lights off and on.

"I know how you feel," Miss Gamelon said to her.

"I don't particularly enjoy it," said Miss Goering, "but I expect in the future to be under control."

Over wine at dinner Miss Gamelon told Miss Goering that it was only correct that she should be thus. "What do you expect, dear," she said, "coming from the kind of family you come from? You're all tuned high, all of you. You've got to allow yourself things that other people haven't any right to allow themselves."

Miss Goering began to feel a little tipsy. She looked dreamily at Miss Gamelon, who was eating her second helping of chicken cooked in wine. There was a little spot of grease in the corner of her mouth.

"I love to drink," said Miss Gamelon, "but there isn't much point to it when you have to work. It's fine enough when you have plenty of leisure time. I have a lot of leisure time now."

"Have you a guardian angel?" asked Miss Goering.

"Well, I have a dead aunt, maybe that's what you mean; she might be watching over me."

"That is not what I mean—I mean something quite different."

"Well, of course . . ." said Miss Gamelon.

"A guardian angel comes when you are very young, and gives you special dispensation."

"From what?"

"From the world. Yours might be luck; mine is money. Most people have a guardian angel; that's why they move slowly."

"That's an imaginative way of talking about guardian angels. I guess my guardian angel is what I told you about heeding my warnings. I think maybe she could warn me about both of us. In that way I could keep you out of trouble. Of course, with your consent," she added, looking a little confused.

Miss Goering had a definite feeling at that moment that Miss Gamelon was not in the least a nice woman, but she refused to face this because she got too much enjoyment from the sensation of being nursed and pampered. She told herself that it would do no harm for a little while.

"Miss Gamelon," said Miss Goering, "I think it would be a very fine idea if you were to make this your home—for the time being, at least. I don't think you have any pressing business that would oblige you to remain elsewhere, have you?"

"No, I haven't any business," said Miss Gamelon. "I don't see why I couldn't stay here—I'd have to get my things at my sister's house. Outside of that I don't know of anything else."

"What things?" asked Miss Goering impatiently. "Don't go back at all. We can get things at the stores." She got up and walked quickly up and down the room.

"Well," said Miss Gamelon, "I think I had better get my things."

"But not tonight," said Miss Goering, "tomorrow—tomorrow in the car."

"Tomorrow in the car," repeated Miss Gamelon after her.

Miss Goering made arrangements to give Miss Gamelon a room near her own, to which she led her shortly after dinner was over.

"This room," said Miss Goering, "has one of the finest views in the entire house." She drew the curtains apart. "You've got your moon and your stars tonight, Miss Gamelon, and a very nice silhouette of trees against the sky."

Miss Gamelon was standing in semi-darkness near the dressing-table. She was fingering the brooch on her blouse. She wished that Miss Goering would leave so that she could think about the house and Miss Goering's offer, in her own way.

There was a sudden scrambling in the bushes below the window. Miss Goering jumped.

"What's that?" Her face was very white and she put her hand to her forehead. "My heart hurts so for such a long time afterwards whenever I'm frightened," she said in a small voice.

"I think I'd better go to bed now and go to sleep," said Miss Gamelon. She was suddenly overcome by all the wine that she had drunk. Miss Goering took her leave reluctantly. She had been prepared to talk half the night. The following morning Miss Gamelon went home to collect her things and give her sister her new address.

Three months later Miss Goering knew little more about Miss Gamelon's ideas than she had on the first night that they had dined together. She had learned quite a lot about Miss Gamelon's personal characteristics, however, through careful observation. When Miss Gamelon had first arrived she had spoken a great deal about her love of luxury and beautiful objects, but Miss Goering had since then taken her on innumerable shopping trips; and she had never seemed interested in anything more than the simplest necessities.

She was quiet, even a little sullen, but she seemed to be fairly contented. She enjoyed dining out at large, expensive restaurants, particularly if dinner music accompanied the meal. She did not seem to like the theater. Very often Miss Goering would buy tickets for a play, and at the last moment Miss Gamelon would decline to go.

"I feel so lazy," she would say, "that bed seems to be the most beautiful thing in the world at this moment."

When she did go to the theater, she was easily bored. Whenever the action of the play was not swift, Miss Goering would catch her looking down into her lap and playing with her fingers.

She seemed now to feel more violently about Miss Goering's activities than she did about her own, although she did not listen so sympathetically to Miss Goering's explanations of herself as she had in the beginning.

On Wednesday afternoon Miss Gamelon and Miss Goering were sitting underneath the trees in front of the house. Miss Goering was drinking whisky and Miss Gamelon was reading. The maid came out and announced to Miss Goering that she was wanted on the telephone.

The call was from Miss Goering's old friend Anna, who invited her to a party the following night. Miss Goering came back out on the lawn, very excited.

"I'm going to a party tomorrow night," she said, "but I don't see how I can wait until then—I look forward to going to parties so much and I am invited to so few that I scarcely know how to behave about them. What will we do to make the hours pass until then?" She took both Miss Gamelon's hands in her own.

It was getting a little chilly. Miss Goering shivered and smiled. "Do you enjoy our little life?" she asked Miss Gamelon.

"I'm always content," said Miss Gamelon, "because I know what to take and what to leave, but you are always at the mercy."

Miss Goering arrived at Anna's looking flushed and a little overdressed. She was wearing velvet and Miss Gamelon had fastened some flowers in her hair.

The men, most of whom were middle-aged, were standing together in one corner of the room, smoking and listening to each other attentively. The ladies, freshly powdered, were seated around the room, talking very little. Anna seemed to be a little tense, although she was smiling. She wore a hostess gown adapted from a central European peasant costume.

"You will have drinks in a minute," she announced to her guests, and then, seeing Miss Goering, she went over to her and led her to a chair next to Mrs. Copperfield's without saying a word.

Mrs. Copperfield had a sharp little face and very dark hair. She was unusually small and thin. She was nervously rubbing her bare arms and looking around the room when Miss Goering seated herself in the chair beside her. They had met for many years at Anna's parties and they occasionally had tea with each other.

"Oh! Christina Goering," cried Mrs. Copperfield, startled to see her friend suddenly seated beside her, "I'm going away!"

"Do you mean," said Miss Goering, "that you are leaving this party?"

"No, I am going on a trip. Wait until I tell you about it. It's terrible."

Miss Goering noticed that Mrs. Copperfield's eyes were brighter than usual. "What is wrong, little Mrs. Copperfield?" she asked, rising from her seat and looking around the room with a bright smile on her face.

"Oh, I'm sure," said Mrs. Copperfield, "that you wouldn't want to hear about it. You can't possibly have any respect for me, but that doesn't make any difference because I have the utmost respect for you. I heard my husband say that you had a religious nature one day, and we almost had a very bad fight. Of course he is crazy to say that. You are gloriously unpredictable and you are afraid of no one but yourself. I hate religion in other people."

Miss Goering neglected to answer Mrs. Copperfield because for the last second or two she had been staring at a stout dark-haired man who was walking heavily across the room in their direction. As he came nearer, she saw that he had a pleasant face with wide jowls that protruded on either side but did not hang down as they do on most obese persons. He was dressed in a blue business suit.

"May I sit beside you?" he asked them. "I have met this young lady before," he said shaking hands with Mrs. Copperfield, "but I am afraid that I have not yet met her friend." He turned and nodded to Miss Goering.

Mrs. Copperfield was so annoyed at the interruption that she neglected to introduce Miss Goering to the gentleman. He drew up a chair next to Miss Goering's and looked at her.

"I have just come from a most wonderful dinner," he said to her, "moderate in price, but served with care and excellently prepared. If it would interest you I can write down the name of the little restaurant for you."

He reached into his vest pocket and pulled out a leather bill-fold. He found only one slip of paper which was not already covered with addresses.

"I will write this down for you," he said to Miss Goering. "Undoubtedly you will be seeing Mrs. Copperfield and then you can pass the information on to her, or perhaps she can telephone to you."

Miss Goering took the slip of paper in her hand and looked carefully at the writing.

He had not written down the name of a restaurant at all; instead he had asked Miss Goering to consent to go home with him later to his apartment. This pleased her greatly as she was usually delighted to stay out as late as possible once she had left her home.

She looked up at the man, whose face was now inscrutable. He sipped his drink with calm, and looked around the room like someone who has finally brought a business conversation to a close. However, there were some sweat beads on his forehead.

Mrs. Copperfield stared at him with distaste, but Miss Goering's face suddenly brightened. "Let me tell you," she said to them, "about a strange experience I had this morning. Sit still, little Mrs. Copperfield, and listen to me." Mrs. Copperfield looked up at Miss Goering and took her friend's hand in her own.

"I stayed in town with my sister Sophie last night," said Miss Goering, "and this morning I was standing in front of the window drinking a cup of coffee. The building next to Sophie's house is being torn down. I believe that they are intending to put an apartment house in its place. It was not only extremely windy this morning, but it was raining intermittently. From my window I could see into the rooms of this building, as the wall opposite me had already been torn down. The rooms were still partially furnished, and I stood looking at them, watching the rain spatter the wallpaper. The wallpaper was flowered and already covered with dark spots, which were growing larger."

"How amusing," said Mrs. Copperfield, "or perhaps it was depressing."

"I finally felt rather sad watching this and I was about to go away when a man came into one of these rooms and, walking deliberately over to the bed, took up a coverlet which he folded under his arm. It was undoubtedly a personal possession which he had neglected to pack and had just now returned to fetch. Then he walked around the room aimlessly for a bit and finally he stood at the very edge of his room looking down into the yard with his arms akimbo. I could see him more clearly now, and I could easily tell that he was an artist. As he stood there, I was increasingly filled with horror, very much as though I were watching a scene in a nightmare."

At this point Miss Goering suddenly stood up.

"Did he jump, Miss Goering?" Mrs. Copperfield asked with feeling.

"No, he remained there for quite a while looking down into the courtyard with an expression of pleasant curiosity on his face."

"Amazing, Miss Goering," said Mrs. Copperfield. "I do think it's such an interesting story, really, but it has quite scared me out of my wits and I shouldn't enjoy hearing another one like it." She had scarcely finished her sentence when she heard her husband say:

"We will go to Panama and linger there awhile before we penetrate into the interior." Mrs. Copperfield pressed Miss Goering's hand.

"I don't think I can bear it," she said. "Really, Miss Goering, it frightens me so much to go."

"I would go anyway," said Miss Goering.

Mrs. Copperfield jumped off the arm of the chair and ran into the library. She locked the door behind her carefully and then she fell in a little heap on the sofa and sobbed bitterly. When she had stopped crying she powdered her nose, seated herself on the window-sill, and looked down into the dark garden below.

An hour or two later Arnold, the stout man in the blue suit, was still talking to Miss Goering. He suggested to her that they leave the party and go to his own house. "I think that we will have a much nicer time there," he said to her. "There will be less noise and we will be able to talk more freely."

As yet Miss Goering had no desire at all to leave, she enjoyed so much being in a room full of people, but she did not quite know how to get out of accepting his invitation.

"Certainly," she said, "let's be on our way." They rose and left the room together in silence.

"Don't say anything to Anna about our leaving," Arnold told Miss Goering. "It will only cause a commotion. I promise you I'll send some sweets to her tomorrow, or some flowers." He pressed Miss Goering's hand and smiled at her. She was not sure that she did not find him a bit too familiar.

After leaving Anna's party, Arnold walked awhile with Miss Goering and then hailed a cab. The road to his home led through many dark and deserted streets. Miss Goering was so nervous and hysterical about this that Arnold was alarmed.

"I always think," said Miss Goering, "that the driver is only waiting for the passengers to become absorbed in conversation in order to shoot down some street, to an inaccessible and lonely place where he will either torture or murder them. I am certain that most people feel the same way about it that I do, but they have the good taste not to mention it."

"Since you live so far out of town," said Arnold, "why don't you spend the night at my house? We have an extra bedroom."

"I probably shall," said Miss Goering, "although it is against my entire code, but then, I have never even begun to use my code, although I judge everything by it." Miss Goering looked a little morose after having said this and they drove on in silence until they reached their destination.

Arnold's flat was on the second floor. He opened the door and they walked into a room lined to the ceiling with bookshelves. The couch had been made up and Arnold's slippers were lying on the rug beside it. The furniture was heavy and some small Oriental rugs were scattered here and there.

"I sleep in here," said Arnold, "and my mother and father occupy the bedroom. We have a small kitchen, but generally we prefer to eat out. There is another tiny bedroom, originally intended for a maid's room, but I would rather sleep in here and let my eye wander from book to book; books are a great solace to me." He sighed heavily and laid both his hands on Miss Goering's shoulders. "You see, my dear lady," he said, "I'm not exactly doing the kind of thing that I would like to do. . . . I'm in the real-estate business."

"What is it that you would like to do?" asked Miss Goering, looking weary and indifferent.

"Something, naturally," said Arnold, "in the book line, or in the painting line."

"And you can't?"

"No," said Arnold, "my family doesn't believe that such an occupation is serious, and since I must earn my living and pay for my share of this flat, I have been obliged to accept a post in my uncle's office, where I must say I very quickly have become his prize salesman. In the evenings, however, I have plenty of time to move among people who have nothing to do with real estate. As a matter of fact, they think very little about earning money at all. Naturally, these people are interested in having enough to eat. Even though I am thirty-nine years old I still am hoping very seriously that I will be able to make a definitive break with my family. I do not see life through the same pair of eyes that they do. And I feel more and more that my life here with them is becoming insupportable in spite of the fact that I am free to entertain whom I please since I pay for part of the upkeep of the flat."

He sat down on the couch and rubbed his eyes with his hands.

"You'll forgive me, Miss Goering, but I'm feeling very sleepy suddenly. I'm sure the feeling will go away."

Miss Goering's drinks were wearing off and she thought it high time that she got back to Miss Gamelon, but she had not the courage to ride all the way out to her home by herself.

"Well, I suppose this is a great disappointment to you," said Arnold, "but you see I have fallen in love with you. I wanted to bring you here and tell you about my whole life, but now I don't feel like talking about anything."

"Perhaps some other time you'll tell me about your life," said Miss Goering, beginning to walk up and down very quickly. She stopped and turned towards him. "What do you advise me to do?" she asked him. "Do you advise me to go home or stay here?"

Arnold studied his watch. "Stay here by all means," he said.

Just then Arnold's father came in, wearing a lounging-robe and carrying a cup of coffee in his hand. He was very slender and he wore a small pointed beard. He was a more distinguished figure than Arnold.

"Good evening, Arnold," said his father. "Will you introduce me, please, to this young lady?"

Arnold introduced them and then his father asked Miss Goering why she did not take off her cloak.

"As long as you are up so late at night," he said, "and not enjoying the comfort and the security of your own bed, you might as well be at ease. Arnold, my son, never thinks of things like this." He took Miss Goering's cloak off and complimented her on her lovely dress.

"Now tell me where you have been and what you have done. I myself don't go out in society, being content with the company of my wife and son."

Arnold shrugged his shoulders and pretended to look absently around the room. But any person even a little observant could have seen that his face was decidedly hostile.

"Now tell me about this party," said Arnold's father adjusting the scarf that he was wearing around his neck. "*You* tell me." He pointed at Miss Goering, who was beginning to feel much gayer already. She had instantly preferred Arnold's father to Arnold himself.

"I'll tell you about it," said Arnold. "There were many people there, the majority of whom were creative artists, some successful and rich, others rich simply because they had inherited money from some member of the family, and others with just barely enough to eat. None of these people, however, were interested in money as an objective but would have been content, all of them, with just enough to eat."

"Like wild animals," said his father, rising to his feet. "Like wolves! What separates a man from a wolf if it is not that a man wants to make a profit?"

Miss Goering laughed until the tears streamed down her face. Arnold took some magazines from the table and began looking through them very quickly.

Just then Arnold's mother came into the room carrying in one hand a plate heaped with cakes and in the other a cup of coffee.

She was dowdy and unimpressive and of very much the same build as Arnold. She was wearing a pink wrapper.

"Welcome," said Miss Goering to Arnold's mother. "May I have a piece of your cake?"

Arnold's mother, who was a very gauche woman, did not offer Miss Goering any of the cake; instead, hugging the platter close to her, she said to Miss Goering: "Have you known Arnold for long?"

"No, I met your son tonight, at a party."

"Well," said Arnold's mother, putting the tray down and sitting on the sofa, "I guess that isn't long, is it?"

Arnold's father was annoyed with his wife and showed it plainly in his face.

"I hate that pink wrapper," he said.

"Why do you talk about that now when there is company?"

"Because the company doesn't make the wrapper look any different." He winked broadly at Miss Goering and then burst out laughing. Miss Goering again laughed heartily at his remark. Arnold was even glummer than he had been a moment before.

"Miss Goering," said Arnold, "was afraid to go home alone, so I told her that she was welcome to sleep in the extra room. Although the bed isn't very comfortable in there, I think that she will at least have privacy."

"And *why*," said Arnold's father, "was Miss Goering afraid to go home alone?"

"Well," said Arnold, "it is not really very safe for a lady to wander about the streets or even to be in a taxi without an escort at so late an hour. Particularly if she has very far to go. Of course if she hadn't had so far to go I should naturally have accompanied her myself."

"You sound like a sissy, the way you talk," said his father. "I thought that you and your friends were not afraid of such things. I thought you were wild ones and that rape meant no more to you than flying a balloon."

"Oh, don't talk like that," said Arnold's mother, looking really horrified. "Why do you talk like that to them?"

"I wish you would go to bed," Arnold's father said. "As a matter of fact, I am going to order you to go to bed. You are getting a cold."

"Isn't he terrible?" said Arnold's mother, smiling at Miss Goering. "Even when there is company in the house he can't control his lion nature. He *has* a nature like a lion, roaring in the apartment all day long, and he gets so upset about Arnold and his friends."

Arnold's father stamped out of the room and they heard a door slam down the hall.

"Excuse me," said Arnold's mother to Miss Goering, "I didn't want to upset the party."

Miss Goering was very annoyed, for she found the old man quite exhilarating, and Arnold himself was depressing her more and more.

"I think I'll show you where you're going to sleep," said Arnold, getting up from the sofa and in so doing allowing some magazines to slide from his lap to the floor. "Oh, well," he said, "come this way. I'm pretty sleepy and disgusted with this whole affair."

Miss Goering followed Arnold reluctantly down the hall.

"Dear me," she said to Arnold, "I must confess that I am not sleepy. There is really nothing worse, is there?"

"No, it's dreadful," said Arnold. "I personally am ready to fall down on the carpet and lie there until tomorrow noon, I am so completely exhausted."

Miss Goering thought this remark a very inhospitable one and she began to feel a little frightened. Arnold was obliged to search for the key to the spare room, and Miss Goering was left standing alone in front of the door for some time.

"Control yourself," she whispered out loud, for her heart was beginning to beat very quickly. She wondered how she had ever allowed herself to come so far from her house and Miss Gamelon. Arnold returned finally with the key and opened the door to the room.

It was a very small room and much colder than the room in which they had been sitting. Miss Goering expected that Arnold would be extremely embarrassed about this, but although he shivered and rubbed his hands together, he said nothing. There were no curtains at the window, but there was a yellow shade, which had already been pulled down. Miss Goering threw herself down on the bed.

"Well, my dear," said Arnold, "good night. I'm going to

bed. Maybe we'll go and see some paintings tomorrow, or if you like I'll come out to your house." He put his arms around her neck and kissed her very lightly on the lips and left the room.

She was so angry that there were tears in her eyes. Arnold stood outside of the door for a little while and then after a few minutes he walked away.

Miss Goering went over to the bureau and leaned her head on her hands. She remained in this position for a long time in spite of the fact that she was shivering with the cold. Finally there was a light tap on the door. She stopped crying as abruptly as she had begun and hurried to open the door. She saw Arnold's father standing outside in the badly lighted hall. He was wearing pink striped pajamas and he gave her a brief salute as a greeting. After that he stood very still, waiting apparently for Miss Goering to ask him in.

"Come in, come in," she said to him, "I'm delighted to see you. Heavens! I've had such a feeling of being deserted."

Arnold's father came in and balanced himself on the foot of Miss Goering's bed, where he sat swinging his legs. He lit his pipe in rather an affected manner and looked around him at the walls of the room.

"Well, lady," he said to her, "are you an artist too?"

"No," said Miss Goering. "I wanted to be a religious leader when I was young and now I just reside in my house and try not to be too unhappy. I have a friend living with me, which makes it easier."

"What do you think of my son?" he asked, winking at her.

"I have only just met him," said Miss Goering.

"You'll discover soon enough," said Arnold's father, "that he's a rather inferior person. He has no conception of what it is to fight. I shouldn't think women would like that very much. As a matter of fact, I don't think Arnold has had many women in his life. If you'll forgive me for passing this information on to you. I myself am used to fighting. I've fought my neighbors all my life instead of sitting down and having tea with them like Arnold. And my neighbors have fought me back like tigers too. Now that's not Arnold's kind of thing. My life's ambition always has been to be a notch higher on the tree than my neighbors and I was willing to admit complete disgrace too when I ended up perching a notch lower than anybody else I knew. I haven't been out in a good many years. Nobody comes to see me and I don't go to see anybody. Now, with Arnold and his friends nothing ever really begins or finishes. They're like fish in dirty water to me. If life don't please them one way and nobody likes them one place, then they go someplace else. They aim to please and be pleased; that's why it's so easy to come and bop them on the head from behind, because they've never done any serious hating in their lives."

"What a strange doctrine!" said Miss Goering.

"This is no doctrine," said Arnold's father. "These are my own ideas, taken from my own personal experience. I'm a great believer in personal experience, aren't you?"

"Oh, yes," said Miss Goering, "and I do think you're right about Arnold." She felt a curious delight in running down Arnold.

"Now Arnold," continued his father, and he seemed to grow gayer as he talked, "Arnold could never bear to have anyone catch him sitting on the lowest notch. Everyone knows how big your house is, and men who are willing to set their happiness by that are men of iron."

"Arnold is not an artist, anyway," put in Miss Goering.

"No, that is just it," said Arnold's father, getting more and more excited. "That's just it! He hasn't got the brawn nor the nerve nor the perseverance to be a good artist. An artist must have brawn and pluck and character. Arnold is like my wife," he continued. "I married her when she was twenty years old because of certain business interests. Every time I tell her that, she cries. She's another fool. She doesn't love me a bit, but it scares her to think of it, so that she cries. She's green-eyed with jealousy too and she's coiled around her family and her house like a python, although she doesn't have a good time here. Her life, as a matter of fact, is a wretched one, I must admit. Arnold's ashamed of her and I knock her around all day long. But in spite of the fact that she is a timid woman, she is capable of showing a certain amount of violence and brawn. Because she too, like myself, is faithful to one ideal, I suppose."

Just then there was a smart rap on the door. Arnold's father did not say a word, but Miss Goering called out in a clear voice: "Who is it?"

"It's me, Arnold's mother," came the answer. "Please let me in right away."

"Just one moment," said Miss Goering, "and I certainly shall."

"No," said Arnold's father. "Don't open the door. She has no right whatsoever to command anyone to open the door."

"You had better open it," said his wife. "Otherwise, I'll call the police, and I mean that very seriously. I have never threatened to call them before, you know."

"Yes, you did threaten to call them once before," said Arnold's father, looking very worried.

"The way I feel about my life," said Arnold's mother, "I'd just as soon open all the doors and let everyone come in the house and witness my disgrace."

"That's the last thing she'd ever do," said Arnold's father.

"She talks like a fool when she's angry. I'll let her in," said Miss Goering, walking towards the door. Miss Goering went to open the door. She did not feel very frightened because Arnold's mother, judging from her voice, sounded more as though she was sad than angry. But when Miss Goering opened the door she was surprised to see that, on the contrary, her face was blanched with anger and her eyes were little narrow slits.

"Why do you pretend always to sleep so well?" said Arnold's father. This was the only remark he was able to think of, although he realized himself how inadequate it must have sounded to his wife.

"You're a harlot," said his wife to Miss Goering. Miss Goering was gravely shocked by this remark, and very much to her own amazement, for she had always thought that such things meant nothing to her.

"I am afraid you are entirely on the wrong track," said Miss Goering, "and I believe that some day we shall be great friends."

"I'll thank you to let me choose my own friends," Arnold's mother answered her. "I already have my friends, as a matter of fact, and I don't expect to add any more to my list, and least of all, you."

"Still, you can't tell," said Miss Goering rather weakly backing up a bit, and trying to lean in an easy manner against the bureau. Unfortunately, in calling Miss Goering a harlot Arnold's mother had suggested to her husband the stand that he would take to defend himself.

"How dare you!" he said. "How dare you call anyone that is staying in our house a harlot! You are violating the laws of hospitality to the hundredth degree and I am not going to stand for it."

"Don't bully me," said Arnold's mother. "She's got to go right away this minute or I will make a scandal and you'll be sorry."

"Look, my dear," said Arnold's father to Miss Goering. "Perhaps it would be better if you did go, for your own sake. It is beginning to grow light, so that you needn't be at all frightened."

Arnold's father looked around nervously and then hurried out of the room and down the hall, followed by his wife. Miss Goering heard a door slam and she imagined that they would continue their argument in private.

She herself ran headlong down the hall and out of the house. She found a taxicab after walking a little while and she hadn't been riding more than a few minutes before she fell asleep.

On the following day the sun was shining and both Miss Gamelon and Miss Goering were sitting on the lawn arguing. Miss Goering was stretched out on the grass. Miss Gamelon seemed the more discontented of the two. She was frowning and looking over her shoulder at the house, which was behind them. Miss Goering had her eyes shut and there was a faint smile on her face.

"Well," said Miss Gamelon turning around, "you know so little about what you're doing that it's a real crime against society that you have property in your hands. Property should be in the hands of people who like it."

"I think," said Miss Goering, "that I like it more than most people. It gives me a comfortable feeling of safety, as I have explained to you at least a dozen times. However, in order to work out my own little idea of salvation I really believe that it is necessary for me to live in some more tawdry place and particularly in some place where I was not born."

"In my opinion," said Miss Gamelon, "you could perfectly well work out your salvation during certain hours of the day without having to move everything."

"No," said Miss Goering, "that would not be in accordance with the spirit of the age."

Miss Gamelon shifted in her chair.

"The spirit of the age, whatever that is," she said, "I'm sure it can get along beautifully without you—probably would prefer it."

Miss Goering smiled and shook her head.

"The idea," said Miss Goering, "is to change first of our own volition and according to our own inner promptings before they impose completely arbitrary changes on us."

"I have no such promptings," said Miss Gamelon, "and I think you have a colossal nerve to identify yourself with anybody else at all. As a matter of fact, I think that if you leave this house, I shall give you up as a hopeless lunatic. After all, I am not the sort of person that is interested in living with a lunatic, nor is anyone else."

"When I have given you up," said Miss Goering, sitting up and throwing her head back in an exalted manner, "when I have given you up, I shall have given up more than my house, Lucy."

"That's one of your nastinesses," said Miss Gamelon. "It goes in one of my ears and then out the other."

Miss Goering shrugged her shoulders and went inside the house.

She stood for a while in the parlor rearranging some flowers in a bowl and she was just about to go to her room and sleep when Arnold appeared.

"Hello," said Arnold, "I meant to come and see you earlier, but I couldn't quite make it. We had one of those long family lunches. I think flowers look beautiful in this room."

"How is your father?" Miss Goering asked him.

"Oh," said Arnold, "he's all right, I guess. We have very little to do with each other." Miss Goering noticed that he was sweating again. He had evidently been terribly excited about arriving at her house, because he had forgotten to remove his straw hat.

"This is a really beautiful house," he told her. "It has a quality of past splendor about it that thrills me. You must hate to leave it ever. Well, Father seemed to be quite taken with you. Don't let him get too cocky. He thinks the girls are crazy about him."

"I'm devoted to him," said Miss Goering.

"Well, I hope that the fact that you're devoted to him," said Arnold, "won't interfere with our friendship, because I have decided to see quite a bit of you, providing of course that it is agreeable to you that I do."

"Of course," said Miss Goering, "whenever you like."

"I think that I shall like being here in your home, and you needn't feel that it's a strain. I'm quite happy to sit alone and think, because as you know I'm very anxious to establish myself in some other way than I am now established, which is not satisfactory to me. As you can well imagine, it is even impossible for me to give a dinner party for a few friends because neither Father nor Mother ever stirs from the house unless I do."

Arnold seated himself in a chair by a big bay window and stretched his legs out.

"Come here!" he said to Miss Goering, "and watch the wind rippling through the tops of the trees. There is nothing more lovely in the world." He looked up at her very seriously for a little while.

"Do you have some milk and some bread and marmalade?" he asked her. "I hope there is to be no ceremony between us."

Miss Goering was surprised that Arnold should ask for something to eat so shortly after his luncheon, and she decided that this was undoubtedly the reason why he was so fat.

"Certainly we have," she said sweetly, and she went away to give the servant the order.

Meanwhile Miss Gamelon had decided to come inside and if possible pursue Miss Goering with her argument. When Arnold saw her he realized that she was the companion about whom Miss Goering had spoken the night before.

He rose to his feet immediately, having decided that it was very important for him to make friends with Miss Gamelon.

Miss Gamelon herself was very pleased to see him, as they seldom had company and she enjoyed talking to almost anyone better than to Miss Goering.

They introduced themselves and Arnold pulled up a chair for Miss Gamelon near his own.

"You are Miss Goering's companion," he said to Miss Gamelon. "I think that's lovely."

"Do you think it's lovely?" asked Miss Gamelon. "That's very interesting indeed."

Arnold smiled happily at this remark of Miss Gamelon's and sat on without saying anything for a little while.

"This house is done in exquisite taste," he said finally, "and it is filled with rest and peace."

"It all depends on how you look at it," said Miss Gamelon quickly, jerking her head around and looking out of the window.

"There are certain people," she said, "who turn peace from the door as though it were a red dragon breathing fire out of its nostrils and there are certain people who won't leave God alone either."

Arnold leaned forward trying to appear deferential and interested at the same time.

"I think," he said gravely, "I think I understand what you mean to say."

Then they both looked out of the window at the same time and they saw Miss Goering in the distance wearing a cape over her shoulders and talking to a young man whom they were scarcely able to distinguish because he was directly against the sun.

"That's the agent," said Miss Gamelon. "I suppose there is nothing to look forward to from now on."

"What agent?" asked Arnold.

"The agent through whom she's going to sell her house," said Miss Gamelon. "Isn't it all too dreadful for words?"

"Oh, I'm sorry," said Arnold. "I think it's very foolish of her, but I suppose it's not my affair."

"We're going to live," added Miss Gamelon, " in a four-room frame house and do our own cooking. It's to be in the country surrounded by woods."

"That does sound gloomy, doesn't it?" said Arnold, "but why should Miss Goering have decided to do such a thing?"

"She says it is only a beginning in a tremendous scheme."

Arnold seemed to be very sad. He no longer spoke to Miss Gamelon but merely pursed his lips and looked at the ceiling.

"I suppose the most important thing in the world," he said at length, "is friendship and understanding." He looked at Miss Gamelon questioningly. He seemed to have given up something.

"Well, Miss Gamelon," he said again, "do you not agree

with me that friendship and understanding are the most important things in the world?"

"Yes," said Miss Gamelon, "and keeping your head is, too."

Soon Miss Goering came in with a batch of papers under her arm.

"These," she said, "are the contracts. My, they are lengthy, but I think the agent is a sweet man. He said he thought this house was lovely." She held out the contracts first to Arnold and then to Miss Gamelon.

"I should think," said Miss Gamelon, "that you would be afraid to look in the mirror for fear of seeing something too wild and peculiar. I don't want to have to look at these contracts. Please take them off my lap right away. Jesus God Almighty!"

Miss Goering, as a matter of fact, did look a little wild, and Miss Gamelon with a wary eye had noticed immediately that the hand in which she held the contracts was trembling.

"Where is your little house, Miss Goering?" Arnold asked her, trying to introduce a more natural note into the conversation.

"It's on an island," said Miss Goering, "not far from the city by ferryboat. I remember having visited this island as a child and always having disliked it because one can smell the glue factories from the mainland even when walking through the woods or across the fields. One end of the island is very well populated, although you can only buy third-rate goods in any of the stores. Farther out the island is wilder and more old-fashioned; nevertheless there is a little train that meets the ferry frequently and carries you out to the other end. There you land in a little town that is quite lost and looks very tough, and you feel a bit frightened, I think, to find that the mainland opposite the point is as squalid as the island itself and offers you no protection at all."

"You seem to have looked the situation over very carefully and from every angle," said Miss Gamelon. "My compliments to you!" She waved at Miss Goering from her seat, but one could easily see that she was not feeling frivolous in the least.

Arnold shifted about uneasily in his chair. He coughed and then he spoke very gently to Miss Goering.

"I am sure that the island has certain advantages too, which you know about, but perhaps you prefer to surprise us with them rather than disappoint us."

"I know of none at the moment," said Miss Goering. "Why, are you coming with us?"

"I think that I would like to spend quite a bit of time with you out there; that is, if you will invite me."

Arnold was sad and uneasy, but he felt that he must at any cost remain close to Miss Goering in whatever world she chose to move.

"If you will invite me," he said again, "I will be glad to come out with you for a little while anyway and we will see how it goes. I could continue to keep up my end of the apartment that I share with my parents without having to spend all my time there. But I don't advise you to sell your beautiful house; rather rent it or board it up while you are away. Certainly you might have a change of heart and want to return to it."

Miss Gamelon flushed with pleasure.

"That would be too human a thing for her to consider doing," she said, but she looked a little more hopeful.

Miss Goering seemed to be dreaming and not listening to what either of them was saying.

"Well," said Miss Gamelon, "aren't you going to answer him? He said: why not board your house up or rent it and then if you have a change of heart you can return to it."

"Oh, no," said Miss Goering. "Thank you very much, but I couldn't do that. It wouldn't make much sense to do that."

Arnold coughed to hide his embarrassment at having suggested something so obviously displeasing to Miss Goering.

"I mustn't," he said to himself, "I mustn't align myself too much on the side of Miss Gamelon, or Miss Goering will begin to think that my mind is of the same caliber."

"Perhaps it is better after all," he said aloud, "to sell everything."

Part Two

MR. AND MRS. Copperfield stood on the foredeck of the boat as it sailed into the harbor at Panama. Mrs. Copperfield was very glad to see land at last.

"You admit now," she said to Mr. Copperfield, "that the land is nicer than the sea." She herself had a great fear of drowning.

"It isn't only being afraid of the sea," she continued, "but it's boring. It's the same thing all the time. The colors are beautiful, of course."

Mr. Copperfield was studying the shore line.

"If you stand still and look between the buildings on the docks," he said, "you'll be able to catch a glimpse of some green trains loaded with bananas. They seem to go by every quarter of an hour."

His wife did not answer him; instead she put on the sun-helmet which she had been carrying in her hand.

"Aren't you beginning to feel the heat already? I am," she said to him at last. As she received no answer she moved along the rail and looked down at the water.

Presently a stout woman whose acquaintance she had made on the boat came up to talk with her. Mrs. Copperfield brightened.

"You've had your hair marcelled!" she said. The woman smiled.

"Now remember," she said to Mrs. Copperfield, "the minute you get to your hotel, stretch yourself out and rest. Don't let them drag you through the streets, no matter what kind of a wild time they promise you. Nothing but monkeys in the streets anyway. There isn't a fine-looking person in the whole town that isn't connected with the American Army, and the Americans stick pretty much in their own quarter. The American quarter is called Cristobal. It's separated from Colon. Colon is full of nothing but half-breeds and monkeys. Cristobal is nice. Everyone in Cristobal has got his own little screened-in porch. They'd never dream of screening themselves in, the monkeys in Colon. They don't know when a mosquito's biting them anyway, and even if they did know they wouldn't lift their arm up to shoo him off. Eat plenty of fruit and be careful of the stores. Most of them are owned by Hindus. They're just like Jews, you know. They'll gyp you right and left."

"I'm not interested in buying anything," said Mrs. Copperfield, "but may I come and visit you while I'm in Colon?"

"I love you, dear," answered the woman, "but I like to spend every minute with my boy while I'm here."

"That's all right," said Mrs. Copperfield.

"Of course it's all right. You've got that beautiful husband of yours."

"That doesn't help," said Mrs. Copperfield, but no sooner had she said this than she was horrified at herself.

"Well now, you've had a tussle?" said the woman.

"No."

"Then I think you're a terrible little woman talking that way about your husband," she said, walking away. Mrs. Copperfield hung her head and went back to stand beside Mr. Copperfield.

"Why do you speak to such dopes?" he asked.

She did not answer.

"Well," he said, "for Heaven's sake, look at the scenery now, will you?"

They got into a taxicab and Mr. Copperfield insisted on going to a hotel right in the center of town. Normally all tourists with even a small amount of money stayed at the Hotel Washington, overlooking the sea, a few miles out of Colon.

"I don't believe," Mr. Copperfield said to his wife, "I don't believe in spending money on a luxury that can only be mine for a week at the most. I think it's more fun to buy objects which will last me perhaps a lifetime. We can certainly find a hotel in the town that will be comfortable. Then we will be free to spend our money on more exciting things."

"The room in which I sleep is so important to me," Mrs. Copperfield said. She was nearly moaning.

"My dear, a room is really only a place in which to sleep and dress. If it is quiet and the bed is comfortable, nothing more is necessary. Don't you agree with me?"

"You know very well I don't agree with you."

"If you are going to be miserable, we'll go to the Hotel Washington," said Mr. Copperfield. Suddenly he lost his dignity. His eyes clouded over and he pouted. "But I'll be wretched there, I can assure you. It's going to be so God-damned dull." He was like a baby and Mrs. Copperfield was obliged to comfort him. He had a trick way of making her feel responsible.

"After all, it's mostly my money," she said to herself. "I'm footing the bulk of the expenditures for this trip." Nevertheless, she was unable to gain a sense of power by reminding herself of this. She was completely dominated by Mr. Copperfield, as she was by almost anyone with whom she came in contact. Still, certain people who knew her well affirmed that she was capable of suddenly making a very radical and independent move without a soul to back her up.

She looked out the window of the taxicab and she noticed that there was a terrific amount of activity going on around her in the streets. The people, for the most part Negroes and uniformed men from the fleets of all nations, were running in and out and making so much noise that Mrs. Copperfield wondered if it was not a holiday of some kind.

"It's like a city that is being constantly looted," said her husband.

The houses were painted in bright colors and they had wide porches on the upper floors, supported beneath by long wooden posts. Thus they formed a kind of arcade to shade the people walking in the street.

"This architecture is ingenious," remarked Mr. Copperfield. "The streets would be unbearable if one had to walk along them with nothing overhead."

"You could not stand that, mister," said the cab-driver, "to walk along with nothing over your head."

"Anyway," said Mrs. Copperfield, "do let's choose one of these hotels quickly and get into it."

They found one right in the heart of the red-light district and agreed to look at some rooms on the fifth floor. The manager had told them that these were sure to be the least noisy. Mrs. Copperfield, who was afraid of lifts, decided to go up the stairs on foot and wait for her husband to arrive with the luggage. Having climbed to the fifth floor, she was surprised to find that the main hall contained at least a hundred straight-backed dining-room chairs and nothing more. As she looked around, her anger mounted and she could barely wait for Mr. Copperfield to arrive on the lift in order to tell him what she thought of him. "I must get to the Hotel Washington," she said to herself.

Mr. Copperfield finally arrived, walking beside a boy with the luggage. She ran up to him.

"It's the ugliest thing I've ever seen," she said.

"Wait a second, please, and let me count the luggage; I want to make sure it's all here."

"As far as I'm concerned, it could be at the bottom of the sea—all of it."

"Where's my typewriter?" asked Mr. Copperfield.

"Talk to me this minute," said his wife, beside herself with anger.

"Do you care whether or not you have a private bath?" asked Mr. Copperfield.

"No, no. I don't care about that. It's not a question of comfort at all. It's something much more than that."

Mr. Copperfield chuckled. "You're so crazy," he said to her with indulgence. He was delighted to be in the tropics at last and he was more than pleased with himself that he had managed to dissuade his wife from stopping at a ridiculously expensive hotel where they would have been surrounded by tourists. He realized that this hotel was sinister, but that was what he loved.

They followed the bellhop to one of the rooms, and no sooner had they arrived there than Mrs. Copperfield began pushing the door backwards and forwards. It opened both ways and could only be locked by means of a little hook.

"Anyone could break into this room," said Mrs. Copperfield.

"I dare say they could, but I don't think they would be very likely to, do you?" Mr. Copperfield made a point of never reassuring his wife. He gave her fears their just due. However, he did not insist, and they decided upon another room, with a stronger door.

Mrs. Copperfield was amazed at her husband's vivacity. He had washed and gone out to buy a papaya.

She lay on the bed thinking.

"Now," she said to herself, "when people believed in God

they carried Him from one place to another. They carried Him through the jungles and across the Arctic Circle. God watched over everybody, and all men were brothers. Now there is nothing to carry with you from one place to another, and as far as I'm concerned, these people might as well be kangaroos; yet somehow there must be someone here who will remind me of something . . . I must try to find a nest in this outlandish place."

Mrs. Copperfield's sole object in life was to be happy, although people who had observed her behavior over a period of years would have been surprised to discover that this was all.

She rose from her bed and pulled Miss Goering's present, a manicuring set, from her grip. "Memory," she whispered. "Memory of the things I have loved since I was a child. My husband is a man without memory." She felt intense pain at the thought of this man whom she liked above all other people, this man for whom each thing he had not yet known was a joy. For her, all that which was not already an old dream was an outrage. She got back on her bed and fell sound asleep.

When she awoke, Mr. Copperfield was standing near the foot of the bed, eating a papaya.

"You must try some," he said. "It gives you lots of energy and besides it's delicious. Won't you have some?" He looked at her shyly.

"Where have you been?" she asked him.

"Oh, walking through the streets. As a matter of fact, I've walked for miles. You should come out, really. It's a madhouse. The streets are full of soldiers and sailors and whores. The women are all in long dresses . . . incredibly cheap dresses. They'll all talk to you. Come on out."

They were walking through the streets arm in arm. Mrs. Copperfield's forehead was burning hot and her hands were cold. She felt something trembling in the pit of her stomach. When she looked ahead of her the very end of the street seemed to bend and then straighten out again. She told this to Mr. Copperfield and he explained that it was a result of their having so recently come off the boat. Above their heads the children were jumping up and down on the wooden porches and making the houses shake. Someone bumped against Mrs.

Copperfield's shoulder and she was almost knocked over. At the same time she was very much aware of the strong and fragrant odor of rose perfume. The person who had collided with her was a Negress in a pink silk evening dress.

"I can't tell you how sorry I am. I can't tell you," she said to them. Then she looked around her vaguely and began to hum.

"I told you it was a madhouse," Mr. Copperfield said to his wife.

"Listen," said the Negress, "go down the next street and you'll like it better. I've got to meet my beau over at that bar." She pointed it out to them. "That's a beautiful barroom. Everyone goes in there," she said. She moved up closer and addressed herself solely to Mrs. Copperfield. "You come along with me, darling, and you'll have the happiest time you've ever had before. I'll be your type. Come on."

She took Mrs. Copperfield's hand in her own and started to drag her away from Mr. Copperfield. She was bigger than either of them.

"I don't believe that she wants to go to a bar just now," said Mr. Copperfield. "We'd like to explore the town awhile first."

The Negress caressed Mrs. Copperfield's face with the palm of her hand. "Is that what you want to do, darling, or do you want to come along with me?" A policeman stopped and stood a few feet away from them. The Negress released Mrs. Copperfield's hand and bounded across the street laughing.

"Wasn't that the strangest thing you've ever seen?" said Mrs. Copperfield, breathlessly.

"You better mind your own business," said the policeman. "Why don't you go over and look at the stores? Everybody walks along the streets where the stores are. Buy something for your uncle or your cousin."

"No, that's not what I want to do," said Mrs. Copperfield.

"Well, then, go to a movie," said the policeman, walking away.

Mr. Copperfield was hysterical with laughter. He had his handkerchief up to his mouth. "This is the sort of thing I love," he managed to say. They walked along farther and turned down another street. The sun was setting and the air was still and hot. On this street there were no balconies, only little one-story houses. In front of every door at least one woman was seated. Mrs. Copperfield walked up to the window of one house and looked in. The room inside was almost entirely filled by a large double bed with an extremely bumpy mattress over which was spread a lace throw. An electric bulb under a lavender chiffon lamp shade threw a garish light over the bed, and there was a fan stamped *Panama City* spread open on the pillow.

The woman seated in front of this particular house was rather old. She sat on a stool with her elbows resting on her knees, and it seemed to Mrs. Copperfield, who had now turned to look at her, that she was probably a West Indian type. She was flat-chested and raw-boned, with very muscular arms and shoulders. Her long, disgruntled-looking face and part of her neck were carefully covered with a light-colored face powder, but her chest and arms remained dark. Mrs. Copperfield was amused to see that her dress was of lavender theatrical gauze. There was an attractive gray streak in her hair.

The Negress turned around, and when she saw that both Mr. and Mrs. Copperfield were watching her, she stood up and smoothed the folds of her dress. She was almost a giantess.

"Both of you for a dollar," she said.

"A dollar," Mrs. Copperfield repeated after her. Mr. Copperfield, who had been standing near by at the curb, came closer to them.

"Frieda," he said, "let's walk down some more streets."

"Oh, please!" said Mrs. Copperfield. "Wait a minute."

"A dollar is the best price I can make," said the Negress.

"If you care to stay here," suggested Mr. Copperfield, "I'll walk around a bit and come back for you in a little while. Maybe you'd better have some money with you. Here is a dollar and thirty-five cents, just in case. . . ."

"I want to talk to her," said Mrs. Copperfield, looking fixedly into space.

"I'll see you, then, in a few minutes. I'm restless," he announced, and he walked away.

"I love to be free," Mrs. Copperfield said to the woman after he had left. "Shall we go into your little room? I've been admiring it through the window. . . ."

Before she had finished her phrase the woman was pushing her through the door with both hands and they were inside the room. There was no rug on the floor, and the walls were bare. The only adornments were those which had been visible from the street. They sat down on the bed.

"I had a little gramophone in that corner over there," said the woman. "Someone who came off a ship lent it to me. His friend came and took it back."

"Tee-ta-ta-tee-ta-ta," she sang and tapped her heels for a few seconds. She took both Mrs. Copperfield's hands in her own and pulled her off the bed. "Come on now, honey." She hugged Mrs. Copperfield to her. "You're awful little and very sweet. You *are* sweet, and maybe you are lonesome." Mrs. Copperfield put her cheek on the woman's breast. The smell of the theatrical gauze reminded her of her first part in a school play. She smiled up at the Negress, looking as tender and as gentle as she was able.

"What do you do in the afternoons?" she asked the woman.

"Play cards. Go to a movie. . . ."

Mrs. Copperfield stepped away from her. Her cheeks were flame-red. They both listened to the people walking by. They could now hear every word that was being said outside the window. The Negress was frowning. She wore a look of deep concern.

"Time is gold, honey," she said to Mrs. Copperfield, "but maybe you're too young to realize that."

Mrs. Copperfield shook her head. She felt sad, looking at the Negress. "I'm thirsty," she said. Suddenly they heard a man's voice saying:

"You didn't expect to see me back so soon, Podie?" Then several girls laughed hysterically. The Negress's eyes came to life.

"Give me one dollar! Give me one dollar!" she screamed excitedly at Mrs. Copperfield. "You have stayed your time here anyway." Mrs. Copperfield hurriedly gave her a dollar and the Negress rushed out into the street. Mrs. Copperfield followed her.

In front of the house several girls were hanging onto a heavy man who was wearing a crushed linen suit. When he saw Mrs. Copperfield's Negress in the lavender dress, he broke away from the others and put his arms around her. The Negress rolled her eyes joyously and led him into the house, without so much as nodding good-by to Mrs. Copperfield. Very shortly the others ran down the street and Mrs. Copperfield was left alone. People passed by on either side of her, but none of them interested her yet. On the other hand, she herself was of great interest to everyone, particularly to those women who were seated in front of their doors. She was soon accosted by a girl with fuzzy hair.

"Buy me something, Momma," said the girl.

As Mrs. Copperfield did not answer but simply gave the girl a long sad look, the girl said:

"Momma, you can pick it out yourself. You can buy me even a feather, I don't care." Mrs. Copperfield shuddered. She thought she must be dreaming.

"What do you mean, a feather? What do you mean?"

The girl squirmed with delight.

"Oh, Momma," she said in a voice which broke in her throat. "Oh, Momma, you're funny! You're so funny. I don't know what is a feather, but anything you want with your heart, you know."

They walked down the street to a store and came out with a little box of face powder. The girl said good-by and disappeared round the corner with some friends. Once again Mrs. Copperfield was alone. The hacks went past filled with tourists. "Tourists, generally speaking," Mrs. Copperfield had written in her journal, "are human beings so impressed with the importance and immutability of their own manner of living that they are capable of traveling through the most fantastic places without experiencing anything more than a visual reaction. The hardier tourists often find that one place resembles another."

Very soon Mr. Copperfield came back and joined her. "Did you have a wonderful time?" he asked her.

She shook her head and looked up at him. Suddenly she felt so tired that she began to cry.

"Cry-baby," said Mr. Copperfield.

Someone came up behind them. A low voice said: "She was lost?" They turned around to see an intelligent-looking girl with sharp features and curly hair standing right behind them. "I wouldn't leave her in the streets here if I were you," she said.

"She wasn't lost; she was just depressed," Mr. Copperfield explained.

"Would you think I was fresh if I asked you to come to a nice restaurant where we can all eat dinner?" asked the girl. She was really quite pretty.

"Let's go," said Mrs. Copperfield vehemently. "By all means." She was now excited; she had a feeling that this girl would be all right. Like most people, she never really believed that one terrible thing would happen after another.

The restaurant wasn't really nice. It was very dark and very long and there was no one in it at all.

"Wouldn't you rather eat somewhere else?" Mrs. Copperfield asked the girl.

"Oh no! I would never go anywhere else. I'll tell you if you are not angry. I can get a little bit of money here when I come and bring some people."

"Well, let me give you the money and we'll go somewhere else. I'll give you whatever he gives you," said Mrs. Copperfield.

"That's silly," said the girl. "That's very silly."

"I have heard there is a place in this city where we can order wonderful lobster. Couldn't we go there?" Mrs. Copperfield was pleading with the girl now.

"No—that's silly." She called a waiter who had just arrived with some newspapers under his arm.

"Adalberto, bring us some meat and some wine. Meat first." This she said in Spanish.

"How well you speak English!" said Mr. Copperfield.

"I always love to be with Americans when I can," said the girl.

"Do you think they're generous?" asked Mr. Copperfield.

"Oh, sure," said the girl. "Sure they're generous. They're generous when they have the money. They're even more generous when they've got their family with them. I once knew a man. He was an American man. A real one, and he was staying at the Hotel Washington. You know that's the most beautiful hotel in the world. In the afternoon every day his wife would take a siesta. He would come quickly in a taxicab to Colon and he was so excited and frightened that he would not get back to his wife on time that he would never take me into a room and so he would go with me instead to a store and he would say to me: ‘Quick, quick—pick something—anything that you want, but be in a hurry about it.’”

“How terrifying!” said Mrs. Copperfield.

“It was terrible,” said the Spanish girl. “I always went so crazy that once I was really crazy and I said to him: ‘All right, I will buy this pipe for my uncle.’ I don’t like my uncle, but I had to give it to him.”

Mr. Copperfield roared with laughter.

“Funny, isn’t it?” said the girl. “I tell you if he ever comes back I will never buy another pipe for my uncle when he takes me to the store. She’s not a bad-looker.”

“Who?” asked Mr. Copperfield.

“Your wife.”

“I look terrible tonight,” said Mrs. Copperfield.

“Anyway it does not matter because you are married. You have nothing to worry about.”

“She’ll be furious with you if you tell her that,” said Mr. Copperfield.

“Why will she be furious? That is the most beautiful thing in the whole world, not to have something to worry about.”

“That is not what beauty is made of,” interposed Mrs. Copperfield. “What has the absence of worry to do with beauty?”

“That has everything to do with what is beautiful in the world. When you wake up in the morning and the first minute you open your eyes and you don’t know who you are or what your life has been—that is beautiful. Then when you know who you are and what day in your life it is and you still think you are sailing in the air like a happy bird—that is beautiful. That is, when you don’t have any worries. You can’t tell me you like to worry.”

Mr. Copperfield simpered. After dinner he suddenly felt very tired and he suggested that they go home, but Mrs. Copperfield was much too nervous, so she asked the Spanish girl if she would not consent to spend a little more time in her company. The girl said that she would if Mrs. Copperfield did not mind returning with her to the hotel where she lived.

They said good-by to Mr. Copperfield and started on their way.

The walls of the Hotel de las Palmas were wooden and painted a bright green. There were a good many birdcages standing in the halls and hanging from the ceilings. Some of them were empty. The girl's room was on the second floor and had brightly painted wooden walls the same as the corridors.

"Those birds sing all day long," said the girl, motioning to Mrs. Copperfield to sit down on the bed beside her. "Sometimes I say to myself: 'Little fools, what are you singing about in your cages?' And then I think: 'Pacifica, you are just as much a fool as those birds. You are also in a cage because you don't have any money. Last night you were laughing for three hours with a German man because he had given you some drinks. And you thought he was stupid.' I laugh in my cage and they sing in their cage."

"Oh well," said Mrs. Copperfield, "there really is no rapport between ourselves and birds."

"You don't think it is true?" asked Pacifica with feeling. "I tell you it is true."

She pulled her dress over her head and stood before Mrs. Copperfield in her underslip.

"Tell me," she said, "what do you think of those beautiful silk kimonos that the Hindu men sell in their shops? If I were with such a rich husband I would tell him to buy me one of those kimonos. You don't know how lucky you are. I would go with him every day to the stores and make him buy me pretty things instead of standing around and crying like a little baby. Men don't like to see women cry. You think they like to see women cry?"

Mrs. Copperfield shrugged her shoulders. "I can't think," she said.

"You're right. They like to see women laugh. Women have got to laugh all night. You watch some pretty girl one time. When she laughs she is ten years older. That is because she does it so much. You are ten years older when you laugh."

"True," said Mrs. Copperfield.

"Don't feel bad," said Pacifica. "I like women very much. I like women sometimes better than men. I like my grandmother and my mother and my sisters. We always had a good time together, the women in my house. I was always the best one. I was the smartest one and the one who did the most work. Now I wish I was back there in my nice house, contented. But I still want too many things, you know. I am lazy but I have a terrible temper too. I like these men that I meet very much. Sometimes they tell me what they will do in their future life when they get off the boat. I always wish for them that it will happen very soon. The damn boats. When they tell me they just want to go around the world all their life on a boat I tell them: 'You don't know what you're missing. I'm through with you, boy.' I don't like them when they are like that. But now I am in love with this nice man who is here in business. Most of the time he can pay my rent for me. Not always every week. He is very happy to have me. Most of the men are very happy to have me. I don't hold my head too high for that. It's from God that it comes." Pacifica crossed herself.

"I once was in love with an older woman," said Mrs. Copperfield eagerly. "She was no longer beautiful, but in her face I found fragments of beauty which were much more exciting to me than any beauty that I have known at its height. But who hasn't loved an older person? Good Lord!"

"You like things which are not what other people like, don't you? I would like to have this experience of loving an older woman. I think that is sweet, but I really am always in love with some nice man. It is lucky for me, I think. Some of the girls, they can't fall in love any more. They only think of money, money, money. You don't think so much about money, do you?" She asked Mrs. Copperfield.

"No, I don't."

"Now we rest a little while, yes?" The girl lay down on the bed and motioned to Mrs. Copperfield to lie down beside her. She yawned, folded Mrs. Copperfield's hand in her own, and fell asleep almost instantly. Mrs. Copperfield thought that she might as well get some sleep too. At that moment she felt very peaceful.

They were awakened by a terrific knocking at the door. Mrs. Copperfield opened her eyes and in a second she was a prey to the most overwhelming terror. She looked at Pacifica, and her friend's face was not very much more reassuring than her own.

"Callate!" she whispered to Mrs. Copperfield reverting to her native tongue.

"What is it? What is it?" asked Mrs. Copperfield in a harsh voice. "I don't understand Spanish."

"Don't say a word," repeated Pacifica in English.

"I can't lie here without saying a word. I know I can't. What is it?"

"Drunken man. In love with me. I know him well. He hurt me very bad when I sleep with him. His boat has come in again."

The knocking grew more insistent and they heard a man's voice saying:

"I know you are there, Pacifica, so open the bloody door."

"Oh, open it, Pacifica!" pleaded Mrs. Copperfield, jumping up from the bed. "Nothing could be worse than this suspense."

"Don't be crazy. Maybe he is drunk enough and he will go away."

Mrs. Copperfield's eyes were glazed. She was becoming hysterical.

"No, no—I have always promised myself that I would open the door if someone was trying to break in. He will be less of an enemy then. The longer he stays out there, the angrier he will get. The first thing I will say to him when I open the door is: 'We are your friends,' and then perhaps he will be less angry."

"If you make me even more crazy than I am I don't know what to do," said Pacifica. "Now we just wait here and see if he goes away. We might move this bureau against the door. Will you help me move it against the door?"

"I can't push anything!" Mrs. Copperfield was so weak that she slid along the wall onto the floor.

"Have I got to break the God-damned door in?" the man was saying.

Mrs. Copperfield rose to her feet, staggered over to the door, and opened it.

The man who came in was hatchet-faced and very tall. He had obviously had a great deal to drink.

"Hello, Meyer," said Pacifica. "Can't you let me get some sleep?" She hesitated a minute, and as he did not answer her she said again: "I was trying to get some sleep."

"I was tight asleep," said Mrs. Copperfield. Her voice was higher than usual and her face was very bright. "I am sorry we did not hear you right away. We must have kept you waiting a long time."

"Nobody ever kept me waiting a long time," said Meyer, getting redder in the face. Pacifica's eyes were narrowing. She was beginning to lose her temper.

"Get out of my room," she said to Meyer.

In answer to this, Meyer fell diagonally across the bed, and the impact of his body was so great that it almost broke the slats.

"Let's get out of here quickly," said Mrs. Copperfield to Pacifica. She was no longer able to show any composure. For one moment she had hoped that the enemy would suddenly burst into tears as they do sometimes in dreams, but now she was convinced that this would not happen. Pacifica was growing more and more furious.

"Listen to me, Meyer," she was saying. "You go back into the street right away. Because I'm not going to do anything with you except hit you in the nose if you don't go away. If you were not such hot stuff we could sit downstairs together and drink a glass of rum. I have hundreds of boy friends who just like to talk to me and drink with me until they are stiffs under the table. But you always try to bother me. You are like an ape-man. I want to be quiet."

"Who the hell cares about your house!" Meyer bellowed at her. "I could put all your houses together in a row and shoot at them like they were ducks. A boat's better than a house any day! Any time! Come rain, come shine! Come the end of the world!"

"No one is talking about houses except you," said Pacifica, stamping her foot, "and I don't want to listen to your foolish talk."

"Why did you lock the door, then, if you weren't living in this house like you were duchesses having tea together, and praying that none of us were ever going to come on shore again. You were afraid I'd spoil the furniture and spill something on the floor. My mother had a house, but I always slept in the house next door to her house. That's how much I care about houses!"

"You misunderstand," said Mrs. Copperfield in a trembling voice. She wanted very much to remind him gently that this was not a house but a room in a hotel. However, she felt not only afraid but ashamed to make this remark.

"Jesus Christ, I'm disgusted," Pacifica said to Mrs. Copperfield without even bothering to lower her voice.

Meyer did not seem to hear this, but instead he leaned over the edge of the bed with a smile on his face and stretched one arm towards Pacifica. He managed to get hold of the hem of her slip and pull her towards him.

"Not as long as I live!" Pacifica screamed at him, but he had already wrapped his arms around her waist and he was kneeling on the bed, pulling her towards him.

"Housekeeper," he said, laughing, "I'll bet if I took you out to sea you'd vomit. You'd mess up the boat. Now lie down here and stop talking."

Pacifica looked darkly at Mrs. Copperfield for a moment. "Well then," she said, "give me first the money, because I don't trust you. I will sleep with you only for my rent."

He dealt her a terrific blow on the mouth and split her lip. The blood started to run down her chin.

Mrs. Copperfield rushed out of the room. "I'll get help, Pacifica," she yelled over her shoulder. She ran down the hall and down the stairs, hoping to find someone to whom she could report Pacifica's plight, but she knew she would not have the courage to approach any men. On the ground floor she caught sight of a middle-aged woman who was knitting in her room with the door ajar. Mrs. Copperfield rushed in to her.

"Do you know Pacifica?" she gasped.

"Certainly I know Pacifica," said the woman. She spoke like an Englishwoman who has lived for many years among Americans. "I know everybody that lives here for more than two nights. I'm the proprietor of this hotel."

"Well then, do something quickly. Mr. Meyer is in there and he's very drunk."

"I don't do anything with Meyer when he's drunk." The woman was silent for a moment and the idea of doing something with Meyer struck her sense of humor and she chuckled. "Just imagine it," she said, "'Mr. Meyer, will you kindly leave the room? Pacifica is tired of you. Ha-ha-ha—*Pacifica* is tired of you.' Have a seat, lady, and calm down. There's some gin in that cut-glass decanter over there next to the avocados. Would you like some?"

"You know I'm not used to violence," Mrs. Copperfield

said. She helped herself to some gin, and repeated that she was not used to violence. "I doubt that I shall ever get over this evening. The stubbornness of that man. He was like an insane person."

"Meyer isn't insane," said the proprietress. "Some of them are much worse. He told me he was very fond of Pacifica. I've always been decent to him and he's never given me any trouble."

They heard screams from the next floor. Mrs. Copperfield recognized Pacifica's voice.

"Oh, please, let's get the police," pleaded Mrs. Copperfield.

"Are you crazy?" said the woman. "Pacifica doesn't want to get mixed up with the police. She would rather have both legs chopped off. I can promise you that is true."

"Well then, let's go up there," said Mrs. Copperfield. "I'm ready to do anything."

"Keep seated, Mrs.—what's your name? My name is Mrs. Quill."

"I'm Mrs. Copperfield."

"Well, you see, Mrs. Copperfield, Pacifica can take care of herself better than we can take care of her. The fewer people that get involved in a thing, the better off everybody is. That's one law I have here in the hotel."

"All right," said Mrs. Copperfield, "but meanwhile she might be murdered."

"People don't murder as easy as that. They do a lot of hitting around but not so much murdering. I've had some murders here, but not many. I've discovered that most things turn out all right. Of course some of them turn out bad."

"I wish I could feel as relaxed as you about everything. I don't understand how you can sit here, and I don't understand how Pacifica can go through things like this without ending up in an insane asylum."

"Well, she's had a lot of experience with these men. I don't think she's scared really. She's much tougher than us. She's just bothered. She likes to be able to have her room and do what she likes. I think sometimes women don't know what they want. Do you think maybe she has a little yen for Meyer?"

"How could she possibly? I don't understand what you mean."

"Well now, that boy she says she's in love with; now, I don't really think she's in love with him at all. She's had one after another of them like that. All nice dopes. They worship the ground she walks on. I think she gets so jealous and nervous while Meyer's away that she likes to pretend to herself that she likes these other little men better. When Meyer comes back she really believes she's mad at him for interfering. Now, maybe I'm right and maybe I'm wrong, but I think it goes a little something like that."

"I think it's impossible. She wouldn't allow him to hurt her, then, before she went to bed with him."

"Sure she would," said Mrs. Quill, "but I don't know anything about such things. Pacifica's a nice girl, though. She comes from a nice family too."

Mrs. Copperfield drank her gin and enjoyed it.

"She'll be coming down here soon to have a talk," said Mrs. Quill. "It's balmy here and they all enjoy themselves. They talk and they drink and they make love; they go on picnics; they go to the movies; they dance, sometimes all night long. . . . I need never be lonely unless I want to. . . . I can always go and dance with them if I feel like it. I have a fellow who takes me out to the dancing places whenever I want to go and I can always string along. I love it here. Wouldn't go back home for a load of monkeys. It's hot sometimes, but mostly balmy, and nobody's in a hurry. Sex doesn't interest me and I sleep like a baby. I am never bothered with dreams unless I eat something which sits on my stomach. You have to pay a price when you indulge yourself. I have a terrific yen for lobster à la Newburg, you see. I know exactly what I'm doing when I eat it. I go to Bill Grey's restaurant I should say about once every month with this fellow."

"Go on," said Mrs. Copperfield, who was enjoying this.

"Well, we order lobster à la Newburg. I tell you it's the most delicious thing in the world. . . ."

"How do you like frogs' legs?" asked Mrs. Copperfield.

"Lobster à la Newburg for me."

"You sound so happy I have a feeling I'm going to nestle right in here, in this hotel. How would you like that?"

"You do what you want to with your own life. That's my motto. For how long would you want to stay?"

"Oh, I don't know," said Mrs. Copperfield. "Do you think I'd have fun here?"

"Oh, no end of fun," said the proprietress. "Dancing, drinking . . . all the things that are pleasant in this world. You don't need much money, you know. The men come off the ships with their pockets bulging. I tell you this place is God's own town, or maybe the Devil's." She laughed heartily.

"No end of fun," she repeated. She got up from her chair with some difficulty and went over to a box-like phonograph which stood in the corner of the room. After winding it up she put on a cowboy song.

"You can always listen to this," she said to Mrs. Copperfield, "whenever your little heart pleases. There are the needles and the records and all you've got to do is wind it up. When I'm not here, you can sit in this rocker and listen. I've got famous people singing on those records like Sophie Tucker and Al Jolson from the United States, and I say that music is the ear's wine."

"And I suppose reading would be very pleasant in this room—at the same time that one listened to the gramophone," said Mrs. Copperfield.

"Reading—you can do all the reading you want."

They sat for some time listening to records and drinking gin. After an hour or so Mrs. Quill saw Pacifica coming down the hall. "Now," she said to Mrs. Copperfield, "here comes your friend."

Pacifica had on a little silk dress and bedroom slippers. She had made up her face very carefully and she had perfumed herself.

"Look what Meyer brought me," she said, coming towards them and showing them a very large wrist watch with a radium dial. She seemed to be in a very pleasant mood.

"You have been talking here one to the other," she said, smiling at them kindly. "Now suppose we all three of us go and take a walk through the street and get some beer or whatever we want."

"That would be nice," said Mrs. Copperfield. She was beginning to worry a bit about Mr. Copperfield. He hated her to disappear this way for a long time because it gave him an unbalanced feeling and interfered very much with his sleep. She promised herself to drop by the room and let him know that she was still out, but the very idea of going near the hotel made her shudder.

"Hurry up, girls," said Pacifica.

They went back to the quiet restaurant where Pacifica had taken Mr. and Mrs. Copperfield to dinner. Opposite was a very large saloon all lighted up. There was a ten-piece band playing there, and it was so crowded that the people were dancing in the streets.

Mrs. Quill said: "Oh boy, Pacifica! There's the place where you could have the time of your life tonight. Look at the time *they're* having."

"No, Mrs. Quill," said Pacifica. "We can stay here fine. The light is not so bright and it is more quiet and then we will go to bed."

"Yes," said Mrs. Quill, her face falling. Mrs. Copperfield thought she saw in Mrs. Quill's eyes a terribly pained and thwarted look.

"I'll go there tomorrow night," said Mrs. Quill softly. "It doesn't mean a thing. Every night they have those dances. That's because the boats never stop coming in. The girls are never tired either," she said to Mrs. Copperfield. "That's because they sleep all they want in the day-time. They can sleep as well in the day-time as they do at night. They don't get tired. Why should they? It doesn't make you tired to dance. The music carries you along."

"Don't be a fool," said Pacifica. "They're always tired."

"Well, which is it?" asked Mrs. Copperfield.

"Oh," said Mrs. Quill, "Pacifica is always looking on the darkest side of life. She's the gloomiest thing I ever knew."

"I don't look at the dark side, I look at the truth. You're a little foolish sometimes, Mrs. Quill."

"Don't talk to me that way when you know how much I love you," said Mrs. Quill, her lips beginning to tremble.

"I'm sorry, Mrs. Quill," said Pacifica gravely.

"There is something very lovable about Pacifica," Mrs. Copperfield thought to herself. "I believe she takes everyone quite seriously."

She took Pacifica's hand in her own.

"In a minute we're going to have something nice to drink," she said, smiling up at Pacifica. "Aren't you glad?"

"Yes, it will be nice to have something to drink," said Pacifica politely; but Mrs. Quill understood the gaiety of it. She rubbed her hands together and said: "I'm with you."

Mrs. Copperfield looked out into the street and saw Meyer walking by. He was with two blondes and some sailors.

"There goes Meyer," she said. The other two women looked across the street and they all watched him disappear.

Mr. and Mrs. Copperfield had gone over to Panama City for two days. The first day after lunch Mr. Copperfield proposed a walk towards the outskirts of the city. It was the first thing he always did when he arrived in a new place. Mrs. Copperfield hated to know what was around her, because it always turned out to be even stranger than she had feared.

They walked for a long time. The streets began to look all alike. On one side they went gradually uphill, and on the other they descended abruptly to the muddy regions near the sea. The stone houses were completely colorless in the hot sun. All the windows were heavily grilled; there was very little sign of life anywhere. They came to three naked boys struggling with a football, and turned downhill towards the water. A woman dressed in black silk came their way slowly. When they had passed her she turned around and stared at them shamelessly. They looked over their shoulders several times and they could still see her standing there watching them.

The tide was out. They made their way along the muddy beach. Back of them there was a huge stone hotel built in front of a low cliff, so that it was already in the shade. The mud flats and the water were still in the sunlight. They walked along until Mr. Copperfield found a large, flat rock for them to sit on.

"It's so beautiful here," he said.

A crab ran along sideways in the mud at their feet.

"Oh, look!" said Mr. Copperfield. "Don't you love them?"

"Yes, I do love them," she answered, but she could not suppress a rising feeling of dread as she looked around her at the landscape. Someone had painted the words *Cerveza—Beer* in green letters on the façade of the hotel.

Mr. Copperfield rolled up his trousers and asked if she would care to go barefoot to the edge of the water with him.

"I think I've gone far enough," she said.

"Are you tired?" he asked her.

"Oh, no. I'm not tired." There was such a pained expression on her face as she answered him that he asked her what the trouble was.

"I'm unhappy," she said.

"Again?" asked Mr. Copperfield. "What is there to be unhappy about now?"

"I feel so lost and so far away and so frightened."

"What's frightening about this?"

"I don't know. It's all so strange and it has no connection with anything."

"It's connected with Panama," observed Mr. Copperfield acidly. "Won't you ever understand that?" He paused. "I don't think really that I'm going to try to make you understand anything any more. . . . But I'm going to walk to the water's edge. You spoil all my fun. There's absolutely nothing anyone can do with you." He was pouting.

"Yes, I know. I mean go to the water's edge. I guess I am tired after all." She watched him picking his way among the tiny stones, his arms held out for balance like a tight-rope walker's, and wished that she were able to join him because she was so fond of him. She began to feel a little exalted. There was a strong wind, and some lovely sailboats were passing by very swiftly not far from the shore. She threw her head back and closed her eyes, hoping that perhaps she might become exalted enough to run down and join her husband. But the wind did not blow quite hard enough, and behind her closed eyes she saw Pacifica and Mrs. Quill standing in front of the Hotel de las Palmas. She had said good-by to them from the old-fashioned hack that she had hired to drive her to the station. Mr. Copperfield had preferred to walk, and she had been alone with her two friends. Pacifica had been wearing the satin kimono which Mrs. Copperfield had bought her, and a pair of bedroom slippers decorated with pompons. She had stood near the wall of the hotel squinting, and complaining about being out in the street dressed only in a kimono, but Mrs. Copperfield had had only a minute to say good-by to them and she would not descend from the carriage.

"Pacifica and Mrs. Quill," she had said to them, leaning out of the victoria, "you can't imagine how I dread leaving you even for only two days. I honestly don't know how I'll be able to stand it."

"Listen, Copperfield," Mrs. Quill had answered, "you go and have the time of your life in Panama. Don't you think about us for one minute. Do you hear me? My, oh my, if I was young enough to be going to Panama City with my husband, I'd be wearing a different expression on my face than you are wearing now."

"That means nothing to be going to Panama City with your husband," Pacifica had insisted very firmly. "That does not mean that she is happy. Everyone likes to do different things. Maybe Copperfield likes better to go fishing or buy dresses." She had then smiled gratefully at Pacifica.

"Well," Mrs. Quill had retorted somewhat feebly, "I'm sure you would be happy, Pacifica, if you were going to Panama City with your husband. . . . It's beautiful over there."

"Anyway, she has been in Paris," Pacifica had answered.

"Well, promise me you will be here when I get back," Mrs. Copperfield had begged them. "I'm so terrified that you might suddenly vanish."

"Don't make up such stories to yourself, my dear; life is difficult enough. Where are we going away?" Pacifica had said to her, yawning and starting to go inside. Then she had blown a kiss to Mrs. Copperfield from the doorway and waved her hand.

"Such fun, to be with them," she said audibly, opening her eyes. "They are a great comfort."

Mr. Copperfield was on his way back to the flat rock where she was sitting. He had a stone of strange texture and formation in his hand. He was smiling as he came towards her.

"Look," he said, "isn't this an amusing stone? It's really quite beautiful. I thought you would like to see it, so I brought it to you." Mrs. Copperfield examined the stone and said: "Oh, it is beautiful and very strange. Thanks ever so much." She looked at it lying in the palm of her hand. As she examined it Mr. Copperfield pressed her shoulder and said: "Look at the big steamer plowing through the water. Do you see it?" He twisted her neck slightly so that she might look in the right direction.

"Yes, I see it. It's wonderful too. . . . I think we had better be walking back home. It's going to be dark soon."

They left the beach and started walking through the streets again. It was getting dark, but there were more people standing around now. They commented openly on Mr. and Mrs. Copperfield as they passed by.

"It's really been the most wonderful day," Mr. Copperfield said. "You must have enjoyed some of it, because we've seen such incredible things." Mrs. Copperfield squeezed his hand harder and harder.

"I don't have wingèd feet like you," she said to him. "You must forgive me. I can't move about so easily. At thirty-three I have certain habits."

"That's bad," he answered. "Of course, I have certain habits too—habits of eating, habits of sleeping, habits of working—but I don't think that is what you meant, was it?"

"Let's not talk about it. That isn't what I meant, no."

The next day Mr. Copperfield said that they would go out and see some of the jungle. Mrs. Copperfield said they hadn't the proper equipment and he explained that he hadn't meant that they would go exploring into the jungle but only around the edges where there were paths.

"Don't let the word 'jungle' frighten you," he said. "After all it only means tropical forest."

"If I don't feel like going in I won't. It doesn't matter. Tonight we are going back to Colon, aren't we?"

"Well, maybe we'll be too tired and we'll have to stay here another night."

"But I told Pacifica and Mrs. Quill that we would be back tonight. They'll be so disappointed if we aren't."

"You aren't really considering *them*, are you? . . . After all, Frieda! Anyway, I don't think they'll mind. They'll understand."

"Oh, no, they won't," answered Mrs. Copperfield. "They'll be disappointed. I told them I would be back before midnight and that we would go out and celebrate. I'm positive that Mrs. Quill will be very disappointed. She loves to celebrate."

"Who on earth is Mrs. Quill?"

"Mrs. Quill . . . Mrs. Quill and Pacifica."

"Yes, I know, but it's so ridiculous. It seems to me you wouldn't care to see them for more than one evening. I should think it would be easy to know what they were like in a very short time."

"Oh, I know what they're like, but I do have so much fun with them." Mr. Copperfield did not answer.

They went out and walked through the streets until they came to a place where there were some buses. They inquired about schedules, and boarded a bus called *Shirley Temple.* On the insides of the doors were painted pictures of Mickey Mouse. The driver had pasted postcards of the saints and the holy Virgin on the windshield above his head. He was drinking a Coca-Cola when they got in the bus.

"*¿En que barco vinieron?*" asked the driver.

"*Venimos de Colon,*" said Mr. Copperfield.

"What was that?" Mrs. Copperfield asked him.

"Just what boat did we come on, and I answered we have just arrived from Colon. You see, most people have just come off a boat. It corresponds to asking people where they live, in other places."

"*J'adore Colon, c'est tellement* . . ." began Mrs. Copperfield. Mr. Copperfield looked embarrassed. "Don't speak in French to him. It doesn't make any sense. Speak to him in English."

"I adore Colon."

The driver made a face. "Dirty wooden city. I am sure you have made a big mistake. You will see. You will like Panama City better. More stores, more hospitals, wonderful cinemas, big clean restaurants, wonderful houses in stone; Panama City is a big place. When we drive through Ancon I will show you how nice the lawns are and the trees and the sidewalks. You can't show me anything like that in Colon. You know who likes Colon?" He leaned way over the back of his seat, and as they were sitting behind him he was breathing right in their faces.

"You know who likes Colon?" He winked at Mr. Copperfield. "They're all over the streets. That is what it is there; nothing else much. We have that here too, but in a separate place. If you like that you can go. We have everything here."

"You mean the whores?" asked Mrs. Copperfield in a clear voice.

"*Las putas*," Mr. Copperfield explained in Spanish to the driver. He was delighted at the turn in the conversation and fearful lest the driver should not get the full savor of it.

The driver covered his mouth with his hand and laughed.

"She loves that," said Mr. Copperfield, giving his wife a push.

"No—no," said the driver, "she could not."

"They've all been very sweet to me."

"*Sweet!*" said the driver, almost screaming. "There is not this much sweet in them." He made a tiny little circle with his thumb and forefinger. "No, not sweet—someone has been fooling you. He knows." He put his hand on Mr. Copperfield's leg.

"I'm afraid I don't know anything about it," said Mr. Copperfield. The driver winked at him again, and then he said, "She thinks she knows *las*—I will not say the word, but she has never met one of them."

"But I have. I have even taken a siesta with one."

"*Siesta!*" the driver roared with laughter. "Don't make fun please, lady. That is not very nice, you know." He suddenly looked very sober. "No, no, no." He shook his head sadly.

By now the bus had filled up and the driver was obliged to start off. Every time they stopped he would turn around and wag a finger at Mrs. Copperfield. They went through Ancon and passed several long low buildings set up on some small hills.

"Hospitals," yelled the driver for the benefit of Mr. and Mrs. Copperfield. "They have doctors here for every kind of thing in the world. The Army can go there for nothing. They eat and they sleep and they get well all for nothing. Some of the old ones live there for the rest of their lives. I dream to be in the American Army and not driving this dirty bus."

"I should hate to be regimented," said Mr. Copperfield with feeling.

"They are always going to dinners and balls, balls and dinners," commented the driver. There was a murmuring from the back of the bus. The women were all eager to know what the driver had said. One of them who spoke English explained rapidly to the others in Spanish. They all giggled about it for fully five minutes afterwards. The driver started to sing *Over There*, and the laughter reached the pitch of hysteria. They were now almost in the country, driving alongside a river. Across the river was a very new road and behind that a tremendous thick forest.

"Oh, look," said Mr. Copperfield, pointing to the forest. "Do you see the difference? Do you see how enormous the trees are and how entangled the undergrowth is? You can tell that even from here. No northern forests ever look so rich."

"That's true, they don't," said Mrs. Copperfield.

The bus finally stopped at a tiny pier. Only three women and the Copperfields remained inside by now. Mrs. Copperfield looked at them hoping that they were going to the jungle, too.

Mr. Copperfield descended from the bus and she followed reluctantly. The driver was already in the street smoking. He was standing beside Mr. Copperfield, hoping that he would start another conversation. But Mr. Copperfield was much too excited at being so near the jungle to think of anything else. The three women did not get out. They remained in their seats talking. Mrs. Copperfield looked back into the bus and stared at them with a perplexed expression on her face. She seemed to be saying: "Please come out, won't you?" They were embarrassed and they started to giggle again.

Mrs. Copperfield went over to the driver and said to him: "Is this the last stop?"

"Yes," he said.

"And they?"

"Who?" he asked, looking dumb.

"Those three ladies in the back."

"They ride. They are very nice ladies. This is not the first time they are riding on my bus."

"Back and forth?"

"Sure," said the driver.

Mr. Copperfield took Mrs. Copperfield's hand and led her onto the pier. A little ferry was coming towards them. There seemed to be no one on the ferry at all.

Suddenly Mrs. Copperfield said to her husband: "I just don't want to go to the jungle. Yesterday was such a strange, terrible day. If I have another day like it I shall be in an awful state. Please let me go back on the bus."

"But," said Mr. Copperfield, "after you've come all the way here, it seems to me so silly and so senseless to go back. I can assure you that the jungle will be of some interest to you. I've been in them before. You see the strangest-shaped leaves and flowers. And I'm sure you would hear wonderful noises. Some of the birds in the tropics have voices like xylophones, others like bells."

"I thought maybe when I arrived here I would feel inspired; that I would feel the urge to set out. But I don't in the least. Please let's not discuss it."

"All right," said Mr. Copperfield. He looked sad and lonely. He enjoyed so much showing other people the things he liked best. He started to walk away towards the edge of the water and stared out across the river at the opposite shore. He was very slight and his head was beautifully shaped.

"Oh, please don't be sad!" said Mrs. Copperfield, hurrying over to him. "I refuse to allow you to be sad. I feel like an ox. Like a murderer. But I would be such a nuisance over on the other side of the river in the jungle. You'll love it once you're over there and you will be able to go much farther in without me."

"But my dear—I don't mind . . . I only hope you will be able to get home all right on the bus. Heaven knows when I'll get home. I might decide to just wander around and around . . . and you don't like to be alone in Panama."

"Well then," said Mrs. Copperfield, "suppose I take the train back to Colon. It's a simple trip, and I have only one grip with me. Then you can follow me tonight if you get back early from the jungle, and if you don't you can come along tomorrow morning. We had planned to go back tomorrow anyway. But you must give me your word of honor that you will come."

"It's all so complicated," said Mr. Copperfield. "I thought we were going to have a nice day in the jungle. I'll come back tomorrow. The luggage is there, so there is no danger of my not coming back. Good-by." He gave her his hand. The ferry was scraping against the dock.

"Listen," she said, "if you're not back by twelve tonight, I shall sleep at the Hotel de las Palmas. I'll phone our hotel at twelve and see if you're there, in case I'm out."

"I won't be there until tomorrow."

"I'm at the Hotel de las Palmas if I'm not home, then."

"All right, but be good and get some sleep."

"Yes, of course I will."

He got into the boat and it pulled out.

"I hope his day has not been spoiled," she said to herself. The tenderness that she was feeling for him now was almost overwhelming. She got back on the bus and stared fixedly out the window because she did not want anyone to see that she was crying.

Mrs. Copperfield went straight to the Hotel de las Palmas. As she descended from the carriage she saw Pacifica walking towards her alone. She paid the driver and rushed up to her.

"Pacifica! How glad I am to see you!"

Pacifica's forehead had broken out. She looked tired.

"Ah, Copperfield," she said, "Mrs. Quill and I did not think we would ever see you again and now you are back."

"But, Pacifica, how can you say a thing like that? I'm surprised at both of you. Didn't I promise you I would be back before midnight and that we would celebrate?"

"Yes, but people often say this. After all, nobody gets angry if they don't come back."

"Let's go and say hello to Mrs. Quill."

"All right, but she has been in a terrible humor all the day, crying a lot and not eating anything."

"What on earth is the matter?"

"She had some fight, I think, with her boy friend. He don't like her. I tell her this but she won't listen."

"But the first thing she told me was that sex didn't interest her."

"To go to bed she don't care so much, but she is terribly sentimental, like she was sixteen years old. I feel sorry to see an old woman making such a fool."

Pacifica was still wearing her bedroom slippers. They went past the bar, which was filled with men smoking cigars and drinking.

"My God! how in one minute they make a place stink," said Pacifica. "I wish I could go and have a nice little house with a garden somewhere."

"I'm going to live here, Pacifica, and we'll all have lots of fun."

"The time for fun is over," said Pacifica gloomily.

"You'll feel better after we've all had a drink," said Mrs. Copperfield.

They knocked on Mrs. Quill's door.

They heard her moving about in her room and rattling some papers. Then she came to the door and opened it. Mrs. Copperfield noticed that she looked weaker than usual.

"Do come in," she said to them, "although I have nothing to offer you. You can sit down for a while."

Pacifica nudged Mrs. Copperfield. Mrs. Quill went back to her chair and took up a handful of bills which had been lying on the table near her.

"I must look over these. You will excuse me, but they're terribly important."

Pacifica turned to Mrs. Copperfield and talked softly.

"She can't even see them, because she does not have her glasses on. She is behaving like a child. Now she will be mad at us because her boy friend, like she calls him, has left her alone. I will not be treated like a dog very long."

Mrs. Quill overheard what Pacifica was saying, and reddened. She turned to Mrs. Copperfield.

"Do you still intend to come and live in this hotel?" she asked her.

"Yes," said Mrs. Copperfield buoyantly, "I wouldn't live anywhere else for the world. Even if you do growl at me."

"You probably will not find it comfortable enough."

"Don't growl at Copperfield," put in Pacifica. "First, she's been away for two days, and second, she doesn't know, like I do, what you are like."

"I'll thank you to keep your common little mouth shut," retorted Mrs. Quill, shuffling the bills rapidly.

"I am sorry to have disturbed you, Mrs. Quill," said Pacifica, rising to her feet and going towards the door.

"I wasn't yelling at Copperfield, I just said that I didn't think she would be comfortable here." Mrs. Quill laid down the bills. "Do you think she would be comfortable here, Pacifica?"

"A common little thing does not know anything about these questions," answered Pacifica and she left the room, leaving Mrs. Copperfield behind with Mrs. Quill.

Mrs. Quill took some keys from the top of her dresser and

motioned to Mrs. Copperfield to follow her. They walked through some halls and up a flight of stairs and Mrs. Quill opened the door of one of the rooms.

"Is it near Pacifica's?" asked Mrs. Copperfield.

Mrs. Quill without answering led her back through the halls and stopped near Pacifica's room.

"This is dearer," said Mrs. Quill, "but it's near Miss Pacifica's room if that's your pleasure and you can stand the noise."

"What noise?"

"She'll start yammering away and heaving things around the minute she wakes up in the morning. It don't affect her any. She's tough. She hasn't got a nerve in her body."

"Mrs. Quill—"

"Yes."

"Could you have someone bring me a bottle of gin to my room?"

"I think I can do that. . . . Well, I hope you are comfortable." Mrs. Quill walked away. "I'll have your bag sent up," she said, looking over her shoulder.

Mrs. Copperfield was appalled at the turn of events.

"I thought," she said to herself, "that they would go on the way they were forever. Now I must be patient and wait until everything is all right again. The longer I live, the less I can foresee anything." She lay down on the bed, put her knees up, and held onto her ankles with her hands.

"Be gay . . . be gay . . . be gay," she sang, rocking back and forth on the bed. There was a knock on the door and a man in a striped sweater entered the room without waiting for an answer to his knock.

"You ask for a bottle of gin?" he said.

"I certainly did—hooray!"

"And here's a suitcase. I'm putting it down here."

Mrs. Copperfield paid him and he left.

"Now," she said, jumping off the bed, "now for a little spot of gin to chase my troubles away. There just isn't any other way that's as good. At a certain point gin takes everything off your hands and you flop around like a little baby. Tonight I want to be a little baby." She took a hookerful, and shortly after that another. The third one she drank more slowly.

The brown shutters of her window were wide open and a

small wind was bringing the smell of frying fat into the room. She went over to the window and looked down into the alleyway which separated the Hotel de las Palmas from a group of shacks.

There was an old lady seated in a chair in the alleyway, eating her dinner.

"Eat every bit of it!" Mrs. Copperfield said. The old lady looked up dreamily, but she did not answer.

Mrs. Copperfield put her hand over her heart. "*Le bonheur*," she whispered, "*le bonheur* . . . what an angel a happy moment is—and how nice not to have to struggle too much for inner peace! I know that I shall enjoy certain moments of gaiety, willy-nilly. No one among my friends speaks any longer of character—and what interests us most, certainly, is finding out what we are like."

"Copperfield!" Pacifica burst into the room. Her hair was messy and she seemed to be out of breath. "Come on downstairs and have some fun. Maybe they are not the kind of men you like to be with, but if you don't like them you just walk away. Put some rouge on your face. Can I have some of your gin, please?"

"But a moment ago you said the time for fun was over!"

"What the hell!"

"By all means what the hell," said Mrs. Copperfield. "That's music to anyone's ears. . . . If you could only stop me from thinking, always, Pacifica."

"You don't want to stop thinking. The more you can think, the more you are better than the other fellow. Thank your God that you can think."

Downstairs in the bar Mrs. Copperfield was introduced to three or four men.

"This man is Lou," said Pacifica, pulling out a stool from under the bar and making her sit next to him.

Lou was small and over forty. He wore a light-weight gray suit that was too tight for him, a blue shirt, and a straw hat.

"She wants to stop thinking," said Pacifica to Lou.

"Who wants to stop thinking?" asked Lou.

"Copperfield. The little girl who is sitting on a stool, you big boob."

"Boob yourself. You're gettin' just like one of them New York girls," said Lou.

"Take me to Nueva York, take me to Nueva York," said Pacifica, bouncing up and down on her stool.

Mrs. Copperfield was shocked to see Pacifica behaving in this kittenish manner.

"Remember the belly buttons," said Lou to Pacifica.

"The belly buttons! The belly buttons!" Pacifica threw up her arms and screeched with delight.

"What about the belly buttons?" asked Mrs. Copperfield.

"Don't you think those two are the funniest words in the whole world? Belly and button—belly and button—in Spanish it is only *ombligo*."

"I don't think anything's *that* funny. But you like to laugh, so go ahead and laugh," said Lou, who made no attempt to talk to Mrs. Copperfield at all.

Mrs. Copperfield pulled at his sleeve. "Where do you come from?" she asked him.

"Pittsburgh."

"I don't know anything about Pittsburgh," said Mrs. Copperfield. But Lou was already turning his eyes in Pacifica's direction.

"Belly button," he said suddenly without changing his expression. This time Pacifica did not laugh. She did not seem to have heard him. She was standing up on the rail of the bar waving her arms in an agitated and officious manner.

"Well, well," she said, "I see that nobody has yet bought for Copperfield a drink. Am I with grown men or little boys? No, no . . . Pacifica will find other friends." She started to climb down from the bar, commanding Mrs. Copperfield to follow her. In the meantime she knocked off the hat of the man who was seated next to her with her elbow.

"Toby," she said to him, "you ought to be ashamed." Toby had a sleepy fat face and a broken nose. He was dressed in a dark brown heavy-weight suit.

"What? Did you want a drink?"

"Of course I wanted a drink." Pacifica's eyes were flashing.

Everyone was served and she settled back on her stool. "Come on now," she said, "what are we going to sing?"

"I'm a monotone," said Lou.

"Singing ain't in my line," said Toby.

They were all surprised to see Mrs. Copperfield throw her head back as though filled with a sudden feeling of exaltation and start to sing.

"Who cares if the sky cares to fall into the sea
Who cares what banks fail in Yonkers
As long as you've got the kiss that conquers
Why should I care?
Life is one long jubilee
As long as I care for you
And you care for me."

"Good, fine . . . now another one," said Pacifica in a snappy voice.

"Did you ever sing in a club?" Lou asked Mrs. Copperfield. Her cheeks were very red.

"Actually, I didn't. But when I was in the mood, I used to sing very loudly at a table in a restaurant and attract a good bit of attention."

"You wasn't such good friends with Pacifica the last time I was in Colon."

"My dear man, I wasn't here. I was in Paris, I suppose."

"She didn't tell me you were in Paris. Are you a screwball or were you really in Paris?"

"I was in Paris. . . . After all, stranger things have happened."

"Then you're fancy?"

"What do you mean, fancy?"

"Fancy is what fancy does."

"Well, if you care to be mysterious it's your right, but the word 'fancy' doesn't mean a thing to me."

"Hey," said Lou to Pacifica, "is she tryin' to be high-hat with me?"

"No, she's very intelligent. She's not like you."

For the first time Mrs. Copperfield sensed that Pacifica was proud of her. She realized that all this time Pacifica had been waiting to show her to her friends and she was not so sure that she was pleased. Lou turned to Mrs. Copperfield again.

"I'm sorry, Duchess. Pacifica says you got something on the ball and that I shouldn't address myself to you."

Mrs. Copperfield was bored with Lou, so she jumped down and went and stood between Toby and Pacifica. Toby was talking in a thick low voice with Pacifica.

"I'm tellin' you if she gets a singer in here and paints the place up a little she could make a lot of money on the joint. Everybody knows it's a good place to hit the hay in, but there ain't no music. You're here, you got a lot of friends, you got a way with you. . . ."

"Toby, I don't want to start with music and a lot of friends. I'm quiet. . . ."

"Yeah, you're quiet. This week you're quiet and maybe next week you won't want to be so quiet."

"I don't change my mind like that, Toby. I have a boy friend. I don't want to live in here much longer, you know."

"But you're livin' here now."

"Yes."

"Well, you want to make a little money. I'm tellin' you, with a little money we could fix up the joint."

"But why must I be here?"

"Because you got contacts."

"I never saw such a man. Talking all the time about business."

"You're not such a bad one for business yourself. I saw you hustlin' up a drink for that pal of yours. You get your cut, don't you?"

Pacifica kicked Toby with her heel.

"Listen, Pacifica, I like to have fun. But I can't see somethin' that could be coinin' the money takin' in petty cash."

"Stop being so busy." Pacifica pushed his hat off his head. He realized there was nothing to be done and sighed.

"How's Emma?" he asked her listlessly.

"Emma? I have not seen her since that night on the boat. She looked so gorgeous dressed up like a sailor."

"Women look fantastic dressed up in men's clothes," put in Mrs. Copperfield with enthusiasm.

"That's what you think," said Toby. "They look better to me in ruffles."

"She was only talking for a *minute* they look nice," said Pacifica.

"Not for me," said Toby.

"All right, Toby, maybe not for you, but for her they look nice that way."

"I still think I'm right. It ain't only a matter of opinion."

"Well, you can't prove it mathematically," said Mrs. Copperfield. Toby looked at her with no interest in his face.

"What about Emma?" said Pacifica. "You are really not interested finally in somebody?"

"You asked me to talk about somethin' besides business, so I asked you about Emma, just to show how sociable I am. We both know her. We were on a party together. Ain't that the right thing to do? How's Emma, how's your momma and your poppa. That's the kind of talk you like. Next I tell you how my family is gettin' along and maybe I bring in another friend who we both forgot we knew, and then we say prices are goin' up and comes the revolution and we all eat strawberries. Prices are goin' up fast and that's why I wanted you to cash in on this joint."

"My God!" said Pacifica, "my life is hard enough and I am all alone, but I can still enjoy myself like a young girl. *You*, you are an old man."

"Your life don't have to be hard, Pacifica."

"Well, your life is still very hard and you are always trying to make it easy. That's the hardest part even of your life."

"I'm just waitin' to get a break. With my ideas and a break my life can be easy overnight."

"And then what will you do?"

"Keep it that way or maybe make it even easier. I'll be plenty busy."

"You will never have any time for anything."

"What's a guy like me want time for—plantin' tulips?"

"You don't enjoy to talk to me, Toby."

"Sure. You're friendly and cute and you got a good brain aside from a few phony ideas."

"And what about me? Am I friendly and cute too?" asked Mrs. Copperfield.

"Sure. You're all friendly and cute."

"Copperfield, I think we have just been insulted," said Pacifica, drawing herself up.

Mrs. Copperfield started to march out of the room in mock anger, but Pacifica was already thinking of something else and Mrs. Copperfield found herself to be in the ridiculous position of the performer who is suddenly without an audience. She came back to the bar.

"Listen," said Pacifica, "go upstairs and knock on Mrs. Quill's door. Tell her that Mr. Toby wants to meet her very much. Don't say Pacifica sent you. She will know this anyway and it will be easier for her if you don't say it. She will love to come down. That I know like if she was my mother."

"Oh, I'd love to, Pacifica," said Mrs. Copperfield, running out of the room.

When Mrs. Copperfield arrived in Mrs. Quill's room, Mrs. Quill was busy cleaning the top drawer of her dresser. It was very quiet in her room and very hot.

"I never have the heart to throw these things away," said Mrs. Quill, turning around and patting her hair. "I suppose you've met half of Colon," she said sadly, studying Mrs. Copperfield's flushed face.

"No, I haven't, but would you care to come down and meet Mr. Toby?"

"Who is Mr. Toby, dear?"

"Oh, please come, please come just for me."

"I will, dear, if you'll sit down and wait while I change into something better."

Mrs. Copperfield sat down. Her head was spinning. Mrs. Quill pulled out a long black silk dress from her closet. She drew it over her head and then selected some strings of black beads from her jewel-box, and a cameo pin. She powdered her face carefully and stuck several more hairpins into her hair.

"I'm not going to bother to take a bath," she said when she had finished. "Now, do you really think that I should meet this Mr. Toby, or do you think perhaps another night would be better?"

Mrs. Copperfield took Mrs. Quill's hand and pulled her out of the room. Mrs. Quill's entrance into the barroom was gracious and extremely formal. She was already using the hurt that her beau had caused her to good advantage.

"Now, dear," she said quietly to Mrs. Copperfield, "tell me which one is Mr. Toby."

"That one over there, sitting next to Pacifica," Mrs. Copperfield said hesitantly. She was fearful lest Mrs. Quill should find him completely unattractive and leave the room.

"I see. The stout gentleman."

"Do you hate fat people?"

"I don't judge people by their bodies. Even when I was a young girl I liked men for their minds. Now that I'm middle-aged I see how right I was."

"I've always been a body-worshipper," said Mrs. Copperfield, "but that doesn't mean that I fall in love with people who have beautiful bodies. Some of the bodies I've liked have been awful. Come, let's go over to Mr. Toby."

Toby stood up for Mrs. Quill and took off his hat.

"Come sit down with us and have a drink."

"Let me get my bearings, young man. Let me get my bearings."

"This bar belongs to you, don't it?" said Toby, looking worried.

"Yes, yes," said Mrs. Quill blandly. She was staring at the top of Pacifica's head. "Pacifica," she said, "don't you drink too much. I have to watch out for you."

"Don't you worry, Mrs. Quill. I have been taking care of myself for a long time." She turned to Lou and said solemnly: "Fifteen years." Pacifica was completely natural. She behaved as though nothing had occurred between her and Mrs. Quill. Mrs. Copperfield was enchanted. She put her arms around Mrs. Quill's waist and hugged her very tight.

"Oh," she said, "oh, you make me so happy!"

Toby smiled. "The girl's feelin' good, Mrs. Quill. Now don't you want a drink?"

"Yes, I'll have a glass of gin. It pains me the way these girls come away from their homes so young. I had my home and my mother and my sisters and my brothers until the age of twenty-six. Even so, when I got married I felt like a scared rabbit. As if I was going out into the world. Mr. Quill was like a family to me, though, and it wasn't until he died that I really got out into the world. I was in my thirties then, and more of a scared rabbit than ever. Pacifica's really been out in the world much longer than I have. You know, she is like an old sea captain. Sometimes I feel very silly when she tells me of some of her experiences. My eyes almost pop right out of my head. It isn't so much a question of age as it is a question of experience. The Lord has spared me more than he has spared Pacifica. She hasn't been spared a single thing. Still, she's not as nervous as I am."

"Well, she certainly don't know how to look out for herself for someone who's had so much experience," said Toby. "She don't know a good thing when she sees it."

"Yes, I expect you're right," said Mrs. Quill, warming up to Toby.

"Sure I'm right. But she's got lots of friends here in Panama, ain't she?"

"I dare say Pacifica has a great many friends," said Mrs. Quill.

"Come on, you know she's got lots of friends, don't you?"

As Mrs. Quill looked as though she had been somewhat startled by the pressing tone in his voice, Toby decided he was hurrying things too much.

"Who the hell cares, anyway?" he said, looking at her out of the corner of his eye. This seemed to have the right effect on Mrs. Quill, and Toby breathed a sigh of relief.

Mrs. Copperfield went over to a bench in the corner and lay down. She shut her eyes and smiled.

"That's the best thing for her," said Mrs. Quill to Toby. "She's a nice woman, a dear sweet woman, and she's had a little too much to drink. Pacifica, she can really take care of herself like she says. I've seen her drink as much as a man, but with her it's different. As I said, she's had all the experience in the world. Now, Mrs. Copperfield and me, we have to watch ourselves more carefully or else have some nice man watching out for us."

"Yeah," said Toby, twisting around on his stool. "Bartender, another gin. You want one, don't you?" he asked Mrs. Quill.

"Yes, if you'll watch out for me."

"Sure I will. I'll even take you home in my arms if you fall down."

"Oh, no." Mrs. Quill giggled and flushed. "You wouldn't try that, young man. I'm heavy, you know."

"Yeah. . . . Say—"

"Yes?"

"Would you mind telling me something?"

"I'd be delighted to tell you anything you'd like to hear."

"How is it you ain't never bothered to fix this place up?"

"Oh, dear, isn't it awful? I've always promised myself I would and I never get around to it."

"No dough?" asked Toby. Mrs. Quill looked vague. "Haven't you got no money to fix it up with?" he repeated.

"Oh yes, certainly I have." Mrs. Quill looked around at the bar. "I even have some things upstairs that I always promised myself to hang up on the walls here. Everything is so dirty, isn't it? I feel ashamed."

"No, no," said Toby impatiently. He was now very animated. "That ain't what I mean at all."

Mrs. Quill smiled at him sweetly.

"Listen," said Toby, "I been handlin' restaurants and bars and clubs all my life, and I can make them go."

"I'm certain that you can."

"I'm tellin' you that I can. Listen, let's get out of here; let's go some place else where we can really talk. Any place in town you name I'll take you to. It's worth it to me and it'll be worth it to you even more. You'll see. We can have more to drink or maybe a little bite to eat. Listen"—he grabbed hold of Mrs. Quill's upper arm—"would you like to go to the Hotel Washington?"

At first Mrs. Quill did not react, but when she realized what he had said, she answered that she would enjoy it very much, in a voice trembling with emotion. Toby jumped off the stool, pulled his hat down over his face, and started walking out of the bar, saying: "Come on, then," over his shoulder to Mrs. Quill. He looked annoyed but resolute.

Mrs. Quill took Pacifica's hand in her own and told her that she was going to the Hotel Washington.

"If there was any possible way I would take you with us, I would, Pacifica. I feel very badly to be going there without you, but I don't see how you can come, do you?"

"Now, don't you worry about that, Mrs. Quill. I'm having a very good time here," said Pacifica in a sincerely world-weary tone of voice.

"That's a hocus-pocus joint," said Lou.

"Oh no," said Pacifica, "it is very nice there, very beautiful.

She will have a lovely time." Pacifica pinched Lou. "You don't know," she said to him.

Mrs. Quill walked out of the bar slowly and joined Toby on the sidewalk. They got into a hack and started for the hotel. Toby was silent. He sprawled way back in his seat and lighted a cigar.

"I regret that automobiles were ever invented," said Mrs. Quill.

"You'd go crazy tryin' to get from one place to another if they wasn't."

"Oh, no. I always take my time. There isn't anything that can't wait."

"That's what you think," said Toby in a surly tone of voice, sensing that this was just the thing that he would have to combat in Mrs. Quill. "It's just that extra second that makes Man O'War or any other horse come in first," he said.

"Well, life isn't a horse race."

"Nowadays that's just what life is."

"Well, not for me," said Mrs. Quill.

Toby was disgusted.

The walk which led up to the veranda of the Hotel Washington was lined with African date-palms. The hotel itself was very impressive. They descended from the carriage. Toby stood in the middle of the walk between the scraping palms and looked towards the hotel. It was all lighted up. Mrs. Quill stood beside Toby.

"I'll bet they soak you for drinks in there," said Toby. "I'll bet they make two hundred per cent profit."

"Oh, please," said Mrs. Quill, "if you don't feel you can afford it let's take a carriage and go back. The ride is so pleasant anyway." Her heart was beating very quickly.

"Don't be a God-damn fool!" Toby said to her, and they headed for the hotel.

The floor in the lobby was of imitation yellow marble. There was a magazine stand in one corner where the guests were able to buy chewing gum and picture postcards, maps, and souvenirs. Mrs. Quill felt as though she had just come off a ship. She wandered about in circles, but Toby went straight up to the man behind the magazine stand and asked him where he could get a drink. He suggested to Toby that they go out on the terrace.

"It's generally where everyone goes," he said.

They were seated at a table on the edge of the terrace, and they had a very nice view of a stretch of beach and the sea.

Between them on the table there was a little lamp with a rose-colored shade. Toby began at once to twirl the lamp shade. His cigar by now was very short and very wet.

Here and there on the terrace small groups of people were talking together in low voices.

"Dead!" said Toby.

"Oh, I think it's lovely," said Mrs. Quill. She was shivering a little, as the wind kept blowing over her shoulder, and it was a good deal cooler than in Colon.

A waiter was standing beside them with his pencil poised in the air waiting for an order.

"What do you want?" asked Toby.

"What would you suggest, young man, that's really delicious?" said Mrs. Quill, turning to the waiter.

"Fruit punch à la Washington Hotel," said the waiter abruptly.

"That *does* sound good."

"O.K.," said Toby, "bring one of them and a straight rye for me."

When Mrs. Quill had sipped quite a bit of her drink Toby spoke to her. "So you got the dough, but you never bothered to fix it up."

"Mmmmmm!" said Mrs. Quill. "They've got every kind of fruit in the world in this drink. I'm afraid I'm behaving just like a baby, but there's no one who likes the good things in this world better than me. Of course, I've never had to do without them, you know."

"You don't call livin' the way you're livin' havin' the good things in life, do you?" said Toby.

"I live much better than you think. How do you know how I live?"

"Well, you could have more style," said Toby, "and you could have that easy. I mean the place could be better very easy."

"It probably would be easy, wouldn't it?"

"Yeah." Toby waited to see if she would say anything more by herself before he addressed her again.

"Take all these people here," said Mrs. Quill. "There aren't many of them, but you'd think they'd all get together instead of staying in twos and threes. As long as they're all living here in this gorgeous hotel, you'd think they'd have on their ball dresses and be having a wonderful time every minute, instead of looking out over the terrace or reading. You'd think they'd always be dressed up to the hilt and flirting together instead of wearing those plain clothes."

"They got on sport clothes," said Toby. "They don't want to be bothered dressin'. They probably come here for a rest. They're probably business people. Maybe some of them belong to society. They got to rest too. They got so many places they got to show up at when they're home."

"Well, I wouldn't pay out all that money just to rest. I'd stay in my own house."

"It don't make no difference. They got plenty."

"That's true enough. Isn't it sad?"

"I don't see nothin' sad about it. What looks sad to me," said Toby, leaning way over and crushing his cigar out in the ash-tray, "what looks sad to me is that you've got that bar and hotel set-up and you ain't makin' enough money on it."

"Yes, isn't it terrible?"

"I like you and I don't like to see you not gettin' what you could." He took hold of her hand with a certain amount of gentleness. "Now, I know what to do with your place. Like I told you before. Do you remember what I told you before?"

"Well, you've told me so many things."

"I'll tell you again. I've been working with restaurants and bars and hotels all my life and makin' them go. I said makin' them go. If I had the dough right now, if it wasn't that I'm short because I had to help my brother and his family out of a jam, I'd take my own dough before you could say Jack Robinson and sink it into your joint and fix it up. I know that I'd get it right back anyway, so it wouldn't be no act of charity."

"Certainly it wouldn't," said Mrs. Quill. Her head was swaying gently from side to side. She looked at Toby with luminous eyes.

"Well, I got to go easy now until next October, when I got a big contract comin'. A contract with a chain. I could use a little money now, but that ain't the point."

"Don't bother to explain, Toby," said Mrs. Quill.

"What do you mean, don't bother to explain? Ain't you interested in what I've got to tell you?"

"Toby, I'm interested in every word you have to say. But you must not worry about the drinks. Your friend Flora Quill tells you that you needn't worry. We're out to enjoy ourselves and Heaven knows we're going to, aren't we, Toby?"

"Yeah, but just let me explain this to you. I think the reason you ain't done nothin' about the place is because you didn't know where to begin, maybe. Understand? You don't know the ropes. Now, I know all about gettin' orchestras and carpenters and waiters, cheap. I know how to do all that. You got a name, and lots of people like to come there even now because they can go right from the bar upstairs. Pacifica is a big item because she knows every bloke in town and they like her and they trust her. The trouble is, you ain't got no atmosphere, no bright lights, no dancin'. It ain't pretty or big enough. People go to the other places and then they come to your place late. Just before they go to bed. If I was you, I'd turn over in my grave. It's the other guys that are gettin' the meat. You only get a little bit. What's left near the bone, see?"

"The meat nearest the bone is the sweetest," said Mrs. Quill.

"Hey, is there any use my talkin' to you or are you gonna be silly? I'm serious. Now, you got some money in the bank. You got money in the bank, ain't you?"

"Yes, I've got money in the bank," said Mrs. Quill.

"O.K. Well, you let me help you fix up the joint. I'll take everything off your hands. All you got to do is lie back and enjoy the haul."

"Nonsense," said Mrs. Quill.

"Now come on," said Toby, beginning to get angry. "I'm not askin' you for nothin' except maybe a little percentage in the place and a little cash to pay expenses for a while. I can do it all for you cheap and quick and I can manage the joint for you so that it won't cost you much more than it's costin' you now."

"But I think that's wonderful, Toby. I think it's so wonderful."

"You don't have to tell me it's wonderful. I know it's wonderful. It ain't wonderful, it's swell. It's marvelous. We ain't got no time to lose. Have another drink."

"Yes, yes."

"I'm spendin' my last cent on you," he said recklessly.

Mrs. Quill was drunk by now and she just nodded her head.

"It's worth it." He sat back in his chair and studied the horizon. He was very busy calculating in his head. "What percentage in the place do you think I ought to get? Don't forget I'm gonna manage the whole thing for you for a year."

"Oh, dear," said Mrs. Quill, "I'm sure I haven't got any idea." She smiled at him blissfully.

"O.K. How much advance will you give me just so I can stay on here until I get the place goin'?"

"I don't know."

"Well, we'll figure it this way," said Toby cautiously. He was not sure yet that he had taken the right move. "We'll figure it this way. I don't want you to do more than you can. I want to go in this deal with you. You tell me how much money you got in the bank. Then I'll figure out how much fixin' the place up will cost you and then how much I think is a minimum for me. If you ain't got much I'm not gonna let you go busted. You be honest with me and I'll be honest with you."

"Toby," said Mrs. Quill seriously, "don't you think I'm an honest woman?"

"What the hell," said Toby, "do you think I'd put a proposition like that to you if I didn't think you were?"

"No, I guess you wouldn't," said Mrs. Quill sadly.

"How much you got?" asked Toby, looking at her intently.

"What?" asked Mrs. Quill.

"How much money you got in the bank?"

"I'll show you, Toby. I'll show you right away." She started to fumble in her big black leather pocketbook.

Toby had his jaw locked and his eyes averted from the face of Mrs. Quill.

"Messy—messy—messy," Mrs. Quill was saying. "I have everything in this pocketbook but the kitchen stove."

There was a very still look in Toby's eyes as he stared first at the water and then at the palm trees. He considered that he had already won, and he was beginning to wonder whether or not it was really a good thing.

"Dear me," said Mrs. Quill, "I live just like a gypsy. Twenty-two fifty in the bank and I don't even care."

Toby snatched the book from her hands. When he saw that the balance was marked twenty-two dollars and fifty cents, he rose to his feet and, clutching his napkin in one hand and his hat in the other, he walked off the terrace.

After Toby had left the table so abruptly, Mrs. Quill felt deeply ashamed of herself.

"He's just so disgusted," she decided, "that he can't even look me in the face without feeling like throwing up. It's because he thinks I'm balmy to go around gay as a lark with only twenty-two fifty in the bank. Well, well, I expect I'd better start worrying a little more. When he comes back I'll tell him I'll turn over a new leaf."

Everyone had left the terrace by now with the exception of the waiter who had served Mrs. Quill. He stood with his hands behind his back and stared straight ahead of him.

"Sit down for a bit and talk to me," said Mrs. Quill to him. "I'm lonesome on this dark old terrace. It's really a beautiful terrace. You might tell me something about yourself. How much money have you got in the bank? I know you think I'm fresh to ask you, but I'd really like to know."

"Why not?" answered the waiter. "I've got about three hundred and fifty dollars in the bank." He did not sit down.

"Where did you get it?" asked Mrs. Quill.

"From my uncle."

"I guess you feel pretty secure."

"No."

Mrs. Quill began to wonder whether or not Toby would come back at all. She pressed her hands together and asked the young waiter if he knew where the gentleman who had been sitting next to her had gone.

"Home, I guess," said the waiter.

"Well, let's just have one look in the lobby," said Mrs. Quill nervously. She beckoned to the waiter to follow her.

They went into the lobby and together they searched the faces of the guests, who were either standing around in groups or sitting along the wall in armchairs. The hotel was much livelier now than it had been when Mrs. Quill first arrived with Toby. She was deeply troubled and hurt at not seeing Toby anywhere.

"I guess I'd better go home and let you get some sleep," she said absentmindedly to the waiter, "but not before I've bought something for Pacifica. . . ." She had been trembling a little, but the thought of Pacifica filled her with assurance.

"Such an awful, dreadful, mean thing to be alone in the world even for a minute," she said to the waiter. "Come with me and help me choose something, nothing important, just some remembrance of the hotel."

"They're all the same," said the waiter, following her reluctantly. "Just a lot of junk. I don't know what your friend wants. You might get her a little pocketbook with *Panama* painted on it."

"No, I want it to be specially marked with the name of the hotel."

"Well," said the waiter, "most people don't go in for that."

"Oh my—oh my," said Mrs. Quill emphatically, "must I always be told what other people do? I've had just about enough of it." She marched up to the magazine stand and said to the young man behind the counter: "Now, I want something with *Hotel Washington* written on it. For a woman."

The man looked through his stock and pulled out a handkerchief on the corner of which were painted two palm trees and the words: *Souvenir of Panama.*

"Most people prefer this, though," he said, drawing a tremendous straw hat from under the counter and placing it on his own head.

"You see, it gives you as much shadow as an umbrella and it is very becoming." There was nothing written on the hat at all.

"That handkerchief," continued the young man, "most people consider it kind of, you know . . ."

"My dear young man," said Mrs. Quill, "I expressly told you that I wanted this gift to bear the words *Hotel Washington* and if possible also a picture of the hotel."

"But, lady, nobody wants that. People don't want pictures of hotels on their souvenirs. Palm trees, sunsets, sometimes even bridges, but not hotels."

"Do you or do you not have anything that bears the words *Hotel Washington*?" said Mrs. Quill, raising her voice.

The salesman was beginning to get angry. "I *do* have," he said, his eyes flashing, "if you will wait one minute please, madam." He opened a little gate and went out into the lobby.

He was back in a short time carrying a heavy black ash-tray which he set on the counter in front of Mrs. Quill. The name of the hotel was stamped in the center of the ash-tray in yellow lettering.

"Is this the type of thing you wanted?" asked the salesman.

"Why, yes," said Mrs. Quill, "it is."

"All right, madam, that'll be fifty cents."

"That's not worth fifty cents," whispered the waiter to Mrs. Quill.

Mrs. Quill looked through her purse; she was able to find no more than a quarter in change and no bills at all.

"Look," she said to the young man, "I'm the proprietress of the Hotel de las Palmas. I will show you my bank book with my address written in the front of it. Are you going to trust me with this ash-tray just this once? You see, I came with a gentleman friend and we had a falling out and he went home ahead of me."

"I can't help that, madam," said the salesman.

Meanwhile one of the assistant managers who had been watching the group at the magazine stand from another corner of the lobby thought it time to intervene. He was exceedingly suspicious of Mrs. Quill, who did not appear to him to measure up to the standard of the other guests in any way, not even from a distance. He also wondered what could possibly be keeping the waiter standing in front of the magazine stand for such a long while. He walked over to them looking as serious and as thoughtful as he was able.

"Here's my bank book," Mrs. Quill was saying to the salesman.

The waiter, seeing the assistant manager approaching, was frightened and immediately presented Mrs. Quill with the check for the drinks that she and Toby had consumed together.

"You owe six dollars on the terrace," he said to Mrs. Quill.

"Didn't he pay for them?" she said. "I guess he must have been in an awful state."

"Can I help you?" the assistant manager asked of Mrs. Quill.

"I'm sure you can," she said. "I'm the owner of the Hotel de las Palmas."

"I'm sorry," the manager said, "but I'm not familiar with the Hotel de las Palmas."

"Well," said Mrs. Quill, "I have no money with me. I came here with a gentleman, we had a falling out, but I have my bank book here with me which will prove to you that I will have the money as soon as I can run over to the bank tomorrow. I can't sign a check because it's in the savings bank."

"I'm sorry," said the assistant manager, "but we extend credit only to guests residing in the hotel."

"I do that too, in my hotel," said Mrs. Quill, "unless it is something out of the ordinary."

"We make a rule of never extending credit . . ."

"I wanted to take this ash-tray home to my girl friend. She admires your hotel."

"That ash-tray is the property of the Hotel Washington," said the assistant manager, frowning sternly at the salesman, who said quickly: "She wanted something with *Hotel Washington* written on it. I didn't have anything so I thought I'd sell her one of these—for fifty cents," he added, winking at the assistant manager, who was standing farther and farther back on his heels.

"These ash-trays," he repeated, "are the property of the Hotel Washington. We have only a limited number of them in stock and every available tray is in constant use."

The salesman, not caring to have anything more to do with the ash-tray lest he lose his job, carried it back to the table from which he had originally removed it and took up his position again behind the counter.

"Do you want either the handkerchief or the hat?" he asked Mrs. Quill as though nothing had happened.

"She's got all the hats and the hankies she needs," said Mrs. Quill. "I suppose I'd better go home."

"Would you care to come to the desk with me and settle the bill?" asked the assistant manager.

"Well, if you'll just wait until tomorrow—"

"I'm afraid it is definitely against the rules of the hotel, madam. If you'll just step this way with me." He turned to the waiter, who was following the conversation intently. "*Te necesitan afuera*," he said to him, "go on."

The waiter was about to say something, but he decided against it and walked slowly away towards the terrace. Mrs. Quill began to cry.

"Wait a minute," she said, taking a handkerchief from her bag. "Wait a minute—I would like to telephone to my friend Pacifica."

The assistant manager pointed in the direction of the telephone booths, and she hurried away, her face buried in her handkerchief. Fifteen minutes later she returned, crying more pitifully than before.

"Mrs. Copperfield is coming to get me—I told her all about it. I think I'll sit down somewhere and wait."

"Does Mrs. Copperfield have the necessary funds with which to cover your bill?"

"I don't know," said Mrs. Quill, walking away from him.

"You mean you don't know whether or not she will be able to pay your bill?"

"Yes, yes, she'll pay my bill. Please let me sit down over there."

The manager nodded. Mrs. Quill fell into an armchair that stood beside a tall palm tree. She covered her face with her hands and continued to cry.

Twenty minutes later Mrs. Copperfield arrived. In spite of the heat she was wearing a silver-fox cape which she had brought with her for use only in higher altitudes.

Although she was perspiring and badly made up, she felt assured of being treated with a certain amount of deference by the hotel employees because of the silver-fox cape.

She had awakened quite some time before and was again a little drunk. She rushed up to Mrs. Quill and kissed her on the top of her head.

"Where's the man who made you cry?" she asked.

Mrs. Quill looked around through her tear-veiled eyes and pointed to the assistant manager. Mrs. Copperfield beckoned to him with her index finger.

He came over to them and she asked him where she could get some flowers for Mrs. Quill.

"There's nothing like flowers when you're either sick at heart or physically ill," she said to him. "She's been under a terrible strain. Would you get some flowers?" she asked, taking a twenty-dollar bill from her purse.

"There is no florist in the hotel," said the assistant manager.

"That's not very luxurious," said Mrs. Copperfield.

He did not reply.

"Well then," she continued, "the next best thing to do is to buy her something nice to drink. I suggest that we all go to the bar."

The assistant manager declined.

"But," said Mrs. Copperfield, "I insist that you come along. I want to talk things over with you. I think you've been horrid."

The assistant manager stared at her.

"The most horrid thing about you," continued Mrs. Copperfield, "is that you're just as grouchy now that you know your bill will be paid as you were before. You were mean and worried then and you're mean and worried now. The expression on your face hasn't changed one bit. It's a dangerous man who reacts more or less in the same way to good news or bad news."

Since he still made no effort to speak, she continued: "You've not only made Mrs. Quill completely miserable for no reason at all, but you've spoiled my fun too. You don't even know how to please the rich." The assistant manager raised his eyebrows.

"You won't understand this but I shall tell it to you anyway. I came here for two reasons. The first reason, naturally, was in order to get my friend Mrs. Quill out of trouble; the second reason was in order to see your face when you realized that a bill which you never expected to be paid was to be paid after all. I expected to be able to watch the transition. You understand —enemy into friend—that's always terribly exciting. That's why in a good movie the hero often hates the heroine until the very end. But you, of course, wouldn't dream of lowering your standards. You think it would be cheap to turn into an affable human being because you discovered there was money where you had been sure there was no money to be forthcoming. Do you think the rich mind? They never get enough of it. They want to be liked for their money too, and not only for themselves. You're not even a good hotel manager. You're definitely a boor in every way."

The assistant manager looked down with loathing at Mrs. Copperfield's upturned face. He hated her sharp features and her high voice. He found her even more disgusting than Mrs. Quill. He was not fond of women anyway.

"You have no imagination," she said, "*none whatever!* You are missing everything. Where do I pay my bill?"

All the way home Mrs. Copperfield felt sad because Mrs. Quill was dignified and remote and did not give her the lavish thanks which she had been expecting.

Early the next morning Mrs. Copperfield and Pacifica were together in Pacifica's bedroom. The sky was beginning to grow light. Mrs. Copperfield had never seen Pacifica this drunk. Her hair was pushed up on her head. It looked now somewhat like a wig which is a little too small for the wearer. Her pupils were very large and slightly filmed. There was a large dark spot on the front of her checked skirt, and her breath smelled very strongly of whisky. She stumbled over to the window and looked out. It was quite dark in the room. Mrs. Copperfield could barely discern the red and purple squares in Pacifica's skirt. She could not see her legs at all, the shadows were so deep, but she knew the heavy yellow silk stockings and the white sneakers well.

"It's so lovely," said Mrs. Copperfield.

"Beautiful," said Pacifica, turning around, "beautiful." She moved unsteadily around the room. "Listen," she said, "the most wonderful thing to do now is to go to the beach and swim in the water. If you have enough money we can take a taxicab and go. Come on. Will you?"

Mrs. Copperfield was very startled indeed, but Pacifica was already pulling a blanket from the bed. "Please," she said. "You cannot know how much pleasure this would give me. You must take that towel over there."

The beach was not very far away. When they arrived, Pacifica told the cab-driver to come back in two hours.

The shore was strewn with rocks; this was a disappointment to Mrs. Copperfield. Although the wind was not very strong, she noticed that the top branches of the palm trees were shaking.

Pacifica took her clothes off and immediately walked into the water. She stood for a time with her legs wide apart, the water scarcely reaching to her shins, while Mrs. Copperfield sat on a rock trying to decide whether or not to remove her own clothes. There was a sudden splash and Pacifica started to swim. She swam first on her back and then on her stomach, and Mrs. Copperfield was certain that she could hear her singing. When at last Pacifica grew tired of splashing about in the water, she stood up and walked towards the beach. She took tremendous strides and her pubic hair hung between her legs sopping wet. Mrs. Copperfield looked a little embarrassed, but Pacifica plopped down beside her and asked her why she did not come in the water.

"I can't swim," said Mrs. Copperfield.

Pacifica looked up at the sky. She could see now that it was not going to be a completely fair day.

"Why do you sit on that terrible rock?" said Pacifica. "Come, take your clothes off and we go in the water. I will teach you to swim."

"I was never able to learn."

"I will teach you. If you cannot learn I will let you sink. No, this is only a joke. Don't take it serious."

Mrs. Copperfield undressed. She was very white and thin, and her spine was visible all the way along her back. Pacifica looked at her body without saying a word.

"I know I have an awful figure," said Mrs. Copperfield.

Pacifica did not answer. "Come," she said, getting up and putting her arm around Mrs. Copperfield's waist.

They stood with the water up to their thighs, facing the beach and the palm trees. The trees appeared to be moving behind a mist. The beach was colorless. Behind them the sky was growing lighter very rapidly, but the sea was still almost black. Mrs. Copperfield noticed a red fever sore on Pacifica's lip. Water was dripping from her hair onto her shoulders.

She turned away from the beach and pulled Mrs. Copperfield farther out into the water.

Mrs. Copperfield held onto Pacifica's hand very hard. Soon the water was up to her chin.

"Now lie on your back. I will hold you under your head," said Pacifica.

Mrs. Copperfield looked around wildly, but she obeyed, and floated on her back with only the support of Pacifica's open hand under her head to keep her from sinking. She could see her own narrow feet floating on top of the water. Pacifica started to swim, dragging Mrs. Copperfield along with her. As she had only the use of one arm, her task was an arduous one and she was soon breathing like a bull. The touch of her hand underneath the head of Mrs. Copperfield was very light—in fact, so light that Mrs. Copperfield feared that she would be left alone from one minute to the next. She looked up. The sky was packed with gray clouds. She wanted to say something to Pacifica, but she did not dare to turn her head.

Pacifica swam a little farther inland. Suddenly she stood up and placed both her hands firmly in the small of Mrs. Copperfield's back. Mrs. Copperfield felt happy and sick at once. She turned her face and in so doing she brushed Pacifica's heavy stomach with her cheek. She held on hard to Pacifica's thigh with the strength of years of sorrow and frustration in her hand.

"Don't leave me," she called out.

At this moment Mrs. Copperfield was strongly reminded of a dream that had recurred often during her life. She was being chased up a short hill by a dog. At the top of the hill there stood a few pine trees and a mannequin about eight feet high. She approached the mannequin and discovered her to be fashioned out of flesh, but without life. Her dress was of black velvet, and tapered to a very narrow width at the hem. Mrs. Copperfield wrapped one of the mannequin's arms tightly around her own waist. She was startled by the thickness of the arm and very pleased. The mannequin's other arm she bent upward from the elbow with her free hand. Then the mannequin began to sway backwards and forwards. Mrs. Copperfield clung all the more tightly to the mannequin and together they fell off the top of the hill and continued rolling for quite a distance until they landed on a little walk, where they remained locked in each other's arms. Mrs. Copperfield loved this part of the dream best; and the fact that all the way down the hill the mannequin acted as a buffer between herself and the broken bottles and little stones over which they fell gave her particular satisfaction.

Pacifica had resurrected the emotional content of her dream for a moment, which Mrs. Copperfield thought was certainly the reason for her own peculiar elation.

"Now," said Pacifica, "if you don't mind I will take one more swim by myself." But first she helped Mrs. Copperfield to her feet and led her back to the beach, where Mrs. Copperfield collapsed on the sand and hung her head like a wilted flower. She was trembling and exhausted as one is after a love experience. She looked up at Pacifica, who noticed that her eyes were more luminous and softer than she had ever seen them before.

"You should go in the water more," said Pacifica; "you stay in the house too much."

She ran back into the water and swam back and forth many times. The sea was now blue and much rougher than it had been earlier. Once during the course of her swimming Pacifica rested on a large flat rock which the outgoing tide had uncovered. She was directly in the line of the hazy sun's pale rays. Mrs. Copperfield had a difficult time being able to see her at all and soon she fell asleep.

Upon arriving back at the hotel, Pacifica announced to Mrs. Copperfield that she was going to sleep like a dead person. "I hope I don't wake up for ten days," she said.

Mrs. Copperfield watched her stumble down the bright green corridor, yawning and tossing her head.

"Two weeks I'll sleep," she said again, and then she went into her room and shut the door behind her. In her own room Mrs. Copperfield decided that she had better call up Mr. Copperfield. She went downstairs and walked out into the street, which seemed to be moving as it had on the first day of her arrival. There were a few people already seated on their balconies who were looking down at her. A very thin girl, wearing a red silk dress which hung down to her ankles, was crossing the street towards her. She looked surprisingly young and fresh. When Mrs. Copperfield was nearer to her she decided that she was a Malayan. She was rather startled when the girl stopped directly in front of her and addressed her in perfect English.

"Where have you been that you got your hair all wet?" she said.

"I've been taking a swim with a friend of mine. We—we went early to the beach." Mrs. Copperfield didn't feel much like talking.

"What beach?" asked the girl.

"I don't know," said Mrs. Copperfield.

"Well, did you walk there or did you ride?"

"We rode."

"There isn't any beach really near enough to walk to, I guess," said the girl.

"No, I guess there isn't," said Mrs. Copperfield, sighing and looking around her. The girl was walking along with her.

"Was the water cold?" asked the girl.

"Yes and no," said Mrs. Copperfield.

"Did you swim in the water naked with your friend?"

"Yes."

"Then there weren't any people around, I suppose."

"No, there wasn't a soul there. Do you swim?" Mrs. Copperfield asked the girl.

"No," she said, "I never go near the water." The girl had a shrill voice. She had light hair and brows. She could easily have been partly English. Mrs. Copperfield decided not to ask her. She turned to the girl.

"I'm going to make a telephone call. Where is the nearest place with a phone?"

"Come to Bill Grey's restaurant. They keep it very cool. I generally spend my mornings there drinking like a fish. By the time it's noon I'm cockeyed drunk. I shock the tourists. I'm half Irish and half Javanese. They make bets about what I am. Whoever wins has to buy me a drink. Guess how old I am."

"God knows," said Mrs. Copperfield.

"Well, I'm sixteen."

"Very possible," said Mrs. Copperfield. The girl seemed peeved. They walked in silence to Bill Grey's restaurant, where the girl pushed Mrs. Copperfield through the door and along the floor towards a table in the middle of the restaurant.

"Sit down and order whatever you like. It's on me," said the girl.

There was an electric fan whirling above their heads.

"Isn't it delicious in here?" she said to Mrs. Copperfield.

"Let me make my phone call," said Mrs. Copperfield, who was terrified lest Mr. Copperfield should have come in a few hours ago and be waiting impatiently for her call even at this very moment.

"Make all the phone calls you like," said the girl.

Mrs. Copperfield went into the booth and phoned her husband. He said that he had arrived a short time ago, and that he would have breakfast and join her afterwards at Bill Grey's. He sounded cold and tired.

The girl, while waiting anxiously for her return, had ordered two old-fashioneds. Mrs. Copperfield came back to the table and flopped into her seat.

"I never can sleep late in the mornings," said the girl. "I don't even like to sleep at night if I have anything better to do. My mother told me that I was as nervous as a cat, but very healthy. I went to dancing school but I was too lazy to learn the steps."

"Where do you live?" asked Mrs. Copperfield.

"I live alone in a hotel. I've got plenty of money. A man in the Army is in love with me. He's married but I never go with anyone else. He gives me plenty of money. He's even got more money at home. I'll buy you what you want. Don't tell anyone around here, though, that I've got money to spend on other people. I never buy them anything. They give me a pain. They live such terrible lives. So cheap; so stupid; so very stupid! They don't have any privacy. I have two rooms. You can use one of them if you like."

Mrs. Copperfield said she wouldn't need to, very firmly. She wasn't fond of this girl in the least.

"What is your name?" the girl asked her.

"Frieda Copperfield."

"My name is Peggy—Peggy Gladys. You looked kind of adorable to me with your hair all wet and your little nose as shiny as it was. That's why I asked you to drink with me."

Mrs. Copperfield jumped. "Please don't embarrass me," she said.

"Oh, let me embarrass you, adorable. Now finish your drink and I'll get you some more. Maybe you're hungry and would like some steak."

The girl had the bright eyes of an insatiable nymphomaniac. She wore a ridiculous little watch on a black ribbon around her wrist.

"I live at the Hotel de las Palmas," said Mrs. Copperfield. "I am a friend of the manager there, Mrs. Quill, and one of her guests, Pacifica."

"That's no good, that hotel," said Peggy. "I went in there with some fellows for drinks one night and I said to them: 'If you don't turn right around and leave this hotel, I'll never allow you to take me out again.' It's a cheap place; awful place; it's filthy dirty besides. I'm surprised at you living there. My hotel is much nicer. Some Americans stay there when they come off the boat if they don't go to the Hotel Washington. It's the Hotel Granada."

"Yes, that is where we were staying originally," said Mrs. Copperfield. "My husband is there now. I think it is the most depressing place I have ever set foot in. I think the Hotel de las Palmas is a hundred million times nicer."

"But," said the girl, opening her mouth wide in dismay, "I think you have not looked very carefully. I've put all my own things around in my room of course, and that makes a lot of difference."

"How long have you been living there?" asked Mrs. Copperfield. She was completely puzzled by this girl and a little bit sorry for her.

"I have been living there for a year and a half. It seems like a lifetime. I moved in a little while after I met the man in the Army. He's very nice to me. I think I'm smarter than he is. That's because I'm a girl. Mother told me that girls were never dumb like men, so I just go ahead and do whatever I think is right."

The girl's face was elfin and sweet. She had a cleft chin and a small snub-nose.

"Honestly," she said, "I've got lots of money. I can always get more. I'd love to get you anything you like, because I love the way you talk and look and the way you move; you're elegant." She giggled and put her own dry rough hand in Mrs. Copperfield's.

"Please," she said, "be friendly to me. I don't often see people I like. I never do the same thing twice, really I don't. I haven't asked anyone up to my rooms in the longest while because I'm not interested and because they get everything so dirty. I know you wouldn't get everything dirty because I can tell that you come from a nice class of people. I love people with a good education. I think it's wonderful."

"I have so much on my mind," said Mrs. Copperfield. "Generally I haven't."

"Well, forget it," said the young girl imperiously. "You're

with Peggy Gladys and she's paying for your drinks. Because she wants to pay for your drinks with all her heart. It's such a beautiful morning. Cheer up!" She took Mrs. Copperfield by the sleeve and shook her.

Mrs. Copperfield was still deep in the magic of her dream and in thoughts of Pacifica. She was uneasy and the electric fan seemed to blow directly on her heart. She sat staring ahead of her, not listening to a word the girl was saying.

She could not tell how long she had been dreaming when she looked down and saw a lobster lying on a plate in front of her.

"Oh," she said, "I can't eat this. I can't possibly eat this."

"But I ordered it for you," said Peggy, "and there is some beer coming along. I had your old-fashioned taken away because you weren't touching it." She leaned across the table and tucked Mrs. Copperfield's napkin under her chin.

"Please eat, dearest," said Peggy, "you'll give me such great pleasure if you do."

"What do you think you're doing?" said Mrs. Copperfield fretfully. "Playing house?"

Peggy laughed.

"You know," said Mrs. Copperfield, "my husband is coming here to join us. He'll think we're both stark raving mad to be eating lobster in the morning. He doesn't understand such things."

"Well, let's eat it up quickly, then," said Peggy. She looked wistfully at Mrs. Copperfield. "I wish he wasn't coming," she said. "Couldn't you telephone him and tell him not to come?"

"No, my dear, that would be impossible. Besides, I don't have any reason to tell him not to come. I am very anxious to see him." Mrs. Copperfield could not resist being just a little bit sadistic with Peggy Gladys.

"Of course you want to see him," said Peggy, looking very shy and demure. "I'll be quiet while he's here, I'll promise you."

"That's just what I don't want you to do. Please continue to prattle when he's here."

"Of course, darling. Don't be so nervous."

Mr. Copperfield arrived as they were eating their lobster. He was wearing a dark green suit and looking extremely well. He came over to them smiling pleasantly.

"Hello," said Mrs. Copperfield. "I'm very glad to see you. You look very well. This is Peggy Gladys; we've just met."

He shook hands with her and seemed very pleased. "What on earth are you eating?" he asked them.

"Lobster," they answered. He frowned. "But," he said, "you'll have indigestion, and you're drinking beer too! Good God!" He sat down.

"I don't mean to interfere, of course," said Mr. Copperfield, "but it's very bad. Have you had breakfast?"

"I don't know," said Mrs. Copperfield purposely. Peggy Gladys laughed. Mr. Copperfield raised his brows.

"You must know," he murmured. "Don't be ridiculous."

He asked Peggy Gladys where she was from.

"I'm from Panama," she told him, "but I'm half Irish and half Javanese."

"I see," said Mr. Copperfield. He kept smiling at her.

"Pacifica's asleep," said Mrs. Copperfield suddenly.

Mr. Copperfield frowned. "Really," he said, "are you going back there?"

"What do you think I'm going to do?"

"There isn't any point of staying here much longer. I thought we'd pack. I've made arrangements in Panama. We can sail tomorrow. I have to phone them tonight. I've found out a lot about the various countries in Central America. It might be possible for us to stay on a kind of cattle ranch in Costa Rica. A man told me about it. It's completely isolated. You have to get there on a river boat."

Peggy Gladys looked bored.

Mrs. Copperfield put her head in her hands.

"Imagine red and blue guacamayos flying over the cattle," Mr. Copperfield laughed. "Latin Texas. It must be completely crazy."

"Red and blue guacamayos flying over the cattle," Peggy Gladys repeated after him. "What are guacamayos?" she asked.

"They're tremendous red and blue birds, more or less like parrots," said Mr. Copperfield. "As long as you are eating lobster I think I shall have ice cream with whipped cream on top."

"He's nice," said Peggy Gladys.

"Listen," said Mrs. Copperfield, "I feel sick. I don't think I can sit through the ice cream."

"I won't take long," said Mr. Copperfield. He looked at her. "It must be the lobster."

"Maybe I'd better take her to my Hotel Granada," said Peggy Gladys, jumping to her feet with alacrity. "She'll be very comfortable there. Then you can come after you've eaten your ice cream."

"That seems sensible, don't you think so, Frieda?"

"No," said Mrs. Copperfield vehemently, clutching at the chain she wore around her neck. "I think I'd better go right straight back to the Hotel de las Palmas. I *must* go. I must go immediately. . . ." She was so distraught that she rose from the table, forgetting her pocketbook and her scarf, and started to leave the restaurant.

"But you've left everything behind you," Mr. Copperfield called out after her.

"I'll take them," exclaimed Peggy Gladys. "You eat your ice cream and come later." She rushed after Mrs. Copperfield and together they ran down the suffocatingly hot street towards the Hotel de las Palmas.

Mrs. Quill was standing in the doorway drinking something out of a bottle.

"I'm on the cherry-pop wagon until dinner time," she said.

"Oh, Mrs. Quill, come up to my room with me!" said Mrs. Copperfield, putting her arms around Mrs. Quill and sighing deeply. "Mr. Copperfield is back."

"Why don't you come upstairs with *me*?" said Peggy Gladys. "I promised your husband I'd take care of you."

Mrs. Copperfield wheeled round. "Please be quiet," she shouted, looking fixedly at Peggy Gladys.

"Now, now," said Mrs. Quill, "don't upset the little girl. We'll have to be giving her a honey bun to quiet her. Of course it took more than a honey bun to quiet me at her age."

"I'm all right," said Peggy Gladys. "Will you kindly take us to her room? She's supposed to be flat on her back."

The young girl sat on the edge of Mrs. Copperfield's bed with her hand on Mrs. Copperfield's forehead.

"I'm sorry," she said. "You look very badly. I wish you wouldn't be so unhappy. Couldn't you possibly not think about it now and think about it some other day? Sometimes if you let things rest . . . I'm not sixteen, I'm seventeen. I feel like a child. I can't seem to say anything unless people think I'm very young. Maybe you don't like the fact that I'm so fresh. You're white and green. You don't look pretty. You looked much prettier before. After your husband has been here I'll take you for a ride in a carriage if you like. My mother's dead," she said softly.

"Listen," said Mrs. Copperfield. "If you don't mind going away now . . . I'd like to be by myself. You can come back later."

"What time can I come back?"

"I don't know; come back later; can't you see? I don't know."

"All right," said Peggy Gladys. "Maybe I should just go downstairs and talk to that fat woman, or drink. Then when you're ready you can come down. I have nothing to do for three days. You really want me to go?"

Mrs. Copperfield nodded.

The girl left the room reluctantly.

Mrs. Copperfield started to tremble after the girl had closed the door behind her. She trembled so violently that she shook the bed. She was suffering as much as she had ever suffered before, because she was going to do what she wanted to do. But it would not make her happy. She did not have the courage to stop from doing what she wanted to do. She knew that it would not make her happy, because only the dreams of crazy people come true. She thought that she was only interested in duplicating a dream, but in doing so she necessarily became the complete victim of a nightmare.

Mr. Copperfield came very quietly into her room. "How do you feel now?" he asked.

"I'm all right," she said.

"Who was that young girl? She was very pretty—from a sculptural point of view."

"Her name is Peggy Gladys."

"She spoke very well, didn't she? Or am I wrong?"

"She spoke beautifully."

"Have you been having a nice time?"

"I've had the most wonderful time in my whole life," said Mrs. Copperfield, almost weeping.

"I had a nice time too, exploring Panama City. But my room was so uncomfortable. There was too much noise. I couldn't sleep."

"Why didn't you take a nicer room in a better hotel?"

"You know me. I hate to spend money. I never think it's worth it. I guess I should have. I should have been drinking too. I'd have had a better time. But I didn't."

They were silent. Mr. Copperfield drummed on the bureau. "I guess we should be leaving tonight," he said, "instead of staying on here. It's terribly expensive here. There won't be another boat for quite a few days."

Mrs. Copperfield did not answer.

"Don't you think I'm correct?"

"I don't want to go," she said, twisting on the bed.

"I don't understand," said Mr. Copperfield.

"I can't go. I want to stay here."

"For how long?"

"I don't know."

"But you can't plan a trip that way. Perhaps you don't intend to plan a trip."

"Oh, I'll plan a trip," said Mrs. Copperfield vaguely.

"You will?"

"No, I won't."

"It's up to you," said Mr. Copperfield. "I just think you'll be missing a great deal by not seeing Central America. You're certain to get bored here unless you start to drink. You probably will start to drink."

"Why don't you go, and then come back when you've seen enough?" she suggested.

"I won't come back because I can't look at you," said Mr. Copperfield. "You're a horror." So saying, he took an empty pitcher from the bureau, threw it out of the window into the alley, and left the room.

An hour later Mrs. Copperfield went downstairs into the bar. She was surprised and glad to see Pacifica there. Although Pacifica had powdered her face very heavily, she looked tired. She was sitting at a little table holding her pocketbook in her hands.

"Pacifica," said Mrs. Copperfield, "I didn't know that you were awake. I was certain that you were asleep in your room. I'm so glad to see you."

"I could not close my eyes. I was sleeping for fifteen minutes and then after that I could not close my eyes. Someone came to see me."

Peggy Gladys walked over to Mrs. Copperfield. "Hello," she said, running her fingers through Mrs. Copperfield's hair. "Are you ready to take that ride yet?"

"What ride?" asked Mrs. Copperfield.

"The ride in the carriage with me."

"No, I'm not ready," said Mrs. Copperfield.

"When will you be?" asked Peggy Gladys.

"I'm going to buy some stockings," said Pacifica. "You want to come with me, Copperfield?"

"Yes. Let's go."

"Your husband looked upset when he left the hotel," said Peggy Gladys. "I hope you didn't have a fight."

Mrs. Copperfield was walking out of the door with Pacifica. "Excuse us," she called over her shoulder to Peggy Gladys. She was standing still and looking after them like a hurt animal!

It was so hot out that even the most conservative women tourists, their faces and chests flame-red, were pulling off their hats and drying their foreheads with their handkerchiefs. Most of them, to escape the heat, were dropping into the little Hindu stores where, if the shop wasn't too crowded, the salesman offered them a little chair so that they might view twenty or thirty kimonos without getting tired.

"*Qué calor!*" said Pacifica.

"To hell with stockings," said Mrs. Copperfield, who thought she was about to faint. "Let's get some beer."

"If you want, go and get yourself some beer. I must have stockings. I think bare legs on a woman is something terrible."

"No, I'll come with you." Mrs. Copperfield put her hand in Pacifica's.

"Ay!" cried Pacifica, releasing her hand. "We are both too wet, darling. *Qué barbaridad!*"

The store into which Pacifica took Mrs. Copperfield was very tiny. It was even hotter in there than on the street.

"You see you can buy many things here," said Pacifica. "I come here because he knows me and I can get my stockings for very little money."

While Pacifica was buying her stockings Mrs. Copperfield looked at all the other little articles in the store. Pacifica took such a long time that Mrs. Copperfield grew more and more bored. She stood first on one foot and then on the other.

Pacifica argued and argued. There were dark perspiration stains under her arms, and the wings of her nose were streaming.

When it was all over and Mrs. Copperfield saw that the salesman was wrapping the package, she went over and paid the bill. The salesman wished her good luck and they left the store.

There was a letter for her at home. Mrs. Quill gave it to her.

"Mr. Copperfield left this for you," she said. "I tried to urge him to stay and have a cup of tea or some beer, but he was in a hurry. He's one handsome fellow."

Mrs. Copperfield took the letter and started towards the bar.

"Hello, sweet," said Peggy Gladys softly.

Mrs. Copperfield could see that Peggy was very drunk. Her hair was hanging over her face and her eyes were dead.

"Maybe you're not ready yet . . . but I can wait a long time. I love to wait. I don't mind being by myself."

"You'll excuse me a minute if I read a letter which I just received from my husband," said Mrs. Copperfield.

She sat down and tore open the envelope.

Dear Frieda [she read],

I do not mean to be cruel but I shall write to you exactly what I consider to be your faults and I hope sincerely that what I have written will influence you. Like most people, you are not able to face more than one fear during your lifetime. You also spend your life fleeing from your first fear towards your first hope. Be careful that you do not, through your own wiliness, end up always in the same position in which you began. I do not advise you to spend your life surrounding yourself with those things which you term necessary to your existence, regardless of whether or not they are objectively interesting in themselves or even to your own particular intellect. I believe sincerely that only those men who reach the stage where it is possible for them to combat a second tragedy within themselves, and not the first over again, are worthy of being called mature. When you think someone is going ahead, make sure that he is not really standing still. In order to go ahead, you must leave things behind which most people are unwilling to do. Your first pain, you carry it with you like a lodestone in your breast because all tenderness will come from there. You must carry it with you through your whole life but you must not circle around it. You must give up the search for those symbols which only serve to hide its face from you. You will have the illusion that they are disparate and manifold but they are always the same. If you are only interested in a bearable life, perhaps this letter does not concern you. For God's sake, a ship leaving port is still a wonderful thing to see.

J. C.

Mrs. Copperfield's heart was beating very quickly. She crushed the letter in her hand and shook her head two or three times.

"I'll never bother you unless you ask me to bother you," Peggy Gladys was saying. She did not seem to be addressing anyone in particular. Her eyes wandered from the ceiling to the walls. She was smiling to herself.

"She is reading a letter from her husband," she said, letting her arm fall down heavily on the bar. "I myself don't want a husband—never—never—never. . . ."

Mrs. Copperfield rose to her feet.

"*Pacifica*," she shouted, "*Pacifica!*"

"Who is Pacifica?" asked Peggy Gladys. "I want to meet her. Is she as beautiful as you are? Tell her to come here. . . ."

"Beautiful?" the bartender laughed. "Beautiful? Neither of them is beautiful. They're both old hens. You're beautiful even if you are blind drunk."

"Bring her in here, darling," said Peggy Gladys, letting her head fall down on the bar.

"Listen, your pal's been out of the room two whole minutes already. She's gone to look for Pacifica."

Part Three

IT WAS several months later, and Miss Goering, Miss Gamelon, and Arnold had been living for nearly four weeks in the house which Miss Goering had chosen.

This was gloomier even than Miss Gamelon had expected it would be, since she hadn't much imagination, and reality was often more frightening to her than her wildest dreams. She was now more incensed against Miss Goering than she had been before they had changed houses, and her disposition was so bad that scarcely an hour went by that she did not complain bitterly about her life, or threaten to leave altogether. Behind the house was a dirt bank and some bushes, and if one walked over the bank and followed a narrow path through some more bushes, one soon came to the woods. To the right of the house was a field that was filled with daisies in the summertime. This field might have been quite pleasant to look at had there not been lying right in the middle of it the rusted engine of an old car. There was very little place to sit out of doors, since the front porch had rotted away, so they had, all three of them, got into the habit of sitting close by the kitchen door, where the house protected them from the wind. Miss Gamelon had been suffering from the cold ever since she had arrived. In fact, there was no central heating in the house: only a few little oil stoves, and although it was still only early fall, on certain days it was already quite chilly.

Arnold returned to his own home less and less frequently, and more and more often he took the little train and the ferry boat into the city from Miss Goering's house and then returned again after his work was done to have his dinner and sleep on the island.

Miss Goering never questioned his presence. He became more careless about his clothing, and three times in the last week he had neglected to go in to his office at all. Miss Gamelon had made a terrible fuss over this.

One day Arnold was resting upstairs in one of the little bedrooms directly under the roof and she and Miss Goering were seated in front of the kitchen door warming themselves in the afternoon sun.

"That slob upstairs," said Miss Gamelon, "is eventually going to give up going to the office at all. He's going to move in here completely and do nothing but eat and sleep. In another year he's going to be as big as an elephant and you won't be able to rid yourself of him. Thank the Lord I don't expect to be here then."

"Do you really think that he will be so very, very fat in one year?" said Miss Goering.

"I know it!" said Miss Gamelon. There was a sudden blast of wind which blew the kitchen door open. "Oh, I hate this," said Miss Gamelon vehemently, getting up from her seat to fix the door.

"Besides," she continued, "who ever heard of a man living together with two ladies in a house which does not even contain one extra bedroom, so that he is obliged to sleep fully clothed on the couch! It is enough to take one's appetite away, just to walk through the parlor and see him there at all hours of the day, eyes open or shut, with not a care in the world. Only a man who is a slob could be willing to live in such a way. He is even too lazy to court either of us, which is a most unnatural thing you must admit—if you have any conception at all of the male physical make-up. Of course he is not a man. He is an elephant."

"I don't think," said Miss Goering, "that he is as big as all that."

"Well, I told him to rest in my room because I couldn't stand seeing him on the couch any more. And as for you," she said to Miss Goering, "I think you are the most insensitive person that I have ever met in my life."

At the same time Miss Gamelon was really worried—although she scarcely admitted this to herself—that Miss Goering was losing her mind. Miss Goering seemed thinner and more nervous and she insisted on doing most of the housework all by herself. She was constantly cleaning the house and polishing the doorknobs and the silver; she tried in many small ways to make the house livable without buying any of the things which were needed to make it so; she had in these last few weeks suddenly developed an extreme avarice and drew only enough money from the bank to enable them to live in the simplest manner possible. At the same time she seemed to think nothing of paying for Arnold's food, as he scarcely ever offered to contribute anything to the upkeep of the house. It was true that he went on paying his own share in his family's apartment, which perhaps left him very little to pay for anything else. This made Miss Gamelon furious, because although she did not understand why it was necessary for Miss Goering to live on less than one tenth of her income, she had nevertheless adjusted herself to this tiny scale of living and was trying desperately to make the money stretch as far as possible.

They sat in silence for a few minutes. Miss Gamelon was thinking seriously about all these things when suddenly a bottle broke against her head, inundating her with perfume and making quite a deep cut just above her forehead. She started to bleed profusely and sat for a moment with her hands over her eyes.

"I didn't actually mean to draw blood," said Arnold leaning out of the window. "I just meant to give her a start."

Miss Goering, although she was beginning to regard Miss Gamelon more and more as the embodiment of evil, made a swift and compassionate gesture towards her friend.

"Oh, my dear, let me get you something to disinfect the cut with." She went into the house and passed Arnold in the hall. He was standing with his hand on the front door, unable to decide whether to stay in or go out. When Miss Goering came down again with the medicine, Arnold had disappeared.

It was near evening, and Miss Gamelon, with a bandaged head, was standing in front of the house. She could see the road between the trees, from where she was standing. Her face was very white and her eyes were swollen because she had been weeping bitterly. She was weeping because it was the first time in her life that anyone had ever struck her physically. The more she thought about it, the more serious it became in her mind, and while she stood in front of the house she was suddenly frightened for the first time in her life. How far she had traveled from her home! Twice she had begun to pack her bags and twice she had decided not to do so, only because she could not bring herself to leave Miss Goering, since in her own way, though she scarcely knew it herself, she was deeply attached to her. It was dark before Miss Gamelon went into the house.

Miss Goering was terribly upset because Arnold had not yet returned, although she did not care for him very much more than she had in the beginning. She, too, stood outside in the dark for nearly an hour because her anxiety was so great that she was unable to remain in the house.

While she was still outside, Miss Gamelon, seated in the parlor before an empty fireplace, felt that all of God's wrath had descended upon her own head. The world and the people in it had suddenly slipped beyond her comprehension and she felt in great danger of losing the whole world once and for all—a feeling that is difficult to explain.

Each time that she looked over her shoulder into the kitchen and saw Miss Goering's dark shape still standing in front of the door, her heart failed her a little more. Finally Miss Goering came in.

"Lucy!" she called. Her voice was very clear and a little higher than usual. "Lucy, let's go and find Arnold." She sat opposite Miss Gamelon, and her face looked extraordinarily bright.

Miss Gamelon said: "Certainly not."

"Well, after all," said Miss Goering, "he lives in my house."

"Yes, that he does," said Miss Gamelon.

"And it is only right," said Miss Goering, "that people in the same house should look after each other. They always do, I think, don't they?"

"They're more careful about who gets under the same roof with them," said Miss Gamelon, coming to life again.

"I don't think so, really," said Miss Goering. Miss Gamelon breathed a deep sigh and got up. "Never mind," she said, "soon I'll be in the midst of real human beings again."

They started through the woods along a path which was a short cut to the nearest town, about twenty minutes from their house on foot. Miss Goering screeched at every strange noise and clutched at Miss Gamelon's sweater all the way. Miss Gamelon was sullen and suggested that they take the long way around on their way back.

At last they came out of the woods and walked a short stretch along the highway. On either side of the road were restaurants which catered mainly to automobilists. In one of these Miss Goering saw Arnold seated at a table near the window, eating a sandwich.

"There's Arnold," said Miss Goering. "Come along!" She took hold of Miss Gamelon's hand and almost skipped in the direction of the restaurant.

"It is really almost too good to be true," said Miss Gamelon; "he is eating again."

It was terribly hot inside. They removed their sweaters and went to sit with Arnold at his table.

"Good evening," said Arnold. "I didn't expect to see you here." This he said to Miss Goering. He avoided looking in the direction of Miss Gamelon.

"Well," said Miss Gamelon, "are you going to explain yourself?"

Arnold had just taken quite a large bite of his sandwich so that he was unable to answer her. But he did roll his eyes in her direction. It was impossible to tell with his cheeks so full whether or not he looked angry. Miss Gamelon was terribly annoyed at this, but Miss Goering sat smiling at them because she was glad to have them both with her again.

Finally Arnold swallowed his food.

"I don't have to explain myself," he said to Miss Gamelon, looking very grouchy indeed now that he had swallowed his food. "You owe a profound apology to me for hating me and telling Miss Goering about it."

"I have a perfect right to hate whom I please," said Miss Gamelon, "and also, since we live in a free country, I can talk about it on the street corner if I want to."

"You don't know me well enough to hate me. You've misjudged me anyway, which is enough to make any man furious, and I *am* furious."

"Well then, get out of the house. Nobody wants you there anyway."

"That's incorrect; Miss Goering, I am sure, wants me there, don't you?"

"Yes, Arnold, of course," said Miss Goering.

"There is no justice," said Miss Gamelon; "you are both outrageous." She sat up very straight, and both Arnold and Miss Goering stared at her bandage.

"Well," said Arnold, wiping his mouth and pushing his plate

away, "I am sure there is some way whereby we can arrange it so we can both live in the house together."

"Why are you so attached to the house?" screamed Miss Gamelon. "All you ever do when you're in it is to stretch out in the parlor and go to sleep."

"The house gives me a certain feeling of freedom."

Miss Gamelon looked at him.

"You mean an opportunity to indulge your laziness."

"Now look," said Arnold, "suppose that I am allowed to use the parlor after dinner and in the morning. Then you can use it the rest of the time."

"All right," said Miss Gamelon, "I agree, but see that you don't set your foot in it during the entire afternoon."

On the way home both Miss Gamelon and Arnold seemed quite contented because they had evolved a plan. Each one thought he had got the better of the bargain and Miss Gamelon was already outlining to herself several pleasant ways of spending an afternoon in the parlor.

When they arrived home she went upstairs to bed almost immediately. Arnold lay on the couch, fully dressed, and pulled a knitted coverlet over him. Miss Goering was sitting in the kitchen. After a little while she heard someone sobbing in the parlor. She went inside and found Arnold crying into his sleeve.

"What's the matter, Arnold?"

"I don't know," said Arnold, "it's so disagreeable to have someone hate you. I really think I had perhaps better leave and go back to my house. But I dislike doing that more than anything in the world and I hate the real-estate business and I hate for her to be angry with me. Can't you tell her it's just a period of adjustment for me—to please wait a little bit?"

"Certainly, Arnold, I shall tell her that the very first thing in the morning. Maybe if you went to business tomorrow, she might feel better about you."

"Do you think so?" asked Arnold, sitting bolt upright in his eagerness. "Then I will." He got up and stood by the window with his feet wide apart. "I just can't stand to have anyone hate me during this period of adjustment," he said, "and then of course I'm devoted to you both."

The next evening, when Arnold came home with a box of

chocolates apiece for Miss Goering and Miss Gamelon, he was surprised to find his father there. He was sitting in a straight-backed chair next to the fireplace, drinking a cup of tea, and he had on a motoring cap.

"I came out to see, Arnold, how well you were providing for these young ladies. They seem to be living in a dung-heap here."

"I don't see where you have any right to say such a thing as a guest, Father," said Arnold, gravely handing a box of candy to each of the women.

"Certainly, because of age, my dear son, I am allowed to say a great many things. Remember you are all children to me, including Princess over here." He hooked Miss Goering's waist with the top of his cane and drew her over to him. She had never imagined she would see him in such a rollicking good humor. He looked to her smaller and thinner than on the night they had met.

"Well, where do you crazy bugs eat?" he asked them.

"We have a square table," said Miss Gamelon, "in the kitchen. Sometimes we put it in front of the fireplace, but it's never very adequate."

Arnold's father cleared his throat and said nothing. He seemed to be annoyed that Miss Gamelon had spoken.

"Well, you're all crazy," he said, looking at his son and at Miss Goering, and purposely excluding Miss Gamelon, "but I'm rooting for you."

"Where is your wife?" Miss Goering asked him.

"She's at home, I gather," said Arnold's father, "and as sour as a pickle and just as bitter to taste."

Miss Gamelon giggled at this remark. It was the kind of thing that she found amusing. Arnold was delighted to see that she was brightening up a bit.

"Come out with me," said Arnold's father to Miss Goering, "into the wind and the sunshine, my love, or shall I say into the wind and the moonlight, never forgetting to add 'my love.'"

They left the room together and Arnold's father led Miss Goering a little way into the field.

"You see," he said, "I've decided to go back to a number of my boyish tastes. For instance, I took a certain delight in nature when I was young. I can frankly say that I have decided to throw away some of my conventions and ideals and again get a kick out of nature—that is, of course if you are willing to be by my side. It all depends on that."

"Certainly," said Miss Goering, "but what does this involve?"

"It involves," said Arnold's father, "your being a true woman. Sympathetic and willing to defend all that I say and do. At the same time prone to scolding me just a little." He put his ice-cold hand in hers.

"Let's go in," said Miss Goering. "I want to go inside." She began tugging at his arm, but he would not move. She realized that although he looked terribly old-fashioned and a little ridiculous in his motoring cap, he was still very strong. She wondered why he had seemed so much more distinguished the first night that they had met.

She tugged at his arm even harder, half in play, half in earnest, and in so doing she quite unwittingly scratched the inside of his wrist with her nail. She drew a little blood, which seemed to upset Arnold's father quite a lot, because he began stumbling through the field as quickly as he could towards the house.

Later he announced to everyone his intention of staying the night in Miss Goering's house. They had lighted a fire and they were all seated around it together. Twice Arnold had fallen asleep.

"Mother would be terribly worried," said Arnold.

"Worried?" said Arnold's father. "She will probably die of a heart attack before morning, but then, what is life but a puff of smoke or a leaf or a candle soon burned out anyway?"

"Don't pretend you don't take life seriously," said Arnold, "and don't pretend, just because there are women around, that you are light-hearted. You're the grim, worrying type and you know it."

Arnold's father coughed. He looked a little upset.

"I don't agree with you," he said.

Miss Goering took him upstairs to her own bedroom.

"I hope you will sleep in peace," she said to him. "You know that I'm delighted to have you in my house any time."

Arnold's father pointed to the trees outside the window.

"Oh, night!" he said. "Soft as a maiden's cheek, and as

mysterious as the brooding owl, the Orient, the turbaned sultan's head. How long have I ignored thee underneath my reading lamp, occupied with various and sundry occupations which I have now decided to disregard in favor of thee. Accept my apology and let me be numbered among thy sons and daughters. You see," he said to Miss Goering, "you see what a new leaf I have really turned over; I think we understand each other now. You mustn't ever think people have only one nature. Everything I said to you the other night was wrong."

"Oh," said Miss Goering, a little dismayed.

"Yes, I am now interested in being an entirely new personality as different from my former self as A is from Z. This has been a very lovely beginning. It augurs well, as they say."

He stretched out on the bed, and while Miss Goering was looking at him he fell asleep. Soon he began to snore. She threw a cover over him and left the room, deeply perplexed.

Downstairs she joined the others in front of the fire. They were drinking hot tea into which they had poured a bit of rum.

Miss Gamelon was relaxing. "This is the best thing in the world for your nerves," she said, "and also for softening the sharp angles of your life. Arnold has been telling me about his progress in his uncle's office. How he started as a messenger and has now worked his way up to being one of the chief agents in the office. We've had an extremely pleasant time just sitting here. I think Arnold has been hiding from us a very excellent business sense."

Arnold looked a little distressed. He was still fearful of displeasing Miss Goering.

"Miss Gamelon and I are going to inquire tomorrow whether or not there is a golf course on the island. We have discovered a mutual interest in golf," he said.

Miss Goering could not understand Arnold's sudden change of attitude. It was as though he had just arrived at a summer hotel and was anxious to plan a nice vacation. Miss Gamelon also surprised her somewhat, but she said nothing.

"Golf would be wonderful for you," said Miss Gamelon to Miss Goering; "probably would straighten you out in a week."

"Well," said Arnold apologetically, "she might not like it."

"I don't like sports," said Miss Goering; "more than anything else, they give me a terrific feeling of sinning."

"On the contrary," said Miss Gamelon, "that's exactly what they never do."

"Don't be rude, Lucy dear," said Miss Goering. "After all, I have paid sufficient attention to what happens inside of me and I know better than you about my own feelings."

"Sports," said Miss Gamelon, "can never give you a feeling of sinning, but what is more interesting is that you can never sit down for more than five minutes without introducing something weird into the conversation. I certainly think you have made a study of it."

The next morning Arnold's father came downstairs with his shirt collar open and without a vest. He had rumpled his hair up a bit so that now he looked like an old artist.

"What on earth is Mother going to do?" Arnold asked him at breakfast.

"Fiddlesticks!" said Arnold's father. "You call yourself an artist and you don't even know how to be irresponsible. The beauty of the artist lies in the childlike soul." He touched Miss Goering's hand with his own. She could not help thinking of the speech he had made the night he had come into her bedroom and how opposed it had been to everything he was now saying.

"If your mother has a desire to live, she will live, providing she is willing to leave everything behind her as I have done," he added.

Miss Gamelon was slightly embarrassed by this elderly man who seemed to have just recently made some momentous change in his life. But she was not really curious about him.

"Well," said Arnold, "I imagine you are still providing her with money to pay the rent. I am continuing to contribute my share."

"Certainly," said his father. "I am always a gentleman, although I must say the responsibility weighs heavy on me, like an anchor around my neck. Now," he continued, "let me go out and do the marketing for the day. I feel able to run a hundred-yard dash."

Miss Gamelon sat with furrowed brow, wondering if Miss Goering would permit this crazy old man to live on in the already crowded house. He set out towards town a little while later. They called after him from the window, entreating him to return and put on his coat, but he waved his hand at the sky and refused.

In the afternoon Miss Goering did some serious thinking. She walked back and forth in front of the kitchen door. Already the house, to her, had become a friendly and familiar place and one which she readily thought of as her home. She decided that it was now necessary for her to take little trips to the tip of the island, where she could board the ferry and cross back over to the mainland. She hated to do this as she knew how upsetting it would be, and the more she considered it, the more attractive the life in the little house seemed to her, until she even thought of it as humming with gaiety. In order to assure herself that she would make her excursion that night, she went into her bedroom and put fifty cents on the bureau.

After dinner, when she announced that she was taking a train ride alone, Miss Gamelon nearly wept with indignation. Arnold's father said he thought it was a wonderful idea to take "a train ride into the blue," as he termed it. When Miss Gamelon heard him encouraging Miss Goering, she could no longer contain herself and rushed up into her bedroom. Arnold hastily left the table and lumbered up the steps after her.

Arnold's father begged Miss Goering to allow him to go with her.

"Not this time," she said, "I must go alone"; and Arnold's father, although he said he was very much disappointed, still remained elated. There seemed to be no end to his good humor.

"Well," he said, "setting out into the night like this is just in the spirit of what I'd like to do, and I think that you are cheating me prettily by not allowing me to accompany you."

"It is not for fun that I am going," said Miss Goering, "but because it is necessary to do so."

"Still, I beg you once more," said Arnold's father, ignoring the implications of this remark and getting down on his knees with difficulty, "I beg you, take me with you."

"Oh, please, my dear," said Miss Goering, "please don't make it hard for me. I have a weakish personality."

Arnold's father jumped to his feet. "Certainly," he said, "I would not make anything hard for you." He kissed her wrist and wished her good luck. "Do you think the two turtle doves will talk to me?" he asked her, "or do you think they will remain cooped up together all night? I rather hate to be alone."

"So do I," said Miss Goering. "Bang on their door; they'll talk to you. Good-by. . . ."

Miss Goering decided to walk along the highway, as it was really too dark to walk through the woods at this hour. She had proposed this to herself as a stint, earlier in the afternoon, but had later decided that it was pure folly even to consider it. It was cold and windy out and she pulled her shawl closer around her. She continued to affect woolen shawls, although they had not been stylish for a good many years. Miss Goering looked up at the sky; she was looking for the stars and hoping very hard to see some. She stood still for a long time, but she could not decide whether it was a starlit night or not because even though she fixed her attention on the sky without once lowering her eyes, the stars seemed to appear and disappear so quickly that they were like visions of stars rather than like actual stars. She decided that this was only because the clouds were racing across the sky so quickly that the stars were obliterated one minute and visible the next. She continued on her way to the station.

When she arrived she was surprised to find that there were eight or nine children who had got there ahead of her. Each one carried a large blue and gold school banner. The children weren't saying much, but they were engaged in hopping heavily first on one foot and then on the other. Since they were doing this in unison, the little wooden platform shook abominably and Miss Goering wondered whether she had not better draw the attention of the children to this fact. Very shortly, however, the train pulled into the station and they all boarded it together. Miss Goering sat in a seat across the aisle from a middle-aged stout woman. She and Miss Goering were the only occupants of the car besides the children. Miss Goering looked at her with interest.

She was wearing gloves and a hat and she sat up very straight. In her right hand she held a long thin package which looked like a fly-swatter. The woman stared ahead of her and not a muscle in her face moved. There were some more packages that she had piled neatly on the seat next to her. Miss Goering looked at her and hoped that she too, was going to the tip of the island. The train started to move and the woman put her free hand on top of the packages next to her so that they would not slide off the seat.

The children had mostly crowded into two seats and those who would have had to sit elsewhere preferred to stand around the already occupied seats. Soon they began to sing songs, which were all in praise of the school from which they had come. They did this so badly that it was almost too much for Miss Goering to bear. She got out of her seat and was so intent upon getting to the children quickly that she paid no attention to the lurching of the car and consequently in her hurry she tripped and fell headlong on the floor right next to where the children were singing.

She managed to get on her feet again although her chin was bleeding. She first asked the children to please stop their singing. They all stared at her. Then she pulled out a little lace handkerchief and started to mop the blood from her chin. Soon the train stopped and the children got off. Miss Goering went to the end of the car and filled a paper cup with water. She wondered nervously, as she mopped her chin in the dark passage, whether or not the lady with the fly-swatter would still be in the car. When she got back to her seat she saw with great relief that the lady was still there. She still held the fly-swatter, but she had turned her head to the left and was looking out at the little station platform.

"I don't think," said Miss Goering to herself, "that it would do any harm if I changed my seat and sat opposite her. After all, I suppose it's quite a natural thing for ladies to approach each other on a suburban train like this, particularly on such a small island."

She slid quietly into the seat opposite the woman and continued to occupy herself with her chin. The train had started again and the woman stared harder and harder out of the window in order to avoid Miss Goering's eye, for Miss Goering was a little disturbing to certain people. Perhaps because of her red and exalted face and her outlandish clothes.

"I'm delighted that the children have left," said Miss Goering; "now it is really pleasant on this train."

It began to rain and the woman pressed her forehead to the

glass in order to stare more closely at the slanting drops on the window-pane. She did not answer Miss Goering. Miss Goering began again, for she was used to forcing people into conversation, her fears never having been of a social nature.

"Where are you going?" Miss Goering asked, first because she was really interested in knowing whether or not the woman was traveling to the tip of the island, and also because she thought it a rather disarming question. The woman studied her carefully.

"Home," she said in a flat voice.

"And do you live on this island?" Miss Goering asked her. "It's really enchanting," she added.

The woman did not answer, but instead she started to gather all her packages up in her arms.

"Where exactly do you live?" asked Miss Goering. The woman's eyes shifted about.

"Glensdale," she said hesitatingly, and Miss Goering, although she was not sensitive to slights, realized that the woman was lying to her. This pained her very much.

"Why do you lie to me?" she asked. "I assure you that I am a lady like yourself."

The woman by then had mustered her strength and seemed more sure of herself. She looked straight into Miss Goering's eyes.

"I live in Glensdale," she said, "and I have lived there all my life. I am on my way to visit a friend who lives in a town a little farther along."

"Why do I terrify you so?" Miss Goering asked her. "I would like to have talked to you."

"I won't stand for this another moment," the woman said, more to herself than to Miss Goering. "I have enough real grief in my life without having to encounter lunatics."

Suddenly she grabbed her umbrella and gave Miss Goering a smart rap on the ankles. She was quite red in the face and Miss Goering decided that in spite of her solid bourgeois appearance she was really hysterical, but since she had met many women like this before, she decided not to be surprised from now on at anything that the woman might do. The woman left her seat with all of her packages and her umbrella and walked down the aisle with difficulty. Soon she returned, followed by the conductor.

They stopped beside Miss Goering. The woman stood behind the conductor. The conductor, who was an old man, leaned way over Miss Goering so that he was nearly breathing in her face.

"You can't talk to anyone on these here trains," he said, "unless you know them." His voice sounded very mild to Miss Goering.

Then he looked over his shoulder at the woman, who still seemed annoyed but more calm.

"The next time," said the conductor, who really was at a loss for what to say, "the next time you're on this train, stay in your seat and don't molest anybody. If you want to know the time you can ask them without any to-do about it or you can just make me a little signal with your hand and I'll be willing to answer all your questions." He straightened up and stood for a moment trying to think of something more to say. "Remember also," he added, "and tell this to your relatives and to your friends. Remember also that there are no dogs allowed on this train or people in masquerade costume unless they're all covered up with a big heavy coat; and no more hubbubs," he added, shaking a finger at her. He tipped his hat to the woman and went on his way.

A minute or two later the train stopped and the woman got off. Miss Goering looked anxiously out of the window for her, but she could see only the empty platform and some dark bushes. She held her hand over her heart and smiled to herself.

When she arrived at the tip of the island the rain had stopped and the stars were shining again intermittently. She had to walk down a long narrow boardwalk which served as a passage between the train and the landing pier of the ferry. Many of the boards were loose and Miss Goering had to be very careful where she was stepping. She sighed with impatience, because it seemed to her that as long as she was still on this boardwalk it was not certain that she would actually board the ferry. Now that she was approaching her destination she felt that the whole excursion could be made very quickly and that she would soon be back with Arnold and his father and Miss Gamelon.

The boardwalk was only lighted at intervals and there were long stretches which she had to cross in the dark. However, Miss Goering, usually so timorous, was not frightened in the least. She even felt a kind of elation, which is common in certain unbalanced but sanguine persons when they begin to approach the thing they fear. She became more agile in avoiding the loose boards, and even made little leaps around them. She could now see the landing dock at the end of the boardwalk. It was very brightly lighted and the municipality had erected a good-sized flagpole in the center of the platform. The flag was now wrapped around the pole in great folds, but Miss Goering could distinguish easily the red and white stripes and the stars. She was delighted to see the flag in this far-off place, for she hadn't imagined that there would be any organization at all on the tip of the island.

"Why, people have been living here for years," she said to herself. "It is strange that I hadn't thought of this before. They're here naturally, with their family ties, their neighborhood stores, their sense of decency and morality, and they have certainly their organizations for fighting the criminals of the community." She felt almost happy now that she had remembered all this.

She was the only person waiting for the ferry. Once she had got on, she went straight to the prow of the boat and stood watching the mainland until they reached the opposite shore. The ferry dock was at the foot of a road which joined the main street at the summit of a short steep hill. Trucks were still obliged to stop short at the top of the hill and unload their freight into wheelbarrows, which were then rolled cautiously down to the dock. Looking up from the dock, it was possible to see the side walls of the two stores at the end of the main street but not very much more. The road was so brightly lighted on either side that it was possible for Miss Goering to distinguish most of the details on the clothing of the persons who were coming down the hill to board the ferry.

She saw coming towards her three young women holding onto one another's arms and giggling. They were very fancily dressed and were trying to hold onto their hats as well as one another. This made their progress very slow, but half-way down the hill they called to someone on the dock who was standing near the post to which the ferry had been moored.

"Don't you leave without us, George," they yelled to him, and he waved his hand back in a friendly manner.

There were many young men coming down the hill and they too, seemed to be dressed for something special. Their shoes were well shined, and many of them wore flowers in their buttonholes. Even those who had started long after the three young women quickly trotted past them. Each time this happened the girls would go into gales of laughter, which Miss Goering could hear only faintly from where she stood. More and more people kept appearing over the top of the hill and most of them, it seemed to Miss Goering, did not exceed the age of thirty. She stepped to the side and soon they were talking and laughing together all over the foredeck and the bridge of the ferry. She was very curious to know where they were going, but her spirits had been considerably dampened by witnessing the exodus, which she took as a bad omen. She finally decided that she would question a young man who was still on the dock and standing not very far away from her.

"Young man," she said to him, "would you mind telling me if you are all actually going on some lark together in a group or if it's a coincidence?"

"We're all going to the same place," said the boy, "as far as I know."

"Well, could you tell me where that is?" asked Miss Goering.

"Pig Snout's Hook," he answered. Just then the ferry whistle blew. He hastily took leave of Miss Goering and ran to join his friends on the foredeck.

Miss Goering struggled up the hill entirely alone. She kept her eye on the wall of the last store on the main street. An advertising artist had painted in vivid pinks a baby's face of giant dimensions on half the surface of the wall, and in the remaining space a tremendous rubber nipple. Miss Goering wondered what Pig Snout's Hook was. She was rather disappointed when she arrived at the top of the hill to find that the main street was rather empty and dimly lighted. She had perhaps been misled by the brilliant colors of the advertisement of the baby's nipple and had half hoped that the entire town would be similarly garish.

Before proceeding down the main street she decided to examine the painted sign more closely. In order to do this she had to step across an empty lot. Very near to the advertisement she noticed that an old man was bending over some crates and trying to wrench the nails loose from the boards. She decided that she would ask him whether or not he knew where Pig Snout's Hook was.

She approached him and stood watching for a little while before asking her question. He was wearing a green plaid jacket and a little cap of the same material. He was terribly busy trying to pry a nail from the crate with only a thin stick as a tool.

"I beg your pardon," said Miss Goering to him finally, "but I would like to know where Pig Snout's Hook is and also why anyone would go there, if you know."

The man continued to bother with the nail, but Miss Goering could tell that he was really interested in her question.

"Pig Snout's Hook?" said the man. "That's easy. It's a new place, a cabaret."

"Does everyone go there?" Miss Goering asked him.

"If they are the kind who are fools, they go."

"Why do you say that?"

"Why do I say that?" said the man, getting up finally and putting his stick in his pocket. "Why do I say that? Because they go there for the pleasure of being cheated out of their last penny. The meat is just horsemeat, you know. This size and it ain't red. It's a kind of gray, without a sign of a potato near it, and it costs plenty too. They're all as poor as church mice besides, without a single ounce of knowledge about life in the whole crowd of them. Like a lot of dogs straining at the leash."

"And then they all go together to Pig Snout's Hook every single night?"

"I don't know when they go to Pig Snout's Hook," said the man, "any more than I know what cockroaches are doing every night."

"Well, what's so wrong about Pig Snout's Hook?" Miss Goering asked him.

"There's one thing wrong," said the man growing more and more interested, "and that's that they've got a nigger there that jumps up and down in front of a mirror in his room all day long until he sweats and then he does the same thing in front of these lads and lassies and they think he's playing them music. He's got an expensive instrument all right, because I know where he bought it and I'm not saying whether or not he paid for it, but I know he sticks it in his mouth and then starts moving around with his long arms like the arms of a spider and they just won't listen to nothin' else but him."

"Well," said Miss Goering, "certain people do like that type of music."

"Yes," said the man, "certain people do like that type of music and there are people who live together and eat at table together stark naked all the year long and there are others who we both know about"—he looked very mysterious—"but," he continued, "in my day money was worth a pound of sugar or butter or lard any time. When we went out we got what we paid for plus a dog jumpin' through burning hoops, and steaks you could rest your chin on."

"What do you mean?" asked Miss Goering—"a dog jumping through burning hoops?"

"Well," said the man, "you can train them to do anything with years of real patience and perseverance and lots of headaches too. You get a hoop and you light it all around and these poodles, if they're the real thing, will leap through them like birds flying in the air. Of course it's a rare thing to see them doing this, but they've been right here in this town flying right through the centers of burning hoops. Of course people were older then and they cared for their money better and they didn't want to see a black jumping up and down. They would rather prefer to put a new roof on their house." He laughed.

"Well," said Miss Goering, "did this go on in a cabaret that was situated where the Pig Snout's Hook place is now situated? You understand what I mean."

"It surely didn't!" said the man vehemently. "The place was situated right on this side of the river in a real theater with three different prices for the seats and a show every night and three times a week in the afternoon."

"Well, then," said Miss Goering, "that's quite a different thing, isn't it? Because, after all, Pig Snout's Hook is a cabaret, as you said yourself a little while ago, and this place where the poodles jumped through the burning hoops was a theater, so in actuality there is really no point of comparison."

The old man knelt down again and continued to pry the

nails from the boards by placing his little stick between the head of the nail and the wood.

Miss Goering did not know what to say to him, but she felt that it was pleasanter to go on talking than to start off down the main street alone. She could tell that he was a little annoyed, so that she was prepared to ask her next question in a considerably softer voice.

"Tell me," she said to him, "is that place at all dangerous, or is it merely a waste of time."

"Surely, it's as dangerous as you want," said the old man immediately, and his ill humor seemed to have passed. "Certainly it's dangerous. There are some Italians running it and the place is surrounded by fields and woods." He looked at her as if to say: "That is all you need to know, isn't it?"

Miss Goering for an instant felt that he was an authority and she in turn looked into his eyes very seriously. "But can't you," she asked, "can't you tell very easily whether or not they have all returned safely? After all, you have only if necessary to stand at the top of the hill and watch them disembark from the ferry." The old man picked up his stick once more and took Miss Goering by the arm.

"Come with me," he said, "and be convinced once and for all." He took her to the edge of the hill and they looked down the brightly lighted street that led to the dock. The ferry was not there, but the man who sold the tickets was clearly visible in his booth, and the rope with which they moored the ferry to the post, and even the opposite shore. Miss Goering took in the entire scene with a clear eye and waited anxiously for what the old man was about to say.

"Well," said the old man, lifting his arm and making a vague gesture which included the river and the sky, "you can see where it is impossible to know anything." Miss Goering looked around her and it seemed to her that there could be nothing hidden from their eyes, but at the same time she believed what the old man said to her. She felt both ashamed and uneasy.

"Come along," said Miss Goering, "I'll invite you to a beer."

"Thank you very much, ma'am," said the old man. His tone had changed to that of a servant, and Miss Goering felt even more ashamed of having believed what he had told her.

"Is there any particular place that you would like to go?" she asked him.

"No, ma'am," he said, shuffling along beside her. He no longer seemed in the least inclined to talk.

There was no one walking along the main street except Miss Goering and the old man. They did pass a car parked in front of a dark store. Two people were smoking on the front seat.

The old man stopped in front of the window of a bar and grill and stood looking at some turkey and some old sausages which were on display.

"Shall we go in here and have something to eat with our little drink?" Miss Goering asked him.

"I'm not hungry," the man said, "but I'll go in with you and sit down."

Miss Goering was disappointed because he didn't seem to have any sense of how to give even the slightest festive air to the evening. The bar was dark, but festooned here and there with crepe paper. "In honor of some recent holiday, no doubt," thought Miss Goering. There was a particularly nice garland of bright green paper flowers strung up along the entire length of the mirror behind the bar. The room was furnished with eight or nine tables, each one enclosed in a dark brown booth.

Miss Goering and the old man seated themselves at the bar.

"By the way," said the old man to her, "wouldn't you like better to seat yourself at a table where you ain't so much in view?"

"No," said Miss Goering, "I think this is very, very pleasant indeed. Now order what you want, will you?"

"I will have," said the man, "a sandwich of turkey and a sandwich of pork, a cup of coffee, and a drink of rye whisky."

"What a curious psychology!" thought Miss Goering. "I should think he would be embarrassed after just having finished saying that he wasn't hungry."

She looked over her shoulder out of curiosity and noticed that behind her in a booth were seated a boy and a girl. The boy was reading a newspaper. He was drinking nothing. The girl was sipping at a very nice cherry-colored drink through a straw. Miss Goering ordered herself two gins in succession, and when she had finished these she turned around and looked at the girl again. The girl seemed to have been expecting this because she already had her face turned in Miss Goering's direction. She smiled softly at Miss Goering and opened her eyes wide. They were very dark. The whites of her eyes, Miss Goering noticed, were shot with yellow. Her hair was black and wiry and stood way out all over her head.

"Jewish, Rumanian, or Italian," Miss Goering said to herself. The boy did not lift his eyes from his newspaper, which he held in such a way that his profile was hidden.

"Having a nice time?" the girl asked Miss Goering in a husky voice.

"Well," said Miss Goering, "it wasn't exactly in order to have a good time that I came out. I have more or less forced myself to, simply because I despise going out in the night-time alone and prefer not to leave my own house. However, it has come to such a point that I am forcing myself to make these little excursions—"

Miss Goering stopped because she actually did not know how she could go on and explain to this girl what she meant without talking a very long time indeed, and she realized that this would be impossible right at that moment, since the waiter was constantly walking back and forth between the bar and the young people's booth.

"Anyway," said Miss Goering, "I certainly think it does no harm to relax a bit and have a lovely time."

"Everyone must have a wonderfully marvelous time," said the girl, and Miss Goering noticed that there was a trace of an accent in her speech. "Isn't that true, my angel Pussycat?" she said to the boy.

The boy put his newspaper down; he looked rather annoyed. "Isn't what true?" he asked her. "I didn't hear a word that you said." Miss Goering knew perfectly well that this was a lie and that he was only pretending not to have noticed that his girl friend had been speaking with her.

"Nothing very important, really," she said, looking tenderly into his eyes. "This lady here was saying that after all it did nobody any harm to relax and have a lovely time."

"Perhaps," said the boy, "it does more harm than anything else to date to have a lovely time." He said this straight to the girl and completely ignored the fact that Miss Goering had been mentioned at all. The girl leaned way over and whispered into his ear.

"Darling," she said, "something terrible has happened to that woman. I feel it in my heart. Please don't be bad-tempered with her."

"With whom?" the boy asked her.

She laughed because she knew there was nothing else much that she could do. The boy was subject to bad moods, but she loved him and was able to put up with almost anything.

The old man who had come with Miss Goering had excused himself and had taken his drinks and sandwiches over to a radio, where he was now standing with his ear close to the box.

Away in the back of the room a man was bowling up a small alley all by himself; Miss Goering listened to the rumble of the balls as they rolled along the wooden runway, and she wished that she were able to see him so that she could be at peace for the evening with the certainty that there was no one who could be considered a menace present in the room. Certainly there was a possibility that more clients would enter through the door, but this had entirely slipped her mind. Hard though she tried, it was impossible for her to get a look at the man who was rolling the balls.

The young boy and the girl were having a fight. Miss Goering could tell by the sound of their voices. She listened to them carefully without turning her head.

"I don't see why," said the girl, "that you must be furious immediately just because I have mentioned that I always like to come in here and sit for a little while."

"There is absolutely no reason," said the boy, "why you should want to come in here and sit more than in any other place."

"Then why—then why do you come in?" the girl asked hesitantly.

"I don't know," said the boy; "maybe because it's the first thing we hit after we leave our room."

"No," said the girl, "there are other places. I wish you would just say that you liked it here; I don't know why, but it would make me so happy; we've been coming here for a long time."

"I'll be God-damned if I'll say it, and I'll be God-damned if

I'll come here any more if you're going to invest this place with witches' powers."

"Oh, Pussycat," said the girl, and there was real anguish in her tone, "Pussycat, I am not talking about witches and their powers; not even thinking about them. Only when I was a little girl. I should never have told you the story."

The boy shook his head back and forth; he was disgusted with her.

"For God's sake," he said, "that isn't anything near what I mean, Bernice."

"I do not understand *what* you mean," said Bernice. "Many people come into this place or some other place every night for years and years and without doing much but having a drink and talking to each other; it is only because it is like home to them. And we come here only because it is little by little becoming a home to us; a second home if you can call our little room a home; it is to me; I love it very much."

The boy groaned with discontent.

"And," she added, feeling that her words and her tone of voice could not help working a spell over the boy, "the tables and the chairs and the walls here have now become like the familiar faces of old friends."

"What old friends?" said the boy, scowling more and more furiously. "What old friends? To me this is just another shit-house where poor people imbibe spirits in order to forget the state of their income, which is nonexistent."

He sat up very straight and glared at Bernice.

"I guess that is true, in a way," she said vaguely, "but I feel that there is something more."

"That's just the trouble."

Meanwhile Frank, the bartender, had been listening to Bernice's conversation with Dick. It was a dull night and the more he thought about what the boy had said, the angrier he felt. He decided to go over to the table and start a row.

"Come on, Dick," he said, grabbing him by the collar of his shirt. "If that's the way you feel about this place, get the hell out of here." He yanked him out of his seat and gave him a terrific shove so that Dick staggered a few steps and fell headlong over the bar.

"You big fat-head," Dick yelled at the bartender, lunging

out at him. "You hunk of retrogressive lard. I'll push your white face in for you."

The two were now fighting very hard. Bernice was standing on the table and pulling at the shirts of the fighters in an attempt to separate them. She was able to reach them even when they were quite a distance from the table because the benches terminated in posts at either end, and by grabbing hold of one of them she could swing out over the heads of the fighters.

Miss Goering, from where she was now standing, could see the flesh above Bernice's stocking whenever she leaned particularly far out of her booth. This would not have troubled her so much had she not noticed that the man who had been rolling the wooden balls had now moved away from his post and was staring quite fixedly at Bernice's bare flesh whenever the occasion presented itself. The man had a narrow red face, a pinched and somewhat inflamed nose, and very thin lips. His hair was almost orange in color. Miss Goering could not decide whether he was of an exceedingly upright character or of a criminal nature, but the intensity of his attitude almost scared her to death. Nor was it even possible for Miss Goering to decide whether he was looking at Bernice with interest or with scorn.

Although he was getting in some good punches and his face was streaming with sweat, Frank the bartender appeared to be very calm and it seemed to Miss Goering that he was losing interest in the fight and that actually the only really tense person in the room was the man who was standing behind her.

Soon Frank had a split lip and Dick a bloody nose. Very shortly after this they both stopped fighting and walked unsteadily towards the washroom. Bernice jumped off the table and ran after them.

They returned in a few minutes, all washed and combed and holding dirty handkerchiefs to their mouths. Miss Goering walked up to them and took hold of each man by the arm.

"I'm glad that it's all over now, and I want each of you to have a drink as my guest."

Dick looked very sad now and very subdued. He nodded his head solemnly and they sat down together and waited for Frank to fix them their drinks. He returned with their drinks, and after he had served them, he too seated himself at the table. They all drank in silence for a little while. Frank was dreamy and seemed to be thinking of very personal things that had nothing to do with the events of the evening. Once he took out an address book and looked through its pages several times. It was Miss Goering who first broke the silence.

"Now tell me," she said to Bernice and Dick, "tell me what you are interested in."

"I'm interested in the political struggle," said Dick, "which is of course the only thing that any self-respecting human being could be interested in. I am also on the winning side and on the right side. The side that believes in the redistribution of capital." He chuckled to himself and it was very easy to tell that he thought he was conversing with a complete fool.

"I've heard all about that," said Miss Goering. "And what are you interested in?" she asked the girl.

"Anything he is interested in, but it is true that I had believed the political struggle was very important before I met him. You see, I have a different nature than he has. What makes me happy I seem to catch out of the sky with both hands; I only hold whatever it is that I love because that is all I can really see. The world interferes with me and my happiness, but I never interfere with the world except now since I am with Dick." Bernice put her hand out on the table for Dick to take hold of it. She was already a little drunk.

"It makes me sad to hear you talk like this," said Dick. "You, as a leftist, know perfectly well that before we fight for our own happiness we must fight for something else. We are living in a period when personal happiness means very little because the individual has very few moments left. It is wise to destroy yourself first; at least to keep only that part of you which can be of use to a big group of people. If you don't do this you lose sight of objective reality and so forth, and you fall plunk into the middle of a mysticism which right now would be a waste of time."

"You are right, darling Dickie," said Bernice, "but sometimes I would love to be waited on in a beautiful room. Sometimes I think it would be nice to be a bourgeois." (She said the word "bourgeois," Miss Goering noticed, as though she had just learned it.) Bernice continued: "I am such a human person. Even though I am poor I will miss the same things that they do, because sometimes at night the fact that they are sleeping in their houses with security, instead of making me angry, fills me with peace like a child who is scared at night likes to hear grown people talking down in the street. Don't you think there is some sense in what I say, Dickie?"

"None whatsoever!" said the boy. "We know perfectly well that it is this security of theirs that makes us cry out at night."

Miss Goering by now was very anxious to get into the conversation.

"You," she said to Dick, "are interested in winning a very correct and intelligent fight. I am far more interested in what is making this fight so hard to win."

"They have the power in their hands; they have the press and the means of production."

Miss Goering put her hand over the boy's mouth. He jumped. "This is very true," she said, "but isn't it very obvious that there is something else too that you are fighting? You are fighting their present position on this earth, to which they are all grimly attached. Our race, as you know, is not torpid. They are grim because they still believe the earth is flat and that they are likely to fall off it at any minute. That is why they hold on so hard to the middle. That is, to all the ideals by which they have always lived. You cannot confront men who are still fighting the dark and all the dragons, with a new future."

"Well, well," said Dick, "what should I do then?"

"Just remember," said Miss Goering, "that a revolution won is an adult who must kill his childhood once and for all."

"I'll remember," said Dick, sneering a bit at Miss Goering.

The man who had been rolling the balls was now standing at the bar.

"I better go see what Andy wants," said Frank. He had been whistling softly all through Miss Goering's conversation with Dick, but he seemed to have been listening nevertheless, because as he was leaving the table he turned to Miss Goering.

"I think that the earth is a very nice place to be living on," he said to her, "and I never felt that by going one step too far I was going to fall off it either. You can always do things two or three times on the earth and everybody's plenty patient till you get something right. First time wrong doesn't mean you're sunk."

"Well, I wasn't talking about anything like that," said Miss Goering.

"That's what you're talking about all right. Don't try to pussyfoot it out now. But I tell you it's perfectly all right as far as I'm concerned." He was looking with feeling into Miss Goering's eyes. "My life," he said, "is my own, whether it's a mongrel or a prince."

"What on earth is he talking about?" Miss Goering asked Bernice and Dick. "He seems to think I've insulted him."

"God knows!" said Dick. "At any rate I am sleepy. Bernice, let's go home."

While Dick was paying Frank at the bar, Bernice leaned over Miss Goering and whispered in her ear.

"You know, darling," she said, "he's not really like this when we are home together alone. He makes me really happy. He is a sweet boy and you should see the simple things that delight him when he is in his own room and not with strangers. Well"—she straightened up and seemed to be a little embarrassed at her own burst of confidence—"well, I am very glad indeed that I met you and I hope we did not give you too much of a rough time. I promise you that it has never happened before, because underneath, Dick is really like you and me, but he is in a very nervous state of mind. So you must forgive him."

"Certainly," said Miss Goering, "but I do not see what for."

"Well, good-by," said Bernice.

Miss Goering was far too embarrassed and shocked by what Bernice had said behind Dick's back to notice at first that she was now the only person in the barroom besides the man who had been rolling the wooden balls and the old man, who had by now fallen asleep with his head on the bar. When she did notice, however, she felt for one desolate moment that the whole thing had been prearranged and that although she had forced herself to take this little trip to the mainland, she had somehow at the same time been tricked into taking it by the powers above. She felt that she could not leave and that even if she tried, something would happen to interfere with her departure.

She noticed with a faint heart that the man had lifted his drink from the bar and was coming towards her. He stopped about a foot away from her table and stood holding his glass in mid-air.

"You will have a drink with me, won't you?" he asked her without looking particularly cordial.

"I'm sorry," said Frank from behind the bar, "but we're going to close up now. No more drinks served, I'm afraid."

Andy said nothing, but he went out the door and slammed it behind him. They could hear him walking up and down outside of the saloon.

"He's going to have his own way again," said Frank, "damn it all."

"Oh, dear," said Miss Goering, "are you afraid of him?"

"Sure I'm not," said Frank, "but he's disagreeable—that's the only word I can think up for him—disagreeable; and after it's all said and done, life is too short."

"Well," said Miss Goering, "is he dangerous?"

Frank shrugged his shoulders. Soon Andy came back.

"The moon and the stars are out now," he said, "and I could almost see clear to the edge of the town. There are no policemen in sight, so I think we can have our drink."

He slid in, onto the bench opposite Miss Goering.

"It's cold and lifeless without a living thing on the street," he began, "but that's the way I like it nowadays; you'll forgive me if I sound morose to a gay woman like yourself, but I have a habit of never paying attention to whoever I am talking to. I think people would say about me: 'lacking in respect for other human beings.' *You* have great respect for your friends, I'm sure, but that is only because you respect yourself, which is always the starting-off point for everything: yourself."

Miss Goering did not feel very much more at ease now that he was talking to her than she had before he had sat down. He seemed to grow more intense and almost angry as he talked, and his way of attributing qualities to her which were not in any way true to her nature gave his conversation an eerie quality and at the same time made Miss Goering feel inconsequential.

"Do you live in this town?" Miss Goering asked him.

"I do, indeed," said Andy. "I have three furnished rooms in a new apartment house. It is the only apartment house in this town. I pay rent every month and I live there all alone. In the afternoon the sun shines into my apartment, which is one of the finest ironies, in my opinion, because of all the apartments in the building, mine is the sunniest and I sleep there all day with my shades drawn down. I didn't always live there. I lived before in the city with my mother. But this is the nearest thing I could find to a penal island, so it suits me; it suits me fine." He fumbled with some cigarettes for a few minutes and kept his eyes purposely averted from Miss Goering's face. He reminded her of certain comedians who are at last given a secondary tragic role and execute it rather well. She also had a very definite impression that one thing was cleaving his simple mind in two, causing him to twist between his sheets instead of sleeping, and to lead an altogether wretched existence. She had no doubt that she would soon find out what it was.

"You have a very special type of beauty," he said to her; "a bad nose, but beautiful eyes and hair. It would please me in the midst of all this horror to go to bed with you. But in order to do this we'll have to leave this bar and go to my apartment."

"Well, I can't promise you anything, but I will be glad to go to your apartment," said Miss Goering.

Andy told Frank to call the hackstand and tell a certain man who was on duty all night to come over and get them.

The taxi drove down the main street very slowly. It was very old and consequently it rattled a good deal. Andy stuck his head out of the window.

"How do you do, ladies and gentlemen?" he shouted at the empty street, trying to approximate an English accent. "I hope, I certainly hope that each and every one of you is having a fine time in this great town of ours." He leaned back against his seat again and smiled in such a horrid manner that Miss Goering felt frightened again.

"You could roll a hoop down this street, naked, at midnight and no one would ever know it," he said to her.

"Well, if you think it is such a dismal place," said Miss Goering, "why don't you move somewhere else, bag and baggage?"

"Oh, no," he said gloomily, "I'll never do that. There's no use in my doing that."

"Is it that your business ties you down here?" Miss Goering asked him, although she knew perfectly well he was speaking of something spiritual and far more important.

"Don't call me a business man," he said to her.

"Then you are an artist?"

He shook his head vaguely as though not quite sure what an artist was.

"Well, all right," said Miss Goering, "I've had two guesses; now won't you tell me what you are?"

"A bum!" he said stentoriously, sliding lower in his seat. "You knew that all the time, didn't you, being an intelligent woman?"

The taxicab drew up in front of the apartment house, which stood between an empty lot and a string of stores only one story high.

"You see, I get the afternoon sun all day long," he said, "because I have no obstructions. I look out over this empty lot."

"There is a tree growing in the empty lot," said Miss Goering. "I suppose that you are able to see it from your window?"

"Yes," said Andy. "Weird, isn't it?"

The apartment house was very new and very small. They stood together in the lobby while Andy searched his pockets for the keys. The floor was of imitation marble, yellow in color except in the center where the architect had set in a blue peacock in mosaic, surrounded by various long-stemmed flowers. It was hard to distinguish the peacock in the dim light, but Miss Goering crouched down on her heels in order to examine it better.

"I think those are water lilies around that peacock," said Andy, "but a peacock is supposed to have thousands of colors in him, isn't he? Multicolored, isn't that the point of a peacock? This one's all blue."

"Well," said Miss Goering, "perhaps it is nicer this way."

They left the lobby and went up some ugly iron steps. Andy lived on the first floor. There was a terrible odor in the hall, which he told her never went away.

"They're cooking in there for ten people," he said, "all day long. They all work at different hours of the day; half of them don't see the other half at all, except on Sundays and holidays."

Andy's apartment was very hot and stuffy. The furniture was brown and none of the cushions appeared to fit the chairs properly.

"Here's journey's end," said Andy. "Make yourself at home. I'm going to take off some of my clothes." He returned in a minute wearing a bathrobe made of some very cheap material. Both ends of his bathrobe cords had been partially chewed away.

"What happened to your bathrobe cords?" Miss Goering asked him.

"My dog chewed them away."

"Oh, have you a dog?" she asked him.

"Once upon a time I had a dog and a future, and a girl," he said, "but that is no longer so."

"Well, what happened?" Miss Goering asked, throwing her shawl off her shoulders and mopping her forehead with her handkerchief. The steam heat had already begun to make her sweat, particularly as she had not been used to central heating for some time.

"Let's not talk about my life," said Andy, putting his hand up like a traffic officer. "Let's have some drinks instead."

"All right, but I certainly think we should talk about your life sooner or later," said Miss Goering. All the while she was thinking that she would allow herself to go home within an hour. "I consider," she said to herself, "that I have done quite well for my first night." Andy was standing up and pulling his bathrobe cord tighter around his waist.

"I was," he said, "engaged to be married to a very nice girl who worked. I loved her as much as a man can love a woman. She had a smooth forehead, beautiful blue eyes, and not so good teeth. Her legs were something to take pictures of. Her name was Mary and she got along with my mother. She was a plain girl with an ordinary mind and she used to get a tremendous kick out of life. Sometimes we used to have dinner at midnight just for the hell of it and she used to say to me: 'Imagine us, walking down the street at midnight to have our dinner. Just two ordinary people. Maybe there isn't any sanity.' Naturally, I didn't tell her that there were plenty of people like the people who live down the hall in 5D who eat dinner at midnight, not because they are crazy, but because they've got jobs that cause them to do so, because then maybe she wouldn't have got so much fun out of it. I wasn't going to spoil it and tell her that the world wasn't crazy, that the world was medium fair; and I didn't know either that a couple of months later her sweetheart was going to become one of the craziest people in it."

The veins in Andy's forehead were beginning to bulge, his face was redder, and the wings of his nostrils were sweaty.

"All this must really mean something to him," thought Miss Goering.

"Often I used to go into an Italian restaurant for dinner; it was right around the corner from my house; I knew mostly all the people that ate there, and the atmosphere was very convivial. There were a few of us who always ate together. I always bought the wine because I was better fixed than most of them. Then there were a couple of old men who ate there, but we never bothered with them. There was one man too who wasn't so old, but he was solitary and didn't mix in with the others. We knew he used to be in the circus, but we never found out what kind of a job he had there or anything. Then one night, the night before he brought her in, I happened to be gazing at him for no reason on earth and I saw him stand up and fold his newspaper into his pocket, which was peculiar-looking because he hadn't finished his dinner yet. Then he turned towards us and coughed like he was clearing his throat.

"'Gentlemen,' he said, 'I have an announcement to make.' I had to quiet the boys because he had such a thin little voice you could hardly hear what he was saying.

"'I am not going to take much of your time,' he continued, like someone talking at a big banquet, 'but I just want to tell you and you'll understand why in a minute. I just want to tell you that I'm bringing a young lady here tomorrow night and without any reservations I want you all to love her: This lady, gentlemen, is like a broken doll. She has neither arms nor legs.' Then he sat down very quietly and started right in eating again."

"How terribly embarrassing!" said Miss Goering. "Dear me, what did you answer to that?"

"I don't remember," said Andy, "I just remember that it was embarrassing like you say and we didn't feel that he had to make the announcement anyway.

"She was already in her chair the next night when we got there; nicely made up and wearing a very pretty, clean blouse pinned in front with a brooch shaped like a butterfly. Her hair was marcelled too and she was a natural blonde. I kept my ear cocked and I heard her telling the little man that her appetite got better all the time and that she could sleep fourteen hours a day. After that I began to notice her mouth. It was like a rose petal or a heart or some kind of a little shell. It was really beautiful. Then right away I started to wonder what she would be like; the rest of her, you understand—without any legs." He stopped talking and walked around the room once, looking up at his walls.

"It came into my mind like an ugly snake, this idea, and curled there to stay. I looked at her head so little and so delicate against the dark grimy wall and it was the apple of sin that I was eating for the first time."

"Really for the first time?" said Miss Goering. She looked bewildered and was lost in thought for a moment.

"From then on I thought of nothing else but finding out; every other thought left my head."

"And before what were your thoughts like?" Miss Goering asked him a little maliciously. He didn't seem to hear her.

"Well, this went on for some time—the way I felt about her. I was seeing Belle, who came to the restaurant often, after that first night, and I was seeing Mary too. I got friendly with Belle. There was nothing special about her. She loved wine and I actually used to pour it down her throat for her. She talked a little bit too much about her family and was a little too good. Not exactly religious, but a little too full of the milk of human kindness sort of thing. It grew and grew, this terrible curiosity or desire of mine until finally my mind started to wander when I was with Mary and I couldn't sleep with her any more. She was swell all the way through it, though, patient as a lamb. She was much too young to have such a thing happen to her. I was like a horrible old man or one of those impotent kings with a history of syphilis behind him."

"Did you tell your sweetheart what was getting on your nerves?" asked Miss Goering, trying to hurry him up a bit.

"I didn't tell her because I wanted the buildings to stay in place for her and I wanted the stars to be over her head and not cockeyed—I wanted her to be able to walk in the park and feed the birdies in years to come with some other fine human being hanging onto her arm. I didn't want her to have to lock something up inside of her and look out at the world through a nailed window. It was not long before I went to bed with Belle and got myself a beautiful case of syphilis, which I spent the next two years curing. I took to bowling along about then and I finally left my mother's house and my work and came out to No-man's Land. I can live in this apartment all right on a little money that I get from a building I own down in the slums of the city."

He sat down in a chair opposite Miss Goering and put his face in his hands. Miss Goering judged that he had finished and she was just about to thank him for his hospitality and wish him good-night when he uncovered his face and began again.

"The worst of all I remember clearly; more and more I couldn't face my mother. I'd stay out bowling all day long and half the night. Then on the fourth day of July I decided that I would make a very special effort to spend the day with her. There was a big parade supposed to go by our window at three in the afternoon. Very near to that time I was standing in the parlor with a pressed suit on, and Mother was sitting as close to the window as she could get. It was a sunny day out and just right for a parade. The parade was punctual because about a quarter to three we began to hear some faint music in the distance. Then soon after that my country's red, white, and blue flag went by, held up by some fine-looking boys. The band was playing *Yankee Doodle.* All of a sudden I hid my face in my hands; I couldn't look at my country's flag. Then I knew, once and for all, that I hated myself. Since then I have accepted my status as a skunk. 'Citizen Skunk' happens to be a little private name I have for myself. You can have some fun in the mud, though, you know, if you just accept a seat in it instead of trying to squirm around."

"Well," said Miss Goering, "I certainly think you could pull yourself together with a bit of an effort. I wouldn't put much stock in that flag episode either."

He looked at her vaguely. "You talk like a society lady," he said to her.

"I am a society lady," said Miss Goering. "I am also rich, but I have purposely reduced my living standards. I have left my lovely home and I have moved out to a little house on the island. The house is in very bad shape and costs me practically nothing. What do you think of that?"

"I think you're cuckoo," said Andy, and not at all in a friendly tone. He was frowning darkly. "People like you shouldn't be allowed to have money."

Miss Goering was surprised to hear him making such a show of righteous indignation.

"Please," she said, "could you possibly open the window?"

"There will be an awfully cold wind blowing through here if I do," said Andy.

"Nevertheless," said Miss Goering, "I think I would prefer it."

"I'll tell you," said Andy, moving uncomfortably around his chair. "I just put in a bad spell of grippe and I'm dead afraid of getting into a draft." He bit his lip and looked terribly worried. "I could go and stand in the next room if you want while you get your breath of fresh air," he added, brightening up a bit.

"That's a jolly good idea," said Miss Goering.

He left and closed the bedroom door softly behind him. She was delighted with the chance to get some cool air, and after she had opened the window she placed her two hands on the sill far apart from each other and leaned out. She would have enjoyed this far more had she not been certain that Andy was standing still in his room consumed with boredom and impatience. He still frightened her a little and at the same time she felt that he was a terrible burden. There was a gas station opposite the apartment house. Although the office was deserted at the moment, it was brightly lighted and a radio on the desk had been left on. There was a folksong coming over the air. Soon there was a short rap at the bedroom door, which was just what she had been expecting to hear. She closed the window regretfully before the tune had finished.

"Come in," she called to him, "come in." She was dismayed to see when Andy opened the door that he had removed all of his clothing with the exception of his socks and his underdrawers. He did not seem to be embarrassed, but behaved as though they had both tacitly understood that he was to appear dressed in this fashion.

He walked with her to the couch and made her sit down beside him. Then he flung his arm around her and crossed his legs. His legs were terribly thin, and on the whole he looked inconsequential now that he had removed his clothing. He pressed his cheek to Miss Goering's.

"Do you think you could make me a little happy?" he asked her.

"For Heaven's sake," said Miss Goering, sitting bolt upright, "I thought you were beyond that."

"Well, no man can really look into the future, you know." He narrowed his eyes and attempted to kiss her.

"Now, about that woman," she said, "Belle, who had neither arms nor legs?"

"Please, darling, let's not discuss her now. Will you do me that favor?" His tone was a little sneering, but there was an undercurrent of excitement in his voice. He said: "Now tell me whatever it is that you like. You know . . . I haven't lost all my time these two years. There are a few little things I pride myself on."

Miss Goering looked very solemn. She was thinking of this very seriously, because she suspected that were she to accept Andy's offer it would be far more difficult for her to put a stop to her excursions, should she feel so disposed. Until recently she had never followed too dangerously far in action any course which she had decided upon as being the morally correct one. She scarcely approved of this weakness in herself, but she was to a certain extent sensible and happy enough to protect herself automatically. She was feeling a little tipsy, however, and Andy's suggestion rather appealed to her. "One must allow that a certain amount of carelessness in one's nature often accomplishes what the will is incapable of doing," she said to herself.

Andy looked towards the bedroom door. His mood seemed to have changed very suddenly and he seemed confused. "This does not mean that he is not lecherous," thought Miss Goering. He got up and wandered around the room. Finally he pulled an old gramophone out from behind the couch. He took up a good deal of time dusting it off and collecting some needles that were scattered around and underneath the turntable. As he knelt over the instrument he became quite absorbed in what he was doing and his face took on an almost sympathetic aspect.

"It's a very old machine," he mumbled. "I got it a long, long time ago."

The machine was very small and terribly out of date, and had Miss Goering been sentimental, she would have felt a little sad watching him; however, she was growing impatient.

"I can't hear a word that you are saying," she shouted at him in an unnecessarily loud voice.

He got up without answering her and went into his room. When he returned he was again wearing his bathrobe and holding a record in his hand.

"You'll think I'm silly," he said, "bothering with that machine so long, when all I've got to play for you is this one record. It's a march; here." He handed it to her in order that she might read the title of the piece and the name of the band that was executing it.

"Maybe," he said, "you'd rather not hear it. A lot of people don't like march music."

"No, do play it," said Miss Goering. "I'll be delighted, really."

He put the record on and sat on the edge of a very uncomfortable chair at quite a distance from Miss Goering. The needle was too loud and the march was the *Washington Post.* Miss Goering felt as uneasy as one can feel listening to parade music in a quiet room. Andy seemed to be enjoying it and he kept time with his feet during the entire length of the record. But when it was over he seemed to be in an even worse state of confusion than before.

"Would you like to see the apartment?" he asked her.

Miss Goering leaped up from the couch quickly lest he should change his mind.

"A woman who made dresses had this apartment before me, so my bedroom is kind of sissyish for a man."

She followed him into the bedroom. He had turned the bed down rather badly and the slips of the two pillows were gray and wrinkled. On his dresser were pictures of several girls, all of them terribly unattractive and plain. They looked more to Miss Goering like the church-going type of young woman than like the mistresses of a bachelor.

"They're nice-looking girls, aren't they?" said Andy to Miss Goering.

"Lovely-looking," she said, "lovely."

"None of these girls live in this town," he said. "They live in different towns in the vicinity. The girls here are guarded and they don't like bachelors my age. I don't blame them. I go take one of these girls in the pictures out now and then when I feel like it. I even sit in their living-rooms of an evening with them, with their parents right in the house. But they don't see much of me, I can tell you that."

Miss Goering was growing more and more puzzled, but she didn't ask him any more questions because she was suddenly feeling weary.

"I think I'll be on my way now," she said, swaying a little on her feet. She realized immediately how rude and unkind she was being and she saw Andy tightening up. He put his fists into his pockets.

"Well, you can't go now," he said to her. "Stay a little longer and I'll make you some coffee."

"No, no, I don't want any coffee. Anyway, they'll be worrying about me at home."

"Who's they?" Andy asked her.

"Arnold and Arnold's father and Miss Gamelon."

"It sounds like a terrible mob to me," he said. "I couldn't stand living with a crowd like that."

"I love it," said Miss Goering.

He put his arms around her and tried to kiss her, but she pulled away, "No, honestly, I'm much too tired."

"All right," he said, "all right!" His brow was deeply furrowed and he looked completely miserable. He took his bathrobe off and got into his bed. He lay there with the sheet up to his neck, threshing his feet about and looking up at the ceiling like someone with a fever. There was a small light burning on the table beside the bed which shone directly into his face, so that Miss Goering was able to distinguish many lines which she had not noticed before. She went over to his bed and leaned over him.

"What *is* the matter?" she asked him. "Now it's been a very pleasant evening and we all need some sleep."

He laughed in her face. "You're some lunatic," he said to her, "and you sure don't know anything about people. I'm all right here, though." He pulled the sheet up farther and lay there breathing heavily. "There's a five o'clock ferry that leaves in about a half hour. Will you come back tomorrow evening? I'll be where I was tonight at that bar."

She promised him that she would return on the following evening, and after he had explained to her how to get to the dock, she opened his window for him and left.

Stupidly enough, Miss Goering had forgotten to take her key with her and she was obliged to knock on the door in order to get into her house. She pounded twice, and almost immediately she heard someone running down the steps. She could tell that it was Arnold even before he had opened the door. He was wearing a rose-colored pajama jacket and a pair of trousers. His suspenders were hanging down over his hips. His beard had grown quite a bit for such a short time and he looked sloppier than ever.

"What's the matter with you, Arnold?" said Miss Goering. "You look dreadful."

"Well, I've had a bad night, Christina. I just put Bubbles to sleep a little while ago; she's terribly worried about you. As a matter of fact, I don't think you've shown us much consideration."

"Who is Bubbles?" Miss Goering asked him.

"Bubbles," he said, "is the name I have for Miss Gamelon."

"Well," said Miss Goering, going into the house and seating herself in front of the fireplace, "I took the ferry back across to the mainland and I became very much involved. I might return tomorrow night," she added, "although I don't really want to very much."

"I don't know why you find it so interesting and intellectual to seek out a new city," said Arnold, cupping his chin in his hand and looking at her fixedly.

"Because I believe the hardest thing for me to do is really move from one thing to another, partly," said Miss Goering.

"Spiritually," said Arnold, trying to speak in a more sociable tone, "spiritually I'm constantly making little journeys and changing my entire nature every six months."

"I don't believe it for a minute," said Miss Goering.

"No, no, it is true. Also I can tell you that I think it is absolute nonsense to move physically from one place to another. All places are more or less alike."

Miss Goering did not answer this. She pulled her shawl closer around her shoulders and of a sudden looked quite old and very sad indeed.

Arnold began to doubt the validity of what he had just said, and immediately resolved to make exactly the same excursion from which Miss Goering had just returned, on the following night. He squared his jaw and pulled out a notebook from his pocket.

"Now, will you give me the particulars on how to reach the mainland?" said Arnold. "The hours when the train leaves, and so forth."

"Why do you ask?" said Miss Goering.

"Because I'm going to go there myself tomorrow night. I should have thought you would have guessed that by this time."

"No, judging by what you just finished saying to me, I would not have guessed it."

"Well, I talk one way," said Arnold, "but I'm really, underneath, the same kind of maniac that you are."

"I would like to see your father," Miss Goering said to him.

"I think he's asleep. I hope he will come to his senses and go home," said Arnold.

"Well, I am hoping the contrary," said Miss Goering. "I'm terribly attached to him. Let's go upstairs and just look into his room."

They went up the stairs together and Miss Gamelon came out to meet them on the landing. Her eyes were all swollen and she was wrapped in a heavy wool bathrobe.

She began speaking to Miss Goering in a voice that was thick with sleep. "Once more, and it will be the last you will see of Lucy Gamelon."

"Now, Bubbles," said Arnold, "remember this is not an ordinary household and you must expect certain eccentricities on the part of the inmates. You see, I have dubbed us all inmates."

"Arnold," said Miss Gamelon, "now don't you begin. You know what I told you this afternoon about talking drivel."

"Please, Lucy," said Arnold.

"Come, come, let's all go and take a peek at Arnold's father," suggested Miss Goering.

Miss Gamelon followed them only in order to continue admonishing Arnold, which she did in a low voice. Miss Goering pulled the door open. The room was very cold and she realized for the first time that it was already bright outdoors. It had all happened very quickly while she was talking to Arnold in the parlor, but there it was nearly always dark because of the thick bushes outside.

Arnold's father was sleeping on his back. His face was still and he breathed regularly without snoring. Miss Goering shook him a few times by the shoulder.

"The procedures in this house," said Miss Gamelon, "are what amount to criminal. Now you're waking up an old man who needs his sleep, at the crack of dawn. It makes me shudder to stand here and see what you've become, Christina."

At last Arnold's father awakened. It took him a little while to realize what had happened, but when he had, he leaned on his elbows and said in a very chipper manner to Miss Goering:

"Good morning, Mrs. Marco Polo. What beautiful treasures have you brought back from the East? I'm glad to see you, and if there's anywhere you want me to go with you, I'm ready." He fell back on his pillow with a thump.

Miss Goering said that she would see him later, that at the moment she was badly in need of some rest. They left the room, and before they had closed the door behind them, Arnold's father was already asleep. On the landing Miss Gamelon began to cry and she buried her face for a moment in Miss Goering's shoulder. Miss Goering held her very tightly and begged her not to cry. Then she kissed both Arnold and Miss Gamelon good-night. When she arrived in her room she was overcome with fright for a few moments, but shortly she fell into a deep sleep.

At about five thirty on the following afternoon Miss Goering announced her intention of returning again that evening to the mainland. Miss Gamelon was standing up, sewing one of Arnold's socks. She was dressed more coquettishly than was her habit, with a ruffle around the neck of her dress and a liberal coating of rouge on her cheeks. The old man was in a big chair in the corner reading the poetry of Longfellow, sometimes aloud, sometimes to himself. Arnold was still dressed in the same fashion as the night before, with the exception of a sweater which he had pulled on over his pajama top. There was a big coffee stain on the front of his sweater, and the ashes of his cigarette had spilled over his chest. He was lying on the couch half asleep.

"You will go back there again over my dead body," said Miss Gamelon. "Now, please, Christina, be sane and do let us all have a pleasant evening together."

Miss Goering sighed. "Well, you and Arnold can have a perfectly pleasant evening together without me. I am sorry. I'd love to stay, but I really feel that I must go."

"You drive me wild with your mysterious talk," said Miss Gamelon. "If only some member of your family were here! Why don't we phone for a taxi," she said hopefully, "and go to the city? We might eat some Chinese food and go to the theater afterwards, or a picture show, if you are still in your pinch-penny mood."

"Why don't you and Arnold go to the city and eat some Chinese food and then go to the theater? I will be very glad to have you go as my guests, but I'm afraid I can't accompany you."

Arnold was growing annoyed at the ease with which Miss Goering disposed of him. Her manner also gave him a very bad sense of being inferior to her.

"I'm sorry, Christina," he said from his couch, "but I have no intention of eating Chinese food. I have been planning all along to take a little jaunt to the mainland opposite this end of the island too, and nothing will stop me. I wish you'd come along with me, Lucy; as a matter of fact, I don't see why we can't all go along together. It is quite senseless that Christina should make such a morbid affair out of this little saunter to the mainland. Actually there is nothing to it."

"Arnold!" Miss Gamelon screamed at him. "You're losing your mind too, and if you think I am going on a wild-goose chase aboard a train and a ferry just to wind up in some little rat-trap, you're doubly crazy. Anyway, I've heard that it is a very tough little town, besides being dreary and without any interest whatsoever."

"Nevertheless," said Arnold, sitting up and planting his two feet on the floor, "I'm going this evening."

"In that case," said Arnold's father, "I'm going too."

Secretly Miss Goering was delighted that they were coming and she did not have the courage to deter them, although she felt that it would have been the correct thing for her to do. Her excursions would be more or less devoid of any moral value in her own eyes if they accompanied her, but she was so delighted that she convinced herself that perhaps she might allow it just this time.

"You had better come along, Lucy," said Arnold; "otherwise you are going to be here all alone."

"That's perfectly all right, my dear," said Lucy. "I'll be the only one that comes out whole, in the end. And it might be very delightful to be here without any of you."

Arnold's father made an insulting noise with his mouth, and Miss Gamelon left the room.

This time the little train was filled with people and there were quite a few boys going up and down the aisle selling candy and fruit. It had been a curiously warm day and there had been a shower of short duration, one of those showers that are so frequent in summer but so seldom occur in the fall.

The sun was just setting and the shower had left in its wake quite a beautiful rainbow, which was only visible to those people who were seated on the left side of the train. However, most of the passengers who had been seated on the right side were now leaning over the more fortunate ones and getting quite a fair view of the rainbow too.

Many of the women were naming aloud to their friends the colors that they were able to distinguish. Everyone on the train seemed to love it except Arnold, who, now that he had asserted himself, felt terribly depressed, partly as a result of having had to move from his couch and consider the prospect of a dull evening and partly also because he doubted very much whether he would be able to make it up with Lucy Gamelon. She was, he felt certain, the type of person who could remain angry for weeks.

"Oh, I think this is terribly, terribly gay," said Miss Goering. "This rainbow and this sunset and all these people jabbering away like magpies. Don't you think it's gay?" Miss Goering was addressing Arnold's father.

"Oh, yes," he said. "It's a real magic carpet."

Miss Goering searched his face because his voice sounded a little sad to her. He did, as a matter of fact, appear to be slightly uneasy. He kept looking around at the passengers and pulling his tie.

They finally left the train and boarded the ferry. They all stood at the prow together as Miss Goering had done on the previous night. This time when the ferry landed, Miss Goering looked up and saw no one coming down the hill.

"Usually," she said to them, forgetting that she herself had only made the trip once before, "this hill is swarming with people. I cannot imagine what has happened to them tonight."

"It's a steep hill," said Arnold's father. "Is there no way of getting into the town without climbing that hill?"

"I don't know," said Miss Goering. She looked at him and noticed that his sleeves were too long for him. As a matter of fact, his overcoat was about a half-size too large.

If there had been no one on the hill going to or from the ferry, the main street was swarming with people. The cinema was all lighted up and there was a long line forming in front of the box office. There had obviously been a fire, because there were three red engines parked on one side of the street, a few blocks up from the cinema. Miss Goering judged that it had been of no consequence since she could see neither traces of smoke nor charred buildings. However, the engines added to the gaiety of the street as there were many young people crowded around them making jokes with the firemen who remained in the trucks. Arnold walked along at a brisk pace, carefully examining everything on the street and pretending to be very much lost in his own impressions of the town.

"I see what you mean," he said to Miss Goering, "it's glorious."

"What is glorious?" Miss Goering asked him.

"All this." Suddenly Arnold stopped dead. "Oh look, Christina, what a beautiful sight!" He had made them stop in front of a large empty lot between two buildings. The empty lot had been converted into a brand-new basket-ball court. The court was very elegantly paved with gray asphalt and brightly lighted by four giant lamps that were focused on the players and on the basket. There was a ticket office at one side of the court where the participants bought their right to play in the game for one hour. Most of the people playing were little boys. There were several men in uniform and Arnold judged that they worked for the court and filled in when an insufficient number of people bought tickets to form two complete teams. Arnold flushed with pleasure.

"Look, Christina," he said, "you run along while I try my hand at this; I'll come and get Pop and you later."

She pointed the bar out to him, but she had the feeling that Arnold was not paying much attention to what she was saying. She stood for a moment with Arnold's father and they watched him rush up to the ticket office and hurriedly push his change through the wicket. He was on the court in no time, running around in his overcoat and jumping up in the air with his arms apart. One of the uniformed men had stepped quickly out of the game in order to cede his place to Arnold. But he was now trying desperately to attract his attention because Arnold had been in such a hurry at the ticket office that the agent had not had time to give him the colored arm-band by which the players were able to distinguish the members of their own team.

"I suppose," said Miss Goering, "that we had better go along. Arnold, I imagine, will follow us shortly."

They walked down the street. Arnold's father hesitated a moment before the saloon door.

"What kind of men come in here?" he asked her.

"Oh," said Miss Goering, "all sorts of men, I guess. Rich and poor, workers and bankers, criminals and dwarfs."

"Dwarfs," Arnold's father repeated uneasily.

The minute they were inside Miss Goering spotted Andy. He was drinking at the farther end of the bar with his hat pulled down over one eye. Miss Goering hastily installed Arnold's father in a booth.

"Take your coat off," she said, "and order yourself a drink from that man over there behind the bar."

She went over to Andy and stretched her hand out to him. He was looking very mean and haughty.

"Hello," he said. "Did you decide to come over to the mainland again?"

"Why, certainly," said Miss Goering. "I told you I would."

"Well," said Andy, "I've learned in the course of years that it doesn't mean a thing."

Miss Goering felt a little embarrassed. They stood side by side for a little while without saying a word.

"I'm sorry," said Andy, "but I have no suggestions to make to you for the evening. There is only one picture show in town and they are showing a very bad movie tonight." He ordered himself another drink and gulped it down straight. Then he turned the dial of the radio very slowly until he found a tango.

"Well, may I have this dance?" he asked, appearing to brighten up a bit.

Miss Goering nodded her head.

He held her very straight and so tightly that she was in an extremely awkward and uncomfortable position. He danced with her into a far corner of the room.

"Well," he said, "are you going to try and make me happy? Because I have no time to waste." He pushed her away from him and stood up very straight facing her, with his arms hanging down along his sides.

"Step back a little farther, please," he said. "Look carefully at your man and then say whether or not you want him."

Miss Goering did not see how she could possibly answer anything but yes. He was standing now with his head cocked to one side, looking very much as though he were trying to refrain from blinking his eyes, the way people do when they are having snapshots taken.

"Very well," said Miss Goering, "I do want you to be my man." She smiled at him sweetly, but she was not thinking very hard of what she was saying.

He held his arms out to her and they continued to dance. He was looking over her head very proudly and smiling just a little. When they had finished their dance, Miss Goering remembered with a pang that Arnold's father had been sitting in his booth alone all this time. She felt doubly sorry because he seemed to have saddened and aged so much since they had boarded the train that he scarcely resembled at all the chipper, eccentric man he had been for a few days at the island house, or even the fanatical gentleman he had appeared to Miss Goering on the first night that they had met.

"Dear me, I must introduce you to Arnold's father," she said to Andy. "Come over this way with me."

She felt even more remorse when she arrived at the booth because Arnold's father had been sitting there all the while without having ordered himself a drink.

"What's the matter?" asked Miss Goering, her voice rising way up in the air like the voice of an excited mother. "Why on earth didn't you order yourself something to drink?"

Arnold's father looked around him furtively. "I don't know," he said, "I didn't feel any desire to."

She introduced the two men to each other and they all sat down together. Arnold's father asked Andy very politely whether or not he lived in this town and what his business was. During the course of their conversation they both discovered that not only had they been born in the same town, but they had, in spite of a difference in age, also lived there once at the same time without ever having met. Andy, unlike most people, did not seem to become more lively when they both happened upon this fact.

"Yes," he answered wearily to the questions of Arnold's father, "I did live there in 1920."

"Then certainly," said Arnold's father sitting up straighter, "then certainly you were well acquainted with the McLean family. They lived up on the hill. They had seven children, five girls and two boys. All of them, as you must remember, were the possessors of a terrific shock of bright red hair."

"I did not know them," said Andy quietly, beginning to get red in the face.

"That's very strange," said Arnold's father. "Then you must have known Vincent Connelly, Peter Jacketson, and Robert Bull."

"No," said Andy, "no, I didn't." His good spirits seemed to have vanished entirely.

"They," said Arnold's father, "controlled the main business interests of the town." He studied Andy's face carefully.

Andy shook his head once more and looked off into space.

"Riddleton?" Arnold's father asked him abruptly.

"What?" said Andy.

"Riddleton, president of the bank."

"Well, not exactly," said Andy.

Arnold's father leaned back against the bench and sighed. "Where did you live?" he asked finally of Andy.

"I lived," said Andy, "at the end of Parliament Street and Byrd Avenue."

"It was terrible around there before they started tearing it up, wasn't it?" Arnold's father said, his eyes filled with memories.

Andy pushed the table roughly aside and walked quickly over to the bar.

"He didn't know anyone decent in the whole blooming town," said Arnold's father. "Parliament and Byrd was the section—"

"Please," said Miss Goering. "Look, you've insulted him. What a shame; because neither one of you cares about this sort of thing at all! What nasty little devil got into you both?"

"I don't think he has very good manners, and he is clearly not the type of man I would expect to find you associating with."

Miss Goering was a little peeved with Arnold's father, but instead of saying anything to him she went over to Andy and consoled him.

"Please don't mind him," she said. "He's really a delightful old thing and quite poetic. It's just that he's been through some radical changes in his life, all in the last few days, and I guess he's feeling the strain now."

"Poetic is he?" Andy snapped at her. "He's a pompous old monkey. That's what he is." Andy was really very angry.

"No," said Miss Goering, "he is not a pompous old monkey."

Andy finished his drink and swaggered over to Arnold's father with his hands in his pockets.

"You're a pompous old monkey!" he said to him. "A pompous old good-for-nothing monkey!"

Arnold's father slid out of his seat with his eyes cast downward and walked towards the door.

Miss Goering, who had overheard Andy's remark, hurried after him, but she whispered to Andy as she passed him, that she intended to come right back.

When they were outside they leaned together against a lamp post. Miss Goering could see that Arnold's father was trembling.

"I have never in my life encountered such rudeness," he said. "That man is worse than a gutter puppy."

"Well, I wouldn't worry about it," said Miss Goering. "He was just ill-tempered."

"Ill-tempered?" said Arnold's father. "He's the kind of cheaply dressed brute that is more and more thickly populating the world today."

"Oh, come," said Miss Goering, "that is neither here nor there."

Arnold's father looked at Miss Goering. Her face was very lovely on this particular evening, and he sighed with regret. "I suppose," he said, "that you are deeply disappointed in me in your own particular way, and that you are able to have respect in your heart for him while you are unable to find it within that very same heart for me. Human nature is mysterious and very beautiful, but remember that there are certain infallible signs that I, as an older man, have learned to recognize. I would not trust that man too far. I love you, my dear, with all my heart, you know."

Miss Goering stood in silence.

"You are very close to me," he said after a little while, squeezing her hand.

"Well," she said, "would you care to step back into the saloon or do you feel that you've had enough?"

"It would be literally impossible for me to return to that saloon even should I have the slightest desire to. I think I had better go along. You won't come with me, will you, my dear?"

"I'm very sorry," said Miss Goering, "but unfortunately this was a previous engagement. Would you like me to walk down to the basket-ball court? Perhaps Arnold will have wearied of his game by this time. If not, you can easily sit and watch the players for a little while."

"Yes, that would be very kind of you," said Arnold's father, in such a sad voice that he almost broke Miss Goering's heart.

Very shortly they arrived at the basket-ball court. Things had changed quite a bit. Most of the small boys had dropped out of the game and a great many young men and women had taken the place of both the small boys and the guards. The women were screaming with laughter and quite a large crowd had gathered to watch the players. After Miss Goering and Arnold's father had stood there for a minute they realized that Arnold himself was the cause of most of the merriment. He had removed his coat and his sweater and, to their surprise, they saw that he was still wearing his pajama top. He had pulled it outside of his pants in order to appear more ridiculous. They watched him run across the court with the ball in his arms roaring like a lion. When he arrived at a strategic position, however, instead of passing the ball on to another member of his team he merely dropped it on the court between his feet and proceeded to butt one of his opponents in the stomach like a goat. The crowd roared with laughter. The uniformed guards were particularly delighted because it was a pleasant and unexpected break in the night's routine. They were all standing in a row, smiling very broadly.

"I shall try and see if I can find a chair for you," said Miss Goering. She returned shortly and led Arnold's father to a folding chair that one of the guards had obligingly set up right outside of the ticket office. Arnold's father sat down and yawned.

"Good-by," said Miss Goering. "Good-by, darling, and wait here until Arnold has finished his game."

"But wait a moment," said Arnold's father. "When will you return to the island?"

"I might not return," she said. "I might not return right away, but I will see that Miss Gamelon receives enough money to manage the house and the food."

"But I must certainly see you. This is not a very human way to make a departure."

"Well, come along a minute," said Miss Goering, taking hold of his hand and pulling him with difficulty through the crowd over to the sidewalk.

Arnold's father remonstrated that he would not return to the saloon for a million dollars.

"I'm not taking you to the saloon. Don't be silly," she said. "Now, do you see that ice-cream parlor across the street?" She pointed to a little white store almost directly opposite them. "If I don't come back, which is very probable, will you meet me there on Sunday morning? That will be in eight days, at eleven o'clock in the morning."

"I will be there in eight days," said Arnold's father.

When she returned with Andy to his apartment that night, she noticed that there were three long-stemmed roses on a table next to the couch.

"Why, what lovely flowers!" she exclaimed. "This reminds me that my mother had once the loveliest garden for miles around her. She won many prizes with her roses."

"Well," said Andy, "no one in my family ever won a prize with a rose, but I bought these for you in case you came."

"I'm deeply touched," said Miss Goering.

Miss Goering had been living with Andy for eight days. He was still very nervous and tense, but he seemed on the whole to be much more optimistic. To Miss Goering's surprise, he had begun on the second day to talk of the business possibilities in town. He surprised her very much too by knowing the names of the leading families of the community and moreover by being familiar with certain details concerning their private lives. On Saturday night he had announced to Miss Goering his intention of having a business conference the next morning with Mr. Bellamy, Mr. Schlaegel, and Mr. Dockerty. These men controlled most of the real estate not only in the town itself but in several neighboring towns. Besides these interests they also had a good many of the farms of the surrounding country. He was terribly excited when he told her his plans, which were mainly to sell the buildings he owned in the city, for which he had already been offered a small sum, and buy a share in their business.

"They're the three smartest men in town," he said, "but they're not gangsters at all. They come from the finest families here and I think it would be nice for you too."

"That is not the kind of thing that interests me in the least," said Miss Goering.

"Well, naturally, I wouldn't expect it to interest you or me," said Andy, "but you've got to admit we're living in the world, unless we want to behave like crazy kids or escaped lunatics or something like that."

For several days it had been quite clear to Miss Goering that Andy was no longer thinking of himself as a bum. This would have pleased her greatly had she been interested in reforming her friends, but unfortunately she was only interested in the course that she was following in order to attain her own salvation. She was fond of Andy, but during the last two nights she had felt an urge to leave him. This was also very much due to the fact that an unfamiliar person had begun to frequent the bar.

This newcomer was of almost mammoth proportions, and both times that she had seen him he had been wearing a tremendous black overcoat well cut and obviously made of very expensive material. She had seen his face only fleetingly once or twice, but what she had seen of it had so frightened her that she had been able to think of very little else for two days now.

This man, they had noticed, drove up to the saloon in a very beautiful big automobile that resembled more a hearse than a private car. Miss Goering had examined it one day when the man was drinking in the saloon. It appeared to be almost brand-new. She and Andy had looked in through the window and had been a little surprised to see a lot of dirty clothes on the floor. Miss Goering was completely preoccupied now with what course to take should the newcomer be willing to make her his mistress for a little while. She was almost sure that he would, because several times she had caught him looking at her in a certain way which she had learned to recognize. Her only hope was that he would disappear before she had the chance to approach him. If he did, she would be exempt and thus able to fritter away some more time with Andy, who now seemed so devoid of anything sinister that she was beginning to scrap with him about small things the way one does with a younger brother.

On Sunday morning Miss Goering woke up to find Andy in his shirt sleeves, dusting off some small tables in the living-room.

"What is it?" she asked him. "Why are you bustling around like a bride?"

"Don't you remember?" he asked, looking hurt. "Today is the big day—the day of the conference. They are coming here bright and early, all three of them. They live like robins, those business men. Couldn't you," he asked her, "couldn't you do something about making this room prettier? You see, they've all got wives, and even if they probably couldn't tell you what the hell they've got in their living-rooms, their wives have all got plenty of money to spend on little ornaments and their eyes are probably used to a certain amount of fuss."

"Well, this room is so hideous, Andy, I don't see that anything would do it any good."

"Yes, I guess it's a pretty bad room. I never used to notice it much." Andy put on a navy-blue suit and combed his hair very neatly, rubbing in a little brilliantine. Then he paced up and down the living-room floor with his hands in his hip pockets. The sun was pouring in through the window, and the radiator was whistling in an annoying manner while it overheated the room as it had done constantly since Miss Goering had arrived.

Mr. Bellamy, Mr. Schlaegel, and Mr. Dockerty had received Andy's note and were on their way up the stairs, having accepted the appointment more out of curiosity and from an old habit of never letting anything slip by than because they actually believed that their visit would prove fruitful. When they smelled the terrible stench of the cheap cooking in the halls, they put their hands over their mouths in order not to laugh too loudly and performed a little mock pantomime of retreating towards the staircase again. They really didn't care very much, however, because it was Sunday and they preferred being together than with their families, so they proceeded to knock on Andy's door. Andy quickly wiped his hands because they were sweaty and ran to open the door. He stood in the doorway and shook hands with each man vigorously before inviting them to come in.

"I'm Andrew McLane," he said to them, "and I'm sorry that we have not met before." He ushered them into the room and all three of them realized at once that it was going to be abominably hot. Mr. Dockerty, the most aggressive of the three men, turned to Andy.

"Would you mind opening the window, fellow?" he said in a loud voice. "It's boiling in here."

"Oh," said Andy blushing, "I should have thought of it." He went over and opened the windows.

"How do you stand it, fellow?" said Mr. Dockerty. "You trying to hatch something in here?"

The three men stood in a little group near the couch and pulled out some cigars, which they examined together and discussed for a minute.

"Two of us are going to sit on this couch, fellow," said Mr. Dockerty, "and Mr. Schlaegel can sit here on this little armchair. Now where are you going to sit?"

Mr. Dockerty had decided almost immediately that Andy was a complete boob and was taking matters into his own hands. This so disconcerted Andy that he stood and stared at the three men without saying a word.

"Come," said Mr. Dockerty, carrying a chair out of a corner of the room and setting it down near the couch, "come, you sit here."

Andy sat down in silence and played with his fingers.

"Tell me," said Mr. Bellamy, who was a little more soft-spoken and genteel than the other two. "Tell me how long you have been living here."

"I have been living here two years," said Andy listlessly.

The three men thought about this for a little while.

"Well," said Mr. Bellamy, "and tell us what you have done in these three years."

"Two years," said Andy.

Andy had prepared quite a long story to tell them because he had suspected that they might question him a bit about his personal life in order to make certain what kind of man they were dealing with, and he had decided that it would not be wise to admit that he had done absolutely nothing in the past two years. But he had imagined that the meeting was to be conducted on a much more friendly basis. He had supposed that the men would be delighted to have found someone who was willing to put a little money into their business, and would be more than anxious to believe that he was an upright, hard-working citizen. Now, however, he felt that he was being cross-questioned and made a fool of. He could barely control his desire to bolt out of the room.

"Nothing," he said, avoiding their eyes, "nothing."

"It always amazes me," said Mr. Bellamy, "how people are able to have leisure time—that is, if they have more leisure time than they need. Now I mean to say that our business has been running for thirty-two years. There hasn't been a day gone by that I haven't had at least thirteen or fourteen things to attend to. That might seem a little exaggerated to you or maybe even very much exaggerated, but it isn't exaggerated, it's true. In the first place I attend personally to every house on our list. I check the plumbing and the drainage and the what-not. I see whether or not the house is being kept up properly and I also visit it in all kinds of weather to see how it fares during a storm or a blizzard. I know exactly how much coal it takes to heat every house on our list. I talk personally to our clients and I try to influence them on the price they are asking for their house, whether or not they are trying to rent or to sell. For instance, if they are asking a price that I know is too high because I am able to compare it with every price on the market, I try to persuade them to lower their price a little bit so that it will be nearer the norm. If, on the other hand, they are cheating themselves and I know . . ."

The other two men were getting a little bored. One could easily see that Mr. Bellamy was the least important of the three, although he might easily have been the one that accomplished all the tedious work. Mr. Schlaegel interrupted him.

"Well, my man," he said to Andy, "tell us what this is all about. In your letter you stated that you had some suggestions whereby you thought we could profit, as well as yourself, of course."

Andy got up from his chair. It was evident to the men now that he was under a terrific tension, so they were doubly on their guard.

"Why don't you come back some other time?" said Andy very quickly. "Then I will have thought it out more clearly."

"Take your time, take your time, now, fellow," said Mr. Dockerty. "We are all here together and there's no reason why we shouldn't talk it over right away. We don't really live in town, you know. We live twenty minutes out in Fairview. We developed Fairview ourselves, as a matter of fact."

"Well," said Andy, coming back and sitting on the edge of his chair, "I have a little property myself."

"Where's that?" said Mr. Dockerty.

"It's a building, in the city, way down, near the docks." He gave Mr. Dockerty the name of the street and then sat biting his lips. Mr. Dockerty didn't say anything.

"You see," continued Andy, "I thought I might hand my rights to this building over to the corporation in return for an interest in your business—at least a right to work for the firm and get my share out of the selling I do. I wouldn't need to have equal rights with you immediately, naturally, but I thought I'd discuss these details with you later if you were interested."

Mr. Dockerty shut his eyes and then after a little while he addressed himself to Mr. Schlaegel.

"I know the street he is talking about," he said. Mr. Schlaegel shook his head and made a face. Andy looked at his shoes.

"For a long time," said Mr. Dockerty, still addressing Mr. Schlaegel, "for a long time the buildings in that district have been a drag on the market. Even as slums they're pretty bad and the profit from any one of them is just enough to keep body and soul together. That's because, as you remember, Schlaegel, there is no means of transportation at any convenient distance and it's surrounded by fish markets.

"Besides that," went on Mr. Dockerty, turning to Andy, "we have in our charter a clause that prohibits our taking on any more men except on a strict salary basis, and, my friend, there's a list as long as my arm waiting for a job in our offices, if there should be a vacancy. Their tongues are hanging out for any job we can offer them. Fine young men too, the majority of them just out of college, raring to work, and to put into use every modern trick of selling that they have learned about. I know some of their families personally and I'm sorry I can't help these lads out more than I am able to."

Just then Miss Goering came rushing through the room. "I'm an hour or two late for Arnold's father," she screamed over her shoulder as she went out the door. "I will see you later."

Andy had got up and was facing the window with his back to the three men. His shoulder blades were twitching.

"Was that your wife?" Mr. Dockerty called to him.

Andy did not answer, but in a few seconds Mr. Dockerty repeated his question, mainly because he had a suspicion it had not been Andy's wife and he was anxious to know whether or not he had guessed correctly. He kicked Mr. Schlaegel's foot with his own and they winked at each other.

"No," said Andy, turning around and revealing his flame-red face. "No, she is not my wife. She's my girl friend. She's been living here with me for a week nearly. Is there anything else you men want to know?"

"Now look here, fellow," said Mr. Dockerty, "there's nothing for you to get excited about. She's a very pretty woman, very pretty, and if you're upset about the little business talk we had together, there's no reason for that either. We explained everything to you clearly, like three pals." Andy looked out of the window.

"You know," said Mr. Dockerty, "there are other jobs you can get that will be far more suited to you and your background and that'll make you lots happier in the end. You ask your girl friend if that isn't so." Still Andy did not answer them.

"There are other jobs," Mr. Dockerty ventured to say again, but since there was still no answer from Andy, he shrugged his shoulders, rose with difficulty from the couch, and straightened his vest and his coat. The others did likewise. Then all three of them politely bade good-by to Andy's back and left the room.

Arnold's father had been sitting in the ice-cream parlor one hour and a half when Miss Goering finally came running in. He looked completely forlorn. It had never occurred to him to buy a magazine to read and there had been no one to look at in the ice-cream parlor because it was still morning and people seldom dropped in before afternoon.

"Oh, I can't tell you, my dear, how sorry I am," said Miss Goering, taking both his hands in hers and pressing them to her lips. He was wearing woolen gloves. "I can't tell you how these gloves remind me of my childhood," Miss Goering continued.

"I've been cold these last few days," said Arnold's father, "so Miss Gamelon went into town and bought me these."

"Well, and how is everything going?"

"I will tell you all about that in a little while," said Arnold's father, "but I would like to know if you are all right, my dear woman, and whether or not you intend to return to the island."

"I—I don't think so," said Miss Goering, "not for a long time."

"Well, I must tell you of the many changes that have taken place in our lives, and I hope that you will not think of them as too drastic or sudden or revolutionary, or whatever you may call it."

Miss Goering smiled faintly.

"You see," he continued, "it has been growing colder and colder in the house these last few days. Miss Gamelon has had the sniffles terribly, I must concede, and also, as you know, she's been in a wretched test about the old-fashioned cooking equipment right from the beginning. Now, Arnold doesn't really mind anything if he has enough to eat, but recently Miss Gamelon has refused to set foot in the kitchen."

"Now what on earth has been the outcome of all this? Do hurry up and tell me," Miss Goering urged him.

"I can't go any faster than I'm going," said Arnold's father. "Now, the other day Adele Wyman, an old school friend of Arnold's, met him in town and they had a cup of coffee together. In the course of the conversation Adele mentioned that she was living in a two-family house on the island and that she liked it but she was terribly worried about who was going to move into the other half."

"Well, then, am I to gather that they have moved into this house and are living there?"

"They have moved into that house until you come back," said Arnold's father. "Fortunately, it seemed that you had no lease on the first little house; therefore, since it was the end of the month, they felt free to move out. Miss Gamelon wonders if you will send the rent checks to the new house. Arnold has volunteered to pay the difference in rent, which is very slight."

"No, no, that is not necessary. Is there anything more that is new?" said Miss Goering.

"Well, it might interest you to know," said Arnold's father, "that I have decided to return to my wife and my original house."

"Why?" Miss Goering asked.

"A combination of circumstances, including the fact that I am old and feel like going home."

"Oh my," said Miss Goering, "it's a shame to see things breaking up this way, isn't it?"

"Yes, my dear, it is a pity, but I have come here to ask you a favor besides having come because I loved you and wanted to say good-by to you."

"I will do anything for you," said Miss Goering, "that I can possibly do."

"Well," said Arnold's father, "I would like you to read over this note that I have written to my wife. I want to send it to her and then I will return on the following day to my house."

"Certainly," said Miss Goering. She noticed there was an envelope on the table in front of Arnold's father. She picked it up.

Dear Ethel [she read],

I hope that you will read this letter with all that indulgence and sympathy which you possess so strongly in your heart.

I can only say that there is, in every man's life, a strong urge to leave his life behind him for a while and seek a new one. If he is living near to the sea, a strong urge to take the next boat and sail away no matter how happy his home or how beloved his wife or mother. It is true also if the man is living near a road that he may feel the strong urge to strap a knapsack on his back and walk away, again leaving a happy home behind him. Very few people follow this urge once they have passed their youth without doing so. But it is my idea that sometimes age affects us like youth, like strong champagne that goes to our heads, and we dare what we have never dared before, perhaps also because we feel that it is our last chance. However, while as youths we might continue in such an adventure, at my age one very quickly finds out that it is a mere chimera and that one has not the strength. Will you take me back?

Your loving husband,

Edgar

"It is simple," said Arnold's father, "and it expresses what I felt."

"Is that really the way you felt?" asked Miss Goering.

"I believe so," said Arnold's father. "It must have been. Of course I did not mention to her anything concerning my sentiments about you, but she will have guessed that, and such things are better left unsaid. . . ."

He looked down at his woolen gloves and said no more for a little while. Suddenly he reached in his pocket and pulled out another letter.

"I'm sorry," he said, "I almost forgot. Here is a letter from Arnold."

"Now," said Miss Goering opening the letter, "what can this be about?"

"Surely a lot about nothing and about the trollop he is living with, which is worse than nothing." Miss Goering opened the letter and proceeded to read it aloud:

Dear Christina,

I have told Father to explain to you the reasons for our recent change of domicile. I hope he has done so and that you are satisfied that we have not behaved rashly nor in a manner that you might conclude was inconsiderate. Lucy wants you to send her check to this present address. Father was supposed to tell you so but I thought that perhaps he might forget. Lucy, I am afraid, has been very upset by your present escapade. She is constantly in either a surly or melancholic mood. I had hoped that this condition would ameliorate after we had moved, but she is still subject to long silences and often weeps at night, not to mention the fact that she is exceedingly cranky and has twice had a set-to with Adele, although we have only been here two days. I see in all this that Lucy's nature is really one of extreme delicateness and morbidity and I am fascinated to be by her side. Adele on the other hand has a very equable nature, but she is terribly intellectual and very much interested in every branch of art. We are thinking of starting a magazine together when we are more or less settled. She is a pretty blonde girl.

I miss you terribly, my dear, and I want you to please believe that if I could only somehow reach what was inside of me I would break out of this terrible cocoon I am in. I expect to some day really. I will always remember the story you told me when we first met, in which I always felt was buried some strange significance, although I must admit to you now that I could not explain what. I must go and take Bubbles some hot tea to her room now. Please, please *believe in me.*

Love and kisses,

Arnold

"He's a nice man," said Miss Goering. For some reason Arnold's letter made her feel sad, while his father's letter had annoyed and puzzled her.

"Well," said Arnold's father, "I must be leaving now if I want to catch the next ferry."

"Wait," said Miss Goering, "I will accompany you to the dock." She quickly unfastened a rose that she had been wearing on the collar of her coat and pinned it on the old man's lapel.

When they arrived at the dock the gong was being sounded and the ferry was all ready to leave for the island. Miss Goering was relieved to see this, for she had feared a long sentimental scene.

"Well, we made it in the nick of time," said Arnold's father, trying to adopt a casual manner. But Miss Goering could see that his blue eyes were wet with tears. . . . She could barely restrain her own tears and she looked away from the ferry up the hill.

"I wonder," said Arnold's father, "if you could lend me fifty cents. I sent all my money to my wife and I didn't think of borrowing enough from Arnold this morning."

She quickly gave him a dollar and they kissed each other good-by. While the ferry pulled out, Miss Goering stood on the dock and waved; he had asked her to do this as a favor to him.

When she returned to the apartment she found it empty, so that she decided to go to the bar and drink, feeling certain that if Andy was not already there, he would arrive sooner or later.

She had been drinking there a few hours and it was beginning to grow dark. Andy had not yet arrived and Miss Goering felt a little relieved. She looked over her shoulder and saw that the heavy-set man who owned the hearse-like car was coming through the door. She shivered involuntarily and smiled sweetly at Frank, the bartender.

"Frank," she said, "don't you ever get a day off?"

"Don't want one."

"Why not?"

"Because I want to keep my nose to the grindstone and do something worth while later on. I don't get much enjoyment out of anything but thinking my own thoughts, anyway."

"I just hate thinking mine, Frank."

"No, that's silly," said Frank.

The big man in the overcoat had just climbed up on a stool and thrown a fifty-cent piece down on the bar. Frank served him his drink. After he had drunk it he turned to Miss Goering.

"Will you have a drink?" he asked her.

Much as she feared him, Miss Goering felt a peculiar thrill at the fact that he had at last spoken to her. She had been expecting it for a few days now, and felt she could not refrain from telling him so.

"Thank you so much," she said in such an ingratiating manner that Frank, who approved little of ladies who spoke to strangers, frowned darkly and moved over to the other end of the bar, where he began to read a magazine. "Thank you so much, I'd be glad to. It might interest you to know that I have imagined our drinking together like this for some time now and I am not at all surprised that you asked me. I had rather imagined that it would happen at this time of day too, and when there was no one else here." The man nodded his head once or twice.

"Well, what do you want to drink?" he asked her. Miss Goering was very disappointed that he had made no direct answer to her remark.

After Frank had served the drink the man snatched it from in front of her.

"Come on," he said, "let's go and sit in a booth."

Miss Goering clambered down from her stool and followed him to the booth that was farthest from the door.

"Well," he said to her after they had been sitting there for a little while, "do you work here?"

"Where?" said Miss Goering.

"Here, in this town."

"No," said Miss Goering.

"Well, then, do you work in another town?"

"No, I don't work."

"Yes, you do. You don't have to try to fool me, because no one ever has."

"I don't understand."

"You work as a prostitute, after a fashion, don't you?"

Miss Goering laughed. "Heavens!" she said. "I certainly never thought I looked like a prostitute merely because I had red hair; perhaps like a derelict or an escaped lunatic, but never a prostitute!"

"You don't look like no derelict or escaped lunatic to me. You look like a prostitute, and that's what you are. I don't mean a real small-time prostitute. I mean a medium one."

"Well, I don't object to prostitutes, but really I assure you I am no such thing."

"I don't believe you."

"But how are we to form any kind of friendship at all," said Miss Goering, "if you don't believe anything I say?"

The man shook his head once more. "I don't believe you when you say you're not a prostitute because I know you're a prostitute."

"All right," said Miss Goering, "I'm tired of arguing." She had noticed that his face, unlike most other faces, seemed not to take on any added life when he was engaged in conversation and she felt that all her presentiments about him had been justified.

He was now running his foot up her leg. She tried to smile at him but she was unable to.

"Come now," she said, "Frank is very apt to see what you are doing from where he is standing behind the bar and I should feel terribly embarrassed."

He seemed to ignore her remark completely and continued to press on her leg more and more vigorously.

"Would you want to come home with me and have a steak dinner?" he asked her. "I'm having steak and onions and coffee. You could stay a few days if everything worked out, or longer. This other little girl, Dorothy, just went away about a week ago."

"I think that would be nice," said Miss Goering.

"Well," he said, "It's almost an hour's drive there in a car. I have to go now to see someone here in town, but I'll be back in half a hour or so; if you want some steak you better be here too."

"All right, I will," said Miss Goering.

He had not been gone more than a few minutes when Andy arrived. He had both hands in his pockets and his coat collar turned up. He was looking down at his feet.

"Lord God Almighty!" Miss Goering said to herself. "I have to break the news to him right away and I have not seen him so dejected in a week."

"What on earth happened to you?" she asked him.

"I have been to a movie, giving myself a little lesson in self-control."

"What does that mean?"

"I mean that I was upset; my soul was turned inside out this morning and I had but two choices, to drink and continue drinking or to go to a movie. I chose the latter."

"But you still look terribly morose."

"I am less morose. I am just showing the results of the terrific fight that I have waged inside of myself, and you know that the face of victory often resembles the face of defeat."

"Victory fades so quickly that it is scarcely apparent and it is always the face of defeat that we are able to see," said Miss Goering. She did not want to tell him, in front of Frank, that she was leaving, because she was certain that Frank would know where she was going. "Andy," she said, "would you mind coming across the street with me, to the ice-cream parlor? I have something that I want to talk to you about."

"All right," said Andy rather more casually than Miss Goering had expected. "But I want to come back right away for a drink."

They went across the street to the little ice-cream parlor and sat down at a table opposite each other. There was no one in the store with the exception of themselves and the boy who served the customers. He nodded at them when they came in.

"Back again?" he said to Miss Goering. "That old man sure waited for you a long time this morning."

"Yes," said Miss Goering, "it was dreadful."

"Well, you gave him a flower, anyway, when you left. He must have been tickled about that."

Miss Goering did not answer him as she had very little time to waste.

"Andy," she said, "I'm going in a few minutes to a place that's about an hour away from here and I probably won't be coming back for quite some time."

Andy seemed to understand the situation immediately. Miss Goering sat back and waited while he pressed his palms tighter and tighter to his temples.

Finally he looked up at her. "You," he said, "as a decent human being, cannot do this to me."

"Well, I'm afraid I can, Andy. I have my own star to follow, you know."

"But do you know," said Andy, "how beautiful and delicate a man's heart is when he is happy for the first time? It is like the thin ice that has imprisoned those beautiful young plants that are released when the ice thaws."

"You have read that in some poem," said Miss Goering.

"Does that make it any the less beautiful?"

"No," said Miss Goering, "I admit that it is a very beautiful thought."

"You don't dare tear the plant up now that you have melted the ice."

"Oh, Andy," said Miss Goering, "you make me sound so dreadful! I am merely working out something for myself."

"You have no right to," said Andy. "You're not alone in the world. You've involved yourself with me!" He was growing more excited perhaps because he realized that it was useless saying anything to Miss Goering at all.

"I'll get down on my knees," said Andy, shaking his fist at her. No sooner had he said this than he was down on his knees near her feet. The waiter was terribly shocked and felt that he had better say something.

"Look, Andy," he said in a very small voice, "Why don't you get up off your knees and think things over?"

"Because," said Andy, raising his own voice more and more, "because she daren't refuse a man who is down on his knees. She daren't! It would be sacrilege."

"I don't see why," said Miss Goering.

"If you refuse," said Andy, "I'll disgrace you, I'll crawl out into the street, I'll put you to shame."

"I really have no sense of shame," said Miss Goering, "and I think your own sense of shame is terribly exaggerated, besides being a terrific sap on your energies. Now I must go, Andy. Please get up."

"You're crazy," said Andy. "You're crazy and monstrous—*really*. Monstrous. You are committing a monstrous act."

"Well," said Miss Goering, "perhaps my maneuvers do seem a little strange, but I have thought for a long time now that often, so very often, heroes who believe themselves to be monsters because they are so far removed from other men turn around much later and see really monstrous acts being committed in the name of something mediocre."

"Lunatic!" Andy yelled at her from his knees. "You're not even a Christian."

Miss Goering hurried out of the ice-cream parlor after having kissed Andy lightly on the head, because she realized that if she did not leave him very quickly she would miss her appointment. As a matter of fact, she had judged correctly, because her friend was just coming out of the saloon when she arrived.

"Are you coming out with me?" he said. "I got through a little sooner that I thought and I decided I wasn't going to wait around, because I didn't think you'd come."

"But," said Miss Goering, "I accepted your invitation. Why didn't you think I'd come?"

"Don't get excited," said the man. "Come on, let's get in the car."

As they drove past the ice-cream parlor on their way out of town, Miss Goering looked through the window to see if she could catch a glimpse of Andy. To her surprise, she saw that the store was filled with people, so that they overflowed into the street and quite crowded the sidewalk, and she was unable really to see into the store at all.

The man was sitting in front with the chauffeur, who was not in uniform, and she was sitting alone in the back seat. This arrangement had surprised her at first, but she was pleased. She understood shortly why he had arranged the seating in this manner. Soon after they had left the town behind them he turned around and said to her:

"I'm going to sleep now. I'm more comfortable up here

because I don't bounce around so much. You can talk to the chauffeur if you want."

"I don't think I care to talk with anyone," said Miss Goering.

"Well, do whatever the hell you want," he said. "I don't want to be waked up until those steaks are on the grill." He promptly pulled his hat down over his eyes and went to sleep.

As they drove on, Miss Goering felt sadder and lonelier than she had ever felt before in her life. She missed Andy and Arnold and Miss Gamelon and the old man with all her heart and very soon she was weeping silently in the back of the car. It was only with a tremendous exertion of her will that she refrained from opening the door and leaping out into the road.

They passed through several small towns and at last, just as Miss Goering was dozing off, they arrived in a medium-sized city.

"This is the town we were heading for," said the chauffeur, assuming that Miss Goering had been watching the road impatiently. It was a noisy town and there were many tramways all heading in different directions. Miss Goering was astonished that the noise did not awaken her friend in the front seat. They soon left the center of town, although they were still in the city proper when they drove up in front of an apartment building. The chauffeur had quite a difficult time awakening his employer, but at last he succeeded by yelling the man's own address close to his ear.

Miss Goering was waiting on the sidewalk, standing first on one foot and then on the other. She noticed that there was a little garden that ran the length of one side of the apartment house. It was planted with evergreen trees and bushes, all of small dimensions because it was obvious that both the garden and the apartment house were very new. A string of barbed wire surrounded the garden and there was a dog trying to crawl under it. "I'll go put the car away, Ben," said the chauffeur.

Ben got out of the car and pushed Miss Goering ahead of him into the lobby of the apartment.

"Fake Spanish," Miss Goering said more to herself than to Ben.

"This isn't fake Spanish," he said glumly, "this is real Spanish."

Miss Goering laughed a little. "I don't think so," she said. "I have been to Spain."

"I don't believe you," said Ben. "Anyhow, this is real Spanish, every inch of it."

Miss Goering looked around her at the walls, which were made of yellow stucco and ornamented with niches and clusters of tiny columns.

Together they entered a tiny automatic elevator and Miss Goering's heart nearly failed her. Her companion pressed a button, but the elevator remained stationary.

"I could tear the man to pieces who made this gadget," he said, stamping on the floor.

"Oh, please," said Miss Goering, "please let me out."

He paid no attention to her, but stamped even harder than before, and pressed on the button over and over again as though the fear in her voice had excited him. At last the elevator started to rise. Miss Goering hid her face in her hands. They reached the second floor, where the elevator stopped, and they got out. They waited together in front of one of three doors that opened on a narrow hall.

"Jim has the keys with him," said Ben; "he'll be up in a minute. I hope you understand that we won't go dancing or any nonsense. I can't stand what people call fun."

"Oh, I love all that," said Miss Goering. "Fundamentally I am a light-hearted person. That is, I enjoy all the things that light-hearted people enjoy."

Ben yawned.

"He's never going to listen to me," Miss Goering said to herself.

Presently the chauffeur returned with the keys and let them into the apartment. The living-room was small and unattractive. Someone had left an enormous bundle in the middle of the floor. Through some rents in the paper Miss Goering could see that the bundle contained a pretty pink quilt. She felt a little heartened at the sight of the quilt and asked Ben whether or not he had chosen it himself. Without answering her question he called to the chauffeur, who had gone into the kitchen adjoining the living-room. The door between the two rooms was open, and Miss Goering could see the chauffeur standing next to the sink in his hat and coat and slowly unwrapping the steaks.

"I told you to see that they called for that damn blanket," Ben shouted to him.

"I forgot."

"Then carry one of those reminder pads with you and pull it out of your pocket once in a while. You can buy one at the corner."

Ben threw himself down on the couch next to Miss Goering, who had seated herself, and put his hand on her knee.

"Why? Don't you want the quilt now that you have bought it?" Miss Goering asked him.

"I didn't buy it. That girl who was here with me last week bought it, to throw over us in bed."

"And you don't like the colour?"

"I don't like a lot of extra stuff hanging around."

He sat brooding for a few minutes and Miss Goering, whose heart began to beat much too quickly each time that he lapsed into silence, searched her mind for another question to ask.

"You're not fond of discussions," she said to him.

"You mean talking?"

"Yes."

"No, I'm not."

"Why aren't you?"

"You say too much when you talk," he answered absently.

"Well, aren't you anxious to find out about people?"

He shook his head. "I don't need to find out about people, and, what's more important, they don't need to find out about me." He looked at her out of the corner of his eye.

"Well," she said a little breathlessly, "there must be something you like."

"I like women a lot and I like to make money if I can make it quickly." Without warning he jumped to his feet and pulled Miss Goering up with him, grabbing hold of her wrist rather roughly. "While he's finishing the steaks let's go inside for a minute."

"Oh, please," Miss Goering pleaded, "I'm so tired. Let's rest here a little before dinner."

"All right," said Ben. "I'm going to my room and stretch out till the steaks are cooked. I like them overdone."

While he was gone, Miss Goering sat on the couch pulling at her sweating fingers. She was torn between an almost overwhelming desire to bolt out of the room and a sickening compulsion to remain where she was.

"I do hope," she said to herself, "that the steaks will be ready before I have a chance to decide."

However, by the time the chauffeur awakened Ben to announce that the steaks were cooked, Miss Goering had decided that it was absolutely necessary for her to stay.

They sat together around a small folding table and ate in silence. They had barely finished their meal when the telephone rang. Ben answered, and when he had finished his conversation he told Miss Goering and Jim that they were all three of them going into the city. The chauffeur looked at him knowingly.

"It doesn't take long from here," said Ben, pulling on his coat. He turned to Miss Goering. "We are going to a restaurant," he said to her. "You'll sit patient at a separate table while I talk business with some friends. If it gets terribly late you and me will spend the night in the city at a hotel where I always go, downtown. Jim will drive the car back out and sleep here. Now is everything understood by everybody?"

"Perfectly," said Miss Goering, who was naturally delighted that they were leaving the apartment.

The restaurant was not very gay. It was in a large square room on the first floor of an old house. Ben led her to a table near the wall and told her to sit down.

"Every now and then you can order something," he said, and went over to three men who were standing at a makeshift bar improvised of thin strips of wood and papier-mâché.

The guests were nearly all men, and Miss Goering noticed that there were no distinguished faces among them, although not one of them was shabbily dressed. The three men to whom Ben was talking were ugly and even brutal-looking. Presently she saw Ben make a sign to a woman who was seated not far from her own table. She went and spoke to him and then walked quickly over to Miss Goering's table.

"He wants you to know he's going to be here a long time, maybe over two hours. I am supposed to get you what you want. Would you like some spaghetti or a sandwich? I'll get you whichever you want."

"No, thank you," said Miss Goering. "But won't you sit down and have a drink with me?"

"To tell you the truth, I won't," said the woman, "although I thank you very much." She hesitated a moment before saying good-by. "Of course, I would like to have you come over to our table and join us, but the situation is hard to explain. Most of us here are close friends, and when we see each other we tell each other everything that has happened."

"I understand," said Miss Goering, who was rather sad to see her leave because she did not fancy sitting alone for two or three hours. Although she was not anxious to be in Ben's company, the suspense of waiting all that time with so little to distract her was almost unbearable. It occurred to her that she might possibly telephone to a friend and ask her to come and have a drink at the restaurant. "Certainly," she thought. "Ben can't object to my having a little chat with another woman." Anna and Mrs. Copperfield were the only two people she knew well enough to invite on such short notice. Of the two she preferred Mrs. Copperfield and thought her the most likely to accept such an invitation. But she was not certain that Mrs. Copperfield had returned yet from her trip through Central America. She called the waiter and requested that he take her to the phone. After asking a few questions he showed her into a drafty hall and called the number for her. She was successful in reaching her friend, who was terribly excited the moment she heard Miss Goering's voice.

"I am flying down immediately," she said to Miss Goering. "I can't tell you how terrific it is to hear from you. I have not been back long, you know, and I don't think I'll stay."

Just as Mrs. Copperfield was telling her this, Ben came into the hall and snatched the receiver from Miss Goering's hand. "What's this about, for Christ's sake?" he demanded.

Miss Goering asked Mrs. Copperfield to hold on a moment. "I am calling a woman friend," she said to Ben, "a woman whom I haven't seen in quite some time. She is a lively person and I thought she might like to come down and have a drink with me. I was growing lonely at my table."

"Hello," Ben shouted into the phone, "are you coming down here?"

"By all means and *tout de suite*," Mrs. Copperfield answered. "I adore her."

Ben seemed satisfied and returned the receiver to Miss Goering without saying a word. Before leaving the hall, however, he announced to Miss Goering that he was not going to take on two women. She nodded and resumed her conversation with Mrs. Copperfield. She told her the address of the restaurant which the waiter had written down for her, and said good-by.

About half an hour later Mrs. Copperfield arrived, accompanied by a woman whom Miss Goering had never seen before. She was dismayed at the sight of her old friend. She was terribly thin and she appeared to be suffering from a skin eruption. Mrs. Copperfield's friend was fairly attractive, Miss Goering thought, but her hair was far too wiry for her own taste. Both women were dressed expensively and in black.

"There she is," Mrs. Copperfield screamed, grabbing Pacifica by the hand and running over to Miss Goering's table.

"I can't tell you how delighted I am that you called," she said. "You are the one person in the world I wanted to have see me. This is Pacifica. She is with me in my apartment."

Miss Goering asked them to sit down.

"Listen," said Pacifica to Miss Goering, "I have a date with a boy very far uptown. It is wonderful to see you, but he will be very nervous and unhappy. She can talk to you and I'll go and see him now. You are great friends, she told me."

Mrs. Copperfield rose to her feet. "Pacifica," she said, "you must stay here and have drinks first. This is a miracle and you must be in on it."

"It is so late now that I will be in a damned mess if I don't go right away. She would not come here alone," Pacifica said to Miss Goering.

"Remember, you promised to come and get me afterwards," said Mrs. Copperfield. "I will telephone you as soon as Christina is ready to leave."

Pacifica said good-by and hurried out of the room.

"What do you think of her?" Mrs. Copperfield asked Miss Goering, but without waiting for an answer she called for the waiter and ordered two double whiskies. "What do you think of her?" she repeated.

"Where's she from?"

"She is a Spanish girl from Panama, and the most wonderful character that has ever existed. We don't make a move without each other. I am completely satisfied and contented."

"I should say, though, that you are a little run down," said Miss Goering, who was frankly worried about her friend.

"I'll tell you," said Mrs. Copperfield, leaning over the table and suddenly looking very tense. "I am a little worried—not terribly worried, because I shan't allow anything to happen that I don't want to happen—but I am a little worried because Pacifica has met this blond boy who lives way uptown and he has asked her to marry him. He never says anything and he has a very weak character. But I think he has bewitched her because he pays her compliments all the time. I've gone up to his apartment with her, because I won't allow them to be alone, and she has cooked dinner for him twice. He's crazy for Spanish food and eats ravenously of every dish she puts in front of him."

Mrs. Copperfield leaned back and stared intently into Miss Goering's eyes.

"I am taking her back to Panama as soon as I am able to book passage on a boat." She ordered another double whisky. "Well, what do you think of it?" she asked eagerly.

"Perhaps you'd better wait and see whether or not she really wants to marry him."

"Don't be insane," said Mrs. Copperfield. "I can't live without her, not for a minute. I'd go completely to pieces."

"But you have gone to pieces, or do I misjudge you dreadfully?"

"True enough," said Mrs. Copperfield, bringing her fist down on the table and looking very mean. "I *have* gone to pieces, which is a thing I've wanted to do for years. I know I am as guilty as I can be, but I have my happiness, which I guard like a wolf, and I have authority now and a certain amount of daring, which, if you remember correctly, I never had before."

Mrs. Copperfield was getting drunk and looking more disagreeable.

"I remember," said Miss Goering, "that you used to be somewhat shy, but I dare say very courageous. It would take a good deal of courage to live with a man like Mr. Copperfield, whom I gather you are no longer living with. I've admired you very much indeed. I am not sure that I do now."

"That makes no difference to me," said Mrs. Copperfield. "I feel that you have changed anyway and lost your charm. You seem stodgy to me now and less comforting. You used to be so gracious and understanding; everyone thought you were light in the head, but I thought you were extremely instinctive and gifted with magic powers." She ordered another drink and sat brooding for a moment.

"You will contend," she continued in a very clear voice, "that all people are of equal importance, but although I love Pacifica very much, I think it is obvious that I am more important."

Miss Goering did not feel that she had any right to argue this point with Mrs. Copperfield.

"I understand how you feel," she said, "and perhaps you are right."

"Thank God," said Mrs. Copperfield, and she took Miss Goering's hand in her own.

"Christina," she pleaded, "please don't cross me again, I can't bear it."

Miss Goering hoped that Mrs. Copperfield would now question her concerning her own life. She had a great desire to tell someone everything that had happened during the last year. But Mrs. Copperfield sat gulping down her drink, occasionally spilling a little of it over her chin. She was not even looking at Miss Goering and they sat for ten minutes in silence.

"I think," said Mrs. Copperfield at last, "that I will telephone Pacifica and tell her to call for me in three quarters of an hour."

Miss Goering showed her to the phone and returned to the table. She looked up after a moment and noticed that another man had joined Ben and his friends. When her friend returned from the telephone, Miss Goering saw immediately that something was very much the matter. Mrs. Copperfield fell into her seat.

"She says that she does not know when she is coming down, and if she is not here by the time you feel like leaving, I am to return home with you, or all alone by myself. It's happened to me now, hasn't it? But the beauty of me is that I am only a step from desperation all the time and I am one of the few people I know who could perform an act of violence with the greatest of ease."

She waved her hand over her head.

"Acts of violence are generally performed with ease," said Miss Goering. She was at this point completely disgusted with Mrs. Copperfield, who rose from her seat and walked in a crooked path over to the bar. There she stood taking drink after drink without turning her little head which was almost completely hidden by the enormous fur collar on her coat.

Miss Goering went up to Mrs. Copperfield just once, thinking that she might persuade her friend to return to the table. But Mrs. Copperfield showed a furious tear-stained face to Miss Goering and flung her arm out sideways, striking Miss Goering in the nose with her forearm. Miss Goering returned to her seat and sat nursing her nose.

To her great surprise, about twenty minutes later Pacifica arrived, accompanied by her young man. She introduced him to Miss Goering and then hurried over to the bar. The young man stood with his hands in his pockets and looked around him rather awkwardly.

"Sit down," said Miss Goering. "I thought that Pacifica was not coming."

"She was not coming," he answered very slowly, "but then she decided that she would come because she was worried that her friend would be upset."

"Mrs. Copperfield is a highly strung woman, I am afraid," said Miss Goering.

"I don't know her very well," he answered discreetly.

Pacifica returned from the bar with Mrs. Copperfield, who was now terribly gay and wanted to order drinks for everyone. But neither the boy nor Pacifica would accept her offer. The boy looked very sad and soon excused himself, saying that he had only intended to see Pacifica to the restaurant and then return to his home. Mrs. Copperfield decided to accompany him to the door, patting his hand all the way and stumbling so badly that he was obliged to slip his arm around her waist to keep her from falling. Pacifica, meanwhile, leaned over to Miss Goering.

"It is terrible," she said. "What a baby your friend is! I can't leave her for ten minutes because it almost breaks her heart, and she is such a kind and generous woman, with such a beautiful apartment and such beautiful clothes. What can I do with her? She is like a little baby. I tried to explain it to my young man, but I can't explain it really to anyone."

Mrs. Copperfield returned and suggested that they all go elsewhere to get some food.

"I can't," said Miss Goering, lowering her eyes. "I have an appointment with a gentleman." She would have liked to talk to Pacifica a little longer. In some ways Pacifica reminded her of Miss Gamelon although certainly Pacifica was a much nicer person and more attractive physically. At this moment she noticed that Ben and his friends were putting on their coats and getting ready to leave. She hesitated only a second and then hurriedly said good-by to Pacifica and Mrs. Copperfield. She was just drawing her wrap over her shoulders when, to her surprise, she saw the four men walk very rapidly towards the door, right past her table. Ben made no sign to her.

"He must be coming back," she thought, but she decided to go into the hall. They were not in the hall, so she opened the door and stood on the stoop. From there she saw them all get into Ben's black car. Ben was the last one to get in, and just as he stepped on the running board, he turned his head around and saw Miss Goering.

"Hey," he said, "I forgot about you. I've got to go big distances on some important business. I don't know when I'll be back. Good-by."

He slammed the door behind him and they drove off. Miss Goering began to descend the stone steps. The long staircase seemed short to her, like a dream that is remembered long after it has been dreamed.

She stood on the street and waited to be overcome with joy and relief. But soon she was aware of a new sadness within herself. Hope, she felt, had discarded a childish form forever.

"Certainly I am nearer to becoming a saint," reflected Miss Goering, "but is it possible that a part of me hidden from my sight is piling sin upon sin as fast as Mrs. Copperfield?" This latter possibility Miss Goering thought to be of considerable interest but of no great importance.

IN THE SUMMER HOUSE

For

Oliver Smith

CHARACTERS

GERTRUDE EASTMAN CUEVAS
MOLLY, *her daughter*
MR. SOLARES
MRS. LOPEZ, *Mr. Solares' sister*
FREDERICA, *Mrs. Lopez' daughter*
ESPERANZA, *the Solares' family servant*
LIONEL
VIVIAN, *Gertrude's young boarder*
MRS. CONSTABLE, *Vivian's mother*
INEZ
CHAUFFEUR
TWO HAGS
TWO FIGURE BEARERS

SCENES

Act One

Scene 1: Gertrude Eastman Cuevas' garden on the coast, Southern California
Scene 2: The beach. One month later
Scene 3: The garden. One month later

Act Two

Scene 1: The Lobster Bowl. Ten months later, before dawn
Scene 2: The same. Two months later, late afternoon

Time: The Present

ACT ONE

SCENE I

GERTRUDE EASTMAN CUEVAS' *garden somewhere on the coast of Southern California. The garden is a mess, with ragged cactus plants and broken ornaments scattered about. A low hedge at the back of the set separates the garden from a dirt lane which supposedly leads to the main road. Beyond the lane is the beach and the sea. The side of the house and the front door are visible. A low balcony hangs over the garden. In the garden itself there is a round summer house covered with vines.*

GERTRUDE (*a beautiful middle-aged woman with sharply defined features, a good carriage and bright red hair. She is dressed in a tacky provincial fashion. Her voice is tense but resonant. She is seated on the balcony*): Are you in the summer house?

(MOLLY, *a girl of eighteen with straight black hair cut in bangs and a somnolent impassive face, does not hear* GERTRUDE'*s question but remains in the summer house.* GERTRUDE, *repeating, goes to railing.*)

Are you in the summer house?

MOLLY: Yes, I am.

GERTRUDE: If I believed in acts of violence, I would burn the summer house down. You love to get in there and loll about hour after hour. You can't even see out because those vines hide the view. Why don't you find a good flat rock overlooking the ocean and sit on it? (MOLLY *fingers the vine.*) As long as you're so indifferent to the beauties of nature, I should think you would interest yourself in political affairs, or in music or painting or at least in the future. But I've said this to you at least a thousand times before. You admit you relax too much?

MOLLY: I guess I do.

GERTRUDE: We already have to take in occasional boarders to help make ends meet. As the years go by the boarders will increase, and I can barely put up with the few that come here now; I'm not temperamentally suited to boarders. Nor am I interested in whether this should be considered a character defect or not. I simply hate gossiping with strangers and I don't want to listen to their business. I never have and I never will. It disgusts me. Even my own flesh and blood saps my vitality—particularly you. You seem to have developed such a slow and gloomy way of walking lately . . . not at all becoming to a girl. Don't you think you could correct your walk?

MOLLY: I'm trying. I'm trying to correct it.

GERTRUDE: I'm thinking seriously of marrying Mr. Solares, after all. I would at least have a life free of financial worry if I did, and I'm sure I could gradually ease his sister, Mrs. Lopez, out of the house because she certainly gets on my nerves. He's a manageable man and Spanish men aren't around the house much, which is a blessing. They're almost always out . . . not getting intoxicated or having a wild time . . . just out . . . sitting around with bunches of other men . . . Spanish men . . . Cubans, Mexicans . . . I don't know . . . They're all alike, drinking little cups of coffee and jabbering away to each other for hours on end. That was your father's life anyway. I minded then. I minded terribly, not so much because he left me alone, but he wasn't in his office for more than a few hours a day . . . and he wasn't rich enough, not like Mr. Solares. I lectured him in the beginning. I lectured him on ambition, on making contacts, on developing his personality. Often at night I was quite hoarse. I worked on him steadily, trying to make him worry about sugar. I warned him he was letting his father's interests go to pot. Nothing helped. He refused to worry about sugar; he refused to worry about anything. (*She knits a moment in silence.*) I lost interest finally. I lost interest in sugar . . . in him. I lost interest in our life together. I wanted to give it all up . . . start out fresh, but I couldn't. I was carrying you. I had no choice. All my hopes were wrapped up in you then, all of them. You were my reason for going on, my one and only hope . . . my love. (*She knits furiously. Then, craning her neck to look in the summer house, she gets up and goes to the rail.*) Are you asleep in there, or are you reading comic strips?

MOLLY: I'm not asleep.

GERTRUDE: Sometimes I have the strangest feeling about you. It frightens me . . . I feel that you are plotting something. Especially when you get inside that summer house. I think your black hair helps me to feel that way. Whenever I think of a woman going wild, I always picture her with black hair, never blond or red. I know that what I'm saying has no connection with a scientific truth. It's very personal. They say red-haired women go wild a lot but I never picture it that way. Do you?

MOLLY: I don't guess I've ever pictured women going wild.

GERTRUDE: And why not? They do all the time. They break the bonds . . . Sometimes I picture little scenes where they turn evil like wolves . . . (*Shuddering.*) I don't choose to, but I do all the same.

MOLLY: I've never seen a wild woman.

GERTRUDE (*music*): On the other hand, sometimes I wake up at night with a strange feeling of isolation . . . as if I'd fallen off the cliffs and landed miles away from everything that was close to my heart . . . Even my griefs and my sorrows don't seem to belong to me. Nothing does—as if a shadow had passed over my whole life and made it dark. I try saying my name aloud, over and over again, but it doesn't hook things together. Whenever I feel that way I put my wrapper on and I go down into the kitchen. I open the ice chest and take out some fizzy water. Then I sit at the table with the light switched on and by and by I feel all right again. (*The music fades. Then in a more matter-of-fact tone.*) There is no doubt that each one of us has to put up with a shadow or two as he grows older. But if we occupy ourselves while the shadow passes, it passes swiftly enough and scarcely leaves a trace on our daily lives . . . (*She knits for a moment. Then looks up the road.*) The girl who is coming here this afternoon is about seventeen. She should be arriving pretty soon. I also think that Mr. Solares will be arriving shortly and that he'll be bringing one of his hot picnic luncheons with him today. I can feel it in my bones. It's disgraceful of me, really, to allow him to feed us on our own lawn, but then, their mouths count up to six, while ours count up to only two. So actually it's only half a disgrace. I hope Mr.

Solares realizes that. Besides, I might be driven to accepting his marriage offer and then the chicken would be in the same pot anyway. Don't you agree?

MOLLY: Yes.

GERTRUDE: You don't seem very interested in what I'm saying.

MOLLY: Well, I . . .

GERTRUDE: I think that you should be more of a conversationalist. You never express an opinion, nor do you seem to have an outlook. What on earth is your outlook?

MOLLY (*uncertainly*): Democracy . . .

GERTRUDE: I don't think you feel very strongly about it. You don't listen to the various commentators, nor do you ever glance at the newspapers. It's very easy to say that one is democratic, but that doesn't prevent one from being a slob if one is a slob. I've never permitted myself to become a slob, even though I sit home all the time and avoid the outside world as much as possible. I've never liked going out any more than my father did. He always avoided the outside world. He hated a lot of idle gossip and had no use for people anyway. "Let the world do its dancing and its drinking and its interkilling without me," he always said. "They'll manage perfectly well; I'll stick to myself and my work." (*The music comes up again and she is lost in a dream.*) When I was a little girl I made up my mind that I was going to be just like him. He was my model, my ideal. I admired him more than anyone on earth. And he admired me of course. I was so much like him—ambitious, defiant, a fighting cock always. I worshipped him. But I was never meek, not like Ellen my sister. She was very frail and delicate. My father used to put his arms around her, and play with her hair, long golden curls . . . Ellen was the weak one. That's why he spoiled her. He pitied Ellen. (*With wonder, and very delicately, as if afraid to break a spell. The music expresses the sorrow she is hiding from herself.*) Once he took her out of school, when she was ten years old. He bought her a little fur hat and they went away together for two whole weeks. I was left behind. I had no reason to leave school. I was healthy and strong. He took her to a big hotel on the edge of a lake. The lake was frozen, and they sat in the sunshine all day long, watching the people skate. When they came back he said, "Look at her, look at Ellen. She has roses in her cheeks." He pitied Ellen, but he was proud of me. I was his true love. He never showed it . . . He was so frightened Ellen would guess. He didn't want her to be jealous, but I knew the truth . . . He didn't have to show it. He didn't have to say anything. (*The music fades and she knits furiously, coming back to the present.*) Why don't you go inside and clean up? It might sharpen your wits. Go and change that rumpled dress.

MOLLY (MOLLY *comes out of the summer house and sniffs a blossom*): The honeysuckle's beginning to smell real good. I can never remember when you planted this vine, but it's sure getting thick. It makes the summer house so nice and shady inside.

GERTRUDE (*stiffening in anger*): I told you never to mention that vine again. You know it was there when we bought this house. You love to call my attention to that wretched vine because it's the only thing that grows well in the garden and you know it was planted by the people who came here before us and not by me at all. (*She rises and paces the balcony.*) You're mocking me for being such a failure in the garden and not being able to make things grow. That's an underhanded Spanish trait of yours you inherit from your father. You love to mock me.

MOLLY (*tenderly*): I would never mock you.

GERTRUDE (*working herself up*): I thought I'd find peace here . . . with these waving palms and the ocean stretching as far as the eye can see, but you don't like the ocean . . . You won't even go in the water. You're afraid to swim . . . I thought we'd found a paradise at last—the perfect place—but you don't want paradise . . . You want hell. Well, go into your little house and rot if you like . . . I don't care. Go on in while you still can. It won't be there much longer . . . I'll marry Mr. Solares and send you to business school. (*The voices of* MR. SOLARES *and his family arriving with a picnic lunch stop her. She leans over the railing of the balcony and looks up the road.*) Oh, here they come with their covered pots. I knew they'd appear with a picnic luncheon today. I could feel it in my bones. We'll put our own luncheon away for supper and have our supper tomorrow for lunch . . . Go and change . . . Quickly . . . Watch that walk. (MOLLY *exits into the house.* GERTRUDE *settles down in her chair to prepare for* MR. SOLARES' *arrival.*) I wish they weren't coming. I'd rather be here by myself really. (*Enter Spanish people.*) Nature's the best company of all. (*She pats her bun and rearranges some hairpins. Then she stands up and waves to her guests, cupping her mouth and yelling at the same time.*) Hello there!

(*In another moment* MR. SOLARES, MRS. LOPEZ *and her daughter,* FREDERICA *and the three servants enter, walking in single file down the lane. Two of the servants are old hags and the third is a young half caste,* ESPERANZA, *in mulberry-colored satin. The servants all carry pots wrapped with bright bandanas.*)

MR. SOLARES (*he wears a dark dusty suit. Pushing ahead of his sister,* MRS. LOPEZ, *in his haste to greet* GERTRUDE *and thus squeezing his sister's arm rather painfully against the gate post*): Hello, Miss Eastman Cuevas! (MRS. LOPEZ *squeals with pain and rubs her arm. She is fat and middle-aged. She wears a black picture hat and black city dress. Her hat is decorated with flowers.* MR. SOLARES *speaks with only a trace of an accent, having lived for many years in this country. Grinning and bobbing around.*) We brought you a picnic. For you and your daughter. Plenty of everything! You come down into the garden.

(*The others crowd slowly through the gate and stand awkwardly in a bunch looking up at* GERTRUDE.)

GERTRUDE (*perfunctorily*): I think I'll stay here on the balcony, thank you. Just spread yourselves on the lawn and we'll talk back and forth this way. It's all the same. (*To the maids*) You can hand me up my food by stepping on that little stump and I'll lean over and get it.

MRS. LOPEZ (*her accent is much thicker than her brother's, smiling up at* GERTRUDE): You will come down into the garden, Miss Eastman Cuevas?

MR. SOLARES (*giving his sister a poke*): Acaba de decirte que se queda arriba. Ya no oyes? (*The next few minutes on the stage have a considerable musical background. The hags and* ESPERANZA *start spreading bandanas on the lawn and emptying the baskets. The others settle on the lawn.* ESPERANZA *and the hags sing a raucous song as they work, the hags just joining in at the chorus and a bit off key.* ESPERANZA *brings over a pot wrapped in a Turkish towel and serves the family group. They all take enormous helpings of spaghetti.* MR. SOLARES *serves himself.*) Italian spaghetti with meat balls! Esperanza, serve a big plate to Miss Eastman Cuevas up on the porch. You climb on that.

(*He points to a fake stump with a gnome carved on one side of it.*)

ESPERANZA (*disagreeably*): Caramba!

(*She climbs up on the stump after filling a plate with spaghetti and hands it to* GERTRUDE, *releasing her hold on the plate before* GERTRUDE *has secured her own grip.* ESPERANZA *jumps out of the way immediately and the plate swings downward under the weight of the food, dumping the spaghetti on* MRS. LOPEZ' *head.*)

GERTRUDE: Oh! (*To* ESPERANZA.) You didn't give me a chance to get a firm hold on it!

MR. SOLARES: Silencio!

(ESPERANZA *rushes over to the hags and all three of them become hysterical with laughter. After their hysterics they pull themselves together and go over to clean up* MRS. LOPEZ *and to restore* GERTRUDE*'s plate to her filled with fresh spaghetti. They return to their side of the garden in a far corner and everyone starts to eat.*)

MR. SOLARES (*to* GERTRUDE): Miss Eastman Cuevas, you like chop suey?

GERTRUDE: I have never eaten any.

MRS. LOPEZ (*eager to get into the conversation and expressing great wonder in her voice*): Chop suey? What is it?

MR. SOLARES (*in a mean voice to* MRS. LOPEZ): You know what it is. (*In Spanish.*) Que me dejes hablar con la Señora Eastman Cuevas por favor. (*To* GERTRUDE.) I'll bring you some chop suey tomorrow in a box, or maybe we better go out to a restaurant, to a dining and dancing. Maybe you would go to try out some chop suey . . . Would you?

GERTRUDE (*coolly*): That's very nice of you but I've told you before that I don't care for the type of excitement you get when you go out . . . You know what I mean—entertainment, dancing, etc. Why don't you describe chop suey to me and I'll try and imagine it? (MRS. LOPEZ *roars with laughter for no apparent reason.* GERTRUDE *cranes her neck and looks down at her over the balcony with raised eyebrows.*) I could die content without ever setting foot in another restaurant. Frankly, I would not care if every single one of them burned to the ground. I really love to sit on my porch and look out over the ocean.

MRS. LOPEZ: You like the ocean?

GERTRUDE: I love it!

MRS. LOPEZ (*making a wild gesture with her arm*): I hate it!

GERTRUDE: I love it. It's majestic . . .

MRS. LOPEZ: I hate!

GERTRUDE (*freezing up*): I see that we don't agree.

MR. SOLARES (*scowling at* MRS. LOPEZ): Oh, she loves the ocean. I don't know what the hell is the matter with her today. (GERTRUDE *winces at his language.*) Myself, I like ocean, land, mountain, all kinds of food, chop suey, chile, eel, turtle steak . . . Everything. Solares like everything. (*In hideous French accent.*) Joie de vivre! (*He snaps his fingers in the air.*)

GERTRUDE (*sucking some long strands of spaghetti into her mouth*): What is your attitude toward your business?

MR. SOLARES (*happily*): My business is dandy.

GERTRUDE (*irritably*): Yes, but what is your attitude toward it?

MR. SOLARES (*with his mouth full*): O.K.

GERTRUDE: Please try to concentrate on my question, Mr. Solares. Do you like business or do you really prefer to stay home and lazy around?

MRS. LOPEZ (*effusively*): He don't like no business—he likes to stay home and sleep—and eat. (*Then in a mocking tone intended to impress* MR. SOLARES *himself.*) "Fula, I got headache . . . I got bellyache . . . I stay home, no?" (*She jabs her brother in the ribs with her elbow several times rolling her eyes in a teasing manner and repeats.*) "Fula, I got headache . . . I got bellyache . . . I stay home, no?" (*She jabs him once again even harder and laughs way down in her throat.*)

MR. SOLARES: Fula! Esta es la última vez que sales conmigo. Ya déjame hablar con la Señora *Eastman Cuevas*!

MRS. LOPEZ: Look, *Miss* Eastman Cuevas?

GERTRUDE (*looking disagreeably surprised*): Yes?

MRS. LOPEZ: You like to talk to me?

GERTRUDE (*as coolly as possible short of sounding rude*): Yes, I enjoy it.

MRS. LOPEZ (*triumphantly to* MR. SOLARES): Miss Eastman Cuevas *like* talk to me, so you shut your mouth. He don't want no one to talk to you, Miss Eastman Cuevas because he think he gonna marry you.

(FREDERICA *doubles over and buries her face in her hands. Her skinny shoulders shake with laughter.*)

MR. SOLARES (*embarrassed and furious*): Bring the chicken and rice, Esperanza.

ESPERANZA: You ain't finished what you got!

MR. SOLARES: Cállate, y traigame el arroz con pollo.

(ESPERANZA *walks across the lawn with the second pot wrapped in a Turkish towel. She walks deliberately at a very slow pace, throwing a hip out at each step, and with a terrible sneer on her face. She serves them all chicken and rice, first removing the spaghetti plates and giving them clean ones. Everyone takes enormous helpings again, with the exception of* GERTRUDE *who refuses to have any.*)

GERTRUDE (*while* ESPERANZA *serves the others*): If Molly doesn't come out soon she will simply have to miss her lunch. It's very tiring to have to keep reminding her of the time and the other realities of life. Molly is a dreamer.

MRS. LOPEZ (*nodding*): That's right.

GERTRUDE (*watching* FREDERICA *serve herself*): Do you people always eat such a big midday meal? Molly and I are in the habit of eating simple salads at noon.

MRS. LOPEZ (*wiping her mouth roughly with her napkin. Then without pausing and with gusto*): For breakfast: chocolate and sugar bread; for lunch: soup, beans, eggs, rice, roast pork with potatoes and guava paste . . . (*She pulls on a different finger for each separate item.*) Next day: soup, eggs, beans, rice, chicken with rice and guava paste—other day: soup, eggs, beans, rice, stew meat, roasted baby pig and guava paste. Other day: soup, rice, beans, grilled red snapper, roasted goat meat and guava paste.

FREDERICA (*speaking for the first time, rapidly, in a scarcely audible voice*): Soup, rice, beans, eggs, ground-up meat and guava paste.

GERTRUDE (*wearily*): We usually have a simple salad.

MR. SOLARES: She's talkin' about the old Spanish custom. She only come here ten years ago when her old man died. I don't like a big lunch neither. (*In a sudden burst of temerity.*) Listen, what my sister said was true. I hope I am gonna marry you some day soon. I've told you so before. You remember?

MRS. LOPEZ (*laughing and whispering to* FREDERICA, *who goes off into hysterics, and then delving into a shopping bag which lies beside her on the grass. In a very gay voice*): This is what you gonna get if you make a wedding. (*She pulls out a paper bag and hurls it at* GERTRUDE*'s head with the gesture of a baseball pitcher. The bag splits and spills rice all over* GERTRUDE. *There is general hilarity and even a bit of singing on the part of* ESPERANZA *and the hags.* MRS. LOPEZ *yells above the noise.*) Rice!

GERTRUDE (*standing up and flicking rice from her shoulders*): Stop it! Please! Stop it! I can't stand this racket . . . Really. (*She is genuinely upset. They subside gradually. Bewildered, she looks out over the land toward the road.*) Something is coming down the road . . . It must be my boarder . . . No . . . She would be coming in an automobile. (*Pause.*) Gracious! It certainly is *no* boarder, but what is it?

MRS. LOPEZ: Friend come and see you?

GERTRUDE (*bewildered, staring hard*): No, it's not a friend. It's . . . (*She stares harder.*) It's some sort of king—and others.

MRS. LOPEZ (*to her brother*): Qué?

MR. SOLARES (*absently absorbed in his food*): King. Un rey y otros mas . . .

MRS. LOPEZ (*nodding*): Un rey y otros mas.

(*Enter* LIONEL, *bearing a cardboard figure larger than himself, representing Neptune, with flowing beard, crown and sceptre, etc. He is followed by two or more other figure bearers, carrying representations of a channel swimmer and a mermaid.* LIONEL *stops at the gate and dangles into the garden a toy lobster which he has tied to the line of a real fishing rod. The music dies down.*)

LIONEL: Advertisement. (*He bobs the lobster up and down.*)

GERTRUDE: For what?

LIONEL: For the Lobster Bowl . . . It's opening next week. (*Pointing.*) That figure there represents a mermaid and the other one is Neptune, the sea god. This is a lobster . . . (*He shakes the rod.*) Everything connected with the sea in some capacity. Can we have a glass of water?

GERTRUDE: Yes. (*Calling.*) Molly! Molly!

MOLLY (*from inside the house*): What is it?

GERTRUDE: Come out here immediately. (*To* LIONEL) Excuse me but I think your figures are really awful. I don't like advertising schemes anyway.

LIONEL: I have nothing to do with them. I just have to carry them around a few more days and then after that I'll be working at the Bowl. I'm sorry you don't like them.

GERTRUDE: I've always hated everything that was larger than life size.

(LIONEL *opens the gate and enters the garden, followed by the other figure bearers. The garden by now has a very cluttered appearance. The servants,* MRS. LOPEZ *and* FREDERICA *have been gaping at the figures in silence since their arrival.*)

MRS. LOPEZ (*finding her tongue*): Una maravilla!

FREDERICA: Ay, sí.

(*She is nearly swooning with delight. Enter* MOLLY. *She stops short when she sees the figures.*)

MOLLY: Oh . . . What are those?

LIONEL: Advertisements. This is Neptune, the old god.

(MOLLY *approaches the figures slowly and touches Neptune.*)

MOLLY: It's beautiful . . .

LIONEL: Here's a little lobster. (*He dangles it into* MOLLY*'s open palm.*)

MOLLY: It looks like a real lobster. It even has those long threads sticking out over its eyes.

GERTRUDE: Antennae.

MOLLY: Antennae.

LIONEL (*pulling another little lobster from his pocket and handing it to* MOLLY): Here. Take this one. I have a few to give away.

MOLLY: Oh, thank you very much.

(*There follows a heated argument between* FREDERICA *and* MRS. LOPEZ, *who is trying to force* FREDERICA *to ask for a lobster too. They almost come to blows and finally* MRS. LOPEZ *gives* FREDERICA *a terrific shove which sends her stumbling over toward* LIONEL *and* MOLLY.)

MRS. LOPEZ (*calling out to* LIONEL): Give my girl a little fish please!

(LIONEL *digs reluctantly into his pocket and hands* FREDERICA *a little lobster. She takes it and returns to her mother, stubbing her toe in her confusion.*)

GERTRUDE (*craning her neck and looking out over the lane toward the road*): There's a car stopping. This really must be my boarder. (*She looks down into the garden with an expression of consternation on her face.*) The garden is a wreck. Mr. Solares, can't your servants organize this mess? Quickly, for heaven's sake. (*She looks with disgust at* MR. SOLARES, *who is still eating, but holds her tongue. Enter* VIVIAN, *a young girl of fifteen with wild reddish gold hair. She is painfully thin and her eyes appear to pop out of her head with excitement. She is dressed in bright colors and wears high heels. She is followed by a chauffeur carrying luggage.*) And get those figures out of sight!

VIVIAN (*stopping in the road and staring at the house intently for a moment*): The house is heavenly!

(MOLLY *exits rapidly.*)

GERTRUDE: Welcome, Vivian Constable. I'm Gertrude Eastman Cuevas. How was your trip?

VIVIAN: Stinky. (*Gazing with admiration into the garden packed with people.*) And your garden is heavenly too.

GERTRUDE: The garden is a wreck at the moment.

VIVIAN: Oh, no! It's fascinating.

GERTRUDE: You can't possibly tell yet.

VIVIAN: Oh, but I can. I decide everything the first minute. It's a fascinating garden.

(*She smiles at everyone.* MR. SOLARES *spits chicken skin out of his mouth onto the grass.*)

MRS. LOPEZ: Do you want some spaghetti?

VIVIAN: Not yet, thank you. I'm too excited.

GERTRUDE (*to* MR. SOLARES): Will you show Miss Constable and the chauffeur into the house, Mr. Solares? I'll meet you at the top of the stairs.

(*She exits hurriedly into the house, but* MR. SOLARES *continues gnawing on his bone not having paid the slightest attention to* GERTRUDE*'s request. Enter* MRS. CONSTABLE, VIVIAN*'s mother. She is wearing a distinguished city print, gloves, hat* *and veil. She is frail like her daughter but her coloring is dull.*)

VIVIAN (*spying her mother. Her expression immediately hardens*): Why did you get out of the taxi? You promised at the hotel that you wouldn't get out if I allowed you to ride over with me. You promised me once in the room and then again on the porch. Now you've gotten out. You're dying to spoil the magic. Go back . . . Don't stand there looking at the house. (MRS. CONSTABLE *puts her fingers to her lips entreating silence, shakes her head at* VIVIAN *and scurries off stage after nodding distractedly to the people on the lawn.*) She can't keep a promise.

GERTRUDE (*coming out onto the balcony again and spotting* MR. SOLARES, *still eating on the grass*): What is the matter with you, Mr. Solares? I asked you to show Miss Constable and the chauffeur into the house and you haven't budged an inch. I've been waiting at the top of the stairs like an idiot.

(MR. SOLARES *scrambles to his feet and goes into the house followed by* VIVIAN *and the chauffeur. Enter* MRS. CONSTABLE *again.*)

MRS. CONSTABLE (*coming up to the hedge and leaning over. To* MRS. LOPEZ): Forgive me but I would like you to tell Mrs. Eastman Cuevas that I am at the Herons Hotel. (MRS. LOPEZ *nods absently.* MRS. CONSTABLE *continues in a scarcely audible voice.*) You see, Mrs. Eastman Cuevas comes from the same town that I come from and through mutual friends I heard that she took in boarders these days, so I wrote her that Vivian my daughter was coming.

MRS. LOPEZ: Thank you very much.

MRS. CONSTABLE: My daughter likes her freedom, so we have a little system worked out when we go on vacations. I stay somewhere nearby but not in the same place. Even so, I am the nervous type and I would like Mrs. Eastman Cuevas to know that I'm at the Herons . . . You see my daughter is unusually high spirited. She feels everything so strongly that she's apt to tire herself out. I want to be available just in case she collapses.

MRS. LOPEZ (*ruffling* FREDERICA*'s hair*): Frederica get very tired too.

MRS. CONSTABLE: Yes, I know. I suppose all the young girls do. Will you tell Mrs. Eastman Cuevas that I'm at the Herons?

MRS. LOPEZ: O.K.

MRS. CONSTABLE: Thank you a thousand times. I'll run along now or Vivian will see me and she'll think that I'm interfering with her freedom . . . You'll notice right away what fun she gets out of life. Good-bye.

MRS. LOPEZ: Good-bye, Mrs. Vamos; despiértense. Esperanza. (MRS. CONSTABLE *exits hurriedly. To* MR. SOLARES.) Now we go home.

MR. SOLARES (*sullenly*): All right. (*Spanish group leaves.*) Esperanza! Esperanza! Frederica!

(*Enter from the house* VIVIAN, GERTRUDE *and the chauffeur, who leaves the garden and exits down the lane.*)

VIVIAN (*to* GERTRUDE, *continuing a conversation*): I'm going to be sky high by dinner time. Then I won't sleep all night. I know myself.

GERTRUDE: Don't you use controls?

VIVIAN: No, I never do. When I feel myself going up I just go on up until I hit the ceiling. I'm like that. The world is ten times more exciting for me than it is for others.

GERTRUDE: Still I believe in using controls. It's a part of the law of civilization. Otherwise we would be like wild beasts. (*She sighs.*) We're bad enough as it is, controls and all.

VIVIAN (*hugging* GERTRUDE *impulsively*): You've got the prettiest hair I've ever seen, and I'm going to love it here. (GERTRUDE *backs away a little, embarrassed.* VIVIAN *spots the summer house.*) What a darling little house! It's like the home of a bird or a poet. (*She approaches the summer house and enters it.* MRS. LOPEZ *motions to the hags to start cleaning up. They hobble around one behind the other gathering things and scraping plates very ineffectually. More often than not the hag behind scrapes more garbage onto the plate just cleaned by the hag in front of her. They continue this until the curtain falls. Music begins. Calling to* GERTRUDE.) I can imagine all sorts of things in here, Miss Eastman Cuevas. I could make plans for hours on end in here. It's so darling and little.

GERTRUDE (*coldly*): Molly usually sits in there. But I can't say that she plans much. Just dozes or reads trash. Comic strips. It will do no harm if someone else sits in there for a change.

VIVIAN: Who is Molly?

GERTRUDE: Molly is my daughter.

VIVIAN: How wonderful! I want to meet her right away . . . Where is she?

(*The boys start righting the cardboard figures.*)

LIONEL: Do you think we could have our water?

GERTRUDE: I'm sorry. Yes, of course. (*Calling.*) Molly! (*Silence.*) Molly! (*More loudly.*) Molly! (*Silence.*)

LIONEL: I think we'll go along to the next place. Don't bother your daughter. I'll come back if I may. I'd like to see you all again . . . and your daughter. She disappeared so quickly.

GERTRUDE: You stay right where you are. I'll get her out here in a minute. (*Screaming.*) Molly! Come out here immediately! Molly!

VIVIAN (*in a trilling voice*): Molly! Come on out! . . . I'm in your little house . . . Molly!

GERTRUDE (*furious*): Molly!

(*All the players look expectantly at the doorway.* MOLLY *does not appear and the curtain comes down in silence.*)

SCENE 2

One month later.

A beach and a beautiful backdrop of the water. The SOLARES *family is again spread out among dirty plates as though the scenery had changed around them while they themselves had not stirred since the first act.* GERTRUDE *is kneeling and rearranging her hair near the* SOLARES *family,* VIVIAN *at her feet.* MOLLY *and* LIONEL *a little apart from the other people,* MOLLY *watching* VIVIAN. *The two old bags are wearing white slips for swimming.*

The music is sad and disturbing, implying a more serious mood.

MRS. LOPEZ (*poking her daughter who is lying next to her*): A ver si tú y Esperanza nos cantan algo . . .

FREDERICA (*from under handkerchief which covers her face*): Ay, mamá.

MRS. LOPEZ (*calling to* ESPERANZA): Esperanza, a ver si nos cantan algo, tú y Frederica.

(*She gives her daughter a few pokes. They argue a bit and* FREDERICA *gets up and drags herself wearily over to the bags. They consult and sing a little song. The bags join in at the chorus.*)

ESPERANZA: Bueno—sí . . .

GERTRUDE (*when they have finished*): That was nice. I like sad songs.

VIVIAN (*still at her feet and looking up at her with adoration*): So do I . . . (MOLLY *is watching* VIVIAN, *a beam of hate in her eye.* VIVIAN *takes* GERTRUDE*'s wrist and plays with her hand just for a moment.* GERTRUDE *pulls it away, instinctively afraid of* MOLLY*'s reaction. To* GERTRUDE.) I wish Molly would come swimming with me. I thought maybe she would. (*Then to* MOLLY, *for* GERTRUDE*'s benefit.*) Molly, won't you come in, just this once. You'll love it once you do. Everyone loves the water, everyone in the world.

GERTRUDE (*springing to her feet, and addressing the Spanish people*): I thought we were going for a stroll up the beach after lunch. (*There is apprehension behind her words.*) You'll never digest lying on your backs, and besides you're sure to fall asleep if you don't get up right away. (*She regains her inner composure as she gives her commands.*)

MRS. LOPEZ (*groaning*): Ay! Caray! Why don't you sleep, Miss Eastman Cuevas?

GERTRUDE: It's very bad for you, really. Come on. Come on, everybody! Get up! You too, Alta Gracia and Quintina, get up! Come on, everybody up! (*There is a good deal of protesting while the servants and the* SOLARES *family struggle to their feet.*) I promise you you'll feel much better later on if we take just a little walk along the beach.

VIVIAN (*leaping to* GERTRUDE*'s side in one bound*): I *love* to walk on the beach!

(MOLLY *too has come forward to be with her mother.*)

GERTRUDE (*pause. Again stifling her apprehension with a command*): You children stay here. Or take a walk along the cliffs if you'd like to. But be careful!

FREDERICA: I want to be with my mother.

GERTRUDE: Well, come along, but we're only going for a short stroll. What a baby you are, Frederica Lopez.

MR. SOLARES: I'll run the car up to my house and go and collect that horse I was telling you about. Then I'll catch up with you on the way back.

GERTRUDE: You won't get much of a walk.

(FREDERICA *throws her arms around her mother and gives her a big smacking kiss on the cheek.* MRS. LOPEZ *kisses* FREDERICA. *They all exit slowly, leaving* VIVIAN, LIONEL, MOLLY *and the dishes behind.* MOLLY, *sad that she can't walk with her mother, crosses wistfully back to her former place next to* LIONEL, *but* VIVIAN—*eager to cut her out whenever she can—rushes to* LIONEL*'s side, and crouches on her heels exactly where* MOLLY *was sitting before.* MOLLY *notices this, and settles in a brooding way a little apart from them, her back to the pair.*)

VIVIAN: Lionel, what were you saying before about policies?

LIONEL: When?

VIVIAN: Today, before lunch. You said, "What are your policies" or something crazy like that?

LIONEL: Oh, yes. It's just . . . I'm mixed up about my own policies, so I like to know how other people's are getting along.

VIVIAN: Well, I'm for freedom and a full exciting life! (*Pointedly to* MOLLY'S *back.*) I'm a daredevil. It frightens my mother out of her wits, but I love excitement!

LIONEL: Do you always do what gives you pleasure?

VIVIAN: Whenever I can, I do.

LIONEL: What about conflicts?

VIVIAN: What do you mean?

LIONEL: Being pulled different ways and not knowing which to choose.

VIVIAN: I don't have those. I always know exactly what I want to do. When I have a plan in my head I get so excited I can't sleep.

LIONEL: Maybe it would be a stroke of luck to be like you. I have nothing but conflicts. For instance, one day I think I ought to give up the world and be a religious leader, and the next day I'll turn right around and think I ought to throw myself deep into politics. (VIVIAN, *bored, starts untying her beach shoes.*) There have been ecclesiastics in my family before. I come from a gloomy family. A lot of the men seem to have married crazy wives. Five brothers out of six and a first cousin did. My uncle's first wife boiled a cat alive in the upstairs kitchen.

VIVIAN: What do you mean, the upstairs kitchen?

LIONEL: We had the top floor fitted out as an apartment and the kitchen upstairs was called the upstairs kitchen.

VIVIAN (*hopping to her feet*): Oh, well, let's stop talking dull heavy stuff. I'm going to swim.

LIONEL: All right.

VIVIAN (*archly*): Good-bye, Molly.

(*She runs off stage in the direction of the cove.* MOLLY *sits on rock.*)

LIONEL (*goes over and sits next to her*): Doesn't the ocean make you feel gloomy when the sky is gray or when it starts getting dark out?

MOLLY: I don't guess it does.

LIONEL: Well, in the daytime, if it's sunny out and the ocean's blue it puts you in a lighter mood, doesn't it?

MOLLY: When it's blue . . .

LIONEL: Yes, when it's blue and dazzling. Don't you feel happier when it's like that?

MOLLY: I don't guess I emphasize that kind of thing.

LIONEL: I see. (*Thoughtfully.*) Well, how do you feel about the future? Are you afraid of the future in the back of your mind?

MOLLY: I don't guess I emphasize that much either.

LIONEL: Maybe you're one of the lucky ones who looks forward to the future. Have you got some kind of ambition?

MOLLY: Not so far. Have you?

LIONEL: I've got two things I think I should do, like I told Vivian. But they're not exactly ambitions. One's being a religious leader, the other's getting deep into politics. I don't look forward to either one of them.

MOLLY: Then you'd better not do them.

LIONEL: I wish it was that simple. I'm not an easygoing type. I come from a gloomy family . . . I dread being a minister in a way because it brings you so close to death all the time. You would get too deep in to ever forget death and eternity again, as long as you lived—not even for an afternoon. I think that even when you were talking with your friends or eating or joking, it would be there in the back of your mind. Death, I mean . . . and eternity. At the same time I think I might have a message for a parish if I had one.

MOLLY: What would you tell them?

LIONEL: Well, that would only come through divine inspiration, after I made the sacrifice and joined up.

MOLLY: Oh.

LIONEL: I get a feeling of dread in my stomach about being a political leader too . . . That should cheer me up more, but it doesn't. You'd think I really liked working at the Lobster Bowl.

MOLLY: Don't you?

LIONEL: Yes, I do, but of course that isn't life. I have fun too, in between worrying . . . fun, dancing, and eating, and swimming . . . and being with you. I like to be with you because you seem to only half hear me. I think I could say just the opposite and it wouldn't sound any different to you. Now why do I like that? Because it makes me feel very peaceful. Usually if I tell my feelings to a person I don't want to see them any more. That's another peculiar quirk of mine. Also there's something very familiar about you, even though I never met you before two months ago. I don't know what it is quite . . . your face . . . your voice . . . (*Taking her hand.*) or maybe just your hand. (*Holds her hand for a moment, deep in thought.*) I hope I'm not going to dread it all for too long. Because it doesn't feel right to me, just working at the Lobster Bowl. It's nice though really . . . Inez is always around if you want company. She can set up oyster cocktails faster than anyone on the coast. That's what she claims, anyway. She has some way of checking. You'd like Inez.

MOLLY: I don't like girls.

LIONEL: Inez is a grown-up woman. A kind of sturdy rock-of-Gibraltar type but very high strung and nervous too. Every now and then she blows up. (MOLLY *rises suddenly and crosses to the rock.*) Well, I guess it really isn't so interesting to be there, but it is outside of the world and gloomy ideas. Maybe it's the decorations. It doesn't always help though, things come creeping in anyway.

MOLLY (*turning to* LIONEL): What?

LIONEL: Well, like what ministers talk about . . . the valley of the Shadow of Death and all that . . . or the world comes creeping in. I feel like it's a warning that I shouldn't stay too long. That I should go back to St. Louis. It would be tough though. Now I'm getting too deep in. I suppose you live mainly from day to day. That's the way girls live mainly, isn't it?

MOLLY (*crossing back to* LIONEL): I don't know. I'm all right as long as I can keep from getting mad. It's hard to keep from getting mad when you see through people. Most people can't like I do. I'd emphasize that all right. The rest of the stuff doesn't bother me much. A lot of people want to yank you out and get in themselves. Girls do anyway. I haven't got anything against men. They don't scheme the way girls do. But I keep to myself as much as I can.

LIONEL: Well, there's that angle too, but my point of view is different. Have you thought any more about marrying me if your mother marries Mr. Solares? I know we're both young, but you don't want to go to business school and she's sure to send you there if she marries him. She's always talking about it. She'd be in Mexico most of the year and you'd be in business school. We could live over the Lobster Bowl and get all the food we wanted free, and it's good food. Mr. Solares and Mrs. Lopez liked it when they went to eat there.

MOLLY: Yes, I know they did.

LIONEL: Well?

MOLLY: I won't think of it until it happens. I can't picture anything being any different than it is. I feel I might just plain die if everything changes, but I don't imagine it will.

LIONEL: You should look forward to change.

MOLLY: I don't want anything different.

LIONEL: Then you *are* afraid of the future just like me.

MOLLY (*stubbornly*): I don't think much about the future.

(VIVIAN *returns from her swim.*)

LIONEL (*to* MOLLY): Well, even if you don't think much about the future you have to admit that . . .

(*He is interrupted by* VIVIAN *who rushes up to them, almost stumbling in her haste.*)

VIVIAN (*plopping down next to* LIONEL *and shaking out her wet hair*): Wait 'til you hear this . . . ! (LIONEL *is startled.* VIVIAN *is almost swooning with delight, to* LIONEL.) It's so wonderful . . . I can hardly talk about it . . . I saw the whole thing in front of my eyes . . . Just now while I was swimming . . .

LIONEL: What?

VIVIAN: Our restaurant.

LIONEL: What restaurant?

VIVIAN: *Our restaurant.* The one we're going to open together, right now, as soon as we can. I'll tell you about it . . . But only on one condition . . . You have to promise you won't put a damper on it, and tell me it's not practical. (*Shaking him.*)

LIONEL (*bored*): All right.

VIVIAN: Well, this is it. I'm going to sell all the jewelry my grandmother left me and we're going on a trip. We're going to some city I don't know which but some big city that will be as far from here as we can get. Then we'll take jobs and when we have enough money we'll start a restaurant. We could start it on credit with just the barest amount of cash. It's not going to be just an ordinary restaurant but an odd one where everyone sits on cushions instead of on chairs. We could dress the waiters up in those flowing Turkish bloomers and serve very expensive oriental foods, all night long. It will be called Restaurant Midnight. Can you picture it?

LIONEL (*very bored*): Well, yes . . . in a way . . .

VIVIAN: Well, I can see the whole thing . . . very small lamps and perfume in the air, no menus, just silent waiters . . . bringing in elaborate dishes one after the other . . . and music. We could call it "Minuit" . . . as it is in French . . . But either way we must leave soon . . . I can't go on this way with my mother snooping around . . . I can't be tied down . . . I've tried running off before, when I felt desperate . . . But things didn't work out . . . maybe because I never had a real friend before . . . But *now* I have *you*— (*She stops, suddenly aware of* MOLLY*—then with a certain diffidence.*) and Molly, of course, she must come too—we understand each other even if she is still waters run deep. She has to escape from her mother too . . .

(MOLLY *starts at the word "mother." Her face blackens.*)

LIONEL: Molly, you're shivering . . . Why didn't you say something? (*Looking up.*) The sun's gone behind a cloud, no wonder you're cold . . . I can go back to the house and get you a jacket, unless you want to come along and go home now too. (MOLLY *does not move.*) I'll go and get it. Sit nearer the rocks you'll be out of the wind. Vivian, do you want something heavier than that? (*Points to her robe.*)

VIVIAN: No, thanks. I'm much too excited about Restaurant Midnight to notice anything. Besides I'm not very conscious of the physical. (LIONEL *exits.* MOLLY *gets up and walks to the rocks leading to the cliff.*) Have you ever eaten Armenian vine leaves with little pine nuts inside of them?

(MOLLY *is climbing the rocks.*)

MOLLY: Don't follow me . . .

VIVIAN: Or their wonderful flaky desserts with golden honey poured . . .

MOLLY: Don't follow me!

VIVIAN (*tapering off*): . . . all over them . . .

MOLLY: The day you came I was standing on the porch watching you. I heard everything you said. You put your arm around my mother, and you told her she had beautiful hair, then you saw my summer house and you told her how much you loved it. You went and sat in it and you yelled, Come out, Molly. I'm in your little house. You've tried in every way since you came to push me out. She hates you.

VIVIAN: What?

MOLLY: My mother hates you! She hates you!

VIVIAN (*after recovering from her shock starts out after her in a rage*): That's a lie, a rotten lie . . . She doesn't hate me . . . She's ashamed of *you* . . . ashamed of you. (*Exits, then repeating several times off stage.*) She's ashamed of you . . . ashamed of you . . .

(*Her voice is muffled by the entrance of the Mexicans and* GERTRUDE. *The servants head the procession, chattering like magpies and singing.* MR. SOLARES *and* FREDERICA *bring up the rear carrying a tremendous pink rubber horse with purple dots. The hindquarters are supported by* FREDERICA.)

MRS. LOPEZ (*signaling to one of the hags who puts a fancy cushion down on the bench, which she sits on, then yelling to* GERTRUDE): Well, how do you like our gorgeous horse? Pretty big, eh?

MR. SOLARES: It's worth thirty-two dollars.

(*They all seat themselves.*)

GERTRUDE: Now that you've asked me I'll tell you quite frankly that I would never dream of spending my money on a thing like that.

MRS. LOPEZ (*popping a mint into her mouth*): Pretty big, eh?

GERTRUDE (*irritably*): Yes, yes, it's big all right but I don't see what that has to do with anything.

MRS. LOPEZ: That right. Big, lots of money. Little not so much.

GERTRUDE (*bitterly*): All the worse.

MRS. LOPEZ (*merrily*): Maybe next year, bigger. You got one? (GERTRUDE, *bored, does not answer.*) You got one?

GERTRUDE: What?

MRS. LOPEZ: A rubber horse?

GERTRUDE: Oh, for heaven's sake! I told you I thought it was silly. I don't believe in toys for grownups. I think they should buy other things, if they have money to spare.

MRS. LOPEZ (*complacently folding her hands*): What?

GERTRUDE: Well, I guess a dresser or a chair or clothing or curtains. I don't know but certainly not a rubber horse. Clothing, of course, one can always buy because the styles change so frequently.

MR. SOLARES: Miss Eastman Cuevas, how many dresses you got?

GERTRUDE (*icily*): I have never counted them.

MRS. LOPEZ (*to her brother*): Cincuenta nueve, dile.

MR. SOLARES: She got fifty-nine back at the house.

GERTRUDE (*in spite of herself*): Fifty-nine!

MR. SOLARES: I bought them all for her, since her husband died. He was a no good fellow. No ambition, no brain, no pep.

MRS. LOPEZ (*smiling, and nodding her head to* GERTRUDE *sweetly*): Fifty-nine dresses. You like to have that many dresses?

(*Enter* MRS. CONSTABLE *carrying a fishing pole and basket, although she is immaculately dressed in a white crocheted summer ensemble. She has on a large hat and black glasses.*)

MRS. CONSTABLE (*trying to smile and appear at ease*): I hope I'm not interrupting a private discussion.

MR. SOLARES: Happy to see you on this beautiful day. Sit down with us. We weren't having no discussion. Just counting up how many dresses the ladies got.

MRS. CONSTABLE (*a little shocked*): Oh! I myself was hunting for a good spot to fish and I passed so near to your house that I dropped in to call, but you weren't there, of course. Then I remembered that you told me about a bathing spot, somewhere in this direction, so I struck out hoping to find you. Where are the children?

GERTRUDE: They were here a little while ago . . . They'll be back.

MRS. CONSTABLE: I think I might sit down for a few minutes and wait for my bird to come back. I call Vivian my bird. Don't you think it suits her, Mrs. Eastman Cuevas?

GERTRUDE (*bored*): Yes.

MRS. CONSTABLE (*she sits down on a cushion*): I miss her very badly already. It's partly because she has so much life in her. She finds so many things of interest to do and think about. (*She speaks with wonder in her voice.*) I myself can't work up very much interest. I guess that's normal at my age. I can't think of much to do really, not being either a moviegoer, or a card player or a walker. Don't you think that makes me miss her more?

GERTRUDE (*icily*): It might.

MRS. CONSTABLE: This morning after I was cleaned and dressed I sat on the porch, but I got so tired of sitting there that I went to the front desk and asked them to tell me how to fish. They did and I bought this pole. The clerk gave me a kit with some bait in it. I think it's a worm. I'm not looking forward to opening the kit. I don't like the old hook either. I'll wager I don't fish after all. (*She sighs.*) So you see what my days are like.

GERTRUDE: Don't you read?

MRS. CONSTABLE: I would love to read but I have trouble with concentration.

MR. SOLARES (*coming over and crouching next to* MRS. CONSTABLE *on his heels*): How are you feeling today, Mrs. Constable? What's new?

MRS. CONSTABLE: Not very well, thank you. I'm a little bit blue. That's why I thought I'd get a look at my bird.

MR. SOLARES (*still to* MRS. CONSTABLE): You're looking real good. (*Studying her crocheted dress.*) That's handwork, ain't it?

MRS. CONSTABLE (*startled*): Why, yes.

MR. SOLARES: You like turtle steak?

MRS. CONSTABLE: What?

MR. SOLARES: Turtle steak. You like it, Mrs. Constable?

MRS. CONSTABLE (*stammering, bewildered*): Oh, yes . . .

GERTRUDE: Mr. Solares!

MR. SOLARES (*looking up*): What is it?

GERTRUDE: Perhaps I might try chop suey with you, after all. Did it originate in China or is it actually an American dish?

MR. SOLARES: I don't know, Miss Eastman Cuevas. (*Quickly turns again to* MRS. CONSTABLE.)

MRS. LOPEZ (*loudly to* GERTRUDE): Now you want to eat chop suey because he's talkin' to the other lady. You be careful, Señora Eastman Cuevas or you gonna lose him. (*She chuckles.*)

GERTRUDE (*furious but ignoring* MRS. LOPEZ): I thought we might try some tonight, Mr. Solares—that is, if you'd like to . . . (*Bitterly.*) Or have you lost your taste for chop suey?

MR. SOLARES: No, it's good. (*Turning to* MRS. CONSTABLE *again.*) I'll call you up in your hotel and we'll go eat a real good turtle steak with fried potatoes one night. One steak would be too big for you, Mrs. Constable. You look like a dainty eater. Am I right?

GERTRUDE (*turns and sees* MOLLY *sitting on the rock*): Molly, we met Lionel. He's bringing the coats. (*She sees* MOLLY*'s stricken face and questions her.*) Molly, what's happened? (MOLLY *doesn't answer.*) What is it Molly? What's happened to you . . . Molly . . . what happened? What is it Molly? (*Looking around for* VIVIAN.) Where's Vivian? (MOLLY *still does not answer.*) Molly . . . Where is she? Where's Vivian?

MOLLY (*in a quavering voice*): She's gathering shells . . .

(MRS. CONSTABLE *rises and starts looking vaguely for* VIVIAN. *Then she sits down again.* GERTRUDE *gathers her composure after a moment and speaks to* MR. SOLARES.)

GERTRUDE (*starts off and meets* LIONEL): Mr. Solares, I'm going home. It's windy and cold . . . The clouds are getting thicker every minute . . . The sun's not coming out again. I'm going back to the house.

LIONEL (*entering with the coats*): I brought these . . . I brought one for Vivian too. . . . Where's Vivian?

GERTRUDE (*takes sweater from* LIONEL): She's gathering shells. (*She puts sweater on* MOLLY*'s shoulders.*) Molly, put this on, you'll freeze. (*She starts off and calls to* MR. SOLARES.) I'm going home.

(MOLLY *rises and starts to leave and comes face to face with* MRS. CONSTABLE. *They look at each other a moment.* MOLLY *then rushes off, following her mother.* MRS. CONSTABLE *goes back to the rock.* MR. SOLARES *and the Spanish people start to gather up their stuff and prepare to leave.*)

MR. SOLARES: We're coming right away Miss Eastman Cuevas. (*He gives the servants orders in Spanish. Then to* MRS. CONSTABLE.) Come on back to the house and I'll mix up some drinks.

MRS. CONSTABLE: No, thank you.

MRS. LOPEZ (*butting into the conversation*): You don't come?

MR. SOLARES (*to* MRS. LOPEZ): Acaba de decir, no thank you . . . no oyes nunca?

(*The Spanish people all exit noisily.*)

LIONEL (*as he leaves, sees* MRS. CONSTABLE *alone*): Aren't you coming Mrs. Constable?

MRS. CONSTABLE: I think I'll sit here and wait for my bird.

LIONEL: But she might climb up the cliffs and go home around the other way. It's getting colder Mrs. Constable . . . I could wait with you . . .

MRS. CONSTABLE: I don't want to talk. No, I'll just sit here and wait a little while.

LIONEL (*going off*): Don't worry, Mrs. Constable. She'll be all right.

MRS. CONSTABLE (*left alone on the stage*): I get so frightened, I never know where she's going to end up.

THE CURTAIN FALLS SLOWLY

SCENE 3

Same as Scene 1. There is an improvised stand in the upper right-hand corner of the garden (the corner from the house), festooned with crepe paper and laden with a number of hot dogs, as well as part of a wedding cake and other things. MOLLY *is leaning against the stand wearing a simple wedding dress with a round shirred neck. She has removed her veil and she looks more like a girl graduating from school than like a bride. She is eating a hot dog. The stage is flooded with sunlight.*

GERTRUDE (*also in bridal costume. She is sitting on a straight-backed chair in the middle of the garden, with her own dress hiked above her ankles, revealing bedroom slippers with pompons. Eyeing* MOLLY): Molly! You don't have to stuff yourself just because the others stuffed so much that they had to go and lie down! After all, you and I are brides even if I did take off my shoes. But they pinched so, I couldn't bear it another minute. Don't get mustard spots all over your dress. You'll want to show it to your grandchildren some day.

(MOLLY*'s mouth is so full that she is unable to answer. The hags and* ESPERANZA *are lying with their heads under the stand, for shade, and their legs sticking way out into the garden.* MRS. CONSTABLE *is wandering around in a widow's outfit, with hat and veil. She holds a champagne glass in her hand.*)

MRS. CONSTABLE (*stopping beside* GERTRUDE*'s chair*): I don't know where to go or what to do next. I can't seem to tear myself away from you or Mr. Solares or Mrs. Lopez or Molly. Isn't that a ridiculous reaction? (*She is obviously tight.*) I feel linked to you. That's the only way I can explain it. I don't ever want to have any other friends. It's as if I had been born right here in this garden and had never lived anywhere before in my life. Isn't that funny? I don't want ever to have any other friends. Don't leave me please. (*She throws her arms around* GERTRUDE.) I don't know where to go. Don't leave me. (*She squeezes* GERTRUDE *for a moment in silence.*)

GERTRUDE: Now you must stop brooding. Can't you occupy yourself with something?

MRS. CONSTABLE (*firmly*): I'm not brooding. I can think about it without feeling a thing, because if you must know it's just not real to me. I can't believe it. Now what does seem real is that you and Mr. Solares are going away and deserting me and Mrs. Lopez and Molly and Lionel too. And I don't want to be anywhere except in this garden with all of you. Isn't it funny? Not that I'm enjoying myself, but it's all that I want to do, just hang around in this garden. (*She goes over to the stand rather unsteadily and pours some champagne into her glass out of a bottle. She takes a few sips, then bitterly in a changed tone.*) I want to stay right here, by this stand.

GERTRUDE (*looking over her shoulder at* MRS. CONSTABLE): Drinking's not the answer to anything.

MRS. CONSTABLE: Answer? Who said anything about answers? I don't want any answers. It's too late for answers. Not that I ever asked much anyway. (*Angrily.*) I never cared for answers. You can take your answers and flush them down the toilet. I *want* to be able to stay here. Right here where I am, and never, never leave this garden. Why don't you have a drink, or one of these lousy hot dogs? (*She brushes a few hot dogs off the stand, onto the grass.* MOLLY *stoops down and picks them up.*) Let's stay here, Gertrude Eastman Cuevas, please.

GERTRUDE: You're being silly, Mrs. Constable. I know you're upset, but still you realize that I've sold the house and that Molly and I are going on honeymoons.

MRS. CONSTABLE (*vaguely*): What about Mrs. Lopez?

GERTRUDE: Well, now, I guess she has her own affairs to attend to, and Frederica. Mrs. Constable, I think a sanatorium would be the best solution for you until you are ready to face the world again.

MRS. CONSTABLE (*thickly*): What world?

GERTRUDE: Come now, Mrs. Constable, you know what I mean.

MRS. CONSTABLE: I know you're trying to be a bitch!

GERTRUDE: Mrs. Constable . . . I . . . (*She turns to* MOLLY *who has come to her side.*) Molly, go inside. At once . . . (MOLLY *runs into the house.*) Mrs. Constable, you ought to be ashamed. I won't tolerate such . . .

MRS. CONSTABLE: You have no understanding or feeling. Mrs. Lopez is much nicer than you are. You're very coarse. I know that even if I do hate to read. You're coarse, coarse and selfish. Two awful things to be. But I'm stuck here anyway so what difference does it make?

GERTRUDE (*refusing to listen to any more of her rambling*): Mrs. Constable, I'm surprised at you. I'm going in. I won't put up with this. What would Vivian think . . .

MRS. CONSTABLE: Vivian was a bird. How do you know what Vivian would feel? Do you know anything about birds?

Vivian understood everything I did. Vivian loved me even if she did answer back and act snippy in company. She was much too delicate to show her true feelings all over the place like you do and like I do.

GERTRUDE (*crossing to* MRS. CONSTABLE): I've never in my life shown my feelings. I don't know what you're talking about!

MRS. CONSTABLE (*reeling about at the wedding table*): I don't know what I'm talking about . . . (*She grabs a bottle of champagne and offers it to* GERTRUDE.) Have another drink, Miss Eastman Cuevas.

GERTRUDE (*in disgust grabs the bottle from her and puts it on the table*): I don't like to drink!

MRS. CONSTABLE: Then have a hot dog. (*She drops it at* GERTRUDE*'s feet.* GERTRUDE *starts toward the house.* MRS. CONSTABLE *stops her.*) You and I grew up believing this kind of thing would never happen to us or to any of ours.

GERTRUDE: What?

MRS. CONSTABLE: We were kept far away from tragedy, weren't we?

GERTRUDE: No, Mrs. Constable. None of us have been kept from it.

MRS. CONSTABLE: Yes, well, now it's close to me, because Vivian hopped off a cliff—just like a cricket.

GERTRUDE: Life is tragic, Mrs. Constable.

MRS. CONSTABLE: I don't want tragic.

GERTRUDE (*can't put up with it any more*): Why don't you lie down on the grass and rest? It's dry. (GERTRUDE *starts toward the door of the house.* MRS. CONSTABLE *takes the suggestion and falls in a heap behind the stump under the balcony of the house.*) Take your veil off. You'll roast! (MRS. CONSTABLE *complies and* GERTRUDE *goes into the house. The two old hags appear from behind the wedding table and start to take some hot dogs. They are stopped by* MOLLY *coming out of the house.* MOLLY *looks for a moment at the garden and then runs into her summer house. A moment later* GERTRUDE *calls to the garden from the balcony.*) Molly? Molly, are you in the summer house?

MOLLY: Yes, I am.

GERTRUDE: They're getting ready. After we've left if Mrs. Constable is still asleep, will you and Lionel carry her inside and put her to bed in my room? Tomorrow when you leave for the Lobster Bowl you can take her along and drop her off at her hotel. Poor thing. Be sure and clean up this mess in the morning. I have a list of things here I want you to attend to. I'll leave it on the table downstairs. Mr. Solares and I will be leaving soon.

MOLLY: No!

GERTRUDE: Yes.

MOLLY: Please don't go away.

GERTRUDE: Now, Molly, what kind of nonsense is this? You know we're leaving, what's the matter with you?

MOLLY: No, I won't let you go!

GERTRUDE: Please, Molly, no mysteries. It's very hard getting everyone started and I'm worn out. And I can't find my pocketbook. I think I left it in the garden. I'm coming down to look. (GERTRUDE *leaves the balcony to come downstairs.* MOLLY *comes out of the summer house and stands waiting with a small bunch of honeysuckle in her hands.* GERTRUDE *comes out of the house and crosses to the wedding table. She looks at* MOLLY *and sees her crying and goes to her.*) What on earth is wrong, Molly? Why are you crying? Are you nervous? You've been so contented all day, stuffing yourself right along with the others. What has happened now?

MOLLY: I didn't picture it.

GERTRUDE: Picture what?

MOLLY: What it would be like when the time came. Your leaving . . .

GERTRUDE: Why not?

MOLLY: I don't know. I don't know . . . I couldn't picture it, I guess. I thought so long as we were here we'd go right on being here. So I just ate right along with the others like you say.

GERTRUDE: Well, it sounds like nonsense to me. Don't be a crybaby, and wipe your tears.

(GERTRUDE *starts toward the table when she is stopped by* MOLLY *who puts the flowers in her hands.*)

MOLLY: Stay!

GERTRUDE: Molly. Put them back. They belong on your wedding dress.

MOLLY: No, they're from the vine. I picked them for you!

GERTRUDE: They're for your wedding. They belong to your dress. Here, put them back . . .

MOLLY: No . . . No . . . They're for you . . . They're flowers for you! (GERTRUDE *does not know what to make of this strange and sudden love and moves across the garden.*) I love you. I love you. Don't leave me. I love you. Don't go away!

GERTRUDE (*shocked and white*): Molly, stop. You can't go on like this!

MOLLY: I love you. You can't go!

GERTRUDE: I didn't think you cared this much. If you really feel this way, why have you tormented me so . . .

MOLLY: I never have. I never have.

GERTRUDE: You have. You have in a thousand different ways. What about the summer house?

MOLLY: Don't leave me!

GERTRUDE: And the vine?

MOLLY: I love you!

GERTRUDE: What about the vine, and the ocean, what about that? If you care this much why have you tormented me so about the water . . . when you knew how ashamed I was . . . Crazy, unnatural fear . . . Why didn't you try to overcome it, if you love me so much? Answer that!

(MOLLY, *in a frenzy of despair, starts clawing at her dress, pulling it open.*)

MOLLY: I will. I will. I'll overcome it. I'm sorry. I'll go in the water right away. I'm going now. I'm going . . .

(MOLLY *rips off her veil and throws it on the wedding table and makes a break for the gate to the ocean.* GERTRUDE *in horror grabs* MOLLY*'s arm and drags her back into the garden.*)

GERTRUDE: Stop it! Come back here at once. Are you insane? Button your dress. They'll see you . . . they'll find you this way and think you're insane . . .

MOLLY: I was going in the water . . .

GERTRUDE: Button your dress. Are you insane! This is what I meant. I've always known it was there, this violence. I've told you again and again that I was frightened. I wasn't sure what I meant . . . I didn't want to be sure. But I was right, there's something heavy and dangerous inside you, like some terrible rock that's ready to explode . . . And it's been getting worse all the time. I can't bear it any more. I've got to get away, out of this garden. That's why I married. That's why I'm going away. I'm frightened of staying here with you any more. I can't breathe. Even on bright days the garden seems like a dark place without any air. I'm stifling!

(GERTRUDE *passes below the balcony on her way to the front door,* MRS. LOPEZ *tilts a vessel containing rice and pours it on* GERTRUDE*'s head.*)

MRS. LOPEZ: That's for you, bride number one! Plenty more when you go in the car with Solares. Ha ha! Frederica, ándele, tú también!

(FREDERICA, *terribly embarrassed, tosses a little rice onto* GERTRUDE *and starts to giggle.*)

GERTRUDE (*very agitated, ill-humoredly flicking rice from her shoulders*): Oh, really! Where is Mr. Solares? Is he ready?

MRS. LOPEZ: My brother is coming right away. Where is bride number two?

GERTRUDE (*looking around for* MOLLY *who is back in the summer house*): She's gone back into the summer house. (*She goes out.*)

MRS. LOPEZ: I got rice for her too! (*Calling down to the servants who are still lying with their heads under the food stand.*) Quinta! Altagracia! Esperanza! Despiértense!

(*The servants wake up and come crawling out from under the food stand.*)

ESPERANZA (*scowling*): Caray!

(*She takes an enormous comb out of her pocket and starts running it through her matted hair. There is a sound of a horn right after* ESPERANZA *begins to comb her hair.*)

FREDERICA (*beside herself with excitement*): It's Lionel back with the automobile, Mama! It must be time. Tell the musicians to start playing!

MRS. LOPEZ: Yes, querida. Música!

(*She kisses her daughter effusively and they both exit from the balcony into the house talking and laughing.* LIONEL *enters from the lane, hurries across the lawn and into the house, just as* FREDERICA *and* MRS. LOPEZ *enter through the front door onto the lawn.* MRS. LOPEZ *calling to the servants.*)

Cuando sale la Señora Eastman Cuevas de la casa, empezerán

a cantar. (*She sings a few bars herself counting the time with a swinging finger and facing the servants, who rise and line up in a row. Calling to* MOLLY.) Bride number two! Bride number two! Molly!

(*She takes a few steps toward the summer house and throws some rice at it. The rice gets stuck in the vines instead of reaching* MOLLY *inside. After a few more failures, she goes around to the front of the summer house and, standing at the entrance, she hurls handful after handful at* MOLLY. *Enter from the house* LIONEL, *and* MR. SOLARES. *The men are carrying grips.* MRS. CONSTABLE *is still stretched out in a corner where she won't interfere with the procession. Some very naive music starts back stage (sounding, if possible, like a Taxco band), as they proceed across the lawn; then the maids begin to sing. While this happens* MRS. LOPEZ *gradually ceases to throw her rice and then disappears in the summer house where she takes the weeping* MOLLY *into her arms.*)

LIONEL: Where's Molly?

MRS. LOPEZ (*over the music, from inside the summer house*): She don't feel good. She's crying in here. I cried too when I had my wedding. Many young girls do. I didn't want to leave my house neither. (*She steps out of the summer house.*)

LIONEL (*calling*): I'll be back, Molly, as soon as I load these bags.

(*Enter* GERTRUDE *as* MRS. LOPEZ *comes out of the summer house. The music swells and the singing is louder.* GERTRUDE *walks rapidly through the garden in a shower of rice and rose petals.* MOLLY *comes out of the summer house and* GERTRUDE *stops. They confront each other for a second without speaking.* GERTRUDE *continues on her way.* MOLLY *goes back into the summer house.*)

GERTRUDE (*from the road, calling over the music*): Good-bye, Molly!

(*The wedding party files out, singing,* MRS. LOPEZ *bringing up the rear. She throws a final handful of rice at the summer house, but it does not reach. They exit.* MOLLY *is left alone on the stage. The music gradually fades.*)

LIONEL (*returning and coming into the garden*): Molly! (*There is no answer. He walks around to the front of the summer house and looks in.*) Molly, I'm sorry you feel bad. (*Pause.*) Why don't you come out? There's a very pretty sunset. (*He reaches in and pulls her out by the hands. He puts his arm around her shoulder and leads her toward the house.*) We can go upstairs on the balcony and look at the sunset.

(*They disappear into the house and reappear on the balcony, where they go to the balustrade and lean over it.*)

MOLLY (*staring down into the garden, in a very small voice*): It looks different.

LIONEL (*after gazing off into the distance very thoughtfully for a minute*): I've always liked it when something that I've looked at every day suddenly seems strange and unfamiliar. Maybe not always, but when I was home I used to like looking out my window after certain storms that left a special kind of light in the sky.

MOLLY (*in a whisper*): It looks different . . .

LIONEL: A very brilliant light that illuminated only the most distant places, the places nearest to the horizon. Then I could see little round hills, and clumps of trees, and pastures that I didn't remember ever seeing before, very, very close to the sky. It always gave me a lift, as if everything might change around me but in a wonderful way that I wouldn't have guessed was possible. Do you understand what I mean?

(MOLLY *shakes her head, negatively. He looks at her for a moment, a little sadly.*)

MOLLY (*anguished, turning away from him*): I don't know. I don't know. It looks so different . . .

CURTAIN

ACT TWO

SCENE I

The Lobster Bowl, ten months later.

Just before dawn. The oyster-shell door is open and the sound of waves breaking will continue throughout this scene. MOLLY *and* LIONEL *are playing cards at one of the tables, Russian Bank or its equivalent. They are sitting in a circle of light. The rest of the stage is in darkness.* MRS. CONSTABLE *is lying on a bench but can't be seen.*

MOLLY: You just put a king on top of another king.

LIONEL: I was looking for an ace.

MOLLY (*smiling*): It's right here, silly, under your nose.

LIONEL: It's almost morning.

MOLLY (*wistful*): Can't we play one more game after this?

LIONEL: All right.

(*They play for a while in silence, then* LIONEL *stops again.*)

MOLLY: What is it?

LIONEL: Nothing.

MOLLY: I don't think you want to play at all. You're thinking about something else.

LIONEL: I had a letter from my brother . . . again.

MOLLY (*tense*): The one who's still in St. Louis?

LIONEL: That's right, the popular one, the one who'd like us to come back there.

MOLLY: He's big and tall.

LIONEL: Yes, he's big and tall, like most boys in this country. I've been thinking a lot about St. Louis, Molly . . .

MOLLY: Inez says we've got bigger men here than they have in Europe.

LIONEL: Well, Swedes are big and so are Yugoslavians . . .

MOLLY: But the French people are little.

LIONEL: Well, yes, but they're not as little as all that. They're not midgets. And they're not the way people used to picture them years ago, silly and carefree and saying Oo . . . la . . . la . . . all the time.

MOLLY: They're not saying Oo . . . la . . . la?

LIONEL: I don't know really, I've never been there. (*Dreaming, neglecting his cards.*) Molly, when you close your eyes and picture the world do you see it dark? (MOLLY *doesn't answer right away.*) Do you, Molly? Do you see the world dark behind your eyes?

MOLLY: I . . . I don't know . . . I see parts of it dark.

LIONEL: Like what?

MOLLY: Like woods . . . like pine-tree woods.

LIONEL: I see it dark, but beautiful like the ocean is right now. And like I saw it once when I was a child . . . just before a total eclipse. Did you ever see a total eclipse?

MOLLY: I never saw any kind of eclipse.

LIONEL: I saw one with my brother. There was a shadow over the whole earth. I was afraid then, but it stayed in my memory like something that was beautiful. It made me afraid but I knew it was beautiful.

MOLLY: It's my game.

(*They start shuffling.*)

LIONEL (*tentative*): Did you ever worry about running far away from sad things when you were young, and then later getting older and not being able to find your way back to them ever again, even when you wanted to?

MOLLY: You would never want to find your way back to sad things.

LIONEL: But you might have lost wonderful things too, mixed in with the sad ones. Suppose in a few years I wanted to remember the way the world looked that day, the day of the eclipse when I saw the shadow.

MOLLY (*stops dealing her cards out very slowly, steeped in a dream*): She had a shadow.

LIONEL: And suppose I couldn't remember it. What Molly?

MOLLY: She had a shadow.

LIONEL: Who?

MOLLY: My mother.

LIONEL: Oh . . . (*He deals his cards out more rapidly, becoming deeply absorbed in his game.*)

MOLLY: It used to come and pass over her whole life and make it dark. It didn't come very often, but when it did she used to go downstairs and drink fizzy water. Once I went down when I was twelve years old. I waited until she was asleep and I sneaked down into the kitchen very quietly. Then I switched the light on and I opened the ice chest and I took out a bottle of fizzy water just like she did. Then I went over to the table and I sat down.

LIONEL (*without looking up from his cards*): And then . . .

MOLLY: I drank a little water, but I couldn't drink any more. The water was so icy cold. I was going to drink a whole bottleful like she did, but nothing . . . really nothing turned out like I thought it would. (LIONEL *mixes all his cards up together in a sudden gesture.* MOLLY *comes out of her dream.*) Why are you messing up the cards? We haven't begun our game . . . (LIONEL *doesn't answer.*) What's the matter?

LIONEL: Nothing.

MOLLY: But you've messed up the cards.

LIONEL: I was trying to tell you something . . . It meant a lot to me . . . I wanted you to listen.

MOLLY: I was listening.

LIONEL: You told me about fizzy water . . . and your mother. (MOLLY *automatically passing her hand over her own cards and messing them up.*) I wanted you to listen. I don't want you to half hear me any more. I used to like it but . . .

MOLLY (*pathetic, bewildered*): I listen to you. We had a nice time yesterday . . . when . . . when we were digging for clams.

LIONEL (*looking back at her unable to be angry, now with compassion*): Yes, Molly, we did. We had a very good time . . . yesterday. I like digging for clams . . . (*They hold, looking at each other for a moment.*) I'm going upstairs. I'm tired. I'm going to bed.

(LIONEL *exits up stairs.* MRS. CONSTABLE *comes out of the darkness, where she has been sleeping on her bench, into the circle of light.*)

MOLLY: You woke up.

MRS. CONSTABLE: I've been awake . . . for a while. I was waiting.

MOLLY: I won the game, but it wasn't much fun. Lionel didn't pay attention to the cards.

MRS. CONSTABLE: I was waiting because I wanted to tell you something . . . a secret . . . I always tell you my secrets

. . . But there's one I haven't told you . . . I've known it all along . . . But I've never said anything to you . . . never before . . . But now I'm going to . . . I must.

MOLLY (*wide-eyed, thinking she is referring to* VIVIAN): It wasn't my fault! I didn't mean to . . .

MRS. CONSTABLE: My husband never loved me . . . Vivian?

MOLLY: Vivian! It wasn't my fault . . . I didn't . . . She . . . I didn't . . . (MOLLY *starts to sob.*)

MRS. CONSTABLE (*clapping her hand over* MOLLY*'s mouth*): Shhhhhh . . . They belonged to each other, my husband and Vivian. They never belonged to me . . . ever . . . But I couldn't admit it . . . I hung on hard to the bitter end. When they died . . . nothing was left . . . no memories . . . Everything vanished . . . all the panic . . . and the strain . . . I hardly remember my life. They never loved me . . . I didn't really love them . . . My heart had fake roots . . . when the strain was over, they dried up . . . they shriveled and snapped and my heart was left empty. There was no blood left in my heart at all . . . They never loved me! Molly . . . your mother . . . It's not too late . . . She doesn't . . .

MOLLY (*interrupting, sensing that* MRS. CONSTABLE *will say something too awful to hear*): My mother wrote me. I got the letter today. She *hates* it down in Mexico. She hates it there.

MRS. CONSTABLE: Molly, if you went away from here, I'd miss you very much. If you went away there wouldn't be anyone here I loved . . . Molly, go away . . . go away with Lionel . . . Don't stay here in the Lobster Bowl . . .

MOLLY (*commenting on her mother's letter and then reading from it*): She doesn't know how long she can stand it . . . She says she doesn't feel very well . . . "The climate doesn't suit me . . . I feel sick all the time and I find it almost impossible to sleep . . . I can't read very much . . . not at night . . . because the light is too feeble here in the mountains. Mrs. Lopez has two of her sisters here at the moment. Things are getting more and more unbearable. Mrs. Lopez is the least raucous of the three. I hope that you are occupying yourself with something constructive. Be careful not to dream and be sure . . ."

MRS. CONSTABLE: Why shouldn't you dream?

MOLLY: I used to waste a lot of time day-dreaming. I guess I still do. She didn't want me to dream.

MRS. CONSTABLE: Why shouldn't you dream? Why didn't she want you to?

MOLLY: Because she wanted me to grow up to be wonderful and strong like she is. Will she come back soon, Mrs. Constable? Will she make them all leave there? Will she?

MRS. CONSTABLE: I don't know dear . . . I don't know . . . I suppose she will . . . If she needs you, she'll come back. If she needs you, I'm sure she will.

MOLLY: Are you going to walk home along the edge of the water?

MRS. CONSTABLE: I like wet sand . . . and I like the spray.

MOLLY: You'll get the bottom of your dress all soaking wet. You'll catch cold.

MRS. CONSTABLE: I love the waves breaking in this early light . . . I run after them. I run after the waves . . . I scoop up the foam and I rub it on my face. All along the way I think it's beginning . . .

MOLLY: What?

MRS. CONSTABLE: My life. I think it's beginning, and then . . .

MOLLY: And then?

MRS. CONSTABLE: I see the hotel. (MRS. CONSTABLE *exits through oyster-shell door.*)

MOLLY (*she reads again part of her mother's letter*): "Two days ago, Fula Lopez went into the city and came back with a hideous white dog. She bought it in the street. The dog's bark is high and sharp. It hasn't stopped yapping since it came. I haven't slept at all for two nights. Now I'm beginning a cold . . ."

THE LIGHTS FADE AS THE CURTAIN FALLS

SCENE 2

The Lobster Bowl. Two months later.

INEZ (*she is middle-aged, full bosomed, spirited but a little coarse. She cannot see into* MOLLY*'s booth from where she stands behind* *the bar*): I'd rather hit myself over the head with a club than drag around here the way you do, reading comic books all day long. It's so damp and empty and quiet in here. (*She shakes a whole tray of glasses in the sink, which makes a terrific racket.*)

MOLLY: It's not a comic book. It's a letter from my mother.

INEZ: What's new?

MOLLY: It came last week.

INEZ: What are you doing reading it now?

MOLLY: She's coming back today. She's coming back from Mexico.

INEZ: Maybe she'll pep things up a little. I hear she's got more personality than you. (*Shifts some oysters.*) You didn't model yourself after her, did you?

MOLLY: No.

INEZ: Ever try modeling yourself after anyone?

MOLLY: No.

INEZ: Well, if you don't feel like you've got much personality yourself, it's an easy way to do. You just pick the right model and you watch how they act. I never modeled myself after anyone, but there were two or three who modeled after me. And they weren't even relatives—just ordinary girls. It's an easy way to do. (*Shifts some oysters.*) Anyway, I don't see poring over comic books. I'd rather have someone tell me a good joke any day. What's really nice is to go out—eight or nine—to an Italian dinner, and sit around afterwards listening to the different jokes. You get a better selection that way! Ever try that?

MOLLY: I don't like big bunches of people.

INEZ: You could at least live in a regular home if you don't like crowds, and do cooking for your husband. You don't even have a hot plate in your room! (*Crash of stool to floor, followed by some high giggles.*) There goes Mrs. Constable again. You'd think she'd drink home, at her hotel, where no one could see her. She's got a whole suite to herself there. It's been over a year since her daughter's accident, so I could say her drinking permit had expired. I think she's just on a plain drunk now. Right? (MOLLY *nods.*) You sure are a button lip. As long as you're sitting there you might as well talk. It don't cost extra. (*She frowns and looks rather mean for a moment. There is more offstage racket.*) I think Mrs. Constable is heading this way. I hope to God she don't get started on Death. Not that I blame her for thinking about it after what happened, but I don't like that topic.

(*Enter* MRS. CONSTABLE.)

MRS. CONSTABLE (*she has been drinking*): How is everyone, this afternoon?

MOLLY: My mother's coming back today.

INEZ: I'm kind of rushing, Mrs. Constable. I've got to have three hundred oyster cocktails ready by tonight and I haven't even prepared the hot sauce yet.

MRS. CONSTABLE: Rushing? I didn't know that people still rushed . . .

INEZ: Here we go, boys!

MRS. CONSTABLE: Then you must be one of the fortunate ones who has not yet stood on the edge of the black pit. There is no rushing after that, only waiting. It seems hardly worthwhile even keeping oneself clean after one has stood on the edge of the black pit.

INEZ: If you're clean by nature, you're clean.

MRS. CONSTABLE: Oh, really? How very interesting!

INEZ: Some people would rather be clean than eat or sleep.

MRS. CONSTABLE: How very interesting! How nice that they are all so terribly interested in keeping clean! Cleanliness is so important really, such a *deep deep* thing. Those people who are so interested in keeping clean must have very deep souls. They must think a lot about life and death, that is when they're not too busy *washing*, but I guess washing takes up most of their time. How right they are! Hoorah for them! (*She flourishes her glass.*)

INEZ (*with a set face determined to ignore her taunts*): The tide's pretty far out today. Did you take a look at the . . .

MRS. CONSTABLE: They say that people can't live unless they can fill their lives with petty details. That's people's way of avoiding the black pit. I'm just a weak, ordinary, *very ordinary* woman in her middle years, but I've been able to wipe all the petty details from my life . . . all of them. I never rush or get excited about anything. I've dumped my entire life out the window . . . like that! (*She tips her whisky glass and pours a little on the floor.*)

INEZ (*flaring up*): Listen here, Mrs. Constable, I haven't got time to go wiping up slops. I've got to prepare three hundred oyster cocktails. That means toothpicks and three hundred little hookers of hot sauce. I haven't got time to talk so I certainly haven't got time to wipe up slops.

MRS. CONSTABLE: I know . . . toothpicks and hot sauce and hookers. Very interesting! How many oysters do you serve to a customer? Please tell me.

INEZ (*only half listening to* MRS. CONSTABLE, *automatically*): Five.

MRS. CONSTABLE (*smirking as much as she can*): Five! How fascinating! Really and truly, I can't believe it!

INEZ: Balls! Now you get out and don't come back here until I finish my work. Not if you know what's good for you. I can feel myself getting ready to blow up! (*Shifts some more oysters.*) I'm going upstairs now and I'm going to put a cold towel on my head. Then, I'm coming down to finish my oyster cocktails, and when I do I want peace and quiet. I've got to have peace and quiet when I'm doing my oyster cocktails. If I don't I just get too nervous. That's all.

MRS. CONSTABLE: I'm going . . . whether you're getting ready to blow up or not. (*She walks unsteadily toward exit. Then from the doorway.*) I happen to be a very independent woman . . . But you are just plain bossy, Mrs. Oyster Cocktail Sauce. (*Exit* MRS. CONSTABLE.)

INEZ: Independent! I could make her into a slave if I cared to. I could walk all over her if I cared to, but I don't. I don't like to walk all over anyone. Most women do . . . they love it. They like to take some other man or woman and make him or her into a slave, but I don't. I don't like slaves. I like everybody to be going his own independent way. Hello. Good-bye. You go your way and I'll go my way, but no slaves. I'll bet you wouldn't find ten men in this town as democratic as I am. (*Shifts some oysters.*) Well, here I go. I guess I'll give myself a fresh apron while I'm up there. Then I'll be ready when they come for their oysters. (*Vaguely touching her head.*) I don't like to eat oysters any more. I suppose I've seen too much of them, like everything else in life.

(*She pulls the chain on the big light behind the bar so that the *scene darkens. There is a little light playing on* MOLLY'*s booth and on the paper flowers and leaves.* MOLLY *puts her book of comics down, sits dreaming for a moment. There is summer house music to indicate a more lyrical mood. She pulls a letter out of her pocket and reads it. Enter* LIONEL.)

LIONEL: Hey.

MOLLY: Where were you?

LIONEL: I was walking along the beach thinking about something. Molly, listen. I got a wire this morning!

MOLLY: A wire?

LIONEL: Yes, from my brother.

MOLLY: The one in St. Louis? The one who wants us to come . . .

LIONEL: Yes, Molly. He has a place for me in his business now. He sells barbecue equipment to people.

MOLLY: To people?

LIONEL: Yes, to people. For their back yards, and he wants my help.

MOLLY: But . . . but you're going to be a religious leader.

LIONEL: I didn't say I wouldn't be, or I may end up religious without leading anybody at all. But wherever I end up, I'm getting out of here. I've made up my mind. This place is a fake.

MOLLY: These oyster shells are real and so is the turtle. He just hasn't got his own head and feet. They're wooden.

LIONEL: To me this place is a fake. I chose it for protection, and it doesn't work out.

MOLLY: It doesn't work out?

LIONEL: Molly, you know that. I've been saying it to you in a thousand different ways. You know it's not easy for me to leave. Places that don't work out are ten times tougher to leave than any other places in the world.

MRS. CONSTABLE: My sisters used to have cherry contests. They stuffed themselves with cherries all week long and counted up the pits on Saturday. It made them feel exuberant.

MOLLY: I can't eat cherries.

MRS. CONSTABLE: I couldn't either. I'd eat a few and I'd feel sick. But that never stopped me. I never missed a single contest. I despised cherry contests, but I couldn't stand being left out. Never. Every week I'd sneak off to the woods with bags full of cherries. I'd sit on a log and pit each cherry with a knife. Then I'd bury the fruit in a deep hole and fill it up with dirt. I cheated so hard to be in them, and I didn't even like them. I was so scared to be left out.

LIONEL: They are harder to leave, Molly, places that don't work out. I know it sounds crazy, but they are. Like it's three times harder for me to leave now than when I first came here, and in those days I liked the decorations. Molly, don't look so funny. I can explain it all some other way. (*Indicates oyster-shell door.*) Suppose I kept on closing that door against the ocean every night because the ocean made me sad and then one night I went to open it and I couldn't even find the door. Suppose I couldn't tell it apart from the wall any more. Then it would be too late and we'd be shut in here forever once and for all. It's not going to happen, Molly. I won't let it happen. We're going away—you and me. We're getting out of here. We're not playing cards in this oyster cocktail bar until we're old.

MOLLY (*turns and looks up the stairs and then back to* LIONEL): If we had a bigger light bulb we could play in the bedroom upstairs.

LIONEL (*walking away*): You're right Molly, dead right. We could do just that. We could play cards up there in that God-forsaken bedroom upstairs. (*Exits.*)

MRS. CONSTABLE (*gets up and goes to* MOLLY): Molly, call him back.

MOLLY: No, I'm going upstairs.

MRS. CONSTABLE: It's time . . . Go . . . go with Lionel.

MOLLY: My mother's coming. I'm going to her birthday supper.

MRS. CONSTABLE: Don't go there . . .

MOLLY: I'm late. I must change my dress. (*She exits up the stairs.*)

MRS. CONSTABLE (*stumbling about and crossing to the bar*): You're hanging on just like me. If she brought you her love you wouldn't know her. You wouldn't know who she was. (MRS. CONSTABLE *sinks into a chair below the bar.* GERTRUDE *enters. She is pale, distraught. She does not see* MRS. CONSTABLE.) Hello, Gertrude Eastman Cuevas.

GERTRUDE (*trying to conceal the strain she is under*): Hello, Mrs. Constable. How are you?

MRS. CONSTABLE: How are you making out?

GERTRUDE: Molly wrote me you were still here. Where is she?

MRS. CONSTABLE: You look tired.

GERTRUDE: Where is Molly? (LIONEL *enters.*) Lionel! How nice to see you! Where's Molly?

LIONEL: I . . . I didn't know you were coming.

GERTRUDE: Didn't you?

LIONEL: I didn't expect to see you. How are you, Mrs. Eastman Cuevas? How was your trip? When did you arrive?

GERTRUDE: Well, around two . . . But I *had* to wait . . . They were driving me here . . . Didn't you *know* I was coming?

LIONEL: No, I didn't.

GERTRUDE (*uneasily*): But I wrote Molly. I told her I was coming. I wanted to get here for my birthday. I wrote Molly that. Didn't she tell you about it? I sent her a letter. The paper was very sweet. I was sure that she would show it to you. There's a picture of a little Spanish dancer on the paper with a real lace mantilla pasted round her head. Didn't she show it to you?

LIONEL (*brooding*): No.

GERTRUDE: That's strange. I thought she would. I have others for her too. A toreador with peach satin breeches and a macaw with real feathers.

LIONEL (*unheeding*): She never said anything about it. She never showed me any letter.

GERTRUDE: That's strange. I thought . . . I thought . . . (*She hesitates, feeling the barrier between them. Tentative.*) Macaws are called guacamayos down there.

LIONEL: Are they?

GERTRUDE: Yes, they are. Guacamayos . . .

LIONEL: What's the difference between them and parrots?

GERTRUDE: They're bigger! Much bigger.

LIONEL: Do they talk?

GERTRUDE: Yes, they do, but parrots have a better vocabulary. Lionel, my birthday supper's tonight. I suppose you can't come. You work late at night, don't you?

LIONEL: I work at night, but not for long . . .

GERTRUDE: You'll work in the day then?

LIONEL: No.

GERTRUDE: Then when will you work?

LIONEL: I'm quitting.

GERTRUDE: What?

LIONEL: I'm quitting this job. I'm getting out.

GERTRUDE: Getting out. What will you do? Where will you work?

LIONEL: I'm quitting. I'm going. (*He exits.*)

GERTRUDE: Lionel . . . Wait . . . Where are you going?

MRS. CONSTABLE: Come on over here and talk to me . . . You need a drink.

GERTRUDE: Where is she? Where's Molly?

MRS. CONSTABLE: She's gone down on the rocks, hunting for mussels.

GERTRUDE: Hunting for mussels? But she knew I was coming. Why isn't she here? I don't understand. Didn't she get my letter?

MRS. CONSTABLE (*dragging* GERTRUDE *rather roughly to a table*): Sit down . . . You look sick.

GERTRUDE: I'm not sick . . . I'm just tired, exhausted, that's all. They've worn me out in a thousand different ways. Even today . . . I wanted to see Molly the second we arrived, but I had to wait. I tried to rest. I had a bad dream. It's hanging over me still. But I'll be all right in a little bit. I'll be fine as soon as I see Molly. I'm just tired, that's all.

MRS. CONSTABLE: I'm glad you're well. How is Mrs. Lopez? If I were a man, I'd marry Mrs. Lopez. She'd be my type. We should both have been men. Two Spanish men, married to Mrs. Lopez.

GERTRUDE: She was part of the whole thing! The confusion . . . the racket . . . the pandemonium.

MRS. CONSTABLE: I like Mrs. Lopez, and I'm glad she's fat.

GERTRUDE: There were twelve of us at table every meal.

MRS. CONSTABLE: When?

GERTRUDE: All these months down in Mexico. Twelve of us at least. Old ladies, babies, men, little girls, everyone jabbering, the noise, the screeching never stopped . . . The cooks, the maids, even the birds . . .

MRS. CONSTABLE: Birds?

GERTRUDE: Dirty noisy parrots, trailing around loose. There was a big one called Pepe, with a frightening beak.

MRS. CONSTABLE (*rather delighted*): Pepe?

GERTRUDE: Their pet, their favorite . . . Crazy undisciplined bird, always climbing up the table leg and plowing through the food.

MRS. CONSTABLE (*ingenuous*): Didn't you like Pepe?

GERTRUDE (*dejected, as if in answer to a sad question, not irritated*): No, I didn't like Pepe. I didn't like anything. Where's Molly? (*Going to oyster-shell door.*)

MRS. CONSTABLE: When are you going back?

GERTRUDE: Back? I'm never going back. I've made up my mind. From now on I'm staying in the house up here. It was a terrible mistake. I told him that. I told him that when he had to be there he could go by himself. We had a terrible fight . . . It was disgusting. When he stood there saying that men should never have given us the vote, I slapped him.

MRS. CONSTABLE: I never voted. I would vote all right if I could only register.

GERTRUDE: He's a barbarian. A subnormal human being. But it doesn't matter. He can stay down there as long as he likes. I'll be up here, where I belong, near Molly. (*Face clouding over.*) What was he saying before? What did he mean?

MRS. CONSTABLE: Who?

GERTRUDE: Lionel. He said he was quitting. He said he was leaving, getting out of here.

MRS. CONSTABLE: Lionel's sick of the Lobster Bowl. I'm not. Molly likes it too, more than Lionel.

GERTRUDE: Molly. She couldn't like it here, not after our life in the ocean house.

MRS. CONSTABLE: Tell me more, Gertrude Eastman Cuevas. Did you enjoy the scenery?

GERTRUDE: What?

MRS. CONSTABLE: Down in Mexico.

GERTRUDE: I didn't enjoy anything. How could I, the way they lived? It wasn't even civilized.

MRS. CONSTABLE: (*merrily*): Great big lunches every day.

GERTRUDE: There were three or four beds in every single room.

MRS. CONSTABLE: Who was in them?

GERTRUDE: Relatives, endless visiting relatives, snapping at each other, jabbering half the night. No wonder I look sick. (*Sadly to herself.*) But I'll be fine soon, I know it. I will . . . as soon as I see Molly. If only she'd come back . . . (*To* MRS. CONSTABLE.) Which way did she go? Do you think I could find her?

MRS. CONSTABLE: She always goes a different way.

GERTRUDE: She couldn't like it in this ugly place. It's not true!

MRS. CONSTABLE: They take long walks down the beach or go digging for clams. They're very polite. They invite me along. But I never accept. I know they'd rather go off together, all by themselves.

GERTRUDE (*alarmed*): All by themselves!

MRS. CONSTABLE: When they play cards at night, I like to watch them. Sometimes I'm asleep on that bench, but either way I'm around. Inez doesn't know about it. She goes to bed early. She thinks I leave here at a reasonable hour. She's never found out. I take off my shoes and I wade home at dawn.

GERTRUDE: I don't know what's happening to the people in this world. (*Leaves* MRS. CONSTABLE.)

MRS. CONSTABLE: Why don't you go back to Mexico, Gertrude Eastman Cuevas, go back to Pepe? (GERTRUDE *looks in disgust at* MRS. CONSTABLE. *More gently.*) Then have a drink.

GERTRUDE (*fighting back a desire to cry*): I don't like to drink.

MRS. CONSTABLE: Then what do you like? What's your favorite pleasure?

GERTRUDE: I don't know. I don't know. I don't like pleasures. I . . . I like idealism and backbone and ambition. I take after my father. We were both very proud. We had the same standards, the same ideals. We both loved grit and fight.

MRS. CONSTABLE: You loved grit and fight.

GERTRUDE: We were exactly alike. I was his favorite. He loved me more than anyone in the world!

MRS. CONSTABLE (*faintly echoing*): More than anyone in the world . . .

GERTRUDE (*picking up one of the two boxes she brought with her and brooding over it*): It was a senseless dream, a nightmare.

MRS. CONSTABLE: What's in the box?

GERTRUDE: Little macaroons. I bought them for Molly on the

way up. I thought she'd like them. Some of them are orange and some are bright pink. (*Shakes the box and broods again, troubled, haunted by the dream.*) They were so pretty . . .

MRS. CONSTABLE: Aren't they pretty any more?

GERTRUDE: I had a dream about them just now, before I came. I was running very fast through the night trying to get to Molly, but I couldn't find the way. I kept losing all her presents. Everything I'd bought her I kept scattering on the ground. Then I was in a cold room with my father and she was there too. I asked him for a gift. I said, "I want something to give to my child," and he handed me this box . . . (*Fingering the actual box.*) I opened it up, and took out a macaroon and I gave it to Molly. (*Long pause. She looks haunted, deeply troubled.*) When she began to eat it, I saw that it was hollow, just a shell filled with dust. Molly's lips were gray with dust. Then I heard him . . . I heard my father. (*Excited.*) He was laughing. He was laughing at *me*! (*She goes away from* MRS. CONSTABLE *to collect herself.*) I've loved him so. I don't know what's happening to me. I've never been this way. I've always thrown things off, but now even foolish dreams hang over me. I can't shake anything off. I'm not myself . . . I . . . (*Stiffening against the weakness.*) When I was in the ocean house . . . (*Covering her face with her hands and shaking her head, very softly, almost to herself.*) Oh, I miss it so . . . I miss it so.

MRS. CONSTABLE: Houses! I hate houses. I like public places. Houses break your heart. Come and be with me in the Lobster Bowl. They gyp you, but it's a great place. They gyp you, but I don't care.

GERTRUDE: It was a beautiful house with a wall and a garden and a view of the sea.

MRS. CONSTABLE: Don't break your heart, Mrs. Eastman dear, don't . . .

GERTRUDE: I was happy in my house. There was nothing wrong. I had a beautiful life. I had Molly. I was busy teaching her. I had a full daily life. Everything was fine. There was nothing wrong. I don't know why I got frightened, why I married again. It must have been . . . it must have been because we had no money. That was it . . . We had so little money, I got frightened for us both . . . I should never have married. Now my life's lost its meaning . . . I have nightmares all the time. I lie awake in the night trying to think of just one standard or one ideal but something foolish pops into my head like Fula Lopez wearing city shoes and stockings to the beach. I've lost my daily life, that's all. I've lost Molly. My life has no meaning now. It's their fault. It's because I'm living their way. But I'm back now with Molly. I'm going to be fine again . . . She's coming with me tonight to my birthday supper . . . It's getting dark out. Where is she? (LIONEL *enters at bar with basket of glasses.*) Lionel. Wait . . .

LIONEL: What is it?

GERTRUDE: What did you mean just now.

LIONEL: When?

GERTRUDE: Before . . . when I came in. You said you were going, getting out.

LIONEL: I am. I sent a wire just now.

GERTRUDE: Wire?

LIONEL: Yes, to my brother. I'm going to St. Louis. He has a business there.

GERTRUDE: But you can't do that! I've come back. You won't have to live in this stupid Lobster Bowl. You're going to be living in a house with *me.*

LIONEL: We'll never make a life, sticking around here. I've made up my mind. We're going away . . .

GERTRUDE: You talk like a child.

LIONEL (*interrupting*): I'm not staying here.

GERTRUDE: You're running away . . . You're running home to your family . . . to your brother. Don't you have any backbone, any fight?

LIONEL: I don't care what you think about me! It's Molly that . . .

GERTRUDE: What about Molly!

LIONEL: I've got to get Molly out of here, far away from everything she's ever known. It's her only chance.

GERTRUDE: You're taking her away from *me*. That's what you're doing.

LIONEL: You're like a wall around Molly, some kind of shadow between us. She lives . . .

GERTRUDE (*interrupting, vehement*): I'm not a shadow any

more. I've come back and I'm staying here, where I belong with Molly! (LIONEL *looks at her with an expression of bitterness and revulsion.*) What is it? Why do you look at me that way?

LIONEL: What way?

GERTRUDE: As if I was some terrible witch . . . That's it, some terrible witch!

LIONEL: You're using her. You need Molly. You don't love her. You're using her . . .

GERTRUDE: You don't know what you're talking about. You don't know anything about me or Molly. You never could. You never will. When she married she was desperate. She cried like a baby and she begged me to stay. But you want to drag her away from me—from her mother. She loves me more than anyone on earth. She needs me. In her heart she's still a child.

LIONEL: If you get what you want she'll stay that way. Let her go, if you love her at all, let her go away . . . Don't stop her . . .

GERTRUDE: I can't stop her. How can I? She'll do what she likes, but I won't stand here watching while you drag her away. I'll talk to her myself. I'll ask her what she wants, what she'd really like to do. She has a right to choose.

LIONEL: To choose?

GERTRUDE: Between going with you and staying with me!

(LIONEL *is silent. After a moment he walks away from* GERTRUDE. *Then to himself as if she were no longer there.*)

LIONEL: This morning she was holding her wedding dress up to the light.

GERTRUDE (*proud*): She's going to wear it to my birthday supper. It's a party dress, after all.

LIONEL (*not really answering*): She didn't say anything to me. She just held her dress up to the light.

GERTRUDE: Go and find her. Get her now. Bring her back . . . tell her I'm here.

LIONEL: If you go half way up those stairs and holler . . .

GERTRUDE: No, Mrs. Constable said she was hunting mussels on the beach.

LIONEL: She's upstairs. (LIONEL *goes up to landing and calls.*) Molly! Your mother's here. She wants you. Come on down. Your mother's back.

(MOLLY *enters down stairs.* LIONEL *backs away and lurks in the shadows near the bar.*)

GERTRUDE (*tentative, starts forward to embrace her, but stops*): Molly, how pretty you look! How lovely . . . and your wedding dress.

MOLLY (*spellbound, as if looking at something very beautiful just behind* GERTRUDE): I took it out this morning for your birthday.

GERTRUDE: I'm glad, darling. How are you? Are you well, Molly? Are you all right?

MOLLY: Yes, I am.

GERTRUDE (*going to table*): I have something for you. A bracelet! (*She hooks necklace around* MOLLY'*s neck.*) And a necklace! They're made of real silver. Oh, how sweet you look! How pretty you look in silver! Just like a little girl, just as young as you looked when we were in the ocean house together. The ocean house, Molly! I miss it so. Don't you?

MOLLY: I knew you'd come back.

(*They sit down.*)

GERTRUDE: I knew it, too, from the beginning. They were strangers—all of them. I couldn't bear it. Nothing, really nothing meant anything to me down there, nothing at all. And you, darling, are you happy? What do you do in this terrible ugly place?

MOLLY: In the afternoon we hunt for mussels, sometimes, and at night we play cards . . . Lionel and me.

GERTRUDE (*uneasily*): I spoke to Lionel just now.

MOLLY: Did you?

GERTRUDE: Yes, about St. Louis.

MOLLY (*darkening*): Oh!

LIONEL (*coming over to them from the bar*): Yes, Molly. I'm arranging things now for the trip tomorrow. My mind's made up. If you're not coming with me, I'm going by myself. I'm coming down in a little while and you've got to tell me what you're going to do. (LIONEL *exits upstairs.*)

GERTRUDE: You see. With or without you he's determined to go. Don't look frightened, Molly. I won't allow you to go. You're coming with me, with your mother, where you belong. I never should have let you marry. I never should have left you. I'll never leave you again, darling. You're mine, the only one I have . . . my own blood . . . the only thing I'm sure of in the world. (*She clasps* MOLLY *greedily to her breast.*) We're going soon, but we've got to wait for them, Mrs. Lopez and Frederica. They're calling for us here. You're coming with me and you're never going back. Tonight, when you go to bed, you can wear my gown, the one you've always loved with the different colored tulips stitched around the neck. (*She notices* MOLLY*'s strange expression and the fact that she has recoiled just a little.*) What is it, dear? Don't you like the gown with the tulips any more? You used to . . .

MOLLY (*as if from far away*): I like it.

GERTRUDE: Tomorrow, after Lionel has gone, I'll come back to pack you up. (*Fingering the necklace.*) Did you like the paper with the dancing girl on it?

MOLLY: I have your letter here.

GERTRUDE: There are different ones at home—a toreador with peach satin breeches and a macaw with real feathers . . . (*It is obvious to her that* MOLLY *is not listening.*) You've seen them, dear . . . Those big parrots . . . (*Anxiously.*) Haven't you?

MOLLY: What?

GERTRUDE (*trying to ignore* MOLLY*'s coldly remote behavior*): How could you bear it here in this awful public place after our life together in the ocean house?

MOLLY: I used to go back and look into the garden . . . over the wall. Then the people moved in and I didn't go there any more. But, after a while . . .

GERTRUDE (*cutting in*): I'll make it all up to you, darling. You'll have everything you want.

MOLLY: It was all right after a while. I didn't mind so much. It was like being there . . .

GERTRUDE: What, Molly? What was like being there?

MOLLY: After a while I could sit in that booth, and if I wanted to I could imagine I was home in the garden . . . inside the summer house.

GERTRUDE: That's over, Molly. That's over now. All over. I have a wonderful surprise for you, darling. Can you guess?

MOLLY (*bewildered*): I don't know. I don't know.

GERTRUDE: I ordered the platform built, and the trellis, and I know where I can get the vines. Fully grown vines, heavy with leaves . . . just like the ones . . . (*She is stopped again by* MOLLY'*s expression. Then, touching her face apologetically.*) I know, I know. I don't look well. I look sick. But I'm not . . . I'm not sick.

MOLLY: No, you don't look sick. You look . . . different.

GERTRUDE: It's their fault. It's because I'm living their way. But soon I'll be the same again, my old self.

(*Enter* MRS. LOPEZ *and* FREDERICA *carrying paper bags.*)

MRS. LOPEZ: Inez! Inez! ya llegamos . . .

GERTRUDE: Here they are.

INEZ (*coming downstairs with a heavy tread*): Something tells me I hear Fula Lopez, the girl I love . . .

MRS. LOPEZ (*grabbing* INEZ *and whirling her around*): Inez . . . Guapa . . . Inez. Aquí estamos . . . que alegría . . . We are coming back from Mexico, Frederica, Fula . . . (*She spots* GERTRUDE.) and Eastman Cuevas. (*Then to* MOLLY, *giving her a big smacking kiss.*) Molly . . . Hello, Molly! Inez, guapa, bring us three limonadas, please . . . two for Fula and one for Frederica. Look, look, Eastman Cuevas. We got gorgeous stuff. (*She pulls a chicken out of a bag she is carrying and dangles it for* GERTRUDE.) Look and see what a nice one we got . . . Feel him!

GERTRUDE: No, later at home.

MRS. LOPEZ: Pinch him, see how much fat he got on him.

GERTRUDE (*automatically touching chicken for a second*): He's very nice . . . (*Then swerving around abruptly and showing a stern fierce profile to the audience.*) Why is he here?

MRS. LOPEZ (*looking stupid*): Who?

GERTRUDE: The chicken. Why is he here?

MRS. LOPEZ: The chicken? He go home. We put him now with his rice and his peas.

GERTRUDE (*in a fury manifestly about the chicken. But her rage conceals panic about* MOLLY): But *what* rice and peas. You know what we're having . . . I ordered it myself . . . It was going to be a light meal . . . something *I* liked . . . for once . . . we're having jellied consommé and little African lobster tails.

MRS. LOPEZ (*crossing back to center tables and stopping near* MRS. CONSTABLE): That's right, jelly and Africa and this one too.

(*She hoists chicken up in the air with a flourish. Enter* MRS. CONSTABLE.)

MRS. CONSTABLE: A chicken. I hate chickens. I'd rather have a dog.

(FREDERICA *pulls a thin striped horn out of one of the paper bags and blows on it.*)

GERTRUDE: Frederica, stop that. Stop that at once! I told you I didn't want to hear a single horn on my birthday. This is a party for adults. Put that away. Come along, we're leaving. We'll leave here at once.

FREDERICA (*in her pallid voice*): And Umberto? My uncle . . .

GERTRUDE: What about him?

FREDERICA: Uncle Umberto say he was calling for us to ride home all together.

GERTRUDE (*automatically*): Where *is* he?

FREDERICA: He is with Pepe Hernández, Frederica Gómez, Pacito Sánchez, Pepito Pita Luga . . .

GERTRUDE: No more names, Frederica . . . Tell him we're coming. We'll be right along . . .

MRS. LOPEZ: And the limonadas . . .

GERTRUDE: Never mind the limonadas. We're leaving here at once . . . Collect your bundles . . . Go on, go along.

(*The Mexicans start to collect everything, and there is the usual confusion and chatter.* FREDERICA *spills some horns out of her bag.* MRS. LOPEZ *screams at her, etc. They reach the exit just as* INEZ *arrives with the limonadas.*)

MRS. LOPEZ (*almost weeping, in a pleading voice to* GERTRUDE): Look, Eastman Cuevas the limonadas!

FREDERICA (*echoing*): The limonadas . . . Ay!

GERTRUDE: No! There isn't time. I said we were leaving. We're leaving at once . . .

INEZ (*to* MRS. LOPEZ *as they exit, including* MRS. CONSTABLE): Take them along . . . Drink them in the car, for Christ's sake.

MRS. LOPEZ (*off stage*): But the glasses . . .

INEZ (*off stage*): To hell with the glasses. Toss them down the cliff.

GERTRUDE: Molly, it's time to go. (MOLLY *starts for stairway.*) Molly, come along. We're going. What is it, Molly? Why are you standing there? You have your silver bracelet on and the necklace to match. We're ready to leave. Why are you waiting? Tonight you'll wear my gown with the tulips on it. I told you that . . . and tomorrow we'll go and I'll show you the vines. When you see how thick the leaves are and the blossoms, you'll know I'm not dreaming. Molly, why do you look at me like that? What is it? What did you forget?

(LIONEL *comes downstairs.* GERTRUDE *stiffens and pulls* MOLLY *to her side with a strong hand, holding her there as a guard holds his prisoner.*)

GERTRUDE: Lionel, we're going. It's all settled. We're leaving at once. Molly's coming with me and she's not coming back.

MOLLY (*her voice sticking in her throat*): I . . .

LIONEL (*seeing her stand there, overpowered by her mother, as if by a great tree, accepts the pattern as utterly hopeless once and for all. Then, after a moment*): Good-bye, Molly. Have a nice time at the birthday supper . . . (*Bitterly.*) You look very pretty in that dress. (*He exits through oyster-shell door.*)

GERTRUDE (*after a moment. Calm and firm, certain of her triumph*): Molly, we're going now. You've said good-bye. There's no point in standing around here any longer.

MOLLY (*retreating*): Leave me alone . . .

GERTRUDE: Molly, what is it? Why are you acting this way?

MOLLY: I want to go out.

GERTRUDE: Molly!

MOLLY: I'm going . . . I'm going out.

GERTRUDE (*blocking her way*): I'll make it all up to you. I'll give you everything you wanted, everything you've dreamed about.

MOLLY: You told me not to dream. You're all changed . . . You're not like you used to be.

GERTRUDE: I will be, darling. You'll see . . . when we're together. It's going to be the same, just the way it was. Tomorrow we'll go back and look at the vines, thicker and more beautiful . . .

MOLLY: I'm going . . . Lionel!

GERTRUDE (*blocking her way, fiendish from now on*): He did it. He changed you. He turned you against me.

MOLLY: Let me go . . . You're all changed.

GERTRUDE: You can't go. I won't let you. I can stop you. I can and I will.

(*There is a physical struggle between them near the oyster-shell door.*)

MOLLY (*straining to get through the door and calling in a voice that seems to come up from the bottom of her heart*): Lionel!

GERTRUDE: I know what you did . . . I didn't want to . . . I was frightened, but I knew . . . You hated Vivian. I'm the only one in the world who knows you. (MOLLY *aghast ceases to struggle. They hold for a moment before* GERTRUDE *releases her grip on* MOLLY. *Confident now that she has broken her daughter's will forever.*) Molly, we're going . . . We're going home.

MOLLY: (*backing away in horror*): No!

GERTRUDE: Molly, we're going! (MOLLY *continues to retreat.*) If you don't (MOLLY, *shaking her head, still retreats*). If you don't, I'll tell her! I'll call Mrs. Constable.

MOLLY (*still retreating*): No . . .

GERTRUDE (*wild, calling like an animal*): Mrs. Constable! Mrs. Constable! (*To* MOLLY, *shaking her.*) Do you see what you're doing to me! Do you? (MRS. CONSTABLE *appears in doorway.* GERTRUDE *drags* MOLLY *brutally out of her corner near the staircase and confronts her with* MRS. CONSTABLE.) I have something to tell you, Mrs. Constable. It's about Molly. It's about my daughter . . . She hated Vivian. My daughter hated yours and a terrible ugly thing happened . . . an ugly thing happened on the cliffs . . .

MRS. CONSTABLE (*defiantly*): Nothing happened . . . Nothing!

GERTRUDE (*hanging on to* MOLLY, *who is straining to go*): It *had* to happen. I know Molly . . . I know her jealousy . . . I was her whole world, the only one she loved . . . She wanted me all to herself . . . I know that kind of jealousy and what it can do to you . . . I know what it feels like to wish someone dead. When I was a little girl . . . I . . . (*She stops dead as if a knife had been thrust in her heart now. The hand holding* MOLLY'*s in its hard iron grip slowly relaxes. There is a long pause. Then, under her breath.*) Go . . . (MOLLY'*s flight is sudden. She is visible in the blue light beyond the oyster-shell door only for a second. The Mexican band starts playing the wedding song from Act One.* GERTRUDE *stands as still as a statue.* MRS. CONSTABLE *approaches, making a gesture of compassion.*) The band is playing on the beach. They're playing their music. Go, Mrs. Constable . . . Please.

(MRS. CONSTABLE *exits through oyster-shell door.*)

FREDERICA (*entering from street, calling, exuberant*): Eastman Cuevas! Eastman Cuevas! Uncle Umberto is ready. We are waiting in the car . . . Where's Molly? (*She falters at the sight of* GERTRUDE*'s white face. Then, with awe.*) Ay dios . . . Qué pasa? Qué tiene? Miss Eastman Cuevas, you don't feel happy? (*She unpins a simple bouquet of red flowers and puts it into* GERTRUDE*'s hand.*) For your birthday, Miss Eastman Cuevas . . . your birthday . . .

(*She backs away into the shadows, not knowing what to do next.* GERTRUDE *is standing rigid, the bouquet stuck in her hand.*)

GERTRUDE (*almost in a whisper, as the curtain falls*): When I was a little girl . . .

STORIES AND OTHER WRITINGS

A Guatemalan Idyll

WHEN THE traveler arrived at the pension the wind was blowing hard. Before going in to have the hot soup he had been thinking about, he left his luggage inside the door and walked a few blocks in order to get an idea of the town. He came to a very large arch through which, in the distance, he could see a plain. He thought he could distinguish figures seated around a far-away fire, but he was not certain because the wind made tears in his eyes.

"How dismal," he thought, letting his mouth drop open. "But never mind. Brace up. It's probably a group of boys and girls sitting around an open fire having a fine time together. The world is the world, after all is said and done, and a patch of grass in one place is green the way it is in any other."

He turned back and walked along quickly, skirting the walls of the low stone houses. He was a little worried that he might not be able to recognize a door of his pension.

"There's not supposed to be any variety in the U.S.A.," he said to himself. "But this Spanish architecture beats everything, it's so monotonous." He knocked on one of the doors, and shortly a child with a shaved head appeared. With a strong American accent he said to her: "Is this the Pension Espinoza?"

"*Sí!*" The child led him inside to a fountain in the center of a square patio. He looked into the basin and the child did too.

"There are four fish inside here," she said to him in Spanish. "Would you like me to try and catch one of them for you?"

The traveler did not understand her. He stood there uncomfortably, longing to go to his room. The little girl was still trying to get hold of a fish when her mother, who owned the pension, came out and joined them. The woman was quite fat, but her face was small and pointed, and she wore glasses attached by a gold chain to her dress. She shook hands with him and asked him in fairly good English if he had had a pleasant journey.

"He wants to see some of the fish," explained the child.

"Certainly," said Señora Espinoza, moving her hands about

in the water with dexterity. "Soon now, soon now," she said, laughing as one of the fish slipped between her fingers.

The traveler nodded. "I would like to go to my room," he said.

The American was a little dismayed by his room. There were four brass beds in a row, all of them very old and a little crooked.

"God!" he said to himself. "They'll have to remove some of these beds. They give me the willies."

A cord hung down from the ceiling. On the end of it at the height of his nose was a tiny electric bulb. He turned it on and looked at his hands under the light. They were chapped and dirty. A barefoot servant girl came in with a pitcher and a bowl.

In the dining room, calendars decorated the walls, and there was an elaborate cut-glass carafe on every table. Several people had already begun their meal in silence. One little girl was speaking in a high voice.

"I'm not going to the band concert tonight, mamá," she was saying.

"Why not?" asked her mother with her mouth full. She looked seriously at her daughter.

"Because I don't like to hear music. I hate it!"

"Why?" asked her mother absently, taking another large mouthful of her food. She spoke in a deep voice like a man's. Her head, which was set low between her shoulders, was covered with black curls. Her chin was heavy and her skin was dark and coarse; however, she had very beautiful blue eyes. She sat with her legs apart, with one arm lying flat on the table. The child bore no resemblance to her mother. She was frail, with stiff hair of the peculiar light color that is often found in mulattoes. Her eyes were so pale that they seemed almost white.

As the traveler came in, the child turned to look at him.

"Now there are nine people eating in this pension," she said immediately.

"Nine," said her mother. "Many mouths." She pushed her plate aside wearily and looked up at the calendar beside her on the wall. At last she turned around and saw the stranger. Having already finished her own dinner, she followed the progress of his meal with interest. Once she caught his eye.

"Good appetite," she said, nodding gravely, and then she watched his soup until he had finished it.

"My pills," she said to Lilina, holding her hand out without turning her head. To amuse herself, Lilina emptied the whole bottle into her mother's hand.

"Now you have your pills," she said. When Señora Ramirez realized what had happened, she dealt Lilina a terrible blow in the face, using the hand which held the pills, and thus leaving them sticking to the child's moist skin and in her hair. The traveler turned. He was so bored and at the same time disgusted by what he saw that he decided he had better look for another pension that very night.

"Soon," said the waitress, putting his meat in front of him, "the musician will come. For fifty cents he will play you all the songs you want to hear. One night would not be time enough. *She* will be out of the room by then." She looked over at Lilina, who was squealing like a stuck pig.

"Those pills cost me three *quetzales* a bottle," Señora Ramirez complained. One of the young men at a nearby table came over and examined the empty bottle. He shook his head.

"A barbarous thing," he said.

"What a dreadful child you are, Lilina!" said an English lady who was seated at quite a distance from everybody else. All the diners looked up. Her face and neck were quite red with annoyance. She was speaking to them in English.

"Can't you behave like civilized people?" she demanded.

"You be quiet, you!" The young man had finished examining the empty pill bottle. His companions burst out laughing.

"O.K., girl," he continued in English. "Want a piece of chewing gum?" His companions were quite helpless with laughter at his last remark, and all three of them got up and left the room. Their guffaws could be heard from the patio, where they had grouped around the fountain, fairly doubled up.

"It's a disgrace to the adult mind," said the English lady. Lilina's nose had started to bleed, and she rushed out.

"And tell Consuelo to hurry in and eat her dinner," her mother called after her. Just then the musician arrived. He was a small man and he wore a black suit and a dirty shirt.

"Well," said Lilina's mother. "At last you came."

"I was having dinner with my uncle. Time passes, Señora Ramirez! *Gracias a Dios!*"

"*Gracias a Dios* nothing! It's unheard-of, having to eat dinner without music."

The violinist fell into a chair, and, bent over low, he started to play with all his strength.

"Waltzes!" shouted Señora Ramirez above the music. "Waltzes!" She looked petulant and at the same time as though she were about to cry. As a matter of fact, the stranger was quite sure that he saw a tear roll down her cheek.

"Are you going to the band concert tonight?" she asked him; she spoke English rather well.

"I don't know. Are you?"

"Yes, with my daughter Consuelo. If the unfortunate girl ever gets here to eat her supper. She doesn't like food. Only dancing. She dances like a real butterfly. She has French blood from me. She is of a much better type than the little one, Lilina, who is always hurting; hurting me, hurting her sister, hurting her friends. I hope that God will have pity on her." At this she really did shed a tear or two, which she brushed away with her napkin.

"Well, she's young yet," said the stranger. Señora Ramirez agreed heartily.

"Yes, she is young." She smiled at him sweetly and seemed quite content.

Lilina meanwhile was in her room, standing over the white bowl in which they washed their hands, letting the blood drip into it. She was breathing heavily like someone who is trying to simulate anger.

"Stop that breathing! You sound like an old man," said her sister Consuelo, who was lying on the bed with a hot brick on her stomach. Consuelo was small and dark, with a broad flat face and an unusually narrow skull. She had a surly nature, which is often the case when young girls do little else but dream of a lover. Lilina, who was a bully without any curiosity concerning the grown-up world, hated her sister more than anyone else she knew.

"Mamá says that if you don't come in to eat soon she will hit you."

"Is that how *you* got that bloody nose?"

"No," said Lilina. She walked away from the basin and her eye fell on her mother's corset, which was lying on the bed. Quickly she picked it up and went with it into the patio, where she threw it into the fountain. Consuelo, frightened by the appropriation of the corset, got up hastily and arranged her hair.

"Too much upset for a girl of my age," she said to herself patting her stomach. Crossing the patio she saw Señorita Córdoba walking along, holding her head very high as she slipped some hairpins more firmly into the bun at the back of her neck. Consuelo felt like a frog or a beetle walking behind her. Together they entered the dining room.

"Why don't you wait for midnight to strike?" said Señora Ramirez to Consuelo. Señorita Córdoba, assuming that this taunt had been addressed to her, bridled and stiffened. Her eyes narrowed and she stood still. Señora Ramirez, a gross coward, gave her a strange idiotic smile.

"How is your health, Señorita Córdoba?" she asked softly, and then feeling confused, she pointed to the stranger and asked him if he knew Señorita Córdoba.

"No, no; he does not know me." She held out her hand stiffly to the stranger and he took it. No names were mentioned.

Consuelo sat down beside her mother and ate voraciously, a sad look in her eye. Señorita Córdoba ordered only fruit. She sat looking out into the dark patio, giving the other diners a view of the nape of her neck. Presently she opened a letter and began to read. The others all watched her closely. The three young men who had laughed so heartily before were now smiling like idiots, waiting for another such occasion to present itself.

The musician was playing a waltz at the request of Señora Ramirez, who was trying her best to attract again the attention of the stranger. "Tra-la-la-la," she sang, and in order better to convey the beauty of the waltz she folded her arms in front of her and rocked from side to side.

"Ay, Consuelo! It is for her to waltz," she said to the stranger. "There will be many people in the plaza tonight, and there is so much wind. I think that you must fetch my shawl, Consuelo. It is getting very cold."

While awaiting Consuelo's return she shivered and picked her teeth.

The traveler thought she was crazy and a little disgusting. He had come here as a buyer for a very important textile concern. Having completed all his work, he had for some reason decided to stay on another week, perhaps because he had always heard that a vacation in a foreign country was a desirable thing. Already he regretted his decision, but there was no boat out before the following Monday. By the end of the meal he was in such despair that his face wore a peculiarly young and sensitive look. In order to buoy himself up a bit, he began to think about what he would get to eat three weeks hence, seated at his mother's table on Thanksgiving Day. They would be very glad to hear that he had not enjoyed himself on this trip, because they had always considered it something in the nature of a betrayal when anyone in the family expressed a desire to travel. He thought they led a fine life and was inclined to agree with them.

Consuelo had returned with her mother's shawl. She was dreaming again when her mother pinched her arm.

"Well, Consuelo, are you coming to the band concert or are you going to sit here like a dummy? I daresay the Señor is not coming with us, but *we* like music, so get up, and we will say good night to this gentleman and be on our way."

The traveler had not understood this speech. He was therefore very much surprised when Señora Ramirez tapped him on the shoulder and said to him severely in English: "Good night, Señor. Consuelo and I are going to the band concert. We will see you tomorrow at breakfast."

"Oh, but I'm going to the band concert myself," he said, in a panic lest they leave him with a whole evening on his hands.

Señora Ramirez flushed with pleasure. The three walked down the badly lit street together, escorted by a group of skinny yellow dogs.

"These old grilled windows are certainly very beautiful," the traveler said to Señora Ramirez. "Old as the hills themselves, aren't they?"

"You must go to the capital if you want beautiful buildings," said Señora Ramirez. "Very new and clean they are."

"I should think," he said, "that these old buildings were your point of interest here, aside from your Indians and their native costumes."

They walked on for a little while in silence. A small boy came up to them and tried to sell them some lollipops.

"Five *centavos*," said the little boy.

"Absolutely not," said the traveler. He had been warned that the natives would cheat him, and he was actually enraged every time they approached him with their wares.

"Four *centavos* . . . three *centavos*. . . ."

"No, no, no! Go away!" The little boy ran ahead of them.

"I would like a lollipop," said Consuelo to him.

"Well, why didn't you say so, then?" he demanded.

"No," said Consuelo.

"She does not mean no," explained her mother. "She can't learn to speak English. She has clouds in her head."

"I see," said the traveler. Consuelo looked mortified. When they came to the end of the street, Señora Ramirez stood still and lowered her head like a bull.

"Listen," she said to Consuelo. "Listen. You can hear the music from here."

"Yes, mamá. Indeed you can." They stood listening to the faint marimba noise that reached them. The traveler sighed.

"Please, let's get going if we *are* going," he said. "Otherwise there is no point."

The square was already crowded when they arrived. The older people sat on benches under the trees, while the younger ones walked round and round, the girls in one direction and the boys in the other. The musicians played inside a kiosk in the center of the square. Señora Ramirez led both Consuelo and the stranger into the girls' line, and they had not been walking more than a minute before she settled into a comfortable gait, with an expression very much like that of someone relaxing in an armchair.

"We have three hours," she said to Consuelo.

The stranger looked around him. Many of the girls were barefoot and pure Indian. They walked along holding tightly to one another, and were frequently convulsed with laughter.

The musicians were playing a formless but militant-sounding piece which came to many climaxes without ending. The drummer was the man who had just played the violin at Señora Espinoza's pension.

"Look!" said the traveler excitedly. "Isn't that the man who was just playing for us at dinner. He must have run all the way. I'll bet he's sweating some."

"Yes, it is he," said Señora Ramirez. "The nasty little rat. I would like to tear him right off his stand. Remember the one at the Grand Hotel, Consuelo? He stopped at every table, señor, and I have never seen such beautiful teeth in my life. A smile on his face from the moment he came into the room until he went out again. This one looks at his shoes while he is playing, and he would like to kill us all."

Some big boys threw confetti into the traveler's face.

"I wonder," he asked himself. "I wonder what kind of fun they get out of just walking around and around this little park and throwing confetti at each other."

The boys' line was in a constant uproar about something. The broader their smiles became, the more he suspected them of plotting something, probably against him, for apparently he was the only tourist there that evening. Finally he was so upset that he walked along looking up at the stars, or even for short stretches with his eyes shut, because it seemed to him that somehow this rendered him a little less visible. Suddenly he caught sight of Señorita Córdoba. She was across the street buying lollipops from a boy.

"Señorita!" He waved his hand from where he was, and then joyfully bounded out of the line and across the street. He stood panting by her side, while she reddened considerably and did not know what to say to him.

Señora Ramirez and Consuelo came to a standstill and stood like two monuments, staring after him, while the lines brushed past them on either side.

Lilina was looking out of her window at some boys who were playing on the corner of the street under the street light. One of them kept pulling a snake out of his pocket; he would then stuff it back in again. Lilina wanted the snake very much. She chose her toys according to the amount of power or responsibility she thought they would give her in the eyes of others. She thought now that if she were able to get the snake, she would perhaps put on a little act called "Lilina and the Viper," and charge admission. She imagined that she would wear a fancy dress and let the snake wriggle under her collar. She left her room and went out of doors. The wind was stronger than it had been, and she could hear the music playing even from where she was. She felt chilly and hurried toward the boys.

"For how much will you sell your snake?" she asked the oldest boy, Ramón.

"You mean Victoria?" said Ramón. His voice was beginning to change and there was a shadow above his upper lip.

"Victoria is too much of a queen for you to have," said one of the smaller boys. "She is a beauty and you are not." They all roared with laughter, including Ramón, who all at once looked very silly. He giggled like a girl. Lilina's heart sank. She was determined to have the snake.

"Are you ever going to stop laughing and begin to bargain with me? If you don't I'll have to go back in, because my mother and sister will be coming home soon, and they wouldn't allow me to be talking here like this with you. I'm from a good family."

This sobered Ramón, and he ordered the boys to be quiet. He took Victoria from his pocket and played with her in silence. Lilina stared at the snake.

"Come to my house," said Ramón. "My mother will want to know how much I'm selling her for."

"All right," said Lilina. "But be quick, and I don't want them with us." She indicated the other boys. Ramón gave them orders to go back to their houses and meet him later at the playground near the cathedral.

"Where do you live?" she asked him.

"Calle de las Delicias number six."

"Does your house belong to you?"

"My house belongs to my Aunt Gudelia."

"Is she richer than your mother?"

"Oh, yes." They said no more to each other.

There were eight rooms opening onto the patio of Ramón's house, but only one was furnished. In this room the family cooked and slept. His mother and his aunt were seated opposite one another on two brightly painted chairs. Both were fat and both were wearing black. The only light came from a charcoal fire which was burning in a brazier on the floor.

They had bought the chairs that very morning and were consequently feeling lighthearted and festive. When the children arrived they were singing a little song together.

"Why don't we buy something to drink?" said Gudelia, when they stopped singing.

"Now you're going to go crazy, I see," said Ramón's mother. "You're very disagreeable when you're drinking."

"No, I'm not," said Gudelia.

"Mother," said Ramón. "This little girl has come to buy Victoria."

"I have never seen you before," said Ramón's mother to Lilina.

"Nor I," said Gudelia. "I am Ramón's aunt, Gudelia. This is my house."

"My name is Lilina Ramirez. I want to bargain for Ramón's Victoria."

"Victoria," they repeated gravely.

"Ramón is very fond of Victoria and so are Gudelia and I," said his mother. "It's a shame that we sold Alfredo the parrot. We sold him for far too little. He sang and danced. We have taken care of Victoria for a long time, and it has been very expensive. She eats much meat." This was an obvious lie. They all looked at Lilina.

"Where do you live, dear?" Gudelia asked Lilina.

"I live in the capital, but I'm staying now at Señora Espinoza's pension."

"I meet her in the market every day of my life," said Gudelia. "Maria de la Luz Espinoza. She buys a lot. How many people has she staying in her house? Five, six?"

"Nine."

"Nine! Dear God! Does she have many animals?"

"Certainly," said Lilina.

"Come," said Ramón to Lilina. "Let's go outside and bargain."

"He loves that snake," said Ramón's mother, looking fixedly at Lilina.

The aunt sighed. "Victoria . . . Victoria."

Lilina and Ramón climbed through a hole in the wall and sat down together in the midst of some foliage.

"Listen," said Ramón. "If you kiss me, I'll give you Victoria for nothing. You have blue eyes. I saw them when we were in the street."

"I can hear what you are saying," his mother called out from the kitchen.

"Shame, shame," said Gudelia. "Giving Victoria away for nothing. Your mother will be without food. I can buy my own food, but what will your mother do?"

Lilina jumped to her feet impatiently. She saw that they were getting nowhere, and unlike most of her countrymen, she was always eager to get things done quickly.

She stamped back into the kitchen, opened her eyes very wide in order to frighten the two ladies, and shouted as loud as she could: "Sell me that snake right now or I will go away and never put my foot in this house again."

The two women were not used to such a display of rage over the mere settlement of a price. They rose from their chairs and started moving about the room to no purpose, picking up things and putting them down again. They were not quite sure what to do. Gudelia was terribly upset. She stepped here and there with her hand below her breast, peering about cautiously. Finally she slipped out into the patio and disappeared.

Ramón took Victoria out of his pocket. They arranged a price and Lilina left, carrying her in a little box.

Meanwhile Señora Ramirez and her daughter were on their way home from the band concert. Both of them were in a bad humor. Consuelo was not disposed to talk at all. She looked angrily at the houses they were passing and sighed at everything her mother had to say. "You have no merriment in your heart," said Señora Ramirez. "Just revenge." As Consuelo refused to answer, she continued. "Sometimes I feel that I am walking along with an assassin."

She stopped still in the street and looked up at the sky. "*Jesu Maria!*" she said. "Don't let me say such things about my own daughter." She clutched at Consuelo's arm.

"Come, come. Let us hurry. My feet ache. What an ugly city this is!"

Consuelo began to whimper. The word "assassin" had affected her painfully. Although she had no very clear idea of an assassin in her mind, she knew it to be a gross insult and contrary to all usage when applied to a young lady of breeding. It so frightened her that her mother had used such a word in connection with her that she actually felt a little sick to her stomach.

"No, mamá, no!" she cried. "Don't say that I am an assassin. Don't!" Her hands were beginning to shake, and already the tears were filling her eyes. Her mother hugged her and they stood for a moment locked in each other's arms.

Maria, the servant, was standing near the fountain looking into it when Consuelo and her mother arrived at the pension. The traveler and Señorita Córdoba were seated together having a chat.

"Doesn't love interest you?" the traveler was asking her.

"No . . . no . . ." answered Señorita Córdoba. "City life, business, the theater. . . ." She sounded somewhat half-hearted about the theater.

"Well, that's funny," said the traveler. "In my country most young girls are interested in love. There are some, of course, who are interested in having a career, either business or the stage. But I've heard tell that even these women deep down in their hearts want a home and everything that goes with it."

"So?" said Señorita Córdoba.

"Well, yes," said the traveler. "Deep down in your heart, don't you always hope the right man will come along some day?"

"No . . . no . . . no. . . . Do you?" she said absent-mindedly.

"Who, me? No."

"No?"

She was the most preoccupied woman he had ever spoken with.

"Look, señoras," said Maria to Consuelo and her mother. "Look what is floating around in the fountain! What is it?"

Consuelo bent over the basin and fished around a bit. Presently she pulled out her mother's pink corset.

"Why, mamá," she said. "It's your corset."

Señora Ramirez examined the wet corset. It was covered with muck from the bottom of the fountain. She went over to a chair and sat down in it, burying her face in her hands. She rocked back and forth and sobbed very softly. Señora Espinoza came out of her room.

"Lilina, my sister, threw it into the fountain," Consuelo announced to all present.

Señora Espinoza looked at the corset.

"It can be fixed. It can be fixed," she said, walking over to Señora Ramirez and putting her arms around her.

"Look, my friend. My dear little friend, why don't you go to bed and get some sleep? Tomorrow you can think about getting it cleaned."

"How can we stand it? Oh, how can we stand it?" Señora Ramirez asked imploringly, her beautiful eyes filled with sorrow. "Sometimes," she said in a trembling voice, "I have no more strength than a sparrow. I would like to send my children to the four winds and sleep and sleep and sleep."

Consuelo, hearing this, said in a gentle tone: "Why don't you do so, mamá?"

"They are like two daggers in my heart, you see?" continued her mother.

"No, they are not," said Señora Espinoza. "They are flowers that brighten your life." She removed her glasses and polished them on her blouse.

"Daggers in my heart," repeated Señora Ramirez.

"Have some hot soup," urged Señora Espinoza. "Maria will make you some—a gift from me—and then you can go to bed and forget all about this."

"No, I think I will just sit here, thank you."

"Mamá is going to have one of her fits," said Consuelo to the servant. "She does sometimes. She gets just like a child instead of getting angry, and she doesn't worry about what she is eating or when she goes to sleep, but she just sits in a chair or goes walking and her face looks very different from the way it looks at other times." The servant nodded, and Consuelo went in to bed.

"I have French blood," Señora Ramirez was saying to Señora Espinoza. "I am very delicate for that reason—too delicate for my husband."

Señora Espinoza seemed worried by the confession of her friend. She had no interest in gossip or in what people had to say about their lives. To Señora Ramirez she was like a man, and she often had dreams about her in which she became a man.

The traveler was highly amused.

"I'll be damned!" he said. "All this because of an old corset. Some people have nothing to think about in this world. It's funny, though, funny as a barrel of monkeys."

To Señorita Córdoba it was not funny. "It's too bad," she said. "Very much too bad that the corset was spoiled. What are you doing here in this country?"

"I'm buying textiles. At least, I was, and now I'm just taking a little vacation here until the next boat leaves for the United States. I kind of miss my family and I'm anxious to get back. I don't see what you're supposed to get out of traveling."

"Oh, yes, yes. Surely you do," said Señorita Córdoba politely. "Now if you will excuse me I am going inside to do a little drawing. I must not forget how in this peasant land."

"What are you, an artist?" he asked.

"I draw dresses." She disappeared.

"Oh, God!" thought the traveler after she had left. "Here I am, left alone, and I'm not sleepy yet. This empty patio is so barren and so uninteresting, and as far as Señorita Córdoba is concerned, she's an iceberg. I like her neck though. She has a neck like a swan, so long and white and slender, the kind of neck you dream about girls having. But she's more like a virgin than a swan." He turned around and noticed that Señora Ramirez was still sitting in her chair. He picked up his own chair and carried it over next to hers.

"Do you mind?" he asked. "I see that you've decided to take a little night air. It isn't a bad idea. I don't feel like going to bed much either."

"No," she said. "I don't want to go to bed. I will sit here. I like to sit out at night, if I am warmly enough dressed, and look up at the stars."

"Yes, it's a great source of peace," the traveler said. "People don't do enough of it these days."

"Would you not like very much to go to Italy?" Señora Ramirez asked him. "The fruit trees and the flowers will be wonderful there at night."

"Well, you've got enough fruit and flowers here, I should say. What do you want to go to Italy for? I'll bet there isn't as much variety in the fruit there as here."

"No? Do you have many flowers in your country?"

The traveler was not able to decide.

"I would like really," continued Señora Ramirez, "to be somewhere else—in your country or in Italy. I would like to be somewhere where the life is beautiful. I care very much whether life is beautiful or ugly. People who live here don't care very much. Because they do not think." She touched her finger to her forehead. "I love beautiful things: beautiful houses, beautiful gardens, beautiful songs. When I was a young girl I was truly wild with happiness—doing and thinking and running in and out. I was so happy that my mother was afraid I would fall and break my leg or have some kind of accident. She was a very religious woman, but when I was a young girl I could not remember to think about such a thing. I was up always every morning before anybody except the Indians, and every morning I would go to market with them to buy food for all the houses. For many years I was doing this. Even when I was very little. It was very easy for me to do anything. I loved to learn English. I had a professor and I used to get on my knees in front of my father that the professor would stay longer with me every day. I was walking in the parks when my sisters were sleeping. My eyes were so big." She made a circle with two fingers. "And shiny like two diamonds, I was so excited all the time." She churned the air with her clenched fist. "Like this," she said. "Like a storm. My sisters called me wild Sofía. At the same time they were calling me wild Sofía, I was in love with my uncle, Aldo Torres. He never came much to the house before, but I heard my mother say that he had no more money and we would feed him. We were very rich and getting richer every year. I felt very sorry for him and was thinking about him all the time. We fell in love with each other and were kissing and hugging each other when nobody was there who could see us. I would have lived with him in a grass hut. He married a woman who had a little money, who also loved him very much. When he was married he got fat and started joking a lot with my father. I was glad for him that he was richer but pretty sad for myself. Then my sister Juanita, the oldest, married a very rich man. We were all very happy about her and there was a very big wedding."

"You must have been brokenhearted, though, about your uncle Aldo Torres going off with someone else, when you had befriended him so much when he was poor."

"Oh, I liked him very much," she said. Her memory seemed suddenly to have failed her and she did not appear to be interested in speaking any longer of the past. The traveler felt disturbed.

"I would love to travel," she continued, "very, very much, and I think it would be very nice to have the life of an actress, without children. You know it is my nature to love men and kissing."

"Well," said the traveler, "nobody gets as much kissing as they would like to get. Most people are frustrated. You'd be surprised at the number of people in my country who are frustrated and good-looking at the same time."

She turned her face toward his. The one little light bulb shed just enough light to enable him to see into her beautiful eyes. The tears were still wet on her lashes and they magnified her eyes to such an extent that they appeared to be almost twice their normal size. While she was looking at him she caught her breath.

"Oh, my darling man," she said to him suddenly. "I don't want to be separated from you. Let's go where I can hold you in my arms." The traveler was feeling excited. She had taken hold of his hand and was crushing it very hard.

"Where do you want to go?" he asked stupidly.

"Into your bed." She closed her eyes and waited for him to answer.

"All right. Are you sure?"

She nodded her head vigorously.

"This," he said to himself, "is undoubtedly one of those things that you don't want to remember next morning. I'll want to shake it off like a dog shaking water off its back. But what can I do? It's too far along now. I'll be going home soon and the whole thing will be just a soap bubble among many other soap bubbles."

He was beginning to feel inspired and he could not understand it, because he had not been drinking.

"A soap bubble among many other soap bubbles," he repeated to himself. His inner life was undefined but well controlled as a rule. Together they went into his room.

"Ah," said Señora Ramirez after he had closed the door behind them, "this makes me happy."

She fell onto the bed sideways, like a beaten person. Her feet stuck out into the air, and her heavy breathing filled the room. He realized that he had never before seen a person behave in this manner unless sodden with alcohol, and he did not know what to do. According to all his standards and the standards of his friends she was not a pleasant thing to lie beside.

She was unfastening her dress at the neck. The brooch with which she pinned her collar together she stuck into the pillow behind her.

"So much fat," she said. "So much fat." She was smiling at him very tenderly. This for some reason excited him, and he took off his own clothing and got into bed beside her. He was as cold as a clam and very bony, but being a truly passionate woman she did not notice any of that.

"Do you really want to go through with this?" he said to her, for he was incapable of finding new words for a situation that was certainly unlike any other he had ever experienced. She fell upon him and felt his face and his neck with feverish excitement.

"Dear God!" she said. "Dear God!" They were in the very act of making love. "I have lived twenty years for this moment and I cannot think that heaven itself could be more wonderful."

The traveler hardly listened to this remark. His face was hidden in the pillow and he was feeling the pangs of guilt in the very midst of his pleasure. When it was all over she said to him: "That is all I want to do ever." She patted his hands and smiled at him.

"Are you happy, too?" she asked him.

"Yes, indeed," he said. He got off the bed and went out into the patio.

"She was certainly in a bad way," he thought. "It was almost like death itself." He didn't want to think any further. He stayed outside near the fountain as long as possible. When he returned she was up in front of the bureau trying to arrange her hair.

"I'm ashamed of the way I look," she said. "I don't look the way I feel." She laughed and he told her that she looked perfectly all right. She drew him down onto the bed again. "Don't send me back to my room," she said. "I love to be here with you, my sweetheart."

The dawn was breaking when the traveler awakened next morning. Señora Ramirez was still beside him, sleeping very soundly. Her arm was flung over the pillow behind her head.

"Lordy," said the traveler to himself. "I'd better get her out of here." He shook her as hard as he could.

"Mrs. Ramirez," he said. "Mrs. Ramirez, wake up. Wake up!" When she finally did wake up, she looked frightened to death. She turned and stared at him blankly for a little while. Before he noticed any change in her expression, her hand was already moving over his body.

"Mrs. Ramirez," he said. "I'm worried that perhaps your daughters will get up and raise a hullabaloo. You know, start whining for you, or something like that. Your place is probably in there."

"What?" she asked him. He had pulled away from her to the other side of the bed.

"I say I think you ought to go into your room now the morning's here."

"Yes, my darling, I will go to my room. You are right." She sidled over to him and put her arms around him.

"I will see you later in the dining room, and look at you and look at you, because I love you so much."

"Don't be crazy," he said. "You don't want anything to show in your face. You don't want people to guess about this. We must be cold with one another."

She put her hand over her heart.

"Ay!" she said. "This cannot be."

"Oh, Mrs. Ramirez. Please be sensible. Look, you go to your room and we'll talk about this in the morning . . . or, at least, later in the morning."

"Cold I cannot be." To illustrate this, she looked deep into his eyes.

"I know, I know," he said. "You're a very passionate woman. But my God! Here we are in a crazy Spanish country."

He jumped from the bed and she followed him. After she had put on her shoes, he took her to the door.

"Good-bye," he said.

She couched her cheek on her two hands and looked up at him. He shut the door.

She was too happy to go right to bed, and so she went over

to the bureau and took from it a little stale sugar Virgin which she broke into three pieces. She went over to Consuelo and shook her very hard. Consuelo opened her eyes, and after some time asked her mother crossly what she wanted. Señora Ramirez stuffed the candy into her daughter's mouth.

"Eat it, darling," she said. "It's the little Virgin from the bureau."

"Ay, mamá!" Consuelo sighed. "Who knows what you will do next? It is already light out and you are still in your clothes. I am sure there is not other mother who is still in her clothes now, in the whole world. Please don't make me eat any more of the Virgin now. Tomorrow I will eat some more. But it is tomorrow, isn't it? What a mix-up. I don't like it." She shut her eyes and tried to sleep. There was a look of deep disgust on her face. Her mother's spell was a little frightening this time.

Señora Ramirez now went over to Lilina's bed and awakened her. Lilina opened her eyes wide and immediately looked very tense, because she thought she was going to be scolded about the corset and also about having gone out alone after dark.

"Here, little one," said her mother. "Eat some of the Virgin."

Lilina was delighted. She ate the stale sugar candy and patted her stomach to show how pleased she was. The snake was asleep in a box near her bed.

"Now tell me," said her mother. "What did you do today?" She had completely forgotten about the corset. Lilina was beside herself with joy. She ran her fingers along her mother's lips and then pushed them into her mouth. Señora Ramirez snapped at the fingers like a dog. Then she laughed uproariously.

"Mamá, please be quiet," pleaded Consuelo. "I want to go to sleep."

"Yes, darling. Everything will be quiet so that you can sleep peacefully."

"I bought a snake, mamá," said Lilina.

"Good!" exclaimed Señora Ramirez. And after musing a little while with her daughter's hand in hers, she went to bed.

In her room Señora Ramirez was dressing and talking to her children.

"I want you to put on your fiesta dresses," she said, "because I am going to ask the traveler to have lunch with us."

Consuelo was in love with the traveler by now and very jealous of Señorita Córdoba, who she had decided was his sweetheart. "I daresay he has already asked Señorita Córdoba to lunch," she said. "They have been talking together near the fountain almost since dawn."

"*Santa Catarina!*" cried her mother angrily. "You have the eyes of a madman who see flowers where there are only cow turds." She covered her face heavily with a powder that was distinctly violet in tint, and pulled a green chiffon scarf around her shoulders, pinning it together with a brooch in the form of a golf club. Then she and the girls, who were dressed in pink satin, went out into the patio and sat together just a little out of the sun. The parrot was swinging back and forth on his perch and singing. Señora Ramirez sang along with him; her own voice was a little lower than the parrot's.

Pastores, pastores, vamos a Belén
A ver a María y al niño también.

She conducted the parrot with her hand. The old señora, mother of Señora Espinoza, was walking round and round the patio. She stopped for a moment and played with Señora Ramirez's seashell bracelet.

"Do you want some candy?" she asked Señora Ramirez.

"I can't. My stomach is very bad."

"Do you want some candy?" she repeated. Señora Ramirez smiled and looked up at the sky. The old lady patted her cheek.

"Beautiful," she said. "You are beautiful."

"Mamá!" screamed Señora Espinoza, running out of her room. "Come to bed!"

The old lady clung to the rungs of Señora Ramirez's chair like a tough bird, and her daughter was obliged to pry her hands open before she was able to get her away.

"I'm sorry, Señora Ramirez," she said. "But when you get old, you know how it is."

"Pretty bad," said Señora Ramirez. She was looking at the traveler and Señorita Córdoba. They had their backs turned to her.

"Lilina," she said. "Go and ask him to have lunch with us . . . go. No, I will write it down. Get me a pen and paper."

"Dear," she wrote, when Lilina returned. "Will you come to

have lunch at my table this afternoon? The girls will be with me, too. All the three of us send you our deep affection. I tell Consuelo to tell the maid to move the plates all to the same table. Very truly yours, Sofía Piega de Ramirez."

The traveler read the note, acquiesced, and shortly they were all seated together at the dining-room table.

"Now this is really stranger than fiction," he said to himself. "Here I am sitting with these people at their table and feeling as though I had been here all my life, and the truth of the matter is that I have only been in this pension about fourteen or fifteen hours altogether—not even one day. Yesterday I felt that I was on a Zulu island, I was so depressed. The human animal is the funniest animal of them all."

Señora Ramirez had arranged to sit close beside the stranger, and she pressed her thigh to his all during the time that she was eating her soup. The traveler's appetite was not very good. He was excited and felt like talking.

After lunch Señora Ramirez decided to go for a walk instead of taking a siesta with her daughters. She put on her gloves and took with her an umbrella to shield her from the sun. After she had walked a little while she came to a long road, completely desolate save for a few ruins and some beautiful tall trees along the way. She looked about her and shook her head at the thought of the terrible earthquake that had thrown to the ground this city, reputed to have been once the most beautiful city in all the Western Hemisphere. She could see ahead of her, way at the road's end, the volcano named Fire. She crossed herself and bit her lips. She had come walking with the intention of dreaming of her lover, but the thought of this volcano which had erupted many centuries ago chased all dreams of love from her mind. She saw in her mind the walls of the houses caving in, and the roofs falling on the heads of the babies . . . and the mothers, their skirts covered with mud, running through the streets in despair.

"The innocents," she said to herself. "I am sure that God had a perfect reason for this, but what could it have been? *Santa María*, but what could it have been! If such a disorder should happen again on this earth, I would turn completely to jelly like a helpless idiot."

She looked again at the volcano ahead of her, and although

nothing had changed, to her it seemed that a cloud had passed across the face of the sun.

"You are crazy," she went on, "to think that an earthquake will again shake this city to the earth. You will not be going through such a trial as these other mothers went through, because everything now is different. God doesn't send such big trials any more, like floods over the whole world, and plagues."

She thanked her stars that she was living now and not before. It made her feel quite weak to think of the women who had been forced to live before she was born. The future too, she had heard, was to be very stormy because of wars.

"Ay!" she said to herself. "Precipices on all sides of me!" It had not been such a good idea to take a walk, after all. She thought again of the traveler, shutting her eyes for a moment.

"*Mi amante! Amante querido!*" she whispered; and she remembered the little books with their covers lettered in gold, books about love, which she had read when she was a young girl, and without the burden of a family. These little books had made the ability to read seem like the most worthwhile and delightful talent to her. They had never, of course, touched on the coarser aspects of love, but in later years she did not find it strange that it was for such physical ends that the heroes and heroines had been pining. Never had she found any difficulty in associating nosegays and couplets with the more gross manifestations of love.

She turned off into another road in order to avoid facing the volcano, constantly ahead of her. She thought of the traveler without really thinking of him at all. Her eyes glowed with the pleasure of being in love and she decided that she had been very stupid to think of an earthquake on the very day that God was making a bed of roses for her.

"Thank you, thank you," she whispered to Him, "from the bottom of my heart. Ah!" She smoothed her dress over her bosom. She was suddenly very pleased with everything. Ahead she noticed that there was a very long convent, somewhat ruined, in front of which some boys were playing. There was also a little pavilion standing not far away. It was difficult to understand why it was so situated, where there was no formal park, nor any trees or grass—just some dirt and a few bushes. It had the strange static look of a ship that has been grounded. Señora

Ramirez looked at it distastefully; it was a small kiosk anyway and badly in need of a coat of paint. But feeling tired, she was soon climbing up the flimsy steps, red in the face with fear lest she fall through to the ground. Inside the kiosk she spread a newspaper over the bench and sat down. Soon all her dreams of her lover faded from her mind, and she felt hot and fretful. She moved her feet around on the floor impatiently at the thought of having to walk all the way home. The dust rose up into the air and she was obliged to cover her mouth with her handkerchief.

"I wish to heaven," she said to herself, "that he would come and carry me out of this kiosk." She sat idly watching the boys playing in the dirt in front of the convent. One of them was a good deal taller than the others. As she watched their games, her head slumped forward and she fell asleep.

No tourists came, so the smaller boys decided to go over to the main square and meet the buses, to sell their lollipops and picture postcards. The oldest boy announced that he would stay behind.

"You're crazy," they said to him. "Completely crazy."

He looked at them haughtily and did not answer. They ran down the road, screaming that they were going to earn a thousand *quetzales.*

He had remained behind because for some time he had noticed that there was someone in the kiosk. He knew even from where he stood that it was a woman because he could see that her dress was brightly colored like a flower garden. She had been sitting there for a long time and he wondered if she were not dead.

"If she is dead," he thought, "I will carry her body all the way into town." The idea excited him and he approached the pavilion with bated breath. He went inside and stood over Señora Ramirez, but when he saw that she was quite old and fat and obviously the mother of a good rich family he was frightened and all his imagination failed him. He thought he would go away, but then he decided differently, and he shook her foot. There was no change. Her mouth, which had been open, remained so, and she went on sleeping. The boy took a good piece of the flesh on her upper arm between his thumb and forefinger and twisted it very hard. She awakened with a shudder and looked up at the boy, perplexed.

His eyes were soft.

"I awakened you," he said, "because I have to go home to my house, and you are not safe here. Before, there was a man here in the bandstand trying to look under your skirt. When you are asleep, you know, people just go wild. There were some drunks here too, singing an obscene song, standing on the ground, right under you. You would have had red ears if you had heard it. I can tell you that." He shrugged his shoulders and spat on the floor. He looked completely disgusted.

"What is the matter?" Señora Ramirez asked him.

"Bah! This city makes me sick. I want to be a carpenter in the capital, but I can't. My mother gets lonesome. All my brothers and sisters are dead."

"Ay!" said Señora Ramirez. "How sad for you! I have a beautiful house in the capital. Maybe my husband would let you be a carpenter there, if you did not have to stay with your mother."

The boy's eyes were shining.

"I'm coming back with you," he said. "My uncle is with my mother."

"Yes," said Señora Ramirez. "Maybe it will happen."

"My sweetheart is there in the city," he continued. "She was living here before."

Señora Ramirez took the boy's long hand in her own. The word sweetheart had recalled many things to her.

"Sit down, sit down," she said to him. "Sit down here beside me. I too have a sweetheart. He's in his room now."

"Where does he work?"

"In the United States."

"What luck for you! My sweetheart wouldn't love him better than she loves me, though. She wants me or simply death. She says so any time I ask her. She would tell the same thing to you if you asked her about me. It's the truth."

Señora Ramirez pulled him down onto the bench next to her. He was confused and looked out over his shoulder at the road. She tickled the back of his hand and smiled up at him in a coquettish manner. The boy looked at her and his face seemed to weaken.

"You have blue eyes," he said.

Señora Ramirez could not wait another minute. She took

his head in her two hands and kissed him several times full on the mouth.

"Oh, God!" she said. The boy was delighted with her fine clothes, her blue eyes, and her womanly ways. He took Señora Ramirez in his arms with real tenderness.

"I love you," he said. Tears filled his eyes, and because he was so full of a feeling of gratitude and kindness, he added: "I love my sweetheart and I love you too."

He helped her down the steps of the kiosk, and with his arm around her waist he led her to a sequestered spot belonging to the convent grounds.

The traveler was lying on his bed, consumed by a feeling of guilt. He had again spent the night with Señora Ramirez, and he was wondering whether or not his mother would read this in his eyes when he returned. He had never done anything like this before. His behavior until now had never been without precedent, and he felt like a two-headed monster, as though he had somehow slipped from the real world into the other world, the world that he had always imagined as a little boy to be inhabited by assassins and orphans, and children whose mothers went to work. He put his head in his hands and wondered if he could ever forget Señora Ramirez. He remembered having read that the careers of many men had been ruined by women who because they had a certain physical stranglehold over them made it impossible for them to get away. These women, he knew, were always bad, and they were never Americans. Nor, he was certain, did they resemble Señora Ramirez. It was terrible to have done something he was certain none of his friends had ever done before him, nor would do after him. This experience, he knew, would have to remain a secret, and nothing made him feel more ill than having a secret. He liked to imagine that he and the group of men whom he considered to be his friends, discoursed freely on all things that were in their hearts and in their souls. He was beginning to talk to women in this free way, too—he talked to them a good deal, and he urged his friends to do likewise. He realized that he and Señora Ramirez never spoke, and this horrified him. He shuddered and said to himself: "We are like two gorillas."

He had been, it is true, with one or two prostitutes, but he had never taken them to his own bed, nor had he stayed with them longer than an hour. Also, they had been curly-headed blond American girls recommended to him by his friends.

"Well," he told himself, "there is no use making myself into a nervous wreck. What is done is done, and anyway, I think I might be excused on the grounds that: one, I am in a foreign country, which has sort of put me off my balance; two, I have been eating strange foods that I am not used to, and living at an unusually high altitude for me; and, three, I haven't had my own kind to talk to for three solid weeks."

He felt quite a good deal happier after having enumerated these extenuating conditions, and he added: "When I get onto my boat I shall wave goodby to the dock, and say good riddance to bad rubbish, and if the boss ever tries to send me out of the country, I'll tell him: 'not for a million dollars!'" He wished that it were possible to change pensions, but he had already paid for the remainder of the week. He was very thrifty, as, indeed, it was necessary for him to be. Now he lay down again on his bed, quite satisfied with himself, but soon he began to feel guilty again, and like an old truck horse, laboriously he went once more through the entire process of reassuring himself.

Lilina had put Victoria into a box and was walking in the town with her. Not far from the central square there was a dry-goods shop owned by a Jewish woman. Lilina had been there several times with her mother to buy wool. She knew the son of the proprietress, with whom she often stopped to talk. He was very quiet, but Lilina liked him. She decided to drop in at the shop now with Victoria.

When she arrived, the boy's mother was behind the counter stamping some old bolts of material with purple ink. She saw Lilina and smiled brightly.

"Enrique is in the patio. How nice of you to come and see him. Why don't you come more often?" She was very eager to please Lilina, because she knew the extent of Señora Ramirez's wealth and was proud to have her as a customer.

Lilina went over to the little door that led into the patio behind the shop, and opened it. Enrique was crouching in the dirt beside the washtubs. She was surprised to see that his head was wrapped in bandages. From a distance the dirty bandages gave the effect of a white turban.

She went a little nearer, and saw that he was arranging some marbles in a row.

"Good morning, Enrique," she said to him.

Enrique recognized her voice, and without turning his head, he started slowly to pick up the marbles one at a time and put them into his pocket.

His mother had followed Lilina into the patio. When she saw that Enrique, instead of rising to his feet and greeting Lilina, remained absorbed in his marbles, she walked over to him and gave his arm a sharp twist.

"Leave those damned marbles alone and speak to Lilina," she said to him. Enrique got up and went over to Lilina, while his mother, bending over with difficulty, finished picking up the marbles he had left behind on the ground.

Lilina looked at the big, dark red stain on Enrique's bandage. They both walked back into the store. Enrique did not enjoy being with Lilina. In fact, he was a little afraid of her. Whenever she came to the shop he could hardly wait for her to leave.

He went over now to a bolt of printed material which he started to unwind. When he had unwound a few yards, he began to follow the convolutions of the pattern with his index finger. Lilina, not realizing that his gesture was a carefully disguised insult to her, watched him with a certain amount of interest.

"I have something with me inside this box," she said after a while.

Enrique, hearing his mother's footsteps approaching, turned and smiled at her sadly.

"Please show it to me," he said.

She lifted the lid from the snake's box and took it over to Enrique.

"This is Victoria," she said.

Enrique thought she was beautiful. He lifted her from her box and held her just below the head very firmly. Then he raised his arm until the snake's eyes were on a level with his own.

"Good morning, Victoria," he said to her. "Do you like it here in the store?"

This remark annoyed his mother. She had slipped down to the other end of the counter because she was terrified of the snake.

"You speak as though you were drunk," she said to Enrique. "That snake can't understand a word you're saying."

"She's really beautiful," said Enrique.

"Let's put her back in the box and take her to the square," said Lilina. But Enrique did not hear her, he was so enchanted with the sensation of holding Victoria.

His mother again spoke up. "Do you hear Lilina talking to you?" she shouted. "Or is that bandage covering your ears as well as your head?"

She had meant this remark to be stinging and witty, but she realized herself that there had been no point to it.

"Well, go with the little girl," she added.

Lilina and Enrique set off toward the square together. Lilina had put Victoria back into her box.

"Why are we going to the square?" Enrique asked Lilina.

"Because we are going there with Victoria."

Six or seven buses had converged in one of the streets that skirted the square. They had come from the capital and from other smaller cities in the region. The passengers who were not going any farther had already got out and were standing in a bunch talking together and buying food from the vendors. One lady had brought with her a cardboard fan intended as an advertisement for beer. She was fanning not only herself, but anyone who happened to come near her.

The bus drivers were racing their motors, and some were trying to move into positions more advantageous for departing. Lilina was excited by the noise and the crowd. Enrique, however, had sought a quiet spot, and was now standing underneath a tree. After a while she ran over to him and told him that she was going to let Victoria out of her box.

"Then we'll see what happens," she said.

"No, no!" insisted Enrique. "She'll only crawl under the buses and be squashed to death. Snakes live in the woods or in the rocks."

Lilina paid little attention to him. Soon she was crouching on the edge of the curbstone, busily unfastening the string around Victoria's box.

Enrique's head had begun to pain him and he felt a little ill. He wondered if he could leave the square, but he decided he did not have the courage. Although the wind had risen, the sun was very hot, and the tree afforded him little shade. He watched Lilina for a little while, but soon he looked away from her, and began to think instead about his own death. He was certain that his head hurt more today than usual. This caused him to sink into the blackest gloom, as he did whenever he remembered the day he had fallen and pierced his skull on a rusty nail. His life had always been precious to him, as far back as he could recall, and it seemed perhaps even more so now that he realized it could be violently interrupted. He disliked Lilina; probably because he suspected intuitively that she was a person who could fall over and over again into the same pile of broken glass and scream just as loudly the last time as the first.

By now Victoria had wriggled under the buses and been crushed flat. The buses cleared away, and Enrique was able to see what had happened. Only the snake's head, which had been severed from its body, remained intact.

Enrique came up and stood beside Lilina. "Now are you going home?" he asked her, biting his lip.

"Look how small her head is. She must have been a very small snake," said Lilina.

"Are you going home to your house?" he asked her again.

"No. I'm going over by the cathedral and play on the swings. Do you want to come? I'm going to run there."

"I can't run," said Enrique, touching his fingers to the bandages. "And I'm not sure that I want to go over to the playground."

"Well," said Lilina. "I'll run ahead of you and I'll be there if you decide to come."

Enrique was very tired and a little dizzy, but he decided to follow her to the playground in order to ask her why she had allowed Victoria to escape under the buses.

When he arrived, Lilina was already swinging back and forth. He sat on a bench near the swings and looked up at her. Each time her feet grazed the ground, he tried to ask her about Victoria, but the question stuck in his throat. At last he stood up, thrust his hands into his pockets, and shouted at her.

"Are you going to get another snake?" he asked. It was not

what he had intended to say. Lilina did not answer, but she did stare at him from the swing. It was impossible for him to tell whether or not she had heard his question.

At last she dug her heel into the ground and brought the swing to a standstill. "I must go home," she said, "or my mother will be angry with me."

"No," said Enrique, catching hold of her dress. "Come with me and let me buy you an ice."

"I will," said Lilina. "I love them."

They sat together in a little store, and Enrique bought two ices.

"I'd like to have a swing hanging from the roof of my house," said Lilina. "And I'd have my dinner and my breakfast served while I was swinging." This idea amused her and she began to laugh so hard that her ice ran out of her mouth and over her chin.

"Breakfast, lunch, and dinner and take a bath in the swing," she continued. "And make *pipi* on Consuelo's head from the swing."

Enrique was growing more and more nervous because it was getting late, and still they were not talking about Victoria.

"Could I swing with you in your house?" he asked Lilina.

"Yes. We'll have two swings and you can make *pipi* on Consuelo's head, too."

"I'd love to," he said.

His question seemed more and more difficult to present. By now it seemed to him that it resembled more a declaration of love than a simple question.

Finally he tried again. "Are you going to buy another snake?" But he still could not ask her why she had been so careless.

"No," said Lilina. "I'm going to buy a rabbit."

"A rabbit?" he said. "But rabbits aren't as intelligent or as beautiful as snakes. You had better buy another snake like Victoria."

"Rabbits have lots of children," said Lilina. "Why don't we buy a rabbit together?"

Enrique thought about this for a while. He began to feel almost lighthearted, and even a little wicked.

"All right," he said. "Let's buy two rabbits, a man and a woman." They finished their ices and talked together more and more excitedly about the rabbits.

On the way home, Lilina squeezed Enrique's hand and kissed him all over his cheeks. He was red with pleasure.

At the square they parted, after promising to meet again that afternoon.

It was a cloudy day, rather colder than usual, and Señora Ramirez decided to dress in her mourning clothes, which she always carried with her. She hung several strands of black beads around her neck and powdered her face heavily. She and Consuelo began to walk slowly around the patio.

Consuelo blew her nose. "Ay, mamá," she said. "Isn't it true that there is a greater amount of sadness in the world than happiness?"

"I don't know why you are thinking about this," said her mother.

"Because I have been counting my happy days and my sad days. There are many more sad days, and I am living now at the best age for a girl. There is nothing but fighting, even at balls. I would not believe any man if he told me he liked dancing better than fighting."

"This is true," said her mother. "But not all men are really like this. There are some men who are as gentle as little lambs. But not so many."

"I feel like an old lady. I think that maybe I will feel better when I'm married." They walked slowly past the traveler's door.

"I'm going inside," said Consuelo suddenly.

"Aren't you going to sit in the patio?" her mother asked her.

"No, with all those children screaming and the chickens and the parrot talking and the white dog. And it's such a terrible day. Why?"

Señora Ramirez could not think of any reason why Consuelo should stay in the patio. In any case she preferred to be there alone if the stranger should decide to talk to her.

"What white dog?" she said.

"Señora Espinoza has bought a little white dog for the children."

The wind was blowing and the children were chasing each other around the back patio. Señora Ramirez sat down on one of the little straight-backed chairs with her hands folded in her lap. The thought came into her mind that most days were likely to be cold and windy rather than otherwise, and that there would be many days to come exactly like this one. Unconsciously she had always felt that these were the days preferred by God, although they had never been much to her own liking.

The traveler was packing with the vivacity of one who is in the habit of making little excursions away from the charmed fold to return almost immediately.

"Wow!" he said joyfully to himself. "I sure have been giddy in this place, but the bad dream is over now." It was nearly bus time. He carried his bags out to the patio, and was confused to find Señora Ramirez sitting there. He prompted himself to be pleasant.

"Señora," he said, walking over to her. "It's goodby now till we meet again."

"What do you say?" she asked.

"I'm taking the twelve o'clock bus. I'm going home."

"Ah! You must be very happy to go home." She did not think of looking away from his face. "Do you take a boat?" she asked, staring harder.

"Yes. Five days on the boat."

"How wonderful that must be. Or maybe it makes you sick." She put her hand over her stomach.

"I have never been seasick in my life."

She said nothing to this.

He backed against the parrot swinging on its perch, and stepped forward again quickly as it leaned to bite him.

"Is there anyone you would like me to look up in the United States?"

"No. You will be coming back in not such a long time?"

"No. I don't think I will come back here again. Well. . . ." He put out his hand and she stood up. She was fairly impressive in her black clothes. He looked at the beads that covered her chest.

"Well, good-bye, señora. I was very happy to have met you."

"*Adios*, señor, and may God protect you on your trip. You will be coming back maybe. You don't know."

He shook his head and walked over to the Indian boy

standing by his luggage. They went out into the street and the heavy door closed with a bang. Señora Ramirez looked around the patio. She saw Señorita Córdoba move away from the half-open bedroom door where she had been standing.

Early 1940s

A Day in the Open

IN THE outskirts of the capital there was a low white house, very much like the other houses around it. The street on which it stood was not paved, as this was a poor section of the city. The door of this particular house, very new and studded with nails, was bolted inside and out. A large room, furnished with some modern chromium chairs, a bar, and an electric record machine, opened onto the empty patio. A fat little Indian boy was seated in one of the chairs, listening to the tune *Good Night, Sweetheart*, which he had just chosen. It was playing at full volume and the little boy was staring very seriously ahead of him at the machine. This was one of the houses owned and run by Señor Kurten, who was half Spanish and half German.

It was a gray afternoon. In one of the bedrooms Julia and Inez had just awakened. Julia was small and monkey-like. She was appealing only because of her extraordinarily large and luminous eyes. Inez was tall and high-breasted. Her head was a bit too small for her body and her eyes were too close together. She wore her hair in stiff waves.

Julia was moaning on her bed.

"My stomach is worse today," she said to Inez. "Come over and feel it. The lump on the right side is bigger." She twisted her head on the pillow and sighed. Inez was staring sternly into space.

"No," she said to Julia. "I cannot bear to feel that lump. *Santa María!* With something like that inside me I should go wild." She made a wry face and shuddered.

"You must not feel it if you do not want to," said Julia drowsily. Inez poured herself some *guaro*. She was a heavy drinker but her vitality remained unimpaired, although her skin often broke out in pimples. She ate violet lozenges to cover the smell of liquor on her breath and often popped six or seven of them into her mouth at once. Being full of enterprise she often made more money outside the whorehouse than she did at her regular job.

Julia was Mexican and a great favorite with the men, who enjoyed feeling that they were endangering her very life by going to bed with her.

"Well," said Inez, "I think that this afternoon I will go to the movies, if you will lend me a pair of your stockings. You had better lie here in your bed. I would sit here with you but it makes me feel very strange now to stay in this room. It is peculiar because, you know, I am a very calm woman and have suffered a great deal since I was born. You should go to a doctor," she added.

"I cannot bear to be out in the street," said Julia. "The sun is too hot and the wind is too cold. The smell of the market makes me feel sick, although I have known it all my life. No sooner have I walked a few blocks than I must find some park to sit in, I am so tired. Then somebody comes and tries to sell me orchids and I buy them. I have been out three times this week and each time I have bought some flowers. Now you know I can't afford to do this, but I am so weak and ill that I am becoming more like my grandmother every day. She had a feeling that she was not wanted here on this earth, either by God or by other people, so she never felt that she could refuse anyone anything."

"Well, if you are going to become like your grandmother," said Inez, "it will be a sad mistake. I should forget this sort of thing. You'll get to the doctor. Meanwhile, sit in the sun more. I don't want to be unkind. . . ."

"No, no. You are not unkind," Julia protested.

"You sit in this dark room all day long even when there is sun and you do not feel so sick."

Julia was feeling more desperately lonely than she had ever felt before in her life. She patted her heart. Suddenly the door pushed open and Señor Kurten came into the room. He was a slight man with a low forehead and a long nose.

"Julia and Inez," he said. "Señor Ramirez just telephoned that he is coming over this afternoon with a friend. He is going to take you both out to the country on a picnic and you are to hurry up and be ready. Try to bring them back to the bar in the evening."

"Hans," said Julia. "I am sick. I can't see Señor Ramirez or anyone else."

"Well, you know I can't do anything if he wants to see you. If he was angry he could make too much trouble. I am sorry." Señor Kurten left the room, closing the door slowly behind him.

"He is so important," said Inez, rubbing some eau de cologne over Julia's forehead. "So important, poor child. You must go." Her hand was hard and dry.

"Inez—" Julia clutched at Inez's kimono just as she was walking away. She struggled out of bed and threw herself into the arms of her friend. Inez was obliged to brace herself against the foot of the bed to keep from being knocked over.

"Don't make yourself crazy," said Inez to Julia, but then Inez began to cry; the sound was high like the squeal of a pig.

"Inez," said Julia. "Get dressed and don't cry. I feel better, my little baby."

They went into the bar and sat down to await the arrival of Señor Ramirez and his friend. Julia's arm was flung over the side of the chair, and her purse was swinging from her hand on an unusually long strap. She had put a little red dot in the corner of each eye, and rouged her cheeks very highly.

"You don't look very good," said Inez. "I'm afraid in my heart for you."

Julia opened her eyes wide and stared fixedly ahead of her at the wall. The Indian boy was polishing a very large alarm clock with care.

Soon Señor Ramirez stuck his head through the doorway. He had a German face but there was something very Spanish in the angle of his slouched fedora hat. His mustaches were blond and abundant. He had just shaved, and the talcum powder was visible on his chin and on his cheeks. He wore a pink shirt and a light tweed jacket, and on the fourth finger of each hand a heavy gold ring studded with a jewel.

"Come on, daughters," he said. "The car is waiting outside, with my friend. Move along."

Señor Ramirez drove very quickly. Julia and Inez sat uncomfortably on the edge of the back seat, hanging onto the straps at the side.

"We are going on a picnic," shouted Señor Ramirez. "I've brought with me five bottles of champagne. They are in the back of the car and they were all packed in ice by my cook. There is no reason why we should not have everything we want with us. They are inside a basket in the back. She wrapped the ice in a towel. That way it doesn't melt so quickly, but still we have to get there in a pretty short time. I drink nothing but

American whiskey, so I brought along a quart of it for myself. What do you think of that?"

"Oh, how nice," said Julia.

"I think we shall have a wonderful time," said Inez.

Señor Ramirez's friend Alfredo looked ill and disgruntled. He did not say anything himself, nor did the angle of his head indicate that he was listening to a word that anyone else was saying.

It was a cold day and the parasols under which the policemen stood were flapping in the wind. They passed a new yellow brick building, high at the top of six or seven flights of yellow brick steps.

"That is going to be a new museum," said Señor Ramirez. "When it opens we are all going to have a big dinner there together. Everyone there will be an old friend of mine. That's nothing. I can have dinner with fifty people every night of my life."

"A life of fiesta," put in Inez.

"Even more than that. They are more than just fiestas," he said, without quite knowing what he meant himself.

The sun was shining into Julia's lap. She felt lightheaded and feverish. Señor Ramirez turned the radio on as loud as he could. They were broadcasting *Madame Butterfly* as the car reached the outskirts of the city.

"I have three radios at home," said Señor Ramirez.

"Ah," said Inez. "One for the morning, one for the night and one for the afternoon." Julia listened to Inez with interest and wonder. They were on the edge of a deep ravine, going round a curve in the road. The mountainside across the ravine was in the shade, and some Indians were climbing toward the summit.

"Walk, walk, walk . . ." said Julia mournfully. "Oh, how tired it makes me feel to watch them."

Inez pinched her friend's arm. "Listen," she whispered to her. "You are not in your room. You daren't say things like that. You must not speak of being tired. It's no fun for them. They wouldn't like it."

"We'll be coming to that picnic spot in a minute," said Señor Ramirez. "Nobody knows where it is but me. I like to have a spot, you know, where all my friends won't come and disturb me. Alfredo," he added, "are you hungry?"

"I don't think this Alfredo is very nice, do you?" Inez asked very softly of Julia.

"Oh, yes," said Julia, for she was not quick to detect a mean nature in anybody, being altogether kind and charitable herself. At last, after driving through a path wide enough for only one car, they arrived at the picnic spot. It was a fair-sized clearing in a little forest. Not far from it, at the bottom of a hill, was a little river and a waterfall. They got out and listened to the noise of the water. Both of the women were delighted with the sound.

"Since it is so sunny out, ladies," said Señor Ramirez, "I am going to walk around in my underpants. I hope that my friend will do the same if he wants to."

"What a lucky thing for us," said Inez in a strident voice. "The day begins right." Señor Ramirez undressed and slipped on a pair of tennis shoes. His legs were very white and freckled.

"Now I will give you some champagne right away," he said to them, a little out of breath because he had struggled so quickly out of his clothes. He went over to where he had laid the basket and took from it a champagne bottle. On his way back he stumbled over a rock; the bottle fell from his hand and was smashed in many pieces. For a moment his face clouded over and he looked as though he were about to lose his temper; instead, seizing another bottle from the basket, he flung it high into the air, almost over the tops of the trees. He returned elated to his friends.

"A gentleman," he said, "always knows how to make fun. I am one of the richest businessmen in this country. I am also the craziest. Like an American. When I am out I always have a wonderful time, and so does everyone who is with me, because they know that while I am around there is always plenty. Plenty to eat, plenty to drink, and plenty of beautiful women to make love to. Once you have been out with me," he pointed his finger at Julia and Inez, "any other man will seem to you like an old-lady schoolteacher."

He turned to Alfredo. "Tell me, my friend, have you not had the time of your life with me?"

"Yes, I have," said Alfredo. He was thinking very noticeably of other things.

"His mind is always on business," Señor Ramirez explained to Julia. "He is also very clever. I have gotten him this job with a German concern. They are manufacturing planes." Alfredo said something to Señor Ramirez in German, and they spoke no longer on the subject. They spread out their picnic lunch and sat down to eat.

Señor Ramirez insisted on feeding Julia with his own fingers. This rather vexed Inez, so she devoted herself to eating copiously. Señor Ramirez drank quantities of whiskey out of a tin folding cup. At the end of fifteen or twenty minutes he was already quite drunk.

"Now, isn't it wonderful to be all together like this, friends? Alfredo, aren't these two women the finest, sweetest women in the world? I do not understand why in the eyes of God they should be condemned to the fires of hell for what they are. Do you?"

Julia moaned and rose to her feet.

"No, no!" she said, looking up helplessly at the branches overhead.

"Come on," said Señor Ramirez. "We're not going to worry about this today, are we?" He took hold of her wrist and pulled her down to the ground beside him. Julia hid her face in her hands and leaned her head against his shoulder. Soon she was smiling up at him and stroking his face.

"You won't leave me alone?" she asked, laughing a little in an effort to bring him to terms with her. If anyone were to be pitted successfully against the Divine, she thought, it would certainly be someone like Señor Ramirez. The presence of such men is often enough to dispel fear from the hearts of certain people for whom God is more of an enemy than a friend. Señor Ramirez's principal struggle in life was one of pride rather than of conscience; and because his successes were numerous each day, replenishing his energy and his taste for life, his strength was easily felt by those around him. Now that he was near her, Julia felt that she was safe from hell, and she was quite happy even though her side still hurt her very badly.

"Now," said Inez, "I think that we should all play a game, to chase gloomy thoughts out of this girl's head."

She rose to her feet and snatched Señor Ramirez's hat from where it lay beside him on the ground, placing it a few feet away upside down on the grass. Then she gathered some acorns in the picnic basket.

"Now," she said. "We will see who can throw these acorns into the hat. He will win."

"I think," said Señor Ramirez, "that the two women should be naked while we are playing this; otherwise it will be just a foolish children's game."

"And we are not children at all," said Inez, winking at him. The two women turned and looked at Alfredo questioningly.

"Oh, don't mind him," said Señor Ramirez. "He sees nothing but numbers in his head."

The two girls went behind some bushes and undressed. When they returned, Alfredo was bending over a ledger and trying to explain something to Señor Ramirez, who looked up, delighted that they had returned so quickly, so that he would not be obliged to listen.

"Ah," he said. "Now this looks much more like friends together, doesn't it, Alfredo?"

"Come on," said Inez. "We will all get into line here with this basket and each one will try to throw the acorn into the hat."

Señor Ramirez grew quite excited playing the game; then he began to get angry because he never managed to get the acorn into the hat. Inez screeched with laughter and threw her acorn wider and wider of the mark, each time purposely, in order to soothe, if possible, the hurt pride of Señor Ramirez. Alfredo refused to play at all.

"Games don't interest me," said Señor Ramirez suddenly. "I'd like to play longer with you, daughters, but I can't honestly keep my mind on the game."

"It is of no importance at all, really," said Inez, busily trying to think up something to do next.

"How are your wife and children?" Julia asked him.

Inez bit her lip and shook her head.

"They are well taken care of. I have sent them to a little town where they are staying in a pension. Quiet women—all three of them—the little girls and the mother. I am going to sleep." He stretched out under a tree and put his hat over his face. Alfredo was absorbed in his ledger. Inez and Julia sat side by side and waited.

"You have the brain of a baby chicken," Inez said to Julia. "I must think for both of us. If I had not had a great deal of practice when I had to keep count of all the hundreds of tortillas that I sold for my mother, I don't know where we would be."

"Dead, probably," said Julia. They began to feel cold.

"Come," said Inez. "Sing with me." They sang a song about leaving and never returning, four or five times through. When Señor Ramirez awakened he suggested to Julia that they go for a walk. She accepted sweetly, and so they started off through the woods. Soon they reached a good-sized field where Señor Ramirez suggested that they sit for a while.

"The first time I went to bed with a woman," he said, "it was in the country like this. The land belonged to my father. Three or four times a day we would come out into the fields and make love. She loved it, and would have come more often if I had asked her to. Some years later I went to her wedding and I had a terrible fight there. I don't even remember who the man was, but in the end he was badly hurt. I can tell you that."

"If you put your arms around me," said Julia, "I will feel less cold. You don't mind my asking you to do this, but I love you very much and I feel very contented with you."

"That's good," said Señor Ramirez, looking off at the mountains and shielding his eyes from the sun. He was listening to the sound of the waterfall, which was louder here. Julia was laughing and touching various parts of his body.

"Ah," she said. "I don't mind my side hurting me so badly if I can only be happy the way I am now with you. You are so sweet and so wonderful."

He gave her a quick loud kiss on the mouth and rose to his feet.

"Listen," he said. "Wouldn't you like to come into the water with me?"

"I am too sick a woman to go into the water, and I am a little bit afraid."

"In my arms you don't have to be afraid. I will carry you. The current would be too strong for you to manage anyway." Señor Ramirez was now as gay as a lark, although he had been bored but a moment before. He liked nothing better than performing little feats that were assured of success from the beginning. He carried her down to the river, singing at the top of his voice.

The noise of the falls was very loud here, and Julia clung tightly to her escort.

"Don't let go, now," she said. But her voice seemed to fly away behind her like a ribbon caught in the wind. They were in the water and Señor Ramirez began to walk in the direction of the falls.

"I will hold tight, all right," he said. "Because the water runs pretty swiftly near the falls." He seemed to enjoy stepping precariously from one stone to another with Julia in his arms.

"This is not so easy, you know. This is damned hard. The stones are slippery." Julia tightened her grip around his neck and kissed him quickly all over his face.

"If I let you go," he said, "the current would carry you along like a leaf over the falls, and then one of those big rocks would make a hole in your head. That would be the end, of course." Julia's eyes widened with horror, and she yelled with the suddenness of an animal just wounded.

"But why do you scream like that, Julia? I love you, sweetheart." He had had enough of struggling through the water, and so he turned around and started back.

"Are we going away from the waterfall?"

"Yes. It was wonderful, wasn't it?"

"Very nice," she said.

He grew increasingly careless as the current slackened, with the result that he miscalculated and his foot slipped between two stones. This threw him off his balance and he fell. He was unhurt, but the back of Julia's head had hit a stone. It started to bleed profusely. He struggled to his feet and carried her to the riverbank. She was not sure that she was not dying, and hugged him all the more closely. Pulling her along, he walked quickly up the hill and back through the woods to where Inez and Alfredo were still sitting.

"It will be all right, won't it?" she asked him a bit weakly.

"Those damn rocks were slippery," he growled. He was sulky, and eager to be on his way home.

"Oh, God of mine!" lamented Inez, when she saw what had happened. "What a sad ending for a walk! Terrible things always happen to Julia. She is a daughter of misfortune. It's a lucky thing that I am just the contrary."

Señor Ramirez was in such a hurry to leave the picnic spot

that he did not even want to bother to collect the various baskets and plates he had brought with him. They dressed, and he yelled for them all to get into the car. Julia wrapped a shawl around her bleeding head. Inez went around snatching up all the things, like an enraged person.

"Can I have these things?" she asked her host. He nodded his head impatiently. Julia was by now crying rhythmically like a baby that has almost fallen asleep.

The two women sat huddled together in the back of the car. Inez explained to Julia that she was going to make presents of the plates and baskets to her family. She shed a tear or two herself. When they arrived at the house, Señor Ramirez handed some banknotes to Inez from where he was sitting.

"*Adios*," he said. The two women got out of the car and stood in the street.

"Will you come back again?" Julia asked him tenderly, ceasing to cry for a moment.

"Yes, I'm coming back again," he said. "*Adios.*" He pressed his foot on the accelerator and drove off.

The bar was packed with men. Inez led Julia around through the patio to their room. When she had shut the door, she slipped the banknotes into her pocket and put the baskets on the floor.

"Do you want any of these baskets?" she asked.

Julia was sitting on the edge of her bed, looking into space. "No, thank you," she said. Inez looked at her, and saw that she was far away.

"Señor Ramirez gave me four drinking cups made out of plastic," said Inez. "Do you want one of them for yourself?"

Julia did not answer right away. Then she said: "Will he come back?"

"I don't know," Inez said. "I'm going to the movies. I'll come and see you afterwards, before I go into the bar."

"All right," said Julia. But Inez knew that she did not care. She shrugged her shoulders and went out through the door, closing it behind her.

Early 1940s

Song of an Old Woman

Oh, I'm sad for never knowing courage,
And I'm sad for the stilling of fear.
Closer to the sun now and farther from the heart.
I think that my end must be near.

I linger too long at a picnic,
   'cause a picnic's gayer than me.
And I hold to the edge of the table,
   'cause the table's stronger than me,
And I lean on anyone's shoulder
   because anyone's warmer than me.

Oh, I'm sad for never knowing courage,
And I'm sad for the stilling of fear.
Closer to the sun now and farther from the heart.
I think that my end must be near.

1942

Two Skies

Today's a holiday.
The devil walks the beach.
Faintly I see him, and faintly see flowers.
I walk beneath two skies,
Mixing hearts and branches together.

My head is lovely
   when the sun shines through it.
My house is brighter
   with the snow drifts in it.
A boat is sailing through my house
   but the wind is blowing the other way.

Today's a holiday.
I picked a desert rose.
There's mist in the wall, and stone in the flowers.
I walk beneath two skies,
Losing hearts and branches together.

1942

A Quarreling Pair

The two puppets are sisters in their early fifties. The puppet stage should have a rod or string dividing it down the middle to indicate two rooms. One puppet is seated on each side of the dividing line. If it is not possible to seat them, they will have to stand. HARRIET, *the older puppet, is stronger-looking and wears brighter colors.*

HARRIET (*the stronger puppet*): I hope you are beginning to think about our milk.

RHODA (*after a pause*): Well, I'm not.

HARRIET: Now what's the matter with you? You're not going to have a visitation from our dead, are you?

RHODA: I don't have visitations this winter, because I'm too tired to love even our dead. Anyway, I'm disgusted with the world.

HARRIET: Just mind your business. I mind mine, and I *am* thinking about our milk.

RHODA: I'm so tired of being sad. I'd like to change.

HARRIET: You don't get enough enjoyment out of your room. Why don't you?

RHODA: Oh, because the world and its sufferers are always on my mind.

HARRIET: That's not normal. You're not smart enough to be of any use to the outside, anyway.

RHODA: If I were young I'd succor the sick. I wouldn't care about culture, even, if I were young.

HARRIET: You don't have any knack for making a home. There's blessed satisfaction in that, at any rate.

RHODA: My heart's too big to make a home.

HARRIET: No. It's because you have no self-sufficiency. If I wasn't around, you wouldn't have the leisure to worry. You're a lost soul, when I'm not around. You don't even have the pep to worry about the outside when I'm not around. Not that the outside loses by that. (*She sniffs with scorn.*)

RHODA: You're right. But I swear that my heart is big.

HARRIET: I've come to believe that what is inside of people is not so very interesting. You can breed considerable discontent around you with a big heart, and considerable harmony with a small one. Compare your living quarters to mine. And my heart is small like Papa's was.

RHODA: You chill me to the marrow when you tell me that your heart is small. You do love me, though, don't you?

HARRIET: You're my sister, aren't you?

RHODA: Sisterly love is one of the few boons in this life.

HARRIET: Now, that's enough exaggerating. I could enumerate other things.

RHODA: I suppose it's wicked to squeeze love from a small heart. I suppose it's a sin. I suppose God meant for small hearts to be busy with other things.

HARRIET: Possibly. Let's have our milk in my room. It's so much more agreeable to sit in here. Partly because I'm a neater woman than you are.

RHODA: Even though you have a small heart, I wish there were no one but you and me in the world. Then I would never feel that I had to go among the others.

HARRIET: Well, I wish I could hand you my gift for contentment in a box. It would be so lovely if you were like me. Then we could have our milk in *either* room. One day in your room and the next day in mine.

RHODA: I'm sure that's the sort of thing that never happens.

HARRIET: It happens in a million homes, seven days a week. I'm the type that's in the majority.

RHODA: Never, never, never . . .

HARRIET (*very firmly*): It happens in a million homes.

RHODA: *Never, never, never!*

HARRIET (*rising*): Are you going to listen to me when I tell you that it happens in a million homes, or must I lose my temper?

RHODA: You have already lost it.

(HARRIET *exits rapidly in a rage.* RHODA *goes to the chimes and sings.*)

My horse was frozen like a stone
A long, long time ago.
Frozen near the flower bed
In the wintry sun.
Or maybe in the night time,
Or maybe not at all.

My horse runs across the fields
On many afternoons.
Black as dirt and filled with blood
I glimpse him fleeing toward the woods
And then not at all.

HARRIET (*offstage*): I'm coming with your milk, and I hope the excitement is over for today.

(*Enters, carrying two small white glasses.*)

Oh, why do I bring milk to a person who is dead-set on making my life a real hell?

RHODA (*clasping her hands with feeling*): Yes, why? Why? Why? Why? Oh, what a hideous riddle!

HARRIET: You love to pretend that everything is a riddle. You think that's the way to be intellectual. There is no riddle. I am simply keeping up my end of the bargain.

RHODA: Oh, bargains, bargains, bargains!

HARRIET: Will you let me finish, you excitable thing? I'm trying to explain that I'm behaving the way I was molded to behave. I happen to be appreciative of the mold I was cast in, and neither heaven nor earth is going to damage it. Your high-strung emotions are not going to affect me. Here's your milk.

(*She enters* RHODA*'s side of the stage and hands her the milk, but* RHODA *punches the bottom of the glass with her closed fist and sends it flying out of* HARRIET*'s hand.* HARRIET *deals* RHODA *a terrific blow on the face and scurries back to her own room. There is silence for a moment. Then* HARRIET *buries her face in her hands and weeps,* RHODA *exits, and* HARRIET *goes to the chimes and sings.*)

I dreamed I climbed upon a cliff,
My sister's hand in mine.
Then searched the valley for my house
But only sunny fields could see
And the church spire shining.
I searched until my heart was cold
But only sunny fields could see
And the church spire shining.
A girl ran down the mountainside
With bluebells in her hat.

I asked the valley for her name
But only wind and rain could hear
And the church bell tolling.
I asked until my lips were cold
But wakened not yet knowing
If the name she bore was my sister's name
Or if it was my own.

Rhoda?

RHODA: What do you want?

HARRIET: Go away if you like.

RHODA: The moment hasn't come yet, and it won't come today, because the day is finished and the evening is here. Thank God!

HARRIET: I know I should get some terrible disease and die if I thought I did not live in the right. It would break my heart.

RHODA: You do live in the right, sweetie, so don't think about it. (*Pause.*) I'll go and get your milk.

HARRIET: I'll go too. But let's drink it in here, because it really *is* much pleasanter in here, isn't it?

(*They rise.*)

Oh, I'm so glad the evening has come! I'm nervously exhausted.

(*They exit.*)

1945

Plain Pleasures

ALVA PERRY was a dignified and reserved woman of Scotch and Spanish descent, in her early forties. She was still handsome, although her cheeks were too thin. Her eyes particularly were of an extraordinary clarity and beauty. She lived in her uncle's house, which had been converted into apartments, or tenements, as they were still called in her section of the country. The house stood on the side of a steep, wooded hill overlooking the main highway. A long cement staircase climbed halfway up the hill and stopped some distance below the house. It had originally led to a power station, which had since been destroyed. Mrs. Perry had lived alone in her tenement since the death of her husband eleven years ago; however, she found small things to do all day long and she had somehow remained as industrious in her solitude as a woman who lives in the service of her family.

John Drake, an equally reserved person, occupied the tenement below hers. He owned a truck and engaged in free-lance work for lumber companies, as well as in the collection and delivery of milk cans for a dairy.

Mr. Drake and Mrs. Perry had never exchanged more than the simplest greeting in all the years that they had lived here in the hillside house.

One night Mr. Drake, who was standing in the hall, heard Mrs. Perry's heavy footsteps, which he had unconsciously learned to recognize. He looked up and saw her coming downstairs. She was dressed in a brown overcoat that had belonged to her dead husband, and she was hugging a paper bag to her bosom. Mr. Drake offered to help her with the bag and she faltered, undecided, on the landing.

"They are only potatoes," she said to him, "but thank you very much. I am going to bake them out in the back yard. I have been meaning to for a long time."

Mr. Drake took the potatoes and walked with a stiff-jointed gait through the back door and down the hill to a short stretch of level land in back of the house which served as a yard. Here he put the paper bag on the ground. There was a big new incinerator smoking near the back stoop and in the center of the yard Mrs. Perry's uncle had built a roofed-in pigpen faced in vivid artificial brick. Mrs. Perry followed.

She thanked Mr. Drake and began to gather twigs, scuttling rapidly between the edge of the woods and the pigpen, near which she was laying her fire. Mr. Drake, without any further conversation, helped her to gather the twigs, so that when the fire was laid, she quite naturally invited him to wait and share the potatoes with her. He accepted and they sat in front of the fire on an overturned box.

Mr. Drake kept his face averted from the fire and turned in the direction of the woods, hoping in this way to conceal somewhat his flaming-red cheeks from Mrs. Perry. He was a very shy person and though his skin was naturally red all the time it turned to such deep crimson when he was in the presence of a strange woman that the change was distinctly noticeable. Mrs. Perry wondered why he kept looking behind him, but she did not feel she knew him well enough to question him. She waited in vain for him to speak and then, realizing that he was not going to, she searched her own mind for something to say.

"Do you like plain ordinary pleasures?" she finally asked him gravely.

Mr. Drake felt very much relieved that she had spoken and his color subsided. "You had better first give me a clearer notion of what you mean by ordinary pleasures, and then I'll tell you how I feel about them," he answered soberly, halting after every few words, for he was as conscientious as he was shy.

Mrs. Perry hesitated. "Plain pleasures," she began, "like the ones that come without crowds or fancy food." She searched her brain for more examples. "Plain pleasures like this potato bake instead of dancing and whisky and bands. . . . Like a picnic but not the kind with a thousand extra things that get thrown out in a ditch because they don't get eaten up. I've seen grown people throw cakes away because they were too lazy to wrap them up and take them back home. Have you seen that go on?"

"No, I don't think so," said Mr. Drake.

"They waste a lot," she remarked.

"Well, I do like plain pleasures," put in Mr. Drake, anxious that she should not lose the thread of the conversation.

"Don't you think that plain pleasures are closer to the heart of God?" she asked him.

He was a little embarrassed at her mentioning anything so solemn and so intimate on such short acquaintance, and he could not bring himself to answer her. Mrs. Perry, who was ordinarily shut-mouthed, felt a stream of words swelling in her throat.

"My sister, Dorothy Alvarez," she began without further introduction, "goes to all gala affairs downtown. She has invited me to go and raise the dickens with her, but I won't go. She's the merriest one in her group and separated from her husband. They take her all the places with them. She can eat dinner in a restaurant every night if she wants to. She's crazy about fried fish and all kinds of things. I don't pay much mind to what I eat unless it's a potato bake like this. We each have only one single life which is our real life, starting at the cradle and ending at the grave. I warn Dorothy every time I see her that if she doesn't watch out her life is going to be left aching and starving on the side of the road and she's going to get to her grave without it. The farther a man follows the rainbow, the harder it is for him to get back to the life which he left starving like an old dog. Sometimes when a man gets older he has a revelation and wants awfully bad to get back to the place where he left his life, but he can't get to that place—not often. It's always better to stay alongside of your life. I told Dorothy that life was not a tree with a million different blossoms on it." She reflected upon this for a moment in silence and then continued. "She has a box that she puts pennies and nickels in when she thinks she's running around too much and she uses the money in the box to buy candles with for church. But that's all she'll do for her spirit, which is not enough for a grown woman."

Mr. Drake's face was strained because he was trying terribly hard to follow closely what she was saying, but he was so fearful lest she reveal some intimate secret of her sister's and later regret it that his mind was almost completely closed to everything else. He was fully prepared to stop her if she went too far.

The potatoes were done and Mrs. Perry offered him two of them.

"Have some potatoes?" she said to him. The wind was colder now than when they had first sat down, and it blew around the pigpen.

"How do you feel about these cold howling nights that we have? Do you mind them?" Mrs. Perry asked.

"I surely do," said John Drake.

She looked intently at his face. "He is as red as a cherry," she said to herself.

"I might have preferred to live in a warm climate maybe," Mr. Drake was saying very slowly with a dreamy look in his eye, "if I happened to believe in a lot of unnecessary changing around. A lot of going forth and back, I mean." He blushed because he was approaching a subject that was close to his heart.

"Yes, yes, yes," said Mrs. Perry. "A lot of switching around is no good."

"When I was a younger man I had a chance to go way down south to Florida," he continued. "I had an offer to join forces with an alligator-farm project, but there was no security in the alligators. It might not have been a successful farm; it was not the risk that I minded so much, because I have always yearned to see palm trees and coconuts and the like. But I also believed that a man has to have a pretty good reason for moving around. I think that is what finally stopped me from going down to Florida and raising alligators. It was not the money, because I was not raised to give money first place. It was just that I felt then the way I do now, that if a man leaves home he must leave for some very good reason—like the boys who went to construct the Panama Canal or for any other decent reason. Otherwise I think he ought to stay in his own home town, so that nobody can say about him, 'What does he think he can do here that we can't?' At least that is what I think people in a strange town would say about a man like myself if I landed there with some doubtful venture as my only excuse for leaving home. My brother don't feel that way. He never stays in one place more than three months." He ate his potato with a woeful look in his eye, shaking his head from side to side.

Mrs. Perry's mind was wandering, so that she was very much startled when he suddenly stood up and extended his hand to her.

"I'll leave now," he said, "but in return for the potatoes, will you come and have supper with me at a restaurant tomorrow night?"

She had not received an invitation of this kind in many years, having deliberately withdrawn from life in town, and she did not know how to answer him. "Do you think I should do that?" she asked.

Mr. Drake assured her that she should do it and she accepted his invitation. On the following afternoon, Mrs. Perry waited for the bus at the foot of the short cement bridge below the house. She needed help and advice from her sister about a lavender dress which no longer fitted her. She herself had never been able to sew well and she knew little about altering women's garments. She intended to wear her dress to the restaurant where she was to meet John Drake, and she was carrying it tucked under her arm.

Dorothy Alvarez lived on a side street in one half of a two-family house. She was seated in her parlor entertaining a man when Mrs. Perry rang the bell. The parlor was immaculate but difficult to rest in because of the many bright and complicated patterns of the window curtains and the furniture covers, not the least disquieting of which was an enormous orange and black flowerpot design repeated a dozen times on the linoleum floor covering.

Dorothy pulled the curtain aside and peeked out to see who was ringing her bell. She was a curly-headed little person, with thick, unequal cheeks that were painted bright pink.

She was very much startled when she looked out and saw her sister, as she had not been expecting to see her until the following week.

"Oh!" Dorothy exclaimed.

"Who is it?" her guest asked.

"It's my sister. You better get out of here, because she must have something serious to talk to me about. You better go out the back door. She don't like bumping up against strangers."

The man was vexed, and left without bidding Dorothy good-bye. She ran to the door and let Mrs. Perry in.

"Sit down," she said, pulling her into the parlor. "Sit down and tell me what's new." She poured some hard candy from a paper bag into a glass dish.

"I wish you would alter this dress for me or help me do it," said Mrs. Perry. "I want it for tonight. I'm meeting Mr. Drake, my neighbor, at the restaurant down the street, so I thought I could dress in your house and leave from here. If you did the alteration yourself. I'd pay you for it."

Dorothy's face fell. "Why do you offer to pay me for it when I'm your sister?"

Mrs. Perry looked at her in silence. She did not answer, because she did not know why herself. Dorothy tried the dress on her sister and pinned it here and there. "I'm glad you're going out at last," she said. "Don't you want some beads?"

"I'll take some beads if you've got a spare string."

"Well I hope this is the right guy for you," said Dorothy, with her customary lack of tact. "I would give anything for you to be in love, so you would quit living in that ugly house and come and live on some street nearby. Think how different everything would be for me. You'd be jollier too if you had a husband who was dear to you. Not like the last one. . . . I suppose I'll never stop dreaming and hoping," she added nervously because she realized, but, as always, a little too late, that her sister hated to discuss such matters. "Don't think," she began weakly, "that I'm so happy here all the time. I'm not so serious and solemn as you, of course. . . ."

"I don't know what you've been talking about," said Alva Perry, twisting impatiently. "I'm going out to have a dinner."

"I wish you were closer to me," whined Dorothy. "I get blue in this parlor some nights."

"I don't think you get very blue," Mrs. Perry remarked briefly.

"Well, as long as you're going out, why don't you pep up?"

"I am pepped up," replied Mrs. Perry.

Mrs. Perry closed the restaurant door behind her and walked the full length of the room, peering into each booth in search of her escort. He had apparently not yet arrived, so she chose an empty booth and seated herself inside on the wooden bench. After fifteen minutes she decided that he was not coming and, repressing the deep hurt that this caused her, she focused her full attention on the menu and succeeded in shutting Mr. Drake from her mind. While she was reading the menu, she unhooked her string of beads and tucked them away in her purse. She had called the waitress and was ordering pork when Mr. Drake arrived. He greeted her with a timid smile.

"I see that you are ordering your dinner," he said, squeezing into his side of the booth. He looked with admiration at her lavender dress, which exposed her pale chest. He would have preferred that she be bareheaded because he loved women's hair. She had on an ungainly black felt hat which she always wore in every kind of weather. Mr. Drake remembered with intense pleasure the potato bake in front of the fire and he was much more excited than he had imagined he would be to see her once again.

Unfortunately she did not seem to have any impulse to communicate with him and his own tongue was silenced in a very short time. They ate the first half of their meal without saying anything at all to each other. Mr. Drake had ordered a bottle of sweet wine and after Mrs. Perry had finished her second glass she finally spoke. "I think they cheat you in restaurants."

He was pleased she had made any remark at all, even though it was of an ungracious nature.

"Well, it is usually to be among the crowd that we pay large prices for small portions," he said, much to his own surprise, for he had always considered himself a lone wolf, and his behavior had never belied this. He sensed this same quality in Mrs. Perry, but he was moved by a strange desire to mingle with her among the flock.

"Well, don't you think what I say is true?" he asked hesitantly. There appeared on his face a curious, dislocated smile and he held his head in an outlandishly erect position which betrayed his state of tension.

Mrs. Perry wiped her plate clean with a piece of bread. Since she was not in the habit of drinking more than once every few years, the wine was going very quickly to her head.

"What time does the bus go by the door here?" she asked in a voice that was getting remarkably loud.

"I can find out for you if you really want to know. Is there any reason why you want to know now?"

"I've got to get home some time so I can get up tomorrow morning."

"Well, naturally I will take you home in my truck when you

want to go, but I hope you won't go yet." He leaned forward and studied her face anxiously.

"I can get home all right," she answered him glumly, "and it's just as good now as later."

"Well, no, it isn't," he said, deeply touched, because there was no longer any mistaking her distinctly inimical attitude. He felt that he must at any cost keep her with him and enlist her sympathies. The wine was contributing to this sudden aggressiveness, for it was not usually in his nature to make any effort to try to get what he wanted. He now began speaking to her earnestly and quickly.

"I want to share a full evening's entertainment with you, or even a week of entertainment," he said, twisting nervously on his bench. "I know where all the roadside restaurants and dance houses are situated all through the county. I am master of my truck, and no one can stop me from taking a vacation if I want to. It's a long time since I took a vacation—not since I was handed out my yearly summer vacation when I went to school. I never spent any real time in any of these roadside houses, but I know the proprietors, nearly all of them, because I have lived here all of my life. There is one dance hall that is built on a lake. I know the proprietor. If we went there, we could stray off and walk around the water, if that was agreeable to you." His face was a brighter red than ever and he appeared to be temporarily stripped of the reserved and cautious demeanor that had so characterized him the evening before. Some quality in Mrs. Perry's nature which he had only dimly perceived at first now sounded like a deep bell within himself because of her anger and he was flung backward into a forgotten and weaker state of being. His yearning for a word of kindness from her increased every minute.

Mrs. Perry sat drinking her wine more and more quickly and her resentment mounted with each new glass.

"I know all the proprietors of dance houses in the county also," she said. "My sister Dorothy Alvarez has them up to her house for beer when they take a holiday. I've got no need to meet anybody new or see any new places. I even know this place we are eating in from a long time ago. I had dinner here with my husband a few times." She looked around her. "I remember *him*," she said, pointing a long arm at the proprietor, who had just stepped out of the kitchen.

"How are you after these many years?" she called to him.

Mr. Drake was hesitant about what to do. He had not realized that Mrs. Perry was getting as drunk as she seemed to be now. Ordinarily he would have felt embarrassed and would have hastened to lead her out of the restaurant, but he thought that she might be more approachable drunk and nothing else mattered to him. "I'll stay with you for as long as you like," he said.

His words spun around in Mrs. Perry's mind. "What are you making a bid for, anyway?" she asked him, leaning back heavily against the bench.

"Nothing dishonorable," he said. "On the contrary, something extremely honorable if you will accept." Mr. Drake was so distraught that he did not know exactly what he was saying, but Mrs. Perry took his words to mean a proposal of marriage, which was unconsciously what he had hoped she would do. Mrs. Perry looked at even this exciting offer through the smoke of her resentment.

"I suppose," she said, smiling joylessly, "that you would like a lady to mash your potatoes for you three times a day. But I am not a mashed-potato masher and I never have been. I would prefer," she added, raising her voice, "I would prefer to have *him* mash my potatoes for *me* in a big restaurant kitchen." She nodded in the direction of the proprietor, who had remained standing in front of the kitchen door so that he could watch Mrs. Perry. This time he grinned and winked his eye.

Mrs. Perry fumbled through the contents of her purse in search of a handkerchief and, coming upon her sister's string of beads, she pulled them out and laid them in her gravy. "I am not a mashed-potato masher," she repeated, and then without warning she clambered out of the booth and lumbered down the aisle. She disappeared up a dark brown staircase at the back of the restaurant. Both Mr. Drake and the proprietor assumed that she was going to the ladies' toilet.

Actually Mrs. Perry was not specifically in search of the toilet, but rather for any place where she could be alone. She walked down the hall upstairs and jerked open a door on her left, closing it behind her. She stood in total darkness for a minute, and then, feeling a chain brush her forehead, she yanked at it brutally, lighting the room from a naked ceiling bulb, which she almost pulled down together with its fixtures.

She was standing at the foot of a double bed with a high Victorian headboard. She looked around her and, noticing a chair placed underneath a small window, she walked over to it and pushed the window open, securing it with a short stick; then she sat down.

"This is perfection," she said aloud, glaring at the ugly little room. "This is surely a gift from the Lord." She squeezed her hands together until her knuckles were white. "Oh, how I love it here! How I love it! How I love it!"

She flung one arm out over the window sill in a gesture of abandon, but she had not noticed that the rain was teeming down, and it soaked her lavender sleeve in a very short time.

"Mercy me!" she remarked, grinning. "It's raining here. The people at the dinner tables don't get the rain, but I do and I like it!" She smiled benignly at the rain. She sat there half awake and half asleep and then slowly she felt a growing certainty that she could reach her own room from where she was sitting without ever returning to the restaurant. "I have kept the pathway open all my life," she muttered in a thick voice, "so that I could get back."

A few moments later she said, "I am sitting there." An expression of malevolent triumph transformed her face and she made a slight effort to stiffen her back. She remained for a long while in the stronghold of this fantasy, but it gradually faded and in the end dissolved. When she drew her cold shaking arm in out of the rain, the tears were streaming down her cheeks. Without ceasing to cry she crept on to the big double bed and fell asleep, face downward, with her hat on.

Meanwhile the proprietor had come quietly upstairs, hoping that he would bump into her as she came out of the ladies' toilet. He had been flattered by her attention and he judged that in her present drunken state it would be easy to sneak a kiss from her and perhaps even more. When he saw the beam of light shining under his own bedroom door, he stuck his tongue out over his lower lip and smiled. Then he tiptoed down the stairs, plotting on the way what he would tell Mr. Drake.

Everyone had left the restaurant, and Mr. Drake was walking

up and down the aisle when the proprietor reached the bottom of the staircase.

"I am worried about my lady friend," Mr. Drake said, hurrying up to him. "I am afraid that she may have passed out in the toilet."

"The truth is," the proprietor answered, "that she has passed out in an empty bedroom upstairs. Don't worry about it. My daughter will take care of her if she wakes up feeling sick. I used to know her husband. You can't do nothing about her now." He put his hands into his pockets and looked solemnly into Mr. Drake's eyes.

Mr. Drake, not being equal to such a delicate situation, paid his bill and left. Outside he crawled into his freshly painted red truck and sat listening desolately to the rain.

The next morning Mrs. Perry awakened a little after sunrise. Thanks to her excellent constitution she did not feel very sick, but she lay motionless on the bed looking around her at the walls for a long time. Slowly she remembered that this room she was lying in was above the restaurant, but she did not know how she had gotten there. She remembered the dinner with Mr. Drake, but not much of what she had said to him. It did not occur to her to blame him for her present circumstance. She was not hysterical at finding herself in a strange bed because, although she was a very tense and nervous woman, she possessed great depth of emotion and only certain things concerned her personally.

She felt very happy and she thought of her uncle who had passed out at a convention fifteen years ago. He had walked around the town all the morning without knowing where he was. She smiled.

After resting a little while longer, she got out of bed and clothed herself. She went into the hall and found the staircase and she descended with bated breath and a fast-beating heart, because she was so eager to get back down into the restaurant.

It was flooded with sunshine and still smelled of meat and sauce. She walked a little unsteadily down the aisle between the rows of wooden booths and tables. The tables were all bare and scrubbed clean. She looked anxiously from one to the other, hoping to select the booth they had sat in, but she was unable to choose among them. The tables were all identical. In a moment this anonymity served only to heighten her tenderness.

"John Drake," she whispered. "My sweet John Drake."

1946

Camp Cataract

BERYL KNOCKED on Harriet's cabin door and was given permission to enter. She found her friend seated near the window, an open letter in her hand.

"Good evening, Beryl," said Harriet. "I was just reading a letter from my sister." Her fragile, spinsterish face wore a canny yet slightly hysterical expression.

Beryl, a stocky blond waitress with stubborn eyes, had developed a dogged attachment to Harriet and sat in her cabin whenever she had a moment to spare. She rarely spoke in Harriet's presence, nor was she an attentive listener.

"I'll read you what she says; have a seat." Harriet indicated a straight chair and Beryl dragged it into a dark corner where she sat down. It creaked dangerously under the weight of her husky body.

"Hope I don't bust the chair," said Beryl, and she blushed furiously, digging her hands deep into the pockets of the checked plus-fours she habitually wore when she was not on duty.

"'Dear Sister,'" Harriet read. "'You are still at Camp Cataract visiting the falls and enjoying them. I always want you to have a good time. This is your fifth week away. I suppose you go on standing behind the falls with much enjoyment like you told me all the guests did. I think you said only the people who don't stay overnight have to pay to stand behind the waterfall . . . you stay ten weeks . . . have a nice time, dear. Here everything is exactly the same as when you left. The apartment doesn't change. I have something I want to tell you, but first let me say that if you get nervous, why don't you come home instead of waiting until you are no good for the train trip? Such a thing could happen. I wonder of course how you feel about the apartment once you are by the waterfall. Also, I want to put this to you. Knowing that you have an apartment and a loving family must make Camp Cataract quite a different place than it would be if it were all the home and loving you had. There must be wretches like that up there. If you see them, be sure to give them loving because they are the lost souls of the earth. I fear nomads. I am afraid of them and afraid for them too. I don't know what I would do if any of my dear ones were seized with the wanderlust. We are meant to cherish those who through God's will are given into our hands. First of all come the members of the family, and for this it is better to live as close as possible. Maybe you would say, "Sadie is old-fashioned; she doesn't want people to live on their own." I am not old-fashioned, but I don't want any of us to turn into nomads. You don't grow rich in spirit by widening your circle but by tending your own. When you are gone, I get afraid about you. I think that you might be seized with the wanderlust and that you are not remembering the apartment very much. Particularly this trip . . . but then I know this cannot be true and that only my nerves make me think such things. It's so hot out. This is a record-breaking summer. Remember, the apartment is not just a row of rooms. It is the material proof that our spirits are so wedded that we have but one blessed roof over our heads. There are only three of us in the apartment related by blood, but Bert Hoffer has joined the three through the normal channels of marriage, also sacred. I know that you feel this way too about it and that just nerves makes me think Camp Cataract can change anything. May I remind you also that if this family is a garland, you are the middle flower; for me you are anyway. Maybe Evy's love is now flowing more to Bert Hoffer because he's her husband, which is natural. I wish they didn't think you needed to go to Camp Cataract because of your spells. Haven't I always tended you when you had them? Bert's always taken Evy to the Hoffers and we've stayed together, just the two of us, with the door safely locked so you wouldn't in your excitement run to a neighbor's house at all hours of the morning. Evy liked going to the Hoffers because they always gave her chicken with dumplings or else goose with red cabbage. I hope you haven't got it in your head that just because you are an old maid you have to go somewhere and be by yourself. Remember, I am also an old maid. I must close now, but I am not satisfied with my letter because I have so much more to say. I know you love the apartment and feel the way I feel. You are simply getting a tourist's thrill out of being there in a cabin like all of us do. I count the days until your sweet return. Your loving sister, Sadie.'"

Harriet folded the letter. "Sister Sadie," she said to Beryl, "is a great lover of security."

"She sounds swell," said Beryl, as if Harriet were mentioning her for the first time, which was certainly not the case.

"I have no regard for it whatsoever," Harriet announced in a positive voice. "*None.* In fact, I am a great admirer of the nomad, vagabonds, gypsies, seafaring men. I tip my hat to them; the old prophets roamed the world for that matter too, and most of the visionaries." She folded her hands in her lap with an air of satisfaction. Then, clearing her throat as if for a public address, she continued. "I don't give a tinker's damn about feeling part of a community, I can assure you. . . . That's not why I stay on at the apartment . . . not for a minute, but it's a good reason why she does . . . I mean Sadie; she loves a community spirit and she loves us all to be in the apartment because the apartment is in the community. She can get an actual thrill out of knowing that. But of course I can't . . . I never could, never in a thousand years."

She tilted her head back and half-closed her eyes. In the true style of a person given to interminable monologues, she was barely conscious of her audience. "Now," she said, "we can come to whether I, on the other hand, get a thrill out of Camp Cataract." She paused for a moment as if to consider this. "Actually, I don't," she pronounced sententiously, "but if you like, I will clarify my statement by calling Camp Cataract my *tree house.* You remember tree houses from your younger days. . . . You climb into them when you're a child and plan to run away from home once you are safely hidden among the leaves. They're popular with children. Suppose I tell you point-blank that I'm an extremely original woman, but also a very shallow one . . . in a sense, a *very* shallow one. I am afraid of scandal." Harriet assumed a more erect position. "I despise anything that smacks of a bohemian dash for freedom; I know that this has nothing to do with the more serious things in life . . . I'm sure there are hundreds of serious people who kick over their traces and jump into the gutter; but I'm too shallow for anything like that . . . I know it and I enjoy knowing it. Sadie on the other hand cooks and cleans all day long and yet takes her life as seriously as she would a religion . . . myself and the apartment and the Hoffers. By the Hoffers, I mean my sister Evy and her big pig of a husband Bert." She made a wry face. "I'm the only one with taste in the family but I've never even suggested a lamp for the apartment. I wouldn't lower myself by becoming involved. I do however refuse to make an unseemly dash for freedom. I refuse to be known as 'Sadie's wild sister Harriet.' There is something intensively repulsive to me about unmarried women setting out on their own . . . also a very shallow attitude. You may wonder how a woman can be shallow and know it at the same time, but then, this is precisely the tragedy of any person, if he allows himself to be griped." She paused for a moment and looked into the darkness with a fierce light in her eyes. "Now let's get back to Camp Cataract," she said with renewed vigor. "The pine groves, the canoes, the sparkling purity of the brook water and cascade . . . the cabins . . . the marshmallows, the respectable clientele."

"Did you ever think of working in a garage?" Beryl suddenly blurted out, and then she blushed again at the sound of her own voice.

"No," Harriet answered sharply. "Why should I?"

Beryl shifted her position in her chair. "Well," she said, "I think I'd like that kind of work better than waiting on tables. Especially if I could be boss and own my garage. It's hard, though, for a woman."

Harriet stared at her in silence. "Do you think Camp Cataract smacks of the gutter?" she asked a minute later.

"No, sir. . . ." Beryl shook her head with a woeful air.

"Well then, there you have it. It is, of course, the farthest point from the gutter that one could reach. Any blockhead can see that. My plan is extremely complicated and from my point of view rather brilliant. First I will come here for several years . . . I don't know yet exactly how many, but long enough to imitate roots . . . I mean to imitate the natural family roots of childhood . . . long enough so that I myself will feel: "Camp Cataract is *habit*, Camp Cataract is life, Camp Cataract is not escape." Escape is unladylike, habit isn't. As I remove myself gradually from within my family circle and establish myself more and more solidly into Camp Cataract, then from here at some later date I can start making my sallies into the outside world almost unnoticed. None of it will seem to the onlooker like an ugly impetuous escape. I intend to rent the same cabin every year and to stay a little longer each time. Meanwhile I'm learning a great deal about trees and flowers and bushes . . . I am interested in nature." She was quiet for a moment. "It's rather lucky too," she added, "that the doctor has approved of my separating from the family for several months out of every year. He's a blockhead and doesn't remotely suspect the extent of my scheme nor how perfectly he fits into it . . . in fact, he has even sanctioned my request that no one visit me here at the camp. I'm afraid if Sadie did, and she's the only one who would dream of it, I wouldn't be able to avoid a wrangle and then I might have a fit. The fits are unpleasant; I get much more nervous than I usually am and there's a blank moment or two." Harriet glanced sideways at Beryl to see how she was reacting to this last bit of information, but Beryl's face was impassive.

"So you see my plan," she went on, in a relaxed, offhand manner, "complicated, a bit dotty and completely original . . . but then, I *am* original . . . not like my sisters . . . oddly enough I don't even seem to belong socially to the same class as my sisters do. I am somehow"—she hesitated for a second—"more fashionable."

Harriet glanced out of the window. Night had fallen during the course of her monologue and she could see a light burning in the next cabin. "Do you think I'm a coward?" she asked Beryl.

The waitress was startled out of her torpor. Fortunately her brain registered Harriet's question as well. "No, sir," she answered. "If you were, you wouldn't go out paddling canoes solo, with all the scary shoots you run into up and down these rivers. . . ."

Harriet twisted her body impatiently. She had a sudden and uncontrollable desire to be alone. "Good-bye," she said rudely. "I'm not coming to supper."

Beryl rose from her chair. "I'll save something for you in case you get hungry after the dining room's closed. I'll be hanging around the lodge like I always am till bedtime." Harriet nodded and the waitress stepped out of the cabin, shutting the door carefully behind her so that it would not make any noise.

Harriet's sister Sadie was a dark woman with loose features and sad eyes. She was turning slightly to fat in her middle years, and did not in any way resemble Harriet, who was only a few years her senior. Ever since she had written her last letter to Harriet about Camp Cataract and the nomads Sadie had suffered from a feeling of steadily mounting suspense—the suspense itself a curious mingling of apprehension and thrilling anticipation. Her appetite grew smaller each day and it was becoming increasingly difficult for her to accomplish her domestic tasks.

She was standing in the parlor gazing with blank eyes at her new furniture set—two enormous easy chairs with bulging arms and a sofa in the same style—when she said aloud: "I can talk to her better than I can put it in a letter." Her voice had been automatic and when she heard her own words a rush of unbounded joy flooded her heart. Thus she realized that she was going on a little journey to Camp Cataract. She often made important decisions this way, as if some prearranged plot were being suddenly revealed to her, a plot which had immediately to be concealed from the eyes of others, because for Sadie, if there was any problem implicit in making a decision, it lay, not in the difficulty of choosing, but in the concealment of her choice. To her, secrecy was the real absolution from guilt, so automatically she protected all of her deepest feelings and compulsions from the eyes of Evy, Bert Hoffer and the other members of the family, although she had no interest in understanding or examining these herself.

The floor shook; recognizing Bert Hoffer's footsteps, she made a violent effort to control the flux of her blood so that the power of her emotion would not be reflected in her cheeks. A moment later her brother-in-law walked across the room and settled in one of the easy chairs. He sat frowning at her for quite a little while without uttering a word in greeting, but Sadie had long ago grown accustomed to his unfriendly manner; even in the beginning it had not upset her too much because she was such an obsessive that she was not very concerned with outside details.

"God-damned velours," he said finally. "It's the hottest stuff I ever sat on."

"Next summer we'll get covers," Sadie reassured him, "with a flower pattern if you like. What's your favorite flower?" she asked, just to make conversation and to distract him from looking at her face.

Bert Hoffer stared at her as if she'd quite taken leave of her senses. He was a fat man with a red face and wavy hair. Instead of answering this question, which he considered idiotic, he mopped his brow with his handkerchief.

"I'll fix you a canned pineapple salad for supper," she said to him with glowing eyes. "It will taste better than heavy meat on a night like this."

"If you're going to dish up pineapple salad for supper," Bert Hoffer answered with a dark scowl, "you can telephone some other guy to come and eat it. You'll find me over at Martie's Tavern eating meat and potatoes, if there's any messages to deliver."

"I thought because you were hot," said Sadie.

"I was talking about the velvet, wasn't I? I didn't say anything about the meat."

He was a very trying man indeed, particularly in a small apartment, but Sadie never dwelled upon this fact at all. She was delighted to cook and clean for him and for her sister Evelyn so long as they consented to live under the same roof with her and Harriet.

Just then Evelyn walked briskly into the parlor. Like Sadie she was dark, but here the resemblance ceased, for she had a small and wiry build, with a flat chest, and her hair was as straight as an Indian's. She stared at her husband's shirt sleeves and at Sadie's apron with distaste. She was wearing a crisp summer dress with a very low neckline, an unfortunate selection for one as bony and fierce-looking as she.

"You both look ready for the dump heap, not for the dining room," she said to them. "Why do we bother to have a dining room . . . is it just a farce?"

"How was the office today?" Sadie asked her sister.

Evelyn looked at Sadie and narrowed her eyes in closer scrutiny. The muscles in her face tightened. There was a moment of dead silence, and Bert Hoffer, cocking a wary eye in his wife's direction, recognized the dangerous flush on her cheeks. Secretly he was pleased. He loved to look on when Evelyn blew up at Sadie, but he tried to conceal his enjoyment because he did not consider it a very masculine one.

"What's the matter with you?" Evelyn asked finally, drawing closer to Sadie. "There's something wrong besides your dirty apron."

Sadie colored slightly but said nothing.

"You look crazy," Evelyn yelled. "What's the matter with you? You look so crazy I'd be almost afraid to ask you to go to the store for something. Tell me what's happened!" Evelyn was very excitable; nonetheless hers was a strong and sane nature.

"I'm not crazy," Sadie mumbled. "I'll go get the dinner." She pushed slowly past Evelyn and with her heavy step she left the parlor.

The mahogany dining table was much too wide for the small oblong-shaped room, clearing the walls comfortably only at the two ends. When many guests were present some were seated first on one side of the room and were then obliged to draw the table toward themselves, until its edge pressed painfully into their diaphragms, before the remaining guests could slide into their seats on the opposite side.

Sadie served the food, but only Bert Hoffer ate with any appetite. Evelyn jabbed at her meat once or twice, tasted it, and dropped her fork, which fell with a clatter on to her plate.

Had the food been more savory she might not have pursued her attack on Sadie until later, or very likely she would have forgotten it altogether. Unfortunately, however, Sadie, although she insisted on fulfilling the role of housewife, and never allowed the others to acquit themselves of even the smallest domestic task, was a poor cook and a careless cleaner as well. Her lumpy gravies were tasteless, and she had once or twice boiled a good cut of steak out of indifference. She was lavish, too, in spite of being indifferent, and kept her cupboards so loaded with food that a certain quantity spoiled each week and there was often an unpleasant odor about the house. Harriet, in fact, was totally unaware of Sadie's true nature and had fallen into the trap her sister had instinctively prepared for her, because beyond wearing an apron and simulating the airs of other housewives, Sadie did not possess a community spirit at all, as Harriet had stated to Beryl the waitress. Sadie certainly yearned to live in the grown-up world that her parents had established for them when they were children, but in spite of the fact that she had wanted to live in that world with Harriet, and because of Harriet, she did not understand it properly. It remained mysterious to her even though she did all the housekeeping and managed the apartment entirely alone. She couldn't ever admit to herself that she lived in constant fear that Harriet would go away, but she brooded a great deal on outside dangers, and had she tried, she could not have remembered a time when this fear had not been her strongest emotion.

Sometimes an ecstatic and voracious look would come into her eyes, as if she would devour her very existence because she loved it so much. Such passionate moments of appreciation were perhaps her only reward for living a life which she knew in her heart was one of perpetual narrow escape. Although Sadie was neither sly nor tricky, but on the contrary profoundly sincere and ingenuous, she schemed unconsciously to keep the Hoffers in the apartment with them, because she did not want to reveal the true singleness of her interest either to Harriet or to herself. She sensed as well that Harriet would find it more difficult to break away from all three of them (because as a group they suggested a little society, which impressed her sister) than she would to escape from her alone. In spite of her mortal dread that Harriet might strike out on her own, she had never brooded on the possibility of her sister's marrying. Here, too, her instinct was correct: she knew that she was safe and referred often to the "normal channels of marriage," conscious all the while that such an intimate relationship with a man would be as uninteresting to Harriet as it would to herself.

From a financial point of view this communal living worked out more than satisfactorily. Each sister had inherited some real estate which yielded her a small monthly stipend; these stipends, combined with the extra money that the Hoffers contributed out of their salaries, covered their common living expenses. In return for the extra sum the Hoffers gave toward the household expenses, Sadie contributed her work, thus saving them the money they would have spent hiring a servant, had they lived alone. A fourth sister, whose marriage had proved financially more successful than Evy's, contributed generously toward Harriet's support at Camp Cataract, since Harriet's stipend certainly did not yield enough to cover her share of their living expenses at the apartment and pay for a long vacation as well.

Neither Sadie nor Bert Hoffer had looked up when Evy's fork clattered onto her plate. Sadie was truly absorbed in her own thoughts, whereas Bert Hoffer was merely pretending to be, while secretly he rejoiced at the unmistakable signal that his wife was about to blow up.

"When I find out why Sadie looks like that if she isn't going to be crazy, then I'll eat," Evelyn announced flatly, and she folded her arms across her chest.

"I'm not crazy," Sadie said indistinctly, glancing toward Bert Hoffer, not in order to enlist his sympathies, but to avoid her younger sister's sharp scrutiny.

"There's a big danger of your going crazy because of Grandma and Harriet," said Evelyn crossly. "That's why I get so nervous the minute you look a little out of the way, like you do tonight. It's not that you get Harriet's expression . . . but then you might be getting a different kind of craziness . . . maybe worse. She's all right if she can go away and there's not too much excitement . . . it's only in spells anyway. But you—you might get a worse kind. Maybe it would be steadier."

"I'm not going to be crazy," Sadie murmured apologetically.

Evelyn glowered in silence and picked up her fork, but then immediately she let it fall again and turned on her sister with renewed exasperation. "Why don't you ask me why *I'm* not going to be crazy?" she demanded. "Harriet's my sister and Grandma's my grandma just as much as she is yours, isn't she?"

Sadie's eyes had a faraway look.

"If you were normal," Evelyn pursued, "you'd give me an intelligent argument instead of not paying any attention. Do you agree, Hoffer?"

"Yes, I do," he answered soberly.

Evelyn stiffened her back. "I'm too much like everybody else to be crazy," she announced with pride. "At a picture show, I feel like the norm."

The technical difficulty of disappearing without announcing

her plan to Evelyn suddenly occurred to Sadie, who glanced up quite by accident at her sister. She knew, of course, that Harriet was supposed to avoid contact with her family during these vacation months at the doctor's request and even at Harriet's own; but like some herd animal, who though threatened with the stick continues grazing, Sadie pursued her thoughts imperturbably. She did not really believe in Harriet's craziness nor in the necessity of her visits to Camp Cataract, but she was never in conscious opposition to the opinions of her sisters. Her attitude was rather like that of a child who is bored by the tedium of grown-up problems and listens to them with a vacant ear. As usual she was passionately concerned only with successfully dissimulating what she really felt, and had she been forced to admit openly that there existed such a remarkable split between her own opinions and those of her sisters, she would have suffered unbelievable torment. She was able to live among them, listening to their conferences with her dead outside ear (the more affluent sister was also present at these sessions, and her husband as well), and even to contribute a pittance toward Harriet's support at the camp, without questioning the validity either of their decisions or of her own totally divergent attitude. By a self-imposed taboo, awareness of this split was denied her, and she had never reflected upon it.

Harriet had gone to Camp Cataract for the first time a year ago, after a bad attack of nerves combined with a return of her pleurisy. It had been suggested by the doctor himself that she go with his own wife and child instead of traveling with one of her sisters. Harriet had been delighted with the suggestion and Sadie had accepted it without a murmur. It was never her habit to argue, and in fact she had thought nothing of Harriet's leaving at the time. It was only gradually that she had begun writing the letters to Harriet about Camp Cataract, the nomads and the wanderlust—for she had written others similar to her latest one, but never so eloquent or full of conviction. Previous letters had contained a hint or two here and there, but had been for the main part factual reports about her summer life in the apartment. Since writing this last letter she had not been able to forget her own wonderful and solemn words (for she was rarely eloquent), and even now at the dinner table they rose continually in her throat so that she was thrilled over and over again and could not bother her head about announcing her departure to Evelyn. "It will be easier to write a note," she said to herself. "I'll pack my valise and walk out tomorrow afternoon, while they're at business. They can get their own dinners for a few days. Maybe I'll leave a great big meat loaf." Her eyes were shining like stars.

"Take my plate and put it in the warmer, Hoffer," Evelyn was saying. "I won't eat another mouthful until Sadie tells us what we can expect. If she feels she's going off, she can at least warn us about it. I deserve to know how she feels . . . I tell every single thing I feel to her and Harriet . . . I don't sneak around the house like a thief. In the first place I don't have any time for sneaking, I'm at the office all day! Is this the latest vogue, this sneaking around and hiding everything you can from your sister? Is it?" She stared at Bert Hoffer, widening her eyes in fake astonishment. He shrugged his shoulders.

"I'm no sneak or hypocrite and neither are you, Hoffer, you're no hypocrite. You're just sore at the world, but you don't pretend you love the world, do you?"

Sadie was lightheaded with embarrassment. She had blanched at Evy's allusion to her going, which she mistook naturally for a reference to her intention of leaving for Camp Cataract.

"Only for a few days . . ." she mumbled in confusion, "and then I'll be right back here at the table."

Evelyn looked at her in consternation. "What do you mean by announcing calmly how many days it's going to be?" she shouted at her sister. "That's really sacrilegious! Did you ever hear of such a crusty sacrilegious remark in your life before?" She turned to Bert Hoffer, with a horror-stricken expression on her face. "How can I go to the office and look neat and clean and happy when this is what I hear at home . . . when my sister sits here and says she'll only go crazy for a few days? How *can* I go to the office after that? How can I look right?"

"I'm not going to be crazy," Sadie assured her again in a sorrowful tone, because although she felt relieved that Evelyn had not, after all, guessed the truth, hers was not a nature to indulge itself in trivial glee at having put someone off her track.

"You just said you were going to be crazy," Evelyn exclaimed heatedly. "Didn't she, Bert?"

"Yes," he answered, "she did say something like that. . . ."

The tendons of Evelyn's neck were stretched tight as she darted her eyes from her sister's face to her husband's. "Now, tell me this much," she demanded, "do I go to the office every day looking neat and clean or do I go looking like a bum?"

"You look O.K.," Bert said.

"Then why do my sisters spit in my eye? Why do they hide everything from me if I'm so decent? I'm wide open, I'm frank, there's nothing on my mind besides what I say. Why can't they be like other sisters all over the world? One of them is so crazy that she must live in a cabin for her nerves at *my* expense, and the other one is planning to go crazy deliberately and behind my back." She commenced to struggle out of her chair, which as usual proved to be a slow and laborious task. Exasperated, she shoved the table vehemently away from her toward the opposite wall. "Why don't we leave the space all on one side when there's no company?" she screamed at both of them, for she was now annoyed with Bert Hoffer as well as with Sadie. Fortunately they were seated at either end of the table and so did not suffer as a result of her violent gesture, but the table jammed into four chairs ranged on the opposite side, pinning three of them backward against the wall and knocking the fourth onto the floor.

"Leave it there," Evelyn shouted dramatically above the racket. "Leave it there till doomsday," and she rushed headlong out of the room.

They listened to her gallop down the hall.

"What about the dessert?" Bert Hoffer asked Sadie with a frown. He was displeased because Evelyn had spoken to him sharply.

"Leftover bread pudding without raisins." She had just gotten up to fetch the pudding when Evelyn summoned them from the parlor.

"Come in here, both of you," she hollered. "I have something to say."

They found Evelyn seated on the couch, her head tilted way back on a cushion, staring fixedly at the ceiling. They settled into easy chairs opposite her.

"I could be normal and light in any other family," she said,

"I'm normally a gay light girl . . . not a morose one. I like all the material things."

"What do you want to do tonight?" Bert Hoffer interrupted, speaking with authority. "Do you want to be excited or do you want to go to the movies?" He was always bored by these self-appraising monologues which succeeded her explosions.

Evy looked as though she had not heard him, but after a moment or two of sitting with her eyes shut she got up and walked briskly out of the room; her husband followed her.

Neither of them had said good-bye to Sadie, who went over to the window as soon as they'd gone and looked down on the huge unsightly square below her. It was crisscrossed by trolley tracks going in every possible direction. Five pharmacies and seven cigar stores were visible from where she stood. She knew that modern industrial cities were considered ugly, but she liked them. "I'm glad Evy and Bert have gone to a picture show," Sadie remarked to herself after a while. "Evy gets high-strung from being at the office all day."

A little later she turned her back on the window and went to the dining room.

"Looks like the train went through here," she murmured, gazing quietly at the chairs tilted back against the wall and the table's unsightly angle; but the tumult in her breast had not subsided, even though she knew she was leaving for Camp Cataract. Beyond the first rush of joy she had experienced when her plan had revealed itself to her earlier, in the parlor, the feeling of suspense remained identical, a curious admixture of anxiety and anticipation, difficult to bear. Concerning the mechanics of the trip itself she was neither nervous nor foolishly excited. "I'll call up tomorrow," she said to herself, "and find out when the buses go, or maybe I'll take the train. In the morning I'll buy three different meats for the loaf, if I don't forget. It won't go rotten for a few days, and even if it does they can eat at Martie's or else Evy will make bologna and eggs . . . she knows how, and so does Bert." She was not really concentrating on these latter projects any more than she usually did on domestic details.

The lamp over the table was suspended on a heavy iron chain. She reached for the beaded string to extinguish the light. When she released it the massive lamp swung from side to side in the darkness.

"Would you like it so much by the waterfall if you didn't know the apartment was here?" she whispered into the dark, and she was thrilled again by the beauty of her own words. "How much more I'll be able to say when I'm sitting right next to her," she murmured almost with reverence. ". . . And then we'll come back here," she added simply, not in the least startled to discover that the idea of returning with Harriet had been at the root of her plan all along.

Without bothering to clear the plates from the table, she went into the kitchen and extinguished the light there. She was suddenly overcome with fatigue.

When Sadie arrived at Camp Cataract it was raining hard.

"This shingled building is the main lodge," the hack driver said to her. "The ceiling in there is three times higher than average, if you like that style. Go up on the porch and just walk in. You'll get a kick out of it."

Sadie reached into her pocketbook for some money.

"My wife and I come here to drink beer when we're in the mood," he continued, getting out his change. "If there's nobody much inside, don't get panicky; the whole camp goes to the movies on Thursday nights. The wagon takes them and brings them back. They'll be along soon."

After thanking him she got out of the cab and climbed the wooden steps on to the porch. Without hesitating she opened the door. The driver had not exaggerated; the room was indeed so enormous that it suggested a gymnasium. Wicker chairs and settees were scattered from one end of the floor to the other and numberless sawed-off tree stumps had been set down to serve as little tables.

Sadie glanced around her and then headed automatically for a giant fireplace, difficult to reach because of the accumulation of chairs and settees that surrounded it. She threaded her way between these and stepped across the hearth into the cold vault of the chimney, high enough to shelter a person of average stature. The andirons, which reached to her waist, had been wrought in the shape of witches. She fingered their pointed iron hats. "Novelties," she murmured to herself without enthusiasm. "They must have been especially made." Then, peering out of the fireplace, she noticed for the first time that she was not alone. Some fifty feet away a fat woman sat reading by the light of an electric bulb.

"She doesn't even know I'm in the fireplace," she said to herself. "Because the rain's so loud, she probably didn't hear me come in." She waited patiently for a while and then, suspecting that the woman might remain oblivious to her presence indefinitely, she called over to her. "Do you have anything to do with managing Camp Cataract?" she asked, speaking loudly so that she could be heard above the rain.

The woman ceased reading and switched her big light off at once, since the strong glare prevented her seeing beyond the radius of the bulb.

"No, I don't," she answered in a booming voice. "Why?"

Sadie, finding no answer to this question, remained silent.

"Do you think I look like a manager?" the woman pursued, and since Sadie had obviously no intention of answering, she continued the conversation by herself.

"I suppose you might think I was manager here, because I'm stout, and stout people have that look; also I'm about the right age for it. But I'm not the manager . . . I don't manage anything, anywhere. I have a domineering cranium all right, but I'm more the French type. I'd rather enjoy myself than give orders."

"French . . ." Sadie repeated hesitantly.

"Not French," the woman corrected her. "French *type*, with a little of the actual blood." Her voice was cold and severe.

For a while neither of them spoke, and Sadie hoped the conversation had drawn to a definite close.

"Individuality is my god," the woman announced abruptly, much to Sadie's disappointment. "That's partly why I didn't go to the picture show tonight. I don't like doing what the groups do, and I've seen the film." She dragged her chair forward so as to be heard more clearly. "The steadies here—we call the ones who stay more than a fortnight steadies—are all crazy to get into birds-of-a-feather-flock-together arrangements. If you look around, you can see for yourself how clubby the furniture is fixed. Well, they can go in for it, if they want, but I won't. I keep my chair out in the open here, and when I feel like it I take myself over to one circle or another . . .

there's about ten or twelve circles. Don't you object to the confinement of a group?"

"We haven't got a group back home," Sadie answered briefly.

"I don't go in for group worship either," the woman continued, "any more than I do for the heavy social mixing. I don't even go in for individual worship, for that matter. Most likely I was born to such a vigorous happy nature I don't feel the need to worry about what's up there over my head. I get the full flavor out of all my days whether anyone's up there or not. The groups don't allow for that kind of zip . . . never. You know what rotten apples in a barrel can do to the healthy ones."

Sadie, who had never before met an agnostic, was profoundly shocked by the woman's blasphemous attitude. "I'll bet she slept with a lot of men she wasn't married to when she was younger," she said to herself.

"Most of the humanity you bump into is unhealthy and nervous," the woman concluded, looking at Sadie with a cold eye, and then without further remarks she struggled out of her chair and began to walk toward a side door at the other end of the room. Just as she approached it the door was flung open from the other side by Beryl, whom the woman immediately warned of the new arrival. Beryl, without ceasing to spoon some beans out of a can she was holding, walked over to Sadie and offered to be of some assistance. "I can show you rooms," she suggested. "Unless you'd rather wait till the manager comes back from the movies."

When she realized, however, after a short conversation with Sadie, that she was speaking to Harriet's sister, a malevolent scowl darkened her countenance, and she spooned her beans more slowly.

"Harriet didn't tell me you were coming," she said at length; her tone was unmistakably disagreeable.

Sadie's heart commenced to beat very fast as she in turn realized that this woman in plus-fours was the waitress, Beryl, of whom Harriet had often spoken in her letters and at home.

"It's a surprise," Sadie told her. "I meant to come here before. I've been promising Harriet I'd visit her in camp for a long time now, but I couldn't come until I got a neighbor in to cook for Evy and Bert. They're a husband and wife . . . my sister Evy and her husband Bert."

"I know about those two," Beryl remarked sullenly. "Harriet's told me all about them."

"Will you please take me to my sister's cabin?" Sadie asked, picking up her valise and stepping forward.

Beryl continued to stir her beans around without moving.

"I thought you folks had some kind of arrangement," she said. She had recorded in her mind entire passages of Harriet's monologues out of love for her friend, although she felt no curiosity concerning the material she had gathered. "I thought you folks were supposed to stay in the apartment while she was away at camp."

"Bert Hoffer and Evy have never visited Camp Cataract," Sadie answered in a tone that was innocent of any subterfuge.

"You bet they haven't," Beryl pronounced triumphantly. "That's part of the arrangement. They're supposed to stay in the apartment while she's here at camp; the doctor said so."

"They're not coming up," Sadie repeated, and she still wore, not the foxy look that Beryl expected would betray itself at any moment, but the look of a person who is attentive though being addressed in a foreign language. The waitress sensed that all her attempts at starting a scrap had been successfully blocked for the present and she whistled carefully, dragging some chairs into line with a rough hand. "I'll tell you what," she said, ceasing her activities as suddenly as she had begun them. "Instead of taking you down there to the Pine Cones—that's the name of the grove where her cabin is—I'll go myself and tell her to come up here to the lodge. She's got some nifty rain equipment so she won't get wet coming through the groves like you would . . . lots of pine trees out there."

Sadie nodded in silence and walked over to a fantasy chair, where she sat down.

"They get a lot of fun out of that chair. When they're drunk," said Beryl pointing to its back, made of a giant straw disc. "Well . . . so long. . . ." She strode away. "Dear Valley . . ." Sadie heard her sing as she went out the door.

Sadie lifted the top off the chair's left arm and pulled two books out of its woven hamper. The larger volume was entitled *The Growth and Development of the Texas Oil Companies*, and the smaller, *Stories from Other Climes.* Hastily she replaced them and closed the lid.

*

Harriet opened the door for Beryl and quickly shut it again, but even in that instant the wooden flooring of the threshold was thoroughly soaked with rain. She was wearing a lavender kimono with a deep ruffle at the neckline; above it her face shone pale with dismay at Beryl's late and unexpected visit. She feared that perhaps the waitress was drunk. "I'm certainly not hacking out a free place for myself in this world just in order to cope with drunks," she said to herself with bitter verve. Her loose hair was hanging to her shoulders and Beryl looked at it for a moment in mute admiration before making her announcement.

"Your sister Sadie's up at the lodge," she said, recovering herself; then, feeling embarrassed, she shuffled over to her usual seat in the darkest corner of the room.

"What are you saying?" Harriet questioned her sharply.

"Your sister Sadie's up at the lodge," she repeated, not daring to look at her. "Your sister Sadie who wrote you the letter about the apartment."

"But she can't be!" Harriet screeched. "She can't be! It was all arranged that no one was to visit me here."

"That's what I told her," Beryl put in.

Harriet began pacing up and down the floor. Her pupils were dilated and she looked as if she were about to lose all control of herself. Abruptly she flopped down on the edge of the bed and began gulping in great draughts of air. She was actually practicing a system which she believed had often saved her from complete hysteria, but Beryl, who knew nothing about her method, was horrified and utterly bewildered. "Take it easy," she implored Harriet. "Take it easy!"

"Dash some water in my face," said Harriet in a strange voice, but horror and astonishment anchored Beryl securely to her chair, so that Harriet was forced to stagger over to the basin and manage by herself. After five minutes of steady dousing she wiped her face and chest with a towel and resumed her pacing. At each instant the expression on her face was more indignant and a trifle less distraught. "It's the boorishness of it that I find so appalling," she complained, a suggestion of theatricality in her tone which a moment before had not been present. "If she's determined to wreck my schemes, why doesn't she do it with some style, a little slight bit of cunning? I can't picture anything more boorish than hauling oneself onto a train and simply chugging straight up here. She has no sense of scheming, of intrigue in the grand manner . . . none whatever. Anyone meeting only Sadie would think the family raised potatoes for a living. Evy doesn't make a much better impression, I must say. If they met her they'd decide we were all clerks! But at least she goes to business. . . . She doesn't sit around thinking about how to mess my life up all day. She thinks about Bert Hoffer. Ugh!" She made a wry face.

"When did you and Sadie start fighting?" Beryl asked her.

"I don't fight with Sadie," Harriet answered, lifting her head proudly. "I wouldn't dream of fighting like a common fishwife. Everything that goes on between us goes on undercover. It's always been that way. I've always hidden everything from her ever since I was a little girl. She's perfectly aware that I know she's trying to hold me a prisoner in the apartment out of plain jealousy and she knows too that I'm afraid of being considered a bum, and that makes matters simpler for her. She pretends to be worried that I might forget myself if I left the apartment and commit a folly with some man I wasn't married to, but actually she knows perfectly well that I'm as cold as ice. I haven't the slightest interest in men . . . nor in women either for that matter; still if I stormed out of the apartment dramatically the way some do, they might think I was a bum on my way to a man . . . and I won't give Sadie that satisfaction, ever. As for marriage, of course I admit I'm peculiar and there's a bit wrong with me, but even so I shouldn't want to marry: I think the whole system of going through life with a partner is repulsive in every way." She paused, but only for a second. "Don't you imagine, however," she added severely, looking directly at Beryl, "don't you imagine that just because I'm a bit peculiar and different from the others, that I'm not fussy about my life. I *am* fussy about it, and I *hate* a scandal."

"To hell with sisters!" Beryl exclaimed happily. "Give 'em all a good swift kick in the pants." She had regained her own composure watching the color return to Harriet's cheeks and she was just beginning to think with pleasure that perhaps Sadie's arrival would serve to strengthen the bond of intimacy between herself and Harriet, when this latter buried her head in her lap and burst into tears. Beryl's face fell and she blushed at her own frivolousness.

"I can't any more," Harriet sobbed in anguished tones. "I can't . . . I'm old . . . I'm much too old." Here she collapsed and sobbed so pitifully that Beryl, wringing her hands in grief, sprang to her side, for she was a most tenderhearted person toward those whom she loved. "You are not old . . . you are beautiful," she said, blushing again, and in her heart she was thankful that Providence had granted her the occasion to console her friend in a grief-stricken moment, and to compliment her at the same time.

After a bit, Harriet's sobbing subsided, and jumping up from the bed, she grabbed the waitress. "Beryl," she gasped, "you must run back to the lodge right away." There was a beam of cunning in her tear-filled eyes.

"Sure will," Beryl answered.

"Go back to the lodge and see if there's a room left up there, and if there is, take her grip into it so that there will be no question of her staying in my cabin. I can't have her staying in my cabin. It's the only place I have in the whole wide world." The beam of cunning disappeared again and she looked at Beryl with wide, frightened eyes. ". . . And if there's no room?" she asked.

"Then I'll put her in my place," Beryl reassured her. "I've got a neat little cabin all to myself that she can have and I'll go bunk in with some dopey waitress."

"Well, then," said Harriet, "go, and hurry! Take her grip to a room in the upper lodge annex or to your own cabin before she has a chance to say anything, and then come straight back here for me. I can't get through these pine groves alone . . . now . . . I know I can't." It did not occur to her to thank Beryl for the kind offer she had made.

"All right," said the waitress, "I'll be back in a jiffy and don't you worry about a thing." A second later she was lumbering through the drenched pine groves with shining eyes.

When Beryl came into the lodge and snatched Sadie's grip up without a word of explanation, Sadie did not protest. Opposite her there was an open staircase which led to a narrow gallery hanging halfway between the ceiling and the floor. She watched the waitress climbing the stairs, but once she had passed the landing Sadie did not trouble to look up and follow her progress around the wooden balcony overhead.

A deep chill had settled into her bones, and she was like a person benumbed. Exactly when this present state had succeeded the earlier one Sadie could not tell, nor did she think to ask herself such a question, but a feeling of dread now lay like a stone in her breast where before there had been stirring such powerful sensations of excitement and suspense. "I'm so low," she said to herself. "I feel like I was sitting at my own funeral." She did not say this in the spirit of hyperbolic gloom which some people nurture to work themselves out of a bad mood, but in all seriousness and with her customary attitude of passivity; in fact, she wore the humble look so often visible on the faces of sufferers who are being treated in a free clinic. It did not occur to her that a connection might exist between her present dismal state and the mission she had come to fulfill at Camp Cataract, nor did she take any notice of the fact that the words which were to enchant Harriet and accomplish her return were no longer welling up in her throat as they had done all the past week. She feared that something dreadful might happen, but whatever it was, this disaster was as remotely connected with her as a possible train wreck. "I hope nothing bad happens . . ." she thought, but she didn't have much hope in her.

Harriet slammed the front door and Sadie looked up. For the first second or two she did not recognize the woman who stood on the threshold in her dripping rubber coat and hood. Beryl was beside her; puddles were forming around the feet of the two women. Harriet had rouged her cheeks rather more highly than usual in order to hide all traces of her crying spell. Her eyes were bright and she wore a smile that was fixed and hard.

"Not a night fit for man or beast," she shouted across to Sadie, using a voice that she thought sounded hearty and yet fashionable at the same time; she did this, not in order to impress her sister, but to keep her at a safe distance.

Sadie, instead of rushing to the door, stared at her with an air of perplexity. To her Harriet appeared more robust and coarse-featured than she had five weeks ago at the apartment, and yet she knew that such a rapid change of physiognomy was scarcely possible. Recovering, she rose and went to embrace her sister. The embrace failed to reassure her because of Harriet's wet rubber coat, and her feeling of estrangement became more defined. She backed away.

Upon hearing her own voice ring out in such hearty and fashionable tones, Harriet had felt crazily confident that she might, by continuing to affect this manner, hold her sister at bay for the duration of her visit. To increase her chances of success she had determined right then not to ask Sadie why she had come, but to treat the visit in the most casual and natural way possible.

"Have you put on fat?" Sadie asked, at a loss for anything else to say.

"I'll never be fat," Harriet replied quickly. "I'm a fruit lover, not a lover of starches."

"Yes, you love fruit," Sadie said nervously. "Do you want some? I have an apple left from my lunch."

Harriet looked aghast. "Now!" she exclaimed. "Beryl can tell you that I never eat at night; in fact I never come up to the lodge at night, *never*. I stay in my cabin. I've written you all about how early I get up . . . I don't know anything about the lodge at night," she added almost angrily, as though her sister had accused her of being festive.

"You don't?" Sadie looked at her stupidly.

"No, I don't. Are you hungry, by the way?"

"If she's hungry," put in Beryl, "we can go into the Grotto Room and I'll bring her the food there. The tables in the main dining room are all set up for tomorrow morning's breakfast."

"I despise the Grotto," said Harriet with surprising bitterness. Her voice was getting quite an edge to it, and although it still sounded fashionable it was no longer hearty.

"I'm not hungry," Sadie assured them both. "I'm sleepy."

"Well, then," Harriet replied quickly, jumping at the opportunity, "we'll sit here for a few minutes and then you must go to bed."

The three of them settled in wicker chairs close to the cold hearth. Sadie was seated opposite the other two, who both remained in their rubber coats.

"I really do despise the Grotto," Harriet went on. "Actually

I don't hang around the lodge at all. This is not the part of Camp Cataract that interests me. I'm interested in the pine groves, my cabin, the rocks, the streams, the bridge, and all the surrounding natural beauty . . . the sky also."

Although the rain still continued its drumming on the roof above them, to Sadie, Harriet's voice sounded intolerably loud, and she could not rid herself of the impression that her sister's face had grown fatter. "Now," she heard Harriet saying in her loud voice, "tell me about the apartment. . . . What's new, how are the dinners coming along, how are Evy and Bert?"

Fortunately, while Sadie was struggling to answer these questions, which unaccountably she found it difficult to do, the stout agnostic reappeared, and Harriet was immediately distracted.

"Rover," she called gaily across the room, "come and sit with us. My sister Sadie's here."

The woman joined them, seating herself beside Beryl, so that Sadie was now facing all three.

"It's a surprise to see you up at the lodge at night, Hermit," she remarked to Harriet without a spark of mischief in her voice.

"You see!" Harriet nodded at Sadie with immense satisfaction. "I was not fibbing, was I? How are Evy and Bert?" she asked again, her face twitching a bit. "Is the apartment hot?"

Sadie nodded.

"I don't know how long you plan to stay," Harriet rattled on, feeling increasingly powerful and therefore reckless, "but I'm going on a canoe trip the day after tomorrow for five days. We're going up the river to Pocahontas Falls. . . . I leave at four in the morning, too, which rather ruins tomorrow as well. I've been looking forward to this trip ever since last spring when I applied for my seat, back at the apartment. The canoes are limited, and the guides. . . . I'm devoted to canoe trips, as you know, and can fancy myself a red-skin all the way to the Falls and back, easily."

Sadie did not answer.

"There's nothing weird about it," Harriet argued. "It's in keeping with my hatred of industrialization. In any case, you can see what a chopped-up day tomorrow's going to be. I have to make my pack in the morning and I must be in bed by eight-thirty at night, the latest, so that I can get up at four. I'll have only one real meal, at two in the afternoon. I suggest we meet at two behind the souvenir booth; you'll notice it tomorrow." Harriet waited expectantly for Sadie to answer in agreement to this suggestion, but her sister remained silent.

"Speaking of the booth," said Rover, "I'm not taking home a single souvenir this year. They're expensive and they don't last."

"You can buy salt-water taffy at Gerald's Store in town," Beryl told her. "I saw some there last week. It's a little stale but very cheap."

"Why would they sell salt-water taffy in the mountains?" Rover asked irritably.

Sadie was half listening to the conversation; as she sat watching them, all three women were suddenly unrecognizable; it was as if she had flung open the door to some dentist's office and seen three strangers seated there. She sprang to her feet in terror.

Harriet was horrified. "What is it?" she yelled at her sister. "Why do you look like that? Are you mad?"

Sadie was pale and beads of sweat were forming under her felt hat, but the women opposite her had already regained their correct relation to herself and the present moment. Her face relaxed, and although her legs were trembling as a result of her brief but shocking experience, she felt immensely relieved that it was all over.

"Why did you jump up?" Harriet screeched at her. "Is it because you are at Camp Cataract and not at the apartment?"

"It must have been the long train trip and no food . . ." Sadie told herself, "only one sandwich."

"Is it because you are at Camp Cataract and not at the apartment?" Harriet insisted. She was really very frightened and wished to establish Sadie's fit as a purposeful one and not as an involuntary seizure similar to one of hers.

"It was a long and dirty train trip," Sadie said in a weary voice. "I had only one sandwich all day long, with no mustard or butter . . . just the processed meat. I didn't even eat my fruit."

"Beryl offered to serve you food in the Grotto!" Harriet

ranted. "Do you want some now or not? For heaven's sake, speak up!"

"No . . . no." Sadie shook her head sorrowfully. "I think I'd best go to bed. Take me to your cabin . . . I've got my slippers and my kimono and my nightgown in my satchel," she added, looking around her vaguely, for the fact that Beryl had carried her grip off had never really impressed itself upon her consciousness.

Harriet glanced at Beryl with an air of complicity and managed to give her a quick pinch. "Beryl's got you fixed up in one of the upper lodge annex rooms," she told Sadie in a false, chatterbox voice. "You'll be much more comfortable up here than you would be down in my cabin. We all use oil lamps in the grove and you know how dependent you are on electricity."

Sadie didn't know whether she was dependent on electricity or not since she had never really lived without it, but she was so tired that she said nothing.

"I get up terribly early and my cabin's drafty, besides," Harriet went on. "You'll be much more comfortable here. You'd hate the Boulder Dam wigwams as well. Anyway, the wigwams are really for boys and they're always full. There's a covered bridge leading from this building to the annex on the upper floor, so that's an advantage."

"O.K., folks," Beryl cut in, judging that she could best help Harriet by spurring them on to action. "Let's get going."

"Yes," Harriet agreed, "if we don't get out of the lodge soon the crowd will come back from the movies and we certainly want to avoid them."

They bade good night to Rover and started up the stairs.

"This balustrade is made of young birch limbs," Harriet told Sadie as they walked along the narrow gallery overhead. "I think it's very much in keeping with the lodge, don't you?"

"Yes, I do," Sadie answered.

Beryl opened the door leading from the balcony onto a covered bridge and stepped through it, motioning to the others. "Here we go onto the bridge," she said, looking over her shoulder. "You've never visited the annex, have you?" she asked Harriet.

"I've never had any reason to," Harriet answered in a huffy tone. "You know how I feel about my cabin."

They walked along the imperfectly fitted boards in the darkness. Gusts of wind blew about their ankles and they were constantly spattered with rain in spite of the wooden roofing. They reached the door at the other end very quickly, however, where they descended two steps leading into a short, brightly lit hall. Beryl closed the door to the bridge behind them. The smell of fresh plaster and cement thickened the damp air.

"This is the annex," said Beryl. "We put old ladies here mostly, because they can get back and forth to the dining room without going outdoors . . . and they've got the toilet right here, too." She flung open the door and showed it to them. "Then also," she added, "we don't like the old ladies dealing with oil lamps and here they've got electricity." She led them into a little room just at their left and switched on the light. "Pretty smart, isn't it?" she remarked, looking around her with evident satisfaction, as if she herself had designed the room; then, sauntering over to a modernistic wardrobe-bureau combination, she polished a corner of it with her pocket handkerchief. This piece was made of shiny brown wood and fitted with a rimless circular mirror. "Strong and good-looking," Beryl said, rapping on the wood with her knuckles. "Every room's got one."

Sadie sank down on the edge of the bed without removing her outer garments. Here, too, the smell of plaster and cement permeated the air, and the wind still blew about their ankles, this time from under the badly constructed doorsill.

"The cabins are much draftier than this," Harriet assured Sadie once again. "You'll be more comfortable here in the annex." She felt confident that establishing her sister in the annex would facilitate her plan, which was still to prevent her from saying whatever she had come to say.

Sadie was terribly tired. Her hat, dampened by the rain, pressed uncomfortably against her temples, but she did not attempt to remove it. "I think I've got to go to sleep," she muttered. "I can't stay awake any more."

"All right," said Harriet, "but don't forget tomorrow at two by the souvenir booth . . . you can't miss it. I don't want to see anyone in the morning because I can make my canoe pack better by myself . . . it's frightfully complicated. . . . But if I hurried I could meet you at one-thirty; would you prefer that?"

Sadie nodded.

"Then I'll do my best. . . . You see, in the morning I always practice imagination for an hour or two. It does me lots of good, but tomorrow I'll cut it short." She kissed Sadie lightly on the crown of her felt hat. "Good night," she said. "Is there anything I forgot to ask you about the apartment?"

"No," Sadie assured her. "You asked everything."

"Well, good night," said Harriet once again, and followed by Beryl, she left the room.

When Sadie awakened the next morning a feeling of dread still rested like a leaden weight on her chest. No sooner had she left the room than panic, like a small wing, started to beat under her heart. She was inordinately fearful that if she strayed any distance from the main lodge she would lose her way and so arrive late for her meeting with Harriet. This fear drove her to stand next to the souvenir booth fully an hour ahead of time. Fortunately the booth, situated on a small knoll, commanded an excellent view of the cataract, which spilled down from some high rock ledges above a deep chasm. A fancy bridge spanned this chasm only a few feet below her, so that she was able to watch the people crossing it as they walked back and forth between the camp site and the waterfall. An Indian chief in full war regalia was seated at the bridge entrance on a kitchen chair. His magnificent feather headdress curved gracefully in the breeze as he busied himself collecting the small toll that all the tourists paid on returning from the waterfall; he supplied them with change from a nickel-plated conductor's belt which he wore over his deer-hide jacket, embroidered with minute beads. He was an Irishman employed by the management, which supplied his costume. Lately he had grown careless, and often neglected to stain his freckled hands the deep brick color of his face. He divided his time between the bridge and the souvenir booth, clambering up the knoll whenever he sighted a customer.

A series of wooden arches, Gothic in conception, succeeded each other all the way across the bridge; bright banners fluttered from their rims, each one stamped with the initials of the camp, and some of them edged with a glossy fringe. Only a few feet away lay the dining terrace, a huge flagstone pavilion whose entire length skirted the chasm's edge.

Unfortunately, neither the holiday crowds, nor the festooned bridge, nor even the white waters of the cataract across the way could distract Sadie from her misery. She constantly glanced behind her at the dark pine groves wherein Harriet's cabin was concealed. She dreaded to see Harriet's shape define itself between the trees, but at the same time she feared that if her sister did not arrive shortly some terrible catastrophe would befall them both before she'd had a chance to speak. In truth all desire to convince her sister that she should leave Camp Cataract and return to the apartment had miraculously shriveled away, and with the desire, the words to express it had vanished too. This did not in any way alter her intention of accomplishing her mission; on the contrary, it seemed to her all the more desperately important now that she was almost certain, in her innermost heart, that her trip was already a failure. Her attitude was not an astonishing one, since like many others she conceived of her life as separate from herself; the road was laid out always a little ahead of her by sacred hands, and she walked down it without a question. This road, which was her life, would go on existing after her death, even as her death existed now while she still lived.

There were close to a hundred people dining on the terrace, and the water's roar so falsified the clamor of voices that one minute the guests seemed to be speaking from a great distance and the next right at her elbow. Every now and then she thought she heard someone pronounce her name in a dismal tone, and however much she told herself that this was merely the waterfall playing its tricks on her ears she shuddered each time at the sound of her name. Her very position next to the booth began to embarrass her. She tucked her hands into her coat sleeves so that they would not show, and tried to keep her eyes fixed on the foaming waters across the way, but she had noticed a disapproving look in the eyes of the diners nearest her, and she could not resist glancing back at the terrace every few minutes in the hope that she had been mistaken. Each time, however, she was more convinced that she had read their expressions correctly, and that these people believed, not only that she was standing there for no good reason, but that she was a genuine vagrant who could not afford the price of a dinner. She was therefore immensely relieved when she caught sight of Harriet advancing between the tables from the far end of the dining pavilion. As she drew nearer, Sadie noticed that she was wearing her black winter coat trimmed with red fur, and that her marceled hair remained neatly arranged in spite of the strong wind. Much to her relief Harriet had omitted to rouge her cheeks and her face therefore had regained its natural proportions. She saw Harriet wave at the sight of her and quicken her step. Sadie was pleased that the diners were to witness the impending meeting. "When they see us together," she thought, "they'll realize that I'm no vagrant, but a decent woman visiting her sister." She herself started down the knoll to hasten the meeting. "I thought you'd come out of the pine grove," she called out, as soon as they were within a few feet of one another. "I kept looking that way."

"I would have ordinarily," Harriet answered, reaching her side and kissing her lightly on the cheek, "but I went to the other end of the terrace first, to reserve a table for us from the waiter in charge there. That end is quieter, so it will be more suitable for a long talk."

"Good," thought Sadie as they climbed up the knoll together. "Her night's sleep has done her a world of good." She studied Harriet's face anxiously as they paused next to the souvenir booth, and discovered a sweet light reflected in her eyes. All at once she remembered their childhood together and the great tenderness Harriet had often shown towards her then.

"They have Turkish pilaff on the menu," said Harriet, "so I told the waiter to save some for you. It's such a favorite that it usually runs out at the very beginning. I know how much you love it."

Sadie, realizing that Harriet was actually eager for this dinner, the only one they would eat together at Camp Cataract, to be a success, felt the terrible leaden weight lifted from her heart; it disappeared so suddenly that for a moment or two she was like a balloon without its ballast; she could barely refrain from dancing about in delight. Harriet tugged on her arm.

"I think we'd better go now," she urged Sadie, "then after lunch we can come back here if you want to buy some souvenirs for Evy and Bert . . . and maybe for Flo and Carl and Bobby too. . . ."

Sadie bent down to adjust her cotton stockings, which were

wrinkling badly at the ankles, and when she straightened up again her eyes lighted on three men dining very near the edge of the terrace; she had not noticed them before. They were all eating corn on the cob and big round hamburger sandwiches in absolute silence. To protect their clothing from spattering kernels, they had converted their napkins into bibs.

"Bert Hoffer's careful of his clothes too," Sadie reflected, and then she turned to her sister. "Don't you think men look different sitting all by themselves without women?" she asked her. She felt an extraordinary urge to chat—an urge which she could not remember ever having experienced before.

"I think," Harriet replied, as though she had not heard Sadie's comment, "that we'd better go to our table before the waiter gives it to someone else."

"I don't like men," Sadie announced without venom, and she was about to follow Harriet when her attention was arrested by the eyes of the man nearest her. Slowly lowering his corn cob to his plate, he stared across at her, his mouth twisted into a bitter smile. She stood as if rooted to the ground, and under his steady gaze all her newborn joy rapidly drained away. With desperation she realized that Harriet, darting in and out between the crowded tables, would soon be out of sight. After making what seemed to her a superhuman effort she tore herself away from the spot where she stood and lunged after Harriet shouting her name.

Harriet was at her side again almost instantly, looking up at her with a startled expression. Together they returned to the souvenir booth, where Sadie stopped and assumed a slightly bent position as if she were suffering from an abdominal pain.

"What's the trouble?" she heard Harriet asking with concern. "Are you feeling ill?"

Instead of answering Sadie laid her hand heavily on her sister's arm and stared at her with a hunted expression in her eyes.

"Please try not to look so much like a gorilla," said Harriet in a kind voice, but Sadie, although she recognized the accuracy of this observation (for she could feel very well that she was looking like a gorilla), was powerless to change her expression, at least for a moment or two. "Come with me," she said finally, grabbing Harriet's hand and pulling her along with almost brutal force. "I've got something to tell you."

She headed down a narrow path leading into a thickly planted section of the grove, where she thought they were less likely to be disturbed. Harriet followed with such a quick, light step that Sadie felt no pull behind her at all and her sister's hand, folded in her own thick palm, seemed as delicate as the body of a bird. Finally they entered a small clearing where they stopped. Harriet untied a handkerchief from around her neck and mopped her brow. "Gracious!" she said. "It's frightfully hot in here." She offered the kerchief to Sadie. "I suppose it's because we walked so fast and because the pine trees shut out all the wind. . . . First I'll sit down and then you must tell me what's wrong." She stepped over to a felled tree whose length blocked the clearing. Its torn roots were shockingly exposed, whereas the upper trunk and branches lay hidden in the surrounding grove. Harriet sat down; Sadie was about to sit next to her when she noticed a dense swarm of flies near the roots. Automatically she stepped toward them. "Why are they here?" she asked herself—then immediately she spotted the cause, an open can of beans some careless person had deposited inside a small hollow at the base of the trunk. She turned away in disgust and looked at Harriet. Her sister was seated on the fallen tree, her back gracefully erect and her head tilted in a listening attitude. The filtered light imparted to her face an incredibly fragile and youthful look, and Sadie gazed at her with tenderness and wonder. No sound reached them in the clearing, and she realized with a pounding heart that she could no longer postpone telling Harriet why she had come. She could not have wished for a moment more favorable to the accomplishment of her purpose. The stillness in the air, their isolation, the expectant and gentle light in Harriet's eye, all these elements should have combined to give her back her faith—faith in her own powers to persuade Harriet to come home with her and live among them once again, winter and summer alike, as she had always done before. She opened her mouth to speak and doubled over, clutching at her stomach as though an animal were devouring her. Sweat beaded her forehead and she planted her feet wide apart on the ground as if this animal would be born. Though her vision was barred with pain, she saw Harriet's tear-filled eyes, searching hers.

"Let's not go back to the apartment," Sadie said, hearing her own words as if they issued not from her mouth but from a pit in the ground. "Let's not go back there . . . let's you and me go out in the world . . . just the two of us." A second before covering her face to hide her shame Sadie glimpsed Harriet's eyes, impossibly close to her own, their pupils pointed with a hatred such as she had never seen before.

It seemed to Sadie that it was taking an eternity for her sister to leave. "Go away . . . go away . . . or I'll suffocate." She was moaning the words over and over again, her face buried deep in her hands. "Go away . . . please go away . . . I'll suffocate. . . ." She could not tell, however, whether she was thinking these words or speaking them aloud.

At last she heard Harriet's footstep on the dry branches, as she started out of the clearing. Sadie listened, but although one step followed another, the cracking sound of the dry branches did not grow any fainter as Harriet penetrated farther into the grove. Sadie knew then that this agony she was suffering was itself the dreaded voyage into the world—the very voyage she had always feared Harriet would make. That she herself was making it instead of Harriet did not affect her certainty that this was it.

Sadie stood at the souvenir booth looking at some birchbark canoes. The wind was blowing colder and stronger than it had a while ago, or perhaps it only seemed this way to her, so recently returned from the airless clearing. She did not recall her trip back through the grove; she was conscious only of her haste to buy some souvenirs and to leave. Some chains of paper tacked to the side of the booth as decoration kept flying into her face. The Indian chief was smiling at her from behind the counter of souvenirs.

"What can I do for you?" he asked.

"I'm leaving," said Sadie, "so I want souvenirs. . . ."

"Take your choice; you've got birchbark canoes with or without mailing cards attached, Mexican sombrero ashtrays, exhilarating therapeutic pine cushions filled with the regional needles . . . and banners for a boy's room."

"There's no boy home," Sadie said, having caught only these last words.

"How about cushions or . . . canoes?"

She nodded.

"Which do you want?"

"Both," she answered quickly.

"How many?"

Sadie closed her eyes. Try as she would she could not count up the members of the family. She could not even reach an approximate figure. "Eleven," she blurted out finally, in desperation.

"Eleven of each?" he asked raising his eyebrows.

"Yes . . . yes," she answered quickly, batting the paper chains out of her face, "eleven of each."

"You sure don't forget the old folks at home, do you?" he said, beginning to collect the canoes. He made an individual package of each souvenir and then wrapped them all together in coarse brown paper which he bound with thick twine.

Sadie had given him a note and he was punching his money belt for the correct change when her eyes fell on his light, freckled hand. Startled, she shifted her glance from his hand punching the nickel belt to his brick-colored face streaked with purple and vermilion paint. For the first time she noticed his Irish blue eyes. Slowly the hot flush of shame crept along the nape of her neck. It was the same unbearable mortification that she had experienced in the clearing; it spread upward from her neck to the roots of her hair, coloring her face a dark red. That she was ashamed for the Indian this time, and not of her own words, failed to lessen the intensity of her suffering; the boundaries of her pride had never been firmly fixed inside herself. She stared intently at his Irish blue eyes, so oddly light in his brick-colored face. What was it? She was tormented by the sight of an incongruity she couldn't name. All at once she remembered the pavilion and the people dining there; her heart started to pound. "They'll see it," she said to herself in a panic. "They'll see it and they'll know that I've seen it too." Somehow this latter possibility was the most perilous of all.

"They must never know I've seen it," she said, grinding her teeth, and she leaned over the counter, crushing some canoes under her chest. "Quickly," she whispered. "Go out your little door and meet me back of the booth. . . ."

A second later she found him there. "Listen!" She clutched his hand. "We must hurry . . . I didn't mean to see you . . . I'm sorry . . . I've been trying not to look at you for years . . . for years and years and years. . . ." She gaped at him in horror. "Why are you standing there? We've got to hurry. . . . They haven't caught me looking at you yet, but we've got to hurry." She headed for the bridge, leading the Indian behind her. He followed quickly without saying a word.

The water's roar increased in volume as they approached the opposite bank of the chasm, and Sadie found relief in the sound. Once off the bridge she ran as fast as she could along the path leading to the waterfall. The Indian followed close on her heels, his hand resting lightly in her own, as Harriet's had earlier when they'd sped together through the grove. Reaching the waterfall, she edged along the wall of rock until she stood directly behind the water's cascade. With a cry of delight she leaned back in the curve of the wall, insensible to its icy dampness, which penetrated even through the thickness of her woollen coat. She listened to the cataract's deafening roar and her heart almost burst for joy, because she had hidden the Indian safely behind the cascade where he could be neither seen nor heard. She turned around and smiled at him kindly. He too smiled, and she no longer saw in his face any trace of the incongruity that had shocked her so before.

The foaming waters were beautiful to see. Sadie stepped forward, holding her hand out to the Indian.

When Harriet awakened that morning all traces of her earlier victorious mood had vanished. She felt certain that disaster would overtake her before she could start out for Pocahontas Falls. Heavyhearted and with fumbling hands, she set about making her pack. Luncheon with Sadie was an impossible cliff which she did not have the necessary strength to scale. When she came to three round cushions that had to be snapped into their rainproof casings she gave up with a groan and rushed headlong out of her cabin in search of Beryl.

Fortunately Beryl waited table on the second shift and so she found her reading a magazine, with one leg flung over the arm of her chair.

"I can't make my pack," Harriet said hysterically, bursting into Beryl's cabin without even knocking at the door.

Beryl swung her leg around and got out of her chair. "I'll make your pack," she said in a calm voice, knocking some tobacco out of her pipe. "I would have come around this morning, but you said last night you wanted to make it alone."

"It's Sadie," Harriet complained. "It's that cursed lunch with Sadie. I can't go through with it. I know I can't. I shouldn't have to in the first place. She's not even supposed to be here. . . . I'm an ass. . . ."

"To hell with sisters," said Beryl. "Give 'em all a good swift kick in the pants."

"She's going to stop me from going on my canoe trip . . . I know she is. . . ." Harriet had adopted the whining tone of a little girl.

"No, she isn't," said Beryl, speaking with authority.

"Why not?" Harriet asked. She looked at Beryl almost wistfully.

"She'd better not try anything . . ." said Beryl. "Ever hear of jujitsu?" She grunted with satisfaction. "Come on, we'll go make your pack." She was so pleased with Harriet's new state of dependency that she was rapidly overcoming her original shyness. An hour later she had completed the pack, and Harriet was dressed and ready.

"Will you go with me to the souvenir booth?" she begged the waitress. "I don't want to meet her alone." She was in a worse state of nerves than ever.

"I'll go with you," said Beryl, "but let's stop at my cabin on the way so I can change into my uniform. I'm on duty soon."

They were nearly twenty minutes late arriving at the booth, and Harriet was therefore rather surprised not to see Sadie standing there. "Perhaps she's been here and gone back to the lodge for a minute," she said to Beryl. "I'll find out." She walked up to the souvenir counter and questioned the Indian, with whom she was slightly familiar. "Was there a woman waiting here a while ago, Timothy?" she asked.

"A dark middle-aged woman?"

"That's right."

"She was here for an hour or more," he said, "never budged from this stall until about fifteen minutes ago."

"She couldn't have been here an hour!" Harriet argued. "Not my sister. . . . I told her one-thirty and it's not yet two."

"Then it wasn't your sister. The woman who was here stayed more than an hour, without moving. I noticed her because it was such a queer-looking thing. I noticed her first from my chair at the bridge and then when I came up here she was still standing by the booth. She must have stood here over an hour."

"Then it was a different middle-aged woman."

"That may be," he agreed, "but anyway, this one left about fifteen minutes ago. After standing all that time she turned around all of a sudden and bought a whole bunch of souvenirs from me . . . then just when I was punching my belt for the change she said something I couldn't understand—it sounded like Polish—and then she lit out for the bridge before I could give her a penny. That woman's got impulses," he added with a broad grin. "If she's your sister, I'll give you her change, in case she don't stop here on her way back. . . . But she sounded to me like a Polak."

"Beryl," said Harriet, "run across the bridge and see if Sadie's behind the waterfall. I'm sure this Polish woman wasn't Sadie, but they might both be back there. . . . If she's not there, we'll look in the lodge."

When Beryl returned her face was dead white; she stared at Harriet in silence, and even when Harriet finally grabbed hold of her shoulders and shook her hard, she would not say anything.

1949

A Stick of Green Candy

THE CLAY pit had been dug in the side of a long hill. By leaning back against the lower part of its wall, Mary could see the curved highway above her and the cars speeding past. On the other side of the highway the hill continued rising, but at a steeper angle. If she tilted her head farther back, she could glimpse the square house on the hill's summit, with its flight of stone steps that led from the front door down to the curb, dividing the steep lawn in two.

She had been playing in the pit for a long time. Like many other children, she fancied herself at the head of a regiment; at the same time, she did not join in any neighborhood games, preferring to play all alone in the pit, which lay about a mile beyond the edge of town. She was a scrupulously clean child with a strong, immobile face and long, well-arranged curls. Sometimes when she went home toward evening there were traces of clay on her dark coat, even though she had worked diligently with the brush she carried along every afternoon. She despised untidiness, and she feared that the clay might betray her headquarters, which she suspected the other children of planning to invade.

One afternoon she stumbled and fell on the clay when it was still slippery and wet from a recent rainfall. She never failed to leave the pit before twilight, but this time she decided to wait until it was dark so that her sullied coat would attract less attention. Wisely she refrained from using her brush on the wet clay.

Having always left the pit at an earlier hour, she felt that an explanation was due to her soldiers; to announce simply that she had fallen down was out of the question. She knew that her men trusted her and would therefore accept in good faith any reason she chose to give them for this abrupt change in her day's routine, but convincing herself was a more difficult task. She never told them anything until she really believed what she was going to say. After concentrating a few minutes, she summoned them with a bugle call.

"Men," she began, once they were lined up at attention,

"I'm staying an hour longer today than usual, so I can work on the mountain goat maneuvers. I explained mountain-goat fighting last week, but I'll tell you what it is again. It's a special technique used in the mountains around big cliffs. No machine can do mountain-goat fighting. We're going to specialize." She paused. "Even though I'm staying, I want you to go right ahead and have your recreation hour as usual, like you always do the minute I leave. I have total respect for your recreation, and I know you fight as hard as you play."

She dismissed them and walked up to her own headquarters in the deepest part of the pit. At the end of the day the color of the red pit deepened; then, after the sun had sunk behind the hill, the clay lost its color. She began to feel cold and a little uneasy. She was so accustomed to leaving her men each day at the same hour, just before they thronged into the gymnasium, that now lingering on made her feel like an intruder.

It was almost night when she climbed out of the pit. She glanced up at the hilltop house and then started down toward the deserted lower road. When she reached the outskirts of town she chose the darkest streets so that the coat would be less noticeable. She hated the thick pats of clay that were embedded in its wool; moreover she was suffering from a sense of inner untidiness as a result of the unexpected change in her daily routine. She walked along slowly, scuffing her heels, her face wearing the expression of a person surfeited with food. Far underneath her increasingly lethargic mood lurked a feeling of apprehension; she knew she would be reprimanded for returning home after dark, but she never would admit either the possibility of punishment or the fear of it. At this period she was rapidly perfecting a psychological mechanism which enabled her to forget, for long stretches of time, that her parents existed.

She found her father in the vestibule hanging his coat up on a peg. Her heart sank as he turned around to greet her. Without seeming to, he took in the pats of clay at a glance, but his shifting eyes never alighted candidly on any object.

"You've been playing in that pit below the Speed house again," he said to her. "From now on, I want you to play at the Kinsey Memorial Grounds." Since he appeared to have nothing to say, she started away, but immediately he continued.

"Some day you may have to live in a town where the administration doesn't make any provision for children at all. Or it may provide you with a small plot of land and a couple of dinky swings. There's a very decent sum goes each year to the grounds here. They provide you with swings, seesaws and chin bars." He glanced furtively at her coat. "Tomorrow," he said, "I drive past that pit on my way out to Sam's. I'll draw up to the edge of the road and look down. See that you're over at the Memorial Grounds with the other children."

Mary never passed the playgrounds without quickening her step. This site, where the screams of several dozen children mingled with the high, grinding sound of the moving swings, she had always automatically hated. It was the antithesis of her clay pit and the well-ordered barracks inside it.

When she went to bed, she was in such a state of wild excitement that she was unable to sleep. It was the first time that her father's observations had not made her feel either humiliated or ill. The following day after school she set out for the pit. As she was climbing the long hill (she always approached her barracks from the lower road), she slackened her pace and stood still. All at once she had had the fear that by looking into her eyes the soldiers might divine her father's existence. To each one of them she was like himself—a man without a family. After a minute she resumed her climb. When she reached the edge of the pit, she put both feet together and jumped inside.

"Men," she said, once she had blown the bugle and made a few routine announcements, "I know you have hard muscles in your legs. But how would you like to have even harder ones?" It was a rhetorical question to which she did not expect an answer. "We're going to have hurdle races and plain running every day now for two hours."

Though in her mind she knew dimly that this intensified track training was preparatory to an imminent battle on the Memorial playgrounds, she did not dare discuss it with her men, or even think about it too precisely herself. She had to avoid coming face to face with an impossibility.

"As we all know," she continued, "we don't like to have teams because we've been through too much on the battlefield all together. Every day I'll divide you up fresh before the racing, so that the ones who are against each other today, for instance, will be running on the same side tomorrow. The men in our outfit are funny about taking sides against each other, even just in play and athletics. The other outfits in this country don't feel the same as we do."

She dug her hands into her pockets and hung her head sheepishly. She was fine now, and certain of victory. She could feel the men's hearts bursting with love for her and with pride in their regiment. She looked up—a car was rounding the bend, and as it came nearer she recognized it as her father's.

"Men," she said in a clear voice, "you can do what you want for thirty minutes while I make out the racing schedule and the team lists." She stared unflinchingly at the dark blue sedan and waited with perfect outward calm for her father to slow down; she was still waiting after the car had curved out of sight. When she realized that he was gone, she held her breath. She expected her heart to leap for joy, but it did not.

"Now I'll go to my headquarters," she announced in a flat voice. "I'll be back with the team lists in twenty-five minutes." She glanced up at the highway; she felt oddly disappointed and uneasy. A small figure was descending the stone steps on the other side of the highway. It was a boy. She watched in amazement; she had never seen anyone come down these steps before. Since the highway had replaced the old country road, the family living in the hilltop house came and went through the back door.

Watching the boy, she felt increasingly certain that he was on his way down to the pit. He stepped off the curb after looking prudently for cars in each direction; then he crossed the highway and clambered down the hill. Just as she had expected him to, when he reached the edge of the pit he seated himself on the ground and slid into it, smearing his coat—dark like her own—with clay.

"It's a big clay pit," he said, looking up at her. He was younger than she, but he looked straight into her eyes without a trace of shyness. She knew he was a stranger in town; she had never seen him before. This made him less detestable, nonetheless she had to be rid of him shortly because the men were expecting her back with the team lists.

"Where do you come from?" she asked him.

"From inside that house." He pointed at the hilltop.

"Where do you live when you're not visiting?"

"I live inside that house," he repeated, and he sat down on the floor of the pit.

"Sit on the orange crate," she ordered him severely. "You don't pay any attention to your coat."

He shook his head. She was exasperated with him because he was untidy, and he had lied to her. She knew perfectly well that he was merely a visitor in the hilltop house.

"Why did you come out this door?" she asked, looking at him sharply. "The people in that house go out the back. It's level there and they've got a drive."

"I don't know why," he answered simply.

"Where do you come from?" she asked again.

"That's my house." He pointed to it as if she were asking him for the first time. "The driveway in back's got gravel in it. I've got a whole box of it in my room. I can bring it down."

"No gravel's coming in here that belongs to a liar," she interrupted him. "Tell me where you come from and then you can go get it."

He stood up. "I live in that big house up there," he said calmly. "From my room I can see the river, the road down there and the road up here, and this pit and you."

"It's not your room!" she shouted angrily. "You're a visitor there. I was a visitor last year at my aunt's."

"Good-bye."

He was climbing out of the pit. Once outside he turned around and looked down at her. There was an expression of fulfillment on his face.

"I'll bring the gravel some time soon," he said.

She watched him crossing the highway. Then automatically she climbed out of the pit.

She was mounting the tedious stone steps behind him. Her jaw was clamped shut, and her face had gone white with anger. He had not turned around once to look at her. As they were nearing the top it occurred to her that he would rush into the house and slam the door in her face. Hurriedly she climbed three steps at once so as to be directly behind him. When he opened the door, she pushed across the threshold with him; he did not seem to notice her at all. Inside the dimly lit vestibule the smell of fresh paint was very strong. After a few seconds her eyes became more accustomed to the light, and she saw that the square room was packed solid with furniture. The boy was already pushing his way between two identical bureaus which stood back to back. The space between them was so narrow that she feared she would not be able to follow him. She looked around frantically for a wider artery, but seeing that there was none, she squeezed between the bureaus, pinching her flesh painfully, until she reached a free space at the other end. Here the furniture was less densely packed—in fact, three armchairs had been shoved together around an uncluttered area, wide enough to provide leg room for three people, providing they did not mind a tight squeeze. To her left a door opened on to total darkness. She expected him to rush headlong out of the room into the dark in a final attempt to escape her, but to her astonishment he threaded his way carefully in the opposite direction until he reached the circle of chairs. He entered it and sat down in one of them. After a second's hesitation, she followed his example.

The chair was deeper and softer than any she had ever sat in before. She tickled the thick velvet arms with her fingertips. Here and there, they grazed a stiff area where the nap had worn thin. The paint fumes were making her eyes smart, and she was beginning to feel apprehensive. She had forgotten to consider that grown people would probably be in the house, but now she gazed uneasily into the dark space through the open door opposite her. It was cold in the vestibule, and despite her woollen coat she began to shiver.

"If he would tell me now where he comes from," she said to herself, "then I could go away before anybody else came." Her anger had vanished, but she could not bring herself to speak aloud, or even to turn around and look at him. He sat so still that it was hard for her to believe he was actually beside her in his chair.

Without warning, the dark space opposite her was lighted up. Her heart sank as she stared at a green wall, still shiny with wet paint. It hurt her eyes. A woman stepped into the visible area, her heels sounding on the floorboards. She was wearing a print dress and over it a long brown sweater which obviously belonged to a man.

"Are you there, Franklin?" she called out, and she walked into the vestibule and switched on a second light. She stood still and looked at him.

"I thought I heard you come in," she said. Her voice was flat, and her posture at that moment did not inspire Mary with respect. "Come to visit Franklin?" she asked, as if suddenly aware that her son was not alone. "I think I'll visit for a while." She advanced toward them. When she reached the circle she squeezed in and sat opposite Mary.

"I hoped we'd get a visitor or two while we were here," she said to her. "That's why I arranged this little sitting place. All the rest of the rooms are being painted, or else they're still too smelly for visiting. Last time we were here we didn't see anyone for the whole two weeks. But he was a baby then. I thought maybe this time he'd contact when he went out. He goes out a lot of the day." She glanced at her son. "You've got some dirt on that chair," she remarked in a tone which did not express the slightest disapproval. She turned back to Mary. "I'd rather have a girl than a boy," she said. "There's nothing much I can discuss with a boy. A grown woman isn't interested in the same things a boy is interested in." She scratched a place below her shoulder blades. "My preference is discussing furnishings. Always has been. I like that better than I like discussing styles. I'll discuss styles if the company wants to, but I don't enjoy it nearly so well. The only thing about furnishings that leaves me cold is curtains. I never was interested in curtains, even when I was young. I like lamps about the best. Do you?"

Mary was huddling as far back into her chair as she could, but even so, without drawing her legs up and sitting on her feet, it was impossible to avoid physical contact with the woman, whose knees lightly touched hers every time she shifted a little in her chair. Inwardly, too, Mary shrank from her. She had never before been addressed so intimately by a grown person. She closed her eyes, seeking the dark gulf that always had separated her from the adult world. And she clutched the seat cushion hard, as if she were afraid of being wrenched from the chair.

"We came here six years ago," the woman continued, "when the Speeds had their house painted, and now they're having it painted again, so we're here again. They can't be in the house until it's good and dry because they've both got nose trouble —both the old man and the old lady—but we're not related. Only by marriage. I'm a kind of relative to them, but not enough to be really classed as a relative. Just enough so that they'd rather have me come and look after the house than a stranger. They gave me a present of money last time, but this time it'll be clothes for the boy. There's nothing to boys' clothes really. They don't mean anything."

She sighed and looked around her.

"Well," she said, "we would like them to ask us over here more often than they do. Our town is way smaller than this, way smaller, but you can get all the same stuff there that you can here, if you've got the money to pay. I mean groceries and clothing and appliances. We've got all that. As soon as the walls are dry we go back. Franklin doesn't want to. He don't like his home because he lives in an apartment; it's in the business section. He sits in a lot and don't go out and contact at all."

The light shone through Mary's tightly closed lids. In the chair next to her there was no sound of a body stirring. She opened her eyes and looked down. His ankles were crossed and his feet were absolutely still.

"Franklin," the woman said, "get some candy for me and the girl."

When he had gone she turned to Mary. "He's not a rough boy like the others," she said. "I don't know what I'd do if he was one of the real ones with all the trimmings. He's got some girl in him, thank the Lord. I couldn't handle one of the real ones."

He came out of the freshly painted room carrying a box.

"We keep our candy in tea boxes. We have for years," the woman said. "They're good conservers." She shrugged her shoulders. "What more can you expect? Such is life." She turned to her son. "Open it and pass it to the girl first. Then me."

The orange box was decorated with seated women and temples. Mary recognized it; her mother used the same tea at home. He slipped off the two rubber bands that held the cover on, and offered her the open box. With stiff fingers she took a stick of green candy from the top; she did not raise her eyes.

A few minutes later she was running alone down the stone

steps. It was almost night, but the sky was faintly green near the horizon. She crossed the highway and stood on the hill only a few feet away from the pit. Far below her, lights were twinkling in the Polish section. Down there the shacks were stacked one against the other in a narrow strip of land between the lower road and the river.

After gazing down at the sparkling lights for a while, she began to breathe more easily. She had never experienced the need to look at things from a distance before, nor had she felt the relief that it can bring. All at once, the air stirring around her head seemed delightful; she drank in great draughts of it, her eyes fixed on the lights below.

"This isn't the regular air from up here that I'm breathing," she said to herself. "It's the air from down there. It's a trick I can do."

She felt her blood tingle as it always did whenever she scored a victory, and she needed to score several of them in the course of each day. This time she was defeating the older woman.

The following afternoon, even though it was raining hard, her mother could not stop her from going out, but she had promised to keep her hood buttoned and not to sit on the ground.

The stone steps were running with water. She sat down and looked into the enveloping mist, a fierce light in her eyes. Her fingers twitched nervously, deep in the recess of her rubber pockets. It was unbelievable that they should not at any moment encounter something wonderful and new, unbelievable, too, that he should be ignorant of her love for him. Surely he knew that all the while his mother was talking, she in secret had been claiming him for her own. He would come out soon to join her on the steps, and they would go away together.

Hours later, stiff with cold, she stood up. Even had he remained all day at the window he could never have sighted her through the heavy mist. She knew this, but she could never climb the steps to fetch him; that was impossible. She ran headlong down the stone steps and across the highway. When she reached the pit she stopped dead and stood with her feet in the soft clay mud, panting for breath.

"Men," she said after a minute, "men, I told you we were going to specialize." She stopped abruptly, but it was too late.

She had, for the first time in her life, spoken to her men before summoning them to order with a bugle call. She was shocked, and her heart beat hard against her ribs, but she went on. "We're going to be the only outfit in the world that can do real mountain-goat fighting." She closed her eyes, seeking the dark gulf again; this time she needed to hear the men's hearts beating, more clearly than her own. A car was sounding its horn on the highway. She looked up.

"We can't climb those stone steps up there." She was shouting and pointing at the house. "No outfit can, no outfit ever will. . . ." She was desperate. "It's not for outfits. It's a flight of steps that's not for outfits . . . because it's . . . because. . . ." The reason was not going to come to her. She had begun to cheat now, and she knew it would never come.

She turned her cold face away from the pit, and without dismissing her men, crept down the hill.

1949

East Side: North Africa

THE HIGHEST street in this blue Arab town skirted the edge of a cliff. I walked over to the thick protecting wall and looked down. The tide was out and the flat scummy rocks below were swarming with skinny boys. All of them were wearing pleated bloomer-shaped knickers and little skullcaps as bright as colored candies. An Arab woman came up to the blue wall and stood next to me, grazing my hip with her basket. I pretended not to notice and kept my eyes fixed on a white dog that had just slipped down the side of a rock and was plunged up to his belly in a crater filled with sea water. The sound of his bark reverberating against the high cliff was earsplitting. The woman next to me jabbed the basket firmly into my ribs, and I looked down. It was stuffed full with a big dead porcupine; a pair of new yellow socks were folded on top of its pretty quills.

"That one is a porcupine," she said, pointing a finger stained with red henna into the basket.

I looked at her. She was dressed in a haik and the white cloth covering the lower half of her face was loose, about to fall down.

"I am Zodelia," she announced in a high voice, "and you are a friend of Cherifa and Betzoule." She spoke in Arabic. "You sit in their house and you eat in their house and you sleep in their house." The loose cloth slipped down below her chin and hung there like a bib. She did not pull it up.

Her information was correct. With the help of frequent gifts and a smattering of Arabic, I had made friends with two unmarried sisters who worked in the market. It was unheard of for any of these women whose lives were led almost entirely within a large circle of female relatives to associate with someone who was not only a stranger but a Nazarene. Nazarene is the popular term in Morocco for all non-Moslems of Western origin (out of Nazareth). Their association with me was a profitable one and so they were actually not deviating too far from the conventional relationship of any Arab market woman to any Nazarene, resident in the town or tourist.

Despite the fact that no other Nazarene woman had ever sat

about with them before or for that matter with anyone they had ever known, these sisters and the other women in the family very soon took me for granted. They told me over and over again how much I missed my husband and my relatives and how much I enjoyed Moslem food and being with Moslems. They must have considered that this was sufficient reason for my extraordinary behavior, if they considered the situation from my point of view at all, which it is very possible they did not. They were perpetually weaving little plots to outwit me but this never dampened the spontaneity of their moods; they were conniving, generous and hospitable. Sometimes I played the part of a Nazarene fool being outwitted by two shrewd market women and it seemed to me that they were playing the parts of two shrewd market women outwitting a Nazarene fool.

There was considerable speculation about us in the market place and many of the women claimed that when the rest of the family was asleep the three of us sat smoking in the dark. Smoking is strictly forbidden to Moslem women though some of it goes on behind closed doors, even among decent married women and virgins. Cherifa and Betzoule had learned to smoke from a corrupt cousin who was little better than a whore. I did supply them with cigarettes occasionally, but the room which they shared alone (the other sisters who were married slept with their husbands and children) was, more often than not, filled with visiting female relatives and any such scandalous behavior was impossible. These visits often lasted for months.

"You sit in their house and you sleep in their house and you eat in their house," the woman went on, and I nodded in agreement. "Your name is Jeanie and you live in a hotel with other Nazarenes. How much does the hotel cost you?"

Fortunately a round loaf of bread flopped on the ground from inside the folds of her haik and I did not have to answer her question. She picked the bread up and stuffed it between the quills of the porcupine and the basket handle with some difficulty; then she set the basket down on top of the blue wall and turned to me with bright eyes.

"I am the people in the hotel," she said. "Watch me."

I was pleased because I knew she was about to present me with a little sketch. It would be delightful to watch, since almost every Arab speaks and gestures as if he had studied at a Moslem equivalent of the Comédie Française. At times it would seem to me that they were, all of them, acting in some continuous pageant all about life in a Moslem country.

"The people in the hotel," she announced, formally beginning her sketch. "I am the people in the hotel.

"Good-by, Jeanie, good-by. Where are you going?

"I am going to a Moslem house to visit my Moslem friends, Cherifa and Betzoule. I will sit in a Moslem room and eat Moslem food and sleep on a Moslem bed.

"Jeanie, Jeanie, when will you come back to us in the hotel and sleep in your own room?

"I will come back to you in three days. I will come back and sit in a Nazarene room and eat Nazarene food and sleep on a Nazarene bed. I will spend half the week with Moslem friends and half with—Nazarenes."

Her voice had a triumphant ring as she finished her sentence, dividing my time equally between the Moslems and the Nazarenes; then, without formally announcing the end of the sketch, she walked over to the wall and put one arm around her porcupine basket.

I knew that she did not actually believe that I spent exactly half of my life with Moslem friends and the other half with the Christians in the hotel. A story or a sketch about happiness must not be about what actually happens.

I moved along the wall and stood next to her. Down below, just at the edge of the cliff's shadow, an Arab woman was seated on a rock, washing her legs in one of the craters filled with sea water. The folds of her voluminous white haik were piled in her lap and she was huddled over them.

"She is looking at the ocean," Zodelia said to me.

She was not looking at the ocean. Huddled over the piles of cloth in her lap she could not possibly have seen it without straightening up and turning around.

"She is *not* looking at the ocean," I said.

"She is looking at the ocean," Zodelia repeated, as if I had not spoken. I decided to change the subject.

"Why do you have a porcupine with you?" I asked her, though I knew that some of the Arabs, particularly the country people, enjoyed eating them.

"It is a present for my aunt," she told me. "Do you like it?"

"Yes," I said. "I like porcupines. I like big porcupines and little ones too."

She seemed bewildered and then bored. I had somehow ruined the conversation by mentioning little porcupines. I could tell this by her expression.

"Where is your mother?" she asked me.

"My mother is in my country in her own house," I said automatically; I had answered this question a hundred times.

"Why don't you write her a letter and tell her to come here? You can take her on a promenade and show her the ocean. After that she can go back to her own country and sit in her house." She picked up her basket and adjusted the cloth over her mouth. "Would you like to go to a wedding?" she asked me.

I said that I would love to go to a wedding, and we started off down the wavy blue street, heading into the wind.

When we came to a little store, built like a booth, she stopped.

"Stand here," she said, "I want to buy something."

After studying the counter for a minute or two, she poked me and pointed to some cakes inside a square box with glass sides. "Nice," she asked me, "or not nice?"

These cakes were actually not very nice. They were dusty looking and coated with thin, ugly-colored icing. They were called *galletas Ortiz* and they were made in Spain.

"They are very nice," I said to her and bought her a dozen cakes which I gave her as a gift. She thanked me briefly and we walked on.

After a while we turned off the street into a blind alley and started downhill. When we had nearly reached the end of this alley, she stopped at a heavy studded door on our right and lifted the knocker wrought in the shape of Fatima's hand.

"The wedding is here?" I said to her.

"There is no wedding here," she corrected me, shaking her head and looking grave.

A child opened the door for us and quickly hid behind it, covering her face. I followed Zodelia across the black and white tiles of a closed patio. The walls like those outside were washed in blue and a cold light shone through the broken glass panes far above our heads. Zodelia stopped at one of three doors giving onto this patio where a row of pointed slippers barred the threshold. She stepped out of her own slippers and set them down near the others. I followed her example, which took me quite a little time because there was a knot in my laces.

When I was ready, Zodelia took my hand and pulled me with her into a dimly lit room, where she led me over to a mattress against the wall.

"Sit," she told me, and I obeyed her; then without further comment she walked off, heading for the far end of the room, which was shaped like a trolley car.

At first, because my eyes were blinded by daylight, it seemed to me that Zodelia was disappearing down a long corridor, but after a minute or two I made out the short end wall and the brass bars of a bed, glowing weakly in the darkness. Satisfied that she would not vanish entirely, I looked around me.

Only a few feet away an old lady was seated in the middle of the carpet directly underneath the only light bulb in the room, which hung on a long wire from the unbelievably high ceiling. She was wearing a sumptuous green and purple dress made of a heavy material suitable for draperies. It was solidly embroidered with dark, glossy flowers. Through the many rents and holes in the material I could see the printed cotton dress and the tan sweater she was wearing underneath.

On the mattress opposite mine several women were seated under a life-size photograph of the sultan, and farther along on this same mattress, which like mine ran almost the full length of the room, three babies were sleeping in a row. Each one of them lay close to the wall with his head resting on a fancy cushion.

"Is it nice here?" It was Zodelia, returning. She had removed her haik, and I was horrified to see that she was wearing a black crepe afternoon dress of modern European design. It hung unbelted all the way down to her ankles, almost grazing her bare feet. The hem was lopsided. More and more Moroccan women (in the larger cities) are beginning to wear European-made dresses or approximations of these. In the street they are fortunately still concealed by Moorish haiks or jellabas.

"Is it nice here?" Zodelia asked again, crouching on her haunches opposite the old lady and pointing at her. "That one is Tetum," she said to me. The old lady plunged both hands into a bowl on her lap that was filled with raw meat and began shaping the meat into little balls.

"Tetum," echoed the ladies on the mattress. Each one of these women seemed to be wearing several dresses at once and all of them had bound their heads in a variety of different-colored materials. Their clothes did not show any Western influence.

"This Nazarene," said Zodelia, gesturing in my direction, "spends half her time in a Moslem house with Moslem friends and the other half in a Nazarene hotel with other Nazarenes."

"That's nice," said the women opposite. "Half with Moslem friends and half with Nazarenes." The old lady looked very stern and I noticed that her bony cheeks were tattooed with tiny blue crosses. "Why?" she asked abruptly in a deep voice. "*Why* does she spend half her time with Moslem friends and half with Nazarenes?" She fixed her eyes on Zodelia, never ceasing to shape the meat with swift and accurate fingers. Her knuckles, like her cheekbones, were tattooed with blue crosses.

Zodelia stared back at her with a stupid look on her face. "I don't know why," she answered, shrugging one fat shoulder. It was obvious that the picture she had been painting of my life had suddenly lost all its charm for her.

"Is she crazy?" the old lady asked.

"No," Zodelia answered listlessly. "She is not crazy."

There were shrieks of laughter from the mattress.

The old lady fixed her sharp eyes on me. They were heavily outlined in black. "Where is your husband?" she asked.

"He's traveling in the desert."

"Selling things," Zodelia put in.

Among the Arab women this had become the most popular explanation for my husband's trips. I had not tried to contradict it.

"Where is your mother?" the old lady asked.

"My mother is in our country in her own house."

"Why don't you go and sit with your mother in her own house?" she scolded. "The hotel costs lots of money."

I felt a sudden foolish urge, despite my limited vocabulary, to tell these women about New York City; doubly foolish because, even had I been able to speak fluent Arabic, they might have listened to what I told them with polite smiles but all the while, in their hearts, they would have pictured New York as a walled Moslem town with a predominantly Arab population. Nonetheless I was determined to say something about it and so I decided to tell them about the traffic. This was the simplest subject I could have chosen since even the Arabs use either Spanish or French words for all recent mechanical inventions such as automobiles.

"In the city where I was born," I began, "there are many, many automobiles and many, many trucks."

The women on the mattress were smiling pleasantly. "Is that true?" the center one remarked in a social tone.

"I hate trucks," I told them with feeling.

"She hates trucks," Zodelia explained.

The old lady lifted the bowl of meat off her lap and set it down on the carpet. "Trucks are nice," she said severely.

"That's true . . ." the women agreed, after only a moment's hesitation. "Trucks are very nice."

"Do you like trucks?" I asked Zodelia; I thought that perhaps because of our greater intimacy she might agree with me.

"Yes," she said, "they are nice. Trucks are very nice." She seemed lost in meditation but only for a moment. "Everything is nice," she announced with a look of triumph.

"It's the truth," the women joined in from their mattress. "Everything is nice."

They all looked happy with the exception of the old lady who was still frowning. "Aeshcha!" she hollered, twisting her neck so that her voice could be heard in the patio. "Bring the tea!"

In a minute several little girls came into the room carrying the tea things and a low round table.

"Pass the cakes to the Nazarene," the old lady told the smallest child, who was carrying a cut-glass dish. It was filled with the dry Spanish cakes I had bought for Zodelia. I did not want any of them. I wanted to leave.

"Eat," the women called out from their mattress. "Eat the cakes."

The child pushed the glass dish forward.

I knew that it would be rude of me to leave now without

drinking any tea or eating any of the cakes I had myself bought for Zodelia, but it would be equally rude of me to stay just a little while longer and drink only one glass of tea. I would have to stay at least another hour and drink the minimum three glasses, and even after that the women would protest just as loudly when I finally stood up to leave as I knew they were about to now after this brief visit. Moroccan etiquette demands that a host make every effort to keep his guest from leaving, even when the guest has been sitting around for ten or eleven hours, which is very often the case. One is sometimes detained physically but it is a formality. I searched my mind for some excuse, any excuse, for my abrupt departure; though none would be acceptable to them, I knew that it was expected of me to make one.

"The dinner at the hotel is ready," I said, standing up. Since these women do not concern themselves with fixed meal hours this was the most ineffectual apology I could have made. They do not expect the truth, of course, but they expect an excuse to sound like one.

"Drink tea," said the old woman scornfully. "Later you will sit with the other Nazarenes and eat their food."

"The Nazarenes will be furious if I'm late," I lied more and more stupidly. "They will hit me." I tried to look wild and fearful.

"Drink tea. They will not hit you," the old woman said briefly. "Sit down and drink tea."

The child offered the glass dish once more, but I backed away toward the door.

At last, after a long and tiresome exchange of apologies on my part and shrieks of protest on theirs, I walked out of the room backward, raving to them about the delights of my visit.

Outside I sat down on the black and white tiles to lace my shoes. Only Zodelia followed me into the patio.

"Come back," they were calling, "come back into the room."

I noticed that the porcupine basket was standing only a few feet away from me against a wall. "Is that old lady in the room your aunt—the one you were bringing the porcupine to?" I asked her.

"No," she answered, "she is not my aunt."

"Where is your aunt?"

"My aunt is in her own house."

"When will you take the porcupine to her?" I wanted to keep talking so that she would be distracted and forget to fuss about my departure.

"The porcupine sits here," she said firmly, "in my own house."

There are certain Arab fabrications that seem to be utterly without motive, at least none that any Western mind can possibly fathom. Europeans living in Morocco often speak of something they call the "Oriental wall." I decided not to ask her about the wedding.

When we reached the heavy studded door she opened it just enough to let me through. "Good-by," she said. "I shall see you tomorrow, if Allah wills it."

"When?"

"At four o'clock."

It was obvious that she was choosing this hour at random. There was no way of determining whether or not she would actually turn up and if so at what time. One is not safe in assuming that they will be late.

Before closing the door behind me, she pressed two of the dry Spanish cakes into the palm of my hand.

"Eat them," she urged me graciously. "Eat them at the hotel with the other Nazarenes."

I started up the steep alley, headed once again for the walk along the cliff. The houses on either side of me were so close I could smell the dampness of the walls and feel it on my cheeks like thicker air.

When I reached the place where I had met Zodelia I went over to the wall and leaned on it. Although the sun had sunk behind the houses in back of me, the sky was still luminous and the color of the blue wall had deepened. I rubbed my fingers along it; the wash was fresh and a little of the powdery stuff came off; but no matter how often I walked through these streets reaching out to touch the chalky blue wash on the houses . . . on the walls, I could never satisfy my longing for the town.

I remember that once I reached out to touch the beautiful and powdery face of a clown because his face had awakened some longing; it happened at a little circus but not when I was a child.

1951

SCENES AND FRAGMENTS

Señorita Córdoba

ONE MORNING Señorita Córdoba received a letter from her mother. She sat beside the fountain reading it.

My Dear Violeta—

I do hope you are enjoying every minute of your stay in the city of Antigua. It is a great miracle to think that Antigua has been destroyed once by fire and once by water. My father pointed out the beauty of this city to me at an early age. He said to me, "When you go to Europe, you need not bow your head in shame that you have come from a country inhabited almost entirely by Indians, as many Europeans are wont to believe. But say to them proudly, 'If Europe were a crown and in this crown one jewel were missing—the most beautiful jewel of all—you would find it in my country situated between two volcanoes and surrounded by hills. Its name is Antigua.'" At that age I loved to sit among the ruins, but Aunt Mercedes (who has come to agree with me), Aunt Mercedes and I still think it a little unwise for you to have taken such a trip at this particular moment. I realize it is only a few hours away, of course. Did you say that your board was fifty cents a day? For that they should serve you all the chicken you wanted and if they don't I hope you will be sure to demand your just rights. The lady of the pension will understand. I think perhaps that I as your mother have been a little too spiritual all my life. I do not want you to be the same. Perhaps, though, spiritual would not be the correct term to apply to you. Aunt Mercedes and I have been contenting ourselves with eggs and beans. The meat has been unusually hard this week and so very dear. I don't want you to worry about this or let it spoil your lovely holiday. You might try to buy a picture of the All Saints Day parade from someone who has a camera. Try not to buy it—ask for it, nicely. Señora Sanchez was in the other evening. She was riding by on a horse and she stopped in. She was complaining bitterly about prices, and insulted me grossly, I thought, by handing me half a chicken enveloped in some newspaper, which I handed over to the servants, of course. Aunt Mercedes didn't think that was quite wise. She is a great chicken eater, while I myself am more or less indifferent to all foods, as you know. Aunt Mercedes

> thought it dreadful that she should be riding on a horse, so soon after her husband's death. We send you our best wishes for an agreeable holiday. May the Lord bless you and keep you well.
>
> Your mother

Señorita Córdoba frowned and looked into the fountain. "Such an old-fashioned letter," she thought to herself. "My mother and my aunt are living like cliff dwellers. Such people write a letter about a chicken." She took a pencil from her bag and made some figures on a piece of paper. She knew just about how much money she needed to get back to Paris and to live there for a little while, while she was starting her dress establishment. She was going to make dresses with a Latin spirit. There was only one way for her to get hold of this money, she was certain, and that was through a man. She had seen a lot of this going on in Paris, and she thought that she would know how to handle such a situation if she could possibly meet a man rich enough in Guatemala. "It would all be in a first-class way," she had assured herself.

On the following morning Señorita Córdoba overheard Señora Ramirez telling the children that their father would arrive that day. She was delighted to hear this, because she knew Señor Ramirez to be one of the richest men in the country . . . and a great lady lover. It was on the chance that he would come to Antigua to visit his wife and children that she herself had decided to spend the Holy Week in Señora Espinoza's pension. She knew that Señora Ramirez had been spending the Semana Santa there now for many years, or so she had heard tell from her mother and her mother's friends, who had never understood why Señor Ramirez did not send his wife to a more expensive touristic hotel. He had never been seen at the pension with her until the previous year, when he had suddenly appeared in Antigua and stayed there for several days. However, most people said that he had come to spend his time with his friend Alfonso Gutierres, who had opened an unfrequented but very elegant hotel which was reputed to have the best wine cellar and hard liquor stock in the country. Señorita Córdoba, having heard of his former visit, had been very much in hopes that he would return again this season. She had thought the short journey well worth the risk, particularly as she was tired of helping her mother with the coffee finca and the house—two things which interested her less than anything in the world. She was delighted that he was arriving so promptly. She was never able to relax or enjoy anything that was not concerned directly with the making of her life. Now she was in a feverish state, pulling her dresses out of her trunk and examining them for holes. The figure that she had decided was the minimum sum which she would demand for her trip and to cover the initial investment in her dress shop, and of course her first six months living in Paris, she had marked down on a pad which lay on the bureau. She went over and looked at the pad now, and her cheeks were quite flushed with the intensity of her figuring. She stood there for a long time and then she changed the number on the pad. She made it a little lower.

She picked up a long silk ball dress that she had not worn for many years. It was pink, and to the bodice were pinned some shapeless silk flowers. She decided to wear this to dinner, as it was the fanciest thing she had and was certain to please a Spanish man. She lay down on the bed. Her face was strained and stiff. She shut her eyes for a moment and thought of the name of her shop. It was to be called "Casa Córdoba." "Now," she said to herself, "for what the French call beauty sleep. No thoughts—no thoughts—just rest." She could hear marimba music playing over the radio. She loved listening to music, and it made her think of all the things which she considered beautiful—Venice and the opera and the hall of mirrors in the palace at Versailles. To her, luxury and beauty (beauty there was none without at least the luxury of past splendor) were synonymous with morality, and when people lived well she considered them to be good people and when they lived really luxuriously she considered them to be saints. The marimba music and her memory of Venice and her walk through the hall of mirrors gave her such a feeling of the goodness of God that she crossed herself and decided to buy a candle in the church after her siesta.

The diners had all taken their places when Señorita Córdoba

entered the room. The Ramirez daughters, Consuela and Lilina, were seated on either side of their father, wearing their fiesta dresses. The servant stood in confusion before Señor Ramirez because he had ordered her not to bother with the soup but to bring him instead a large portion of meat and some beer right away.

"Wouldn't you like some soup first?" Maria asked him. Ramirez was beginning to lose his temper when he saw Señorita Córdoba enter the room. She had brightened her cheeks with some rouge, and on the whole she looked quite beautiful. Señor Ramirez's mouth hung open. He turned completely around in his chair and stared at Violeta. The traveler rose at the same time and rushed over to Señorita Córdoba as though he had never seen her before. She blushed a bright pink and her eyebrow twitched. To get away from all this attention she went over to the English lady in the corner and began to talk to her. The English lady was very much surprised because she had never received more than a curt nod from Miss Córdoba before this moment.

"Miss," said Violeta, "I wish you would take a walk with me some morning. I think it is a shame that we haven't become better acquainted with one another."

"Yes, it is, isn't it," answered the English lady. Miss Córdoba's armpits were wet with nervous sweat. She was terribly embarrassed since she had entered the room in her ball dress. She was bending over the English lady with one hand placed flat on the table, and she noticed that the English lady was looking into her bodice, a faint expression of disgust visible in her face, the disgust of an English person who does not like to be near to a foreigner.

"You Spanish girls all have such beautiful olive skin," she said. This was a completely hysterical thing for her to say because Violeta's skin was whiter than her own. She continued, "I would be very glad to take a walk with you but I am sure you will still be in the arms of Morpheus when I have already eaten my breakfast and written my letters for the day. I can't walk after ten because the sun tires me so. I have as a matter of fact covered the ground here thoroughly but I am looking forward to the processions. A friend described them to me so beautifully that I've been longing to see them ever since. A wonderful gift, to make other people see things. I am more or less mute myself. I have been impressed by the colors here. What a sense of color the Indians have. They are famous for it, aren't they?"

"Oh yes, very famous. I will see you then soon?"

"Perhaps."

Señorita Córdoba had nothing to do but to go back to the table and submit to the stares of Señor Ramirez and the appraising glances of the traveler. Out of exuberance Señor Ramirez decided to focus his attention on his older, eleven-year-old child, Consuela.

"Now I think it would do you some good if you drank a big glass of beer," he said. "The Germans always give their children beer and look what a fine race of people they are."

"I don't want any beer, thank you, papa."

"You've never tried it so you don't know whether or not you like it." He poured her some beer and put it in front of her but she made no attempt to drink it. "You heard papa say that he wanted you to drink some beer."

"What kind of a crazy idea is this?" asked Señora Ramirez.

"What kind of a crazy girl is that that she won't drink beer?" answered Señor Ramirez.

"Yes, drink, Consuela," said Señora Ramirez. "What is the matter with you?" She pushed the glass up to her daughter's lips but Consuela refused to drink, although her mouth was covered with foam. The girl's eyes were beginning to shine. With a sudden jerking of her arm she knocked the glass out of her mother's hand, and the beer flowed over the table. Then she jumped up and down and screamed. Señorita Córdoba turned halfway around in her chair and looked at her bitterly. And partly for this reason, and partly because Consuela was herself in love with the traveler and certain that the traveler in turn loved Señorita Córdoba, Consuela lunged toward her and started to scratch Señorita Córdoba's face and to tear her coiffure apart. Violeta, with an icy smile on her face, stuck her leg out in order to trip Consuela, but in so doing she miscalculated and slid off her chair on to the floor. Consuela ran from the room, and both the traveler and Señor Ramirez helped Violeta up from the floor. She leaned her head on her hand and cried a little because the incident had so unnerved her. Señor Ramirez ordered a glass of beer for Señorita Córdoba.

"You drink that, Señorita," he said, "and when I am finished eating I will beat my daughter. I promise you that."

"I hope that you will," said Señorita Córdoba.

"Never before," said the English lady, "have I met three such horrid people. The daughter a real Fury, unable to control herself, the father a child-beater, and the young woman full of revenge, willing to have the child beaten. My digestion is spoiled." She threw her napkin onto the table and left the room.

"Who is that one?" Señor Ramirez asked his wife.

"A tourist who eats here every day."

"She takes everything hard," said the traveler, turning to Señorita Córdoba. "Single women of her age do, you know. In our country we call them old maids."

"What is the difference what she is," said Señorita Córdoba. "To me she is no more than a flea."

"That's right," said Señor Ramirez. "That's right. Most people are fleas—fleas with big stomachs but nothing in their heads."

"But those big stomachs have to be fed," said the traveler, thinking that this was going to be a political discussion. "Or do you believe in letting them eat cake?"

"Cake? I don't care what they eat." The traveler decided not to explain about Marie Antoinette. Señorita Córdoba had composed herself completely by now, and she turned to Señor Ramirez.

"I am Señorita Violeta Córdoba," she said to him, disregarding all traditions of ladylike behavior, for she had always been able to throw tradition to the four winds without being in the least revolutionary. "Thank you for having lifted me from the floor onto my seat."

"And what about me?" said the traveler. "Don't I count in this at all?" Señorita Córdoba nodded to him without smiling. Ramirez stood up and toasted Señorita Córdoba with his beer. "To a beautiful lady," he said, "as beautiful as a red rose." They were speaking together in English.

"A thousand thanks," said Señorita Córdoba quickly. "Let us hope that you mean what you say, and are not just a poet."

"I can be a poet when I want to be, but it is only one of twenty or thirty things that I can do."

Señor Gutierres' hotel was austere but very elegant. The patio around which it was built was very small and almost always very dark. Looking down into it from the third floor, it was hard to distinguish the bushes and the few flower beds. Each bedroom was decorated in order to look as much like the bedroom of a Spanish king or nobleman as possible. The beds were on raised daises and the monogram of the hotel was on each pillow slip. The walls were rough and decorated with crossed sabres and blue or gold banners. The chairs were made of a very dark wood with carved narrow backs and little satin cushions tied to the seats by means of four tassels. Off the patio were two small dining rooms for those guests who preferred not to eat in the presence of strangers, and one large dining room that was public. In the public living room there was a veritable collection of sabres with fancy hilts, and chairs with backs that reached halfway up the wall. It was impossible to see in this room at all during the day, and at night the weak electric lamps left the corners of the room in total darkness.

Señor Gutierres was a gloomy businessman born in Spain who claimed to have noble blood. He was out in the back court, a place to which the guests had no access, wrangling with the cook about a chicken which he was holding by its feet and pinching. He was very thin and had deep circles under his eyes. There were a great many badly made rabbit hutches around, and a tremendous chicken coop. He was one of the few people in the country who kept his chickens in a coop. However, there were three large holes in the wiring and the chickens stepped in and out of the coop freely. The courtyard was a mess and it was just beginning to drizzle when Señor Ramirez came out and clapped his friend on the shoulder. "How about coming down to the bar and having a drink with me?" Señor Gutierres nodded and smiled for a second and together they went to the bar, which was underground and smelled very strongly of new wood. The bar stools were made of barrels. Señor Ramirez sat down on one of these and Señor Gutierres dropped the chicken, which he was still holding, onto the floor. The chicken began to strut around the shiny wooden floor, pecking at whatever it saw.

"How do you like my bar now that it is completed?"

"I will like your brandy even better when I have completed a bottle of that."

"Do you like my bar?" Señor Gutierres said again, determined to get an answer out of Señor Ramirez.

"Beautiful."

"I have designed the whole hotel for movie actresses and actors when they are on their vacations. They will be coming down over that highway like flies when it is finished." He looked at Señor Ramirez to see if he was of the same opinion, but his friend was staring hard at the labels on the bottles.

"A lot of people on their honeymoons, too. Rich people who like to go far, far away when they get married." He took down a bottle of brandy from the shelf and served himself and Señor Ramirez.

"You don't think much about this new highway. I dream about it by day and by night. You will see a difference in the hotels in this country when it is built. You won't recognize the place you were born in inside of five years. No?"

Señor Gutierres could never get it through his head that Norberto Ramirez was not interested in anything but having a good time and wielding a certain amount of power. He had inherited most of his money and was successful because he had the character of a bully. Señor Gutierres could not imagine that anyone as important and as impressive as Señor Ramirez should not be interested in business. He believed that his friend's disinclination to talk on any subject of interest was merely a ruse, which he had long ago decided to ignore.

"I have built my hotel purposely so soon because later it will not be so cheap. I have already quite a few guests who come here because they know they get good quality. They are all quality people. Everything has to be right for them. It is just as cheap to be right as to be wrong, my friend, you know that, and with a war coming in Europe, all these with quality who used to go to Biarritz will come here. And I am not going to make cheap prices for them. They mustn't pay anything different from what they were paying at Biarritz, otherwise they will say to themselves, Look, what is this? There is something wrong—so cheap, and they will even get to worry that there might be lower-class people in the same hotel. No, they must be taken like sleeping babies from one bed to another, quietly, so they don't wake up. A little Spanish decoration for a change will be all right. But if you notice this hotel is made to remind you more or less of a palace."

One of the Indian servants appeared in the doorway. She looked to be about forty and she was nursing a baby at her breast and smiling. "What do you want, Luz?" asked Señor Gutierres.

"I have come for the chicken, Señor. He must feel very sad for he is estranged from the other chickens, his brothers and his sisters, and the poor little thing cannot find anything to eat here." She started to chase it. The chicken spread its wings and ran as fast as it could around and around the room. The baby started to howl.

"Stop it, stop it!" shouted Señor Gutierres. "You can come and get him later."

"No, wait a minute, man," said Señor Ramirez, climbing down from his stool. "I will get this chicken." He spread his arms out and chased it from corner to corner, making terrible scratches in the wooden floor with the heels of his shoes, to the horror of Señor Gutierres, who began to rub his nose nervously with the back of his hand. Señor Ramirez was quite red in the face by now and beginning to lose his balance. He made a lunge toward the chicken and managed to corner it, but in so doing he fell sideways onto the floor and managed to crush the chicken beneath him.

"Ay," said the servant. "Now it is dead we shall have to cook it for tomorrow night's supper."

"Take it away, for the love of God," said Señor Gutierres, lifting his friend to his feet and handing the bloody chicken to the servant.

"What a shame, what a shame." The servant shook her head and left the room. They had another brandy together and did not bother to clean up the blood and the feathers which stuck both to one side of Señor Ramirez' coat and to the floor.

Señorita Córdoba meanwhile had had enough of waiting around the patio for the problematic return of Señor Ramirez.

"My God," she said to herself, "I have no time to lose. I am behaving like a person with not a brain in her head." Besides, it had begun to rain and it was incredibly gloomy sitting there under the eaves, which projected a little bit from the house for the purpose of protecting one from the sun and from the rain. She went into her room, painted her face a bit more, and changed to a short dress. Then she decided to knock on Señora Ramirez' door and by some ruse try to find out where this lady's husband was likely to be. This she did and at first received no answer.

She knocked a little harder. "Come in," said Señora Ramirez in a voice that was caught in her throat. Señorita Córdoba opened the door and saw that Señora Ramirez and the two girls were lying on their beds, in a row. Consuela's dark eyes showed intense suffering as she rolled them slowly in the direction of the door. Lilina, seeing that it was Señorita Córdoba, pulled her pillow out from behind her head and buried her face beneath it. Señora Ramirez' eyes were swollen with sleep and she looked very much as though nothing would ever interest her again. Señorita Córdoba decided to ignore the mood that was in the room and she went hastily to the foot of Señora Ramirez' bed.

"I thought perhaps that you would be feeling rather badly as a result of this afternoon's events, and I came in to tell you more or less not to brood about it, and to ask you whether or not I could help you with anything."

Señora Ramirez nodded her head, and closed her eyes. Señorita Córdoba was growing impatient. She looked down at Consuela. "You, young girl," she said, "You should apologize to me." Consuela shook her head from side to side. "No," she said, "no, you are a very bad woman." She patted her heart.

"Well, Señora Ramirez, your daughter is a maniac. I am a religious woman and I am a very busy woman. That is all that anybody can say of me."

"Certainly," agreed Señora Ramirez, opening her eyes. "That is all anyone can say. And of me they can say that I am a mother of two children, and also a woman with a great many heartaches."

"I suppose you are wondering where your husband is at this very moment."

"No, no," said Señora Ramirez. "He is always outside somewhere."

Señorita Córdoba was exasperated. "But *where*? Where could he be?"

"With Gutierres, drinking."

"Who is Gutierres?"

"He is the owner of a hotel. It is called the Hotel Alhambra. My husband has never taken me to meet him and I shall probably never meet him before the day that I die."

Having gathered the information that she had been seeking, Señorita Córdoba hurriedly took her leave, warning Consuela at the door that she had better repent shortly. And then she was on her way, with an even and decided gait, like someone who has been sent on an important mission by the head of an organization. She was not a person who envisioned failure often, but only the interminable steps toward success.

When she arrived at the hotel she found a servant in the patio and inquired of her where she could find Señor Gutierres. "He is in the bar," said the servant, leading the way slowly.

"Good evening," said Señorita Córdoba, entering the room. "I hope that I have not interrupted a serious business conversation. Women have a very bad habit of doing this."

"Women have no bad habits," said Señor Ramirez, climbing down from his stool and taking her by the arm a little roughly.

"I got it into my head," said Señorita Córdoba, "that I would like to look at some rooms here."

"I am sure you will take great pleasure in seeing them." Señor Gutierres had bounded to the door in his eagerness, but Señor Ramirez held his hand up in the air.

"Before the rooms," he said, "we are all going to have a drink together to celebrate the arrival of a lady. Champagne for her, Gutierres. Sit down, Señorita."

Señorita Córdoba complied with this request only too willingly and took her seat at the bar.

"How delightful," she said. "I always like to drink champagne because it reminds me of Paris, where I belong."

"Paris is a very gay city. The night life there is very beautiful," said Señor Gutierres, believing that he was dealing with an elegant client. "Here in this hotel there is everything to remind you of Paris. I have letters from there asking for reservations. Your father no doubt owns a finca, and you no doubt have lived all your life in Paris and in Biarritz. And now you find this country strange, like the jungle—*bien?*"

"This lady," said Señor Ramirez, "lives in the pension where I always put my wife and my two girls. That is how I know her."

Gutierres' face fell. He had hardly expected to draw his customers from Señora Espinoza's pension, which he considered a step below the large touristic hotels.

"I know the lady who owns the pension," he said sadly, "but very little, only to speak to. I know very few people in this town. My servants buy for me, so why should I speak to anyone?"

"You are better off keeping your life to yourself," said Señorita Córdoba, "than having companions that are doing nothing but just sitting and trying to find someone to laugh with."

A shadow seemed to pass across the face of Señor Ramirez. For a moment he thought of going back to the capital right away. "Here, here," he shouted. "What is all this about your life alone? Let's be together, friends—like baby chickens under the wings of the mother hen."

Señor Gutierres was now just a little bit drunk, and he was beginning to wander on to things that he scarcely knew he thought about. "No," he said, "no—no chickens under one wing. Each man alone, proud, acting as he has been taught to act by his family, never living in a house that is lower than the house in which he was born. Each man remembering his father and his mother and what he has been taught is sacred."

"The only thing that is sacred, my poor boy, is money," said the pleasure-seeking Norberto.

"No, it is one's class," insisted Señor Gutierres. "We must love our own class. I cannot talk and be friendly with people whose childhood I know has been different from mine, who did not have the same silver on the table when they sat down to eat."

"You would be glad to talk with me, Gutierres, even if I ate with pigs when I was a little boy."

"No, no, I would not. There is real friendship only between

men who have always been used to the same things. Between two such men no words need be spoken, because each one knows that the other will do nothing to disgust him or upset him, and the pleasure of being with such a friend is quite enough. I have such a friend here, who knows the value of every piece of furniture in the Alhambra. And there is no wine that is familiar to me that is not familiar to him. We don't have to say anything to each other. Each of us remembers the same things. His family and my family come from the same part of Spain. I feel so close to him that I might say that I would even wear his underclothes. Forgive me, Señorita." He bowed his head.

"But *my* underwear you would not put on for five thousand quetzales, eh, señor?" said Ramirez, throwing his chest out.

Señor Gutierres, having started off talking about his thin code which he considered to be a universal and important ideology, had necessarily to go on further. His astute business sense was completely obliterated by the fanaticism that all men feel about whatever it is they believe makes the world an orderly and respectable place in which to live. "No, señor," he said, "I would not wear your underwear, for your education is far below mine and your family, as I know, were not much more than peasants before they came to this country."

"Oh, how rude you are," said Señorita Córdoba, taking hold of Señor Ramirez' hand. "And I am sure it is not true."

"Certainly it is true," said Señor Ramirez, "and this monkey will soon find out what else is true." Señorita Córdoba was surprised that Señor Ramirez had as yet not kicked the bar stools over, but apparently his family was not a sensitive point with him, and perhaps also he was having a very pleasurable reaction from the drinks and was not inclined to fight.

"Let him kiss his chairs," continued Señor Ramirez, "and see how many women he will get to kiss. He is probably a miserable eunuch anyway. Kiss me." He put his hand under Señorita Córdoba's chin and kissed her full on the mouth. Señorita Córdoba wondered whether or not she should resist this kiss, and decided very quickly that it was wiser to pretend to enjoy it. She passed a fluttering hand over his ear, which was one of the few love gestures she knew about.

"This woman is a trollop," said Señor Gutierres in a

trembling voice. Señor Ramirez could not possibly let this remark pass so he stopped kissing Señorita Córdoba and gave Gutierres a sock on the jaw that knocked him off his stool and onto the floor where he lay unconscious.

"Now," he said to Señorita Córdoba, lifting her down from her stool, "let us find an agreeable place in this beautiful Alhambra Hotel." He spat on the floor.

"Oh, well," said Señorita Córdoba, deciding that it was time for her to be a little bit shy. "Shall we stand in the patio a little bit and then go home?"

"No," he said. "I want to go where I can see your beautiful face." He led her upstairs, and with his foot he kicked open the door to one of the bedrooms, and turned on the light. She went and sat down on one of the chairs which Señor Gutierres considered to be beautiful and folded her hands in her lap. "I have always been interested to know a man like you," she said, "with such a wonderful way of knowing how to live."

"There are no disappointments in my life," said Señor Ramirez, "and I love it. I can show you some wonderful things."

"My life is a terrible disappointment to me," said Señorita Córdoba, and her heart beat very quickly as she felt she was approaching her goal.

The room was badly lighted and she searched his eyes avidly to see what effect her words had made on him. It seemed to her that they had a slightly blank look, like the eyes of anyone who is gazing at a particular object without really seeing it.

"You have not had the right kind of love," he said.

"That is not the only reason," said Señorita Córdoba, shaking her head vigorously. Señor Ramirez was feeling suddenly very drunk and he threw himself down on the bed.

"You must not go to sleep," she said nervously, rising to her feet.

"Who in the devil is going to sleep?" Señor Ramirez leaned on his elbows and looked at her like an angry bull.

"Listen," she said, "I'm so miserable on that finca where I am living that I think that if it goes on any longer I will certainly drown myself in the river."

"Drowning is no good," said Ramirez. "That's only good for scared fools, like those little dogs that shiver all the time—they have them in Mexico. You are not on your finca now.

Come here on the bed and stop talking so much." He put his arm out and caught at the air with his hand.

"I want to go away to Paris, where I have friends, and start a dress shop."

"Sure," said Señor Ramirez.

"But I have not got any money."

"I have so much money."

"I need five thousand dollars."

He started to unbutton his pants. Señorita Córdoba remembered that many men were not interested in ladies nearly as much after they had made love to them as they were beforehand, so she decided that she had better make sure that she received a check first. She did not know how to do this tactfully but her own greed and the fact that he was drunk, and that she thought him a coarse person anyway, made her believe that she would be successful. She walked quickly to the window and stood with her back to him.

"What are you looking at outside the window?" asked Señor Ramirez, in a thick voice, smelling trouble.

"I am not looking at anything. On the contrary, I am just thinking about you, and how little you are really interested in whether or not I will open a dress shop."

"You can open a thousand dress shops, my beautiful woman. What is the matter with you?"

"You lie. I cannot even open one dress shop." She turned around and faced him.

"Wildcat," he said to her. She tried to look more touching. "You will not help me to open a dress shop. Must it be someone else that will help me?"

"I am going to help you open fifty dress shops—tomorrow."

"I would not ask you for fifty, only for one. Would you make me happy and give me a check tonight so that I know when I go to sleep I will have my dress shop? I would like to sleep in peace just for once and know that I am not going to have to go back to that terrible finca, and listen to the dogs howling and my mother praying out loud. This one check would banish all these horrible things from my mind right away and I would be eternally grateful to you. I would be so glad that it had been you who did it, too."

"Well, then, come here."

She sat down on the bed beside him and he kissed her, but while he was kissing her she pushed him away and said to him, "Give me the check now."

"What is this?" asked Señor Ramirez. "Are you still talking about this damn foolish check?"

"Yes," said Señorita Córdoba, seeing that it was no use any longer to employ tact. "I will not go to bed with you unless you first give me a check for five thousand quetzales, or a piece of paper saying that you owe this sum of money to me."

Certainly this remark was not having the right effect on Señor Ramirez, who struggled with difficulty down from the bed and buttoned his trousers. She watched him attentively and noticed that the glands in his neck were moving. "Angry again," she said to herself, but she could think of nothing to say that would calm him except "Where are you going?" which she asked in a rather ironical tone of voice, all her false ardor dampened now by her own conviction that she would fail to get her money. Señor Ramirez was trembling and very red in the face. She stood still and appeared to be very calm even when he finally stumbled out of the room, but when she heard him clambering down the stairs she walked out on to the balcony and looked down over the railing into the patio. One light was burning and in a moment Señor Ramirez came into the patio and picked up what she saw was a large urn with a tall plant growing out of it. This he threw to the ground not very far from his feet, because it was very heavy. It smashed in many pieces, but made less noise than she expected to hear because the dirt inside the urn muffled the sound that it would otherwise have made.

She could not understand his fury, knowing so little about deeply outraged feelings and the fact that so much of people's violence is spent in the elaborate and grim protection of a personality as undeveloped as a foetus yet grown quickly to tremendous proportions, like a giant weed. Being stupid herself, she did not recognize the danger inherent in all those whose self-protective instincts are far greater than the personality they are protecting, because their armor can only be timeworn and made up of the most stagnating of human impulses. Señorita Córdoba was unwounded if unintelligent, and her rages were unimportant nervous discharges.

Señor Ramirez was struggling with the big wooden doors that led into the street and making a terrible racket shaking the heavy iron chains, but it was to no avail because the doors were locked from the inside. She could only hear him now without being able to see him, since the bulb threw no light into the front of the patio. Suddenly he stopped rattling the chains and she heard him walking back in the direction of the staircase.

"My God," she thought, "he has murder in his heart, certainly," and she sneaked around to another side of the balcony. Fortunately the servant who had before been looking for the chicken was awakened by the noise and she now came into the patio to find out what the trouble was. "The door is locked," Ramirez shouted at her.

"Yes," she whispered. "I'll fetch the key."

She returned with the key and let Señor Ramirez out of the patio into the street. Señorita Córdoba decided to wait a little while before returning to the pension herself. She was thinking very hard of a way to redeem herself on the following day. She was like certain mediocre politically-minded persons upon whose minds failure leaves no deep impression, not because of any burning belief in the ideal for which they are fighting, but rather because they are accustomed to thinking only of what to do next. These people are often valuable but at the same time so removed from reality that they are ridiculous. After sitting a while in the gloomy Spanish bedroom Señorita Córdoba went downstairs and in turn awakened the Indian servant, who let her out.

Early 1940s

Looking for Lane

THE TOWN of X— was built on six or seven different levels. Right behind it there rose a heavily wooded mountain range, while below it stretched a swampy valley divided in the middle by a dark green river. Big wooden steps with iron handrails served as short cuts between one level of the town and the next. On the bottom level were the main streets, the shops, and the largest houses. On the third level at the end of the street there was a swift little waterfall near which Miss Dora Sitwell lived in a log house with her sister Lane. Lane was the younger but both sisters were in their middle years. Dora was a tall bony woman with bold black hair which she wore straight and pointing in toward her cheeks on either side. Her eye was bright and her nose long. Her sister was the opposite type—rather chunky and a blonde.

One morning in the fall of the year Dora was mending a pair of antique bellows and her sister lay in bed with a light case of grippe. She called in to Dora:

"Winter is coming and the damp is starting to seep in here already from that mountain. It's too near the house. As a matter of fact the whole town should be leveled. What's the point of living built into the side of a mountain? Why don't we go to Florida?"

"I like the change of seasons," Dora said pleasantly. "I love to watch each season come in—"

"We're too old for that winter summer spring stuff," Lane objected. "We should go to Florida and rest."

"I have as much zip as ever," Dora answered, "and I love the different seasons. So do you."

"I don't at all," said Lane.

Dora hung the bellows on their hook and walked into a dark and crowded corner of the room where she picked up a yellow crock designed to imitate a squash. She uncorked it and poured herself some sherry.

She drank sherry very often during the day but never so much that she lost interest in sewing or household work. Actually, she was more industrious and swifter than Lane, who did not drink but sat still dreaming for long periods of time. Dora returned to the couch which she herself had upholstered with two Indian blankets of different designs. There were a number of Indian and Russian objects in the room.

After a long period of silence, Lane called again.

"You can't tell me you enjoy November."

"I have nothing against November," said Dora. "In fact it's likely to make me feel zippy." Lane's feet thrashed angrily under the covers.

"It's not even natural to be as good-tempered as you are," she complained. "Every woman's got to have her humors."

"But I have nothing that makes me sad."

"Your husband died, didn't he?"

"Yes," Dora answered. "But he's so fortunate to be where he is. It's lovely up there."

"Well," Lane continued crossly. "You won't ever get there from this cluttered-up stupid little log house, I can tell you that."

"You don't have any knack for religion, Lane," Dora said. "You don't get what it's about—you never have."

Lane's face darkened. In referring to her lack of religious inclination her sister had touched on a very sore spot. Lane did not have the fear of God.

She felt ashamed of this, and pretended to fear Him and to think about Him. She was free as well from any fear of the night or of wandering among the hills alone, and from any fear of strangers. This lack too she guarded from her sister's knowledge. It is impossible to foretell what a person will be ashamed of when finally grown up. Lane had no admiration at all for the type of woman so often described as "a dauntless woman" or even sometimes as a "she-devil." It had not even occurred to her that such a woman could be attractive, since moral character rather than personality concerned her, even though at a very underdeveloped level.

She also lived in fear that her sister would discover one day that she had never really formed any attachments. She felt attachment neither for her house, for her sister, nor for the town where she had been born. This secret, bitter but small in the beginning when she had first become conscious of it, had slowly come to contain her whole life. Not an hour passed that found her oblivious of the falsity of her position in the world. As a child believes that in five minutes he will have wings and be able to fly, so Lane hoped that she would awaken one day with a feeling of attachment and love for her sister and for the house, and with the fear of God in her heart.

She picked on her sister night and day, but concerning this behavior she felt no remorse.

Now Lane looked over her shoulder out of the window, and saw the wooded hill rising straight up behind the house. The trees were bare. A white dog ran along beneath the trees, with the dry deep autumn leaves almost covering his back each time his paws touched the ground.

"I wonder," Lane said, "if that dog's going to be out all night."

"What dog, dear?"

"There's a white dog running through the forest."

"I guess he's after chipmunks," said Dora, "or just taking the air. Dogs like air, you know."

"I don't believe they care about air," Lane frowned. "They like food and smells . . ."

". . . and their masters," Dora added. "Don't forget their loyalty—their admirable attachment to their masters. I wish we had a dog."

"He might be taking a short cut through the woods and striking out for the next town," Lane said, her heart sinking.

"With nothing but his tail as luggage, instead of a lot of satchels," Dora added. "Human beings don't know it all. Animals have things more conveniently. Think of the fuss a human being makes when he goes on a journey."

The word "journey" struck deep into Lane's heart, and she closed her eyes for a minute, overcome with shame and anxiety. "You are like that dog," a voice inside of her said. She turned away from the window so that the light would be in back of her and her face could not be seen.

Even though Dora had walked to the far corner of the room again and was lifting the yellow crock, she knew that her sister had "passed into darkness"—a phrase she used to describe certain of Lane's moods, but only to herself. A curious reticence had prevented her from ever wondering why her sister did "pass into darkness"—nor had she ever shown by word or expression that she knew anything was amiss with her sister at these moments.

Lane's moods lent a certain dignity to Dora which she would not otherwise have possessed. Dora loved the existence she led with Lane so passionately that she had actually to sit still on the sofa during certain moments of complete awareness of it, the impact of her joy acting upon her like a blow.

She had been pleased at the death of both her parents and her older sister because this left her free to sell the Sitwell homestead and to construct with the proceeds a log house, which she had been planning to do all her life. She had always longed as well to live in a house built on one floor only and to roll her meals into the parlor on a tea-table. This she did with Lane every day, and with unfailing delight. She lived for pleasure alone, which she thought was the way of an artist—it being natural for certain women to love even the word artist. And not all of them feel this way for snobbish motives. Sometimes when she was in particularly high spirits she referred to herself as an artist. At other times she merely mentioned that she lived like one. One afternoon when she was really tipsy in the hotel barroom she had referred to herself many times as "the artist in the little log house." Because of the wild and joyous look in her black eyes, her neighbors could not believe that her pleasures were simple ones.

Dora had started to love Lane one night when Lane was five years old and she herself was eleven. Her mother and father had told her to bathe Lane because they were going to a show. She prepared the tin tub with warm water and told Lane to wait in the kitchen while she went to fetch some soap. When she returned Lane was no longer in the kitchen. She searched throughout the house for nearly three hours, but she could not find Lane anywhere. Finally, bewildered and tired, she sat on the floor in the hall, planning to wait for her parents' return. While she sat there, it suddenly came to her that she loved Lane more than anything else in the world. "Lane," she said aloud. "You angel pie—you're better than Baby Jesus." She began feeling in her heart that Lane's flight from the kitchen was in the nature of a declaration of love and a secret pact, and her own search through the dark cold rooms—some of them empty of everything but dust and unfamiliar to her—had caused her to feel that in Lane were centered the light and the warm colors of the universe. "Lane is a beautiful rose," she thought, thinking of Lane's curls on her short fat neck.

Later with the help of her parents she searched the barn and they found Lane curled up in the sleigh under some filthy horse blankets.

Dora leaned over and picked Lane up in her arms. Lane, groggy with sleep, bit Dora on the chin and made it bleed. Their mother started to scold, but Dora kissed Lane passionately for a long time, squeezing Lane's head against her own skinny chest. Mrs. Sitwell wrenched them apart in a sudden fury and pulled Dora's hair.

"Why do you kiss her, you little maniac? She just bit you!" Dora smiled but she did not answer.

"Why do you kiss her when she just bit you?" Mrs. Sitwell repeated. "Are you a maniac?"

Dora nodded.

"I won't have it," said Mrs. Sitwell, now cold with fury. "You tell her you're mad she bit you." Dora refused. Mrs. Sitwell twisted her arm. "Tell her you're mad she bit you."

"Lane and me are maniacs," said Dora, in a very quiet voice, still smiling. Mrs. Sitwell slapped her hard on the face.

"No one is a maniac," she said, "and you can't speak to Lane for two days." Then she burst into tears. They all went across the grass to the house. Mrs. Sitwell was sobbing freely. She was a very nervous woman and she had drunk a bit too much at the party. This had made her very gay at first, but later she had grown increasingly belligerent. They all went into the parlor, where Mrs. Sitwell sank into a chair and began staring at Lane through her tear-dimmed eyes.

"They should go to bed," her husband said.

"Lane doesn't look like anybody in the family on either side," said Mrs. Sitwell. "Why does she have such a short neck?"

"One of her antecedents most likely had a short neck," Mr. Sitwell suggested. "An aunt or an uncle."

"I don't feel like going on," said Mrs. Sitwell. "Everything is beyond me." She buried her face in her hands. Dora and Lane left the room.

After that Dora organized a game called "Looking for Lane"

which she played with her sister. It was the usual hide-and-seek game that children play but it gave Dora a much keener pleasure than any ordinary game. Finally the search extended over the countryside and Dora allowed her imagination to run wild. For example, she imagined once that she would find Lane's body dismembered on the railroad tracks. Her feelings about this were mixed. The important thing was that the land became a magic one the moment the search began. Sometimes Lane didn't hide at all, and Dora would discover her in the nursery after searching for nearly a whole afternoon. On such occasions she would become so depressed that she wouldn't eat.

Lane never explained anything. She was a quiet child with round grey eyes and a fat face.

This game stopped abruptly when Dora was fourteen, and she never again thought about it.

Each time that Lane "passed into darkness" Dora had a curious reaction that was not unlike that of a person who remembers a sexual gratification when he does not expect to. She was never alarmed, nor did she feel lonely. To live with a person who is something of a lunatic is certainly a lonely experience even if it is not an alarming one, but Dora had never felt loneliness. Sometimes, although she knew Lane was having a spell, she continued talking.

"Suppose," she said on this particular day, "that we plan our itinerary for next spring. There are several mountains that I'd like to visit. As one grows older one has access to many more pleasures than one ever had as a young person. It's as if at a certain age a thick black curtain were wrenched aside, disclosing row upon row of goodies ready to be snatched. We're put on this earth for us to enjoy—although certain others get their thrill out of abstinence and devotion. That's just doing it the other way around. Not that I care at all what others do—too much contact spoils the essence of things. You'll agree to that, because you're a first-class hermit, anyway. Do you want to have dinner at the hotel?"

Lane did not answer, but looked again out of the window.

"If you're looking for that white dog, Lane, he's certainly deep into the woods by this time."

Late 1940s?

Laura and Sally

LAURA SEABROOK was lying in her bed at four in the afternoon. She lived with Sam Brewster, a mechanic trained as an engineer who helped in many different ways around Camp Cataract. He often drove the truck into town for provisions, or the bus that fetched those people who had no cars from the railroad station. He ran the wood-chopping machine and tended all the roofs and defective screens. He was very happy at his different tasks and did not seem to regret his engineering studies. He regretted having disappointed his mother, but he was usually satisfied with what he was doing, as long as his life was among friendly people and out of doors. He could not bear to live in cities but he did not out of this dislike make a cult of nature.

Laura's hair hung to her shoulders and fell over half of her brooding face. No sunlight penetrated through the thick black pine trees into her cabin, but a blue bulb simulating daylight hung over her head. She was a very great beauty.

Sally McBridge was standing on the door sill smiling at Laura. Hers was a delicate pink face with round but fanatical blue eyes. She came every summer to Camp Cataract and the staff considered her to be somewhat of a lunatic and a fool. She dressed in a provincial out-of-date manner and altogether seemed to belong to either another country or another time. At this moment she was wearing a black coat with an orange fur collar and a bonnet-shaped hat. She could not have been much more than thirty-nine or forty.

"How are you?" she asked Laura. "I thought you'd be dressed and ready to have your dinner."

"I can't dress," said Laura without looking at her.

"Do you have your melancholia?" Sally questioned her with a smile. Laura refused to answer.

"I'll tell you one thing," Sally continued. "You have to live in peace whether you have it or not. You can beat life if you want to." Sally's expression at that moment was almost wicked and even calculating. Laura looked at her for the first time.

"And then what's left to you after you've beaten life?" she asked sullenly.

"Happiness is left," Sally said. "Life is chaos and happiness is system—as if in a very delicately wrought but strong cage, while the life chaos remains outside. But remember I said cage and not room. The distinction is tremendous."

"What distinction?"

"Between room and cage. Do you know what I'm implying?"

Laura shrugged her shoulders. "Don't tell me," she said. For she was very aware that Sally's explanation would be wordy and very boring to her. Sally continued, however, ignoring her remark.

"If your happiness system is like a very delicate cage, you can see out and others can see in, even though your protections are as strong as the silver wires of a cage," she said. "But in a room you're really shut off."

Laura covered her face with her hands. "I hate Camp Cataract," she said. "That's all I know."

"I love it," Sally replied in a simple tone. "Perhaps because an evergreen is my favorite tree. It's modest and always there, like a friend or a loyal dog, winter and summer alike. And when its branches are heavy with snow, there is no tree more beautiful in the universe. Do you like evergreens?"

Laura did not answer. Her eyes were brooding.

"I'm certain you would like some place like Hawaii," Sally said to her. "You're such an impatient restless type of person. A palm tree is more your emblem than a pine. Isn't that so?"

"I have never thought of it," Laura replied. "I don't think of any of the things you think of. I don't believe I've ever looked at a tree, much less thought of one. I don't have a light enough heart to sit and think about things like that."

"My heart is not light, Laura," Sally said. "I have to spend many hours in my cabin alone. I'm going there now—I had a fit of nervous irritability this afternoon, and I want to think about it."

"Anyone who can speak of a happiness system is lighthearted," Laura said flatly.

"Don't talk nonsense, Laura. The finest brains have been occupied with such systems since the beginning of time . . . orientals and occidentals alike."

"That's religion you're speaking of," said Laura. "Not a happiness system."

Quite suddenly Sally's face fell apart. She backed away from the cabin door, and Laura could hear her feet moving through the leaves.

Laura cocked an ear, but it was impossible to tell by listening to the rustle of dead leaves whether Sally was advancing deeper into the pine grove towards her cabin or if she had turned back in the direction of the lodge.

"I've hurt Sally's feelings," Laura thought. The brooding expression left her face, and at once a look of gravity and even nobility took its place. She rose to her feet. "I must go and find her."

She pulled a black dress of very thin material over her head and brushed out her stiff hair. Then she set out through the pine grove in search of Sally.

Her gait was a slow rolling one like that of a sailor. Her lips she kept held parted, and to the gravity of her expression was added a look of wonder which deepened as she approached the lodge. There was no longer any trace of apathy in her countenance. When she reached the dining terrace she stood still and looked about for Sally. The wind was blowing hard, somewhat deadening the roar of the waterfalls. Laura saw Sally moving with difficulty between the last row of tables (the row nearest to the precipice) and the heavy chain which separated the dining terrace from its edge.

"Why does she choose to cross there?" Laura asked herself. "There's barely space to get through without brushing against the diners." She hastened across the terrace herself, but at a more convenient place near the lodge steps. Pine groves surrounded the terrace at the other side as well, but through these groves a path had been cut leading to the main road. Laura reached the path first and hid behind a tree until Sally walked past. Then she came out from her hiding place and followed her. Laura knew that Sally was going to Mr. Cassalotti's restaurant in the village. During the last three weeks she had followed Sally several times to the village and joined her there.

Sally's fits of temper and shame were becoming more and more necessary to Laura. They stirred her blood. And while she hated Sally to such an extent at these moments that she wanted to strike her face, her own dignity at once seemed to swoop down upon her like some great and unexpected bird. It was not to comfort Sally, therefore, that she followed her to the village, but to enjoy for a while this calm and noble self born each time out of the other woman's rage.

She kept at a sufficient distance from Sally so that the other did not hear her footsteps. Camp Cataract, although situated in authentically wild country, was not at a very great distance from a little center, which could hardly have been called a town, but which included several stores, a restaurant, and a railroad station.

It was at this restaurant that Sally now stopped and mounted the stairs. She went into the dining room, located at the back of the house and reached only through the store which opened on the front steps. It was a dark room, with only five or six tables. There was no one about, but she could hear the members of the family moving overhead in their apartment. She chose a table next to a glassed-in scene that Mr. Cassalotti had inserted in a large wall niche. The painted drop was of a cottage with lawn and woods and a little stream running to one side of it. Mr. Cassalotti had extended the real lawn by using stage grass, and there were even little trellises about, stuck with old paper roses, too many of them contrasting oddly with the pastel-shaded flowers painted on the drop. Crowding the lawn was an assortment of poorly selected men and women fashioned in different styles and out of different materials, some being brightly painted lead and others carved out of wood. There was also, to complete the pointless staging, a child's miniature orange automobile set down right in the very midst of the lawn gathering and driven by a tiny rubber baby doll. The scene was illuminated from the sides and at this moment supplied the only light in the dining room.

The immediate urge of any diner with even the slightest degree of sensibility, if not to the actual aesthetic offense, then at least to the offense against order and the fulfillment of intention, was to punch through the glass and remove the automobile, if not half the figures. Only to the Cassalotti family and to children there was no disturbing element in this glassed-in scene.

Sally stared for a bit at the familiar lawn group, and even though she was a fanatic with usually one obsession at a time she felt a strong desire to remove the orange truck, which for a second absorbed her completely. She looked around automatically, as everyone else did, for an opening in the glass, although she knew perfectly well that there was none. Then she turned her back upon it and closed her eyes. She was trembling, and the wings of her nostrils were drawn. However, far from taking fright at the hysteria Laura's words had unloosed, or even growing despondent over it, Sally merely underwent the experience very much the way she stood behind the waterfalls each day at Camp Cataract. Far behind her new fit she was smiling to herself, unbeatable and optimistic.

She knew that Laura had intended to upset her by drawing a line between her happiness system and the religions of the world. But it was not the seriousness of this demarcation that Sally was upset about so much as the simple fact that Laura had attacked her at all. Any criticism or show of aggression on Laura's part was enough to set Sally spinning backwards like someone clubbed over the head. This did not alter the fact that Sally considered herself to be the eventual victor. She knew too, without ever having had to reflect upon it, that Laura's connection with the universe was of greater depth and perception than her own—even though Laura was lazy and frankly jeered at life as without purpose. She had merely to speak of a serious subject when immediately the accent of her voice, the expression in her eye, lent to her words the weight of true gold. If Sally had been sincerely interested in becoming a wonderful person, she would have certainly been alarmed at recognizing a deeper accent of truth in Laura's voice than in her own. She would then have known the despair which comes of recognizing that what another understood automatically she herself would have to strive ceaselessly to understand throughout her life, and this would have caused her either to give up her own struggle—even if only temporarily, in a fit of jealous impotence—or, had she the strength, to continue along her own path, but wiser and more humble for her acquaintance with Laura.

She did neither, but instead set herself the task of conquering Laura—although exactly in what sense she meant to conquer her friend she did not herself know. Hers was an instinctive chase with a concealed objective. It is a curious fact that Sally, whose life was a series of tests and rituals of purification imposed upon herself, should have reacted so unscrupulously to the superiority—whether genuine or imagined by herself—of another woman. It was probable that she related the best and most spiritual part of her mind and heart to her life's purpose and only coarser elements in her nature to her friends.

The door opened and Laura entered the dining room. Her beauty was even darker and more mobile than usual, as she stood for a second in the light of the half-open doorway. Sally looked up and noted how the shadows gave to Laura's face its actual dimension, which ordinarily in a cruder light lay behind the features, only half guessed at by the beholder. Now her features and the beauty behind them were the same thing. Sally looked at her beauty but was neither covetous nor jealous. She was conscious only of the effort it cost her to control her own features and even her arms and legs.

"I hate my nervous system," she said to herself, "but I'll get the better of it someday." Laura was approaching slowly towards the table, a look of great sobriety and weariness upon her face. Sally saw this out of the corner of her eye. "That's the way the attack always begins," she commented to herself. "I mustn't let her get started. I'm the one who should attack anyway. But perhaps today is not a very appropriate day for a beginning. Why are the Cassalottis sitting around their rooms in the middle of the afternoon?" Laura was upon her. She could not conceal this from herself any longer.

"Hello, Sally," Laura said to her, and with no further remarks she seated herself at the table. Sally's eyes were stretched wide in their sockets with the strain of attempting to control her nerves while she waited for Laura's assault to begin. These attacks were never overt but on the contrary so disguised that any third person present would not suspect any aggression at all. Even Sally, by some mysterious but compelling rule of conduct, never raised her voice or in any way let it be too apparent in her answers to Laura that she was conscious of any hostility. And although Sally was quite aware that she was being attacked, her temper was held in abeyance by some mysterious rule of manners, and she spoke pleasantly as if she did not understand the hostility behind Laura's words.

Camp Cataract, for so many years a symbol of escape from the strife of difficult human relations, had become since Laura's arrival the very seat of this type of strain for Sally. But it was a strange fact that Sally did not realize this at all. Having divided her life into two parts, she was incapable of including a third, or at least of treating with it in a profound manner. With Laura, although she never let this be apparent, she was greedy, belligerent, and without scruple.

Neither one of them spoke for a little, and then Laura asked where the Cassalottis were.

"Hanging around their apartments, Italian style, I guess," said Sally.

"Well, I would like a beer," said Laura. "So I'm going to go and get them down in a minute. Would you like a beer?"

Sally looked straight with glistening round eyes and a little fixed smile on her lips. "You know I don't drink, Laura," she said.

"I forgot," Laura answered, "and anyway, you might change."

"I don't change."

"Really?" Laura pretended surprise. "Well, you should try to see what it's like to behave like somebody else for a change. Why don't you get drunk?" Laura rested her chin in her hand and looked thoughtfully at Sally.

"You want nothing but havoc and destruction around you, isn't that so?" Sally asked.

"Do you think I do?"

"You're a wrecker—look at your cabin. I'm not criticizing, but please don't ask me to be like you." Sally's head began to jerk a little with excitement. "Please don't ask me to be like you," she repeated.

Laura was surprised—Sally had never been so openly antagonistic before.

"I would not want you to be like me, Sally," she said in her sincere voice, with even a note of tenderness in her tone. "I would not want anyone to be like me. I've got melancholia. You know that." Her beautiful eyes were now so warm and solicitous that Sally could not continue to snap at her without making a fool of herself, so she kept her mouth tightly shut.

After a bit Laura spoke again.

"You like to sit in your cabin alone, don't you?" she asked Sally.

"I love it," said Sally.

"Why don't you get a sterno cooker? Then you could heat cans and make little stews for your dinner in the cabin."

"I like to sit on the terrace and watch the waterfall while I eat," said Sally, immediately feeling on her guard.

"Beryl could choose things from the lodge kitchen and bring them to you. A sterno cooker doesn't cost very much."

"I'd just as soon sit on the dining terrace and watch the waterfall while I eat," Sally repeated. She was almost sure the attack was on again, but not positive.

"Those little cookers are not very smelly either," Laura continued. "And Beryl could easily bring you plates and cutlery from the main dining room. You could tip her and she would even wash the plates each day and return them to you."

"I don't want to eat in my cabin," Sally said. But the spirit which had moved her a while ago to reprimand Laura was gone, and instead the familiar sensation of heaviness and impotence invaded her limbs and her head.

"Well, I think you really do," said Laura casually, turning away and glancing about the room, as if to demonstrate that she was losing interest in the conversation. "I suppose you really do but you haven't got a sterno cooker."

Sally half shut her eyes. "This is the attack, all right," she said to herself. "But I'll sit through it this time and not defend myself. It's nearly over anyway, I think."

Sally was correct in her guess that Laura's attack was nearly over. In fact, no sooner had she voiced this opinion to herself than Laura was on her feet.

"I am going upstairs," she said, "to drag the Cassalottis down here. I want my beer. Come with me."

Sally rose a little uncertainly to her feet. It was difficult for her to get up quickly when she was in a nervous state, and for one awful moment she thought she was going to fall back in her chair once more, but she managed to reach Laura's side looking fairly normal. They left the dining room and went into a small dark hallway. Laura, who was very familiar with the Cassalotti house, pulled on a door which opened onto a closed stairway. The walls of the stairway were papered in a small flower pattern and very dirty. They started to mount the stairs—slowly because of their steepness. Sally felt her head turning a little. The air in the stairway was stale. But her dizziness was more the result of Laura's proximity than of the bad air in the stairway. Since there was no bannister, she let the flat of her palm travel along the cold, flower-papered wall. This comforted her to a certain extent until they reached the landing.

The terrible gloom and boredom that had descended upon Laura earlier in the day, back at Camp Cataract, had now completely vanished, not from her memory but from her feelings. At last the day was cluttered with possibilities and adventures. The ascension of the stairs aided her optimism, and by the time she reached the landing a happy excitement was fully upon her.

"Cassalottis!" she called in her husky voice, now ringing with gaiety.

"Hello, Laura Seabrook." Rita Cassalotti's voice was gentle but without warmth.

Laura fairly galloped down the length of the uncarpeted hallway, knocking into a wrought iron stand that supported a trough of ferns on the way. The stand teetered for a moment on its high legs, but it did not fall over.

"I want beer, you bums," Laura shouted as she flung open the Cassalottis' parlor door. Greetings were exchanged while Sally hung back in the hallway, not caring to move forward or backward. She knew that Laura wanted to be rid of her.

"She's moved on to the Cassalottis and everybody else might as well be dead," Sally reflected. "But I'll stay. Certainly I shan't come and go at her convenience." Her head was beginning to ache as a result of the afternoon's complications.

She promised herself that on the following day she would go down into the chasm a mile south of Camp Cataract, where descent was more gradual, and walk along the river bed. She reminded herself too that she had already gone three quarters of the way towards directing her life current, as she termed it, into a peace stream, in spite of her bad nervous system. "Camp Cataract," she said to herself, "is definitely carrying off the honors, and *not* my sister's apartment." This thought cheered her up and she started down the hall toward the parlor, where the girls were laughing and talking so loudly that they did not even notice her entering the room.

*

Mr. Cassalotti was there, Berenice and Rita—his oldest daughters—an aunt, and some of the younger children. Everyone was dressed, with the exception of Rita Cassalotti, who was wearing a pink wrapper made of an imitation thick velours. There were more ferns here in the upstairs parlor, just like the ones Laura had barely missed knocking over in the hallway. A linoleum stamped with a red and black design covered the floor. The chairs and the sofa were all occupied by the family, with the exception of one odd Victorian chair made of carved black wood in Chinese style, which stood near a window and was seldom used.

Sally seated herself in this chair and folded her hands in her lap. "Now we'll see how far she'll go," she thought, fixing her eyes on Laura, and she felt elated without noticing that she did.

Rita Cassalotti had a small head and eyes a little too close together but she was pretty. Her teeth were very even and the canines beautifully shaped. Men adored her but she was neither vain nor inclined toward flirtation or lovemaking. She loved the food she got at home, her bedroom furniture and her clothing. Her body was unexpectedly heavier than anyone would have guessed just from seeing her small head and slender neck, but she was not fat, merely soft and round, although only a sensitive man—even if a stranger—might have sensed the coldness lurking in her soft frame.

"What brings you here this afternoon, Laura Seabrook?" Rita questioned her pleasantly.

"I was so bored at Camp Cataract," said Laura, "that I thought the world was coming to an end. Then I remembered that you always cheered me up." This statement was true, at least partially. The Cassalottis did cheer Laura up, but she had forgotten that her original intention had been to pursue Sally and not to visit the Cassalottis.

Rita let out a peal of merry laughter. She always reacted more strongly to what seemed to her the grotesque than to situations or states of feeling that might easily have been included in the content of her own life.

"Do you have a sewing machine, there at Camp Cataract?" Rita asked with a twinkle in her eye.

"No . . . I'm not sure," Laura answered her.

Rita thought this was even more hysterically funny than Laura's first statement.

"Rita! Stop being foolish—you sound like a dope." Her younger sister Berenice silenced her with a look from her big flashing eyes. She was a swarthy, short-legged girl with dark bushy hair and a raucous low voice. Her chin was delicately cleft and her nose was Roman and very beautiful. She was enthusiastic and tempestuous, with a warmth not often encountered in a young girl.

"Why are you talking about machines?" she stormed at Rita.

"Well," said Rita, not in the least disturbed by her sister's outburst. "She said she thought the world was coming to an end, and I thought that if she had a sewing machine she could make some dresses when she didn't know what else to do."

"You're crazy," said Berenice.

"No, I'm not," Rita answered, laughing merrily again. "What's crazy about a sewing machine? You're the one who's on the crazy side, not me."

"Laura's got a lot of trouble," said Berenice. "She wouldn't get no relief from a sewing machine."

"No?" Rita raised her eyebrows and looked questioningly at Laura. "Maybe not," she said with half-hearted interest. The conversation seemed to be losing its grotesque quality and turning on the serious. The very prospect of hearing about anyone else's trouble tired Rita and she yawned.

Mr. Cassalotti, who had not bothered to greet either Laura or Sally, was sitting on a small cane chair and staring ahead of him with hands thrust in his pockets. Without warning he got up from his chair and started toward the door.

"Poppa," said Berenice, "where are you going?"

"I'm going to get the beer out and make raviolis. Come on downstairs and we'll have a little party." He looked back over his shoulder at Laura and nodded to her without changing his expression.

"Just plain havoc, with no thought behind it," Sally was thinking. "That's what she likes, instead of the beautiful. She thinks it's exciting and adventurous to sit indoors in the afternoon with people eating raviolis and drinking beer. She doesn't know where real happiness lies. If she could only be persuaded to stay outdoors a little more. It would be at least a beginning."

Laura was hustling the Cassalottis through the parlor door as hastily as she could, in her eagerness to get at the beer. The children remained always silent and strange whenever Laura appeared. They leaned against the wall looking after her with sober brown eyes.

The Cassalotti sisters, followed by Laura and Sally, started down the steep stairway single file.

"Gee, it's nice you came," said Berenice affectionately to Laura, who was behind her. She turned around and squeezed Laura's leg to emphasize her pleasure. "It will only take Poppa a little while to get the raviolis going, and we can drink beer while we wait anyhow . . ." She gave Rita a little shove and pulled her hair. "Why don't you get dressed, you?" she said.

At that moment Laura's joy at being among the Cassalottis reached its peak—and with it came a familiar chill at the bottom of her heart.

"Oh, God," thought Laura. "I had almost forgotten for a moment. I wish I could be really here, having the kind of fun I think it is to be here."

She was quite accustomed to this cold fright that gripped her heart whenever her pleasure was acute, but it was not fright itself that interested her. She was quite sure that most sensitive people were familiar with this feeling. What disturbed her more than the fright was the chain of questions it always awakened in her mind about whatever she was doing, so that she could never wholeheartedly enter into anything for more than a few seconds at a time.

"How exhausting," she said to herself as she felt the chill settling like a thick fog around her heart. The tormenting question which followed in the wake of her anguish was this: should she consider the anguish to be the natural underlying side of life itself, that side which gives depth and gravity to the sense of living from hour to hour, and which is to be endured simply and accepted, or was it on the other hand a signal for a departure —a signal for a decision? It was this last possibility that she found so upsetting, for she was actually, in her thinking at least, a very conscientious person.

They had reached the landing and Laura stood for a second, uncertainly, with Sally waiting behind her on the bottom step.

She wished she had the courage to go out the door onto the wooden porch and thence down the road through the pine woods, instead of sitting down to eat ravioli and to drink beer. The very thought that such an action was incumbent upon her made her feel faint.

"A silly struggle over two silly alternatives—to eat ravioli or to walk in the woods," she whispered to herself, without believing it. She bit her lips hard and a happy thought struck her: "The Cassalottis would be very insulted if I left. How could I have overlooked it?" The relief she felt, having voiced this sentence to herself, was immediate. Her face lost its hunted animal look, and she took long strides in the direction of the dining room.

The others had gone back into the kitchen behind the dining room and were watching Mr. Cassalotti, who was using the ravioli machine. He was very neat and very systematic in his cooking, being a great admirer of both American factory technique and sanitation. He had already selected four cartons and labeled them neatly with the names of friends. "You can take these back to Camp Cataract with you when you go," he said to Laura. "Tell them a ravioli present from Gregorio Cassalotti—and remind them that Wednesday night is Chicken Cassalotti night. Chicken Cacciatore died when Chicken Cassalotti was born." He laughed to himself.

He did not in any way resemble Laura's conception of an Italian, except physically. He was industrious and really only happy when he worked. The girls took the beer into the dining room and they all seated themselves near the glassed-in scene, including Sally, who sat with her chair exaggeratedly far from the table and turned sideways.

"Pull yourself in," said Berenice.

"No, thank you," Sally answered her. "I'm not going to eat or drink. I'm all right here."

Berenice stared at Sally uncomprehendingly, but she felt herself so remote from the other woman that she could not, as she ordinarily would have done, urge her to join them in eating and drinking.

The Cassalotti sisters had brought to the table about fifteen bottles of beer. Laura, so recently released from her small but painful struggle, was giddy as a result of her escape. There still lurked a doubt in her heart but it was a muffled doubt, reserved for a little later. She was determined now to get drunk, and to have the Cassalottis share her renewed gaiety. With Berenice she did not concern herself, for this girl's gaiety, though of a completely different variety (with real joy as its source, rather than pained joy), matched her own. So it was to Rita she addressed herself.

"Rita, do you like Sunday?" she asked her. Rita's face remained closed, and she appeared to have no intention of answering Laura's question at all. Often she did not answer Laura's questions with even so much as a nod of her head. This made Laura all the more determined to find out how Rita felt about everything. She tried formulating her question to Rita differently.

"Do Sundays make you nervous?" she asked this time.

"I don't know," said Rita, without the faintest expression in her voice.

"I like 'em, good weather or bad," put in Berenice. "If it's good weather, I go fishing or hunting for berries and mushrooms, and if it's bad weather I listen to the radio. In the winter, of course, I don't go after berries or mushrooms."

"Do you go after berries and mushrooms too, on Sundays?" Laura asked Rita, interrupting Berenice.

Sally was exasperated with Laura for showing such a keen interest in Rita Cassalotti's Sundays.

"Why doesn't she ask me what I do on Sunday, instead of asking that trollop? She certainly can't do much of any interest if she stays in her wrapper all day."

"If only Berenice would keep her mouth shut for a minute," Laura thought. "I might then be able to drag something out of Rita." She was a little put out with herself for not being able to imagine Rita's attitude toward Sunday. But all the while Berenice continued to fill the glasses with beer the moment they were emptied, so that Laura very soon cared less and less about finding out anything from Rita.

In fact, she was unpleasantly startled when Rita asked Berenice whether she remembered the Sundays at Felicia Kelly's.

"Not as good as you do," said Berenice. "Because I was a little tyke."

"That was ten years ago," Rita said. "I was twenty years old and you were ten. She had her bushes and trees growing so close to the walk there that we used to get soaking wet from the branches after the rain. I used to rub Berenice's hair with a Turkish towel when we got in the house—my own too. It's a mistake to plant them so close." Rita was actually addressing Berenice rather than Laura, for she was never certain that Laura could really understand much of what was said. Berenice, who was interested in almost any topic of conversation, listened attentively.

"She made tutti-frutti ice cream for her family on Sunday, so she always served us some. It was very good quality. You could see the Old Man and the Old Woman on clear days from her kitchen window. I think you could see the Old Man from the parlor window too, but not the Old Woman. I'm sure you couldn't see the Old Woman from the parlor—no, you couldn't have, it wasn't facing right. Berenice used to get a kick out of that. We can't see any mountain peaks from here, just the valley and the woods. But Berenice could see those two peaks very clear from the Kellys', so she was pleased about that, I guess. Do you remember the Old Man and the Old Woman, Berenice?"

Laura was thoroughly bored by the present turn in the conversation, but she felt compelled to question Rita further, since this account about Felicia Kelly's house was a roundabout answer to Laura's original question "Do you like Sundays?", which proved that at least Rita had heard her question, and that the possibility of finding out more concerning Rita and her tastes was not entirely closed to her.

"Did you like going to see Felicia Kelly on Sunday?" Laura asked her, trying to conceal her weariness by tossing her head back and smiling.

Again Rita's face was closed, and instead of answering Laura's question she poured herself some beer very carefully so as to avoid its forming a head.

"Rita doesn't go to see Felicia Kelly any more," said Berenice, and there was such warmth and radiance shining in her eyes even as she made this announcement that Laura felt recompensed, in spite of Rita's queer stubbornness, and was not annoyed with Berenice for interrupting.

"Really?" she said.

"No. One Sunday she went all the way over there—it's about fifteen miles from here—and nobody was home, not even the dog. The cat was there but the dog wasn't. So she never spoke to Felicia Kelly again."

"We drove all the way over there," said Rita, "and then we had to come all the way back without seeing anyone. Poppa was mad too. He used to drive us over there in the truck and call for us every Sunday. She didn't leave a note, either."

"What happened to her?" Laura asked with some degree of real interest.

"I don't know," said Rita. "I never talked to her again."

"She called up once or twice but Poppa just told her Rita wouldn't talk to her, and then he'd hook the receiver on the telephone," put in Berenice.

"Then you never knew why she wasn't home?" Laura asked Rita, looking at her with wonder.

"No," said Rita. "I never talked to her again." She seemed pleased with the end of her story.

At this point Laura gave up thinking about Rita because she was so much of a mystery to her that there seemed to be no hope of her ever understanding any more about how Rita felt than she did that afternoon, even had she persisted in questioning her for the next fifty years. In a sense it was satisfying to know that such mysteries existed and that she did not have to exert herself any further.

Just then, Mr. Cassalotti came in with the raviolis. He had dished out the portions in the kitchen and now carried the full plates over to the table on a tray.

"I got everything ready so all you have to do now is eat. Move your chair in," he said to Sally, putting a plate of raviolis down on the table for her.

They had all forgotten Sally's presence, and looked toward her with surprise. She had moved her chair even further away from the table during the conversation about Felicia Kelly, although no one had noticed it.

"No, thank you," said Sally, her aloof expression changing

quickly into one of vivid revulsion. "I'm going home in a minute."

"Not before you eat your ravioli," said Mr. Cassalotti calmly, and going over to her chair he got behind it and lifted her over to the table, where he set her down, chair and all, in front of her raviolis.

Berenice had a hunted, frightened look in her eyes as she watched her father with amazement. Ordinarily she would have laughed heartily at such playfulness, but being extremely sensitive, she felt that Sally was not a person to be lifted through the air even in jest. Rita wasn't either worried or amused.

"Oh, Poppa," she said. "If she don't want to eat don't force her."

Mr. Cassalotti returned to the kitchen and there was silence in the dining room. Even Rita noticed the queer strained look on Sally's face, and she stared at her shamelessly while Laura and Berenice averted their eyes.

Sally was so insulted by Mr. Cassalotti's gesture that, although she wanted to flee from the room, she remained rooted to her chair by such shame and by an anger so burning that it temporarily blotted from her mind its source, so that only the present moment existed for her. Her eye fixed on a red-and-white checked curtain on the wall opposite, and immediately she felt that to draw this curtain was her only hope against suffocation. Then the fear that she would not reach the curtain gradually stole the place of both her shame and her anger, imparting a more pitiful and appealing expression to her eyes.

"It's so hot in here," said Berenice, whose sensitive nature was becoming more and more aroused.

Sally heard the remark and now her heart started to beat with panic lest Berenice reach the window before she did. She felt it was absolutely necessary that she herself draw the curtains and not Berenice.

With what seemed to her superhuman effort, she rose to her feet and then walked like a person lightheaded with fever over to the window. She drew the curtains aside with a shaky hand. Behind them was a black shade which Mr. Cassalotti had hung there so that no daylight would ever penetrate the restaurant. He thought that to eat by electricity was more elegant, and that all restaurateurs should equip their restaurants so as to appear in a land of perpetual night.

Sally lifted the shade and there at last was the window. It had been pouring outside only a moment before, so that streams of rain were still sliding down the window pane. Through the pane the leaves of the elm, whose branches almost brushed against the side of the house, appeared larger and more glistening than they actually were. The grass, a brilliant green in the afterlight of the storm, seemed particularly so around the thick wet trunk of the tree.

Sally felt that she was losing ground faster and faster every minute, a condition which she qualified at calmer moments as "going too fast for myself." But it was not because she was so much of a lady or even particularly dignified that Mr. Cassalotti's gesture had insulted her so deeply. The insult lay in the suddenness of the actual interruption, which had violated abruptly her precarious state of balance.

"I'll have to get out on the ground," she said to herself three or four times. Behind her she could hear the subdued voices of the two other women and Berenice. But they seemed far away, as if they were speaking in a separate room. She felt along the glass several times as if she would find a way of going through the window to get outside, but in a moment she sighed and turned around, scanning the room for the right door. In order to reach it she had to pass the table where the others were sitting. But she kept her head high and was in truth scarcely aware of their presence at all.

Unfortunately Laura was drinking her eighth beer, which suddenly changed her mood into one of lachrymose affection.

"Sally, sweetheart," she called as Sally stalked past the table. "Sally, darling, where are you going?" Sally already had her hand on the knob and was pulling on it, but Laura sprang to her feet and reached Sally's side before she was able to get through the door.

"You have to come and eat your ravioli, because it's delicious, but if you won't eat you can talk to Berenice and Rita and me," Laura said to her. Putting her arms around Sally she searched her face with tenderly swimming eyes.

Sally looked as though she were about to be sick, but with

unexpected energy she wrenched herself loose from Laura's embrace and fairly flew out of the room.

The evening air was cold and still, now that the storm had passed, and the sky near the horizon was green, the color green that chills the heart of a person of melancholic or tempestuous nature. But Sally did not even notice it. No natural sight ever depressed her and she did not know what it was to be melancholic.

Pine cones, now soggy and darker-colored after the rain, were scattered about underneath the trees. Sally's sister Henrietta liked to paint pine cones different colors and then heap them into a bowl for decoration.

Sally felt infinitely weary as she looked at these cones, which seemed to be scattered about the grass as far as her eye could see. However (and in spite of the fact that pine cones were abundant in all the surrounding region and lay scattered about even at the very door of her own cabin at Camp Cataract), she felt challenged to gather some, soggy as they were, to take back to her sister. She had nothing but her hat to carry them in, which she determined to use. Squatting down on her heels, she was quickly absorbed in selecting the most perfect cones. In her thoughts there was not a shadow of concern about Laura or the Cassalotti sisters. As far as she was concerned, they did not exist.

Laura had never seen Sally out of control before, and she returned to the table worried and yet excited. Although she was drunk enough to behave carelessly, her instincts forbade her to follow Sally out of doors.

"What do you suppose got into her?" Laura asked.

"A jackass," said Berenice.

Rita reprimanded her sister. "You don't have to use such talk," she said to her.

"She was quite beside herself when she left the room," Laura added, ignoring Berenice's language. Laura knew that she should not be discussing Sally with the Cassalottis, who were certain to interpret her more simply than her unbalanced nature merited.

"She's a stuck-up jackass," Berenice said again. "She doesn't want to associate with us or have you associating with us either.

Don't you think I've known it all along? She didn't eat those raviolis just to insult Poppa. I'd like to see the rotten stinking food they got at her house."

"Fried skunk," said Rita placidly, without a smile.

"That's right." Berenice nodded her approval.

Laura had not expected the conversation about Sally to be on such a low level as this. She was particularly surprised to hear Berenice attack Sally so bitterly, since it had never occurred to her that Berenice could be anything but warmhearted and generous toward everyone.

"Poppa took a lot of trouble making that ravioli for her, and he's a very busy man. I didn't care how the crazy loon acted with us, but she's got to be decent with Poppa. She can't come in here anymore now, that's all. . . . Let her go to a stuck-up place."

"Sally isn't stuck-up," said Laura, who could never be dishonest. "She is high-strung but not stuck-up. High and strict. She's got systems for living."

"So have Rita and me got systems, and one of them is not to look like a rat bit us if we are served food in somebody else's house. We say thank you and we eat our food. So do you, Laura. Don't make excuses for her. Anyway, she hates us."

Berenice was calming down. She scraped at her empty plate with her fork for a little while. Then soon the glow returned to her face, and her eyes were once again shining with warmth and enthusiasm.

"Life is too short . . ." she said, smiling at Laura, and she poured some more beer. But Laura felt ashamed now to have referred to Sally's behavior at all, and she was determined to continue the conversation so as to vindicate in some way the cheapness of her original impulse to gossip.

"I don't think Sally hates you," she said to Berenice. "It's very possible that she loves you."

Berenice opened her eyes wide with incomprehension.

"It's not a bit unusual to love and to hate the same person," Laura continued. Her tone was didactic.

"Unusual," said Berenice. "It's impossible." But she spoke hesitatingly because she was really at sea thus far in the conversation.

"No, no," Laura insisted. "That's partly why living is such

trouble. We are likely to love and to hate the very same person at the very same time, and yet neither emotion is more true than the other. You have to decide which you're going to cater to, that's all. Fortunately, if you are at all decent, you manage to keep pushing love a little bit ahead . . . but it can be very, very difficult keeping it that way. I was that way about my mother, and I have been that way about one other person, but particularly my mother."

"Oh, no—" The words escaped Berenice involuntarily.

"Oh, yes!" Laura was vehement. "Sometimes I wanted to hit Mother so hard that it would knock her head right off her body. She's dead now but I think I would feel the same way if she were alive."

Berenice didn't say anything. She clasped both hands tightly around her glass of beer and stared ahead of her. Rita Cassalotti had long since been occupied with some private concern and remained mute.

After a moment Berenice broke the silence. "I've got to go out now," she announced. Cocking her head to one side, she smiled at Laura—a charming smile that showed the dimple in her cheek—and she looked for all the world like a young girl taking leave of her hostess at a tea party.

"But," said Laura, horrified at this unexpected announcement, "I thought we had hours ahead of us still. You didn't say anything. . . ."

Berenice stood up. "I've got to go into town," she said, and once more she tilted her head to one side and smiled enchantingly at Laura, but without meeting Laura's eye.

Berenice was leaving, and Laura knew somehow that she had no appointment, and knew too that no word she could utter would bring Berenice back into the room. Laura's cheeks were hot with shame. She could not bear to have Berenice turn away from her this way, although a moment before she had considered Berenice so shallow that she was ashamed to discuss Sally with her. She was in a panic lest Berenice should cast away their friendship, and her shame sprang from a suspicion that she had ruined something in Berenice's heart—not because of Berenice but because such a misdeed would reflect seriously on her own character.

"Oh, my God," Laura said to herself, "why did I bring up my

theory about love and hate? She'll never, never forgive me." Laura had a wild respect for people who were capable of becoming so offended that they rose from their chairs and left the room where they were sitting, and sometimes even the house. And if it was for an ideal that they showed such offense and not for any egoistic personal reason, Laura regarded them as saints.

"She must forgive me," she repeated to herself, "she must, or it will be a real calamity."

She recalled the moment on the bottom step, when she had not obeyed the seemingly mystical challenge to walk through the wet woods instead of sitting down to eat her raviolis. So now, by not having had the courage to heed this compulsion, she had lost the Cassalottis as well. In moments of stress she was very apt to see connections between her intimate world and the actions of other people, as if the adverse behavior of others was dependent at least indirectly upon an earlier wrong decision concerning a private matter of her own. She realized the idiocy of such reasoning but at the same time she thought that everyone else felt that way without noticing it. Certainly nothing was so personal to her as this way of being. In fact it was impossible for her to give it up.

Even so, to witness the shock Berenice had suffered as a result of her own careless remark was to Laura the worst possible punishment, because in the face of Berenice's distress, which overwhelmed this girl so naturally that any question or doubt as to whether she could choose or not choose to overlook her feelings was unthinkable, Laura's own feelings against herself assumed a grotesque and petty quality which made her blush. She continued, however, even though humiliated, to suspect that had she not eaten raviolis but really gone walking instead through the woods, she would not have found herself faced by the present quandary. How she was able to feel herself to be grotesque and comical, and at the same time so important that the outcome of her decisions controlled somehow the behavior of people not in the least connected to it, was a puzzle to Laura herself.

She saw all these things and even more, for she was educated enough in psychological matters to conceive that the source of Berenice's own violent reaction to her remarks about hating her mother lay not in what she, Laura, had decided earlier on the bottom step, or even in Berenice's genuine moral indignation, but in a hatred that Berenice might have felt and concealed from herself, at one time or another, towards her own mother. Laura knew about such things but they did not help her one bit when she was in the midst of a calamity.

With all these details very clear in her mind, still (like a person who jumps deliberately into a pit) she was falling deeper and deeper by the second into such an abject terror of Berenice's resentment that she longed for forgiveness more than for anything in the world. She appealed to Rita, hoping that after all she had imagined something amiss in Berenice's behavior while actually everything was really just as it had been a little while before. She had often enough imagined that she had horrified a friend when nothing of the kind had occurred.

"Rita, did Berenice have an appointment?" she asked.

"No, she didn't have no appointment," Rita said, shrugging her shoulders.

"Where did she go then, Rita?" Laura insisted, fixing her eyes on Rita's face.

"She went flying away with the birdies," said Rita Cassalotti, and with sudden animation she stretched out both her arms and moved them up and down in imitation of a bird's flight.

To see Rita thus unconcerned and jesting made Laura feel her plight ever more keenly, for she needed someone's sympathy badly right then. She plucked at Rita's pink sleeve, trying to halt the upward motion of her arm.

"Please stop flying, Rita, and talk to me."

She looked so peculiar that Rita burst out laughing.

"Rita," Laura pleaded, "why do you think she went away?"

Rita shrugged her shoulders. She never paid much attention to Berenice's comings and goings, and had actually scarcely taken notice when Berenice left the table. Rita yawned and got up. "I'm going to get dressed," she said. "I've got a real complete appointment tonight, including dinner, movies, drinks and dancing—with a married guy, too." She started to leave the room and Laura followed behind her. They mounted the stairs together in silence. Laura knew that Rita wanted to be left alone but she was far too nervous to remain by herself and her pride was non-existent.

"I've got to get dressed," said Rita when she found Laura was behind her even in the bedroom.

"Oh, but please, Rita, let me stay here," Laura begged her, and she searched her mind rapidly for a topic of conversation that might interest Rita. "Rita," she said, her eyes full of concern, "I'm terribly worried about your going around with a married man."

"Why?" Rita asked with no interest. She took off her wrapper and stood before Laura in her bloomers. "I'm not afraid of his wife," she said, thrusting her chin out.

"But morally it's wrong." Laura searched her brain frantically, trying to remember at least one reasonable argument against adultery, but she couldn't think of any.

"If he don't go with me, he'll go with someone else," Rita said flatly. "Not that I give a hoot whether I go with him or anyone else. They're all alike, the men, and I never cared for their company much."

"Why not, Rita?" Laura asked her with great interest.

"I don't know," Rita said. "I just don't care for them. I wish you'd let me dress by myself," she said. "I can't keep my mind on it with you here."

There was nothing left for Laura to do but leave. She thought it was irritating that a dumbbell like Rita Cassalotti needed her privacy at all, and she went out angry as well as forlorn.

"I've ruined everything," she said to herself, descending the stairway slowly, one step at a time.

Not knowing whether it was useless or not to wait for Berenice's return, she wandered aimlessly about the dining room, straightening chairs and stopping now and then to gaze at the glassed-in scene, so provokingly flooded with light when the dining room itself lay in darkness. The orange truck driven by the celluloid baby held her eye. The doll, not designed to sit up, had been tilted against the back of the seat with its legs curled in the air almost over its head.

In spite of the incongruity apparent in this combination, she was overcome with boredom, looking at it as if she were seeing it not for the first but for the thousandth time. She turned herself away, almost in embarrassment, as though she herself were responsible for what she saw in the glass case. She would have liked to ponder on the mysterious effect these two objects had on her, but just then the full realization that Berenice Cassalotti would never have faith in her again seemed, like an ocean wave, to break over her head and wash all other thoughts away.

She hurried out of the dining room and into the store. It was empty. On all other occasions Berenice had taken her to the door flushed with beer and pleasure, and filled with the anticipation of Laura's next visit, for in Berenice's joyous heart even a departure took on the aspect of a return.

Laura closed the door behind her and started towards the road that led out of the village to Camp Cataract. It was a wide sandy road bordered by such tall pine trees that, with the exception of a few sunny hours at midday, the road lay constantly in the shadows. The sandy earth was cold and no grass grew anywhere.

Far ahead of her, out of hearing but not out of sight, Laura could see Sally walking along, her handbag swinging from her wrist. She was walking slowly, with small steps, her head bent, and at a pace suitable to a city street.

Laura had forgotten about her completely.

Late 1940s

Going to Massachusetts

BOZOE RUBBED away some tears with a closed fist.

"Come on, Bozoe," said Janet. "You're not going to the North Pole."

Bozoe tugged at the wooly fur, and pulled a little of it out.

"Leave your coat alone," said Janet.

"I don't remember why I'm going to Massachusetts," Bozoe moaned. "I knew it would be like this, once I got to the station."

"If you don't want to go to Massachusetts," said Janet, "then come on back to the apartment. We'll stop at Fanny's on the way. I want to buy those tumblers made out of knobby glass. I want brown ones."

Bozoe started to cry in earnest. This caused Janet considerable embarrassment. She was conscious of herself as a public figure because the fact that she owned and ran a garage had given her a good deal of publicity not only in East Clinton but in the neighboring counties. This scene, she said to herself, makes us look like two Italians saying goodbye. Everybody'll think we're Italians. She did not feel true sympathy for Bozoe. Her sense of responsibility was overdeveloped, but she was totally lacking in real tenderness.

"There's no reason for you to cry over a set of whiskey tumblers," said Janet. "I told you ten days ago that I was going to buy them."

"Passengers boarding Bus Number Twenty-seven, northbound. . . ."

"I'm not crying about whiskey tumblers." Bozoe managed with difficulty to get the words out. "I'm crying about Massachusetts. I can't remember my reasons."

"Rockport, Rayville, Muriel. . . ."

"Why don't you listen to the loudspeaker, Bozoe? It's giving you information. If you paid attention to what's going on around you you'd be a lot better off. You concentrate too much on your own private affairs. Try more to be a part of the world."

*

". . . *The truth is that I am only twenty-five miles away from the apartment, as you have probably guessed. In fact, you could not help but guess it, since you are perfectly familiar with Larry's Bar and Grill. I could not go to Massachusetts. I cried the whole way up to Muriel and it was as if someone else were getting off the bus, not myself. But someone who was in a desperate hurry to reach the next stop. I was in mortal terror that the bus would not stop at Muriel but continue on to some further destination where I would not know any familiar face. My terror was so great that I actually stopped crying. I kept from crying all the way. That is a lie. Not an actual lie because I never lie as you know. Small solace to either one of us, isn't it? I am sure that you would prefer me to lie, rather than be so intent on explaining my dilemma to you night and day. I am convinced that you would prefer me to lie. It would give you more time for the garage.*"

"So?" queried Sis McEvoy, an unkind note in her voice. To Janet she did not sound noticeably unkind, since Sis McEvoy was habitually sharp-sounding, and like her had very little sympathy for other human beings. She was sure that Sis McEvoy was bad, and she was determined to save her. She was going to save her quietly without letting Sis suspect her determination. Janet did everything secretly; in fact, secrecy was the essence of her nature, and from it she derived her pleasure and her sense of being an important member of society.

"What's it all about?" Sis asked irritably. "Why doesn't she raise kids or else go to a psychologist or a psychoanalyst or whatever? My ovaries are crooked or I'd raise kids myself. That's what God's after, isn't it? Space ships or no space ships. What's the problem, anyway? How are her ovaries and the rest of the mess?"

Janet smiled mysteriously. "Bozoe has never wanted a child," she said. "She told me she was too scared."

"Don't you despise cowards?" said Sis. "Jesus Christ, they turn my stomach."

Janet frowned. "Bozoe says she despises cowards, too. She worries herself sick about it. She's got it all linked up together with Heaven and Hell. She thinks so much about Heaven and Hell that she's useless. I've told her for years to occupy herself. I've told her that God would like her better if she was occupied. But she says God isn't interested. That's a kind of slam at me, I suppose. At me and the garage. She's got it in for the garage. It doesn't bother me, but it makes me a little sore when she tries to convince me that I wouldn't be interested in the garage unless she talked to me day and night about her troubles. As if I was interested in the garage just out of spite. I'm a normal woman and I'm interested in my work, like all women are in modern times. I'm a little stockier than most, I guess, and not fussy or feminine. That's because my father was my ideal and my mother was an alcoholic. I'm stocky and I don't like pretty dresses and I'm interested in my work. My work is like God to me. I don't mean I put it above Him, but the next thing to Him. I have a feeling that he approves of my working. That he approves of my working in a garage. Maybe that's cheeky of me, but I can't help it. I've made a name for myself in the garage and I'm decent. I'm normal." She paused for a moment to fill the two whiskey tumblers.

"Do you like my whiskey tumblers?" She was being unusually spry and talkative. "I don't usually have much time to buy stuff. But I had to, of course. Bozoe never bought anything in her life. She's what you'd call a dead weight. She's getting fatter, too, all the time."

"They're good tumblers," said Sis McEvoy. "They hold a lot of whiskey."

Janet flushed slightly at the compliment. She attributed the unaccustomed excitement she felt to her freedom from the presence of Bozoe Flanner.

"Bozoe was very thin when I first knew her," she told Sis. "And she didn't show any signs that she was going to sit night and day making up problems and worrying about God and asking me questions. There wasn't any of that in the beginning. Mainly she was meek, I guess, and she had soft-looking eyes, like a doe or a calf. Maybe she had the problems the whole time and was just planning to spring them on me later. I don't know. I never thought she was going to get so tied up in knots, or so fat either. Naturally if she were heavy and happy too it would be better."

"I have no flesh on my bones at all," said Sis McEvoy, as if she had not even heard the rest of the conversation. "The whole family's thin, and every last one of us has a rotten lousy temper inherited from both sides. My father and my mother had rotten tempers."

"I don't mind if you have a temper display in my apartment," said Janet. "Go to it. I believe in people expressing themselves. If you've inherited a temper there isn't much you can do about it except express it. I think it's much better for you to break this crockery pumpkin, for instance, than to hold your temper in and become unnatural. For instance, I could buy another pumpkin and you'd feel relieved. I'd gather that, at any rate. I don't know much about people, really. I never dabbled in people. They were never my specialty. But surely if you've inherited a temper from both sides it would seem to me that you would have to express it. It isn't your fault, is it, after all?" Janet seemed determined to show admiration for Sis McEvoy.

"I'm having fun," she continued unexpectedly. "It's a long time since I've had any fun. I've been too busy getting the garage into shape. Then there's Bozoe trouble. I've kept to the routine. Late Sunday breakfast with popovers and home-made jam. She eats maybe six of them, but with the same solemn expression on her face. I'm husky but a small eater. We have record players and television. But nothing takes her mind off herself. There's no point in my getting any more machines. I've got the cash and the good will, but there's absolutely no point."

"You seem to be very well set up," said Sis McEvoy, narrowing her eyes. "Here's to you." She tipped her glass and drained it.

Janet filled Sister's glass at once. "I'm having a whale of a good time," she said. "I hope you are. Of course I don't want to butt into your business. Bozoe always thought I pored over my account books for such a long time on purpose. She thought I was purposely trying to get away from her. What do you think, Sis McEvoy?" She asked this almost in a playful tone that bordered on a yet unexpressed flirtatiousness.

"I'm not interested in women's arguments with each other," said Sis at once. "I'm interested in women's arguments with men. What else is there? The rest doesn't amount to a row of monkeys."

"Oh, I agree," Janet said, as if she were delighted by this

statement which might supply her with the stimulus she was after. "I agree one thousand percent. Remember I spend more time in the garage with the men than I do with Bozoe Flanner."

"I'm not actually living with my husband because of my temper," said Sis. "I don't like long-standing relationships. They disagree with me. I get the blues. I don't want anyone staying in my life for a long time. It gives me the creeps. Men are crazy about me. I like the cocktails and the compliments. Then after a while they turn my stomach."

"You're a very interesting woman," Janet Murphy announced, throwing caution to the winds and finding it pleasant.

"I know I'm interesting," said Sis. "But I'm not so sure life is interesting."

"Are you interested in money?" Janet asked her. "I don't mean money for the sake of money, but for buying things."

Sis did not answer, and Janet feared that she had been rude. "I didn't mean to hurt your feelings," she said. "After all, money comes up in everybody's life. Even duchesses have to talk about money. But I won't, any more. Come on. Let's shake." She held out her hand to Sis McEvoy, but Sis allowed it to stay there foolishly, without accepting the warm grip Janet had intended for her.

"I'm really sorry," she went on, "if you think I was trying to be insulting and personal. I honestly was not. The fact is that I have been so busy building up a reputation for the garage that I behave like a savage. I'll never mention money again." In her heart she felt that Sis was somehow pleased that the subject had been brought up, but was not yet ready to admit it. Sis's tedious work at the combination tearoom and soda fountain where they had met could scarcely make her feel secure.

Bozoe doesn't play one single feminine trick, she told herself, and after all, after struggling nearly ten years to build up a successful and unusual business I'm entitled to some returns. I'm in a rut with Bozoe and this Sis is going to get me out of it. (By now she was actually furious with Bozoe.) I'm entitled to some fun. The men working for me have more fun than I have.

"I feel grateful to you, Sis," she said without explaining her remark. "You've done me a service. May I tell you that I admire your frankness, without offending you?"

Sis McEvoy was beginning to wonder if Janet were another

nut like Bozoe Flanner. This worried her a little, but she was too drunk by now for clear thinking. She was enjoying the compliments, although it was disturbing that they should be coming from a woman. She was very proud of never having been depraved or abnormal, and pleased to be merely mean and discontented to the extent of not having been able to stay with any man for longer than the three months she had spent with her husband.

"I'll read you more of Bozoe's letter," Janet suggested.

"I can't wait," said Sis. "I can't wait to hear a lunatic's mind at work first-hand. Her letter's so cheerful and elevating. And so constructive. Go to it. But fill my glass first so I can concentrate. I'd hate to miss a word. It would kill me."

Janet realized that it was unkind of her to be reading her friend's letter to someone who so obviously had only contempt for it. But she felt no loyalty—only eagerness to make Sis see how hard her life had been. She felt that in this way the bond between them might be strengthened.

"Well, here it comes," she said. "Stop me when you can't stand it any more. *I know that you expected me to come back. You did not feel I had the courage to carry out my scheme. I still expect to work it out. But not yet. I am more than ever convinced that my salvation lies in solitude, and coming back to the garage before I have even reached Massachusetts would be a major defeat for me, as I'm sure you must realize, even though you pretend not to know what I'm talking about most of the time. I am convinced that you do know what I'm talking about and if you pretend ignorance of my dilemma so you can increase efficiency at the garage you are going to defeat yourself. I can't actually save you, but I can point little things out to you constantly. I refer to your soul, naturally, and not to any success you've had or to your determination. In any case it came to me on the bus that it was not time for me to leave you, and that although going to Massachusetts required more courage and strength than I seemed able to muster, I was at the same time being very selfish in going. Selfish because I was thinking in terms of my salvation and not yours. I'm glad I thought of this. It is why I stopped crying and got off the bus. Naturally you would disapprove, because I had paid for my ticket which is now wasted, if for no other reason. That's the kind of thing you like me to think about, isn't it? It makes you feel that I'm more human. I have never admired being human, I must say. I want to be like God. But I haven't begun yet. First I have to go to Massachusetts and be alone. But I got off the bus. And I've wasted the fare. I can hear you stressing that above all else, as I say. But I want you to understand that it was not cowardice alone that stopped me from going to Massachusetts. I don't feel that I can allow you to sink into the mire of contentment and happy ambitious enterprise. It is my duty to prevent you from it as much as I do for myself. It is not fair of me to go away until you completely understand how I feel about God and my destiny. Surely we have been brought together for some purpose, even if that purpose ends by our being separate again. But not until the time is ripe. Naturally, the psychiatrists would at once declare that I was laboring under a compulsion. I am violently against psychiatry, and, in fact, against happiness. Though of course I love it. I love happiness, I mean. Of course you would not believe this. Naturally darling I love you, and I'm afraid that if you don't start suffering soon God will take some terrible vengeance. It is better for you to offer yourself. Don't accept social or financial security as your final aim. Or fame in the garage. Fame is unworthy of you; that is, the desire for it. Janet, my beloved, I do not expect you to be gloomy or fanatical as I am. I do not believe that God intended you for quite as harrowing a destiny as He did for me. I don't mean this as an insult. I believe you should actually thank your stars. I would really like to be fulfilling humble daily chores myself and listening to a concert at night or television or playing a card game. But I can find no rest, and I don't think you should either. At least not until you have fully understood my dilemma on earth. That means that you must no longer turn a deaf ear to me and pretend that your preoccupation with the garage is in a sense a holier absorption than trying to understand and fully realize the importance and meaning of my dilemma. I think that you hear more than you admit, too. There is a stubborn streak in your nature working against you, most likely unknown to yourself. An insistence on being shallow rather than profound. I repeat: I do not expect you to be as profound as I am. But to insist on exploiting the most shallow side of one's nature, out of stubbornness and merely because it is more pleasant to be shallow, is certainly a sin. Sis McEvoy will help you to express the shallow side of your nature, by the way. Like a toboggan slide."*

Janet stopped abruptly, appalled at having read this last part aloud. She had not expected Bozoe to mention Sis at all. "Gee," she said. "Gosh! She's messing everything up together. I'm awfully sorry."

Sis McEvoy stood up and walked unsteadily to the television set. Some of her drink slopped onto the rug as she went. She faced Janet with fierce eyes. "There's nobody in the world who can talk to me like that, and there's not going to be. Never!" She was leaning on the set and steadying herself against it with both hands. "I'll keep on building double-decker sandwiches all my life first. It's five flights to the top of the building where I live. It's an insurance building, life insurance, and I'm the only woman who lives there. I have boy friends come when they want to. I don't have to worry, either. I'm crooked so I don't have to bother with abortions or any other kind of mess. The hell with television anyway."

She likes the set, Janet said to herself. She felt more secure. "Bozoe and I don't have the same opinions at all," she said. "We don't agree on anything."

"Who cares? You live in the same apartment, don't you? You've lived in the same apartment for ten years. Isn't that all anybody's got to know?" She rapped with her fist on the wood panelling of the television set. "Whose is it, anyhow?" She was growing increasingly aggressive.

"It's mine," Janet said. "It's my television set." She spoke loud so that Sis would be sure to catch her words.

"What the hell do I care?" cried Sis. "I live on top of a life-insurance building and I work in a combination soda-fountain lunch-room. Now read me the rest of the letter."

"I don't think you really want to hear any more of Bozoe's nonsense," Janet said smoothly. "She's spoiling our evening together. There's no reason for us to put up with it all. Why should we? Why don't I make something to eat? Not a sandwich. You must be sick of sandwiches."

"What I eat is my own business," Sis snapped.

"Naturally," said Janet. "I thought you might like something hot like bacon and eggs. Nice crisp bacon and eggs." She hoped to persuade her so that she might forget about the letter.

"I don't like food," said Sis. "I don't even like millionaires' food, so don't waste your time."

"I'm a small eater myself." She had to put off reading Bozoe's letter until Sis had forgotten about it. "My work at the garage requires some sustenance, of course. But it's brainwork now more than manual labor. Being a manager's hard on the brain."

Sis looked at Janet and said: "Your brain doesn't impress me. Or that garage. I like newspaper men. Men who are champions. Like champion boxers. I've known lots of champions. They take to me. Champions all fall for me, but I'd never want any of them to find out that I knew someone like your Bozoe. They'd lose their respect."

"I wouldn't introduce Bozoe to a boxer either, or anybody else who was interested in sports. I know they'd be bored. I know." She waited. "You're very nice. Very intelligent. You *know* people. That's an asset."

"Stay with Bozoe and her television set," Sis growled.

"It's not her television set. It's mine, Sis. Why don't you sit down? Sit on the couch over there."

"The apartment belongs to both of you, and so does the set. I know what kind of a couple you are. The whole world knows it. I could put you in jail if I wanted to. I could put you and Bozoe both in jail."

In spite of these words she stumbled over to the couch and sat down. "Whiskey," she demanded. "The world loves drunks but it despises perverts. Athletes and boxers drink when they're not in training. All the time."

Janet went over to her and served her a glass of whiskey with very little ice. Let's hope she'll pass out, she said to herself. She couldn't see Sis managing the steps up to her room in the insurance building, and in any case she didn't want her to leave. She's such a relief after Bozoe, she thought. Alive and full of fighting spirit. She's much more my type, coming down to facts. She thought it unwise to go near Sis, and was careful to pour the fresh drink quickly and return to her own seat. She would have preferred to sit next to Sis, in spite of her mention of jail, but she did not relish being punched or smacked in the face. It's all Bozoe's fault, she said to herself. That's what she gets for thinking she's God. Her holy words can fill a happy peaceful room with poison from twenty-five miles away.

"I love my country," said Sis, for no apparent reason. "I love it to death!"

"Sure you do, Hon," said Janet. "I could murder Bozoe for upsetting you with her loony talk. You were so peaceful until she came in."

"Read that letter," said Sister. After a moment she repeated, as if from a distance: "Read the letter."

Janet was perplexed. Obviously food was not going to distract Sis, and she had nothing left to suggest, in any case, but some Gorton's Codfish made into cakes, and she did not dare to offer her these.

What a rumpus that would raise, she said to herself. And if I suggest turning on the television she'll raise the roof. Stay off television and codfish cakes until she's normal again. Working at a lunch counter is no joke.

There was nothing she could do but do as Sis told her and hope that she might fall asleep while she was reading her the letter. "Damn Bozoe anyway," she muttered audibly.

"Don't put on any acts," said Sis, clearly awake. "I hate liars and I always smell an act. Even though I didn't go to college. I have no respect for college."

"I didn't go to college," Janet began, hoping Sis might be led on to a new discussion. "I went to commercial school."

"Shut up, God damn you! Nobody ever tried to make a commercial school sound like an interesting topic except you. Nobody! You're out of your mind. Read the letter."

"Just a second," said Janet, knowing there was no hope for her. "Let me put my glasses on and find my place. Doing accounts at the garage year in and year out has ruined my eyes. My eyes used to be perfect." She added this last weakly, without hope of arousing either sympathy or interest.

Sis did not deign to answer.

"Well, here it is again," she began apologetically. "Here it is in all its glory." She poured a neat drink to give herself courage. "*As I believe I just wrote you, I have been down to the bar and brought a drink back with me. (One more defeat for me, a defeat which is of course a daily occurrence, and I daresay I should not bother to mention it in this letter.) In any case I could certainly not face being without one after the strain of actually boarding the bus, even if I did get off without having the courage to stick on it until I got where I was going. However, please keep in mind the second reason I had for stopping short of my destination. Please read it over carefully so that you will not have only contempt for me. The part about the responsibility I feel toward you. The room here over Larry's Bar and Grill is dismal. It is one of several rented out by Larry's sister whom we met a year ago when we stopped here for a meal. You remember. It was the day we took Stretch for a ride and let him out of the car to run in the woods, that scanty patch of woods you found just as the sun was setting, and you kept picking up branches that were stuck together with wet leaves and dirt. . . ."*

Early 1950s

The Children's Party

HE WAS wearing a green sleeveless tunic that buttoned below his knees, and a yellow paper ruff that scratched his chin . . . real corn sprouted out of the cardboard hat . . . He was the only vegetable in the room. He had felt ashamed of his costume and the weight of the corn on his head; but of all the costumes in the room his was the only one that seemed sweet and natural to him. The others were alarming. He wanted to stare at each one forever and at the same time he wanted to hide his face and look away.

His arm grazed the peculiarly dry flank of a papier-maché cow. The painted eye came close to his. Through a hole in the stiff pupil he saw another eye moving: his stomach wobbled and he hurried away, embarrassed and excited, the smell of glue in his nostrils. From a distance he watched the cow. He could still feel the touch of its dry powdery flank on his arm. It was the most important costume in the room. Other costumes clustered near it, one a policeman's suit with a club.

The cow moved backward and forward at the same pace. It stayed near the middle of the room. There were children inside it. He knew that. He gazed at it with a feeling of deep longing and admiration. It had a serene face, whether it walked backward or forward—and everyone was paying attention to it, talking and laughing with it and with the children inside. He longed for the cow and was dreaming a plan of how they would meet, and prayed that it would not come near him.

The cow was millions and millions of miles away from him, across the ocean, across several oceans and another ocean, where instead of land a whole new ocean began . . . When he reached the middle waters of the second ocean he would be able to see the cow's land, where it lived. But that would not be for many many weeks or months or years. When he reached the middle waters of the second ocean, the cow would tell the children that he was coming. Then the children and the cow would go to the water's edge each day and look out to sea . . . they would have a place ready for him inside the cow . . .

While he was deeply absorbed in his long dream a paper costume smashed into his face and chest. When he opened his eyes, everything was pink. He commenced to thrash at the paper but it backed away of itself. A little fat girl stood blinking at him. She was dressed as a big rose. Her face was beet red and her spectacles were gold-rimmed. She pointed her fat finger at his hat and started screaming. It was a happy scream. He watched her jump heavily from one foot to the other and listened to the faint paper crash of her petals . . .

"Corn for the cow—corn for the cow—corn for the cow—" she sang out.

They were coming toward him singing and clapping. He had seen the cow turn around slowly in the middle of the room. It was moving toward him with its serene face and its stiff painted eyes. When the cow was so near that he could smell the cardboard and the glue, he wanted to run from the room. He would have done so had not the paper hat been strapped firmly under his chin and the corn wired to its crown.

They were praising his costume, admiring the lettuce green ruff at his throat and the way the corn sprouted out of his hat. The cow's large and weightless head prodded the corn in a mild simulacrum of a cow eating.

He had his eyes shut when the corn wobbled ever so lightly on his head. He tried not to feel it. He was not ashamed of his costume, but it was not sweet and familiar to him any more. He would have run away but he stood there stiffly waiting because his costume was not his own any more. It belonged to the children inside the cow. . . .

Early 1950s?

Andrew

ANDREW'S MOTHER looked at her son's face. "He wants to get away from us," she thought, "and he will." She felt overcome by a mortal fatigue. "He simply wants to spring out of his box into the world." With a flippant and worldly gesture she described a flight through the air. Then abruptly she burst into tears and buried her face in her hands.

Andrew watched her thin shoulders shaking inside her woollen dress. When his mother cried he felt as though his face were made of marble. He could not accept the weeping as a part of her personality. It did not appear to be the natural climax of a mood. Instead it seemed to descend upon her from somewhere far away, as if she were giving voice to the crying of a child in some distant place. For it was the crying of a creature many years younger than she, a disgrace for which he felt responsible, since it was usually because of him that she cried.

There was nothing he could say to console her because she was right. He wanted to go away, and there was nothing else he wanted at all. "It's natural when you're young to want to go away," he would say to himself, but it did not help; he always felt that his own desire to escape was different from that of others. When he was in a good humor he would go about feeling that he and many others too were *all* going away. On such days his face was smooth and he enjoyed his life, although even then he was not communicative. More than anything he wanted all days to be like those rare free ones when he went about whistling and enjoying every simple thing he did. But he had to work hard to get such days, because of his inner conviction that his own going away was like no other going away in the world, a certainty he found it impossible to dislodge. He was right, of course, but from a very early age his life had been devoted to his struggle to rid himself of his feeling of uniqueness. With the years he was becoming more expert at travesty, so that now his mother's crying was more destructive. Watching her cry now, he was more convinced than ever that he was not like other boys who wanted to go away. The truth bit into him harder, for seeing her he could not believe even faintly that he shared his sin with other young men. He and his mother were isolated, sharing the same disgrace, and because of this sharing, separated from one another. His life was truly miserable compared to the lives of other boys, and he knew it.

When his mother's sobs had quieted down somewhat, his father called the waitress and asked for the check. "That's good tomato soup," he told her. "And ham with Hawaiian pineapple is one of my favorites, as you know." The waitress did not answer, and the engaging expression on his face slowly faded.

They pushed their chairs back and headed for the cloakroom. When they were outside Andrew's father suggested that they walk to the summit of the sloping lawn where some cannonballs were piled in the shape of a pyramid. "We'll go over to the cannonballs," he said. "Then we'll come back."

They struggled up the hill in the teeth of a bitterly cold wind, holding on to their hats. "This is the north, folks!" his father shouted into the gale. "It's hard going at times, but in a hot climate no one develops."

Andrew put his foot against one of the cannonballs. He could feel the cold iron through the sole of his shoe.

He had applied for a job in a garage, but he was inducted into the Army before he knew whether or not they had accepted his application. He loved being in the Army, and even took pleasure in the nickname which his hutmates had given him the second day after his arrival. He was called Buttonlip; because of this name he talked even less than usual. In general he hated to talk and could not imagine talking as being a natural expression of a man's thoughts. This was not shyness, but secretiveness.

One day in the fall he set out on a walk through the pine grove surrounding the camp. Soon he sniffed smoke and stopped walking. "Someone's making a fire," he said to himself. Then he continued on his way. It was dusk in the grove, but beyond, outside, the daylight was still bright. Very shortly he reached a clearing. A young soldier sat there, crouched over a fire which he was feeding with long twigs. Andrew thought he recognized him—he too was undoubtedly a recent arrival—and so his face was not altogether unfamiliar.

The boy greeted Andrew with a smile and pointed to a tree

trunk that lay on the ground nearby. "Sit down," he said. "I'm going to cook dinner. The mess sergeant gives me my stuff uncooked when I want it that way so I can come out here and make a campfire."

Andrew had an urge to bolt from the clearing, but he seated himself stiffly on the end of the tree trunk. The boy was beautiful, with an Irish-American face and thick curly brown hair. His cheeks were blood red from the heat of the flames. Andrew looked at his face and fell in love with him. Then he could not look away.

A mess kit and a brown paper package lay on the ground. "My food is there in that brown bag," the boy said. "I'll give you a little piece of meat so you can see how good it tastes when it's cooked here, out in the air. Did you go in for bonfires when you were a kid?"

"No," said Andrew. "Too much wind," he added, some vague memory stirring in his mind.

"There's lots of wind," he agreed, and Andrew was unreasonably delighted that the boy considered his remark a sensible one. "Lots of wind, but that never need stop you." He looked up at Andrew with a bright smile. "Not if you like a fire and the outdoors. Where I worked they used to call me Outdoor Tommy. Nobody got sore."

Andrew was so disarmed by his charm that he did not find the boy's last statement odd until he had heard the sentence repeated several times inside his head.

"Sore?"

"Yes, sore." He untied the string that bound his food package and set the meat on a little wire grate. "They never got sore at me," he repeated, measuring his words. "They were a right nice bunch. Sometimes guys don't take to it if you like something real well. They get sore. These guys didn't get sore. Never. They saw me going off to the woods with my supper every evening, and sometimes even, one or two of them would come along. And sometimes twenty-five of us would go out with steaks. But mostly I just went by myself and they stayed back playing games in the cottages or going into town. If it had been winter I'd have stayed in the cottages more. I was never there in winter. If I had been, I might have gone out anyway. I like to make a fire in the snow."

"Where were you?" asked Andrew.

"In a factory by a stream." The meat was cooked, and he cut off a tiny piece for Andrew. "This is all you're going to get. Otherwise I won't have enough in me."

"I've eaten. With the others," said Andrew shortly.

"You've got to try this," the boy insisted. "And see if you like eating it this way, cooked on the coals outdoors. Then maybe you can get on the good side of the mess sergeant and bring your food out here, too. They're all right here. I could stay in this outfit. Just as good as I could stay back home in the hotel."

"You live in a hotel?"

"I lived in a hotel except the summer I was in the factory."

"Well, I'll see you," Andrew mumbled, walking away.

One night after he had eaten his supper he found himself wandering among the huts on the other side of the mess hall. It was Saturday night and most of the huts were dark. He was dejected, and thought of going into town and drinking beer by himself. Andrew drank only beer because he considered other forms of alcohol too expensive, although most of the other soldiers, who had less money than he, drank whiskey. As he walked along thinking of the beer he heard a voice calling to him. He looked up and saw Tommy standing in the doorway of a hut only a few feet away. They greeted each other, and Tommy motioned to him to wait. Then he went inside to get something.

Andrew leaned against a tree with his hands in his pockets. When Tommy came out he held a flat box in his hand. "Sparklers," he said. "I bought them after the Fourth, cut-rate. It's the best time to buy them."

"That's good to know," said Andrew. He had never touched fireworks except on the day of the Fourth. He had a brief memory of alleys on summer nights, where boys were grinding red devils under their heels in the dark. Compared to him they were poor, and he was therefore, like all well-off children, both revolted by them and envious of them. The fact that they played with fireworks after the Fourth of July was disgusting in a way. It had a foreign flavor, and made him feel a little sick, just as the Irish did, and the Jews, and circus people. But he was also excited by them. The sick feeling was part of the excitement.

Andrew had never dressed as a ragamuffin on Thanksgiving, and he had once almost fainted when two boys disguised as hags had come begging at the door. His father's rage had contributed greatly to the nightmarish quality of the memory. It was usually his mother, and not his father, who was angry. But he remembered that his father had seemed to attach great importance to the custom of masquerading on Thanksgiving. "He should be dressed up himself and out there with the others!" he had cried. "He has no right to be lying there, white as a sheet. There's no earthly reason for it. This is a holiday. It's time for *fun*. My God, doesn't anyone in this house ever have any fun? I was a ragamuffin every year until I was grown. Why doesn't he tear up an old pair of pants and go out? I'll take the crown out of my straw hat if he wants to wear it. But he should go out!"

Quite naturally Andrew had thought of running away. This was one of his worst memories. He hated to hear his father speak about the poor. His own romantic conception of them made his father's democratic viewpoint unacceptable. It was as incongruous as if he had come into the parlor and found his father offering one of his cigarettes to a pirate or a gypsy. He preferred his mother's disdain for the poor. In fact, she liked nothing but the smell of her intimates. Of course, she made him feel sick, too, but sick in a different way.

"Come on. Take one," Tommy was saying, and he lighted a sparkler. Andrew stared at the needle-like sparks. The hissing sound of the sparkler awakened old sick feelings, and he longed to pull the little stick from between Tommy's fingers and bury the bright sparks in the earth. Instead, he looked gloomy and said nothing. He liked the fact that Tommy was poor, but he did not want him to be so poor that he seemed foreign. Then he realized that others might not see a connection between being a foreigner and playing with sparklers after the Fourth of July, and he was aware that there was really no logical connection. Yet he himself felt that there was one. Sometimes he wondered whether or not other people went about pretending to be logical while actually they felt as he did inside, but this was not very often, since he usually took it for granted that everyone was more honest than he. The fact that it was impossible to say anything of all this to Tommy both depressed and irritated him.

"I saved a whole box of sparklers for you," Tommy said. "I thought you'd be coming to the clearing."

Andrew could not believe he was hearing the words. At the same time his heart had begun to beat faster. He told himself that he must retain a natural expression.

"I don't know if you like to fool around with stuff they make for kids," Tommy went on. "Maybe you think it's not worth your while. But you don't have to pay much attention to these. You light 'em and they burn themselves out. You can swing 'em around and talk at the same time. Or you don't even have to swing 'em. You can stick 'em in the ground and they go on all by themselves, like little pinwheels. There's not much point to 'em, but I get 'em anyway, every summer after the Fourth of July is over with. This isn't the box I saved for you. That one I gave to someone else who had a nephew." He handed the box to Andrew.

Andrew's face was like stone and his mouth was drawn.

"Here." Tommy tapped the back of Andrew's hand with the flat box. "Here are your sparklers."

"No," said Andrew. "I don't want any sparklers." He was not going to offer any explanation for refusing them. Tommy did not seem to want one in any case. He went on tracing designs in the night with his sparkler. "I'll just stash this box away if you don't want 'em. I can use 'em up. It's better to have one of these going than nothing, and sometimes there's no time for me to build a bonfire."

"You take things easy, don't you?" Andrew said.

Early 1950s

Emmy Moore's Journal

On certain days I forget why I'm here. Today once again I wrote my husband all my reasons for coming. He encouraged me to come each time I was in doubt. He said that the worst danger for me was a state of vagueness, so I wrote telling him why I had come to the Hotel Henry—my eighth letter on this subject—but with each new letter I strengthen my position. I am reproducing the letter here. Let there be no mistake. My journal is intended for publication. I want to publish for glory, but also in order to aid other women. This is the letter to my husband, Paul Moore, to whom I have been married sixteen years. (I am childless.) He is of North Irish descent, and a very serious lawyer. Also a solitary and lover of the country. He knows all mushrooms, bushes and trees, and he is interested in geology. But these interests do not exclude me. He is sympathetic towards me, and kindly. He wants very much for me to be happy, and worries because I am not. He knows everything about me, including how much I deplore being the feminine kind of woman that I am. In fact, I am unusually feminine for an American of Anglo stock. (Born in Boston.) I am almost a "Turkish" type. Not physically, at least not entirely, because though fat I have ruddy Scotch cheeks and my eyes are round and not slanted or almond-shaped. But sometimes I feel certain that I exude an atmosphere very similar to theirs (the Turkish women's) and then I despise myself. I find the women in my country so extraordinarily manly and independent, capable of leading regiments, or of fending for themselves on desert islands if necessary. (These are poor examples, but I am getting my point across.) For me it is an experience simply to have come here alone to the Hotel Henry and to eat my dinner and lunch by myself. If possible before I die, I should like to become a little more independent, and a little less Turkish than I am now. Before I go any further, I had better say immediately that I mean no offense to Turkish women. They are probably busy combating the very same Turkish quality in themselves that I am controlling in me. I understand, too (though this is irrelevant), that many Turkish women are beautiful, and I think that they have discarded their veils. Any other American woman would be sure of this. She would know one way or the other whether the veils had been discarded, whereas I am afraid to come out with a definite statement. I have a feeling that they really have got rid of their veils, but I won't swear to it. Also, if they have done so, I have no idea when they did. Was it many years ago or recently?

Here is my letter to Paul Moore, my husband, in which there is more about Turkish women. Since I am writing this journal with a view to publication, I do not want to ramble on as though I had all the space in the world. No publisher will attempt printing an *enormous* journal written by an unknown woman. It would be too much of a financial risk. Even I, with my ignorance of all matters pertaining to business, know this much. But they may print a small one.

My letter (written yesterday, the morrow of my drunken evening in the Blue Bonnet Room when I accosted the society salesman):

Dearest Paul:

I cannot simply live out my experiment here at the Hotel Henry without trying to justify or at least explain in letters my reasons for being here, and with fair regularity. You encouraged me to write whenever I felt I needed to clarify my thoughts. But you did tell me that I must not feel the need to *justify* my actions. However, I *do* feel the need to justify my actions, and I am certain that until the prayed-for metamorphosis has occurred I shall go on feeling just this need. Oh, how well I know that you would interrupt me at this point and warn me against expecting too much. So I shall say in lieu of metamorphosis, the prayed-for *improvement*. But until then I must justify myself every day. Perhaps you will get a letter every day. On some days the need to write lodges itself in my throat like a cry that must be uttered.

As for the Turkish problem, I am coming to it. You must understand that I am an admirer of Western civilization; that is, of the women who are members of this group. I feel myself that I fall short of being a member, that by some curious accident I was not born in Turkey but should have been. Because of my usual imprecision I cannot even tell how many countries belong to what we call Western Civilization, but I believe Turkey is the place where East meets West, isn't it? I can just about imagine the women there, from what I have heard about the country and the pictures I have seen of it. As for being troubled or obsessed by real Oriental women, I am not. (I refer to the Chinese, Japanese, Hindus, and so on.) Naturally I am less concerned with the Far Eastern women because there is no danger of my being like them. (The Turkish women are just near enough.) The Far Eastern ones are so very far away, at the opposite end of the earth, that they could easily be just as independent and masculine as the women of the Western world. The ones living in-between the two masculine areas would be soft and feminine. Naturally I don't believe this for a minute, but still, the real Orientals are so far away and such a mystery to me that it might as well be true. Whatever they are, it couldn't affect me. They look too different from the way I look. Whereas Turkish women don't. (Their figures are exactly like mine, alas!)

Now I shall come to the point. I know full well that you will consider the above discourse a kind of joke. Or if you don't, you will be irritated with me for making statements of such a sweeping and inaccurate nature. For surely you will consider the picture of the world that I present as inaccurate. I myself know that this concept of the women (all three sets—Western, Middle and Eastern) is a puerile one. It could even be called downright idiotic. Yet I assure you that I see things this way, if I relax even a little and look through my own eyes into what is really inside my head. (Though because of my talent for mimicry I am able to simulate looking through the eyes of an educated person when I wish to.) Since I am giving you such a frank picture of myself, I may as well go the whole hog and admit to you that my secret picture of the world is grossly inaccurate. I have completely forgotten to include in it any of the Latin countries. (France, Italy, Spain.) For instance, I have jumped from the Anglo world to the semi-Oriental as if there were no countries in between at all. I know that these exist. (I have even lived in two of them.) But they do not fit into my scheme. I just don't think about the Latins very much, and this is less understandable than my not thinking about the Chinese or Javanese or Japanese women. You can see why without my having to explain it to you. I do know that the French women are more interested in sports than they used to be, and for all I know they may be indistinguishable from Anglo women by now. I haven't been to France recently so I can't be sure. But in any case the women of those countries don't enter into my picture of the world. Or shall I say that the fact of having forgotten utterly to consider them has not altered the way I visualize the division of the world's women? Incredible though it may seem to you, it hasn't altered anything. (My having forgotten all Latin countries, South America included.) I want you to know the whole truth about me. But don't imagine that I wouldn't be capable of concealing my ignorance from you if I wanted to. I am so wily and feminine that I could live by your side for a lifetime and deceive you afresh each day. But I will have no truck with feminine wiles. I know how they can absorb the hours of the day. Many women are delighted to sit around spinning their webs. It is an absorbing occupation, and the women feel they are getting somewhere. And so they are, but only for as long as the man is there to be deceived. And a wily woman alone is a pitiful sight to behold. Naturally.

I shall try to be honest with you so that I can live with you and yet won't be pitiful. Even if tossing my feminine tricks out the window means being left no better than an illiterate backwoodsman, or the bottom fish scraping along the ocean bed, I prefer to have it this way. Now I am too tired to write more. Though I don't feel that I have clarified enough or justified enough.

I shall write you soon about the effect the war has had upon me. I have spoken to you about it, but you have never seemed to take it very seriously. Perhaps seeing in black and white what I feel will affect your opinion of me. Perhaps you will leave me. I accept the challenge. My Hotel Henry experience includes this risk. I got drunk two nights ago. It's hard to believe that I am forty-seven, isn't it?

My love,
Emmy

Now that I have copied this letter into my journal (I had forgotten to make a carbon), I shall take my walk. My scheme included a few weeks of solitude at the Hotel Henry before attempting anything. I did not even intend to write in my journal as soon as I started to, but simply to sit about collecting my thoughts, waiting for the knots of habit to undo themselves. But after only a week here—two nights ago—I felt amazingly alone and disconnected from my past life, so I began my journal.

My first interesting contact was the salesman in the Blue Bonnet Room. I had heard about this eccentric through my in-laws, the Moores, before I ever came up here. My husband's cousin Laurence Moore told me about him when he heard I was coming. He said: "Take a walk through Grey and Bottle's Department Store, and you'll see a man with a lean red face and reddish hair selling materials by the bolt. That man has an income and is related to Hewitt Molain. He doesn't need to work. He was in my fraternity. Then he disappeared. The next I heard of him he was working there at Grey and Bottle's. I stopped by and said hello to him. For a nut he seemed like a very decent chap. You might even have a drink with him. I think he's quite up to general conversation."

I did not mention Laurence Moore to the society salesman because I thought it might irritate him. I lied and pretended to have been here for months, when actually this is still only my second week at the Hotel Henry. I want everyone to think I have been here a long time. Surely it is not to impress them. Is there anything impressive about a lengthy stay at the Hotel Henry? Any sane person would be alarmed that I should even ask such a question. I ask it because deep in my heart I *do* think a lengthy stay at the Hotel Henry is impressive. Very easy to see that I would, and even sane of me to think it impressive, but not sane of me to expect anyone else to think so, particularly a stranger. Perhaps I simply like to hear myself telling it. I hope so. I shall write some more tomorrow, but now I must go out. I am going to buy a supply of cocoa. When I'm not drunk I like to have a cup of cocoa before going to sleep. My husband likes it too.

She could not stand the overheated room a second longer. With some difficulty she raised the window, and the cold wind blew in. Some loose sheets of paper went skimming off the top of the desk and flattened themselves against the bookcase. She shut the window and they fell to the floor. The cold air had changed her mood. She looked down at the sheets of paper. They were part of the letter she had just copied. She picked them up: "*I don't feel that I have clarified enough or justified enough*," she read. She closed her eyes and shook her head. She had been so happy copying this letter into her journal, but now her heart was faint as she scanned its scattered pages. "I have said nothing," she muttered to herself in alarm. "I have said nothing at all. I have not clarified my reasons for being at the Hotel Henry. I have not justified myself."

Automatically she looked around the room. A bottle of whiskey stood on the floor beside one of the legs of the bureau. She stepped forward, picked it up by the neck, and settled with it into her favorite wicker chair.

Early 1950s

Friday

HE SAT at a little table in the Green Mountain Luncheonette apathetically studying the menu. Faithful to the established tradition of his rich New England family, he habitually chose the cheapest dish listed on the menu whenever it was not something he definitely abhorred. Today was Friday, and there were two cheap dishes listed, both of which he hated. One was haddock and the other fried New England smelts. The cheaper meat dishes had been omitted. Finally, with compressed lips, he decided on a steak. The waitress was barely able to hear his order.

"Did you say steak?" she asked him.

"Yes. There isn't anything else. Who eats haddock?"

"Nine tenths of the population." She spoke without venom. "Look at Agnes." She pointed to the table next to his.

Andrew looked up. He had noticed the girl before. She had a long freckled face with large, rather roughly sketched features. Her hair, almost the color of her skin, hung down to her shoulders. It was evident that her mustard-colored wool dress was homemade. It was decorated at the throat with a number of dark brown woollen balls. Over the dress she wore a man's lumber jacket. She was a large-boned girl. The lower half of her face was long and solid and insensitive-looking, but her eyes, Andrew noted, were luminous and starry.

Although it was bitterly cold outside, the lunchroom was steaming hot and the front window had clouded over.

"Don't you like fish?" the girl said.

He shook his head. Out of the corner of his eye he had noticed that she was not eating her haddock. However, he had quickly looked away, in order not to be drawn into a conversation. The arrival of his steak obliged him to look up, and their eyes met. She was gazing at him with a rapt expression. It made him feel uncomfortable.

"My name is Agnes Leather," she said in a hushed voice, as if she were sharing a delightful secret. "I've seen you eating in here before."

He realized that there was no polite way of remaining silent, and so he said in an expressionless voice, "I ate here yesterday and the day before yesterday."

"That's right." She nodded. "I saw you both times. At noon yesterday, and then the day before a little later than that. At night I don't come here. I have a family. I eat home with them like everybody else in a small town." Her smile was warm and intimate, as if she would like to include him in her good fortune.

He did not know what to say to this, and asked himself idly if she was going to eat her haddock.

"You're wondering why I don't touch my fish?" she said, catching his eye.

"You haven't eaten much of it, have you?" He coughed discreetly and cut into his little steak, hoping that she would soon occupy herself with her meal.

"I almost never feel like eating," she said. "Even though I do live in a small town."

"That's too bad."

"Do you think it's too bad?"

She fixed her luminous eyes upon him intently, as if his face held the true meaning of his words, which might only have seemed banal.

He looked at the long horselike lower half of her face, and decided that she was unsubtle and strong-minded despite her crazy eyes. It occurred to him that women were getting entirely too big and bony. "Do I think what's too bad?" he asked her.

"That I don't care about eating."

"Well, yes," he said with a certain irritation. "It's always better to have an appetite. At least, that's what I thought."

She did not answer this, but looked pensive, as if she were considering seriously whether or not to agree with him. Then she shook her head from side to side, indicating that the problem was insoluble.

"You'd understand if I could give you the whole picture," she said. "This is just a glimpse. But I can't give you the whole picture in a lunchroom. I know it's a good thing to eat. I know." And as if to prove this, she fell upon her haddock and finished it off with three stabs of her fork. It was a very small portion. But the serious look in her eye remained.

"I'm sorry if I startled you," she said gently, wetting her lips. "I try not to do that. You can blame it on my being from a small town if you want, but it has nothing to do with that. It really hasn't. But it's just impossible for me to explain it all to you, so I might as well say I'm from a small town as to say my name is Agnes Leather."

She began an odd nervous motion of pulling at her wrist, and to his surprise shouted for some hotcakes with maple syrup.

At that moment a waitress opened the door leading into the street, and put down a cast-iron cat to hold it back. The wind blew through the restaurant and the diners set up a clamor.

"Orders from the boss!" the waitress screamed. "Just hold your horses. We're clearing the air." This airing occurred every day, and the shrieks of the customers were only in jest. As soon as the clouded glass shone clear, so that the words GREEN MOUNTAIN LUNCHEONETTE in reverse were once again visible, the waitress removed the iron cat and shut the door.

Early 1950s

"Curls and a quiet country face"

CURLS AND a quiet country face.

Jennifer-Madeleine. She seems to move in an afternoon light. A brilliantly lighted cold afternoon just before sunset. The melancholy gold color of hayfields from another time, an earlier time, but seen in our day, part of our time. The hay, but not the light. The double heart. Not a drama, but both families. The final painful experience. There must be no more pain like this. Death is better than a long murder.

Might bring into sharper focus what is surrounding and seeming to be outside when the inside is dying. There can be a new joy, a joy so false that one can be shaken with mirth, as one never is, can never be, when the joy is a true one and the inside is not dying.

A play. There comes a moment when there is no possibility of escape, as if the spirit were a box hitting at the walls of the head. Looking at the ocean is the only relief. I have trained my eye to look away from the beach where they are going to build the new docks. I cannot look at that part of the beach unless I think of my own end, curtail my own sense of time, as Paul says that we must all do now. I can do it, but it's like: "You too can live with cancer." When I was little I had to imagine that there was some limit to physical pain in order to enjoy the day. I have never yet enjoyed a day, but I have never stopped trying to arrange for happiness. My present plan to get Tetum into my house is as good as any other. It is at a very pleasant stage of development—still like a daydream. Nothing has changed. My father predicted everything when he said I would procrastinate until I died. I knew then it was true. In America it was terribly painful to know this as a child. Now that I am nearly forty and in North Africa it is still painful.

A play. Is it writing I'm putting off, or was it always something else—a religious sacrifice? The only time I wrote well, when I passed through the inner door, I felt guilt. I must find that again. If I can't, maybe I shall find a way to give it up. I cannot go on this way.

I love Tangier, but like a dying person. When Tetum and

Cherifa die I might leave. But we are all three of us the same age, more or less. Tetum older, Cherifa a bit younger. I'd like to buy them meat and fish and oil so that they will stay alive longer. I don't know which one I like best, or how long I can go on this way, at the point of expectation, yet knowing at the same time that it is all hopeless. Does it matter? It is more the coming home to them that I want than it is they themselves. But I do want them to belong to me, which is of course impossible. I must try to stop thinking of them. Best to spend a month or two at Madame de Marquette's. The hardest time is now.

Early 1950s

Lila and Frank

FRANK PULLED hard on the front door and opened it with a jerk, so that the pane of glass shook in its frame. It was his sister's custom never to go to the door and open it for him. She had an instinctive respect for his secretive nature.

He hung his coat on a hook in the hall and walked into the parlor, where he was certain he would find his sister. She was seated as usual in her armchair. Next to her was a heavy round table of an awkward height which made it useful for neither eating nor writing, although it was large enough for either purpose. Even in the morning Lila always wore a silk dress, stockings, and well-shined shoes. In fact, at all times of the day she was fully dressed to go into the town, although she seldom ventured from the house. Her hair was not very neat, but she took the trouble to rouge her lips.

"How were the men at the Coffee Pot tonight?" she asked when her brother entered the room. There was no variety in the inflection of her voice. It was apparent that, like him, she had never tried, either by emphasis or coloring of tone, to influence or charm a listener.

Frank sat down and rested for a while without speaking.

"How were the men at the Coffee Pot?" she said again with no change of expression.

"The same as they always are."

"You mean by that, hungry and noisy." For an outsider it would have been hard to say whether she was being critical of the men at the Coffee Pot or sincerely asking for information. This was a question she had asked him many times, and he had various ways of answering, depending upon his mood. On this particular night he was uncommunicative. "They go to the Coffee Pot for a bite to eat," he said.

She looked at him. The depths of her dark eyes held neither warmth nor comfort. "Was it crowded?" she asked.

He considered this for a moment while she watched him attentively. He was near the lamp and his face was raspberry-colored, an even deeper red than it would have been otherwise.

"It was."

"Then it must have been noisy." The dropping of her voice at the end of a sentence gave her listener, if he was a stranger, the impression that she did not intend to continue with the conversation. Her brother of course knew this was not the case, and he was not surprised at all when a minute later she went on. "Did you speak with anyone?"

"No, I didn't." He jumped up from his chair and went over to a glass bookcase in the corner. "I don't usually, do I?"

"That doesn't mean that you won't, does it?" she said calmly.

"I wouldn't change my habits from one night to the next," he said. "Not sitting at the Coffee Pot."

"Why not?"

"It's not human nature to do that, is it?"

"I know nothing about human nature at all," she said. "Nor do you, for that matter. I don't know why you'd refer to it. I do suspect, though, that I at least might change very suddenly." Her voice remained indifferent, as though the subject were not one which was close to her. "It's a feeling that's always present with me . . . here." She touched her breast.

Although he wandered around the room for a moment feigning to have lost interest in the conversation, she knew this was not so. Since they lied to each other in different ways, the excitement they felt in conversing together was very great.

"Tell me," she said. "If you don't expect to experience anything new at the Coffee Pot, why do you continue to go there?" This too she had often asked him in the past weeks, but the repetition of things added to rather than detracting from the excitement.

"I don't like to talk to anybody. But I like to go out," he said. "I may not like other men, but I like the world."

"I should think you'd go and hike in the woods, instead of sitting at the Coffee Pot. Men who don't like other men usually take to nature, I've heard."

"I'm not interested in nature, beyond the ordinary amount."

They settled into silence for a while. Then she began to question him again. "Don't you feel uneasy, knowing that most likely you're the only man at the Coffee Pot who feels so estranged from his fellows?"

He seated himself near the window and half smiled. "No," he said. "I think I like it."

"Why do you like it?"

"Because I'm aware of the estrangement, as you call it, and they aren't." This too he had answered many times before. But such was the faith they had in the depth of the mood they created between them that there were no dead sentences, no matter how often repeated.

"We don't feel the same about secrets," she told him. "I don't consider a secret such a great pleasure. In fact, I should hesitate to name what my pleasure is. I simply know that I don't feel the lack of it."

"Good night," said Frank. He wanted to be by himself. Since he very seldom talked for more than ten or fifteen minutes at a time, she was not at all surprised.

She herself was far too excited for sleep at that moment. The excitement that stirred in her breast was familiar, and could be likened to what a traveler feels on the eve of his departure. All her life she had enjoyed it or suffered from it, for it was a sensation that lay between suffering and enjoyment, and it had a direct connection with her brother's lies. For the past weeks they had concerned the Coffee Pot, but this was of little importance, since he lied to her consistently and had done so since early childhood. Her excitement had its roots in the simultaneous rejection and acceptance of these lies, a state which might be compared to that of the dreamer when he is near to waking, and who knows then that he is moving in a dream country which at any second will vanish forever, and yet is unable to recall the existence of his own room. So Lila moved about in the vivid world of her brother's lies, with the full awareness always that just beyond them lay the amorphous and hidden world of reality. These lies which thrilled her heart seemed to cull their exciting quality from her never-failing consciousness of the true events they concealed. She had not changed at all since childhood, when to expose a statement of her brother's as a lie was as unthinkable to her as the denial of God's existence is to most children. This treatment of her brother, unbalanced though it was, contained within it both dignity and merit, and these were reflected faithfully in her voice and manner.

Early 1950s?

The Iron Table

THEY SAT in the sun, looking out over a big new boulevard. The waiter had dragged an old iron table around from the other side of the hotel and set it down on the cement near a half-empty flower bed. A string stretched between stakes separated the hotel grounds from the sidewalk. Few of the guests staying at the hotel sat in the sun. The town was not a tourist center, and not many Anglo-Saxons came. Most of the guests were Spanish.

"The whole civilization is going to pieces," he said.

Her voice was sorrowful. "I know it." Her answers to his ceaseless complaining about the West's contamination of Moslem culture had become increasingly unpredictable. Today, because she felt that he was in a very irritable mood and in need of an argument, she automatically agreed with him. "It's going to pieces so quickly, too," she said, and her tone was sepulchral.

He looked at her without any light in his blue eyes. "There are places where the culture has remained untouched," he announced as if for the first time. "If we went into the desert you wouldn't have to face all this. Wouldn't you love that?" He was punishing her for her swift agreement with him a moment earlier. He knew she had no desire to go to the desert, and that she believed it was not possible to continue trying to escape from the Industrial Revolution. Without realizing he was doing it he had provoked the argument he wanted.

"Why do you ask me if I wouldn't love to go into the desert, when you know as well as I do I wouldn't. We've talked about it over and over. Every few days we talk about it." Although the sun was beating down on her chest, making it feel on fire, deep inside she could still feel the cold current that seemed to run near her heart.

"Well," he said. "You change. Sometimes you say you *would* like to go."

It was true. She did change. Sometimes she would run to him with bright eyes. "Let's go," she would say. "Let's go into the desert." But she never did this if she was sober.

There was something wistful in his voice, and she had to remind herself that she wanted to feel cranky rather than heartbroken. In order to go on talking she said: "Sometimes I feel like going, but it's always when I've had something to drink. When I've had nothing to drink I'm afraid." She turned to face him, and he saw that she was beginning to have her hunted expression.

"Do you think I *ought* to go?" she asked him.

"Go where?"

"To the desert. To live in an oasis." She was pronouncing her words slowly. "Maybe that's what I should do, since I'm your wife."

"You must do what you really want to do," he said. He had been trying to teach her this for twelve years.

"What I really want. . . . Well, if you'd be happy in an oasis, maybe I'd really want to do that." She spoke hesitantly, and there was a note of doubt in her voice.

"What?" He shook his head as if he had run into a spiderweb. "What is it?"

"I meant that maybe if you were happy in an oasis I would be, too. Wives get pleasure out of making their husbands happy. They really do, quite aside from its being moral."

He did not smile. He was in too bad a humor. "You'd go to an oasis because you wanted to escape from Western civilization."

"My friends and I don't feel there's any *way* of escaping it. It's not interesting to sit around talking about industrialization."

"What friends?" He liked her to feel isolated.

"Our friends." Most of them she had not seen in many years. She turned to him with a certain violence. "I think you come to these countries so you can complain. I'm tired of hearing the word *civilization*. It has no meaning. Or I've forgotten what it meant, anyway."

The moment when they might have felt tenderness had passed, and secretly they both rejoiced. Since he did not answer her, she went on. "I think it's uninteresting. To sit and watch costumes disappear, one by one. It's uninteresting even to mention it."

"They are not costumes," he said distinctly. "They're simply the clothes people wear."

She was as bitter as he about the changes, but she felt it would be indelicate for them both to reflect the same sorrow. It would happen some day, surely. A serious grief would silence their argument. They would share it and not be able to look into each other's eyes. But as long as she could she would hold off that moment.

Early 1950s?

At the Jumping Bean

The interior of the Jumping Bean. Booths, colored paper lanterns. The bar will be supplied with bottles as well as with hamburgers and ketchup. Over the doorway there is a neon sign reading THE JUMPING BEAN, which the audience sees backward. Over the bar is a list written in huge letters:

★ ★

Beanburgers . . . Our Jumping Specials. Unique.
Complete Chicken Dinners . . . $1.33
Extra Cole Slaw Cup Free . . . "For them what likes it."
Free Jumpers with every order.
BEANAROO COCKTAIL. *"Swig it down. Then Jump."* . . . 55 cents.

★ ★

BERYL JANE *and* GABRIEL *are seated at a table. She is dressed in a very feminine, pert manner.*

BERYL JANE: They have such tiny little chickens here.
GABRIEL: Yes, but they don't cost much.
BERYL JANE: I know.
GABRIEL: Maybe it's foolish to try and eat chickens at this price.
BERYL JANE: The other kids do. They love them.
GABRIEL: They're busy dancing and flirting. That's why they come here to the Jumping Bean. To dance and flirt. I guess most of the guys buy these little chicken dinners more for show than they do for eating. If guys were alone they'd just stuff themselves on beanburgers and fill up. Some of them do anyhow. Even with a girl along, guys who are low on cash. And some guys who don't give a damn about showing off to a girl, don't care what impression they make on a girl. A lot of them don't even bother talking. Some of them don't even *like* girls.
BERYL JANE: Those are pansies.
GABRIEL: They come in here, too.
BERYL JANE (*thinking of the cabin she has rented*): What do they order?
GABRIEL (*talking through his hat*): I guess they don't bother

with much. They don't sit down to a table and order the dollar thirty-three, I don't guess. They have beers at the bar, and maybe beanburgers. They don't bother much. They're kind of without girls, and folks frown at them.

BERYL JANE: There's everything in this world. Everything under the sun. But you can't spend your whole life worrying about other people.

GABRIEL: Some people do. They worry about humanity.

BERYL JANE: I worry about reality.

GABRIEL: What do you mean?

BERYL JANE: I mean everything that's close to me, that's real. Like my father and my projects, and . . . and . . . my front porch, the swing, and especially my own room, and science. Science is close to me. (*She hesitates.*) It really is. If I start thinking about far-off things, or things that are too different, then I get, like, paralyzed. I get off the track. Like kids thinking about eternity when they're little. We all hated it.

GABRIEL: We hated eternity?

BERYL JANE: But you have to think about those things more than I do, because you're a poet.

(*The chicken dinners arrive and they stop talking while the waitress lays out the various plates.*)

They really are small chickens, aren't they? They're smaller than they were last time.

WAITRESS: But you've got five different items come with that chicken plate. You've got chips, greens, Juliennes, Parkers, and the slaw cup.

(*She holds up the tiniest possible paper cup.* BERYL JANE *and* GABRIEL *look up at it.*)

If you feel like you want your extra slaw cup right off I can bring it to you now. It's coming free with the dollar thirty-three (*pointing to the list over the bar*) "for them what likes it." (*She reads this in a dull routine voice. She has obviously no spirit of fun in her at all.*) And here's your jumpers. (*She tosses some jumping beans onto the table.*) They come free with all items, down to cokes.

GABRIEL: We don't want any jumping beans. We want to talk and eat.

WAITRESS (*ignoring his request*): We're open all night.

GABRIEL: You can have another dollar thirty-three if you want, Beryl Jane. If you're still hungry when you finish this one.

BERYL JANE: You're not a millionaire, Gabriel.

GABRIEL: If I was a millionaire I'd be traveling. I wouldn't be buying these little chicken dinners.

BERYL JANE: If everything works out with the pigs the way it should, we'll have enough money to travel for two months out of the year. Switzerland or Paris. Or we could go and see the Northern Lights, or museums. Then, back home. (*She eats for a moment.*) You'd have your room upstairs for writing poetry. You'd come back from a trip full of inspiration. All those beautiful sights . . .

(GABRIEL *laughs.*)

. . . And you'd be real glad to be home in your own house . . . in your own room.

(*Her own deep unexpressed fear that none of this will come true communicates itself to the audience.*)

We'll leave some of our land wild, with just natural pastures and woods. Your windows, Gabriel . . . (*She searches his face, but she is not sure he is listening.*) While you're writing your poetry you can look out the window at the wild beautiful land. The kind of land you always say you like.

(GABRIEL *continues eating. He looks very sad.*)

And the equipment and the buildings and the pigs. They'll all be on the other side of the house. You won't even know they're there. It will be just like you were off in a log cabin with nobody around. No pigs . . .

GABRIEL: I don't mind pigs. I like them.

BERYL JANE: Well, maybe you don't like them around all the time. Anyway, not when you're writing poetry.

GABRIEL: I don't care. They can all come into my room if they want to. Maybe I won't write poetry.

(*He looks very defeated.*)

BERYL JANE: The pigs aren't going to walk in and out of the house. It's going to be a very modern farm.

GABRIEL: Can't we stop talking about the future? Why don't we dance?

(*He gets up and goes over to the jukebox. It starts to play.*)

BERYL JANE: I love the future. Except when it looks black. Pop says if the world blows up it won't be my fault. But he gets sore if he doesn't think I'm concentrating on my course. He says I should think about people all over the world and crises a normal amount, but he wants me to tend to my own business and follow my goal. He hates people who are wishy-washy, who don't know what they're doing. You know, like should I or shouldn't I.

GABRIEL: He must be nuts about me.

BERYL JANE: I told him you were interested and getting very excited about pig farming. I told him that you were a writer besides. He asked me if you wrote facts and I said you did.

(*They dance for a moment.*)

Gabriel . . .

GABRIEL: What?

BERYL JANE: What time are we going to go back to the cabin?

(*They stop dancing and stand still in the middle of the floor.*)

It's because you've got so much on your mind all the time. You might forget . . . about the cabin. I don't think we should go there so late that we're both so tired, you know.

(*She stops and looks at him, a very peculiar expression on her face. She seems almost frozen, but she is compelled to go on. Then, in a strange childish voice.*)

I get so tired at night. It's because I get up so early. I get so tired.

(*He doesn't answer. His eyes are blank.*)

Like a kid, isn't it? I'm like a little girl?

(*There must be something terrifying about this scene. Her smile is crooked, as if she were being trampled inside.*)

Don't you think so?

(*An almost repulsive innocence.*)

I still play marbles with my brother. And I climb apple trees.

GABRIEL: Do you?

BERYL JANE: Yes. Maybe you do, too.

GABRIEL: No. I don't.

BERYL JANE: Maybe I'll climb apple trees even after I have a baby. People don't get so old any more. My aunt's forty and she plays pool all the time. When it's summer she goes crabbing.

(*He is silent.*)

There's nothing much to having a baby any more, even. They get 'em walking right off, the mothers, I mean. I'll bet my aunt would get up and play pool the day after her baby was born, if she had a baby. But she's frigid. (*She sits down.*) Are we going?

GABRIEL: I'm going to get a drink. Do you want one?

BERYL JANE: Yes. I'll have a drink.

GABRIEL (*calling*): Waitress! Two drinks!

WAITRESS: Two beanaroo cocktails?

GABRIEL: Two whiskeys. And don't bring those jumping beans.

WAITRESS: No jumpers? They come . . .

GABRIEL: I don't want any jumping beans with my drink. That's enough jumping beans.

BERYL JANE (*in panic embarrassment, but with a drive to get to the cabin no matter what, because she has planned it that way*): Why are you so sore about the jumpers? You can just leave them alone. Just leave them alone on the table if you don't want to play with them.

GABRIEL: Why do they treat us like kids on these routes? It's the same way at Larry's Devilburger.

BERYL JANE (*pale, as if he were insulting her*): They have no jumping beans.

GABRIEL: They've got four cages with those little mice inside them, running up and down ladders like maniacs and swinging themselves.

BERYL JANE: They're not mice. They're hamsters. Everybody loves them. Even people's grandparents.

GABRIEL: And the Routeburger.

BERYL JANE: They've got nothing. Nothing but the extra slaw cup free. That's the same as here, but no other attractions. An extra paper slaw cup and Juliennes and Parks and greens and dancing. They've got the dollar thirty-three but no jumpers.

(*She stops and looks at him.* GABRIEL *has drained his drink and wears a black look on his face.*)

Gabriel?

GABRIEL: What?

BERYL JANE: If you don't like these joints we don't have to come to them. I don't care about them.

(*He shrugs his shoulders.*)

But I am beginning to feel tired, like I said. I'm more like a child than most girls. I like cocoa at night, and bread and jam. I like a child's dinner, not a grown-up dinner. If I'm alone . . . Boy! I go straight for the cocoa and soft-boiled eggs and toast. I don't really give a damn about whiskey.

(GABRIEL *takes her glass and finishes off her drink.*)

BERYL JANE: Now? Gabriel, shall we pay our check and go now? I'll go stand in the doorway while you pay the check.

(GABRIEL *goes to the bar.*)

GABRIEL (*to* WAITRESS): Give me the check and I'll pay here.

WAITRESS: I can bring the check to your table. There's no need for you to come here. You got table service.

GABRIEL: I don't want to go back to my table. I want to pay here.

WAITRESS: You're kind of contrary, aren't you?

(GABRIEL *shrugs.*)

I've got a nephew who's contrary. Name is Norman. He came like that. Interferes with his making a living. He thinks nothing of sitting and letting the women work. Just so long as he can go on being his own contrary self. If he didn't come straight out of my only sister I'd boot him in the ass. He and I don't greet unless it's a calendar holiday. Then we greet because it looks too bad if we don't. But we make it short. He knows he's sitting on my sister while I'm bending my elbow at the Beanburger.

(GABRIEL *leaves the bar angrily, and stands next to* BERYL JANE. *They are framed in the doorway.*)

GABRIEL: There's no moon, Beryl. It's very dark out.

BERYL JANE: I know. But there are lights all along the highway.

GABRIEL: Don't you like the moon, though?

BERYL JANE: I don't know. Not as much as some people. I never think about looking up unless someone says: Beryl, look at the moon! When I'm by myself I never look at the moon. I don't know. I guess I'm not too keen on it.

GABRIEL: Well, what do you like?

(*There is a stillness to the scene. The restaurant lights darken and they are illuminated only by the blue light of the backward-reading neon sign. Their faces look white.*)

BERYL JANE: What do I like?

GABRIEL: What beautiful sight? I mean, without traveling. What do you think is beautiful?

BERYL JANE: I like . . . I like tea-roses. And . . . (*She falters.*) Do you mean anything that's beautiful?

GABRIEL: Yes. You never mention much what you think is beautiful.

BERYL JANE (*very quickly, spontaneously, with sparkle and life*): I think snakes are beautiful. Those snakes with diamonds on their backs and very dark colored scales, deep green and purple and black.

GABRIEL (*uncomprehending*): Snakes.

BERYL JANE: Yes, snakes. Some snakes anyway.

(*She looks at him. He has moved away from her. Panic rising again.*)

Maybe that's not the kind of beautiful thing you meant. Maybe you didn't want to hear about snakes. Maybe you meant more like what beautiful things do I love that the world loves.

(*He does not answer.*)

I told you, Gabriel. Tea-roses. And there are other things, but I don't want to talk about them now. Not in front of the Jumping Bean. I can't think here. And don't tell anybody I like snakes. I don't want people to think . . .

(*He has begun to walk. She stands still an instant, and then starts after him.*)

1955

LETTERS

In 1935, at the age of eighteen, Jane Auer was living in the Hyde Park Hotel in New York with her mother, Claire Stajer Auer. Sidney Auer, Jane's father, had died in 1930. From 1932 until 1934 Jane had been in a sanatorium in Leysin, Switzerland, for treatment of tuberculosis in the bone of her knee. On her return to New York she was operated on and her right leg permanently stiffened.

In New York she began a novel in French, *Le Phaéton Hypocrite*, but spent most of her time exploring Greenwich Village.

The first letter is to George McMillan, a young man who was working in a Village club as doorman, bouncer, and cashier. The incident that precipitated the letter was Jane's running away from home after a fight with her mother. She had been found in Greenwich Village by her Aunt Constance and brought back to her mother's apartment.

I
To George McMillan

The Hyde Park Hotel
Twenty-five East Seventy-Seventh Street
New York

Dear George,

Here's what happened when I arrived home. (Connie was lying about taking me to her place but I didn't raise a kick. I knew I'd be with Mother sooner or later anyway.)

Mother was potting around the kitchen (anticlimax) and Aunt Flo was wrapped up in Uncle Carl's bathrobe. Whenever there's grief around, women always accumulate blankets, men's overcoats, hot water bottles, woolen scarfs.

They whisked me into the bedroom while Mother finished gnawing at her roast beef bone. Connie said, "Get undressed, dear." She was at the burping stage and felt very ill as she had told us once or twice in the car.

I remained dressed—they were four against one anyway. Then Mother came in, in the awful black kimono she had on the night you were here. She said, "What's this?"

I took an arrogant stand. I had a "Who are these people" look on my face and "I must get back down to the party."

Then Connie started in: Now Claire, you know I don't feel

well and I've been looking for Jane for four hours and I was cold and—

Mother: Well, what has Jane to say for herself?

Jane: Nothing. I don't know why I'm here.

Connie: Now Jane, you know that's not true! You wanted to come back. She told me she couldn't hurt you, Claire!

Hysterics on my part here—I don't know quite what I said but I know I almost killed the poor woman and started cursing myself because I couldn't hurt her.

Then she kissed me and they all sat down and said what a wonderful girl I was and what a fine young man you were—and that if I still wanted to marry you twenty-five years from now I could—that Mother wouldn't think of standing in the way of my happiness—and that I was a grand normal girl—and that this Lesbian business was just an adolescent phase (adolescence being from seven to thirty-three in our family) and that if only I didn't have such an analytic mind I certainly would throw it off—and if I really were a Lesbian they'd get up a fund for me and send me down to the Village in my own private bus (I suggested that they might organize picnics for all us girls every two weeks), but I really wasn't one so they couldn't let me go to my ruin!

Aunt Flo suggested 130 more men to straighten me out—Aunt Connie 135. The same remedy seems to go for you and the Les's—like 3 in 1 Oil, or bleeding in the Middle Ages.

In two weeks I shall leave for college—Rollins down South (Florida).

They have beautiful low white buildings. "We have the best equipped dorms in the U.S.A.," says Pres. Holt, "and we hope to suck enough of the rich students' blood so as to be able to install a radio in every room, which will look very well in our catalogue."

It is a modern college and you can specialize in anything you please—conferences they have instead of lectures.

I have been writing this letter for three days. Mother always comes in when I get started. George, pardon the tone of all this but I'm trying to counterbalance all the emotion and drama that's been hanging between us so that we could hardly see each other.

You may come to see me! And tell Lupe anything you like. She hasn't called me since the night you were here.

Love to you—
Jane

1935

Miriam Fligelman had been a childhood friend of Jane's in Woodmere, New York. Miriam had visited Jane in 1935 on her honeymoon trip, following her marriage to Irving Levy.

2
To Miriam Fligelman Levy

My Dear Miriam

Trust me—I'm not going to say anything trite such as "Better late than never" or "Excuse the delay, but I've been so busy."

My problem is much bigger and deeper.

I find myself staring at my writing materials from the couch as though they were "Nazis."

I get nauseous at the thought of putting a pen to paper for any purpose, literary or otherwise. This incapability of mine to "act" is spreading. I stare at my corset for hours now before I put it on.

I am perfectly serious and solemn about the whole thing.

I feel particularly badly about not having written you because I remember the emphatic way in which I agreed that we must not—absolutely must not—lose contact this time and that I would certainly write. Either I don't know myself or I'm a confounded skillful liar.

I thought about you for such a long time after you left—your face that looks just like little Miriam's in a magnifying glass—now—your subdued voice and the Russian toque which you were somehow destined to wear.

The silliness of your being married first—you with your inky hands and your ten thousand books and your skinniness—you were so thin you looked like a drawing instead of a person.

To think you would deceive me too—and develop into a real human being.

I'm sitting in my living room with an old purple cover over me. The sun is in the room and the walls (remember they are yellow) glow. Little strips of sky shine thru the Venetian blinds like blue birds' wings and the mirror that stretches between the two windows takes on a green reflection like a pond.

All this is very soothing to a convalescent. I am recovering from a carefully nurtured grippe. It seems as though it just won't linger any longer—too bad.

Soon I shall be back in bed reading. As I look down my life I see one picture: "me in bed reading." The only difference is that the heap under the bedclothes grew larger.

As you see you will get no news from me today. I prefer irrelevant detail. I never will write you any news probably—unless I marry—and then I shall probably insert a sentence or two about it between a description of a rice pudding and a thumbnail sketch of Miss Foulke. I depend on you for facts, Walter Winchell, and plenty of them because I love reading them.

You have noticed my slipshod sentences and my repetition of words and my hundreds of prepositional phrases and my bad handwriting. It is because I am still nothing but a precocious child—and am I even precocious?

You have my sincerest love Miriam dearest—write me.

Jane

Tell Irving, "I like his looks." Don't by any means show him this. I am in one of my less lucid moments.

New York City, 1936

The following letter to nightclub owner Bertha LaVoe was written in January 1937 from Deal Beach, New Jersey, where Jane and her mother had spent several summers. Apparently Jane had gone there to be alone and write, challenged to do so by her friend Genevieve Phillips.

3
To "Spivy" LeVoe

Dear Spivy— Deal Beach, New Jersey

I am all alone in a great big bed, twenty feet wide. Send me homeless Italian family at once. Man and wife retired at ten thirty. She sat all day twirling a long strand of hair round and round her second finger. Had a glassy look in her eye. At dinner they played foot games underneath the table. Neither of them seems to know who I am.

The "apartment-by-the-sea" is very cold, very quiet, and very sad. I know that the janitor has been lying dead in the basement for weeks under ten feet of water. In the field at our left are the corpses of twenty million crickets. They died on Labor Day. There is also a picnic basket with a dead water rat in it. Sorry to report that the ocean is not pink. The house is rocking in the wind. We sail at any minute I'm sure. Did you know that in New Jersey the wind has a pale lavender nose and a big fat pigtail tied with a whip? Well, it doesn't—really. I'm expecting the Morro Castle ghosts in a half an hour. They sank right outside my window.

I am distressed because Mother is taking me to Havana in three weeks—almost definitely. I'll either be eaten by sharks on the way or I'll marry a Latin and all my children will be born with earrings. I don't want to go to Havana, Spivy. I wonder if you've had your coffee yet. I'm starving. I ate meat balls that tasted like German bullets for dinner.

Drop me a note and I'll have them forward it to New York if I suddenly get weak or hungry and come home. I'll try my best not to because Genevieve would be furious—why I don't know. I won't come home—really.

Love to you, Miss Spivy
Jane

Note for La Touche:
How do you do—La Touche

P.S. Give my regards to the Malfis and write me a sad, sad letter if you write at all. It doesn't matter really—just a whim.

I kees you!
Rudolf

January 29, 1937

4
To Miriam Levy

Hotel Meurice
145 West 58th Street
New York City, New York

My Dear Miriam—

Just received the letter and am sitting down in my fur coat answering it. Will probably get "La Grippe." For Heaven's sake don't name any babies Jane—ever—unless you're a sadist. I'm very jittery about this. I simply can't connect you with a baby. Why only a minute ago we were going to school. Life suddenly seems as short as a pistol shot. After this will you please address me as a "Maiden Aunt" or something. My God, I'm not anywhere near getting married. I know I've been a beast again about writing but I guess I always shall be. You ought to know by now that that does not mean I've forgotten you but simply that I hardly know how to spell.

I am having a very lovely time here with many mad people —artists and pseudo-artists but very night-clubby. As usual I am surrounded by musical people, I who dislike everything but "Swing."

I am very very blue at the moment. I wasn't when I started this letter—my moods are getting almost pathological.

It's so cold and the winter's so long and there seems nothing to experience that I haven't experienced before. I'm tired of loving and being loved. I'm sick of my own voice and I hate books. I'm not even hungry.

I hope you have the most beautiful baby in the world, and I wish you lots of luck.

I shall now go and drink myself to death for a few hours and what is more I shall have no hangover, for which all my friends loathe me.

Please write me some more news. I'll write you a real letter soon, this is just a hurry note.

All my Love
Jane

February 1937

In the winter of 1937 Jane met Paul Bowles through John Latouche. Shortly afterwards she went to Mexico with Paul and Kristians Tonny, a Dutch painter, and Tonny's wife, Marie Claire. Jane ended the trip abruptly and went on to Arizona and then California before returning to New York.

5
To Miriam Levy

Hotel Meurice
145 West 58th Street
New York City, New York

My darling darling friend

I have been in Mexico I have been in Arizona I have been in California. I did not know you had a baby—it's beautiful. I am in the middle of a novel—and Big dramas all around me. I'm not sure whether I'll come out on top there are so many things against me. Believe me Miriam I would have written you if I had known. I was very ill in Mexico. I can't write you now—I was on my way out when I got your letter and I was so horrified at what you must think was carelessness on my part that I had to sit down and write. Darling the baby *is* beautiful but is it a boy or a girl—I must know—and the name? I am so glad you were persistent and wrote me. I lost all my addresses in the desert somewhere. I should love to visit you. Will you write me and tell me whether you are really serious or not and how soon or how late I can come? We have all year of course—there is no hurry.

Please believe me I appreciate your loyalty.

Love
Jane—your vagrant friend.

June 1937

6
To Virgil Thomson

Asbury Park, New Jersey
Friday

Dear Virgil—

Il n'y a pas de plume dans ma grande maison. I want to thank you mille fois de m'avoir invitée au prevue. Nous aimons tellement ta musique. I hope you were not sad that Paul and I did not wait at the bar. Il faisait chaud—on n'avait pas d'argent —la valise pesait—Paul dormait debout—but I worried a lot about it once we were in Jamaica. Maybe you would have come with us and maybe you wanted to talk.

I hope you were a good Massachusetts man and that you will come and spend some time with us on your return. And you can bring your Maggie. I send her a big kiss. Do not tell anyone but I have written three chapters of a bad first novel—anyway c'est de la merde—régulière. Je travaille tous les jours cinq ou six heures.

Lots of Love—
Janie

August 31, 1937

In February 1938 Jane married Paul Bowles. Immediately after the wedding they set out on a honeymoon trip to Central America and France.

7
To Virgil Thomson

San Jose, Costa Rica

We are doing what Pavlik used to do to Gertrude, so she said: J'ai rêvé à vous cette nuit. We discuss them in the morning when they occur.

Scarcely any Indian blood here—my darling Virgil. I shall write you all about Costa Rica.

Love,
Jane

March 23, 1938

8
To Virgil Thomson

Dearest Virgil— Guatemala

Think of you once daily at least—Lake—Indians—a couple of more volcanoes. I want to go to *Trinidad*. I like ports best—they're full of negroes and camelote. The inside of the country is always high true and beautiful. I don't know when we'll arrive in Paris—the end of May or the end of June.

So much love to you—
Jane.

April 21, 1938

9
To Virgil Thomson

Dear Virgil,

That was an awfully nice writeup you gave Paul, and such a beautiful picture of him on top. You know how much I would like to see you and how sweet and how clever I always thought you were. Baby there ain't nobody here at all but do they love each other. Some hautes Dykes from Cagnes sur Mer, on the corner of the Avenida Delicias and Las Palmas and otherwise row upon row of pederasts. C'est même pas bon, pour passer le temps. Quand-même un peu. The climate is really beautiful and good for lunatics. J'aime ma maison et j'apprends à faire des gateaux et des puddings. Aussi je suis de temps en temps à la récherche d'une idée. Je t'assure qu'il ny en a pas qui volent autour, ici. Plenty of liquor but don't want it. Perhaps I shall see you soon but I doubt it. I'm so glad that you are a critic.

So much love
Jane

Èze-Village, France, 1938

In September 1938 Jane and Paul returned to the U.S. for Paul to work on music for the Mercury Theater. By the spring of 1939 they had rented an old farmhouse on Woodrow Road in Staten Island. There Jane worked on *Two Serious Ladies* and Paul on his opera *Denmark Vesey.*

10
To Mary Oliver

Dear Mary Oliver,

I would be so delighted to have you and your German maid come to Staten Island (S.I.). First I shall explain about money and then I shall go on. Paul earns at the moment twenty-two dollars a week on W.P.A. (music project) and that is what we live on. I'm perfectly willing to take a chance on our all eating on that if you are. There are many exceedingly cheap foods such as rice, potatoes and faroja—faroja is a strange Brazilian flour which you brown in butter and salt. You receive it by mail from a Mr. Silver in Brooklyn. There are also the excellent Brazilian black beans which when cooked with a lump or two of fatty meat and a great deal of garlic make an exceedingly tasty dish. Two people or rather four people are not twice as expensive to feed as two, strangely enough. And if you ever do get a little money while you are here I might tell you that around eight dollars will feed two people for a week. Paul will probably stop getting his checks suddenly anyway and then we will all be in the soup, which doesn't frighten me. The only people who must eat are Paul and the cats. Paul is extremely desperate and neurotic if he doesn't. I have explained all this to you because I want you to know what you are getting into. We would all have a place to live as the rent has been paid until November the fifteenth. I daresay we might get some friends such as Harry Dunham who has paid half of the rent to keep it with us another month or two. As for room during the week there are two extra beds. On many weekends Harry Dunham comes down with his fiancée, therefore one bed is occupied. I have two very fine mattresses which we bought in Nice and three thick sofa cushions all of which could be made into an adequate bed which I would be glad to sleep on when there were extras. A German man slept on them last summer on the roof for weeks so it would be no hardship for whoever gets them. I myself have a huge inner spring mattress on a straw mat which sleeps at least three and many extra ladies have slept with me on weekends. Paul has one too but he refuses to share it with anyone. You can see that there is enough room presenting no problem at all during the week and really none on the weekend as weekends are always very complicated or terribly simple and rainy and lonely.

We have now dispensed with the purely physical aspects of your visit if there is to be one. Paul is terribly worried that you might not like the house. He wants you to know it is like a little cottage in Glenora. We have no servant and very few rugs. At any rate you can see no other house from our grounds.

We are surrounded by fields rather dry. I do not think it's depressing. There are fruit trees and a rotten vegetable garden. Harry Dunham just arrived, and he is a wonderful person to have around. We go into New York City once a week. One can get there for around forty-five cents so you could if you liked see your friends when you wanted to. And for people with cars it is no effort at all to drive out here nor does it take much time at all. The only thing that worries me is that you might be bored as Paul is working on his opera and I on my book, but he says you love to read. In the evenings we can play games and drink champagne. I am not working every minute of the time but I must finish it while we still have a roof over our heads and I am always tempted to chat and lazy around. If you do not think it will be too awful we would really love to have you. I myself am always completely happy when there are three people in the house and four people will be a real *nest.*

Please let us know if you will come. Elsie Houston, a singer, is here at the moment for a few days. If you do come and she is still here I am sure you will like her. I am looking forward to meeting you. Paul will write you details of how to come. If you can phone long distance from where you are our number is Tottenville 8-1392. It would be the same price as phoning New York City perhaps a dime more.

Yours,
Jane (Bowles)

Staten Island, Summer 1939

II
To Charles Henri Ford

Dear Charles,

I am so glad you and Pavlick are settled in your barn. I went to New York yesterday and I ended up on Columbus Avenue. I started to sweat. No means of locomotion seemed plausible. I will not live in New York. I think we shall try and find a house nearer the other end of the island so as to be able to get in very easily. Mary Oliver will probably take an apartment in New York and the three of us will live between the two places. I think it is very necessary to be able to get out of New York the minute you want to. More important than getting into it. We will only have this place until November first and we shall try and get our things moved a little ahead of our time and then come to your party if you'll let us with free minds. Mary has many friends whom she hasn't seen in a long time near Norwalk and it is possible that we shall be able to get a night's lodging with one or the other of them. Living the way we do it is delightful to be invited to a party a long way off. I am asking your permission for Mary to come although it is hardly necessary as she is the nicest lady in the whole world. You must tell Pavlick that she is the friend of Dilkousha and Katousha. I was rather upset about what you wrote concerning Robeson and the other *Denmark*. I shall take matters into my own hands and phone Juanita Hall immediately because Paul is a slow person. Juanita said earlier in the summer that she would introduce Paul to him as she thought Paul Robeson would be excited about the opera. He was then abroad. I am going to call Juanita this evening. Of course the opera isn't finished. Paul hasn't worked this week because we got into debt. Since the arrival of Mrs. Oliver our life has been quite exciting and there are a lot of changes in the house. I hope Paul will work next week. He wrote another beautiful song in *Denmark* and if you were sweet you and Parker Tyler both, you would weep when you heard it. I will let you know if anything happens as a result of my call to Juanita. Good luck to you both and please write again. I always like your poems. I hope you will like my book. I hope to get it finished this month if too many upsetting things don't happen.

Jane Bowles

Staten Island, Fall 1939

In 1940 Jane and Paul and a friend, Robert Faulkner, went to Mexico. In Taxco Jane met Helvetia Perkins, a forty-five-year old divorcée. By the end of 1941 Jane had finished writing *Two Serious Ladies.*

12
To Virgil Thomson

My dear Virgil, Taxco, Mexico

I hope that you are well and happy and that you are in New York. Mr. Saroyan is not here. Mother writes that you were under the impression that he was but Paul *is* working on a script of his. I have finished my novel—it seems like a long time but I spent two months in a very bad humor rewriting and drinking and finally threw half of it away and wrote half a new novel—which is an experience I should not like to go through again. After a while it was fun but the beginning was dreadful. I intend to come to New York in a month or so and try to publish. Do you have any ideas about the "state of publishing" as a result of the war? Is it hopeless or with little hope? If you know of anyone who does things about books will you smile at them for me if you still love me? Because I have no idea where to begin. I shall write Touche too. He was very nice actually to read the mess I handed to him last year and not to call me on it. I heard a piece of yours, a vocal piece, with Copland this summer and I liked it. I have your copy of *The State of Music* which I shall bring with me when I return. It's been nicer than you'll know having it here in Taxco so forgive me for taking it. Do you still have that nice "Mimi"? I hope so. If you have time could you possibly find out the price of a room and bath at the Chelsea—if possible without salon—and write me a note about it? I'm riding up with a friend called Mrs. Perkins and I *hope* that I can persuade Paul to come too, but he doesn't fancy coming unless he has a job. I do hope I shall be able to see Maurice on this trip and a little of you. We are going to stay at the Chelsea with or without Paul. I shan't write about the parrot as I'm sure Paul has written you *plenty.* I am bringing a fluffy kitten, however.

Love and Kisses—
Jane

Late December 1941

13
To Virgil Thomson

Hotel Carlton

Dearest Virgil— Friday, 9th

Just to inform you that Paul and I are always thinking of you. Thank you so much for your letter about Chelsea rates and your nice attitude about my book. I daresay there is little point in hoping to publish anything right now. That is why I am in no great hurry to return to the States. However I believe we shall be arriving in the beginning of March—in that way we avoid the long hard winter. One thing is certain and that is my decision *not* to stay in Mexico throughout the duration of the war, which naturally has occurred to all of us in view of the unpleasantness in the States. I read a long article about you in *The Nation*. I enjoyed most the quotations. Who is that man?

Paul's attitude is peculiar. He seems lighter-hearted altho' constantly ill. We have both been reading Henry James' novel *Portrait of a Lady* and we have both loved it. I have also been reading C. G. Jung's *Psychological Types* and I am astonished about the past and fairly ashamed at a lack of information which is common to so many of my friends and most of all to me. I shall try in the future not to be so pompous.

I know that you are fond of a letter full of news but I'm not sure whether or not you really mean it.

Paul and Antonio (a very good Mexican artist whom Paul has undoubtedly written to you about) left this morning for Vera Cruz, a tropical port, where Helvetia and I shall join them in a few days. From there we are going to Tehuantepec, which is a distant isthmus inhabited by a special type of Indian. We will all be there for a few days and then we will promptly return to Taxco. Perhaps we will spend another week down at the seashore (Acapulco) and then in the beginning of Feb. leave for New York, travelling slowly and stopping off at various places in the South if they look inviting.

A little card or a note from you is always so welcome to me. This letter springs from real tenderness because I dreamed of you all last night. You can reach me at "Lista de Correos" in Taxco. I shall be back there in another two weeks. Give my love to Maurice if he is still in N.Y. I would like to know just how depressing New York is.

Much Love
Jane

Mexico City, January 1942

14
To Virgil Thomson

My dear Virgil—

I haven't forwarded your letter to Paul because I am expecting him here in Taxco any day. I was glad to read that life is pleasant. Naturally we get nothing but "gloomies" down here—and their reports have been discouraging. I'm finishing reading a book. I wrote two little . . . but I won't tell you what they are. We are leaving here on the 30 of March, gas willing. I hear it has already been rationed on the Atlantic seaboard. At any rate it will be about two or three weeks from that date before we arrive in N.Y. because we are stopping off on the way. I hope you will not be in Kansas.

Much Love
Jane

Taxco, Mexico, Early March 1942

15
To Virgil Thomson

Hotel De Soto
Savannah, Ga.

Dear Virgil—

Just to advise you that I have sent some of Paul's luggage to myself in care of you at the Chelsea. If they bother you about it just tell them to leave it in the cellar.

Paul stayed on after me (in Mexico) because he was to hear about his trip to S.A. within a few weeks. He has heard, he writes me, and apparently the government is no longer appropriating funds for music so that question (the South American trip) has at last been settled. It has been hanging over our heads.

It now remains to be seen whether I cut my trip short and return to Meji or whether Paul comes up here very shortly. This depends largely on tourist visas—the draft, etc. These things I'd like to talk to you about. If you will be around.

Much Love
Jane

April 1942

Two Serious Ladies was published in New York in 1943. The reviews were generally disheartening. From 1943 until 1946 Jane lived most of the time with Helvetia Perkins either on Helvetia's farm in East Montpelier, Vermont, or in an apartment in New York. She completed the first act of *In the Summer House* and a story, "Plain Pleasures."

16
To Virgil Thomson

Dearest Virgil,

I hope you will enjoy being in Paris and that you will come to dinner next year. I'm sorry Paul's off the paper in a way and thank you very much for getting him on. It was lovely while it lasted, for me anyway because I didn't have to worry about Paul's worrying. I wonder what will happen now. Insecurity and a lot of travelling I suppose, which I concede is more fun (for boys anyway). I kiss you and thank you again.

Bon Voyage
Jane

New York City, 1946

In early 1947 Jane went with Libby Holman on a trip to Cuba. On her return she met Helvetia Perkins in Florida.

17
To Libby Holman

Dearest Libby,

Thank you for your wire. Florence is a mine of misinformation and I hope that Paul has not been listening to her reports and ignoring my wires and letters. I sent Paul one "agonizer" by night letter and one by mail the day after I arrived. He must certainly have them both by now, ossir. Must I wreck this letter by telling you what I told him? We are starting off tomorrow morning, willy nilly. I wired Bubble that we would arrive within five days if there was anything imminent, which is the driving time from here, but that we might take a week longer if there wasn't. We thought we might stop at Marine Land,

Savannah, etc. on the way up, if we feel like it. I have of course received no answer yet from Paul and I'm working myself up into a rage already. I shall certainly leave tomorrow and call him from somewhere along the road, but I may die of apoplexy in the booth, I shall be so angry by then. There is no way of contacting anyone from here because of all the radios and the juke boxes. A very cheap crowd.

I think that it is wonderful Doug met you at the plane and I wonder how you carried it off. I could not stop crying the day that I arrived. I felt very ashamed of this because you upon your return had so much more to face than I. I hated the last night in Havana but I have never in my life been so happy as I was in Varadero. (Even though I didn't take many advantages.) Those blue walls were really beautiful. The dog screamed in his box all the way over and we had to sit in quarantine until two-thirty in the afternoon.

I have a new shoulder pad plan which I would like to discuss with you when I return. I have to buy about five thousand snappers and find a dressmaker. It is a plan that you may find useful for your own shirts, bathrobes, brunch coats, etc. The left pad on my blue long sleeved button-down-the-front dress came loose last night. I got a little excited but I controlled myself and sewed it right back on. Helvetia has a good choice of spools, all the basic colors, and not the fantasies that you and I carried around. The orange cat is nice, a little young of course to be really interesting but it is nice to have him because we have that box. I imagine we shall have to buy another cat box for the books and sugar. I am trying to make a shell collection for Paul and if I can get some Cuban money here I'll bring it back to you. It's interesting because it's so darned old. How is Topper and are you driving him up to Putney? As you probably will before my return, I shall give you Jody's address in case you want to stop there for meal . . . I'm sure they would love to see you.

Have you gotten word one out about the trip? I can't even tell Helvetia what side of Cuba Varadero is *on*. I told her about Amelia finally because I was so desperate for a story. She thought it was interesting. Call Paul if you can and find out whether or not he answered my wire.

I think it is wonderful of Larry to have cabled you. Janice is booking us into Marine Land and trying to get the dog and the cat in too. He thinks he can manage all right. If he can't I'll wire Larry to get in touch with his uncle. I miss you terribly.

Much much love,
Jane

Give my love to Clarissa please and Shirley.

I know Doug will be better for having stayed with you. After all—I AM—in spite of having just attacked Helvetia and both animals with an axe.

Florida, March 27, 1947

In July 1947 Paul went to Morocco, which he had visited in the early thirties, with the intention of writing a novel. He had been offered a contract by Doubleday after the successful publication of a short story in *Partisan Review*. Jane stayed in the U.S. at Treetops, the country estate of Libby Holman, where she worked on a second novel.

18
To Paul Bowles

Dearest Bupple,

I am happy to have an address at last, and I hope for your sake that you will decide not to go to Spain. I don't think you will like it there as well as you do in Morocco and certainly I think Portugal would bore you in short order. I do not say this to be mean because actually I should prefer you in Portugal, letters there are very quick flying over and I imagine it is healthy. I should hate it however if you left a place you liked (just because you do always prefer to move on) and ended up with a lot more money spent, in a place that you didn't find nearly as much fun. But perhaps you mean only to take a flying trip through Spain and then return to Morocco, if you leave at all.

It has been hard enough for me to get on with my novel *here* because of four or five tremendous stumbling blocks—none of them however due to the circumstance of my environment. (My novel is entirely in this laborious style.)

The more I get into it, which isn't very far in pages but quite a bit further in thinking and consecutive work the more frightened I become at the isolated position I feel myself in vis-à-vis of all the writers whom I consider to be of any serious mind. Because I think there is no point in using the word talent any longer. Certainly Carson McCullers is as *talented* as Sartre or Simone de Beauvoir but she is not really a serious writer. I am serious but I am isolated and my experience is probably of no interest at this point to anyone. I am enclosing this article entitled "New Heroes" by Simone de Beauvoir, which I have cut out of *Town and Country*, at least a section of it. Read the sides that are marked pages 121 and 123. It is enough for you to get the meaning, since you know the group so well, and their thinking; read particularly what I have underlined. It is what I have been thinking at the bottom of my mind all this time and God knows it is difficult to write the way I do and yet think their way. This problem you will never have to face because you have always been a truly isolated person so that whatever you write will be good because it will be true which is not so in my case because my kind of isolation I think is an accident, and not inevitable. I could go on and on with this and explain to you better what I mean but there is not space for such a discussion. Not only is your isolation a positive and true one but when you do write from it you immediately receive recognition because what you write is in true relation to yourself which is always recognizable to the world outside. With me who knows? When you are capable only of a serious and ponderous approach to writing as I am—I should say solemn perhaps—it is almost more than one can bear to be continually doubting one's sincerity which is tantamount to doubting one's product. As I move along into this writing I think the part I mind the most is this doubt about my entire experience. This is far more important than feeling "out" of it and "isolated," I suppose, but it also accentuates that guilt a thousand times. It is hard to explain this to you and in a sense it is probably really at bottom what this novel will be about if I can ever get it done! Another souris (or is that spelled Tzoris?) I realize now, after these two months at Libby's, that really *Two Serious Ladies* never *was* a novel, so we are both facing the same doubt exactly, although I cannot imagine your not being able to write one. Helvetia is making her way into this novel which is inevitable since I have thought so much about her for the past seven years. I am also in it in the person of her son, Edgar. This is good because I am usually trying to be too removed from my own experience in writing which can be tricked in a short story very well but not in a novel. It is *bad* because it is simply not much fun. It is upsetting and I get confused. You know what a state of confusion Helvetia has put me into anyway so that I am a far more uncertain person today than I was at twenty-three, so you can imagine how difficult it is for me to hammer a novel out of anything she has prompted me to think. Because it is really not Helvetia whom I mind writing about; I have transformed the situation sufficiently so that I am not too certain every second that she is this character but it is difficult, very difficult to put into words all the things she has caused me to brood about which are I think foreign to my nature but which now obsess me. There are *other* elements in the novel, natch.

I am working and I am diligent and faithful about it but I feel it's such a Herculean task that I shall not finish for years! On the other hand it may, if I can just get over having myself in a book, it may go quickly. But I think it is better to prepare for the worst than the best.

My slowness is appalling and the number of hours when I simply lie on the bed without reading or thinking would shock you. If I can get 150 pages typed, corrected and in to a publisher this fall I shall consider myself very lucky. It is natural that I have had to keep dropping material all along the way. I have never been for two months in one place before without being completely uprooted either physically or emotionally. In any case the work I did in Cuba and the spasmodic work I did in New York is all I can really count on using, together with the work I have done this summer. All those other notebooks don't count and it is time you stopped thinking of them because it simply makes me nervous. I shan't chuck them however because there may be material—in fact I'm sure there is—among them for a short story or two. Even the work in Cuba is out of kilter with what I am doing now but during the four weeks that I had down there or five maybe, when I worked, I at least established the atmosphere, but God knows the characters have changed or at least grown considerably—so that the Cuban part has to be retouched. As for the work I did in N.Y. after I returned it was pretty spasmodic and interrupted but I can use some of it. There isn't much I'm sure—but it is not completely of a different texture like the *Pre-Cuban* work. To give you an idea of my slow pace—I have done about thirty-three typewritten pages in the same number of days. One day I do *three* pages but then the next I do nothing—possibly—and this is working *all day* and after dinner! I mean going at it and stopping for a while and then going at it again. Of course I do a great deal of thinking which takes me forever because my mind is apt to wander—every twenty minutes if I have reached an impasse or a complicated thought and then I am apt to dream the whole morning about some flirtation. It is always nice to slip out and escape into the pool at a bad moment but actually I have been conscientious about staying in my room almost all of the time. I don't write much and I don't read but I am at least in my room. And in a few months I will know once and for all whether I can write this novel or whether I have to give up writing anything. I have thus far been saved by an idea or a little run of dialogue at the last minute when I was about to despair.

I flew down with Libby (for a weekend) to Louisa Carpenter's and Sister Bankhead's. The plane—Louisa's mother's it is—was wonderful and I loved every minute of the flight. I drank heavily on the weekend, played poker and did no work.

Louisa C. is the most sexually attractive woman in the whole world but I am alas not alone in thinking this. We went crabbing and we saw two litters of baby pigs—eleven little piglets in each—or maybe nineteen. Also Sister's two *black Pekes*!! Naturally I was "aux anges" with them. They are really pitch black. Can you imagine it? When we flew back we dropped Libby at La Guardia and then in less than ten minutes we were here. I am forwarding this check because I don't know what to do with it. I had hoped I would have an address from you sooner. My mother is coming this Sunday, the ninth, and staying in New York until the nineteenth, so I shall be in New York ten days. Write me here however as Libby will be coming in and out of New York every other day and bringing my mail—if it's important. Then on the 19th or 20th I will be back here anyway. Naturally I hate this break but I hope to get *some* work done while I'm there. I shall write about sailing to Africa later in the summer. Certainly I shouldn't before a much more substantial amount is done on the novel but I'm not certain I should wait until the bitter end. I cannot decide about this right now anymore than I can about when and if to see Helvetia. I shall certainly not go to Africa before late fall—when you will perhaps return. If not you must let me know *what* to do about the apartment. It will be terribly easy to sublet from Sept. or Oct. on I imagine. I know it is hard to keep paying that money out but Oliver has not been able to find anyone who is interested. It would be nice to find a house there, wouldn't it? In Africa, I mean. I am of course delighted that Gordon likes it better than he did. I read Brion Gysin's piece in *Town and Country*?? That strange story, about the Japanese house that was lifted up intact with all the people in it and put down again on some crazy British Isle, is in it. You have undoubtedly heard him tell it—the story—it's one of his myths. It's all not very amusing. My swimming stroke is improving. I am reading *Sons and Lovers* as well as Kierkegaard. I wish you were here. I am by myself more than I have ever been since childhood. I am worried about Helvetia getting me down but otherwise O.K. except when the work is stale. I suppose both you and G. have *written* novels already. I still think that it was a good idea for me not to go to Africa, don't you? Because with outer complications as well as inner ones I don't think I could have got anything done. But then perhaps you are so disgusted with my slow pace that you don't think what I do matters at this point. I do think I might come to Africa before I have entirely *finished* the book but I shall not think of that until November as I said when you will have either returned or not. I shall not move before then unless something awful happens which would make it impossible for me to work here. I must document myself on hurricanes too before long. I hope to have better news on my progress the next time I write, but I want you should always know the worse so that you will have no false idea of me. I loved G.'s postal card. Give him a kiss for me and tell him that Libby is *very much* taken with him in every way.

I am sending you your literary correspondence so that you will be encouraged by your *prowess* in this field. Don't be worried about my losing your mail either. I am very conscientious about it and open only those business letters which I think might require immediate attention. As for packing your passport away—I thought it was mine—I looked to see whose picture was in it and I dimly remember my own face and not yours. As Libby said when I told her, "How psychosomatic can you get." Otherwise I am extremely reliable. The Hilltop theatre has been writing you and I shall send them a card explaining that until now you have been in Africa without an address so that they won't think you rude. They invited you to see the show, etc. Also sign the enclosed check (unless you will be back in time to deposit it yourself) and send it to me so that I may deposit it or it will be lost entirely. Perhaps they will honor it in Africa and you can give a party. I hope you and Gordon will stick close together.

Perhaps Florence would rent your apt. from the middle of Sept. to the middle of Oct. and by then you will know what your plans are—but I don't know how interested she'd be. You will surely have no trouble however from then on. She will move into mine Oct. 23 because it's lower down and she naturally prefers that, unless H. changes her mind about next winter which I seriously doubt.

I hope the books you sent me will arrive soon and your story. Please write.

Much Love
Jane

P.S. I shall write Gordon later. The Delkas Music Co. 625 South Grand Avenue has sent you your proofs to be corrected with *Blue Pencil* only at your earliest convenience. Shall I forward them? I shall try to find a picture of you to give to Pearl Kazin for Bazaar. (I'll ask her about the big one but I'm so afraid they'll *lose* it.) Your story appears in October. There is a letter from Roditi—otherwise nothing interesting. I did not of course read it. Shall I forward all vaguely interesting mail? I think I had better read it first—if not personal—because it's expensive to send airmail as you know.

Love
Jane

P.P.S. You also have a profit of two cents (.02) from some sheet music you sold. I won't look through my files now to locate the document. Peggy Bate sent you the *Age of Reason* in

English, the first book in Sartre's trilogy. I am keeping it for you.

The Fan is my constant friend and I *love* it.

Stamford, CT, Early August 1947

19
To Paul Bowles

Dear Bubble,

Perhaps you are back from Spain and will receive this letter when it arrives. It is disturbing, I find, to write to someone when there is no certainty of their receiving the letter for weeks or months, but I trust you will not stay in Spain that long. On the other hand this may arrive after you have left Tangier, for a second time, and gone off into the desert or on to Fez. I don't imagine you are going to be staying long anywhere, somehow, particularly with no house. I am sorry Gordon left you, naturally, because the whole thing now sounds incredibly gloomy to me. Not that it is gay here either, or anywhere.

Libby is in and out like the wind because she has found an "interest" in New York, for which I am extremely grateful. She was getting terribly despondent and cried herself to sleep every night which I could hear but do nothing about. I am out here a good deal with Topper and Clarisse and Grandma which I like, although I am apt to idle away ten or eleven hours easily. Still with all that time one is bound to get some work done. I wrote you that I was going to spend ten days in New York with Mama which I did. It was a terrible holocaust, worse than I expected, because I did not do one lick of work for ten days. I slept in a different bed every night, including I.B.'s (of film research fame). You know whom I mean; I.B. was pretty annoyed to find me in her place the next morning, I think, which upset me for a good three days. I spent one pleasant afternoon at the little zoo on 59th Street and thought of you all the time. There was a little baby monkey you would have loved. It was so terribly hot that I drank at the public fountain all the time, a thing which I haven't done for a long while. Not since I was ten years old, or younger. I saw several lunatics sitting around waiting for night to fall and I was sure glad it was only four in the afternoon. I have got back on my work again with unbelievable difficulty and continue crawling along. I am so slow it is almost as though I were going backwards. In a sense I am a little less discouraged than in my last letter but I don't dare even say that because by tomorrow I may be in despair. Tonight I read a story by Katherine Anne Porter called "Pale Horse, Pale Rider." It has completely ruined my evening because it is so sad and depressing and moving—and yet I am not sure I like it. If I feel terribly sad and terribly moved by something it is very puzzling not to be able to say I like it. I keep forgetting what writing is supposed to be anyway. I cannot however think of anything that I have really liked that has made me sad or depressed, no matter how depressing or sad it really was. Perhaps you can write me what I mean.

On the day after tomorrow I am taking a train to Pittsfield where Helvetia and Maurice (he is visiting her) are meeting me. I shall be with her for about five days and then I'm coming back here. We have to see each other I suppose to settle certain things, but it is naturally "inquiétant." I'll bet she's written more than I have this summer. I used to read Valéry when I was younger and I loved it but I'm sure I couldn't now. Florence I think is going to take your apartment until October the 23rd. I wired her that she could have it. (I suggested it to her because she wanted to get into mine on the tenth of Sept. but it is rented until the 23rd of Oct., so I suggested yours to her until she could move downstairs.) That will give you a breathing spell and certainly by the end of Oct. we will know whether or not you are returning or staying over there. If you stay I know you could rent the apt. at a profit because things are still impossible in New York, space I mean, and I think even with the additional rent for steam heat which Oliver wrote you about you can come out gaining. Naturally winter rentals are far easier than summer ones, in fact there is no comparison. Of course if you come back we, rather I, won't rent it from Oct. 23rd on, but you will know soon what you intend doing. As for me, I can't stay here at Libby's forever but probably through the fall. I hope that after I do about twenty more pages of this novel, I shall have completed a section, at least psychologically and then I will write a short story and try to sell it to Aswell. I shall need more money eventually, when I leave here, and although I know you would send me some I don't want to ask you to because there is no reason why I shouldn't earn a little, since I am doing no housekeeping whatsoever. If you come back before the twenty-third and Florence is in your apartment we can certainly find a place to stay for a week or so, here or at Helvetia's. I never went to any New Canaan which was merely Oliver's idea of a good joke. He meant Great Barrington, which is actually Salisbury, where the woman who owns the Inn lives. I went there for a weekend almost two months ago. In any case even if I did go somewhere if it were for more than a few days I would certainly leave a forwarding address! In your letters you sound as though it were *I* not you who were disappearing into the wildernesses and the inaccessibles, which is typical of you. Virgil told me that X—a man whom we both know, and who is serious, but I can't remember his name—told him that up at Knopf's they all deny ever having *heard* of me or published my book.

I am plump and in extremely good health though not at all satisfied. I miss you very much indeed and wonder how we are ever going to meet again with all these distances. I feel quite homeless and yet I think in spite of everything maybe it is better I didn't go to Africa. I am not too worried or sad as long as I keep hearing from you because I know that all at once you will be coming here or I shall simply be going there. I might prefer Paris, however, except for the expense. Oliver and I were both horribly worried by the Cadiz explosion, but I gathered from your letter which arrived on the following day that you were most likely not there. I saw Bobby Lewis who almost flirted with me, I think. He was very cute looking and did not talk about his "wecords" once. He and Libby have made up their friendship. I sometimes feed and diaper the baby at midnight, and I have grown to love him very much—the little one.

I mention renting the apartment, if you don't come back, because surely it will be too expensive to keep just for me even if I have a little money. Maybe I could go to Europe with Florence in December and get over to Africa from there if nothing happens before then. Oliver says he's working on jobs for you, (ossir) so I'm sure everything will be fine (ossir). In any case you must do what you see fit to do. Maybe if you came back we could go down to our beloved Mexico. I am being vague and half cocked about plans because I'm trying to fool myself out of an "agonizer." I can feel this letter slipping into one.

I shall see little Puppet anyway in a few days. The fan is my dearest possession and it has been with me every second. I have actually kissed it, which you can believe. It is right here now with its soft harmless little paddles. Do you want me to forward your mail? At least some of it and shall it be airmail, expense and all? I hope the packet of books arrives soon. I am enjoying my *Sickness unto Death* throughout the summer. Please write to me. It is much easier for you to write than for me, because I always feel that unless I present a problem in a letter I have not really written one. Much love

Teresa

P.S. Oliver is perfectly willing to move his things out so that Florence can rent the entire floor if she wants to—otherwise she will merely pay your share, but I'll let you know definitely in a couple of days—if she takes it or not—with or without Ollie in the studio. *Please* be careful of your health. I say I would prefer Paris to Africa but *only* if I had finished my book. I think it would upset me more—and I would prefer it out of masochism maybe.

I have just received your letter about the Perrins' etc. and enjoyed it thoroughly. How I wish I *were* with you, because I find that kind of thing inspiring and not upsetting. I'm sure I could work in Spain in a little hotel better than here, and I do have moments of terrific remorse. Or even in a Tangier hotel. Still it is best not to brood about all of this and I must try to work whether the decision was right or wrong. I'm sure you are way ahead of me already and it makes me nervous, but you will always be faster than I am so it shouldn't. I am glad you are finally working because there is really no time to lose for anybody. It is wonderful to hear from you often, in fact it is very important that I do. Libby is wonderful but I shall never be quite satisfied or easy about being a guest for so long. She said she would tell me if she wanted me to get out and I do think that the place is good for the fall if we don't get together before December. I have no set ideas about anything since you never mention even remotely your intentions. Keep in touch with Oliver in any case since he may have suggestions for you. I wish that I could write you something amusing but I have no adventures to tell you about. Certainly you would be bored hearing about Iris and Jody and Louisa and Sister Bankhead. You know it is always the same old grind with me or "bringue" as they say in French. Of course I think I shall simply never be interested in any one who is Latin or Arab or Semitic. I am more and more crazy about the Scotch and the Irish and think seriously of paying a visit to those countries and getting it over with. It takes days to get a letter from here to the post office after one has written it. I keep asking Johnny to let me know when he is going to town but often he forgets and I am stuck until the next day. You must write me if you know the works of Katherine Anne Porter, and the sequel of the Perrin story at Ronda. I would love to be in Ronda, perhaps you could find a house there. The train trip sounds dreadful, however.

Much love again

T.

You said in your letter the train was "pitching and lurching" so you must want to bar Spain to me forever!—or at least Ronda.

Stamford, CT, Late August 1947

20
To Paul Bowles

My dear Bubble

I should write this single space but then I would have no room for my grammar corrections. Libby is asleep so I am using Mrs. Swazie's typewriter, mine being locked into Libby's sitting room. I am living sort of half on the third floor and half on the second, but I will explain that later. In some other letter—it's not interesting. It is terribly hard for me to type on this machine because I have to use twice as much pressure as I do on my own, and you can see for yourself what it has done to the edge of the paper. I loathe it and would sooner be using Erika, who I thought was the last straw. It is too hot however to use a fountain pen. I can't imagine that Africa can be much worse than it's been this summer on the Atlantic seaboard. I was in New York during the worst of the heat spell and it was unbelievable. I can't remember now whether I wrote you since seeing my mother or not. I must have. As you remember I spent ten days with her and completely stopped working which I think you might have done too considering the heat and the way I was living. Then I came back here and spent a week or ten days, during which time I did get back on my work again after a few days of adjustment and then I went off again to see H. I would have preferred not to see her until October because then I could have worked here for a month, but perhaps it is just as well that I got all the interruptions in at once. I was with her a little under two weeks and we got a great many things settled. There were some things that were indispensable, such as discussions about my apartment and other details. She offered to keep my room for me if someone else paid for the other half of the apartment but I refused because she said that she did not think she would be in New York very much and I saw no reason for her keeping a room all winter mainly for me. D'abord she would in no time feel that she was being used and the psychological dramas would begin all over again. I said that there was no reason why I had to be in New York at all if you weren't there and that she should only take the room for herself if she really wanted it. I can stay in the studio if you *are* here and if not I would only be in New York to visit Oliver and his couch is perfectly good. Helvetia and I are much better seeing each other away from Tenth Street anyway. She would like at this point to have a room to go to there for when she does come to New York, however, and God knows she may decide to take half the apartment after all on her own hook but nothing need be done about it yet. I was satisfied with my visit to her and I know that I can be with her this winter somewhere if you do not come back and if I don't get to Africa. Oliver says your money situation is very bad which naturally it would be. He seems to think he'll be free in January to go somewhere but that doesn't mean he'd take me necessarily and I don't suppose you or I can afford a ticket or will be able to by then. Well, we will see. I shall come to my novel in a second. I wish that you would tell me what you want me to do about the apt. You complain about paying for it, but as I told you Oliver is now willing to get out of it—but how *can* I sublet it if you do not mention for what length of time you want me to do so. Do you want me to rent it for six months, two months or a year? I have a feeling you would like everything to happen without your taking a hand in it so that it would be impossible for you to come back, perhaps. I assure you I don't like you to have to pay out the seventy-five a month anymore than you do but it is difficult to do anything about it unless you decide that you are going to stay over there and want to risk not having any place to stay here. I can sublet it on a two month lease with option to renew but then the people will leave the minute they get a permanent place. Just as Florence decided after I wrote you that she would not take it because someone wired her that she could have a place for a year. Of course she was unusually lucky and one could take a chance on people staying on from month to month without too much risk perhaps. I think you *can* lease it that way but I am not certain and there is the disadvantage of their moving the minute they get a permanent lease. I am not sure that the shortest lease would not be two months either, but perhaps with the unusual apartment situation even a month is considered. I am renewing my lease on Helvetia's suggestion since there is no possibility of getting stuck with the apartment for the next three years at least and since it will on the contrary be profitable to sublet. She may want to pay for it for two months when the present tenants leave and then she would sublet again if she went South in Jan. or Feb. I am going to speak to Oliver next weekend as well who might be interested in taking one of those rooms down on my floor over, if he is flush this winter and you sublet your floor. The other room could be rented separately and I wondered if by any chance your floor was rented at a large enough profit if you would be interested in hanging on to a room on my floor; Helvetia I am sure would rent it from you for part of the time, and at any other time it would certainly be easy to rent with Oliver in the back room because the layout is perfect for sharing whereas your apartment is impossible. I don't imagine you will want to do this but Oliver may take one of the rooms anyway and then I'll rent the other to either a stranger or Helvetia. I think too he'd be willing to get out of his half and rent it to you if you got back while yours was still rented. This is only a possibility but it might mean that you would at least not be out on the street when your apt. was sublet. As for me, upstairs or downstairs I probably will never have a real room of my own again. I am not writing an agonizer but trying to tell you that there *might* be an alternative if you had to come back suddenly and for this reason are hesitating about subletting. I am not at all sure however that he will be willing to pay nearly 80 dollars a month instead of twenty-five! On the other hand if he paints on my floor in the back room and rents the front to a stranger he may make enough profit to overcome the difference. Theoretically the lease is mine but of course since I don't have any money with which to pay for the apartment Oliver would get the profit money for it. I may even suggest transferring the lease to him, in fact I think I will. It is important only to keep it in the family a little longer while space continues to be so unbelievably tight.

About your apartment you must write me what to do and *if you want to sublet even if Oliver DOESN'T* go into such an arrangement or refuses to give the back room on my floor over to you when you do come back. In other words are you willing to take a chance on no place to stay except a hotel and if so for how long should I sublet it? On the shortest possible lease or not. That would mean of course that I would have to be around to *re*lease it at the end of two months unless I could get people who promised to take it on if I wanted them to, for another two months. Second item to consider is the fact that you left of course without considering all this and unless I can get a friend to take it *everything* in the closets will have to be packed away. I am willing to do this as best I can but I will take no responsibility about doing it wrong. Are there grips there wherein I can pack your clothes or not? Third item is that John La Touche is apparently desperate for a place but neither Oliver nor I are willing to take the responsibility of renting to him without your sanction. You know his character and habits of neatness so you cannot blame me for hesitating. I won't even advise you on it but I left word for him to call me here at Libby's and I expect to hear tonight how much he'd want to pay and if he'd be willing to take it on a short basis or a long one. Naturally I wouldn't have to pack everything away for

Touche and if you are interested cable me that he can have it. Of course you know all the histories it might involve. There is Jean Stafford who wants an apartment for a year.

About my work it is a month now (when I include some bad days in between my seeing Helvetia and Mother when I didn't work because of various preparations for moving around and the general anxiety of it) since I have done anything. As I say I did not *choose* to see either one of them at this point but Mother could not change her dates and Helvetia is tied up with well diggers and carpenters from now until the end of October when our tenants leave and we had to talk about things at some point which you will appreciate. I am desperate however at all this time passing and have done little more on my novel than you have in spite of not moving around. I am terribly discouraged and of course the fact that you get these letters from publishers complimenting you on stories is no help to my morale as far as a *career* is concerned. I have never once received a letter from anyone about "Plain Pleasures" or the first act of my play or my little *Cross-Section* stories and *Partisan Review* would laugh and probably does at my work. This does not concern me deeply but I realize that I have no career really whether I work or not and never have had one. You have more of a one after writing a few short stories than I have after writing an entire novel. All this while, I have been slap-happy, not realizing that publishers did write anybody but now I see how completely unnoticed my work has been professionally. Arthur Weinstein told Virgil that at Knopf's they pretend never to have heard of me so I'm sure they will not publish my next novel. I am quite discouraged about all that and must say that if it were not for you and Edwin Denby, I would feel utterly lost. However none of that bothers me except to make me frightened about never making any kind of reputation which means no money and I refuse to have my non-existent career referred to any longer. I feel silly about it. I don't feel like being in New York at all and would like to go and live somewhere in a small town. I am eager to get back on my novel in spite of all this but that is probably because I haven't been writing it for a while and possibly when I begin again I will feel an inner discouragement and boredom compared to which any hurt pride is poppycock. I wish too that you would not refer to *your* work as your "little novel" which you did in your letter as I'm sure it will be very powerful and twice as excellent as mine, as well as more successful, and so are Dostoievsky and Sartre. Oliver says your story is wonderful and I am certainly eager to see it. I don't mind how much better or worse you write than I do as long as you don't insist that I'm the writer and not you. We can both be, after all and it's silly for you to go on this way just because you are afraid to discourage me. I suppose I was irritated and appalled because you referred to your work as your little novel just as Helvetia would do! She has written more than either of us this summer but also she has had more time. Well I hope all the novels will be good novels and published. I must now however write a short story in order to get some money. Perhaps I can. You will have to pay for your apartment for Sept. and part of October as I simply cannot pick up now and go into town to rent it. Whenever I do it will be a holocaust anyway and I would like to write the story and get back on the novel first. It is still hot in New York, Oliver is on the road or will be next week and I could simply not be there alone. You have not asked me to do this of course but I feel responsible for it, naturally, although I wished you'd made some provisions for such an eventuality before leaving—with your clothes I mean, and your perfumes. When I do go in I shall probably have to find someone to stay with me because I hate letting strangers in when I am alone particularly on that top floor which scares me to death anyway. I am going to telephone Dione and see if she will perhaps join me there when I do go in and stay with me while I sublet which should help a lot but I have no idea whether or not she will do this. Touche I have spoken to since I wrote you about him a page or so ago and he is interested in having an apartment for six or eight months. I told him I'd have to write you about it first. He has to move Tuesday and hopes to have a place by then but is going to call me on Monday if he hasn't. I won't know what to say to him about it frankly and he was very irritable with me over the phone already for not knowing what you wanted to do. Naturally I wouldn't rent it to him for six or eight months without hearing from you but I may *have* to let him in there for a few weeks. He seems to think he'll get a place, however. I am weary of thinking of it all and I had hoped that in your letters you would have something definite to say about it. Naturally I would be more than delighted not to have to bother but then on the other hand I feel I should if it is making you terribly strapped—holding on to it. Your concert is not being given this year as you know so you probably have no reason to come back except to see me and find a job which I guess you can do from there. Helvetia refuses to go to Africa and my going will depend mainly on Oliver and your finances I guess, plus my novel if it still exists by then which it either will or won't. At the moment I don't give a hoot where I am but would prefer a place like Gloucester which I visited with H. and loved. I liked certain towns in Maine very much as well. I would of course like to see you right now but you have been so generous with your letters that I have not felt separated from you nor have I thus far had cause for anxiety except when Cadiz blew up. I do hope you will understand if I wait until October to go in about the apartment. I am desperate to do some work and being there with all the packing and seeing people etc. will be death on any work at all. If Dione will join me I will not dread it so much. She may even want to take it herself and perhaps it would be just the thing because I could always tell her to leave when she stopped paying. The last time I spoke to her she had an income that Bergner was giving her but God knows what has happened by now. She wanted to take my apartment with me and said she could afford 110 dollars rent but no more. If it goes to strangers it will be of course more difficult. You must write me what to do and if you would be interested once yours was sublet in sharing mine with Oliver if *he* wants to. It would cost you 75 a month *but* when you weren't there you could sublet your part because the two rooms even have separate entrances. I might leave my present tenants in it in fact, in the front room, I mean, on condition that they would get out when you came back. Perhaps this is all too complicated but I have tried to mention all possibilities to you just because I feel this once that it might be of some interest to you and necessary to your decision. Don't forget to mention to me what kind of sublet you want me to make if any and bear in mind that the short term ones are more difficult but possible and require someone to be around every two months when the lease gives out. Even if I don't have it rented October fifteenth of next month if I do rent it shortly thereafter you will get most of your money back on the October rent I hope, because surely I can rent it at a profit. But I do hope you understand my asking for as much grace in time before going into the subletting horror as I can get. It will take a while before you answer this anyway and before I receive it; I am asking this only because all is not lost as a result of Mother's visit and the Helvetia interlude but I must get another stretch of work in. I shall have to go to New York towards the middle of October anyway and then I will do something about it if you want me to. You have never asked me to in your letters but what else could you mean by mentioning that your life would be cheap there if you didn't have to spend the seventy-five a month? Naturally I understand and I worry about you but I will do nothing unless you write me a letter as clear as this one is (ossir) and as conscientious because surely you must know what a terrible day this has given me. I have been at this for many hours and it has been so very hot too. I have put in a call to Dione so that I might know whether she'd join me in New York and I am calling Maggie to find out if *she* has any tuyaux about friends looking for a place. All the crickets and bugs are singing outside. I daresay O. may want to go to Africa and maybe he'd take me, quién sabe. Are there any Scotch or Irish there because I *must* have a bit of romantic adventure with all that singing and guitar playing going on. I am thinking of Spain now of course but we would probably hop over. Still it sounds very gloomy somehow and rather like trying to live in a dream. But then so is Gloucester a dream because most of the cod fish balls don't really come from there any more but from Canada and the Groton factories there are of minor importance compared to the new Canadian ones. In fact fish are being pulled in by huge nets attached to derricks and the old time fisherman is a thing of the past except for a sportsman. Would my ladies at the Salisbury Inn enjoy Tangier? They are not very imaginative but could they get over by boat and quote to me again the prices in your next letter. I spent a night in Great Barrington as Oliver calls it, on my way down from Helvetia's. There is a jealousy situation there between two people who have yet never been lovers. Not so very unusual I suppose. But it is a nuisance. We had cocktails with two business women who were friends of my ladies and on vacation at the Inn. One of them heads the design department at the Cannon Towel factory. Her name is Dorrit. I suppose the other lady, the jealous one, would never consent to go to Africa if I were going and actually they would both *bore* you and O. to extinction. If I don't go I hope maybe H. will take me to Mexico or Maine or Canada. She has added more rooms to her house and is altogether being quite wonderful. I think she will invite us all up there. Maurice has been with her half the summer, sharing in her grocery bills. I enclose ad from the *Saturday Review of Literature*. I am quite fat and not a pleasure to myself at all. But you would love my face. You must not be testy because I didn't mention the city where the Elkan publishers were—was that Elkan-Vogel? In any case perhaps it wasn't that name at all but the MS is arriving under separate cover and it *is* Los Angeles. How was I to know you didn't even know what city your music was being published in? I find you unfair sometimes particularly as you leave in a cloud of dust and never give me instructions. I didn't dare forward the manuscript without your permission. I shall go through your mail presently after I have fed the baby and diapered it although it is past midnight and I have been at this since morning. It is small wonder that I cannot write as often as you do. Libby is mostly in New York. Gian-Carlo wants to give my play to his producers. Nick Ray is a huge success in Hollywood but there has been not a peep out of him in reply to Oliver's letter about my play. I suppose he is having his revenge now on Oliver's rudeness, and the general disinterest we showed him. The minute I told Oliver that Gian-Carlo was going to take the play to his producers Oliver said he preferred to do it himself although he gave in very quickly—but I can't understand why he would not have done it before this. Gian-Carlo of course would like to direct it but I am not going to worry about that yet. I intend to spend next weekend there if it's O.K. with them and with Oliver. We naturally have a great deal to talk about concerning the winter, apartments, Africa etc. Apparently he looks very poorly, gaunt and ill.

Now that I have gotten this off my mind I shall be able to work tomorrow after a few business letters, one to Nessler. I just returned from my trip with Helvetia and so things have piled up. We visited Florence in Maine and the telegram about the apartment she could rent for a year arrived while we were there. I'm very sorry because I thought I wouldn't have to start worrying about your situation until November, and that you would have decided by then what to do. I hope you don't think I *want* you to sublet. I merely want to help you if you want me to in a month or so because I feel very sorry that you lose that money. But if you want to let it slide and take a chance on friends getting in there when they do, I'd be delighted. I called East Hampton and discovered that Dione is in New York. Perhaps she will come and live with me there while I sublet *or* if by any chance she had any money maybe between us if I make some we could hang on to it, if you were willing to contribute a little too. It would not be then like losing it to strangers who wouldn't move when you got back. She is living at the moment with Verne. Naturally I would prefer that to anything and I am sure Dione will keep me company there if it comes to that but the money I don't know about yet. Don't trouble your head about the complicated section of this letter concerning my *own* apartment and sharing it with Ollie because if you don't understand it right off you never will and I don't know if he'll do it anyway. Just concentrate on your own.

My fan is still a blessing and I loathe and despise this Connecticut sultry heat. Please write soon and thanks a lot for all your entertaining letters. I hope to see your story next week. Oliver of course would never get around to mailing it here. I don't see why you thought I had gone so far away. It certainly would have been simple enough to get my mail if I'd been in New Canaan. I just fed the little baby and by the way I saw about thirty Pekes in a kennel at Gloucester. I am happy that you are not disappointed in your trip. That would make me sadder than anything.

Much Love
Jane

P.S. Have you heard from Gordon—where on earth is he—and with whom? Will he join you again?

I hope Touche doesn't bamboozle us into getting into your place. It will be difficult if he's out on the street but maybe you'd want him there? Donald is not with him. Forwarding mail under separate cover. Some air mail.

Stamford, CT, September 1947

21
To Paul Bowles

Dearest Bubble,

Your letters have been truly wonderful and so profuse. I wish that I could say the same of mine. I must hate the written word no matter how I use it, and you must enjoy writing, or I'm sure you wouldn't do it. I shall get the worst part of this letter over with. Since I went to see my mother on the ninth of August I have never really got back on my novel except for a week. It is terrible, but there it is. I might certainly just as well have gone to Africa—I know that now. When you wrote me on the twenty-sixth of August I had about ten more pages typed than you did at the time, and some more in a notebook (maybe fifteen but in bad condition) and I have not added a page since. It is terrible, but I think you must know it so that you don't keep writing me "Come in January if your novel is finished." I did naturally no work during my two week trip with H. and then when I returned I set to work on a short story after a day or two or three of catching up on my correspondence with you and Mother and Saks Fifth Avenue, my tenants etc. I was going along with that as slowly as usual for a few days and then Ollie came down for the weekend. He stayed in my room with me so there was naturally no work done. We had a great deal to talk about since I have not seen him at all this summer. I started on a short story after my return from the Helvetia trip because I feel I should earn some money. I have a doctor's bill to pay and a Saks bill which would take just about all the money that I have in the bank, and with the fall coming on and the cleaner's bill (he has stored my fur coat, reconditioned it and done the same with my winter suits), I feel that I must make a little money. This is not an appeal for money but an explanation of why I would veer off my novel which I'm sure you don't approve of. I want to be able to take care of those little things myself, because it is a terrible feeling not to be able to earn enough to pay for even the details of one's life at the age of thirty. I am not frightened because it is not as though I were out on the street or could not ask for money. (Even my mother would give it to me but I would never ask her!) It is simply a question of *humiliation*. The Saks bill is something I ran up a year ago very gradually. It amounts to about fifty-nine dollars and was not an extravagance at the time, since I did need shoes etc. However I should have paid it then when I had enough money in the bank to cover it without getting down to my last dollar and I feel that because of this I have to get out of it myself. I have written them and asked them to give me until November for the payment and sent them fifteen dollars on account. I hope by then to have the money by selling (first writing!) a short story. There *is* a chance that George or Mary Lou would buy it, after all. Libby says they can not attach *you* for the money unless we have a joint account, and she's right because I could do nothing about making Mr. Denny pay Mrs. Denny's telephone bill, morally or legally. I hope someday to get back to my novel. Naturally I know yours will be finished years ahead of mine and will be wonderful. Probably mine will never be done so you had better stop writing about it. Still I hope that the month of October however will be a good one and that I can make up some lost time. I work well in the fall. There were some terrible weeks here in August and during the first half of September. Muggy and breathless. The worst possible kind of weather for thinking or writing. In fact the weather man said that this was the worst summer we have had in twenty-five years. I must say that such weather, the really damp heavy kind, does have a particularly bad effect on one's energy and even after writing a letter I would be exhausted. I don't know whether all these things are excuses or whether I simply can't write. It is not, I am *certain*, for lack of trying. But I know you would rather have me blame it on the weather than on a complete lack of talent or imagination—imagination really because if I can imagine anything I can write it. So much for that. Perhaps I wrote all this to you in my last letter, probably did, but in my next I hope that maybe I'll be back on the novel or at least finished the story. After Oliver left I hung about for a day and drank brandy with Mrs. Swazie, the sixty-three year old deaf secretary who is leaving. It was her farewell night and I had to be with her. But that relationship is too long to tell about. I recovered the next day and just as I was getting down to work Libby appeared from New York, sky high and filled with excitement. Viola Rubber had just introduced her to Echols and Gould and given her the *Folle* to read. She read it that night, part of it, and decided it was something I might have written myself. I don't know how in the world she reached such a conclusion because nothing could be farther from me as you will agree—except that there are some crazy old ladies in it, and *that* I suppose is what gave her the idea. Into town she went the next day and out again that night with the fantastic idea that I should do a new adaptation for it. She had finished it by then and seen Echols and Gould once more, who half promised her a part (one of the minor lunatics) in it, when and if they got it on. They are as you know still looking for the perfect adaptation. She had the fantastic conviction that I could do it but not only was it an idea of hers, which would have been easy to waive, but unfortunately Echols and Gould also had me down on their list, although their first choice is S. N. Behrman whom they can't thus far get hold of. I tried to convince her that I never could do it and that they as well as herself were wrong but she finally put it to me as a particular favor to her and with such insistence that I could not or would not refuse to at least try my hand at a few pages. Oy! I don't know exactly why it would be such a favor to her but whatever it is I would do anything for her if only I could. Gould came out here and brought me the two translations, the potpourri that is a combination of yours and their own and one other by a New York lawyer who did it in four days. I told Libby there was naturally no point in trying unless there was some way of improving on either of those scripts without even going a step further than that, so I insisted on seeing them. I can recognize certain sentences in the potpourri one as being yours. The rest they've made a scramble of mostly. I asked them what they didn't like about your version and they seemed to think you hadn't gotten the Giraudoux spirit very well. I should think you would have hated the play in any case, the first act, particularly, the part before the "Folle" appears. Anyway there was nothing for me to do but to give up a few days and translate three or four speeches as a sample of what I could do—mainly the prospectors. It took me forever as you can imagine but I was very surprised to find that I did have some ideas about them. I showed what I did to Gould and he was very noncommittal about it. He said he thought I was on the right track but it was hard for him to say really, because he had thirteen other translations and adaptations whirling around in his head. I am sending in the final version of these speeches (they take up only three typewritten pages) with Libby today and she will meet the boys at her apartment this afternoon. I don't think for a minute they'll accept me because Gould was completely without enthusiasm but at least I know I will have done my best as far as Libby is concerned and that I have not in any way shirked my task. So now I am ready to return to my own writing (ossir). I must mail my play off to Gian-Carlo this afternoon and forward what little dreary mail you have. Before I finish writing about Echols and Gould, *I don't think they are ever going to get what they want*, because I feel they want it to be as elliptical and complicated as Giraudoux's style and yet to be written like a straight detective drama at the same time. If one *is* "fancy" in the adaptation they say it won't "play well" and yet they want to keep Giraudoux's quality. I am sure it won't play well anyway, and find much of it very tedious indeed. Mostly I can't bear it, but there *are* some charming moments and even moving ones. Well, enough of that. I think it's terribly funny that it should have turned up again, and I have a feeling it's going to be like one of those dreadful thick necked people who are seen first with you and then with Buzzy and finally with Touche or Charlie Ford. They are not dreadful people but unattractive. But then I shudder to think of your impression of my friend at the Inn; I would simply love to see your expression. In fact I cannot help laughing aloud when I think of it. Although I myself find her very attractive I can see the whole thing through your eyes.

About coming to Africa, I don't think there is a chance that she and her friend would, although I mentioned it to her. As for the novel influencing my decision, I shall surely not be finished. I can only hope that I shall get as much done during October, November and December as I didn't get done in August and September. If I really do, I should have a pretty strong grip on it and could decide in December whether or not to go. I told Oliver to get passages anyway and then we can always cancel them. You know how likely he is to change his mind the last minute and then too you may have to come home for something or other. With prices as they are I cannot honestly advise you to come here without the assurance of a job, but I can't say what I'll do either. I *won't* go on a small boat in winter and neither will Ollie, but the American Export lines are getting ready and I think if you could pay half my fare Oliver might pay the other and even I might be able to contribute. I would however not count on that and I should keep my money for clothes and the things that I have to get for myself through the years, if the money is very little, and so far of course it's exactly nothing. Helvetia and I will probably spend November and December together in the country if her furnace gets in. We could all then go up there in fact if you were in this country. She's having another bathroom put in and there are three more bedrooms than there used to be. I'm supposed to ask Oliver up there for Thanksgiving or anytime and you of course would be invited too. Naturally if you came back for a job it would be a nice place for you to go to for a month or two and work if you could stand the boredom, particularly if your apartment were occupied. Oliver says you can't wait to get me into the desert. Of course I'm sure that when I get there, if I do, all the part I would have liked will be over—like the wine and the nice hotels. I would like to stay in a hotel in Fez, I think rather than Tangier, and I still refuse to cross the Atlases in a bus. But if O. came maybe we'd take a cab. I wish to hell I could find some woman still so that I wouldn't always be alone at night. I'm sure Arab night life would interest me not in the slightest. As you know I don't consider those races voluptuous or exciting in any way, as I have said—being a part of them almost. The architecture is another thing, and I think I would love the daytime there, and the very early morning, but I'm sure it is just the opposite with you and would be with Oliver. It is hard for me to think of going anywhere by myself of course, and I'm not even *going* to think about it yet. If my novel is not coming along at all by then it would be more painful than pleasant to go over there and see your manuscript almost done or even half done. I don't think I could bear the sense of failure made so palpable, but I couldn't bear it either to have you in such a terrible state about yours as I am about mine. I really am very glad you are coming along with it and I don't believe any of the things you say about the value of it, but aside from that I also think it is very important that you have this extra source of income if you can really develop it substantially, because it will permit you to do much more work out of the country than your music does which is after all what you want, and in a sense a good way to keep alive with prices here the way they are. None of this makes my life any simpler perhaps or maybe it will but that's beside the point. It will all work out, or it will never, I can't imagine. But certainly I don't like to see you miserable and bored, which you are in New York. I myself cannot get into New York at all. It is almost as difficult for me as getting on a boat to Africa. That is why I hate you to send things to Oliver. I did write you that even if I *weren't* here that I could not understand why you imagined they would not forward my mail to me; I wrote that in reference to the story which you sent Oliver because he had written you that I was in New Canaan (which is ten minutes from here, anyway). Now of course he's read the story, promised a hundred times to mail it and will lose it before I ever see it, probably. You must know that much about him. Also, I'm sure I'll never see the books. Half the packages he receives are lost because they're left in the hall forever. He completely mislaid the whole set of silver John something or other in the theatre (C. Wilson) sent him and I am bitter about your having sent the books to him. I did write you too that I would only go in for a while to sublet the apartment if I had to. Even if he does receive the books they'll go into his library and be amalgamated. Don't you *believe* I'm at Libby's, or do you think it's in the mountains and on a mule trail? I wish that you would explain your logic. It is not that Oliver would purposely do these things but his apartment is like the dead letter office. Everything disappears. I do want the books so badly and I've been waiting and looking forward to them so much. I think it was sweet of you to send them too. I am really frantic about the whole thing. When I saw Oliver he said that he thought he had rented your apartment definitely to Paul Godkin who would get out whenever you wanted him to. He was to let me know about it a week ago and hasn't. I wanted to be sure so that I could do something about it if it weren't rented. But then you know Oliver. He said also he was going to try and get you a job in Hollywood and that you shouldn't come rushing back yet because there was nothing in sight. He is supposed to take care of the boats and passages from New York so you might keep in touch with him about it, if he remains interested. I shall spend a week or so with him at some point. After *Bonanza Bound* opens end of November I shall suggest a rest to him in Vermont. Libby heard an audition of it and hated it but then she has very violent dislikes in the theatre and she seemed to hate this because the people in it were so greedy. Both Oliver and I think it would be nice, the next time there is any money around to get a house maybe in the town of Nyack, and give up New York entirely. The subletting business is a real headache and there is never any place to leave one's things. It is nice to have a place to come back to and I think a *house* in Africa or any other country is silly. I think hotels or temporary places are more fun. But we *should* all have a permanent one which could be closed up without being rented every time we moved. Particularly as we grow older and more feeble. I myself never go out of Libby's house very much and am still the same old home body. I asked Louisa Carpenter if she would like to go to North Africa but she said she wanted to go to South Africa and do some big game hunting. If Sister Bankhead goes down to Alabama, Louisa may fly me down to Maryland in her little Bonanza plane for a few days to catch the last of the fishing season (which of course I can't bear to miss). I would only go if I can be there with Louisa alone or with Libby along, but I can't face being there for three days just with Sister and Louisa for several reasons which wouldn't interest you and are not very important to either your life or mine. The little farm down there is charming and I would like to know Louisa better since she is a sportswoman and such a type has never entered my life. Later she will go duck shooting and I imagine she even goes after deer. And then think how jealous John Uihlein would be. (She's a DuPont as you know and you remember the fuss in Southampton about that Ruth Ellen in the big beach house.) She is really a very attractive plain woman and of course terribly broke all the time. Touche is now after my apartment and I worry about that. He was furious when I asked him if he could pay regularly and I feel it would end up in a big fight. Do you think he would? Maggie was cross with me because she said you wrote someone that I had written you she was going to be married. I denied the whole thing and I don't remember writing anything of the kind nor in fact even hearing such a rumor. What could I have said? And do be careful of what you write, although I don't see why the hell Maggie should get so huffy about it; it's not an evil thing to say about anyone. I might have said something jokingly to you, what was it? I can't imagine. Anyway if there was something write it to me but not to Maggie or anyone else and I'll explain what I meant by the remark—if I ever made one. I miss you a great deal and hope to see you here or there but it's hard to say just yet what will happen for the various reasons I have mentioned. I hope Oliver is doing something about boats in any case so that we do at least have passages. And I hope to God I can get back to my novel and that it will move along. If Oliver goes he will have to rest up first, at Helvetia's perhaps, before taking those shots. But don't for heaven's sake count on anything and do whatever you think wisest. I am taken care of as far as my food and living quarters are concerned so don't worry about me. I have not felt you were far away thus far, in fact I feel it's much nearer than Mexico but I'm sorry you're going into the desert. It will take longer to hear from you now I'm sure, or it *will* when you get there if you are not there yet.

The day is windy, at least, which I like more and more as I get older. H. has been terribly sweet but she is very broke until March, having had all those things added to her house and cannot take any kind of trip before then. She will have to stay in Vermont most of the winter to save up so I imagine by next spring she'll be ready to go somewhere, after the asparagus is up. Of course the news about the world is bad these days, and I must read all the papers which I put into my closet week after week and never read. I intend to study the Marshall Plan one of these days but I'm so far behind now it's going to be difficult. Please write me *here* and you might write O. that the books are a *special* present for me and that I want the pleasure of opening them when they arrive so that they won't be scattered to the four winds if he does ever get them out of the front hall. I prefer not to think about it because I get too angry.

I saw Puppet; Helvetia spent the night here day before yesterday. Her sister lives not far from here and was giving a party on her birthday. Now that one can drive, Vermont is no longer so difficult to get to. No distinguished magazine has ever written me and complimented me on a story, or asked for a contribution, nor have I certainly ever won an O. Henry award. I seem to be completely ignored by the whole literary world just as much as by the commercial one. Nevertheless that would not stop me from writing. But I might have heard from someone all these years even though I have a publisher (ossir). I seriously doubt that Knopf will ever take anything of mine again.

Much Love—as ever—

Jane B.

P.S. I sent all the music I had—but can't remember details. I'll call Helen Strauss. Maybe I'll have better news for you next time about my work.

O. says your story wonderful—but I don't ever expect to see it: subject matter sounds fascinating but scarcely material for a magazine! You'll have to wait to bring it out in a book.

I remember there were some either black or green music sheets I sent you from the place in California, I believe.

Stamford, CT, Late September 1947

22
To Paul Bowles

Dearest Bup,

I have been away for a week but shall forward your mail tomorrow. I usually wait until it accumulates somewhat. There is nothing of importance, you'll see. I have waited to write because I have been in such a boiling rage with you having spent most of this week trying to make some order out of the havoc of your clothes and pure junk left around the apt. none of which I dare throw away. The number of filthy articles that were simply stuffed into the closets is unbelievable. It was like cleaning out an old Vermont farmhouse—the dirt left by two generations of maniacs. I am not even speaking of the laundry in the cardboard box which May is going to do gradually, since there are five hundred dirty things. If you did not have so many clothes such a laundry and such dirt could not accumulate. Naturally at this point it *would* cost a fortune to have everything cleaned. Paul Godkin and I packed away all the clean shirts and woolen stuff, clean and dirty, in grips with moth balls and then for the other things we used cartons. We had to have an extra maid in and even so it took three days and the place is still loaded. There is however room for Arthur and Bobby's things and for Paul's who is very kindly allowing five or six of your suits or coats, whatever they are, to hang in the closet. We emptied the bureau completely. However when May has finished with all your laundry there will be enough again to fill another bureau, so she had better keep it at her apartment until I get back eventually because there is no room really for anything more in the apartment not even a pill box and the boys are entitled to a little comfort since they are paying the rent. I thought that perhaps I could ship some cartons up to Vermont with Helvetia's permission. Every book was taken down and dusted and the floors scrubbed. Paul Godkin has sent everything (curtains etc.) to the cleaners and is really going to a good deal of expense. You are indeed fortunate, really born under a lucky star because had the apartment been sublet to a stranger I *don't* think with all the good will in the world I could have handled the job of making room. I would simply have given up in despair and wept, or disappeared for ever. Even without facing strangers, to have made ready for Bobby and Arthur alone would have been hopeless, because Arthur came down while we were in the midst of clearing space for their clothes and almost collapsed, so I don't think they would have helped me the way *Paul* did. Luckily he had this wonderful maid whom he summoned and she did most of the work with May but still it took supervising and organization. And then there were all these junky old dirty vests—costumes—hats—bathing suits—mats: They marvelled at my not throwing them away but of course I didn't dare unless there was something completely hopeless. It is all very well and your business to keep hoarding things and collecting more but then you should not expect to just go away and have it taken care of. You do not live in an apartment but in a *storeroom* with a little space in the middle! You need once and for all to go over your things, to throw out what you don't really want, and find a permanent place for the rest. If they are all packed away in really good strong boxes and nailed shut absolutely air tight we could store them somewhere, either at Helvetia's or somewhere in Vermont for practically nothing. I'm sure she could make room. I don't mean the books but all the junk—masks—extra serapes—papers that are merely keepsakes at this point—clothing you never wear—or half of what you *do* (you couldn't get around to them all in a year), old shoes etc. Then you could move in and out of your apartment more easily or at least it would be easier on everyone else. Until you had enough money to either keep a place on in New York—whether you were in it or not—or else own a house, you would live without this great burden of things. You need a real house with an attic where you could store things to your heart's content but that would of course involve a servant staying in it or some caretaker near by. If Oliver buys a house in New York you will be in luck because there would be a cellar with plenty of space, I suppose, and judging from the kind of lucky solutions you find to your problems—like Paul Godkin—Oliver probably *will* have a house and you can pile in more things. I know you think I am stewing but you wouldn't really, if *because* of your vast accumulation and the state of chaos you walked out on there had been *no* possibility of subletting. I had to get this off my chest obviously or I would not have ever written you—I mean I could not get on to anything else without writing you about this first. Paul Godkin is a wonderfully generous and helpful person and never complained once. He has fine energy and did a thousand little things while *I* sat on the bed in utter dejection and exhaustion. I think you might write him a letter. *Also* if there is one word of complaint about him when you come back—if you ever do—you had better not voice it when I am anywhere near or could possibly even hear a *report* of your remark. Everyone seems to know about your buying a house in Africa except myself—and why on earth you would suddenly have written about it to Bob Faulkner whom you don't ever see I can't understand. I just *happened* to be in town when Oliver got your wire and I of course advised him to send the $500. I knew you were getting a kick out of the house and I cannot help but want your pleasure. I was hurt though that you had written to Oliver and Bob Faulkner about it and yet no word to me. In your letter to Oliver you don't sound at all as though you expected us *both* to come over but only he. He refuses however to go without me and perhaps you didn't expect that he would. I know that you asked me over in a letter to me but that was before this house came on the scene, and possibly now you feel instinctively that it is all wrong for me. Of course you know how I feel about houses—and living in quarters where I might be conspicuous. I don't of course know about the Arab town of Tangier (I *refuse* to use that Arabic word). It may be filled with European and American eccentrics in any case. That is all I would mind, being conspicuous. As for worrying about comforts—as you know or should by now, that is not the kind of thing that concerns me. Have you forgotten Mrs. Copperfield? I would prefer also that there be no food worth eating for the tourist who has dollars or other money that the natives don't have. I have no interest at all in that and I would feel the proximity of starving France too keenly to really enjoy it. I should keep to a simple couscous and some cheap alcoholic beverage or a dope of some kind since it is impossible for me to live without such aids. I have lost interest in all foods, although I am more plump than ever. Recently I have been drinking quantities of buttermilk. Oliver I don't think will want to live in a house without a bathroom but I discouraged him from having one put in before he got there. I think he might better stay at a hotel and see how he likes it all, before making any more expenditures. This way it is still low enough in price to come under the heading of a "lark" because "lark" it is—which is all right—but surely it will end up costing more than not having a house. I don't care naturally how either one of you spend your money because I have no sensible suggestions actually or anything that *I* would like except perhaps a permanent house here with a servant or farmer in it where we could leave our things forever. Something in a small town. I don't see how an Arab house could be even a "headquarters" as you term it unless you keep a permanent servant in it because surely you would be robbed of all your things the moment you left for the desert or any of these "points" it's so convenient to, as you say in your letter. That is why I consider it a "lark" and not a practical arrangement. I will be only too glad to hear that I am mistaken however and that you *can* leave your things there or intend to have a faithful servant. I hope you will write me the details about just how frightening it's all going to be. I am *bitter* that I have missed the hotel part of your sojourn (all for nothing too) and that I shall arrive in time for the mess. I know now it was a mistake to stay here.

Sometimes I am in despair and sometimes very hilarious but I have a terrific urge now to go to Africa in spite of the house, although even the house I would like in the day time I imagine. The plans are to come in Feb. I hope maybe to have done enough writing by then so as not to be completely ashamed and jealous when confronted with your novel. At the moment I can't even think of it without feeling hot all over. And yet if you had *not* been able to do it I would have wrung my hands in grief—I say this sincerely. If by Feb. I *haven't* done enough maybe I shouldn't come because you'll view me with such disgust but *Oliver* keeps saying he won't go without me. Please keep plaguing him about securing boat *passages*. There have really been a series of plane accidents again. I had a letter from Gordon. Oliver seems to think he'll go to Italy and to Egypt. I would like to go to France as well—food or no food—eventually. Maggie Dunham seems to be interested in coming too. I am simply *dying* to be there now and perhaps I would come alone right away if it weren't too exhausting to think of doing the whole thing by myself—and also if it weren't for my work—but I may inquire and wire you.

However little I have done I am pleased with but shall probably throw it in the rubbish heap when I see yours. The story I am working on to get some money is nearly 60 pages long in my notebook already—and they are large pages—so I worked at a good rate but have not touched it in over a week. I flew down to Maryland for two days and when I returned I tended to your things at the studio for three or four days. I feel like getting back to it. It is utterly unsaleable but I like it thus far if I can only work it out! It's coming out much better than the novel did—and I know why: it's because I tried to put myself into the novel—in the guise of a boy—which somehow throws the whole thing off. I shall go back to it eventually but with grave misgivings. Possibly I am meant to write plays—or short stories. *Two Serious Ladies* was after all *not* a novel. I must also spend *some* time with H. who is flat broke because of all the work she had done on the house and therefore obliged to spend until March in Vermont. If I can spend part of Dec. and January with her it will at least pull her through half the winter. I imagine she'll go somewhere actually by February. She *can* borrow on her income after all. Oliver seems to have mislaid your story. He tried to find it for me when I was in New York. Don't scold him because he is so very helpful and caters to your slightest whim. He says he won't go to Hollywood unless you can go with him which I think is very sweet. He is really wonderful to you—and you are *not* wonderful to him. I am grieved however that he has mislaid your story. I want to read it. I am slowly disintegrating I suppose—but all the time marvelling more and more at American womanhood. It is nice to find as many miracles as I do but perhaps it is time I rested my overblown heart and looked at some Arab houses.

Heaven knows I shall be made nervous over there by the absence of any charming possibilities, whereas for you and Ollie it will be just the opposite—or is there a chance? Write me *everything*—including about the house.

My Love, as ever,
Devotedly
J.B.

P.S. I am at R——— Inn for 2 days. I hope to have a letter when I get home. Don't mind my scolding—it is kind of a literary exercise in precision. Perhaps you don't want me to come? I shall naturally not mind the house when there's more than you and me in it. And it does sound beautiful because you can see the water—yes I think I would have worked much better over there. I have had too much the burden of my entire life here but in a sense I have learned far more by staying.

Stamford, CT, October 1947

23
To Paul Bowles

Dearest Bupple,

Your letter from Tangier—the one written on Thanksgiving day—has thrown me into a state. I think it is rather mean of you not to be more careful of what you say when you know how easily upset I am and how quickly guilty even when I know I'm not in the wrong. I don't know where on earth you got the idea that I would arrive suddenly in Tangier. Surely unless it is just wishful thinking—because you were bored and ready to have me arrive—it must have been Oliver who confused you. I enclose a letter (an excerpt from a letter rather) written in September, late September to Helvetia. To come around January if you did not return had always been my plan—at least since I began to plan at all. Before that it was "*le néant*" because to begin with you were originally going to return. Not that I think you should have. It is only in the last six weeks or so that your letters have become so pressing and one in particular written during the period of the "Villa" when you suddenly said that I should not come so late as Xmas because then the hotels would be full. That startled me greatly, because if I had been able to get there as early as Xmas, even if only because of passage difficulty, it would have been a miracle. After that there was a long blank period when you seemed to write Oliver and not me which I mentioned to you in another letter and which I decided was due to the fact that you didn't think I liked the house idea one bit and were temporarily avoiding me. Perhaps Oliver has been announcing all kinds of arrivals that I never even knew about? I told you too that I would spend a month or so with H. before leaving, otherwise that I would not be happy leaving. January always seemed the wisest to me from the time I thought concretely about the possibility of your not returning, and then Oliver put it off until February. I may have nebulously referred to a fall arrival much earlier in the summer but nothing definite I'm sure. Everything took much longer than I thought. Perhaps you have found it so too. But to finish with this so that it is clear in your mind that I don't feel I've kept you waiting for me in Tangier,

I had planned to come possibly in January without Oliver *with your approval* naturally until this operation of Julian's came up. Only because I always felt O. might not get off even in February. But then Julian knocked out the possibility of Jan. until mother suddenly decided it wasn't too serious about J. a few weeks ago—all of which I wrote you about in my last letter. I am again trying to get away in January but the Fern Line holds out no hope at all, they say however that I may as well be down on the list just because of the barest possibility. Now however since the letter about the Clairvoyant I feel no matter what I do I will not go at the last minute and this worries me terribly because I feel that it will concern Julian's illness if I should get a ticket on the Fern Line for January and then not go. I am fortunate in that Jody is now in New York and working on all this for me so that at least I can work. The work seems to be going well at last as though somehow all those little marks like flies' legs in my notebook were at last turning into sentences and paragraphs. That is also why I wish at this particular moment you hadn't worried me about keeping you sitting in Tangier. It is so extremely irritating and unfair and untrue—not untrue that you took it into your imagination but untrue that I said, "I am coming any minute." Naturally all during the summer there were moments when I thought of simply rushing off and other moments when my deep despond about my own work and your reports about the slow but steady progress in yours somehow combined to make me feel "que ce n'était pas le moment encore." Particularly as I knew you would be out all night all the time. In my present more optimistic mood I wouldn't mind a bit. I want to get there and feel I would if it weren't for the Fortune Teller. You should never have written me that of course. I can't imagine what will make me change after I've bought my ticket except the illness or death of someone very close so you see what a mood I'm in about the whole thing. Do you think he's infallible? I may of course not be able to get the money in January anyway because I don't know about Ollie and you'll be in the desert, maybe, but I'm pretty sure I could. However I can't make it before the middle of the month so I wouldn't get to Tangier till Feb. which would give you time to come out of the desert to meet me or soon thereafter. If I come in Jan. Jody will be with me, as I explained, so I could wait in Tangier. If I can't get away by the middle or end of Jan. it will then be the end of Feb. or March. (Have decided definitely against the Feb. 13th sailing which I mentioned in my last letter) I too might take a short trip, six or eight weeks, with Jody by motor. (Or if we could find a little boat that went to Haiti or Jamaica that might do but I expect we will just have to go somewhere around here.) Of course I feel very frustrated when I think of Mother alarming me so about Julian and then turning round and making me think it's silly to stay for that. (Not her fault really since the doctors seem to have made a mistake at first and I'm glad naturally), but I *could* have had my passage by now I think plus a travelling companion and gotten to see you and Africa all at once! It is infuriating. Also if I had only decided or you had been more urgent about my coming earlier in the summer I might have stepped up everything and got going sooner too. But then what is the use of writing all that. If by some miracle I do get off in January we will go straight to Tangier and you will get there when you can. I will wire you. By February you will have had time to see enough I imagine. I hope you understand that if I don't come by then I will skip February. It would mean everything to my new friend and after all only a month or so to us—which God knows seems like nothing at this point. Don't think either that it is because of her that I have been delayed. Au contraire. 1. I never expected until last month that she wouldn't be going to South America with her partner (they have travelled together for sixteen years). 2. She would have *preferred* most to leave on the first of December or as close to it as possible and asked me if I might not get ready by then but alas it was too late when she suggested this. I had not yet seen Helvetia and soon after that Mother's trouble came, so that even January I thought was out. Her partner has gone off to Honolulu in a semi-huff and it would be cruel of me to walk out on her in Feb. to get a month sooner to Tangier. About this I am morally certain. She could not leave in Feb. and be back by March. As for our getting to Tangier somehow in Jan.: I would naturally want you to be there when we arrived if you could but I don't want you to get hysterical if you are way off or if you get this letter (and) decide you can't go off because of my possible arrival, which I wouldn't put past you at this point. You might better just say, Jane will arrive in March (except that at the last minute she will give up her ticket so she won't! I am really furious that you wrote me such a thing.) Oliver has more or less decided on May for his trip unless he flies over quickly in February. He had the idea you should get all your primitive travelling done before we get there. As for Egypt, the *Vulcania* and the *Saturnia* go there so maybe it will have something to do with that, the Fortune Teller's prediction I mean. Oliver refuses to go on any freighter so he may want you to meet him there. I still can't believe that it takes as long to get from Naples to Tangier as it does from New York to Tangier. What are you thinking of? One has only to look at the map—particularly the big boats which call at Gibraltar. I think it would be fun to go that way. *I* can also wait until May and go with Oliver and Maggie *if* you think that's better but then I shall engage a passage for March in any case and we'll see what your mood is by then or mine, and what you're doing. I certainly *will* wait until May if you still want to be in the desert in March and are bored with the idea of coming out to meet me. If I go with Ollie all my expenses I think would be paid, in fact I know it, but he is undependable. I *am* sure however that he will do no more work for a while after this winter because he will certainly have knocked himself out by spring. He wants to do *Ondine* and my play next season and spend the summer around Africa and Italy if possible. I am working very hard this month typing my long story and revising. I hope in January to work on selling it and perhaps getting an advance on some excerpts from my novel, but I must see Leo Lerman about it and also fix them up. He thinks I should switch to Viking. I really should finish all this work before leaving and if I could just sit here until the boat sailed I would, but leaving—even by January—always entails so much. En tout cas, we will see. Your book I have a feeling will be really wonderful. I should not actually worry about you too much. Are you not in the place you most love and writing about it, and do you not have a parrot? I am of course flattered that you want me there too with all those riches. So I will come in January or March but not in February. It is a short month anyway and I'm sure you see my point about that. (She would be in

N.Y. because of me, instead of with her friend in Honolulu, so that for me to leave would be awful—and even Jan. is late for her to leave and get back by March—so Feb. is of course out. I have made no promises to her but I would not be cruel and I am fond of her.) I have as usual precipitated a holocaust and can't walk out just in that month. M. will be back in March when they return to the Inn towards the end of the month. Besides the idea of making this little trip amuses and enchants me though not nearly so much as it would to find a boat and get to Africa. She is getting a passport just in case we do. Do you think the Clairvoyant could have been wrong about my buying the ticket and then not going, and that it could have meant simply all this business about boats (I have the *Journal of Commerce* sent to me here in Vermont), all of which might have come out in his head as actually buying a ticket? I wonder. I shall never forgive him or you, really. I think I have said enough about this for one letter. If you, for some reason by the time you get this, think it advisable for me to wait and *not* leave in January even *if I can*, for God's sake cable in spite of cost. I don't know what reasons you'd have except that suddenly you might be coming back or be expecting to be gone until next June in the wilderness. I certainly hope not because as long as I hear from you I feel all right unless everything else is wrong which often happens but it's going to be awful from now on with you in the desert—and most likely months between letters. I shall never know what is happening or what to do if I should suddenly have to decide something.

I *loved* your story. Everything that happened in it was perfect down to the man who was looking for Riley and her dismal return to her own apartment house (the janitor having to bring the elevator up from the basement!). You write wonderfully about this country I think, as well as you do about any other country. In fact I am convinced that you are a writer down to the marrow of your bone. Certainly I should never have expected this kind of story out of you. It is even more surprising than the one about Prue and the other two women. This is besides *sumamente* saleable I should say. The tension as usual is terrific. It seems like an innocent enough little story when it begins and the way in which you have shaded it so that it becomes steadily more somber, almost as imperceptibly to the reader as to the girl herself, is I should say masterful. I read it twice because I could not quite encompass it. The effect was so much as though it were almost that night itself and not just something written about a night that I had to reread it to see how on earth you did it, and if you really did. Of course I still don't see how, even now, except through the expert and naturally instinctive choice of the detail. The candles, the sound of the log breaking in two, the melting ice cubes, and some perfect word you use concerning her fingers in the ice bowl. I can't think of such a word *even* after reading it. It was simple enough but so accurate. The drawer and her running to the buzzer, and not pushing it, going back again to the drawer and then to the buzzer again and finally the man called "Riley," were so terrible and exciting somehow that I almost threw up. I think the artistry there was her not answering the buzzer the first time it rang, which started the suspense at just the right pitch. It is an exhausting story and the morning was really wonderful. It is even better reading the second time, too, because one notices little indications about the boy's character in the beginning which should actually be just as lightly drawn as they are or the suspense would be ruined and one would expect him not to return or at least expect some calamity. The whole thing is very wily and real short story writing, I should say. (We don't have to go in to your talent and originality because that has never been questioned.) Perhaps writing *will* be a means to nomadic life for you, but I hope you won't slowly stop writing music, altogether. I think you will do both. You have always wanted to go back to writing anyway and I remember your discussing it very solemnly once at the Chelsea. You were standing against a bureau. I am furious of course about your other story but Oliver insists it isn't lost, just mislaid. Unfortunately he has to go down to the customs in person for the books as far as I know and I don't see him ever doing it. It is appalling but when I get down to New York I shall see what I can do. Meanwhile I shall instruct him not to lose the little slip from [ ] in a letter that I shall write now.

Please be good and don't worry me about Africa. In other words don't be slipshod and get mixed up about what I tell you. Your letters can be very confusing too, but I do try to get the meaning out of them and not falsify. In the most recent one you don't mention your trip into the desert, only to Fez, and I understood from the other one you were starting out on a real Safari. I am so worried that I shan't hear from you for months. *Please* take care of yourself and don't for God's sake get sick down there. Also afraid I won't have any place to mail a carbon of my story when it's finished for a long while. Is there any mail delivery in the desert?

The dog is fine. I hope this reaches you. The neighbors (the bores up the road that have the little girls) came by two nights ago. I was a little tight so I insisted that I would love to go with them to a lecture on "Cooperatives in Vermont" or some such subject. Tonight is the night and I'm certainly horrified at having gotten myself into it. They will take me to the high school auditorium and bring me back with them and have a bit to eat here around ten o'clock. I have made noodle ring with beef stew in the middle. I cook little and mostly work and write letters. My energy comes from the fact that winter is here at last. I function badly in the hot muggy summer and this fall was warm all through September and during half of Oct. Libby also would like to go in May to Africa. I am of course torn between seeing you sooner and avoiding the trip alone, so will wait for your advice on that and meanwhile get on the Fern Line list for March as well as January. Helvetia wants to be on the list for July. I have more to write but I will some other time when I hear where you are. I shall forward mail to British Post Office, what little there is of interest.

Much much love, as ever
Teresa

P.S. I miss you very much indeed and want to see you naturally. If ever you are troubled or puzzled about my inertia just imagine everything you feel about "setting out" in reverse!! Of course I vacillate but I have come a long way nonetheless. I can now actually imagine the trip alone without exactly shuddering, whereas this summer I feared it even with you along. I should hate truthfully at this point not to get to Africa at all.

I am going to walk to town and mail this before I throw it away. I have as usual gotten too wound up about some remark which you have by now forgotten. I suppose it was your saying you were now at last "going to lead your own life"—as though you had been hanging about Libby's kitchen all summer. In the next breath you told me about the parrot's Thanksgiving dinner, so I know you realized that you were being unnecessarily petulant. I have noticed that whenever you are cross in a letter you atone for it quite automatically by describing some gesture of the parrot's. He sounds like another lunatic—thank God—how *will* you lug him all over Africa? Be sure to get a strong cage so that he doesn't stick his head and shoulders through the bars. Does he *say* anything? Is he pretty or just crazy? Your hotel sounded charming but whenever I get to Morocco I shall insist on Fez. You must let me know if you think the Fortune Teller infallible. Love again,

J.

P.P.S. It is so beautiful here in Vt. You must come some winter. The furnace is being put in and as you know there are three rooms and two baths extra. H. is wonderful—no dramas—and she is eager to have you and Oliver here for long stretches of time. You will find it a most satisfactory place to spend a month in as far as work goes but undoubtedly you would be bored for longer periods. But it will be good for when you are obliged to be in this country between jobs etc. I do not accept *any* money from her—which has been an excellent idea. At the moment she's broke anyway because of her artesian well, new rooms etc. and could not even afford the Fern Line before July.

Dear Bupple, this letter was written to Perkins in the latter part of Sept. I'm sure I would have been writing you about the same sort of thing—so it must be Ollie who's done the confusing and naturally he has been instrumental in confusing me but I think it will all work out.

Please forgive this letter if it is spotty and does not give you a clear picture of what I want to do. *All I know is that I may go to Africa in Jan.* and I may not *if I am working well, and Paul comes back.* Perhaps we will all be in the Chelsea again. I wouldn't be a bit surprised. Plus ça change—naturally I want to spend some months with you somewhere before leaving you unless you have changed your mind about coming along with me. You know how many hundreds of times we will all change *ours.* It might be a good idea to rent the apartment until January when I will know for sure except that I suppose that is just when you would *not* want to be in New York. Well it is too complicated to write about but you can bear all these things in mind . . . *Nothing being too imminent.* [ ]

Paul's concert was cancelled because Arthur Gold had a gall bladder operation or attack, I'm not quite sure, but he's been ill. He's better however but they are postponing the whole concert because of lost weeks when they could not rehearse the programme. One more thing. We all think we would like a house perhaps in the town of Nyack on the Hudson from where we could commute and give up New York entirely—but this too has been going on indefinitely hasn't it? I would like that but only if it were big enough so that you could always have a room there which would be yours when you wanted it, which is of course not difficult outside of New York but so impossible in an apartment.

There are other little things to write about. As soon as I got over the hot muggy weather this cold spell put me right to sleep for the [ ]

East Montpelier, VT, December 1947

In January 1948 Jane Bowles arrived in Gibraltar with Jody McLean and crossed over to Tangier by ferry. With Paul and Edwin Denby, Jane and Jody went first to Fez, then set out on their own tour of Morocco. In March Jane accompanied Jody to Spain, saw her off to the U.S., and returned to Tangier, where she moved into the Farhar Hotel. Paul joined her there and shortly received a wire from Margo Jones, who was directing Tennessee Williams' *Summer and Smoke*, asking him to return to New York to do the music for the show.

24
To Libby Holman

Libby darling,

The dog is wonderful. Very soft and made of wool inside and out. The waiter thinks he's wicked, and a young Arab boy mistook his pink ribbon for moustaches. Also he said the dog was a woman because the front paws were breasts. He drew a picture of the dog which I'll keep for you or send. I can't decide. I hope I didn't discourage you with all the bus talk. You know how worked up I get. I've worked myself out of any interest in what Paul or Topper do as long as I don't have to be with them. Paul will make a wise decision (ossir) I'm sure. Are you coming? I hope that you and I can just be on a beach. Maybe that is not your intention. Now it looks as though Paul and I would never go back to the States, but there is time to discuss all this. No answer from Margo Jones so far to Paul's last week's wire. I feel it has all gone up in smoke. Perhaps you could find out what's happening through the agent whose address he gave you. I have a dreary feeling that all kinds of communications have been lost.

I hope I hear from you soon and that you are coming. This is just a note partly about the dog. I imagine it *is* the way I look. Is Louisa back—with or without that God Damned Milly? How is everything and what's happened.

Much love,
The Dog

Tangier, March 24, 1948

In early May Jane and Paul went to Fez, where they stayed at the Hotel Belvedere. While there Jane finished her long short story, "Camp Cataract," and Paul finished his novel *The Sheltering Sky.*

25
To Libby Holman

Dearest Libby,

I have been very excited ever since receiving your telegram. Also if for some reason you don't come, after all, I will have had all the pleasure of looking forward to it anyway. (I am not nearly so well adjusted as I sound.) I think it good that Paul and I wrote contradictory letters because now I feel that you know the worst and the best and are deciding on your own hook. Actually I can't imagine Topper not loving it, *even* if he saw only Fez and Tangier. Certainly it will be worth more to him than staying at Treetops. I didn't mean to make him sound like a mechanic to Paul, but I couldn't guarantee any of his interests except the two Paul mentioned in his letter (workshop and camping trips which you'd told me he liked). I didn't know how interested he was in just travelling and looking around. Lots of bright people haven't been, but have preferred to stay in their own country. Marco Polo for instance. Anyway you know what I mean. I am writing this for Topper's benefit more than for yours because you understand, but he might think I misrepresented him if you read him Paul's letter which I'm sure you did. I think when he gets here Topper himself judging from the heat on the coast can decide how much farther into it he wants to go. We can discuss all that. Paul himself is against taking native buses, since they are constantly tipping over and going off cliffs. Since the war they are all broken down, and so few remain that they load the sides and tops with people which is naturally hazardous anyway. The tires are terrible and they are built (the buses) high and narrow, so you can see how risky they are on a curve. Half the time the brakes don't hold. Cars are very cheap to hire, and it is in no way equivalent to hiring a car in the States or Cuba. We could have lived on one hundred dollars a week the two of us, including everything, *and* hired cars, if we'd wanted to spend more and thus stay a shorter time. I am writing this so that Topper will arrive with an open mind about everything, and not dead set on any way of doing things before he sees the country. I think he'll understand when he *does* see it (OY!). He needn't worry about luxury. Except in Tangier and a few beach towns, the good hotels aren't open. I told you that the best hotel in Tangier was about eight dollars a day or less for two people with meals included, and they are *not* like the Chez Roig meals. Four head waiters and the hors d'oeuvres wagon is three stories high. This is to give you the scale. I am hoping that maybe Ollie will arrive and we can all take a trip together, in that way it will come to nothing. But whatever they decide to do will come to nothing anyway. I realize of course that you have to keep Treetops going whether you are there or not and I imagine that you want everything to be as cheap as possible. I think this must be the case because you were sort of worried when I left. I promise you that Africa will satisfy in this respect (a sentence I borrowed from Jody), but I don't want the men (boys?) to do anything really *dangerous*, whether I am along or not.

I finished my story and am typing it in one more than triplicate (quadruplicate?), so that I will have a copy here to show you. The other three go to my agent, Mrs. Aswell, and Helvetia. Paul has finished his novel as he wrote you, I imagine, and will turn out six stories tomorrow. Please telephone my little Jody before you come, if you do come. She always asks about you in her letters; the number is Lakeville 24. Tell her that you're coming here but don't forget to speak to Mary Anne too and make a fuss over her or there will be more strife. If you come will you be kind enough to bring me the two dresses I left in your apartment in New York, unless they make your luggage overweight. I wrote Scotty about them. The navy one with dots and the sheer black one with broken buttons down the front. At least bring "dotty" if you can't bring both. They should have been found in Ray's closet. I would also like a package of "Zip Epilator" just for fun. For God's sake if you should see Jody by accident in the middle of a field, don't show her this letter. She might not like that sentence quoted. I hope your "Tzoris" (correct spelling?) is a little better and that you *do come*. Oliver wrote you had some success at your club. My love, Libby dear, as ever, J.

Tangier, May 10, 1948

At the end of May, Oliver Smith came to Morocco and joined Paul and Jane in Fez. Soon after he arrived he became ill and for some weeks lay in bed with a high fever. During this time Jane too became ill. She went to a local doctor, a Dr. Cheroux, who told her that there was "something organically wrong" with her heart, though her symptoms soon disappeared.

In June Jane and Paul and Oliver Smith returned to Tangier to meet Libby Holman, who had arrived from the U.S. with Topper. Jane stayed in Tangier while the others took a trip south through the desert and across the High Atlas mountains.

After the visitors left, Paul returned to Tangier, but on July 18 he was called to New York to work on *Summer and Smoke*. Jane remained alone in Tangier at the Hotel Villa de France.

Mornings she worked on her novel *Out in the World*. Much of the rest of the time she spent in pursuit of Cherifa, a young Arab peasant woman who sold grain in the market. It was Paul who had introduced Jane to Cherifa, shortly after her arrival in Tangier.

26
To Paul Bowles

Dearest Bup

It is stupid of me to take so long to get down to writing you. There seems too much really to write about—I mean Fez and money and Africa altogether and my failure to like in it what you do and to like what you do at all anywhere. I love Tangier—the market and the Arab language, the Casbah, etc. And I long to go now to Marrakech and Taroudant. It's a pity and since reading your novel I take it very much to heart. I hope you will not complain about me to Peggy Bate. I know you love to talk behind someone's back, just as I do, but oddly enough I don't get any pleasure complaining about you. On the contrary I am horrified and scared when people attack you because you are difficult to defend at times. Now that I've seen you waiting for O. to arrive and witnessed the subsequent disappointment I shudder to think of my own failure to react properly. I have reason to hope that you simply could not have been that excited about my coming or at least that your excitement was of a different nature. I can't believe that after ten years you would have secretly been expecting someone like yourself (or Edwin Denby) to arrive from Gibraltar. (I am sorry you had to stay there for three days.) At the Farhar I was peculiarly disturbed by the fact that you lingered on in Fez with Edwin instead of rushing to the Farhar to see me. I felt very jealous and left out; I sensed that you were really better off with Edwin and that there would be an unfortunate comparison made at some future date. Alas! it came much sooner than I had expected it would and I have not ceased brooding about it yet; also I have never tried harder to be in your world—to see it the way you did which probably is why I was in such a foul temper the whole time. I wanted to be companionable and pleasant—a source of mild pleasure at meal times and otherwise calm and self-effacing. I am really and truly sorry that it turned out so differently. I don't quite know yet what happened but I do know I have never been so near to a crack-up before. It was not pleasant and I prefer not to think about it ever again. I daresay I won't want to be in Fez ever again, either, unless by next year I've forgotten it all. You are happier there without me anyway, but perhaps the Palais Jamai? Also before I go on to new subjects, I hope that you did not really *think* I would "*pull* a heart attack" on the trip, as you said to Libby and Topper. It's the only thing you've ever said that I've minded, that and your Fez remark about visualizing me in a wheelchair or dead. I was so frightened by my heart anyway. I can find only two explanations for such statements—either you never believed for a minute there was anything wrong at all or else you were really worried and therefore mean. I am at my meanest when I feel the greatest tenderness. Seeing you dead in the novel brought out the spitfire in me at the Belvedere in Fez. Perhaps harpy would be a more suitable word. I was not exactly like Lupe Velez, after all, but more like my Aunt Birdie. Sometimes I find nice explanations like the above for your attitude and sometimes I feel that you saw the whole thing, I mean the state of my health, as nothing but a threat to your trip, which mattered to you more than anything. I wonder . . . It must be that you never believed there *was* anything wrong—but then you must have or you wouldn't have gotten so gloomy and had visions of me in a wheelchair. I thought I was *finished*, I assure you. It was different from thinking, "The war is coming so soon—" but I'm glad now that I did think I had so little time left to live. Cheroux should have never worded his diagnosis the way he did. I told him I was "pulling a heart attack," and he told me that on the contrary there was something organically wrong with my heart—that is why I was frightened. Much more frightened than I told you. I would so much rather have been the neurotic faker than someone really ill and I was still not sure whether I was really well when you mentioned my pulling an attack to Libby. Surely the English in this letter has gone to pieces long ago but I just can't worry about it. You can understand with a little effort what I've written.

I shouldn't mention all this perhaps but I can never write

anything else if there is something that must come out and I'm sure you would not like to be without any letters from me at all. I hope that I'm a horror to even *think* of these remarks and that I should not invest them with too much importance but I cannot forget them, or some aspects of your behavior. I think a word from you would put my mind at rest on this subject. You have a way too of saying things easily so that it wouldn't take you much time. I am not attached to you simply because I'm married to you, as you certainly must know. If I were I could pass over these things conveniently. Oliver thinks that I'm "hanging on to you." I hope you don't think that or that it isn't the actual truth even without your thinking it. I shall approach the awful financial question some other time. Maybe not in a letter. I get upset because you say you have enough money for one but not for two etc. It's probably true, unless we live in a house—it's surely true when one is travelling. It is also true that I could have stayed behind in America indefinitely and have cost you nothing. But now that I am here I am damned if I'll ruin it by worrying about these things. I am extremely grateful to you for letting me stay and use the money. I don't believe I have it coming to me because I'm your wife. I just can't bear that idea and yet I'm not sure either that atavistically I don't probably consider myself—partly—entitled to this sojourn because I am your wife? In other words I feel both things at once. That you are completely free and someone who will help me when he can, out of affection, and yet also that you are a husband. I don't think about the husband part very much but I am trying to be *very* honest. I am not sure either that being confined a bit by the social structure is altogether bad for either one of us. We will see.

The view of the Arab town from my window is a source of endless pleasure to me. I cannot stop looking and it is perhaps the first time in my life that I have felt joyous as a result of a purely visual experience. The noise in the Villa is something I must fight constantly but I cannot leave the *lieu*. Certainly it's the only place in Tangier I want to be. If I left it I would go to the States I think. The Mountain, I know, would be bad in summer unless one found a tree to work under far away. I am just beginning to try to work now and the morning noises are very bad. It makes me frantic because I love it here, but I'm sure that I shall find some quiet spot or else reverse and work at night. Or say from five to nine A.M. I am going with Boussif today about the deed. Cherifa, I'm afraid, is never going to work out. I think she's very much in love with Boussif. She's in a rage because she expected that once his wife left he would marry her, and instead he's taken some woman to cook for him whom he also sleeps with. He brought her to the grain market and introduced her to Cherifa. They all sat in the hanootz according to Lantzmann (I was not there), and joked together. Boussif, however, said that his mistress told Cherifa that only *she*, Cherifa, could come to see Boussif while she lived there, because she was not afraid that Boussif would ever marry a woman who wore no veil and sold grain in the market. I asked Boussif if Cherifa were not insulted, and he said, "No, why?" They are definitely confusing people. I think Cherifa is afraid of me. I saw her sneak behind a stall yesterday when I appeared so that I wouldn't see her. Nonetheless I am determined now to learn Arabic. It is good exercise for the mind in any case and there are more chances that I will get pleasure out of it than not. Even if my evenings with Cherifa and Quinza turn out to be a pipe dream. I am so utterly dependent now on Boussif that it is foolish to even think about it. The pronunciation, Dean says, is impossible to master—ever. One can just vaguely approach it enough to be understood because it takes years to develop certain throat muscles. I said my first words yesterday after Cherifa sneaked behind the stall and I suppose I said them in desperation. The older dyke was there, thank God (she comes to the market irregularly), so I walked over to her and somehow spoke. Just a few words actually, but immediately some old men gathered around me and everyone nodded happily. They said to each other that I spoke Arabic. I am slow and stupid but determined. I shall never of course be as clever as you are.

Customarily I will send your letters immediately upon receiving them from the British Post Office. If they are sent within twenty-four hours they are forwarded free. A few times I have not done this. Reasons: I didn't know it in the beginning, and then once or twice got there, couldn't remember address of Morris Agency, brought letters back here, didn't get them back on time. Have now committed address to memory so no mail will return with me to my room from now on. I must know about your contract. I hope and pray that it is all settled. Oy! I hate to think of it. Also keep me posted as to news about your novel. I shall let you know of any progress or total lack of it on my part (in writing) within a month. It is a little soon yet for me to know whether or not this was a wise decision. (Staying here—I mean.) Of course the less I worry about whether it was or not, the wiser it will have been—and I am more and more pleased that I've stayed so far. I am trying to get Helvetia to come over here, and still think she might be persuaded to come with you if you do come back. I am not very worried about all that, but very eager to see whether I can work or not seriously. If I can't I think I'd better just plain give up writing. Conditions here should be ideal. Except for the awful war cloud, I should say I was very very happy. Naturally, I am moody, but I'm savoring more separate minutes than I have in many years. I love this spot geographically and I'm always pleased to have lots of blue around me. Here there's the water and the sky and the mountains in the distance and all the blue in the Casbah; even in the white, there's lots of blue. The grain market is blue—blue and green. I have had a ladder built so that I could get up on our terrace—about seventy pesetas, and certainly worth it. It is the best view from the Casbah I've seen. The white dome cuts out all that Rif section, thank God, so a room there would be magnificent. I think it would always be small to live in for more than a few days except for one person but very useful as a garçonnière and very profitable to rent, if it were really done up properly. Plumbing etc. We should discuss it further when I've got the deed and when we see each other, here or there. There's no rush after all except that we must make sure the house is really ours. I am going there to cook lunch in a few minutes. Just a pot of ratatouille and some sausage—cheap and very nourishing. Quantities of tomatoes now, so that makes eating simple. It is unfortunate that a hole in the kitchen leads to the bathroom because of the smells. I think the whole bottom part would remain smelly but the room on top would be free of odors. In the bottom there should be a kitchen, closet, bath and room for a servant to sleep—caretaker—and on top the room to read, eat and entertain in—sleep in too, naturally, when one felt like it and there would be part of the terrace left as well. We will decide on all this later. I can't tell now really what I want. I might be fed up with Tangier in three months. But it might be a good investment to improve the house rather than to sell it even if we rented it to Arabs. I know we could rent it to Americans. They love to live in the Casbah and there are lots of bachelors wandering around. Also people like Jay, Bill Chase and others. It's a sweet house and I am really beginning to understand now about your buying it very well. I enclose this check (Dutch royalties on *The Glass Menagerie*). The accompanying note was a mere business form. I have received no notice of your checks coming through but will in a few days go and ask about it. You had better write me the particulars in your next letter as I've forgotten the details. The amount etc. Why don't you call Pearl Kazin at the *Bazaar*? Maybe she could have a drink with you and you might find out whether she's optimistic about selling my story or not. Of course I don't even know whether or not she liked it. Thanks for library card, checkbook etc.

Please—Please write me
Much Love
J.

P.S. Could you try to get Edwin's address for me? Please write my mother immediately. She will want to call you I'm sure so give her your number. Tell her you're coming back here and that I'm crazy about Tangier and therefore stayed behind.

Mother's address: c/o Mayor's
3rd and Main Sts.
Dayton

Tangier, July 1948

27
To Paul Bowles

Dearest Bup,

This must be a short one. I owe letters to H., Libby and O., who wrote me a long Swiss one that was very sweet and interesting. "H" stands for Helvetia, whose letters have been getting better and better. I think if I just stay in Africa for a few more years everything will be fine. Even Mother seems to be calming down. This letter is to assure you that I do have everything you handed over to me in the long narrow envelope and that the receipt from the bank said two hundred and eighty dollars not three hundred and ninety seven or whatever the sum you quoted. I hadn't looked at it when I wrote you because I knew that unless I read the papers you left with me carefully—they're in Spanish—I'd get confused about which was the statement and which was the receipt for the checks. There were two things in the envelope besides the checkbook. I hate reading Spanish legal terminology; in fact everything Spanish gets on my nerves. I don't believe Spain would but you know how they are over here. Perhaps I couldn't stick them over there either—it would be depressing but wonderful to see, as you have assured me many times. The slip acknowledging that the checks had come through also said two hundred and eighty dollars so that *must* be it. I hope there isn't a different receipt. You did say something close to that sum before you left—I'm quite sure of it. In other words, both slips, the one you left inside of "long and narrow" as well as the slip that came through the mails last week, are marked two hundred and eighty bucks, so that must be right. No?

I don't know myself what I meant by aspects of your behavior. (?) I've forgotten. It is true that Oliver was a thousand times more solicitous than you which made me feel that you didn't give a fig, whether I collapsed in the street or not; you must remember that whether I brought it on myself or not, whatever it was, I did think I was going to die or have a heart attack and I was terrified, which I don't think you ever got through your head. I think I expected you to be more worried and concerned than you were, whether I brought it on myself or not. I still don't quite know what the hell it was all about and I suppose the less said about it in letters the better. I am *not* brooding about it and take you at your word that there is no reason to. I don't want for there to be a reason to. I couldn't resist that sentence, because it is just the kind of thing I am longing to write all the time. I am glad that Mary Lou's letter pleased you. P.S. Naturally I'm glad I reworked it—without your advice it wouldn't *exist.* Not that you must expect a sale.

There are many old women and old men at the *Bazaar* who must be convinced that it is the proper material for their magazine; even if Frances McFadden did accept it they could still refuse to have it published. Perhaps Pearl can give you an idea of what to expect. I continue loving Tangier—maybe because I have the feeling of being on the edge of something that I will some day enter. This I don't think I could feel if I didn't know Cherifa and the "Mountain Dyke" that yellow ugly one (!?). It is hard for me to separate the place from the romantic possibilities that I have found in it. I cannot separate the two for the first time in my life. Perhaps I shall be perpetually on the edge of this civilization of theirs. When I am in Cherifa's house I am still on the edge of it, and when I come out I can't believe I was really in it—seeing her afterwards, neither more nor less friendly, like those tunes that go on and on or seem to, is enough to make me convinced that I was never there. My professor has disappeared but I daresay he'll be back. Now that I've mastered a few words it's become an ordeal for me to go into the market. I am frightfully shy and embarrassed by the whole thing—my pronunciation, my inability to understand them most of the time. They each speak differently. All that is a terrible strain and I must steel myself before I plunge into it. I do not underestimate the importance of knowing Jay—who is really sweet to me—because I would not be able to just struggle with Arabic all the time. Also there are days when they disappear entirely and it is nice to know someone here. I am terribly happy because the Mountain Dyke asked me to go for a walk with her either on the mountain or by the sea. I was amazed because I had just about given up getting anywhere with any Arab women ever. I was in a terrible state of despond too because Cherifa had just rushed past me leading a mule to the country. She wore a pink embroidered vest and a new red and white striped blanket. She was on her way to visit her family in the country (three feet out of Tangier). She was supposed to leave three or four days ago and be back yesterday which is precisely why I was hanging around there and instead she was just leaving. I wonder too if I would bother with all this if you didn't exist. I don't know. Surely I would not have begun it—got the idea without you, I mean. It is the way I feel about my writing too. Would I bother if you didn't exist? It is awful not to know what one would do if one were utterly alone in the world. You would do just what you've always done and so would Helvetia but I don't exist independently. I am *doubly* delighted with anything that delights me here because I feel that you are able to participate in my pleasure more than in any pleasure I might have in being with Margaret McKean, or Spivy or simply wandering about New York (which I don't like now, but used to). You know too that I am no hypocrite and would not *pretend* to be pleased—in the first place I couldn't. I know you don't like Tangier much so perhaps it's silly for me to think you can be pleased with my taking any pleasure in it. Perhaps you are not at all pleased. But I think you do approve of my having some Arab women friends and you do see how boring it can be otherwise. I loved Fez as long as we were both working but somehow the whole thing went to pieces after that, as you know. If I ever go back there, I think I'd stay at the Jamai. When you complain about New York, for God's sake don't bring up the radios. Nothing could be worse than the radios here and in Fez. For the rest I agree. If you had any sense you would buy yourself some Birdseye corn or asparagus, some hamburger, canned soups etc. and fix yourself food in the house. Frozen strawberries you love and there are other cheaper fruits available. None of that would be any more difficult than making Klim, tea, "chocolate milk mixed with coffee," and handling the endless paraphernalia one travels with in Africa. Instead of complaining like a maniac why don't you try to solve some way of eating so that you will be stronger when you get to the next place you go? Even if it costs you a little more than the Automat, and it needn't, you would be better nourished. Libby says that Willy May would cook lunch for you and she also said you should call up Scotty at any time and go out there to Treetops. You have no right in the world to complain so much when you've been away an entire year, and it's only the fact that you can be there and earn some money that will permit you to live over here. I don't mean this time but any time. You sound more spoiled than ever, ranting against civilization and the Americans and their noise (after having lived among the Spanish—MY GOD!) and in spite of the fact that I see exactly what you mean and that New York must *really* look hideous after this part of the world, it frightens me to think that you have no part of yourself you can retire into, though that is what you advised *me* to do when the noise and confusion got me down in Fez (on our way to lunch in the carriage). I don't like to see you so helpless and so unable to take one minute of something you don't like gracefully. Please do something about Treetops or your food. You can perfectly well and you will be stronger in the next primitive place you visit. If you think of it that way and not simply as spending money or any effort in New York, you might be able to do it. What do you mean by Peggy's ambivalence—about me? or you? I don't understand. Is she really worried about me? Does she think my coming back would keep you there longer? What's it all about? I have no plans. Do you think you'll come back here or do you prefer to go somewhere else. For God's sake go where *you* want to go and don't dare come to NORTH AFRICA just because of me if you'd rather go to West Africa. How can I say yet what I'll do? I refuse to. I am very happy—with moments of depression because I always have them, but very few. I am delighted I stayed. Tangier is wonderful in summer. I have certain ideas but it is all too premature to start trying to work any of them out. I am typing the little story for George and will send it on in a few days. Be good and please get yourself some decent food. All you do with Birdseye food is to plop it in boiling water. One box of corn or peas is enough for two meals and delicious. Then there are the package soups and hamburger you can make. I think too, that you should go out to Treetops. Helvetia is waiting for a letter from me before she writes you. She would like very much to have you out there if and when you can go. I shall write her immediately—and for God's sake get there and eat before you come back here or anywhere else—or don't you want to? At least get to Libby's. Much Love

J.

P.S. This was to be a short one.

If hamburger is too expensive why not tell Willy May to put a stew on for you in the morning when she comes—beef—carrots—onions—vegetables are cheap in summer—celery—corn etc. She could easily do it every day, alternating beef and lamb. Débrouilles toi—enfin!

I don't remember about your coat—ask Scotty if by any chance it's out there—as for the cigarette cases—God knows.

I take for granted that you don't mind my being over here—will come home if money matters make it advisable for me to live at H's or Libby's.

Tangier, c. July/August 1948

28
To Paul Bowles

Dearest Buppie—

I am off to Cherifa's hanootz. Our relationship is completely static: just as I think that at least it is going backwards (on the days when she sneaks behind a stall) I find that it is right back where it was the next day. Nothing seems to move. I have finally, by wasting hours and hours just hanging about mentioning the Aid Es Seghir about every five seconds, managed to get myself invited for tonight. So I shall go soon to the grain market from where we will leave for M'sallah together. I don't know whether I shall walk behind her or in front of her or parallel to her on the other side of the street. I made my invitation secure by suggesting a chicken. I made wings of my arms and flapped them—"djdédda"—your phonetic spelling and mine are different so don't correct the above in your mind.

Later: It would take far too many pages to explain how the Aid Es Seghir came a day sooner than moon experts expected that it would, and how I therefore went to Cherifa's the very night after the carousing was over. Because in a normally arranged world the whole appointment would have evaporated. On the feast day they don't come to the market at all, and on that day we had fixed our rendezvous there which was in everyone's opinion the day *before* the feast. I was to give her the chicken then so that it could be plucked and put with the olives for the following day. It is all so ridiculous—because others said it wouldn't come for five days. Then I worried about the chicken rotting—well how can I ever explain this? But somehow in this peculiar world where nothing is arranged there is a sudden miraculous junctioning, a moment of unraveling when terribly complicated plans—at least what would be a complicated plan anywhere else—work out somehow as if in a dream, where one has only to think of something for it actually to appear (your novel). It would take years to believe in this, and not to see it merely as an amusing mirage—I mean to believe that such things *do* work out for the Arabs *when* they do, not because there is a law of chance but because such a lack of concentration on even the immediate future would allow all sorts of mysterious rhythms to flower, which we are no longer in possession of. I wonder. The Herrera soup coming down through the streets from all the far sections of Tangier to the Arabs who remained in the Socco after dark—always on time, always warm, and always sufficient to serve the number of people gathered—just like Cherifa's tiny blue tea pot with its endless supply of tea.

Well, in any case I wandered down there at 7:30 A.M. just thinking, Well, maybe she has thought of our appointment and come to wait for me at some point. She wasn't there but the old yellow-faced mountain dyke was, and alas I had to eat quantities of perfectly terrible tortilla-like bread soaked in rancid oil, flies and honey!! Then I followed a parade thinking, "Well it's such a funny country, maybe I'll meet her this way." The policeman said the parade was going to M'sallah but of course it stopped a little above the Villa de France, and the next policeman—also an Arab—said they were *not* going to M'sallah but turning 'round and going back down to the Mendoubia. By then I'd already waited around for it an hour, while it just remained in the square behind the Villa. I was planning to follow it to M'sallah. It was thus far the hottest day in the year and the Tangier flies in August are terrific. Funnily enough I don't mind very much because I am having fun. The men in the parade, some of those wonderful old men, were really beautiful in pink chiffon over white, some in pointed red fez and others in the usual square (?) ones. The horses were wildly spirited even in the heat, and there were hundreds of women gathered all on one side of the road in beautiful djellabas. I went back to the market feeling that there was no chance of meeting her, but somehow I went anyway. She *was* there—no glimmer of surprise or pleasure in her eye when she saw me, in spite of the arrangements having been completely bitched up because of the Aid Es Seghir coming a day sooner. Probably because she'd forgotten there were any arrangements. I had to go through the whole thing again about the chicken "dar dialek gadi nimshi maak" etc. and she said I should meet her at 7:00 P.M. there in the grain market. At 10:30 we started for M'sallah with her cousin Mohammed (who is a good musulman), as our escort. He always steps in when she is on the outs with Boussif—which is now the case. I shall tell you the rest of the story some other time. I miss you and I wish that we could once be together some place where we could both be having such foolish days and yet days that are so full of magic too. It would be fun to come back and talk about them. I can see that I would *hate* to have some one waiting here at the hotel for me, with an eye on the watch and feeling very sad. How eleven women wandered in and out of Cherifa's house and all had tea out of the tiny pot in the morning is something I so wish I could make you see in *color*. But I'm afraid I never can.

I was delighted to hear from my mother that you called her up and that you *are* doing the show. I would have felt so terribly responsible if you weren't because I half pushed you into it. I appreciate your calling her tremendously. I imagine you'd be bored to tears staying with her in Dayton—she mentioned a possibility. You needn't put yourself through *that*. If you see her for God's sake don't mention *anything* about my being nervous or thinking my heart was bad—*nothing* remotely connected with that or she'll be right over here. Of course you wouldn't. Perhaps I *am* the "Dorothy Dix" of Tangier. But for the Arabs, the world's biggest "sucker"—I don't know. But I don't mean any "double entendre." I just realized with horror the pun. I have *no* occasion to make one. I am being extremely economical so don't worry about that. I would always be completely scrupulous about your money because you earn it. I continue pleased that I've stayed on but I'm in despair about Arabic. I can speak a little but understanding them when they speak to each other is another cup of *tea*. Much love

Teresa

P.S. Your checks came through so be at peace about that.

Tangier, c. July/August 1948

29
To Natasha von Hoershelman

Natasha dear,

Thank you for the postal card from Fire Island which has practically ruined my life over here in Africa, now that I've decided to stay awhile. There are many reasons why I've stayed but since actually I don't make decisions ever, I am somehow here because I didn't leave. Paul's gone back to do music for the new Tennessee Williams show. He'll return to Africa probably but that won't influence me. My only reason for returning now, as I've said before, or haven't I ever said it, is you and Katharine and as I'm off liquor for a while I don't think it would be wise to rush home to see you yet. I feel that H. can get here, I mean Helvetia. I am learning Arabic although one can't really learn it at all—you could because you're Russian. Still I can say a little. There's a harem I'm trying to get into, after all our joking about that. There really and truly is. Two veiled pitch black women (I've seen one of them only) and a yellow faced savage down from the mountains who is their husband, I think. It is hard not knowing the language to be sure—yet. I am at a great disadvantage being a *Christian* (OY!) also a woman and any of the market women are ashamed to be seen with me in the streets. Actually I know only two of them. The yellow one and my little Cherifa who is about twelve years younger than myself. No one is fond of me at all, but I like to look at them and listen to what they say, even though I don't understand. I see the Arabs in the market mostly. It is right under my window, almost, so I can run out and look at someone whenever I please. I expect maybe to go to the house belonging to the wild yellow one's family for a feast on Saturday that ends Ramadan (the month of fasting)—God knows how I'll get back. It's way off in the poorest Arab section and I shall never find my way home. They will probably just turn me loose at four in the morning after eleven hours of tea and say goodnight. No one I'm sure will accompany me since they seem to wander all over alone. But then it is all right for them and traditional to do so (but not on the beach or in the country—just in the towns). I don't know the yellow one at all but because she's seen me in Cherifa's stall a lot she decided to ask me. The worst of it is I'm so mixed up by the Arabic pronouns and verbs that I don't actually know whether I asked myself to her family's house or whether she asked me. Surely I asked myself because they don't invite one. Not these market ones. She came over to the stall and somehow in my lousy Arabic I must have got myself into the feast without meaning to. It isn't sure that I'll actually go either—they will probably never mention it again.

Will you please send the enclosed letter off to Sylvia immediately. If I were sure Katharine were not suddenly in Vt. I would ask her to do it. You can perfectly well take it to the office and stick a stamp on it. In fact I have decided to send this to the office where you must have all the necessary equipment. I meant to write you days ago about Mary Lou and now if you don't send the letter off it will be too late. Read it and you'll see why I'm sending it. Kiss Katharine for me. I miss you terribly. For God's sake don't send any more cards from Fire Island— Much Much Love

Jane

Kiss Lola—this is for her to read as well. How is she? It is very important that the letter go off to S. immediately.

Tangier, August 1948

30
To Paul Bowles

Dearest Bup—

I started a long letter to you the other day, telling you all about my terrible afternoon with "Tetum" (the Mountain Dyke). We never did go to the mountain—in fact she never had any intention of going there. We went to a dry triangular square, right in Tangier, surrounded by modern villas and near a bus stop. It was too long and sad and funny and involved to write about, so I gave up. All I can say is that I have never been so frustrated by anyone in my life as I am being right now—except by Iris Barry, and that lasted eleven years—so God knows I'll probably stick around here forever, just for an occasional smile from Tetum or Cherifa. I wrote you how exciting it was to feel on the edge of something. Well, it's beginning to make me very nervous. I don't see any way of getting any further into it, since what I want is so particular (as usual); and as for forgetting them altogether, it's too late. For me Africa right now is the grain market and being an obsessive maybe nothing will change that. I am still learning Arabic and I still love Tangier but I cannot tell how long it will take me to admit that I'm beaten. It is not any personal taste that I'm obliged to fight but a whole social structure, so different from the one you know—for certainly there are two distinct worlds here (the men's world and the women's), as you've often said yourself. As for Cherifa, I'm utterly dependent on Boussif as far as seeing her goes, and he's not around much lately.

I still have a dim hope that if I learned to speak Arabic she would be friendly *maybe* and I could sit in the hanootz with her when I chose to. She never asks me in unless Boussif is there and then he does the asking. Either she is ashamed to be seen with me alone or, quite sensibly, doesn't see the point because I cannot really speak to her. I don't know. I am merely trying to know her better socially (having given up hope as far as anything else is concerned). I can't bear to be continually hurled *out* of the Arab world. The rest of Tangier really doesn't interest me *enough*, though I am very grateful to have Jay here and Bill, but most particularly Jay. I would be lonesome otherwise, though I wouldn't be if they would let me sit with them in the market when I wanted to. Perhaps you have never been in this inferior position vis-à-vis the Arabs. I can understand how if one could get all one wanted here and were admired, courted, and feted, that one would *never never* leave. Even so, without all that—and you've had it—I have never felt so strongly about a place in my life, and it is just maddening not to be able to get *more* of it. How I would love to have walked on the mountain with Tetum (I realize it's a ridiculous name). Naturally she couldn't and never will, and I was a fool to believe her. She's a big liar, and each day she says just the *opposite* of what she said the day before. Do any of the men do that? I mean really the *exact* opposite. Whenever I suggest *anything* to her at all—even a glass of tea—she cuts her throat with an imaginary knife and says something about her family—at least she uses the imaginary knife one day, and on the next is prepared to do anything (verbally only). I am puzzled, vexed, and fascinated, but deep inside I have an awful feeling I shall never never find out any more than I know now. Still, it is only August. We'll see—but I haven't much hope. I wept for two hours after my walk with Tetum. So you see I am very different about these things than you are. I didn't realize how much I had hoped for and how vividly I had pictured the walk on the mountain until I started to cry. After I had cried awhile, I began to laugh. And if *only* you had been here it wouldn't have mattered, because frustrating as it all was it was certainly *ridiculous*, and you would have loved hearing about it. I wish to hell I could have the same sort of adventures in Fez or that you liked Tangier. I cannot imagine a better time really than being in a place we both liked and each of us being free and having adventures, even if mine were frustrating—they would be more amusing naturally if you were here. I wonder how I shall ever be able to leave the view of the Casbah. It means so much to me. Enfin—I do not have to leave yet.

I was delighted about H.B. taking my story. Please speak to Pearl about it. She writes that when Mary Lou gets back she will talk price with the top ladies, and that in any case I shall get at *least* $350—and they hope more. I *certainly* think I should get more, don't you? I can do nothing from here. But talk to M.L. when she gets back. Under separate cover I am sending Ivan Von Auw a copy of my story. I want him to show it to Knopf too. Tell him it's going to be published and that I want an advance on a novel. If that fails, I want Ivan to approach another publisher. One of them is already interested (I forget which) and if he can't get me something then I want another agent. It's all too ridiculous—but I feel the time to strike is now. I have written the story for George Davis and am typing it. I don't work nearly enough—as usual—and keep hoping that the next day I will change my habits completely.

Please do get in touch with Ivan (under Harold Ober in the book). Just call Ober and ask for Ivan. Do you hate to do this? After helping me so much with the story, surely you won't mind this final effort. Knopf might be interested in seeing it—though probably not. I think I should get another publisher. Maybe you will have time to do nothing. I shall also write Ivan all this but I would feel better if I knew *you* were looking after my interests there too—that is, if you would speak to both him and Mary Lou. I have often suggested to Ivan that he speak to Carl Van V. about myself and Knopf. Carl's a great friend of Alfred's and an admirer of mine as well. I think the *Bazaar* can certainly afford more than $350. Don't you? But I don't want to make things too difficult for Mary Lou. I hope you'll be there long enough to see her before going on the road. If not, speak to Pearl. I'd rather sell it for 350 however than *not* sell it at all, naturally, so be careful. I suppose there isn't much you can do really. But at least speak to them all, *particularly* Ivan. You must write me about your own novel. I hope you are on the track of a publisher.

Pearl and Mary Lou both have written me wonderful letters about "Camp Cataract." I'm so happy about all that. Now that it has been fixed up, I *know* that it's the best thing I've ever done—and always was latently. But I don't think it would ever have been if you hadn't helped. I wish though that you had liked it more. I would try Knopf for the novel if I were you. He loves composers and that might help him to advertise a bit, though I know you don't want them to plug that. There should be a letter from you soon. *Are* you coming back? It would be so wonderful here with a car. Tangier weather is *perfect* in summer. I would like to buy some little mattresses for the house soon, and then when you come back we will discuss seriously whether or not to build onto it—that is, if you *do* come back. Or have you decided to go to Dakar? If you think the war's coming any minute, let me know. I daresay in that case I should hurry out of here. Try and bring H. back with you—if you are coming. I'm sure if you wrote her to come with you and chose a decent boat, she would come, particularly if you did all the arranging. I hope you have found some friends in New York since you last wrote me.

Much Love—

J.

P.S. Dearest Bup—

Just received your letter and was delighted to have it though furious at your agent for being an idiot. I think you should pick your own publishing houses. She must be mad. How lucky Carson is to have someone in love with her. I feel that no one will ever be in love with me again.

If and when I leave Africa never to return it will be because I saw exactly what I have always wanted and couldn't have it. The house is fine. I now have the name of the owner and have gone twice to the Mendoubia. But the right people weren't there.

Much Love,

J.

P.P.S. Don't see Mary Lou Aswell unless you want to about my story and don't mention the sum she quoted to me originally. She'll do all she can I know. However you can certainly say that you *personally* think I should get a better price than that.

Pearl wrote at *least* $350—which makes me feel they'll pay $400. I don't know. Mary Lou is always on the writer's side so perhaps there is no point in seeing her except for fun—and I would like you to. She's an angel and I miss her very much.

Do what you like. But definitely see Ivan.

Tangier, August 1948

31
To Katharine Hamill and Natasha von Hoershelman

Katharine dear and Natasha,

Will you get this to my agent—immediately? I have lost his address. Naturally you can keep it for one *night* if you want to read it *OR* if you get it before a weekend he will probably be out of town. I am sending it to *Fortune* in case you, K, are in Vermont.

It is important for me to get it to him quickly because I want Paul to speak to him and Paul *may* be *leaving*. The story has been accepted by the *Bazaar* but I'm trying to get more money for it. I want Ivan (the agent) to get the MS to Knopf—who will read it—and if he likes it I want Ivan to try for an advance on a novel. If he can't get it from Knopf I may try to change publishers. In any case Paul knows all this and will discuss it with him—the reason for the haste. *However* call Ivan up and ask him how quickly he can get around to reading it, and if there's a delay it might as well stay with you for a day or two. Naturally I'd like all of you to see it (most of all *Kay* Guinness, the critic). But I daresay if both of you get through it, I will be lucky. If it does arrive on a weekend *OR* if he says to keep it two days, whoever sees it—Lola or Rosalind might want to or Angelica (she's gone?)—please make read it chez toi. (That means in ***your*** house—***fedar dialek*** in Arabic—an impossible language for me to learn. You can see how unlike anything it is.) The agent is named Ivan Von Auw, c/o Harold Ober in the book—in other words not listed under his own name. Call him. I suggest handing him the script—perhaps on the street to avoid elevators. The Ober office is near you.

Love,
J.

P.S. Thank you for letter. Will have Bubble telephone you. Let me know if MS reaches you—the minute it does. I will write more fully soon. Mr. Von Auw is pronounced Mr. Von Ow!

Tangier, August 1948

32
To Paul Bowles and Oliver Smith

Dear Paul and Oliver,

This is a business letter that I am sending both of you in case it does not reach one of you.

One letter is going to Paul in N.Y., the other I shall send to my mother in Dayton, since she may be able to get it to him on the road. She wrote that they might see each other in Cleveland. I believe this matter regards Paul more than you, Oliver, because as I said you will probably never come here again. Still the house *is* half yours and you did say you were interested so I don't consider you out of it either, unless you want to be, in which case you are.

In any case, as it is, it is neither livable nor rentable even to an Arab, nor could I even invite Cherifa or Tetum there, it is so poor compared to their houses. I had a man come and see it, an Arab, very reliable, I *think*—at least the friend who introduced me I *know* is reliable, and he said that they had robbed

Paul prettily on the house. He has lots of property here himself and estimated that you could sell it for twenty-five thousand pesetas, at the most. I know you bought it in francs but I didn't go into that. If you fixed it up you could sell it for that price plus what it cost you to fix it up. In other words you would always have the original three hundred dollar loss, no matter how many rooms you added on. However you could make up the three hundred dollar loss (say that it is *roughly* that) by living in it or renting it. I have a feeling too that it would be far easier to sell once it can accommodate a family. They all demand two rooms because of the segregation business, which means that now it is uninhabitable except by a bachelor. Perhaps I am mad to think of selling it to an Arab, but I know that lots of them buy property and then rent it and sell the key over and over again to other Arabs, which is a good way to live. The man I spoke to seems to know his business perfectly and gave me an estimate of five hundred and seventy dollars with a leeway of two thousand pesetas, including the fireplace. He could not discuss the water since I wasn't able to tell him exactly how far the pipe would have to be laid. Actually the water is the least of anyone's worries because all summer there isn't much anyway. Little boys come to the door all the time and one can keep great cisterns of it in the kitchen just as the Arabs do. This price would not include changing the rooms all around, as Oliver suggested. It would simply be the cheapest easiest way of adding on. I think eventually the present kitchen could be made into a bathroom and the bathroom into a kitchen—they don't really use kitchens anyway—but that could come later and could be done without changing all the plumbing around—or no plumbing—but there is some sort of pipe in the bathroom and kitchen even now. This same man is looking for a house for me to rent in M'sallah. (1000 pesetas a month is about as cheap as they come there or anywhere.) I thought I might try one out. Even if I loved the one in M'sallah I think that our property should be improved. No other place will ever have a view like that and I know that it can be terribly attractive. Once fixed I'm sure we can (if we want to) sell the key for three hundred dollars and rent it for five hundred pesetas a month or sell it. Also if any of us are flat broke it is a place to be. I'm thinking more of Paul or me now—during lean months when we wouldn't want to be paying any rent. I doubt very much that I can find anything in M'sallah but if I do I shall buy some mattresses that can be transferred to the other house *if* it gets fixed up.

I want an answer on whether you and O. or you or O. want to do this or not. I think you should consider it more from a practical point of view than in terms of my plans. To have everything depend on me would frighten me right out of Tangier. I would promise to stay and see it built and even place a reliable servant in it, if you want me to—if I were leaving and you were not coming. Naturally in case of war I don't know what I'd do. If I did find something I preferred in M'sallah I might rent ours once it were fixed up or leave it empty if one of you were returning. Two houses would be ideal of course for many reasons. I doubt that I will find anything in M'sallah, but if I did I would have a much easier time getting into a life with my one or two Arab friends because inviting them to the Medina is like inviting them to New York. I think if they grew to know me and trust me better eventually I could invite them to the Medina but I know that a séjour in M'sallah first would be indicated. If it turned out to be wonderful there it wouldn't interfere with our having fixed our house. After all that does belong to us or rather you and O. and nothing else will ever have that view. I repeat it will not only rent well, once arranged, but be a thousand times more saleable. Still I feel that watching the boats from the top room at night (the lights in the harbor) may be so enchanting that none of us would ever want to give it up—whether, when here, we live in various combinations, hotels and other houses as well, keeping ours for a garçonnière, or when broke if one or two or all of us squeeze in there which would be possible once the room was added. Certainly for short periods it will be perfectly livable à deux ou à trois. I would love to know your opinions on this matter. If you are both interested the investment would come to about three hundred dollars each. Tangier, by the way, is perfect in summer, not a cloud in the sky ever and mostly cool. If the work is to be done it should be done before rains come. I enclose the plans as he suggests them. They are inaccurate but give you an idea of what it will be like.

If he builds a room big enough to cover the whole roof (he

says it *could* take the weight), the downstairs will have no light whatsoever, except from the only window, which would never reach the patio. The plan at present is to have a small room on the top floor (but considerably larger than the one downstairs) with the open terrace in front, as you and Oliver decided before leaving. The new room would cover the patio kitchen and bathroom leaving just a slice of the patio (dark checked space in both diagrams) for heavy glass, the kind you walk on. It will be the only way of lighting the patio once the skylight is destroyed to make the flooring for the new room. Otherwise there would be literally no éclairage at all, except in the front room. Even though he doesn't seem to agree about the front half not supporting the weight, I personally think it better not to render the bottom part of the house almost useless, and I think too that a terrace in front of the room would be very nice. The stairs would lead out of the dark windowless room one door going into the terrace (arrows) and the other into the new room. (I mean "opening into.") I prefer reaching the terrace from the stairs and not through the room. It will be prettier to have three little windows across the room's front than a window on either side of a door. The stairs would be in a turning double flight with space under them for shelves and storage. I think too that storage space could be built into either end of the terrace for practically no money at all. Or a little kitchen or bathroom—but all that could come later. The house would be unbearably messy—small rooms always are—and all Arab houses derive part of their charm from the impeccable order that reigns within them. Naturally if Paul chooses to live in it with everything spread out, it is his privilege. I would not care to be in it under such circumstances, and he *himself* would I hope prefer it neat. There is a radio that plays Egyptian music constantly until about ten thirty at night but it is not very bothersome from the top floor. Please let me know if you want this done. I know that whatever else I find—although it may please me because of size and the fact that I don't want to live alone but eventually with one or two Arab women as well as you and O.—the view from the house we have will never be duplicated. Certainly not in M'sallah and I know how much that means to both of you and myself too. If you think I should sell the house let me know too or if you think I should go ahead on the building I will then use my own judgment about waiting or going ahead. Naturally if I saw something else that seemed perfect it would be silly to go through the bother of building on ours, though the money I'm sure we could get back. The cost in material is low at the moment—the only reason for deciding shortly. If you are definitely sure you want the room built, one or both of you, I will do it even if I decide against it—but I should at least know whether you want me to go ahead should I decide to. I am furious with Paul because he hasn't written to say he was glad my story was accepted. Please write both of you.

Personally, fixed up I know the house would be charming though small. Perfect for love affairs, little parties and to paint or write in. If Paul is returning he should try to get passage back on American Export to Casa. It's only two hundred bucks. I hope you don't take forever to answer this letter. If I could sell another story and get an advance on my book I too would divide the expenses of the new room, which would make it ridiculous to even consider not building because even now by using it for half a year or less we would get our money's worth out of it, if we then sold it, in spite of the loss. You must write soon.

Much much love,
J.

Paul: Just received your letter. Your novel is *not* a bad novel—don't be ridiculous. I will write you further on that. The deed is virtually ours—remains only the signature of the grand Vizir of the Mosquée—he's been ill—purely a matter of form. The deed will tell whether we can build directly on our neighbor's walls or *not*. If not, the cost will be a little higher. I *should* have the deed within a week they say: *Also* if you want me to go ahead before you come back and if for some reason I can't stick Tangier any longer (frustration) I shall go back and leave the work to you. *But* if I start it I will see it through. I will know a great deal more in a few weeks. I can't go into it now. Much Love J.

Tangier, September 1948

33
To Paul Bowles

Dear Bup—

I was naturally very upset when a check I'd made out to the Villa de France bounced back (1000 pesetas). I called the bank up and raised hell and then when I went down there I found out they were right. I spent one hour poring over the accounts and verifying with my own eyes the checks you drew *after* the statement made out on the 30th of June (the only one in my possession and which you left with me in the long envelope, thank heavens—although I know the bank is honest). In any case your balance then was $497.90 and with the additional $280.24 that arrived afterwards, the total added up to $778.14. Your own checks however, cashed after June 30th, added up to $524.00. (I enclose the little slips with the checks jotted down—and I did insist on seeing them though they wouldn't *give* me the cancelled checks.) You probably don't remember now what they were for, but I know two of them were for me (the ten and the fifty). Anyway that left me with exactly $254.14. I'd understood there was much more or I would have known I was soon coming to the end of the supply. I naturally have all the slips that I get each time I draw money but they never send out statements telling you how much your *balance* is. Since I have all my slips in order, I thought eventually I'd ask for a statement and add them up to see if they tallied. When you left you said that you hoped there would be some money left when you came back. I don't understand—you said I should budget myself at 100 pesetas a day. I checked in here on the 18th of July (my hotel bill started then), roughly 11 weeks (75 days), and according to the money allowed me I should have spent in that period of time (counting the peseta at 30) roughly $223.00. (Figure it out yourself if you like—say eleven weeks at 700 pesetas a week—or ten weeks—it's pretty close anyway.) Counting the money ($25) I have left, I find I have now spent 234 dollars of the $254.00 you left for me. In other words I'm about ten, eleven, or twelve dollars over my budget. I bought a skirt for nine, so actually I think I have done very well. When you went away, I thought 100 pesetas a day was an enormous amount but that was during Ramadan when I ate bread and soup every night in Cherifa's stall. (I had done that while you were on the trip.) But then to eat bread in one's room alone every night is quite a different matter. I eat at *least* once a day in my room, and *usually* twice. Anyway whatever extra money I *had* went to Jacques and I have all his pictures in return. I couldn't let him starve—after all—and it was nice having him in the house. I bought him paints three times. Whatever extra money I ever will have, I shall spend, from now on, on presents—maybe. I doubt that I ever will have any extra though. My room with service and breakfast comes to 55 pesetas a day, which leaves me 45 pesetas to live on. When you figure in tips, laundry, drugs, stamps—you can see very well that I can't be throwing money around. A decent meal costs 30 pesetas, as you know, minimum. Still one can get an indecent one for 12, 22, or 18 pesetas, and I have eaten at the Parade *free* and a lot at a special rate. I am not complaining but saying that 100 pesetas (unless one is in a house) is less than I *thought* it was. There are days when I spend only 10 of my 45 pesetas. But then suddenly the next day I spend sixty for one reason or another—laundry or the maid is due for a tip or drugs—or plain boredom with eating junk in my room, and I go out and have a decent meal. I think the Farhar would amount to the same money or more but I'd get fed. However I would prefer eating the way I do to spending every cent on their awful cooking. With the ten percent service there I'd have about seven pesetas leftover a day to spend (within the budget), and the truck down to town costs five. Still I may go there, though I would gain nothing financially. I cannot decide whether to come back or stay on here. Naturally I can live at Libby's in the States and I would not be such a drag on you.

Still I am not sure you wouldn't prefer me to wait if you are coming. I have done no work lately because I am in a very poor frame of mind, suffering from what you suffer from in New York—except that it does not seem to interfere with *your* work. I find I can think of nothing else and yet I cannot *bring* myself to leave. I refuse to face the fact that there is no hope for me other than a *slightly* increasing social life with Tetum and Cherifa. By offering a present at the right moment, I manage to keep my oar in. Perhaps if I were here long enough and I really learned the language thoroughly (I now speak I suppose about the way you did—or less—which is hardly conversation), I suppose I might get further, though I doubt it. Tetum has her friend Zodelia, and Cherifa is mad about Boussif. That no longer bothers me since I am crazy mad about Tetum—a hopeless hopeless situation. I feel a kind of fever and I even wonder if she hasn't given me a gri-gri to eat—a gri-gri made for Europeans and which prompts them to give away everything they own. Fortunately I restrain myself. But it's the war situation that has been driving me frantic, mainly because I think at every second that I should go home before it's too late, if it isn't too late already. I shall write you again about all that but please, if you are in New York, go down to the bank (address enclosed) immediately and deposit at least $100 to your Hassan account. Then tell them to wire Hassan (deferred) that the money has been deposited. Until then I shall be eating not very well because I don't want to borrow, and my hotel bill will be coming up soon—still they will carry me. But it's awful being here with only twenty-five dollars. So don't delay. Enclosed are the dates when Hassan will be closed, so you can judge whether an air mail letter won't be just as expedient as a wire. In case you can reach Tangier just before a holiday (several are coming up), I would appreciate a wire. The cheapest rate won't be so expensive. I am writing Scotty to do this for me, if she finds out you're not in town, which she can find out easily enough by ringing you. I feel better about the war today, but I've had a very bad unsettling week. You must write what *you* think. Oliver seems willing to go into building on to the house. Get together with him about it. He seems to be doing it to please me but how do I *know* how pleased I'd be? I think it should be on an investment basis. I'll try to find the old man at the Embassy when I've got the deed or maybe before. Are you sure the radio won't drive you crazy? There is one quite near. I know exactly how I'd like to fix the little room downstairs. I may wire you—suddenly—but God knows where you are. I don't see *how* you could have made such a miscalculation on the money really or why you didn't think to warn me but then you thought your checks amounted to much more than they did too—the ones on the New York bank. I feel very deserted and unadvised somehow. Have you seen Ivan? I wish you would help me on a talk with Knopf or *get* me another agent if you think Ivan hopeless. I can't bring myself to send the story to George. I suppose if I were dead sure I could never have Tetum I'd leave but it is the nature of Cupid not to allow those who are stricken to see the truth, so that I do see and I refuse to all at once. Still socially I am making some headway, particularly in a new role that started last week—that is of a procurer for Cherifa. I procure Boussif for her when he disappears, which he does for days at a time. Tetum doesn't touch liquor by the way. If she did it would have made things easier. Still my being European makes everything almost impossible. Are you coming here or not? I know you'll go on to French Morocco and I might go along for a while anyway, depending on where you were headed. It is all too mixed up for words. Naturally if I started building the room, I *would* stay until it was finished—no matter how unhappy I was. Then if everything was awful, you could decide whether you wanted to keep it or not. There's an Arab who wants to buy it now—Mohammed Ouezzani told me—but he looked very doubtful when I told him how tiny it was at present. What about this Mohammed Ouezzani—is he honest? Jay swears by him. He did his contracting for him. I think that I shall spend the two feast days (the Ayd El Kebir) at Cherifa's house—except that it's going to mean buying a sheep. She's trying to get one out of me already. She makes a horn out of her hand and says "Baaa" and then "Thank you." I shall certainly try to avoid buying a whole sheep, even if I have some money from Mary Lou by then, though I expect to have to invest a little money in the Arab part of my life—the *only* reason for being here, at least the most important one—though the view of the Casbah and being able to see the ocean remain very important to me. And somehow I do *love* Tangier. I might be just horrified to wake up and find myself not in Africa. It is all very odd. I shall write again.

Love,
Jane

P.S. Please, please attend to the money—I don't want to be embarrassed at the hotel.

I've started on my novel and as usual getting back into it is hell! The new war crisis doesn't help either. In two weeks or three I should feel more definite about things (ossir).

There is a Jewish holiday a week from Wednesday. I *really* would love it if you had the bank wire Hassan, as I'll be getting jittery if I have to wait very long and the hotel may raise hell. Letters can take nine days!

Tangier, October 1, 1948

34
To Libby Holman and Scotty

Dearest Scotty and Libby or one of you or nobody,

Through some awful miscalculation on the checks he cashed, Paul left me with the impression that I had twice as much money here as I actually do. I think he forgot that he'd drawn out about five hundred dollars of the seven hundred he left. Anyway I'm overdrawn and sitting in Africa without cent one. I've written Paul about it naturally and expect to have the money soon, but in case he's on the road would one of you send me some immediately? He may be in Vermont too. He'll pay you the minute he sees you (ossir). I could try Oliver on this too but you know what reaching him is like and Paul said something about *his* going on the road.

If Libby is away, Scotty, call her and get the O.K. on it or if you can't get hold of her would you advance me the money yourself. I assure you you'll really get it right back from Paul. Libby said I could do this if I got stuck and couldn't reach anyone. In fact she told me to write Polly, but I think this is better and more intimate. The only trouble is that the banks are closed *here* today and tomorrow. Stupidly enough I lost the address they gave me of their corresponding bank in New York; I didn't lose it but sent it off in my letter to Paul and now have to wait until Wednesday before I can find out what it is. The point is this: by depositing the money there you can have them wire the bank here that the money has been deposited to Paul's account and then I can draw it out here. Otherwise the money has to be wired which costs a fortune. This way you can just have them send a deferred cable (cheaper rate that way) saying the money has been deposited, but the *actual money* doesn't have to be wired.

I'm almost certain their bank in New York is the Irving Trust Co., Number something Wall Street (number one I *think*). Please call them and ask them if they are the ones who handle the accounts for Salvador Hassan and Sons, Tangier, Morocco. If they say yes, please have someone deposit one hundred dollars to the account of Paul Bowles, Salvador Hassan and Sons, Tangier, Morocco and ask them to wire Salvador Hassan and Sons, Tangier, that the money has been deposited. As soon as the Hassan bank here gets the wire I can draw on it. The Irving Trust Company sends the wire of course and pays for it out of the money deposited. The only other thing to do is to wire the money straight off. If the Irving Trust Co. has never heard of Salvador Hassan, then I'm really stuck. In that case take out of the hundred whatever it costs to wire the money. (Twelve or thirteen dollars I *think*, which is why I want to avoid it.) If I'm wrong on that it would be simpler to wire the money straight off—I mean if the sum isn't that important. I don't know who could go to the Irving Trust Co. for me, unless Polly has runners in his office. I don't understand much about those things or what a runner would wear if he did go down to the Irving Trust Co. Be sure and tell the runner to tell the Irving Trust Co. to wire that the money has been deposited. They must not write a letter and then toss it out to sea in a bottle. I should be uneasy if they did that. Naturally try and call Paul first (at Libby's) because he has probably done it all already. If he *hasn't*, although you do reach him and he is in New York, give him hell and tell him to please hurry. I need the money in time for the feast of the lamb which is twelve days from today (or eleven if the moon shows early). You can also try to reach Oliver who will pay you back if Paul's away but it might be easier to come over here with the money and we can spend it together. I am terrible sorry to bother whomever I am bothering and frightfully annoyed at this whole thing. I have no idea what to do, whether to come home or stay here and I am not in a very good humor. I would like Libby's itinerary which I have lost. Are you—is she on tour now or not? I miss everybody. When I do return I don't think I'll leave again.

Much love,
Jane

P.S. Please reread this carefully and call in an expert if you don't understand and do hurry if you can. I really have no money.

I hope it's clear that if you do this and the Irving Trust Co. *is* the right bank that *they* must wire El Banco Salvador Hassan and not *me*. Nor must you wire me or Hassan. *They must wire Hassan* that the money has been deposited.

I will explain to Libby why I haven't written. I've been in a kind of funk though different from the one she saw me in before and incapable of doing *anything*.

Tangier, October 1948

35
To Paul Bowles

Dearest Bup,

Just an extra letter because the other was written in haste and agitation. I am still very agitated and wondering if you or Libby will get some money here to me by the Ayd el Kebir. These feasts are so important since the social lives of the Arab women are otherwise reduced to the family and immediate neighbors. One is so rarely invited to their houses and it is certainly necessary for me to make some little gift. I am also worried that you are going to write either a scolding letter or a "I couldn't have cashed that many checks, the bank is wrong" letter. Knowing you and your inaccuracy I was therefore careful and made sure to see the checks as I wrote you, so don't write me anything like that. If you now feel that one hundred pesetas a day is too high as a *budget* please say so. Perhaps when you stated such a sum you had imagined that it was less in dollars than it actually is. Recently the exchange has been at thirty-three—this week I mean. Also don't imagine that I've been *trying* to spend that just because you allowed it to me. I assure you by balancing two lean days against one extravagant one I just about manage. I *could* manage on less at a different hotel (*not* the Farhar) naturally, but I would only do that if I were *dying* to stay in Tangier. As for that, I can say merely that I am playing possum still—and the less I say about it the better. I will soon have the use of Jay's upstairs room and I will try and see if Cherifa and Tetum will come to tea. I don't think Cherifa will come with Tetum but then perhaps Tetum will come with her own friend Zodelia (another blackie, much *darker* than Quinza). I would lose face inviting anyone to our house in its present condition. I find myself in a constant state of inferiority vis-à-vis these women. Of course they live in wonderful long high rooms (the kind I used to hate and now love). Their beds are massive and covered with printed spreads (very Matisse) and white couches line the blue walls. They have hundreds of white frilly cushions too and they put very beautiful seashells into the water pitchers. The room we sit in when I visit Tetum is always the color of early evening because of the blue walls. I know only that room actually but I imagine it rightly as many rooms—there must be hundreds like it. It must be like Ahmed's house, so much more beautiful than the Ktiris'. I know I have written all about this before. Never mind. It is a result of the repetitive note in the Arab life here. In any case even if she does come to tea several times, I have little hope that she will ever come to tea *alone*, and if she did—even so . . . The average American woman would be revolted I suppose by a Negro man, and I think I suffer from the disadvantage of being "different"—all of which made your success years ago. Naturally I admire the women for being this way, so much more dignified than the men, or are they just more conventional? I don't know. I suppose I could banish all hope from my heart and get it over with but I hate to and I never regret being with them. I can't quite explain to you or anyone what it is like to be in one of those rooms—I mean how I feel about it. I suspected I would in the beginning at the wedding, and I loved Cherifa's little house. Mr. Ktiri's on the other hand never had any magic for me really. Perhaps he was too rich, and all those men. The women look wonderful in their homes. I had not intended writing this sort of letter at all. But briefly:

(1) *Please* get in touch with Mary Lou. I am so frightened now that she won't publish the story at all. I have heard nothing from Ivan. Have you helped me on that? If not I think you're mean. He should try to get me an advance from Knopf or a different publisher. If you haven't done anything about all this then who will? I should have a different agent if Ivan won't help me. But please, speak to Mary Lou anyway. I am awfully worried really. Also the Berlin crisis drove me out of my wits last week. What do you think of the war at this point?

(2) I can't reach the carpenter for the Embassy, he is

apparently loaded with work for the moment. Perhaps it is best to wait. I don't know.

(3) Are you coming here or going elsewhere, or don't you know?

(4) I have a way for us to live in Spain for as long as one year on a cultural passport twenty-five pesetas a day minimum *au lieu de cent* and all the pesetas we want sent us from Tangier. I met some Spanish "Intellectuals" who live in Madrid and are dying to meet you. They expect us to come this fall or winter and I think it might be fun. They will help us. (Very good families—Franquistos, I suppose—at least they have to pretend they are, I never asked them.) They are only twenty-three or four. I gave Jacques a few hundred pesetas, the only way he had of leaving Tangier. As I said whatever extra money I had left over from Libby and Oliver's donations and whatever I saved skimping went to him. *Perhaps* you feel I had no right to do this. Personally I have no regrets. It would have gone on something else. I don't think I'd want to stay here and never have any extra money at all. I mean I think it would get very dreary. I have very cheap big lunches now. The Parade is closed to the public at noon but several of us have got together and by chipping in I can eat there for what it would cost if I had a home. I live entirely on starch and vegetables and fish. I have forgotten what meat tastes like and I don't care, except that right now I don't have supper. I don't need it really but it makes an awfully *long* day. About 6:30 or 7:00 they leave the market, so I can either go to the Parade or home to bed. At the Parade I have a special price when I do drink, so don't worry about that. I am always so terribly gloomy when Tetum ties up the grain sacks and says goodbye. Often she and Cherifa leave the market together and we part in front of the hotel. I watch them disappearing up the road in the beautiful soft night and I just can't *yet* go to my room. The Parade is a warm spot to go to thank God, otherwise I would be too lonely I think—I *know*. My breakfast comes in at six and as usual any work that isn't done by twelve isn't done at all. I rarely get tight, in fact I can't digest much liquor in Tangier. I am buckling down on the work but I daresay something will upset it. I wish you'd write.

Much love,
Jane

P.S. By all means try to get your book away from Doubleday-Doran.

Tangier, October 1948

36
To Paul Bowles

Dearest Paul, Tangier

Thank you very much for the money which arrived so very quickly, I was amazed. I still had money in my purse and needn't have worried at all. I hope that you have found the accounts I sent you satisfactory and that you were not too disagreeably surprised at my needing more money. I am waiting to hear what *you* would prefer me to do. There isn't any use in my going into the reasons I would have for staying here or returning to New York (at least for the winter). There are too many pros and cons and all of it would bore you. If I spend the winter with Jody and she *is* willing to be with me, I should like best in one way to be where I had friends: Paris or New York. I think the idea of being with her in Marrakech or the desert is a little frightening and I don't think Tangier's winter weather would please her. Still, I might decide to do that. I don't want to be with Jody in Africa really unless you are coming back here and it is convenient for me because of that. I mean perhaps we could discuss the house and do something about it in the spring. I shall never stray very far from Tangier, my idea being neither to travel a great deal nor to live in Fez or Marrakech. I think we should decide one way or another about the house. Mohammed Ouezzani has a buyer for it, supposedly, and I have been advised by my dearest friend here, Kouche Saïd, to sell whenever I had a chance because you were really rooked, *unless* you want it for your own pleasure. Well I guess we know by now that it was not a good investment, but still if we ever get any fun out of it I think it will have been worth the expense. I personally would prefer a house in M'sallah eventually but then my reasons are all mixed up with people as usual, as I've written you, but I do like M'sallah very much besides and the kind of house one gets there. I heard of one for fifteen hundred dollars with Arab bath, patio and I think little garden (two stories); so you see considering that property in M'sallah is far more expensive than in the Casbah, it must be a bargain. I think however it will be sold long before this reaches you. Houses there are impossible to get and the rents run very high. I cannot get hold of your old man. He is busy working on a palace somewhere. By the time I reach him I suppose the rains will have started and it will be too late to do anything. Perhaps his estimate was lower because he was going to use poor material. The man who estimated it for me was going to make no profit whatsoever. He suggested that I buy my own material and only gave me the estimate as a friend. He has a great deal of property and actually advised me not to build but to sell. Kouche Saïd introduced me to him. Kouche I love and trust as I would any of my really close friends. One cannot compare him to Boussif or to anyone else here in fact. I would put every cent I had into his hands gladly. I know your concert is being given on the fourteenth of November. I don't know whether I could get back on time for that or not. I would appreciate it very much if you would let me know how you feel about it. If you would prefer me to hang on here until you return, I will probably do it, or if you prefer me to return and go to Libby's or somewhere where the financial burden will be reduced to a minimum, then I will start thinking about that. If I should decide I want to stay anyway for a little longer I could use my own money. I mean that I should know at what point I would be staying here against your will or at least contrary to a preference you might have. Perhaps you are never coming near here again. That would naturally influence me immensely. Or perhaps since you will always be in Fez you'd prefer me back in the States. I don't know. All this needn't be decided by mail. We can talk about it if you come here but I should know now at least whether you are coming or not and whether you'd prefer me to be still in Tangier or if you are utterly indifferent one way or another. If the house were livable I could be in it and would be right now. Meanwhile I may move to Jay's in November *if* I don't return which will make things cheaper. I would soon know if I could *ever* hope to have any visits from Tetum. Once I am more certain of that I shall be very decisive, one way or another. Well you will probably be writing me soon. I would have felt better if I'd heard from you.

It is difficult being so very much in the dark—financially too. If I can't depend for *anything* on you here in Tangier next winter, or shall we say Africa, I might feel better and less embarrassed in New York. Unless of course I had a house here to live in. I am thinking again of Jody because I should write her what I can afford. Libby told me earlier I could stay in her apartment in New York with Jody. In that case I know Jody would foot the other bills. But I don't want to get her all the way over here, find out that sentimentally it doesn't work very well, and be financially dependent on her besides for everything. Thank heavens I have some money but if I have to spend it *all* on being in a hotel with Jody I'm not sure I wouldn't prefer returning to the U.S.A. and then coming here again, perhaps in the spring. I don't know what in the devil to do really, and the more I think about it the more complicated the whole mess gets. I *will* stay here to supervise the house *en tout cas* if you *want* it built now, and they say there is still time. I doubt seriously however that the old man, in any case, will be available before spring, and probably the whole thing will be delayed. Please answer me soon. Throw some light on the house, what you expect of me financially if I remain here, if you'd prefer me to remain here, or if you think I should leave forever or leave and return here in the spring. Maybe financially, with the passage, *ça reviendrai au même.* I have four hundred dollars, roughly, and I would like to keep some out for clothes. You can understand that—for a few little follies. I hope that you are well and that your book is with New Directions. Believe it or not I am working. I get up at seven or eight and work between nine and twelve, which is all I can manage a day. But it is best doing it this way. I am still amused by Tetum and Cherifa, also in love. Jane

P.S. I am going to Cherifa's house for the night and Tetum's house tomorrow. The mutton festival is in full swing. I am simply terrified of the food I'll have to eat. Will write all about it. Tell Oliver and Helvetia, can't write everyone the same thing.

October 1948

37
To Paul Bowles and Oliver Smith

Dearest Paul and Oliver,

Today I saw the house I would like. I daresay you will be not interested, but I think it is a real bargain. In francs it comes to a little under two thousand dollars, the lawyer's fee included (the 5 percent that the city takes out for transference of ownership). It has two floors, each with large patio (about four times the size of the one in our house) and each with two rooms, one smaller and one larger giving on to a closed patio. There is a generously sized room on the ground floor which is now a "Moorish" bathroom, in other words the floor is constructed to permit steam baths—a private Turkish bath, I gather. The room was warm when I went into it, so someone must have been in there just before we arrived. I would much prefer that to having a lot of plumbing that doesn't work. The slaves bring in buckets of hot water and the whole room heats up. It could be converted into a bathroom with modern tub, but I think it is foolishness. The Arabs are extremely clean without all that nonsense. The best feature of all is a little garden space off the ground floor. It has a grape arbor and with a few hundred pesetas one could have wonderful flowers growing in it, and it would be charming to eat out there. There are excellent stairs already going up to the terrace which is about three times the size of our present one, and a room could be built there eventually very cheaply since actually the stairs are nearly half the cost, for some reason, of the entire thing. It is a real honest to God house that we could all live in very happily right now.

The disadvantages: The view is not as spectacular as the one from the present house (one can see an apartment house), though one does see the "Charf," which I think is pretty, and a lot of surrounding Moorish houses. The color of the Arab quarter, which is what I care about, is all around one. The Charf is a kind of hilly section in the distance. I love the house and the garden is so very unusual and to me such a great luxury. It is also very important to own actual ground. We don't, you know, in our present house since it is over someone else's, so if in the future it were torn down to be replaced by a *modern* building we wouldn't get any money because we don't own the actual ground. Our house, now, begins in the *air*. I would love to have this house and would certainly live in it often with Moors while you were all on your various trips. Jay says it's the cheapest buy he's ever heard of, but I would certainly make sure there was no hitch in it. The tiles on the stairs are not pretty as are the ones in our present house. The patios however are just plain black and white tiles. It is in excellent condition and the stairway tiles could eventually be changed. Though it is on the edge of M'sallah and therefore valuable as property because right near the European sections of town, one has to go down some narrow winding streets to reach it, and so it is, thank heavens, not accessible by car. It is at a dead end and would therefore be quiet. With an extra room or even two on the terrace it would be large enough for four of us and servants. It could be a place to live for some months out of the year, whereas our present house could never be that. Still it is naturally more of an investment than adding a room on to ours, but that will *never* be big enough for you, Oliver and myself, let alone Helvetia at one time. I know she too will be sold on spending some time in this part of the world once she gets over here. If she cared to join us in the investment it would come to about six hundred to six hundred and fifty dollars apiece for all three of you, and whereas I think that to buy jointly is usually a poor idea, in a place like this it is an excellent one since we would probably not all be in it together very often, hélas.

Any *hole* in M'sallah rents for about eight hundred to one thousand pesetas a month. God knows even at that rate there *is* nothing. The market is being moved down there by the way, and I fear that in ten or fifteen years, or twenty, they will be widening all the streets and tearing the properties down. I am going to see the plans for M'sallah if you are interested. Some of the streets are already being widened, but this one won't be for a long while. By then we will have got our money's worth a hundred times and can sell at a huge profit because we own quite a large plot, including the garden. Perhaps Libby might be interested if Helvetia isn't, although I doubt it. She already has two places anyway and she is not alone like Helvetia. I *really* think that if the three of you got together then whatever happened wouldn't be so very tragic. As we couldn't move in for three months *anyway*, I would only need to make a down payment now to hold it. He has had one offer of 750,000 francs but is holding out for 800,000 (about). I fear that this letter will reach you too late, but if you are at all interested you should wire me and I will get a lawyer at the Embassy to look into it *thoroughly*. Helvetia, if she is *not* in Vermont, is at the San Jacinto Hotel (East 60th). But most likely she has got in touch with you. Perhaps she would hate living Arab style for a few months out of the year but it would be a marvelous contrast to Vermont. I would eventually find the right servant or servants to leave in it when none of us were here. Anyway I have written you about it, so do what you can, but if you are at all interested do it immediately and wire me. I hesitated one day on renting a horrid black cellar-like place in M'sallah (with a horrid toilet one had to *crawl* into), and it was rented for double the amount right from under my nose. I have no doubt that some other house might turn up eventually but probably twenty times as expensive. There's someone trying to buy our little one now who hasn't seen it yet, but we can discuss that later.

Much love,
Jane

P.S. You can get this letter to H. if you think it's simpler than explaining.

Will send my story to George. If I could sell that I would actually have earned enough to buy a third of the house, and I would prefer that really. Then H. could simply be there when she wanted to be. If she liked it she could help towards a room on the third floor. Naturally if you are through with Morocco and moving on to West Africa, there would be no point, as I think of it as a focal point for you and one which would be possible for me, much more than the desert, for some of the year anyway and for the others as well.

Write me Villa de France, Tangier.

Love again,
J.

Tangier, October 1948

38
To Paul Bowles

Dearest Paul,

I had certainly hoped for a letter from you before this, but either you or the British post office is impossible. I have some ideas again for my novel which stopped dead after the Aid, and the wedding that I missed, because I was so bitter and because I'd reached an impasse anyway. Now I feel like working again. It will always be this way I imagine, so I must take advantage of these brief oases. Helvetia's letter upset me very much and so did and (still does) the fact of missing your concert. It began to obsess me, but I didn't dare leave until I heard from you and besides I felt the least I could do was to clear up the house matter. I thought you would be furious if I came home without the deed or at least the assurance that it was waiting for you, because I am not sure they will let me sign it. That finally decided me and of course the fact that there was nothing left on the *Saturnia* by the time I inquired, still hoping I might get a wire from you or a letter from you in answer to mine, but of course you have all disappeared again. To finish with the house: after weeks of going to the Mendoubia they told me I was to go to the qadi where everything would be ready, then started a real Kafka in fancy dress that went on for several days. I wandered between the adoul, the qadi and Mr. Lairini's store from which he had suddenly vanished. I can't go into it, but the whole thing seemed to be moving backward instead of forward as in *Through the Looking Glass.* The adoul kept asking where the Rue Maimouni *was* with a kind of dreamy interest, as though the deed were tucked under the cobbles there. It was all ridiculous and Boussif was divorcing in the next booth. It made me love Tangier. Fortunately a very nice gentleman, an Arab belonging to one of the richest and best families here, took the matter into his own hands and started running about for me the other day. He was worried that something *louche* was going on because he did not think very highly of Mr. Lairini. He doubted however that he would dare do anything really dishonest to an American beyond charging twice too much for the house; *enfin*, his brother being the Nadir of the

Mosques himself, he jumped right into the very thick of it. It seems that the Mendoubia lost the Nadir's letter and therefore the number to the house (210) but now it's all beginning again. They are writing everybody and soon I should be ready to go down to the qadi and the adoul. I hope they don't ask where the Rue Maimouni is. No one ever seems to have heard of it and yet it is an endless and important street. The important thing is that my friend has seen Mr. Lairini and he says that happily there is nothing *louche* going on and that the deed should soon be ours. He has been perfectly charming and accurate in all his appointments. He wants nothing, being very rich himself and not interested in women. I know that I am not explaining it very well but then I have never understood any of it. I think it is important to get the thing over with and registered and I'm sure you will be pleased that I have stayed to attend to it. Meanwhile I have calmed down and am again in good spirits. There was a terrible time there however when I could perhaps have got the boat and tried to guess which you'd prefer me to do when I almost went mad. I am looking forward to your next letter but for God's sake don't just say "do what you like." Jody writes that she will be coming over here the earlier part of December (unless of course I go back). I will put whatever money I've earned toward being here or my passage back and just forget about ever getting any clothes. I don't feel I deserve them anyway, for various reasons. I am deeply disgusted with myself. I don't know what will occur financially with Jody here actually, perhaps the same thing as last year, but I do think I should have some base to live on and therefore perhaps it might be better in New York because there I wouldn't need to fall on your hands at all. I know you hate to figure out anything in advance which is maddening, of course, because there are certain things that must be. If I only got a word from you I would fix up the house even as is (without another room) and move in. Naturally Mr. Bucurri has upset my plans of doing anything since he is *introuvable.* If we had a place to live Jody could join me in it, and then if she insisted on travelling or living in hotels she could pay for it. I know she probably plans to pay for anything we do anyway but then maybe I might better be somewhere else. I shall write and ask her what she prefers. I suppose instead of going into all these complications I might just say that there is a boat leaving on the twenty-first and one on the third of December. If you have any opinions about it you had better write me immediately as there are already no cabins available on the one sailing on the twenty-first. One has to know the captain by the way as far as the American Export ships are concerned, but Miss Fried is inquiring about it for me. I'm almost sure they won't take a woman. Otherwise all ships are about three hundred dollars minimum. I hate in one way the idea of returning. If you were interested in really establishing a headquarters here in Tangier I would be delighted to fix it up, either this house or buy another one and live in it part of the time. If however you are merely dashing through Morocco and starting off on one of your trips around the world, never to return here, then what is the use? Perhaps now is a good time for me to return, as I should otherwise go in the spring (Mother is getting terribly lonely), but I can't bear the idea of leaving Morocco unless I *can* return. I can't explain it at all. I met a man yesterday who has lived in Egypt for years and knows the Near East very well. He was delighted with Tangier and said it was so very much more Oriental than anything around there. Strange. I too feel it very strongly here, though you don't find it exotic at all. I prefer M'sallah to the Casbah. Many things may have happened too, and you yourself may not be returning yet. If however I am to take the boat on the twenty-first there may not be any cabin class left and the one on December third is either first class or third; I shall probably need another hundred dollars to get myself out of here with a margin, or maybe more. I haven't figured it out. Perhaps I should just not think of going any way but second class. I shall try to work now, whichever I do, but my success will depend on knowing whether or not I am staying or leaving very shortly and how much money you think I should allow myself for passage. I am sorry to involve you at all, but as you say yourself one is somehow not alone in the world and if it weren't for you I would never have come to Tangier. I do not regret it and hope when my heart is healed to resume my Arabic lessons if I stay, or when I come back. I did not go near the market for a week, then the other day I went and spoke to Tetum for a while. She is so very beautiful to me. I don't care how crafty or mean she is. I am happy just to look at her. I know you think she is a hiddy. If we go to Fez later I am going to take Cherifa and her sister along for a few days. She would naturally not come alone. Her sister has elephantiasis and wants to go to Moulay Yacoub. I am considerably cheered by the fact that Truman was reelected which I think is better than Dewey, don't you? Mary Oliver is supposedly arriving here today. Mr. McMicking reported this to me. He came through on his way to Fez from Gib, having spent all summer in England. I have developed a great feeling for him and I believe he likes me too. It is *pénible* to be with him of course because of his affliction. Please write me here at the Villa de France, Tangier and immediately. The suspense of not knowing whether you care or not what I do or have any opinion on the subject at all that might help is too much. If I came back would you wait and go up with me to Helvetia's for a fortnight before being on your way? I would cook wonderful things for you and then you could leave and I'd join Jody. I shall see presently whether she has any preference about where to be. If in America we would, I think, go for a month or so down to New Mexico. If you were here I'd come back in March or April and perhaps build onto the house then.

Much love,
Jane

P.S. Oliver's money order has not arrived: I still have some hope because they told me that it took twenty-five or thirty days to get through London. Please thank O. and explain I've been waiting to write him when it arrived to thank him. When did he send it? Is it over a month now? If so we must take steps.

Tangier, November 1948

39
To Paul Bowles

Dear Paul,

Since I wrote you a twenty page letter last night which of course I shan't send, I feel better, and more important still I think this one can be brief and to the point. I must ask you to please keep it for answering purposes because everything I write you seems to go down the drain and I do take pains to keep you au courant and make it easier for you to answer me. Since the end of October I have been waiting in vain for a letter, some indication of what you wanted to do and what you hoped I would do. You say casually that you have neglected your correspondence because of your work but surely you could have found time to scribble a line. I hate to think anyway that I am part of that correspondence of yours and that you only write me when you pull out the list. I am being nasty because I have suffered intolerably for four weeks—anyway, ever since I might have taken the November fifth boat. I received your wire which I appreciated very much. It said letter following and of course that took another ten days. "Will you wait Tangier?" I interpreted in a million different ways. If it had only said *hope* you'll wait Tangier, or *please* wait Tangier, but I suppose you worded it that way purposely. Also I didn't know whether you meant wait and then leave after we've seen each other or what. I didn't worry much because I thought the letter would come in a few days since you announced it and I would know more precisely what you meant. That last bit of waiting finished me off I guess and when Mary came and there was this sudden opportunity to leave I suddenly thought well, why not? It was a good excuse anyway to wire and I suppose I hoped you'd answer that you weren't impartial or that you were because "leaving for Timbuktu upon arrival," but mainly I hoped you weren't impartial. Still, *that* is not your fault and I don't expect you to have guessed that. You may very well not want to be with me this winter because of Jody and would *prefer* me to come back in the spring. I had hoped you would express yourself on that in a letter but you didn't. I asked you about it before. Because you mention really nothing about all this I have a feeling that you have something up your sleeve and are therefore just not saying anything. I know you want to go to Timbuktu but I don't know *when* or if you are planning to go with Gore and Tennessee or what. Between Spain, Marrakech, Fez, the desert, etc., I think we could have a wonderful time either three of us or five of us. (I have no idea about

Tennessee's plans of course.) But you don't even mention this possibility in your letter and probably for good reason. If you are going off alone with Gore and Tennessee for the winter, then I must decide whether I would rather be here with Jody or in New York. She has a car there after all. Maybe Tennessee won't be staying long. You have either mentioned him in your wire to indicate that you had a travelling companion and were more or less making your plans with him and would not be lonely, or else you were mentioning it as a temptation. I can't imagine why you would have stuck him into your wire otherwise. I'm inclined to think you were showing me that I needn't be involved in your arrival at all. I don't know. A car is always a temptation to me as you know. You mention it in your letter but you don't say whether either of us or three of us would ever have a chance to get into it. Perhaps it would be too small for five people and that would leave me out because of Jody. Of course Jody is the whole complication in this. If you think the three of us or five of us or twenty of us (Gordon is in Tunis) can have some fun together for part of Jody's stay here anyway, I shall remain, but if I shan't be seeing you much then I think Jody should decide what she would prefer doing. I personally think it would then be better for me to take the bull by the horns and leave, but maybe she doesn't have the car in the States this winter and maybe she would hate to change her plans. If I don't go back on February third, I mean December third, I shall return in March and try to get over again with Helvetia in summer. Otherwise I shall return here with Libby and Helvetia in the spring. Do you think it's silly that I should have spent all this time here and not see you, which will happen if I leave on the *Saturnia*, December the third? I have missed my chance to return with Mary and in any case she may not be returning. I will know today whether she is or not. As by now I have pains in my head from this problem and I am in a pathological state I may try at the last minute to do something anyway. I keep interpreting your telegrams differently. All at once I think you are trying to influence me to come home and then again I think well no, he is trying to make me feel I *can* return if I like without guilt. I think this time I feel more guilty about staying than I would about returning. Why? Whatever it is it's terribly neurotic but once the cycle starts there is no stopping it—only the departure of the boat—and then I have a few days rest until the next one comes along. I wish I knew what I could do to help myself but when I reason myself out of it for awhile and enjoy a few hours of false peace I am even more tormented afterwards for having forgotten my pain. If you read this carefully you will certainly be able to advise me. Did you understand when I wired I was "miserable" that it was because you seemed to *want* me to come back which confused me? I don't understand also your last telegram. I asked you to wire me if you were *pleased* that I was remaining but you wired in answer: WAS MERELY CLARIFYING SITUATION IF MISERABLE BY ALL MEANS COME IMMEDIATELY. Well, I can't come immediately now but you know this time how I feel and if you think because of Jody and your own plans I'd be better off home right now then wire so in answer to this but first call Jody and give her a chance to say what she'd like. She may *hate* at this point not to leave. Once she gets started on one track she usually can't conceive of a volte-face. As for her boring Tennessee if he's around (or Vidal) she could never bore anyone. She is a character and has fine sentiments. The trouble is I don't know how it will work between Jody and me. I have promised to take Cherifa and Quinza to Fez. I have to buy Cherifa a djellaba and shoes eventually. Also I am taking her to the doctor's right now which is ruining me. She has a skin disease from grain. I have to spend money on something that's "fun!" It's all too ridiculous. I don't know about fixing up the peseta thing from here with you in Gibraltar. The Madrileños will be in Tangier for Christmas and actually suggested February for our meeting in Spain as a good time. That would be perfect if Libby would come then. Couldn't you suggest to Tennessee that he come here first or is he going to drive to Tunis and then go to Italy? I suppose so. I'm sure they could fix the peseta thing for Tennessee too if he was interested. In any case they want records of yours so that they can play them on some radio program. Also they can arrange to give you a concert, they think, so bring sheet music. I imagine I mean scores! A visiting celebrity always has many privileges so I think you should take advantage of their interest in you. They are mad about Tennessee too. Naturally you can do this whether I am here or not. Poor Jody, I suppose, will have to pay the full rate but maybe we could manage something. But if she must I don't expect her to pay for *all* my expenses in Spain. Whatever money I have left will naturally go into the pot, whatever pot I'm in next winter. My tapeworm was yards long but we are not sure of whether I've got rid of the head or not. It didn't come out with the rest but it may have got lost. Since I'm gaining weight I daresay I have got rid of it. *On verra, il n'y a qu'à recommencer autrement.* It's a revolting thing. I feel like a total failure and will try to work for the last time right now, and according to your letter, I will either sail or not on the *Saturnia.* Naturally you don't know exactly what will happen, one never does, but you have a little better idea than I do at this point. Will there be any chance of staying somewhere and working for a month? Jacqueline Cramer, by the way, is taking the Ede house or rather an old man is, and she is going there with her daughter to keep him company and run the house. She is throwing in a lot of beds and some of us or all of us could stay there. Three or four of us anyway I think. She has a little car and would like to drive down to Marrakech in January, or somewhere. Personally I'd like to drive to Colomb-Bechar and into the desert a little way. If Mary Oliver isn't leaving she's going to take a house in Marrakech. She's a holy mess. What about the house in M'sallah? I wrote you about that but now I suppose I won't hear because of all those wires. I wouldn't visit Carson now because I can't write. I'm sorry she's ill and why does she send me her love? She doesn't know me. I suppose it doesn't really matter what I do. For God's sake write or wire soon, and consult Jody. Oliver's money never came. He must do something about it. For heaven's sake reach him and thank him for me. I miss him but I am too upset to write just now. With George gone there is no point in sending my story. I enclose an errand Mr. Ede wants you to do. I hope you will, they have a wonderful new house and may invite us to stay eventually, if you're nice. Mrs. Ede adores you. They think I'm a yenta but I don't think it matters. It will mean everything to me, to my peace of mind and my chances of working, if I hear from you immediately. If you think it is worth the money you can send me a deferred wire, unless you feel that what you have to say cannot be formulated in a wire.

Because of the God damned Gibraltar problem, I should start leaving a week ahead, which does not leave so much time after all. I won't be annoyed if you think Jody and I are better off not here this winter. The whole clue is in your wire—whether you mentioned Tennessee to warn me off or to entice me and whether you are going off to Timbuktu now. God knows. Surely you could not have stuck an extra word in for no reason at all, or did you mean that because of him you couldn't change your passage? In your letter you said you were sharing a cabin with Gore? Perhaps you thought I wouldn't know who Gore was (I know only too well) and would therefore understand better if you mentioned Tennessee. *Kif-kif.* In other words, you might have been trying to show that you were involved with someone in a cabin and could therefore not wait over in New York. That would explain your mentioning Tennessee. In other words, neither as an enticement nor as a hint that you were off with a group of men and that I should make my own separate plans with Jody. Perfectly understandable if you are by the way, it is just that I would prefer knowing so, if it *is* so and I am not going to be seeing much of you. That is the marrow of this letter. Please answer quickly as I said. The horror of it is that if I do come back it will have been wildly ridiculous to have missed your concert. Give my love to Libby, Oliver and Helvetia. Tell Helvetia she must come here later with her car. Perhaps the whole thing will pan out better if I go back in December, but after you've read this carefully you can surely write or wire me something helpful. I shall stop now before I get into an agonizer. How was the concert?

Much love,
Jane

P.S. It is too bad you didn't get back sooner. I guess suddenly I just got lonely and now everything has gone to pieces. I won't mind whatever you decide and please if you want to have this winter free for a land trip that *can't* include Jody and me, then say so and I'll return in spring. I just feel in my bones that Tennessee has a small car! If you can go anywhere with them you *must*, but let me know in time! A letter won't reach me in time unless you write it very quickly! Don't forget, if there is a possibility of a trip by car, other than over that road to Marrakech, we'd like that, but you would have mentioned it if there were.

If I have left anything out, for God's sake try to imagine what I'd like to know yourself.

Tangier, November 1948

40
To Paul Bowles

Dearest Paul,

I feel so happy and relaxed now that I feel I am staying. Perhaps you have written me not to because you don't think you'll see me for more than a week or two? I seriously doubt that, though it may be so and I hope you will be truthful if it is. It is not your fault after all that Jody is coming. Perhaps she will prefer being here in any case, so I might not be leaving whether you are with me or not. I would take a train to Marrakech or the desert, but I don't like the "idea" of train travel in Spain—it will doubtless go through many tunnels—still I can *force* myself on one. The Sicres, by the way, are driving to Madrid in time for Christmas. You mentioned Tennessee and Gore driving through Spain before coming here. Did you want to go with them? Or did you want us both to (or isn't there room for two)? Perhaps you and I being in Spain had nothing to do with them, in that case come here first. If you have a chance to go alone with them for heaven's sake do. I don't want to spoil *that* possibility. Jody gets here ten days after you or eleven so I'd have to be in Gibraltar at that point anyway. I shall find out if there's any possibility of fixing the pesetas *here*, without you. You would want the rate for yourself as well wouldn't you, or are you willing to spend one hundred a day at their official rate—whatever it is? I shall find out what I can do. I hope to God I hear from you soon this time. As I said in my other letter I shan't feel really at peace until I do.

I am so worried that you will think I want to come *home* because of that wire, but it was just a result of being fed up with not hearing a word from you and not knowing what on earth your intentions were. Actually it was meant to get some reassurance from you, but of course you did just the opposite. Well, I'll see what you have to say in your letter. I would like very much to have the house in M'sallah. Have you talked to Oliver about it, or Helvetia? I just don't expect her to be interested, but it's a good investment. Quinza and Cherifa will live with me, I know, but probably Quinza will refuse to climb up into the Casbah. It is quite a pull. If I live in a house here I *insist* on a harem. There is no other way of doing it. They cope with all the details and keep one company (I am quite happy with them without any kind of romance). We can discuss all that when we see one another, but I wish some one of you would be interested in the house. I suppose you think I have quite lost my mind. I missed living in a kind of basement right next to Cherifa's house by hesitating. It was during the days when I was so wretched at having missed the *wedding* in the country with Tetum. I didn't care about anything I was so miserable so someone else took it while I sulked in my room. I am afraid every move I make is wrong, at least recently I have been running in bad luck. I hope it won't continue. Had I moved into that house I would have had quite a nice life, eating every night with Cherifa and Quinza. I am slowly becoming part of their household, but I *must* study my Arabic again. It has gone all to pieces these past weeks.

Living here I have to walk back around eleven at night, or sleep there, which I must say is not amusing after a while. The hip I sleep on is always black and blue in the morning, my couch is so hard. I seem to be the only European woman walking out of there at that hour of the night, and often I carry back my empty briefcase (I take them one bottle of wine in that). I don't know what the Arabs think, and it is very unlike me to be doing something like this.

Naturally some call out to me, but I am not too upset by it. Still I would prefer living in the quarter. I am terribly upset about Oliver's money not arriving. I am afraid I've gone way over my budget what with doctor's bills and food being more of an item now that it's cold, and then when I got very depressed I bought some things, and I have also contributed money to the sheep, as you know. It will come out of my own money, but then I suppose that is just the same as if it came out of yours. I don't know. However, I think now and then when I make some I should get some fun out of it. It just can't support me anyway. I wish you would bring me two large size cakes of *Zip*—wax hair remover (not the tubes)—the one that advertises "It's off because it's out!" It's called Zip "Epilator" and a bottle of "Adalin" (Bayers). It's very expensive but unlike aspirin it does not affect the heart nor is it habit forming. It is a "calmant," quiets the awful turmoil in the solar plexus created by panic, and will be excellent for trips. One does not need a prescription for it so you can see that it's not dangerous. I think it would be a good thing for me to have around.

Don't let Mother load you up with a lot of things. There's nothing else you can bring me really. If I need things for winter I can pick them up here.

If you have advised me to return I shall regret terribly missing your concert. It will seem too utterly ridiculous for words and I shall probably brood for years because it was just the time here when everything was going so *wrong* that if it hadn't been for a feeling I had that you would like to find me here I would have fled. Of course now with Tennessee coming everything is changed for you, though *my pleasure* in seeing *you* will be very great. I shall write Libby and Helvetia, and you keep Oliver informed about everything. I have avoided all the bars where I might run into Mary for the last two days, although she invites me to meals. I felt terribly like some real food for a few days but I never enjoyed a bite of it, and part of my hysteria was due to being around her at all. Any drinks I had with her just made me frightfully ill. Don't forget, if possible bring whatever records you have.

Love,
Jane

P.S. Have just wired Jody. Her letter received this morning made me feel you'd be glad to see me here. It clarified your wires so I shall just take a chance and stay even if I do see you for only a little while. I'm wiring her because I'm afraid she may be upset. Thank God for Jody!

You may think I'm crazy, but I was terribly hurt and just more and more and more depressed at not hearing from you, and your first wire which was clear to me in the beginning wasn't after a while, and the promised letter took forever arriving.

I really don't understand about the pesetas. You had better wire me if and what you want me to do about them. For me? For you? For both of us? It is quite a different question if we don't start off from Tangier together. You must forgive my wires and when I see you I can explain more about it. This morning I walked through M'sallah. I am longing to walk through it with you. Maybe you'll understand why I want some day to live there. I can't imagine ever being away from Morocco very long and I know now that in my heart I have *never* wanted to leave. Otherwise I wouldn't feel so happy. I hope to God you haven't sent for me. Love again,

Jane

Tangier, December 1948

41
To Libby Holman

Dearest Libby,

Your letter was one of the sweetest and most inclusive I have ever received, in great contrast to Paul who must have entered the secret service he's been so mute about everything. You must have heard all about our wild cables back and forth. Your suggestion that I decide everything on my own hook without him was a good one, but you did say that I should wait over here and see him first (at least you suggested it), and alas I had to decide to either be here or there before seeing him or else come home before he left because of Jody's plans. I could not keep her waiting on a perpetual hook. Well why go into it? I had an opportunity to come home with Mary Oliver (I thought), and John Willis—you know how I loathe travelling alone—and it would have helped a bit financially, at least I could have sat in their suite all the way back and just taken any old bunk myself. (She wanted me to come in the suite with them in fact, *if they got one*, since she said the difference in my ticket and the extra amount she would have had to pay to keep me in there would have amounted to a night's drinks, so I might even have done that.) Actually she gave a five hundred dollar tip to a taxi driver just before coming here (100 pounds) so I had no scruples about it. She's quite insane and ordered up fifty sandwiches for the two of us the minute I saw her. That impressed me most. Touche can tell you about her, except that she's such a mess that I thank my stars not to be on the boat with her. Aside from that she finally the other day decided not to leave, after all, so it is a wonderful thing that I did not decide to take advantage of the opportunity presented me. I have not been able to decide from Paul's cables yet whether or not he liked the idea that I was staying but wasn't saying so because he had gathered that I really *wanted* to come home. I got awfully tired of not hearing from him and then when your letter came I thought it *might* be better to come back. It was a terrible strain and just last week I thought maybe this time I really was going to crack, but I made a very big effort and I'm working again. That's all I can do to save my brain. It just gets going around in too many circles. Maybe I shouldn't be staying but it seems to me it's too late now. My only hope is that you will come to Spain in February. I will certainly join you there. Jody is meeting Mary Anne on the Riviera, so she writes, after her stay with me, and then the two of them are going on up to Paris and then on to the boat bound for New York. It's too exhausting. By then I suppose I'll be just stuck in the middle of Spain or back in Tangier again. Paul will be off to Timbuktu, if he isn't on his way there now. Had I known all this shit about Mary Anne I would have come home now and alone. I would have it behind me instead of hanging over me. I was so pleased to have my own private travelling companion (Jody) to return with. I have written her asking her to ask Mary Anne if she would mind terribly, in case that I was alone by then, if we all met on the Riviera or in Paris and I returned with them. It is a very undignified thing to do, but I think it wouldn't hurt Mary Anne to spend a little time with me just to see how it works out. If I'm to be with Jody every year for the rest of her life, I think it would be more convenient for all of us if M.A. took a more friendly attitude, don't you? But she won't; please, please try to come. I may even just plain fly back with *you* as I daresay that's the way you'll do it. Oh! My God! An entirely new *tsuris* has come up! I see seven possibilities. Please call Jody and ask her to reach you in New York. She leaves the Inn on the eighth or ninth of December and writes that she can't give me her New York address. (She leaves New York the 13th of December by the way.) That means of course that she's with her brother. I feel that it would be better to have some way of contacting her. Would you ask Scotty to call Canal 6-8050 and ask for the doctor there? She'll get him eventually (I forget his name, it's a Jewish one and very common) and when she does would she ask for Mrs. Bowles's eyeglass prescription, and have her inquire if it's all right to make a lens and have it poked into the frame over here: I need my *right* lens. If he says you can't do that then I'll just have to go on the prescription (I don't know how good the glasses are here but I can try). If he says it's better to have the whole thing made then I suppose I'd better do that, but I doubt that he knows my size of frame and naturally the other way would be less expensive. I do have two mediocre frames over here which will last out the winter and anyway he might get the wrong size and just *say* it's better that way to make more money. Be very *careful* of him. The address is 191 Canal Street. It has a very sort of Left sounding name, the store, like the People's Eyeglass Store or something like that but I'm not sure that this isn't entirely in my imagination.

I can get chicken heads and giblets for a penny a pile but have no eating companion so what's the use? I'm God-damned sick of having no one to eat with except on odd nights, and no reason to eat at one time more than at another. I don't see how Helvetia makes out on her farm. I have hit the bottom here but that's as it should be. I shall really have a fit if you don't come over because part of my decision to stay was based on the knowledge that God willing I would see you either way. I realize too, Darling, that many things might prevent you from coming so don't *worry* about it. I just hope I will see you, that's all, and I know how you long to spend a little time with Jody. If you can get the lens to her in New York, which would mean communicating with her right now at R——— Inn before she leaves, it would be a great help. Also if you could see her and make lots of charm to her it would help our being in Madrid when you are—*if* you are to be there. You can also tell her about when it will be so she can warn Mary Anne about meeting her in Paris rather than on the Riviera if the time of your stay there works out that way. Madrid is nearer Paris than the Riviera as you probably don't know—mapless. Or isn't it? Oy! She will suggest reaching you probably because of her brother, though don't let on that you realize that because she's very embarrassed about it. Just say "How will we reach each other?" in a very offhand natural voice. I think it would be a very *clever* move to ask *both* of them up for a drink. You can give Mary Anne an Alexander. I want you to start thinking about this and preparing for it. You might bring Claudia and Johnny in for the occasion. Try to find out the dates of Jody's departure so that if I can't go back with her I can go back with you maybe, or at least be left with you, that is if you plan to spend only a certain number of weeks in Europe and it doesn't matter you might as well arrange it so that you don't go back *before* Jody. I don't know of course when your tour begins and what other reasons would prevent you from arranging things that way, but just in case when you see her or talk to her you can get the details. The last time she left me alone here I was truly desperate and the mere thought of it is ruining whatever pleasure I have in her coming. I do find that I am very eager to see her and excited. If only I don't have that awful departure on my head—at least I hope it can be arranged differently this time. Paul hasn't written me yet and I'm just plain puzzled.

Now that I've got all the complications over with I must tell you how happy I am about your tour. Paul told me too about the raves you got. I'm terribly excited about it and I know you are happy. I don't like what you wrote about "that certain party" being highly psychopathic. Were you exaggerating a little—I hope. I am worried now and hope you can give me some reassurance. Also did you really mean that your ulcer is back? You must write me about that at once. Paul of course will tell me what the Lorca plans are (if he recognizes me or has time to call at the hotel). I am glad that you have respect for him and that you like him. I love him very much though I could smack him at the moment. I probably confused the poor thing with my wires but I do wish I had known long ago how I felt. Do you like Tennessee? I like the sound of your beau and am glad he continues to make you happy. You wrote in a previous letter that Helvetia didn't like him? Did she tell you so? She said she saw you at Oliver's party and touched your cold dress. Who is this Wanda? Did you meet her? Was H.

drunk as a hoot owl? I am ill about missing Paul's concert and think he should have somehow—*if* he doesn't care about whether I'm here or not—said something so that I could have arranged to come back for it. Helvetia writes that it was wonderful. I don't think being anywhere near Louisa with Jody around would have been exactly fair to Jody. I might have just become obsessed by Louisa which would have spoiled everything. Won't she keep? Anyway I think it is very dangerous for me to make any plans with *her* in mind. I feel that she is just as hopeless and unattainable as Tetum whom I have finally given up. I could not keep up a friendship with both Tetum and Cherifa. Cherifa just made it impossible. I go to Cherifa's house three times a week with food and wine. She is my sister. Between her and Tetum they have all my scarves, most of my money, my watch, and I am now taking Cherifa to the doctor's twice a week. I shall have to stop however unless he is willing to make me a price. I think he will. I have promised her a cloak (djellaba) for the Mouloud and shoes. I don't mind being liked for my money one bit. Being the richest woman in the world has certain disadvantages but I accept them. I feel that I have done everything, absolutely everything wrong, but perhaps something nice will happen anyway. I *would* like to have some fun again some day.

There is a very nice man in Madrid who knows all of Lorca in Spanish. He is the head of the Trans-World Airlines there, has an apartment and can show us everything we need to see. I think you will like him. He has a fireplace and serves cocktails. I think it would be lots of fun. We can fix up the money thing, tell Jody, so that she needn't spend more than six dollars a day for living. The "Parade" is booming with business but Jay only gets two hundred pesetas a week out of it and his food. Bill keeps the accounts and Jay's too lazy to ask for more money, he says he doesn't care. (That's about seven bucks!) He's quite wonderful really but I shall put the bite on him because he owes me five hundred pesetas (four), and I refuse to have Bill keep it if they've got the money in the box there—it will buy Cherifa's cloak. Ira Bellin got thousands and thousands of pesetas out of Mary Oliver, enough to send for her Russian family. She sold her jackets and pictures. Mary fell in love with her and has gone to buy a house in Marrakech. Cherifa wants me to buy her a taxi, after the djellaba. However I do save a penny a week on eggs. She gets them for me a little less and also knows how to look into them to see whether or not they are rotten. She is getting quite plump because of my affluence and every now and then instead of looking like a boy she looks like a complete Oriental woman. The minute Tetum saw that I was taking Cherifa to the doctor's she wanted to go too. I asked her what was wrong, and as far as I could gather she merely wanted a *thorough checkup*. Last month they were burning crocodile dung and pig's bristles and now they all want x-rays. Cherifa was wild and said I couldn't take Tetum to the doctor because it would be a disgrace and that the doctor would be horrified if I came with a *second* Moorish woman. I have never understood why, but I am terrified of going against her orders and have therefore made an enemy of Tetum. I have more fun at Cherifa's house (the food is divine, ossir), so I thought I'd better give up Tetum. She is more of a conniver and mean all the way through. Besides that, she's too damned conventional and penny-pinching. She brings her own coal to the market and other equipment for making tea. Cherifa is much more grand and orders hers from the tea house, though she has actually less money, I believe. I am working because there is no sense in my brooding about whether I have done right or wrong in staying here. I, too, am *only* happy when I work and of course now that Paul's arriving I feel like it. Perhaps Helvetia and I can accompany you on your spring tour. Write me soon.

Much much love,

Jane

P.S. If the doctor isn't there at the "People's Eyeglass Store?" surely they have my name on their files. I want my prescription whether they can get me the lens on time for you or not. Jody might go and pick it up there. But mail prescription in any case!

Tangier, December 1948

42
To Katharine Hamill and Natasha von Hoershelman

Dearest Katharine and Natasha,

I can't tell you everything that's happened because if I tried to I wouldn't write at all. I have tried to before and simply stopped writing because it was too exhausting. No one could have been happier than I was to receive your Xmas wire. It was wonderful to know you thought of me. (I sound like a real cripple or "Public Charge.") Certainly you were the only ones who did. Then I started many grateful letters and Jody was with me and—it was all very complicated. Now I am in the Sahara desert. I got to Marseille in February, stayed four days and came back to Africa, scared to go to Paris because there is a very long tunnel outside of Marseille. Lola can appreciate this. Of course I'm not neurotic any more, which is a good thing, but I do find it very hard to go *North.* This place we're in is an oasis—a very small one. We had to walk to it from a bus, with donkey carriers for our luggage. It is not a bus but a very interesting and solidly built *truck* that goes to Timbuktu. The dunes are extremely high, and I shall not attempt to climb them again—well maybe I will—because it is so beautiful up there. Nothing but mountains and valleys of sand as far as the eye can see. And to know it stretches for literally hundreds of miles is a very strange feeling. The sand here is a wonderful beige color. It turns bright pink in the evening light. I am impressed. It is not like anything else anywhere in the world (and I do remember New Mexico), not the sand—or the oasis. Anyway the rest is all rocks and rather terrifying. We saw a mirage called "Lake Michigan and the New Causeway" on the way here. I suppose there are mirages in New Mexico but I can't remember. We are going on to Beni Abbes (Paul and I) next Friday. The hotel here is kept up for the army since no tourists ever come but occasionally army people stop by for lunch. There are just Paul and me, the Arab who runs the hotel, and the three soldiers in the fort, and the natives—but *they* are just a little too native—and frightfully underfed. It is very very quiet, no electricity, no cars. Just *Paul* and *me*. And many empty rooms. The great sand desert begins just outside my window. I might almost stroke the first dune with my hand. Friday we are going further "in." (Oy!) But I am looking forward to the next place, though I doubt that it will be as beautiful as this oasis—nothing could be. The little inn there is run by a woman, a *Mademoiselle* Jury. Paul says she's a yenti old maid. Hoorah! I think there are eight or nine "whites" there—a real mob. Paul thinks there will be too much traffic because the truck goes through twice a week. There is no road leading *here* at all, so he's gotten used to it. We plan to be in the desert about a month and then back to Fez. Then to Tangier, where I can resume my "silly" life with the grain market group: Tetum, Zodelia, Cherifa and Quinza. You remember them. I have gotten nowhere—but Cherifa calls me her "sister" and I eat with them several times a week. I bring the food and the two heavy quarts of thick sweet wine. I had Tetum x-rayed. She was determined to go to the doctor's because I'd taken Cherifa ten times about her foot. I spent all morning in the doctor's waiting room among women wrapped in sheets. But I love to be with her—anywhere. She was happy because she had caught up with Cherifa. She felt the x-ray equalled the foot treatments Cherifa got out of me. It is all really about prestige—their life I mean—but I cannot tell them even that I know they are making an ass of me. I am always scared that they might find out I know. I'll tell you about it when I see you. Forgive this disjointed letter, please, I have had a fly after me and then in the middle of it the Arab who runs the hotel asked me to write a letter for him (naturally he can't write) to a man living in a place called "Oil Pump Number Five." It's a famous hell hole south of here. I hope we don't go there to live.

I spent five or six weeks with Jody. I shall always be very devoted to her. The business partner is quite a problem but I shan't have to face it until I get back—if then. I don't know where I live at this point. If I ever have any money I shall buy a place near the one in Delaware. How far is it from New York? Can Natasha and you *really* get out there for weekends? Can we go to Fire Island just once? But only if Kay Guinness is there. I am determined to be famous because of her and Janet Flanner, and I am simply sitting here in Africa biding my time.

I am actually full of plots and plans and have forgotten none of my enemies in the United States. I shall not be here forever. I refuse to spend fewer than three days with you both at a time. I am sure that I am now *utterly* incapable of getting around New York. I have written some, recently, and hope to see "Camp Cataract" appear in summer. How much land is there in Delaware? I am interested and surprised by this purchase of yours. Oliver wants to build a house with the next money he gets, and he is more likely to have some than I am. It would be nice to be settled near you—or would you hate it? I want to know where Dione is and Miss McBride. Please Katharine call up the *main* Y.W.C.A. headquarters and ask if Miss McBride is there. Tell her Jane Bowles was trying to locate her in order to write her a postal card. If you get her, *or* if they say she's out, at least I'll know she still works there (50 something street East, I believe), and you can write me her address. I keep thinking about her. Give my love to Lola and to my dear Florence, whom I should have written. I wrote Lola once—she never answered. Tell Florence I am going to be in Paris by the 24th of June to hear a piece of Paul's. I expect to come back home (?) next summer—middle or end—it will depend. Miss McBride used to be my teacher when I was fourteen. I've seen her a few times since. I miss you still—if anything, more than ever—and am getting rather eager to return for some nice evenings. (Three nights in a row at least—*please.*) Write me British Post Office, Tangier. If I'm still here they'll forward the mail. But I think it will take quite a while to reach you. I don't know. But much love—as ever— Jane

P.S. Tennessee Williams got me a thousand dollars from the "Author's League"—$100 a month for ten months. He liked my play. I love him. Send me Rosalind's address if possible. Will write Tennessee to give her a message via Natalia, whom he's naturally met. Oh! my God—it suddenly occurred to me Janet Flanner is over on this side of the water and *not* in the States at all. I *know* I shall run into her. I'm sure she'll ask about the Arab nationalists and what their attitude was about Palestine. I shall certainly go into a dead faint right over again. I suppose Rosy will be back before I can reach her. And why get excited because she's in Italy when I'm four days away from Tangier—nearer ten days actually because the train to

Colomb-Bechar only runs three times a week and trucks once or twice? Oh well. Give her my love in New York. Ask her for Esther's program. I should so much like to be somewhere when she was. Is Sybil with her? Please write about land or a house near yours. Maybe you could sell a couple of acres or do you want every *inch* of it? I'm furious already because I feel you're going to be difficult. Will mail this from Beni Abbes (six hours from here) when we get there, and you can judge by the postmark whether you're to answer me there or in Tangier. I daresay Tangier is best. We won't be down here more than a month, and we will have spent about twenty days of it by the time this goes, so unless it reaches you fast, write me British Post Office, Tangier. I love you for writing me and I love you anyway. The picture of Natasha is a dream. I have it with me. Please write again. Miss McBride might also be in the book under her name, Mary Frances, but try the Y. first. Kiss Betty and Lola and Florence—haven't Betty's exact address.

Much love again,

J.

Taghit, Algeria, March 1949

43
To Katharine Hamill

Dearest Katharine,

I was very surprised and distressed to hear about your operation but happy you are getting along so well. Has it affected your drinking or eating? Since writing you I have come out of the desert and am back in Tangier—or have I written you *twice*? Now I'm confused so you see it is better really if I don't write at all—then there can be no mix-ups. *Who* is sending me the cards about Palestine? Is it Billie Abelle or all of you? Please let me know at once. If you don't know about them, take Billie aside and ask her if she has sent me two postal cards asking me what I intend to do about Palestine. I smell Janet Flanner of course but does Billie know about that? If not, you must have been up there or told her about it. I think of Billie very often but hesitate to write her because I can't remember whether I'm supposed to or not—because of Virginia. Does Virginia care? I don't know any more. But give her—Billie—my love when you see her, and I will send them both an official postal card.

Katharine dear, I am still sitting here in Africa and have given up the idea of going to Paris—too expensive—too complicated—and I want to work for a few months at a stretch now before returning, which I daresay will be in the fall. You will be without Natasha in August but I daresay you have sewed yourself up with your sister and several others for that month by now but if not why don't you call Helvetia? She'll be on her farm if she doesn't come here (and I doubt that she will) and you can certainly visit her or perhaps she'd visit you. I would like to think of her with you but I'm sure you will have other plans. Why doesn't Natasha retire too when you do? We are having some little rooms built on our roof so that we could all live in my little house in Tangier. (The taxes are $1.20 a year.) It costs nothing for the food, and liquor slightly less than in the States. Wine of course—nothing. We could be here for part of a year or one year and in the States the next. I think you *must* come to Africa sooner or later. There is a Russian woman here with her father and brother (all of them over 8 feet) and her four dogs (each dog bigger than two Arab houses put together), and she wishes she could make 1500 pesetas ($43) a month, which is what she needs to live on for all of them. Seven hundred a month rent and 800 for food—that's 21 dollars monthly for food; rent of course is non-existent in my house.

This "estimate" does not include meat *or* "Mrs. Crocker's Vegetable-Noodle Soup." But it does include fish, vegetable oil, and stones. Also please continue hunting around for Oliver's Pennsylvania country seat. What is all this about gardening? You are going to be gardening all the time. Helvetia's getting her garden in now and I'm furious. She goes right on with her life and here I am year after year in Africa.

When the rooms are built I shall have Cherifa and Quinza over to sleep. Tetum won't come I'm sure but this time when the rooms are ready I shall offer her a present if she lives with me for a day, two days or a week or more. One month—she gets a whole sheep. One night is going to be a toothbrush or a key ring. Two nights—socks, one week—pyjamas. The addition to the house (it is unlivable now) will cost 350 dollars roughly and we will have one more decent room and two more little rooms large enough for beds. There is one decent room downstairs—well not very decent—but long enough to contain Oliver, and another tiny room large enough for a bed. The bed however would fit only a Latin man or most women but no cowboys can get in there. I had planned to come back sooner thinking that I would go to Paris and then on to New York but it hasn't worked out that way, particularly since we're adding on to the house. I would like that done before I leave and then I will know it's there. I expect I'll come back here in summer very often. In any case it is not a great investment! And it can be sold at any time so I do not feel tied to it either. I am trying to get on with my novel and if it isn't reasonably far advanced by fall I shall chuck writing forever—but I am working now and did in the desert but then I stopped again for three weeks in Fez and one week here, so I've decided no moving about for the moment. The trip back was awful! You must be very excited about your house. I am not neurotic except about hooking the bathroom door (we have hooks and slide-bolts in most W.C.s here) but otherwise O.K.

A boy called Themistocles Hoetis has come here to join us. He hated France, particularly Paris. He is twenty-three and was shot down in a plane during the war. He edits a magazine called *Zero* and had corresponded with Paul though he'd never met him. Well—here he is, and he can get out of his body whenever he wants to and turn around and look at it. His name is *really* Themistocles. I am toying with the idea of having diphtheria shots. We are in a hotel up on the "Old Mountain" (an elevated part of Tangier). The straits are below us and across the way Spain. It is unbelievably beautiful here. How is Lola? Are you continuing to get stronger? Will you kiss my darling Natasha and yourself. I have no one to sleep with as usual.

Much love and *write* me—

Jane

Tangier, Late Spring 1949

44
To Libby Holman

Dear Libby,

My letter and Paul's should arrive at the same time. If I don't get an answer *too* this trip I shall kill myself. "Cold actress thwarts comic writer." Tell *Ollie* to recall all pink and blue scripts of my play, am writing a new third act, cutting out that "treatise" at the end which stinks and has been holding us all up for two years. Cecil Beaton thinks I look like Gloria Swanson. I told you I got old out here. *Please*, darling, will you do me a great favor? Cut out "Camp Cataract" *if* it's in this issue and send it to me airmail. I don't know how much it will cost, but it won't be exorbitant like sending the whole magazine, which they will undoubtedly send me, but by boat and it won't get here for two months. That's O.K. if only you will airmail me the story. Scotty can cut it out. Give her my love. Naturally we are waiting to hear *what* you are going to do about Spain. If you do come over call Helvetia up and her Pekingese and ask her if she wants to come along. *Do* run in and see Jody, and fuss over Mary Anne if you are up that way. Kiss Touchie and Ollie. Delighted about T's play.

Love as ever,

J.

Tangier, August 29, 1949

45
To Katharine Hamill

Katharine dear (and N. *if* she's there—but I doubt it):

What a *Beast* I am not writing. I've become very British, by the way, these last weeks. Our English summer crowd is here (2 people), one of them Cecil Beaton, and the locals are all going to a masquerade very soon given by C. dressed as *events.* Isn't it awful? For me, I mean, because as usual I don't remember what's happened. We have a fifty year range. I can think only of Lindbergh's return but need New York City for my costume. I wrote Oliver an alarming letter about the house next to yours and I've not heard a word since. I have no plans—more mixed up than ever, writing off and on—mostly off—when it's hot. Also have my drinking stomach back—God knows why—probably because I stayed off it for so long. Everything has changed since Truman Capote arrived. I wrote you about his staying here. Then all we needed was "Cecil" on the opposite hill for Africa to pick up its skirts and run. So I feel that though I have not gone to Paris it has come here, which is perhaps a good thing. Happy to find myself as uncomfortable, shy and insecure as ever—I mean it almost makes me feel young again to know that I must still have 4 drinks to feel at ease. I am as indestructible as an armored truck, in that sense, and it is a kind of relief to know that it will never change. Cecil Beaton is shy too, tell Natasha. I had a letter from Helvetia which worried me badly. It did not sound to me as if she were very well. I have no idea *exactly* when I will come home —March the latest—but most *likely* in the fall. I am afraid to see Helvetia and also don't know how on earth I shall get from one place to another in New York. Will you *please* write me whether or not I can *always* stay with you or N. or both for 3 days whenever I visit? I've asked you this in every letter. I just simply won't start that shunting back and forth anymore. Anyway where on earth am I going to be? Oy! I wish you would make a casual visit to R——— Inn. There's Jody too, in the middle of winter. I wish we could have a little apartment together just for a couple of months. My love Katharine darling and to Natasha when she returns. J

P.S. I had a letter from Iris Barry, the first in the twelve years of my *courtship*. A friendly note. Do write any news you hear of Margaret and of yourselves of course. Do you play cards? Paul bought a mah jongg set. Can't you both get sabbaticals? Give my love to Billie Abelle always—she is a wonderful girl—and Rosie and Betty and Frances.

Tangier, Late Summer 1949

46
To Libby Holman

Dearest Libby,

I was horrified to read in your letter to Paul that you had not heard from me. I've written *twice* now without answers from you and have been waiting and waiting for a reply. My last letter gave you an address for Paris *and* London, as I was not sure you would reach me in Tangier. I shall repeat that I am spending the winter in Paris, which is now arranged with Jody, who has probably called you up about my coat by now. Paul (I wrote you this too) is hell bent on going to Ceylon. I think it would be fatal if he hung around until February—for Spain. It is the wrong season there, and he doesn't have any place he wants to be in winter except the Sahara where there really is no piano. He can surely find one in Ceylon. He wants to meet you in spring, either in the U.S. if you can't leave there or Spain and Tangier. Surely unless you have a tour you can forfeit the Connecticut spring—just once. I am speaking entirely against myself, as actually I shall probably return in the early spring (late March) and then come back to the old world just as fast as I can get out of the new one—late spring. It would be ideal of course—May and June in Spain—for you and Paul, and we could come back together but wouldn't that be too late for you? I mean wouldn't April suit you better though it wouldn't *me*? Of course I don't know what mid-April plans you have in the new world, but if it's the tulips or Easter I shall be furious. If you do come over—early spring—please let me know. I shall then probably wait for you. I am terribly confused now as to where I live, Libby, it scares me just a little to think of it, so I don't think of it. If you would only move the entire *shebang* to Tangier I'd be happy. Paris was beautiful and depressing, and despite a really wonderful reception in England and here in North Wales I am eager to get back to the "soupe hôtel" in Paris. I stayed there a few days on my way here and am returning on November the 28th to Paris with David Herbert and Michael Duff. I think you know David—at least he's met you—but it was many years ago. You probably know Michael too. Oliver would love this house. It is still run on a pre-war scale. I mean the "staff" are all here, but I feel that tomorrow they may vanish. I shall tell Oliver about it, the luxury of it will make him furious, and he will never dare to mention those bells at Jack Wilson's house again and those two wretched servants of his. As for myself I am almost dead from having my little scarf pressed which is all I brought for three days. It's the little pink one you gave me. I don't know what "Nanny" thought when she unpacked me and found Olive Oyl—Popeye's girl friend—in my suitcase, but she laid her out diagonally on the dressing table. Olive Oyl is made of wood. If I can judge by the few British I have met—who have been either of the aristocracy or the theater or of the "servant class"—I am all out for them. Paul is a *great* success here. He said that naturally his trip to England and the preparations for it slowed down his progress on *Yerma* and he is sorry about that but after all one only writes a first novel once and I don't think he's ever had such a success before in his life and so I am happy he came here and I'm sure you will be too. Parties were given for him every second in London, and though he was very tired after a week of it I know it has done him an enormous amount of good. I think when he gets down to work again it will go very quickly. Please write me. I wish to hell you could come to Paris but I guess you wouldn't.

Much love, Libby darling,
Jane

P.S. Forgot to write you that Paul is all for my allowing Audrey Wood to represent me on *Summer House*. He thinks it will help both me and Oliver and that I'd be a fool not to. Oliver wired me that he thought the new third act wonderful and that he had definite plans for the play, but Paul thinks he is more than likely just keeping up my morale. Audrey Wood wrote me last week (probably prompted by Tenn). Love to Touchie.

North Wales, November 1949

47
To Libby Holman

Dearest Libby,

At last! I won't go on about how puzzled I've been by your silence—and worried. My reason for not thanking you immediately for the clothes (which did arrive)—there was still no letter from you, only a more than confusing message from Jody, namely that you had not heard from *me*. All right that's over and I shall write without going backwards which is always a bore. I did write a long one from England and so did Paul explaining about Ceylon, and there was a lot in it about the Lorca opera too. He did lose some time on it in London but he will catch up now on the boat and I know it did him a great moral good to be at last a *lion* which he has deserved for many years and had somehow never gotten in music. He is now a famous literary figure in England (well-known anyway) and probably will soon be in New York if he isn't already. He took the translation with him on the boat to finish and expects to find a piano in Ceylon so that enough songs are written by spring for you to work on. He would like you to join him in Spain then. He is returning to Tangier around March, approximately. All this was written to you in a long long letter that I saw and which was sent from England (Wilton-Salisbury). From the sound of *your* letter I would judge that you never received it. If this is the case, I *can* write almost everything he said to you in detail since we discussed whether or not it was fair or right of him to go to Ceylon for hours on end, and he was against waiting around until February for several reasons. Please let me know Libby whether or not you received this letter. It's the one in which he even suggests your joining him in Ceylon (!) but is most in favor of meeting you in Spain this spring. In my letter I scolded you and said for once you could miss part of April at Treetops. It's a far better month for Spain and Paul will have enough music done by then to make it worth your while and his too. Now I've gone and repeated all this but I do have a feeling you've received no letters or only half of them. *NO*, Paul did not leave from Tangier, he left from Antwerp, and if Gore goes to Tangier he will not see him there. What *are* all these hog-wild rumors anyway? According to Audrey Wood, Ollie was going to take out an option on my play again beginning January 1st but now there is no *word.* I have overspent myself a little too, thinking the money was coming, so I hope it will. I think it will but if you see Ollie please ask him whether it is coming or not so that at least I know if it is coming. There are a few little things I'd like to buy and also my spring plans depend a little on that and also on whether you want to visit Paul in spring or not. He's already bought his passage back for March. I thought you might come over a little earlier, pick me up in Paris and then we could all go down to Tangier, or you could go from here direct to Spain. Anyway something could be worked out. I wrote Oliver that I was sad to hear you felt you couldn't take a "pleasure" trip, but I think that's one of your big troubles—that everything has to be connected and too complicated to unravel—it may even be necessary for you. I may share this trouble though it expresses itself differently. I forget how!

My plan is either to return to America in early spring, late spring or summer, for a while anyway. This depends on my work, money, you and my play. If Oliver did manage to get a fall production going then I might, if I can, just stay on in Paris or even go down to Tangier before returning to New York and being stuck there for a long period of time—maybe ten years?

As for my life I don't know where I live and I am sorry in a way that you *do.* I am having a very quiet time naturally with Jody here. I saw quickly enough that lots of parties would be out even if I *did* want them and even if I were invited. I know I could get about through Peggy Reille, but I can't put Jody through such evenings and perhaps even not myself. I work and I walk a little and I see a few friends who live nearby. (About 850 of them.) Paris is very beautiful and the only city I think to live in. Except to see you, I have no desire to return to the States ever. Not that I *love* it here, I just hate it there. I love Morocco best I guess. I don't know what will happen to me—not really. *Please, please* write—if only a card. How I wish you could come over, perhaps in February or March. After all, perhaps I could count as "business" and it could be on your way to meeting Paul. Force Ollie to give you a third act, or else ask Audrey Wood to lend you her copy. I had one letter from you which I got (about three weeks after it was written) at American Express disapproving of her, but by then I was pretty well up to my neck. Don't worry about it. Much much love Libby darling and please let us keep in close touch. You *must* come in February. J.

P.S. Will certainly buy Van Gogh if you want me to.

I don't go to nightclubs since Jody came so I haven't seen G. Lloyd except once when I first got here and was taken to the Boeuf.

Expect to have Paul's address any minute, soon as he reaches Ceylon. I'll forward any letter, just send it c/o Mrs. Jane Bowles here.

Paris, January 11, 1950

48
To Paul Bowles

Dearest Bupple,

I suppose I should single-space this, though I hate to. There is no room for corrections. I shall get all the disagreeable things off my mind first. My work went well last week. I had got into a routine, but this week it's all shot to hell again . . . not because of my life really, but because I have come to the male character again. I must change all that I wrote about him in Tangier. Not all, but it must become real to me, otherwise I can't write it. I have decided not to become hysterical, however. If I cannot write my book, then I shall give up writing, that's all. Then either suicide or another life. It is rather frightening to think of. I don't believe I would commit suicide, though intellectually it seems the only way out. I would never be brave enough, and it would upset everybody. But where would I go? I daresay the most courageous thing to do would be nothing. I mean, to continue as I am, but not as a writer. As the wife of a writer? I don't think you'd like that, and could I do it well? I think I'd nag and be mean, and then I would be ashamed. Oh, what a black future it could be! That is why I have to use some control, otherwise I get in a panic. I am trying to write. Jody's being here is a hindrance and a help. A help because she gives a center to my day, and a hindrance because if I read, and wrote the letters I should write, and simply wandered around chewing my cud as one does when one's writing, I would have very little time left for her. We have been seeing too many people . . . not many different ones, but the same few over and over again. There have been very few dinners alone, and it has taken me some weeks to realize that Jody just doesn't want to have anyone much around. Though if they must be around, she prefers them to be men. Gordon she likes, and Frank Price. I have miraculously avoided a real bust-up drama, and have kept the most severe check on myself. I think now that things are well adjusted, and I am clear in my mind about how to conduct the rest of the winter until she leaves: in solitary confinement as much as possible. Strange that when she first arrived I thought we had a whole lifetime together; I guess that threw me into a panic. And now I feel I've done it all wrong. It would have been pleasanter and better for my work seeing no one else (the strain of wondering whether she was enjoying an evening or not gave me a headache), and instead getting into the habit of eating dinner in silence (unless I talk) which is, after all, not so bad. I don't know what I was afraid of. Despair, I guess, as usual. Now there seems to be not enough time left. I have grown used to her again, and fond of her, and we have moved into Frank Price's flat, which will be much better. I had taken my own room on the other floor because our room was not suitable for working; and because of a scene she made about my "walking out" on her, I felt guilty every time I was in my room and was not strictly working. She later explained how she felt, and tried to reassure me that she no longer felt that way about it, yet I could never be in my own room with any serenity. The fairies on the other side of the wall drove me crazy anyway, and turned out to be almost as bad as the children in the courtyard who had made work impossible for me in the room we had shared together (the same arrangement you and I had). It wasn't big enough anyway for actual living, though it was fine just for a week.

I want desperately to get another "clump" of work done in the next four or five weeks. There is simply no time for anything, ever. I know that I shall be terribly upset when she leaves. There will be a week of agony, I suppose. Changing from this charming flat into a cheap room, financial insecurity which I don't have now, and so on. I am sending you O.'s letter so that you know what's going on. If this option does get to me, instead of tearing up roots again, I may spend part of the spring in Paris . . . how long I don't know. I may also go to Tangier, depending on whether you're there or not and a few other unpredictables. If however the play does go into rehearsal this summer, I *would* prefer, as Oliver suggests, to go back in July rather than in the spring. It would be better sailing, would give me longer to work on Yenti, if I'm still working by then, and I'd see you sooner, as I'd most likely get down to Africa eventually.

I see Alice Toklas now and then, but I'm afraid that each time I do I am stiffer and more afraid. She is charming, and will probably see me less and less as a result of my inability to converse. This is not a result of my shyness alone, but of a definite absence of intellect, or should I say of ideas that can be expressed, ideas that I am in any way certain about. I have no opinions really. This is not just neurotic. It is very true. And Alice Toklas gives one plenty of opportunity to express an idea or an opinion. She is sitting there waiting to hear one. She admires your book tremendously. In fact, she talked of little else the last time I saw her. She won't serve me those little bread sandwiches in different colors any more because she says I like them more than the cake, and so eat them instead of the cake. I do like them better. And now I must go there and eat only sweets, which makes me even more nervous. Maybe she'll never speak to me again. Eudora Welty came over to dinner with Mary Lou Aswell and told me she was a great admirer of yours. She asked for *Camp Cataract* and took it home with her. After nearly a month she returned it with a note explaining that she failed on it, but would like to try something else of mine some day. I had met her on the street in the middle of the month, and she said then that she was having trouble with it, and so she never did finish it. I was disturbed by that as I have, since seeing you last, turned into an admirer of hers, and it would be nice for me to be admired by an established and talented American writer, instead of by my friends and no one else. That was upsetting, and also the fact that a friend in the hotel didn't like it really. (A very brilliant and charming girl called

Natika Waterbury, who is now in Paris but whom I met long ago in New York.) This evening Sonia Sekula is giving a small party in her room. Mary Reynolds will come, and Lionel Abel and Pegeen. (Pegeen has two babies, apparently by her husband Hélion.) Jody will attend, perhaps, but I can't, because I am dining with, of all people, Sidéry, who was very excited when he heard I was your wife. I met him at one of the few cocktails I've been to, at Peggy's. He is quite charming, I think. I wrote you about Manchester, but you must simply have forgotten. I gave him to Truman, not because T. wanted him (though if he did it was for my sake, not his) but because I didn't like his face or his nature when I returned. Though Donald was never a real Peke, he was cute from the very first minute, and this one was cute only because he was a little fluffy ball. His muzzle had gotten much whiter, and his face definitely more pointed, and his eyes closer together. I thought I had better give him away while I disliked his looks, as I'm sure he would have been a nuisance. I have a few clippings which I'll enclose, though I'm sure you have them already. The book, though second from the bottom, made the best-seller list, which I think is wonderful. Your literary success is a fact now, and it is not only distinguished but widespread. I think to have Connolly and Toklas and a host of other literary people, plus a public, is really remarkable and wonderful. You should soon write another book. I hope that you are pleased at last, and not simply because it is a way to make some money. You do deserve a success of this kind, and I think you are at the right age for it. I can get no news out of anyone in Tangier. Have written Ira and Jacqueline and the fact that I hear from no one confirms me in my belief that Esterhazy has gone. It is rather horrid not knowing what is going on. I am glad I have a little money down there because if anyone ever writes me I should like to send checks for Fathma. I have just about nothing left here, and I know this will horrify you, but it just happened, and without my going to nightclubs either. I am waiting from day to day for the option money to arrive from Audrey Wood via Oliver, rather than send for more from Tangier. Naturally I would have been more careful if I hadn't had a letter from Wood that sounded pretty definite about the option. *Blondes* is not only a hit but a smash hit. Laurence Olivier's head reader saw my play and wrote that it was morbid and depressing, and though not something to be dismissed, certainly nothing they could think of doing. Truman hates New York, and wrote: "Honey, even if your play is done I hope you won't have to come back for it." Alice T. was delighted that you didn't really care for him very much. (I told her.) She said it was the one thing that really worried her. She could not understand how an intelligent person like you etc. She doesn't seem to worry in the least, however, about my liking him. So I'm insulted . . . again.

Paris is so very beautiful, particularly in this dark winter light. I'm surprised you don't love it more. I still love Africa best I guess, but there one must shut one's eyes against a great many things too. Here there is the Right Bank, and there the Villes Nouvelles, the buses, and the European shoes. You know what I mean. To cross the river never ceases to excite me. I went to see *Phèdre* at the Comédie Française with Natika. I am wildly excited about it. The only thing I have enjoyed thoroughly in years. I have never heard French *grand théâtre* before. I don't know how good the players were, but one must be good to do Racine at all. I shall go there now as often as possible.

I have gotten rounder in the face from the nourishing food. I'm upset about it, but perhaps it is becoming. Poor Michael Duff's son was born dead. I don't hear from them. Just a funny postcard now and then. I am terribly sorry that I can't give you more information about your book. Certainly friends in New York can do better. I might as well be in Ceylon with you. I love the descriptions of it, by the way, though at the moment I feel no need of adding any country to my list. I am puzzled enough with the Seine River and the Grand Socco. Oddly enough I still love Morocco best, though I do not admire it more. I think and think about what it means to me, and as usual have come to no conclusion. I dream about it too, in color, all the time.

Much much love, Bupple dear. I miss you very much. Write me your plans and don't stay away forever. I hope you'll return sometime this spring. Will you?

P.S. I had my tooth fixed. The dentist hurt like hell. Is Gore really joining you?

Paris, January 17, 1950

49
To Paul Bowles

Dear Bup:

I don't know who else is sending you the enclosed, most likely everybody, but rather than take a chance on your missing out on it (or them), I shall send them along. I'm deeply sorry that I have not been nearer to the source of your criticisms, publicity etc. I should certainly have seen to it, that you received them immediately. I enclose Oliver's letter so that you keep up with the plans which as you see are in the air, but not very worrying. I have a feeling that Libby will be coming to Spain in spring. We should have a charming reunion in Morocco, all of us, if it ever works out. Of course nothing will be charming if I can't get my novel written. Yesterday the whole thing dried up on me again and I had the terrible pain in my head that I get—not a pain exactly but a feeling of tightness in my scalp, as if it were drawn tight over an empty drum. (My head is the drum.) It happens too often really and I'm afraid that it is the physical expression of sterility. I go on trying though it is a terrible fight. I had suggested this suite to Oliver (Frank's rooms) for himself though he seems to have misunderstood me. Because of my work, I don't think I could be even in a suite with anyone. I am sorry that he is not coming in early March, particularly for such gloomy reasons. If however he were delayed by something pleasant I should in one sense be glad. I think it will be good to have a few weeks completely to myself. I do feel very strongly that I should give up writing if I can't get further into it than I have. I cannot keep losing it the way I do, much longer. This is hard to explain to you who work so differently. I may really have said all I have to say. Last night I felt so bad about it, I drank almost an entire bottle of gin. I had gone back to my desk after the most terrible *crise* of despair and forced myself to work after I had very nearly thrown everything in the fire (mentally). It was an effort and after that I just started drinking. I felt better as a result and by eleven o'clock I was very cheery indeed. Natika, who lives in the hotel, came by, and we all three of us went out to the Monocle. It has gone down terribly and the tough proprietress I was so crazy about whose name was Bobby and because of whom I hung around Paris for weeks (you remember) after you had left for the South has gone. "Elle n'est plus dans le métier," the bartender told me; he had known her too. "Elle s'est mariée et elle est propriétaire de deux énormes châteaux." Why would she have *two* castles? She was the most masculine woman I had ever seen. I would have been depressed if I hadn't been drunk. Ironically enough I had not been there twenty minutes when "La Zöora" appeared on the little dance floor doing an Algerian belly dance. I was wildly excited and spent the rest of the evening talking Arabic with her though God knows how, because there is practically nothing left of mine. She said *Gol* by the way instead of using the correct *Tangier k*. I wanted so badly to rush somewhere and tell you about it. It was certainly not what I had expected of the Monocle. And to think twelve years ago I sat in that place night after night drunk as a lord and partly because I didn't want to go to Africa—in the beginning entirely for that reason—until I met Bobby "aux deux châteaux." Last night I was more excited finding the Algérienne than I was by anything else. We talked about Colomb-Bechar and the Aid el Kebir. She said she couldn't live in Algiers because her family wouldn't allow her to dance. I can just see them. We are going out to eat cous-cous together one of these days. I have her address. She was the only entraineuse who did not ask for a tip—and I danced with her more than with any of the others—and she warned me against a restaurant that one of them was taking us to after the place closed. She said in Arabic, to me "matimshishi temma—Fluz besef—hamsa miat francs." And so I warned Natika and Jody and we went home instead. She seemed so delighted with me. We were two yenti Algerians meeting in Paris, and helping each other out. Of course she would be called Zöora. I think she might be able to give me the real low down on Arab women and their habits though Algerians may be very different, but surely they have almost everything in common with Moroccans. Alas she is neither a Cherifa nor a Tetum, she's the other type, but terribly nice. Jody ended up the evening dancing with an entraineuse from Martinique, quite fat and dark. Isn't it all ridiculous? The evening cost roughly about ten thousand francs though it needn't have, but we were suckers. It wasn't my money so don't get excited.

Ira has told Tommy Esterhazy to fetch your package. He *is* in the house. Both Jay and Ira have written saying everything is fine though I can't understand why Esterhazy doesn't pull himself together and write. It seems to me that (unless he has written you) it is a piece of uncommon rudeness. I don't understand. Two heartbreaking news items. One: they have sold the space between the Place de France and the B.P.O. and an enormous apartment building is going up. It will be the end of my enjoyment on that end of town. I loved that view so terribly—the rugs on the wall, the Algeciras boat coming in; the whole thing is too damn upsetting. I shall never go to the British Post Office again. The second item is even more horrible. Cherifa, Jay writes, is planning to move to the *new* market. So that will be the real end of everything. I just can't bear to think of her empty stall. Do you think he could be teasing? I am awfully upset and am writing Kouche Saïd about it. I shall enclose a letter to her which I'll ask him to translate, saying that I dreamed a terrible misfortune would befall her should she change her stall. Do you think it would be a sin to try and play the Deus Ex Machina in this? You think I am joking probably, but I am not. I am terribly upset. If one by one all the things I loved about Tangier disappear even in a few months, how can I even look forward to going back ever? The terrible thing is that I love it still just as I did when I left. I am no less hysterical. What is it do you suppose? The fact that I do not rush back at once is no indication of how I feel. It is in my heart and we do own the house. As I wrote you, now that I'm here there are things I must benefit by and that I hope to enjoy—always of course if I'm working well.

I hope you get a good boat, Bupple, otherwise I shall worry. Write me please.

Much love, as ever
Jane

P.S. Terribly worrying about O's mother. What on earth will happen to Ivan if something does happen to her. I hope NOT. And what about Oliver? Will he take it terribly hard if something does? All the more reason for him to come over.

I really can't get *over* the French cats and that is why I keep writing you and O. about them. Do you like them? Toklas has given me up. A blow I scarcely need at the moment. I hate the writing paper you used last. Think of the money I spend happily on overweight for you and then *you* save a few—pence, I suppose—by using those HORRORS—you know I *hate* them.

Paris, Late January 1950

50
To Paul Bowles

Dearest Buppie,

I am happy to have news of you again, though I'm sorry you feel a bit lonesome. There is nothing I would like more than to be alone at the moment (or with you) but then when it happens (my separation from Jody) I probably shall miss her. It is going to be ghastly this time since she knows by now that everything is all washed up. I have never been through anything quite like this winter. How I ever got myself into it, I don't know. But by the time I reached England it seemed too late to wire her and too cruel. I was not *sure* either how really over it was. Perhaps even recently I thought something might be saved. I see no one now but Jody; this I wrote you was my plan, but I had counted somehow on routine and solitude hiding the absence of love or even inviting it again. I was quite wrong, but at least I think Jody can stand it better this way and there is less drinking. My close friends know the reasons for my seclusion and others think I've become a hermit, I imagine. Peggy Guggenheim has called me several times since my one lunch with her but I have more or less told her to try me in March! I could not be more isolated in Beni-Abbes, in fact Bidon 5 is probably a better parallel. Today I had lunch with Sybille Bedford because Jody went to see her friend at the other end of Paris, the only one, a WAC with a new born baby. It was wonderful to have someone to talk to. Sybille, though you hate her, is one of the better minds, I think, and very entertaining. She is rosy cheeked and gay too. God, I just can't take many more gloompots. I am not complaining really about my life, at the moment. I would not mind anything if only Jody did not look so sad. I am doing everything I can, but nothing will make up for the one terrible lack. She is often pleasant but most of the time gloomy and if even slightly drunk, vindictive. If her partner were here it would be better to split it up quickly, but I would not dare let her go off somewhere to wait for Mary Anne alone. I do not think she can take it, and is happier here with me despite the difficult and dismal situation. I put all the blame on myself naturally, and feel now that perhaps I should never start anything with the innocent again. I am not hard enough to take it, myself, not to speak of them. I have still not had a decent time in Paris. Will I in the spring? I daresay the second Jody leaves everyone else I would like to see will leave too. I know Oliver will come but then that is not what I mean. I should love to be able to work here by myself and read and yet have a few appointments which I would look forward to with excitement. I am sorry that I went to England despite what I saw, but on the other hand I am more than pleased at the new development which will permit me to spend some time in Paris, after all. I would have been pretty mad going back to New York in March having got about two days fun out of the whole grand tour. Also I want to get much more work done before returning to the U.S.A. You mention that I shall get more work done in Tangier or New York, but it will be Tangier or Paris or both. I have no plans except to do what I want to do. If you are forced to take a boat to England we can all meet in England or in Paris. I'm sure David would love to have you and Oliver (and me too) at his house for a while. Oliver has ideas of visiting the Cliffords in Italy and wanted to take me there too. I'm sure he'd just as soon take you. Or we might all go, if there's a way to get there for me. You could eventually get to Gib. from Naples. I have a feeling Libby will be meeting you in April in Spain. She says she will either meet you then or in June after Topper's graduation on June the 12th, which she must be back for. I shall enclose the paragraph in case letters go astray. If you get a boat to London why don't you write Libby to take the Queen and we'll all meet here? I'm sure she'd enjoy a week or two in Paris or London and then we could all stick together or separate and meet later again. As usual unless a car materializes I won't want to go skipping around. I'll stick in one place and work, wherever it happens to be. Maybe Paris, maybe Tangier (if I have any work by then that I can call my own). Oliver wants to go back on a French Line, by the way, because he thinks he can get us passage at a very reduced rate. He advertised for them in the [ ]

P.S. I would be perfectly happy to go to England again. I just felt that I went at a wrong moment—though now that I can stay here longer it is less wrong than it was.

Paris, February 13, 1950

51
To Paul Bowles

Dearest Bup: Monday

I enclose Esterhazy's letter. I don't know what to write him, except that I think he should do the work while he is there (*have* it done) rather than while he is away. I am having my money sent to Tangier and the bank can send me ten thousand at a time (mandat-carte). The exchange there is three ninety-five. It will be a nuisance but certainly worth it. I am going to buy some shoes, which I need desperately, a pleated skirt, infroissable, which will go beautifully with my shirts, a gay scarf and a white blouse or two. Mine are coming to pieces, the white ones, and I need some for dressier occasions. When I have bought these few things and paid my five thousand franc dentist bill, I suppose I will have spent about thirty thousand francs at least. I shall spend as little money as possible, though I shan't stay on here very long if it's going to be *la misère.* At the moment I hope to find a cheap, or a cheaper, room here or at the Quai Voltaire, as Jody is leaving in ten days. I would like to continue with my work in peace. None of the two hundred fifty franc rooms is very livable in winter, I'm afraid, and March can be quite cold. I'll pay more for my room and less for food, I guess. I am going over to the École des Langues Étrangères or whatever the hell it's called, and look into a course in Maghrebin-Arabic. I don't think I can go much further in it alone, or with Cherifa. As for Kouch, he can do no more for me, I'm sure. I just can't accept having gotten this far in the damn language, and not getting any further. I think too that it makes my being in Morocco seem somehow more connected with my work. With me, as you know, it is always the dialogue that interests me, and not the paysages so much or the atmosphere. In any case, I cannot express these ever in writing. I feel that some day I might write *Automobile* if I ever finish *this* thing. I will write you what happens with the course. I shall be bitterly disappointed if it turns out to be hopeless.

Now that Gore is with you I suppose you are less lonely and you may even put off your return. Do let Libby know definitely what you are doing, and Esterhazy too. I know either one of us or both of us will want the house to be empty for us when we are there, whether we live in it entirely or just eat in it, work in it, etc. I think it might be a squeeze for both of us unless we're flat broke. I am sorry you have been so worried about the house. I read a letter of yours written to Gordon. Sorry, but pleased, too, that you think of it. It means that you will come home now and then to roost, and not be perpetually wandering around. I am delighted that I am not in Ceylon because of your snake letter to Gordon. In his "desk," indeed, and I spend half the day at a desk. My God!

Eventually I should like to go to Venice and to Ireland. If it were not getting even further away from Tangier I would go there this spring—to Ireland, I mean—by myself (ossir). If life becomes unbearable here and my Arabic course doesn't work out, I may just go to Tangier . . . if I can get Natika to go with me. I don't want to rush off rashly though, and then feel that I have missed my chance of enjoying Paris, forever. God knows when I'll get here again.

Having refused so many invitations to Peggy's, I finally went with Jody and Natika at eight o'clock last night. We were late, invited for six thirty, and most of the people had gone. It was disastrous. Peggy took me over to Marie-Laure de Noailles and introduced me. I kept glancing over my shoulder at Jody to see if she was all right (engaged in conversation) and she was. Madame de Noailles dragged me into a different room so that we could talk quietly. I was uneasy, but Jody was still in a group with Natika and some man when I left her. We talked mostly about Cecil and Truman, and then since we had no cigarettes, I went back into the big room to get them. I was horrified to see Jody standing quite alone, framed in the doorway. I rushed up to her: she was in a rage with Natika and me, a little drunk, too. I tried to calm her down, but alas, by the time I had, Marie-Laure had wandered back into the big room. I started running about like a maniac, looking for cigarettes. It was sort of like a Kafka. I never did get back to Marie-Laure because I was terrified of leaving Jody's side even for a minute. I am sure Madame de Noailles thinks I staged the whole thing, as I never did get back to speak to her at all, and had interrupted a conversation that was obviously unfinished just to bring back some cigarettes. It was all ridiculous, and I'm glad I haven't been out with Jody more. It's hopeless, and I told Peggy not to invite me. I don't care really. Supposedly Mme. de Noailles is an old collaborationist, but she is also Peggy's guest and she must think me nuts or rude. She liked your book immensely.

Perhaps you can write Esterhazy. I don't know what to tell him. Audrey Wood thinks your book *is* a movie and regrets your tie-up with Helen Strauss. Have you written Strauss about it? I imagine they automatically think of those things, don't they? I'm going to see Brion today at the Quai Voltaire. He is leaving for Italy and says he has never been so desperate in his life. The Fulbright seems to have blown up, or he has. I couldn't quite understand, but I shall know more by tonight.

I have met Dilkusha de Rohan. She is really the end, but God knows I shall probably be seen sitting with her in a few weeks. I would have shot myself, however, had I waited in Tangier for her. Mary has disappeared, according to Dil. She was last seen in La Linea. Dil said she was supposed to be coming into another nine thousand pounds, which I suppose might explain Dil's trip there. She only saw Mary *once*, in Tangier, though they did spend three weeks together in Gib. I don't know what it's all about. Sylvia Marlowe is arriving in May. I am getting rather excited about my play again. Do you think that this time it will get on? We went to the zoo and saw a whole monkey village. They lived in little Arab houses. The younger monkeys kept yanking the tiny babies away from the mothers, and then they would run with them all over the rocks. Other young monkeys were the pursuers. Rather like a wild-west movie, except that they almost tore one of the babies apart. You would have loved it. I wish I could take one of these fat (French) cats back to Tangier. Much love

P.S. Please be careful of the snakes and insects. And what are those elephant trips you are going to make? I am frantic too about your going eventually to the place where the plague broke out. There might be a little left even when they do allow visitors. Or will it be safe?

Keep writing me here. Probably won't move but in any case will pick up my mail.

Decided to write Esterhazy not to let anyone work on the house while he's gone.

Paris, February 13, 1950

52
To Libby Holman

Dearest Libby, L'Étape, Pacy-sur-Eure, France

I don't know how everything got into such a mess or what Paul has written you. I should have written you myself but did not dream that you would still want to come over to Spain even if Paul were going to Westport with me—or shortly afterwards.

Since he is coming anyway to do the music, we thought the earlier the better. He has been wonderful since his return from Ceylon and is even willing to risk his fare over, which Oliver won't pay him in case the Westport production never comes off. If it does he'll get his fare out of it one way. I myself am terrified of the whole thing and want him with me very much to help on decisions. I know more or less what you think of this production but I can't possibly decide from here to call it off. Once there the responsibility of deciding such a thing without Paul would be ghastly if it did come to that, and if not there will be a million other things to decide. Paul should be a perfect balance for Oliver and me. I shudder to think too that you won't be around. I had hoped that you would work with Paul at Treetops and that he would be there for me to consult as well. I wouldn't dream of pitching my needs against yours if they were equal but I think in this case they are not. The play has been banging around for five years, no director seems to be willing to do it except this Garson Kanin. If he is a yenti and awful then a decision to give the whole thing up may be the *only* solution. I mean give it up forever because I don't feel that this play can go trailing around any longer—Oliver will be worn out. To decide all this by myself will be a terrific responsibility. Also without the music the play would not have a fair tryout and Paul wants to do it. I naturally am delighted he does. I don't know what Spanish arrangements you've made. Even if he waits to meet you he can only see you for a short while—a few days—and then he'll have to leave. I think that your European plans are wonderful, but I don't feel that it is wildly essential for you to sop up Spanish atmosphere in July and August. Is it? Couldn't you stay at Treetops and spend that time with Paul and learning from records? You'll not only be helping me, but Paul will get much more work done on the opera that way. Have you a Spanish trip worked out with some other people—or what? I realize that if you do, you might want to meet Paul just for a few days in Spain, as you would, if he sails on the 8th, miss him en route. I have understood that you arrive on the 15th.

Changing his passage is going to be difficult, and his being in Connecticut without you will be grim—for him and for me.

I feel the Spanish trip would be a pleasure for both of you, though not an actual *necessity*. There are records that you can listen to and I think Paul could leave after the Westport production is over (August 28th) so you could go to Spain then. I was with Bud and so I know that your Paris concert should not take place before October or November. You may naturally have some plan about Spain that I know nothing about, but please, if you *don't*, consider staying behind just for another six or seven weeks. It would make all the difference in the world to me.

It is not easy for me to take the responsibility of dragging Paul back and I have even suggested his allowing someone else to do the music. He wouldn't dream of it and I think I would have been mortally wounded if he had accepted the suggestion. I know how much he longs to remain over here and have even written him in answer to a wire he sent yesterday about you and Spain, namely "Libby *insists* I be in Spain for her arrival," that I *suspected* him of writing you a letter that would spur you on to come to Spain rather than the reverse, to give him an automatic excuse for remaining an extra week or ten days. I could not imagine your being so insistent otherwise. He would have done so *unconsciously* of course, and perhaps he didn't. You may have, as I said, some new project worked out in Spain that makes going there and speaking to Paul even if only for a few days absolutely essential. If it is, and this really is a terribly important moment in your career, as important as it is in mine to be in America—even if only to *drop* the play—then *forgive* me for even writing this letter. It will only cause you anguish and it is not meant for this—the letter. I am writing it only because I am not at all certain that the picture has been presented to you clearly, that you even know how much it means to me that you be there, which of course is quite beside the point if your Spanish visit has become more than a useful and pleasant project and is now essential and even *if* essential is it essential that you be there right *now* and for the major part of your visit without Bubble? I am writing in the dark of course and now I wish that we had kept in closer touch with each other. I did not gather from Bud Williams (whom I love) that you had any other project except to travel through Spain with Paul and listen to music? Naturally if he *can* get a later boat which will nonetheless bring him back on time to do the music I would wire him if the whole thing blew up and thus save him his fare (he can't get over for under $500). There is an advantage in this but Oliver does not seem to think it is going to blow up at all. The difficult question is this: if I am there and you and Paul are here (in Spain) and I am 90 percent sure that the Westport production *mustn't* go on (I don't *think* that they will do it there unless I consent to let it go on in New York too), then won't I be in a frenzy without Paul there to back me up in my decision to either let it go on or stop it (there will be naturally one thousand other decisions to make but this will be the big one)? Ollie and I must necessarily be on opposite ends in this thing, not always, but it *will* happen. In fact it has already about something and Paul agrees with me. I don't of course know whether or not his arrival around the 15th (if he does sail the 8th) will save *much*. I can be certain however that if he arrives just in time to do the music all will be set. If he comes over sooner as planned he might be a great help, but then he might miss you and also the opportunity of canceling his passage if it does fizzle out within a week or ten days of my arrival in Connecticut.

This whole problem is driving me quite mad, and the fact that Paul won't be living at Treetops and working with you and with me has changed everything. I am sure he can stay with the Kanins or Wilson once the rehearsals start in August but will he like that? I *know* he's okay with you, but if he's nervous and unhappy he's going to drive me crazy and it would be better not to have him there at all, but he wouldn't think of letting anyone else do the score and I am deeply happy about that of course. I know that you probably don't *want* to be around because you don't like the setup, but why leave me then to face it all alone? No one we like will do the damn thing anyway.

Please reconsider your decision about Spain. I know you'll be fair and if it means a great deal more to you than I can imagine, *wire me at once* that you're coming. I shall have to tend to changing Paul's passage from here. I am about one hour and a half out of Paris and shall not move from this Inn until I hear from you, except to go to Paris for the day, but I will even try to delay that so that if your wire says that he should try and change his passage I can attend to it in person rather than on this telephone which has to be *cranked* on with a handle. Don't let me get on that now for another ten pages. The operator is usually in a different town having a glass of wine.

I hope to God you will put off the Spanish extravaganza for just a while longer. You *have* before this for lesser reasons (*hélas*). *If* you do, do you think I ought to try and get Paul a sailing a week or ten days later than his present one? In any case that would give him the extra margin he might need if the show blew up. I will be able to tell so much more about it when I get there (ossir). I suggest this because I feel that you perhaps have some grapevine on it and might not think that the project is nearly as certain as Oliver makes it out. In that case you could advise us quite *apart* from your own plans. You could then wait in Connecticut for that extra week or ten days and if in the interim the whole thing *was* called off you could join him in Spain. If not you would stay in Connecticut and go to Spain later? I could run the same risk that way, of having to sign everything without his presence, or call it off, etc., but if you think that would be the wisest I'll take the chance. Oliver sounds very certain of everything but now he is in Rome, I am here, and Paul is in Tangier if he hasn't fled to the desert by now.

I wish to hell all this had come up while Paul was in Paris. I begged him *daily* to cable you and I'm rather furious that I have to cope with telegrams now and the horror of letters such as these. I really feel terribly discouraged and sad about it. I wouldn't write you this if I didn't feel you could get as much out of being with Paul at Treetops as you could being (with whom?) in Spain. It would naturally make a tremendous difference to me and I have felt foolishly certain and calm about his return because it didn't even occur to me that you would consider Spain if he could not be with you there for any serious length of time. When I received his wire yesterday I was terribly shocked—horrified really. Now I am wondering what it is all about. I feel somehow that something is being kept from me. By Oliver? By Paul? By Bud? By you? What is it? Will you wire me at once here at the Inn? The address is: L'Étape, Pacy-sur-Eure, France. You should say whether or not your Spanish trip still stands and whether I should try therefore to change Paul's passage for a later boat—which may easily be impossible (it would have to be within a week or so of your arrival anyway, if not less).

If not—if you do see your way to staying there without feeling that you have given up a main chance—then please wire me whether or not you think he should even so try to get a slightly later passage which would give you the opportunity of meeting him in Spain a *little* later should it all blow up. I am going under the assumption that you *may* know more about the plans for Westport than I do. Knowing me *too* you may feel sure that I myself will stop them from doing it, and that it would be far better for me to decide this by myself and save Paul $500 and his trip through Spain with you rather than to get him over there. The responsibility of course is enormous and I don't really *expect* you to advise me, unless you want to. I mean, you needn't decide anything except about what concerns you directly, which is utterly impossible since you are in love with me.

Please, please wire me immediately for God's sake. I am wiring Africa that I'm waiting here for your answer before seeing the travel man. The boats will be wildly difficult as you know. If he leaves on the 8th he should be back the 15th or 16th.

I could say much more but I think thus far my letter has been a fair one and not like a beggar's letter or even wily. I am in a wonderful garden so don't feel sorry for me.

Much love, as ever
J.

P.S. Please advise me what to bring Claudia and Johnny, and is Willie-May there and Scotty. I won't get anything for the boys. Isn't this hell?

The Westport date is August 28th by the way, so you see that there is very little time. Naturally I would be more than delighted if they could put it off. You might have spies who could telephone Jack Wilson and sniff what's going on.

June 17, 1950

53
To Libby Holman

Dearest Libby, L'Étape, Pacy-sur-Eure, France

I am surprised and worried that you have not answered my wires—either one of them. I am of course worried about this mess from every point of view. I hope my wire, the last one, did not confuse you: it was meant to help your plans. Ever since I received a letter from Paul with yours enclosed about your Spanish plans and Oliver's statement concerning Paul and the music being sent from Spain, my feelings have become much more definite. I couldn't believe that you would come all the way over here to see Paul only for a week or so unless you had other plans for Spain, but now that I know it is still the *same* plan I really think you'd be a fool to come now. I wouldn't dare to influence you if I did not sincerely believe that the Lorca opera would benefit more by Paul's return, where he would be near a piano, than by a flash meeting in Spain. Also though you have bookings in the fall and winter, I'm certain that there must be some space between these, and considering that Paris is only four hours from Madrid, a meeting later could surely be arranged. I keep thinking of Ira Bellin's flower shop in Tangier. The flowers came three times a week from Holland by plane, all dead. Does this prove my point? In any case distances are short here and I feel that Paul can come back more easily, *probably* after the Westport opening (if there is one) when things will be all set. Naturally he can't write the music in Spain when he hasn't even spoken to the director yet. I am *appalled* at Oliver's muddled thinking and I am really furious that he gave neither of us an inkling of what he'd said to you. Because of this when I meet him in Paris on the 29th I shall *assure* him that unless I am guaranteed that Paul's music will be used in Westport with the minimum number of pieces required I shall refuse to allow the show to go on. I shall insist on this in writing the very day of my arrival there so that there will be no misunderstandings. I was referring to this in my wire to you so that in case you have been thinking all along that there would be some hitch in the music arrangement which would leave you and Paul free to spend a month or more in Spain you would not any longer count on it. I would not blame you in the least for suspecting this hitch knowing the theater as you do, etc. However, I have a chance of avoiding it because I think they are too far in to want to get out entirely just because of the extra money involved in using music and I will refuse to sign anything before Paul is signed up. Paul is coming over for nothing except his passage *one way*. If it doesn't go on even in Westport I believe he's out both passages though I could not swear to this. Oliver was probably *sure* that he wouldn't come on such bad terms, not until New York. (But I don't think the play should be shown without music anywhere.) Probably Oliver by the time we discussed all this in Paris had either forgotten his remarks to you or was too frightened to mention them. I kept saying, "How can Libby send such a *definite* wire to Paul when she knows he's returning, or *might* be?" and Oliver simply said he didn't know—that he had told you Paul might be coming over.

It gives a smack on the head with a rolling pin when he

comes back from Rome. I am really angry with you and I have taken the brunt, I with these agonizing letters and wires. It has been a real headache and has ruined these last weeks entirely. As for your plans, what a mess, and so easily avoidable. You should always keep in touch with me because I am the only one besides yourself who has a sense of responsibility. I can see nothing ahead that will change my plans or Paul's unless he didn't *do* the music. I mean whether he takes the next boat or not I think you'd both gain more by meeting there. Without you there he's less likely to work—I suppose. Anyway you have things to discuss but that is all up to you. I can only state the plans *clearly*. Oy! I don't know how possible the next boat is. The travel agent told me to wire Paul to try to change his tickets in Tangier. The next boat I could see leaving from Gib was as expensive as the one he's on and utterly unknown. Also I think it would be too late. It would give you eight days together, two of which would be spent on traveling (travel in Spain is slow and he must get up and down to Gib). I don't expect him to be busy on my show the *whole* time he's in America—naturally—and it will be over the end of August. After that you could work together if not in Spain somewhere near—Cuba? Anyway, you figure it out. My last letter must have sounded like a loony's letter, but knowing you I was much more careful, at least I thought I was. I didn't want you to sacrifice yourself if you had some concrete Spanish plan other than to meet Paul and that letter was about seeing him or not for a week. Now however it seems crazy if you wanted to go to Spain only to be with him, as I knew you did originally. I shall leave Paris July 7th and sail that day on the Queen Mary. Please don't meet my boat, I loathe it, but you might wire me to tell me what's up. I can't understand why you haven't so far. I know you think it is best to speak to Paul or Oliver. Someday you'll learn that it ain't. I begged Paul daily to answer your wire in Paris but he was waiting for the letter. It would have saved all this three-way tsouris. Love as ever,

J.

P.S. I hope my letters haven't sounded awful. Naturally I *want* you there, but even without that I now feel *honestly*, and I am honest even when greedy, that you must remain.

My address through Saturday the 30th of June will be Hotel de L'Université.

June 26, 1950

54
To Mike Kahn

Dear Mikey,

Oliver wants my agent to send you a regular contract giving you permission to use the play in repertory for two years etc. She is in Chicago but you will get it by next week. Anyway he says it's O.K. The contract will state as well that the Chekov theatre (I mean Hedgerow) has no rights on the play if it should be given anywhere else. I don't think Oliver believes for a minute that Jasper Deeter would claim rights but I guess he's used to doing everything in a formal businesslike way. This will give you the legal right to use the play in case I go to a lunatic asylum in which case a letter from me might have been invalid.

Please give my best love to Shirley and for yourself keep a great deal.

Your friend out of another century
Jane Bowles

New York City, January 1951

55
To Carl Van Vechten

Dear Carlo—

How about Wednesday night after the ballet at Oliver's? He's going to the ballet too, the 14th. Let us KNOW.

Love—
Jane—

P.S. You could bring whoever you're with.

New York City, February 8, 1951

To Carl Van Vechten

Dear Carlo—

Certainly bring Fania Marinoff and Saul Mauriber. I hope you have not understood that it is a party however—I wish it was! I like them. Maybe two or three other friends will come too but it won't be a real and big party. Unless you happen to run into Oliver at the ballet why don't you just come on down? 28 west 10th St. Ring the bell.

New York City, February 12, 1951

56

To Libby Holman

Dearest Libby,

I was appalled to receive this letter from my mother today and I have a terrible cold too. I guess it is best to send it on to you. I do not mean to make you feel sad, but it does explain the business situation rather concisely and it's easier for me to send the letter than it is for me to explain the whole thing.

I feel that in any case you will either lend me the money if you have it and you won't if you don't. I did not think from Mother's last letter that it would all happen so quickly but I guess the letter of warning was just sent to prepare me for this letter which she knew she was going to send for a few days. It's all just too awful, for her I mean, and naturally a hideous worry for me. I won't really start worrying however until I hear that you are broke, or at least incapable of laying your hands on any money right now.

I have been otherwise happy and peaceful this week. Marty is wonderful. It all works out she will be a resident—next year in Switzerland—near enough to Paris for weekends. But it is a dead secret so tear this letter up. I hope you write soon.

All love as ever,

J.

New York City, February 12, 1951

57
To Libby Holman

Dearest Libby,

Marty has given me a little Hermes Rocket typewriter for my birthday and I am very happy about it. She is wonderful to me and I think really loves me devotedly. I know it. It is extraordinary that I should have found at last someone so sweet and trusting and gay and brave and beautiful. She has moments of being extraordinarily beautiful. Particularly in black evening dresses cut low and with long sleeves. She looks not only beautiful but distinguished and as if she could not even possibly have ever met me. Her friend Priscilla is so much more brilliant than I am and she is better looking too and quite rich so I just cannot understand my good fortune. As I have told you there is a great amount of pain in this situation, mostly because of Paul, but it is not insoluble and something will work out eventually. I have been having mild flu which makes me hang around the house, but I do that anyway. I suppose I'll only get out of my room to go to Fire Island or Africa or Europe. I heard from Heber who is making slip covers and curtains for Ollie that you were going to sing in Italy in the spring, though I wish you were working on *Yerma* with Paul. I am glad that you are getting out of that house at least. I don't have a good feeling about it. Also I have been worrying about sending you the end of mother's letter and exposing you to this Valentine remark of hers. Though I really love her it is the kind of thing that makes me shudder and it is like that more or less in all of her letters, but I had not intended to expose you to it. I meant to tear it off and then hurriedly mailed it all at the last minute. I have been worrying about it ever since naturally, though I am not thank God upset about the money thing, as far as you and I are concerned. If you have written that you can't send any I shall try to think up something. If you can suggest anything, write, but I don't see how you could really. I shall try to get to work tomorrow, Monday, before the whole thing crashes on my head. The director of *Come Back Little Sheba* wants to do my play I think but I will know more about it in two weeks. He is coming down to confer with me because he wants certain changes made in the script. I am afraid these changes are big ones and that perhaps he just doesn't understand the play at all. He seemed puzzled by the Spanish servants for instance, at least so he said at lunch. I am hoping that actually he has forgotten the play and only pretended to have reread it because he was supposed to have done so before this luncheon arranged by Audrey Wood. I don't see how he would have had time to reread it when he has been working so hard on Tennessee's *Rose Tattoo*, which is a huge success. Most of the people I speak to seem to be against his directing my play and I am once again in a most monstrous quandary. Probably no one is right for it, except, as Priscilla says, Charlie Chaplin. Anyway I hope the play is coming along down at Hedgerow. I have not heard lately from Mikey and wonder what is going on. Touche has gone down to see his mother in Virginia. Actually I think he is spending twenty minutes with his mother and going on to someone else's "room" also down in Virginia. He telephones in to Alice Bouverie and she gives me the news. His last remark was that he did not intend to come back ever. I don't know whether or not his flight is a sincere effort to get down to work and stop drinking or a rendezvous with a friend of his who goes to college in the South. He has been drinking like a tank lately, emptying bottle after bottle all through the night. You've seen him do it; I think that his situation with Alice has been a strain. I think she would like to marry him and he is probably tempted though ashamed because of her wealth and position. Also there is his other love life who would be crushed by the marriage, so Touche thinks. None of this really exists to me but I repeat it to you because you are interested in Touche. I like Alice more and more though she is tedious beyond belief. It is just so very hard to listen to her. She talks and talks and one is conscious only of the strain. Margaret McKean is in and out of town all of the time and has finally understood I think that I don't want to see her. Aside from being totally uninterested in her romantically I can't bear her wit or the delivery of it. I find her presence really intolerable. There is no doubt that her wit is keener than anyone's in New York but it is frightening more than it is amusing because it seems to operate only as a kind of smokescreen for an endless plot which she herself ignores. She called me up today and whispered to me that she was telephoning from the Algonquin as if she was revealing the formula for the hydrogen bomb. The poor woman is just hunted and haunted all of the time. She is of course drinking like a fish, gallons of cider in public and alone in the bathroom, gin out of her purse, I'm convinced. Naturally she is disturbing because of her disembodied talent. Maureen Stapleton was overwhelmed by her. Do you think there is something wrong with me that I am able to turn so on someone I once liked as much as I did Margaret? In those days of course she was selfish as hell and a fat tyrant but now she is just humble and could be slavish if she had the energy or sobriety to run errands and she is fatter than ever. The terrible thing is that while all along I thought she liked my feeling for *her* but never *me*, I now feel that perhaps I was wrong because she seems dead set on me, though she behaves in a most distinguished manner and never makes me feel either guilty or uncomfortable. I think maybe she just likes my looks. Small and dark. Peter gave a party last night and Ollie and I just sat here without being able to get up enough energy to cross the street. We kept calling Peter up and asking for his guest list. Ollie got sore because Peter had used some of *his* guest list, Ollie claimed, and he scolded him over the telephone. Ollie never drags himself out of the apartment either and the whole thing I suppose is terribly unhealthy. We reinfect each other with our colds and I am in a bathrobe for life. Somewhere deep inside my heart is a tiny picture of Tangier in color. I miss it desperately and it will be for a while at least impossible to really live there. If Marty gets away next year because of her work she will be centered in Switzerland, which will be near enough to Italy and France but not terribly near Africa. However I shall certainly get down there to spend some time with Paul. I look forward to a day when Marty would have some part time work which would allow her to spend half her time in Morocco. I think this work she may do in Europe (the only hope I have of ever living with her) is very likely to be only for part of the year. I hope so. It is silly of course to plan anything. Some days I am in misery because I seem to feel two equally strong destinies and one of them is to be with Paul. I miss him of course terribly. My life would have been simpler if I had never returned here but having known Marty I will not die still searching and feeling cheated. I don't know what I write you about, but you asked me to write, so I do—when it is not too impossible.

Much love always,

J.

New York City, February 18, 1951

In the Summer House was performed in Ann Arbor, Michigan, in May 1953. It opened on Broadway in December and closed the following February. Soon after, Jane returned to Tangier, accompanied by Katharine Hamill and Natasha von Hoershelman. The three of them toured Morocco and then Katharine and Natasha returned to the U.S.

58
To Natasha von Hoershelman and Katharine Hamill

Darling Natasha and Katharine,

I never stop thinking about you but too much happened. Please forgive me if this is not an amusing letter. I tried last night to write you in detail but I had filled two pages just with Ellie and some clothes that the ladies and babies were wearing down in M'sallah, the day you left. I think I had better simply write you a gross factual résumé of what has happened. Then if I have any sense I shall keep notes. Because what is happening is interesting and funny in itself. I am a fool to have lost two whole months of it. I have no memory—only a subconscious memory which I am afraid translates everything into something else, and so I shall have to take notes. I have a very pretty leather book for that purpose.

The day you left I was terribly terribly sad. I still miss you—in the sense that I keep thinking through it all that you should be here and how sorry I am that you left before I could truly take you into some of the life that I love. I turned sour on Ellie about half way up the pier. I could still see the boat. I worried about having exposed Katharine to all those tedious stories—touching in a way but tedious. Ice cream, herring, and the Chico Tax scandal with the brother. Of course it could only happen here on a trip for *Fortune*. I went down that long street, way down in, and landed in a room filled with eighteen women and a dozen or two little babies wearing knitted capes and hoods. One lady had on a peach satin evening dress and over it the jacket of a man's business suit. (A Spanish business suit.) I had been searching for Cherifa, and having been to about three houses all belonging to her family, I finally landed there. I thought I was in a bordello. The room was very plush, filled with hideous blue and white chenille cushions made in Manchester, England. Cherifa wore a pale blue sateen skirt down to the ground and a grayish Spanish sweater, a kind of school sweater but not sporty. She seemed to be constantly flirting with a woman in a pale blue kaftan (our hostess), and finally she sat next to her and encircled her waist. C. looked like a child. The woman weighed about 160 pounds and was loaded with rouge and eye makeup. Now I know her. An alcoholic named Fat Zohra, and one of two wives. She is married to a kind of criminal who I believe knifed his own brother over a card game and spent five years in jail. The other wife lives in a different house and does all the child bearing. Fat Zohra is barren. There was one pale-looking girl (very light green), who I thought was surely the richest and the most distinguished of the lot. She wore a wonderful embroidered kaftan, a rich spinach green with a leaf design. Her face was rather sour: thin compressed lips and a long mean-looking nose. I was sad while they played drums and did their lewd belly dances because I thought: My God if you had only stayed a day longer. But of course if you had, perhaps they wouldn't have asked you in (Cherifa I mean); they are so leery of strangers. In any case at the end of the afternoon (and part of my sadness was an aching jealousy of the woman in the blue kaftan), Cherifa took me to the doorway and into the blue courtyard where two boring pigeons were squatting, and asked me whether or not I was going to live in my house. The drums were still beating and I had sticky cakes in my hand—those I couldn't eat. (I stuffed down as many as I could. I loathe them.) But I was really too jealous and also sad because you had left to get down very many. I said I would of course but not before I found a maid. She told me to wait and a minute later came out with the distinguished pale green one. "Here's your maid," she said. "A very poor girl."

Anyway, a month and a half later she became my maid. I call her Sour Pickle, and she has stolen roughly about one thousand four hundred pesetas from me. I told C. about it who advised me not to keep any money in the house. She is a wonderful maid, an excellent cook, and sleeps with me here. I will go on about this later but I cannot remotely begin to get everything into this letter. You will want to know what happened about Paul, Ellie, Xauen.

Paul went to Xauen for one night, having sworn that he would not spend more than one or two nights at the Massilia. He came back disgusted with Xauen and then started a hopeless series of plans—plans for three of us in one house, and, as I wrote Lyn, I even planned to live in the bottom half of a policeman's house in Tangier Balia (the place with the corrugated tin roofs) while Paul and Ahmed lived in the little house in the Casbah. I felt Cherifa was a hopeless proposition, and had no particular desire to be in my house unless there was some hope of luring her into it. (Maid or no maid.) In the hotel I did try to work a little. But it is always impossible the first month and the wind and the rain continued. The rooms were very damp and cold and one could scarcely sit down in them. I became very attached to the French family who ran the hotel. We stayed on and on in an unsettled way. In the beginning Ellie would come by every day with her loud insensitive battering on the door, and her poor breezy efficient manner and I would try desperately not to smack her. I felt I could not simply drop her and so would make some half-hearted date with her always before lunch so that we could go to Georgette's. Ellie filled me with such a feeling of revulsion that I almost fell in love with Georgette. I never allowed Ellie within a foot of my bed from the moment you stepped on the boat. I have never in my life had such an experience. Nor will I quite understand what possessed me. Some devil but not my usual one. Someone else's devil. In any case she started taking trips. The first time she came back, when I heard the rapping, I said, "Who?" and she said, "The family!" That was it. From then on I could barely stand to be in the same room with her and I hated myself for it. All this revulsion and violence was on a far greater scale than the incident deserved but it must have touched something inside me—something in my childhood. I have never been quite such a horror. Some of it showed outwardly but thank God only a bit of what I was really feeling. She always asked after you. Every time I saw her, "Any letter today?" Also madly irritating for some reason. Finally she got the message and in any case she was away so much that I managed to sneak up here into the Casbah—and I don't believe she knows where I live, though surely she could find out. I hope by now that she is off on a new adventure. Sonie (a pal who takes in the cash at a whorehouse behind the Socco Chico), sees her occasionally and reported that she had left Chico Tax and was driving her own car.

Paul had typhoid in the hotel and that was a frightening mess for two weeks. We were both about to move into our houses. He had found one on a street called Sidi Bouknadel (overlooking the sea) and I was coming here. Then he had typhoid, and then Tennessee came for two whole weeks. I moved in here while Paul was still in the hotel. For a while Ahmed and I were living together while Paul lingered on at the hotel in a weakish state. He is all right now. Ahmed stayed here during the whole month of Ramadan (the month when they eat at night) and I was with him during the last two weeks. Not very interesting except that every night I woke up choking with charcoal smoke, and then he would insist that I eat with him. Liver or steak or whatever the hell it was. At first I minded terribly. Then I began to expect it, and one night he didn't buy really enough for the two of us, and I was grieved. Meanwhile in the daytime I was in the hotel preparing special food for Paul, to bring his appetite back. There were always four or five of us cooking at once in the long narrow hotel kitchen, the only room that looked out on the sea. Meeting Tennessee for dinner and Frankie (they were at the Rembrandt) was complicated too. Synchronizing took up most of the time. We were all in different places.

I have kept out of the David life very successfully except on occasion. I could not possibly manage from here nor do I want to very much though I love him and would hate never to see him. I couldn't go it. The ex-Marchioness of Bath is here for the moment (married her lover, Mister Fielding, a charming man). I went to a dinner party for her in slacks—a thing that I did not do on purpose. They gave a party on the beach which

I wiggled out of but Tuesday I must go to a big ball. However if one only turns up once every two weeks or so it's nice. Or occasionally one goes out twice in a row. They are all constantly at it. David suggested a pool of money so that I might have a telephone. Only Jaime seemed to understand that I didn't want one. The Fieldings are enchanting people and are off to write about pirates in the old days. They have some kind of little car they are going to live in. They will be gone six or eight months. By then Enid Bagnold should be back. Her play was the end or wasn't it? Please write me what you think, now that some time has passed. I scarcely ever go to the Parade. Too depressing. Then came the ghastly Indo-China Oppenheimer period which dovetailed with Tennessee's last days here and also a pitch black boy called George Broadfield who called himself "The New American Negro," and attached himself to me and Paul. I liked him but almost went mad because he was determined to stay in Tangier, and thought nothing of talking for seven or eight hours in a row. I told him he should go and live where there were other artists because there were so few of them here. (He himself is a young writer, or is going to be??) He said that Paul and I were enough for him and I was horrified. It was all my fault. The night I got *Vogue* in the mail, which quoted the remark you might have since seen about writing for one's five hundred goony friends etc., I went out and got drunk. I was terribly upset about it. Though I knew what I had meant I had certainly not made the remark expecting it to be quoted or I would have elaborated. I hate being interviewed and something wrong always does pop out, everytime. I meant "intellectual" which Walter Kerr in the Trib seems to have understood, but at the time I was worried about my friends—the real supporters of the play and the contributors to whatever chance it had financial and otherwise. Anyway I was sick at my stomach. I did go to the Parade and did get very drunk. This pitch black boy seemed charming so I latched on to him as one does occasionally. He was a kind of God-sent antidote to the quotation which I was ashamed of. Paul tried to console me saying that nobody much read *Vogue* and that it would be forgotten. Of course later Walter Kerr devoted a column to it in New York and it appeared in Paris as well where there is no other paper for Americans, so if anyone missed it in

New York they have seen it in Paris or Rome. I now think of it as a kind of joke. Every letter I receive has the article (Kerr's article) enclosed, with its title "Writing Plays for Goons." They come in from all over Europe and the United States. I keep teasing Paul about the scarcely read copy of *Vogue* lying on the floor of the beauty parlor. So much for that. But I did inherit George Broadfield for a while and because it was my doing had to see him constantly for a week. I was a wreck—nervously, because he talked so much. Then he shifted on to Paul, finally ran out of money and moved on to Casablanca.

One day before Ramadan and before Paul had paratyphoid, I went to the market and sat in a gloom about Indo-China and the Moroccan situation and every other thing in the world that was a situation outside my own. Soon I cheered up a little. I was in the part where Tetum sits in among the coal and the mules and the chickens. Two little boy musicians came by. I gave them some money and Tetum ordered songs. Soon we had a big crowd around us, one of those Marrakech circles. Everybody stopped working (working?) and we had one half hour of music, myself and everybody else, in that part of the market (you know). And people gathered from round about. Just like Tiflis. Tetum was in good spirits. She told me that Cherifa had a girl friend who was fat and white. I recognized Fat Zohra, though I shall never know whether I put the fat white picture in her mind or not. I might have said "Is she fat and white?" I don't know. Then she asked me if I wouldn't drive her out to Sidi Menari, one of the sacred groves around here where Sidi Menari (a saint) is buried. They like to visit as many saints as possible, of course, because it gives them extra gold stars for heaven. I thought: "Natasha and Katharine will be angry. They told me to stick to Cherifa but then, they didn't know about fat Zohra." After saying this in my head I felt free to offer Tetum a trip to the grove without making you angry.

Of course it turned out that she wanted to take not only one, but two neighbors and their children. We were to leave at eight thirty A.M., she insisted. The next day when I got to Tetum's house on the Marshan with Temsamany (nearly an hour late) Tetum came to the door in a grey bathrobe. I was very surprised. Underneath she was dressed in a long Zigdoun and under that she wore other things. I can't describe a Zigdoun but it is quite enough to wear without adding on a bathrobe. But when they wear our night clothes they wear them over or under their own (which are simply the under-peelings or first three layers of their day clothes. Like in Tiflis). She yanked me into her house, tickled my palm, shouted to her neighbor (asleep on the other side of a thin curtain) and in general pranced about the room. She dressed me up in a hideous half-Arab, half-Spanish cotton dress which came to my ankles and had no shape at all. Just a little round neck. She belted it and said "Now go back to the hotel and show your husband how pretty you look." I said I would some other day, and what about our trip to the saint's tomb. She said yes, yes, but she had to go and fetch the other two women who both lived in a different part of the town. I said would they be ready, and she said something like: "Bacai shouay." Which means just nothing. Finally I arranged to come back for her at three. Rather infuriated because I had gotten Temsamany up at the crack. But I was not surprised, nor was he. Tetum took me to her gate. "If you are not here at three," she said in sudden anger, "I shall walk to the grove myself on my own legs." (Five hours, roughly.) We went back at three and the laundry bags were ready, and the children, and Tetum.

"We are going to two saints," Tetum said. "First Sidi Menari and then we'll stop at the other saint's on the way back. He's buried on the edge of town and we've got to take the children to him and cut their throats because they have whooping cough." She poked one of the laundry bundles, who showed me a knife. I was getting rather nervous because Paul of course was expecting us back roughly around seven, and I know how long those things can take. We drove along the awful road (the one that frightened you) toward the grove, only we went on and on, much further out, and the road began to bother me a little after a while. You would have hated it. The knife of course served for the symbolic cutting of the children's throat, though at first I had thought they were going to draw some blood, if not a great deal. I didn't think they were actually going to kill the children or I wouldn't have taken them on the ride.

We reached the sacred grove which is not far from the lighthouse one can see coming into the harbor. Unfortunately they have built some ugly restaurants around and about the lighthouse, and not far from the sacred grove so that sedans are now constantly passing on the highway. The grove itself is very beautiful, and if one goes far enough inside it, far away from the road, one does not see the cars passing. We didn't penetrate very far into the grove because being a Christian (Oy!) I can't sit within the vicinity of the saint's tomb. Temsamany spread the tarpaulin on the ground and the endless tea equipment they had brought with them, and they were off to the saint's leaving Temsamany and myself behind. He said: "I shall make a fire, and then when they come back the water will be boiling." They came back. God knows when. The water was boiling. We had used up a lot of dead olive branches. They sat down and lowered their veils so that they hung under their chins like ugly bibs. They had bought an excellent sponge cake. As usual something sweet. I thought: "Romance here is impossible." Tetum's neighbors were ugly. One in particular. "Like a turtle," Temsamany said. She kept looking down into her lap. Tetum, the captain of the group, said to the turtle: "Look at the world, look at the world." "I am looking at the world," the other woman said, but she kept looking down into her lap. They cut up all the sponge cake. I said: "Stop! Leave it. We'll never eat it all." Temsamany said: "I'm going to roller skate." He went off and we could see him through the trees. After a while the conversation stopped. Even Tetum was at a loss. There was a little excitement when they spotted the woman who runs the toilets under the grain market, seated not far off with a group, somewhat larger than ours but nothing else happened.

I went to look for Temsamany on the highway. He had roller skated out of sight. I felt that all my pursuits here were hopeless. I looked back over my shoulder into the grove. Tetum was swinging upside down from an olive tree her knees hooked over a branch, and she is, after all, forty-five and veiled and a miser.

There is more to this day but I see now that I have done exactly what I did not want to do. I have gone into great detail about one incident, which is probably of no interest.

But as a result of that day Cherifa and I have been much closer. In fact she spends two or three nights here a week in dungarees and Haymaker shirts. She asked for five thousand pesetas (about one hundred and fifteen dollars) so that she could fill her grain stall to the brim. I have given her, so far, fifteen hundred pesetas. She sleeps in dungarees and several things underneath. I shall have to write you a whole other letter about this. In fact I waited and waited before writing because foolishly I hoped that I could write you: "I have or have not—Cherifa." The awful thing is that I don't even know. I don't know what they do. I don't know how much they feel. Sometimes I think that I am just up against that awful hard to get virgin block. Sometimes I think they just don't know. I—it is difficult to explain. So hard to know what is clever manoeuvering on her part, what is a lack of passion, and what is fear—just plain fear of losing all her marketable value and that I won't care once I've had her. She is terribly affectionate at times and kissing is heaven. However I don't know quite how soon or if I should clamp down. I simply don't know. All the rules for playing the game are given me by Paul or else Temsamany. Both are men. T. says if you don't get them the first two times you never will. A frightening thought. But then he is a man. I told Paul one couldn't buy desire, and he said desire can come but only with habit. And never does it mean what it means to us—rather less than holding hands supposedly. Everything is very preliminary and pleasant like the beginning of a love affair between a virgin and her boy friend in some automobile. Then when we are finally in bed she says: "Now sleep." Then comes either "Goodbye" or a little Arabic blessing which I repeat after her. There we lie like two logs—one log with open eyes. I take sleeping pill after sleeping pill. Yet I'm afraid to strike the bargain. "If you do this, I will give you all of the money, if not—" It is very difficult for me. Particularly as her affection and tenderness seem so terribly real. I'm not even sure that this isn't the most romantic experience in a sense that I have ever had—and it is all so miraculous compared to what little went on before. I hesitate to rush it, to be brutal in my own eyes, even if she would understand it perfectly. I think love and *sex*, that is tenderness and sex, beyond kissing and les caresses, may be forever separate in their minds, so that one might be going toward something less rather than more than what one had in the beginning. According to the few people I have spoken to—among them P.M. (the Englishman who wrote the book)—I hate mentioning names—they have absolutely no aftermath. Lying back, relaxing, all that which is more pleasant than the thing itself, if one is in love (and only then) is non-existent. Just quickly "O.K. Now we sleep," or a rush for six water bowls to wash the sin away. I'm not even sure I haven't in a way slept with C. Because I did get "Safi-naasu." ("O.K. Now we sleep.") But it does not mean always the same thing. I am up too many trees and cannot write you all obviously. Since I cannot seem to bring myself to the point of striking a verbal bargain (cowardice? delicacy? love?) I don't know—but I simply can't—not yet. I shall have to wait until I find the situation more impossible than pleasant, until my nerves are shot and I am screaming with exasperation. It will come. But I don't believe I can say anything before I feel that way. It would only sound fake. My hunch is she would go away saying "Never." Then eventually come back. At the moment, no matter what, I am so much happier than I was. She seems to be getting a habit of the house. Last night she said, "It's strange that I can't eat eggs in my own house. But here I eat them." Later she said that her bed at home was not as good as mine. Mine by the way is *something*. Lumpy with no springs. Just on straw. A thin wool mattress, on straw. At home she sleeps in a room with her great aunt. The great aunt on the floor, Cherifa on the bed, natch. She's that kind. I find her completely beautiful. A little smaller than myself but with strong shoulders, strong legs with a good deal of hair on them. At the same time soft soft skin—and twenty-eight years old. Last night we went up on the topmost terrace and looked at all of Tangier. The boats and the stars and the long curved line of lights along the beach. There was a cold wind blowing and Cherifa was shivering. I kissed her just a little. Later downstairs she said the roof was very beautiful, and she wondered whether or not God had seen us. I wonder. I could go on about this, dear Katharine and Natasha, and I will some other time. I wish to Christ you were here. I can talk to Paul and he is interested but not that interested because we are all women. We see each other almost daily. His house is not far from here. And it is a lovely walk. Outside the walls of the Casbah, overlooking the beach and the ocean. Most of my time is taken up with him or Cherifa or the house and now work. I am beginning again to work. Before she came I was such a nervous wreck I couldn't do anything. Also I was in despair about all the world news and as I told you Paul's illness. Everything was a mess. Now I am in a panic about money and though I will write a play, I must write other things too for immediate cash. Not that I don't have any for a while but I must not use it all up before I have completed at least enough of a play for an advance. Thank God I am in a house and not in a hotel. Although the house has cost me a good deal until now, it won't henceforth because I've bought most everything I needed except a new bed for upstairs. I shall fill the house with beds—traps for a virgin. I feel happier now that I've written you. All the time I have been saying: I should write about *this* to N. and K. But it seemed impossible, utterly impossible to make a résumé of all that happened before. And as you see, it was impossible. I have not even found it possible to write in this letter why Tetum swinging from an olive tree in her cloak and hood should have precipitated all this but it did. I think Cherifa got worried about losing me to Tetum. She was so worried she asked me for a kaftan right off. Then started a conversation, a bargaining conversation, which resulted in her coming here after Ramadan to spend the night. But I can't go into that now. I always let Fatima (Sour Pickle) decide what we are to eat. It is all so terribly simple—all in one dish. Either lamb with olives or with raisins, and onions, or chicken with the same or ground meat on skewers or beef or lamb on skewers. (You remember how wonderful they taste). Or a fried potato omelet with onions, or boiled noodles with butter or eggs fried in oil, and always lots of black bread and wine at five pesetas a quart (excellent). I've had guests once, Tennessee in fact. White beans in oil and with salt pork like the ones I cooked for you. Lots of salad: cucumber, tomato and onion, all chopped up, almost daily. Fresh figs, bananas, cherries. Whatever fruit is in season. Wonderful bowls of Turkish coffee in the morning which are brought to our bed (when she is here as she happens to be now for a kind of weekend) or to me alone and piles of toast soaked in butter. At noon we eat very little. Usually, if Cherifa isn't here (she supposedly comes twice a week but that can include two afternoons) I go over to Paul's for lunch. Except that he never eats until three thirty—sometimes four. I get up at seven and by then I am so hungry I don't even care. But I like seeing him. We eat soup and bread and butter and cheese and tuna fish. For me tuna fish is the main diet.

I love this life and I'm terrified of the day when my money runs out. The sex thing aside, it is as if I had dreamed this life before I was born. Perhaps I will work hard to keep it. I cannot keep Cherifa without money, or even myself, after all. Paul told Cherifa that without working I would never have any money so she is constantly sending me up into my little work room. A good thing. Naturally I think of her in terms of a long long time. How one can do this and at the same time fully realize the fact that money is of paramount importance to one's friend and etc., etc.—that if there is to be much sleeping it will most likely be against their will or something they will do to please one, I simply don't know. Possibly, if it came to that, I might lose interest in the sleeping part, possibly why I keep putting off the bargaining—but the money I know is paramount. Yet they are not like we are. Someone behaving in the same way who was not an Arab I couldn't bear. All this will have to wait for some other letter. Perhaps it is all a bore; if so tell me. But I thought since you have seen her and Tangier that it would interest you. Please do me a great favor and save this letter. I cannot write more than one letter on this subject. If you think Lyn would be interested in bits and snatches of the letter read them to her because I can't, as I said write about it more than once. Not having seen Tangier or Cherifa, perhaps it would mean nothing to her. But we are on an intimate enough basis—she and Polly and myself—and they went through Marty with me a bit. I shall simply write her about my work and my health and I will tell her that you have a letter about "more stuff," if she wants to see it. And I shall tell her to call you, at the office. Perhaps you can meet some day for a drink if you all want to. I long to know Oliver's address. Lyn wrote me that he was in Calif. That's all. No address. Please write. I shall worry now about this messy letter.

All my love, always,
J. Bowles.

P.S. This letter I shall now correct. I am sure it is unreadable but I'll do the best I can. Received your copy of "Confessions of an Honest Playwright" today. Thank you. In Paris it has the other title, "Writing Plays for Goons." It's the end.

Tangier, June 1954

In December 1954 Jane went with Paul and Ahmed Yacoubi and the Bowleses' driver, Temsamany, to Taprobane, a minute island off the shore of Weligama, Ceylon. Paul had purchased Taprobane in 1952. Upon the island was an ornate octagonal house, without water or electricity, and a botanical garden. Each night the island and the house were invaded by bats.

At Taprobane Paul was working on his novel *The Spider's House*. Jane, who had hoped to write a play, could not work at all. Her hair began to fall out in great hanks and she became terrified that she was becoming bald. She suffered from alternate periods of depression and hysteria, even as she continued to consume large quantities of gin.

In early March she left Ceylon for Tangier, accompanied by Temsamany.

59
To Paul Bowles

Dearest Bupple:

It has been very difficult for me to write you. I have covered sheet after sheet, but now I am less troubled in my head for some reason. Maybe because I hit bottom, I think. And now I feel that the weight is lifting. I am not going back in that wild despairing way over my departure from Ceylon, my missing the end of your novel, the temple of Madura, that terrible trip back alone (a nightmare to the end because it was the twin of the other trip I might have made with you). It was better toward the end, but I hit bottom again in Tangier. The house reeked of medicine and there was the smell of other people's stale soup in the velvet *haeti* and even in the blue wall. I put my nose on the wall. It was cold and I could smell soup. The first day I was in the house the whole Casbah reeked of some sweet and horrible chemical smell which doubled its intensity with each new gust of the east wind. The Arabs were holding their noses, but I didn't know that. On the first day I thought I alone could smell it, and it was like the madness I had been living in. A nightmare smell coming up from the port, and a special punishment for me, for my return. I really felt very bad. I can't even remember whether or not Cherifa came to me here that first night in the house. Truly, I can't. On the second day the barber came over to me in his white and black hood and asked me to go to the Administration about the smell. He was holding his nose. "There are microbes in the air. We will all perish," he said. As he spends his entire time in the mosque and is one of the few old-fashioned Arabs left in the quarter, I was amused. The smell is gone now. The sewer pipes had broken, and they were dumping some chemical into the sea while they were mending them. And from that day on I felt better. And the house smells better—at least, to me. Fathma said: "Naturally. Filthy Nazarene cooking. Everything made of pork. Pork soup, pork bread, pork coffee, an all-pork house." But now there is kaimon, and charcoal, in the air. I feel so much better. But I am terrified of beginning to work. I don't know what I'll do if that nightmare closes in on me again. I am sorry too that you have to live through it. I won't go near you if it happens again. Actually I cannot allow it to happen again. But I must work. I had some shattering news when I returned . . . *le coup de grâce* . . . my taxes. Clean out of my mind from the first second that I banked the money. Somewhere way back, someone, either you or Audrey, warned me not to consider the money all mine, and I was a fool to forget. Having never paid taxes. . . . However, I suppose it is understandable. The slip of paper doesn't say much, not even what percent I am to be taxed. Perhaps all that has gone off to you. In view of the condition I was in this winter and on the boat, I should think this blow would have landed me in the hospital. In fact I went to bed and waited. But I got up again the next day alive and sane still, though my head was pounding with blood-pressure symptoms. I had to get out of that state, obviously, and I did. I tried writing you, but the letters were *magillahs*, and all about Madura and the tax and Mrs. Trimmer and Cherifa in one *tajine*. Senseless and anguished, and they weighed a ton. Not the moment to start that, if I am to "resort to airmail." Anyway, I think I have enough money in the bank to cover the tax, and if not, I have a Fabergé gold bracelet. And I have (if I must sell it, and if Oliver has made full payment on it) my beautiful Berman painting. Naturally, if I had known this was going to be waiting for me I would not have returned, because surely I should like to have discussed the thing with you. It's a terrible bore writing about it. There are so many angles to it: what exemptions I can get . . . maybe a lot . . . maybe none. Is it best to get off the double income-tax and pay direct to the government, or should I pay to you? Anyway, for God's sake don't do anything about it until you see me. I shall wait in Tangier and I shall lead my life as if it would go on. I cannot face the possibility of its not going on. Yet I would be unwilling to stay here if it meant your giving up Temsamany and the car. I consider them essentials, just as there seem to be essentials to my life here without which I might as well be somewhere else. Maybe I'll have to be, but it is best to face that when it comes, in two months or with luck, later. I have pulled every string possible in the sense of looking for a job. I can only do it through friends. There is a terrible depression in Tangier. Hotels empty, the Massilia closing, and ten people waiting for every job. Most people think I am mad, and that I should write or live on you, or both. It is not easy to make friends take my plight seriously. Not easy at all, unless I were to say that I was starving to death, which would be shameful and untrue. I spent just a little too much in every direction. The top floor expenses in New York which I took over for a few months, taxis, restaurants, coming over travelling with Natasha and Katharine, the Rembrandt, the Massilia, extravagances with C., I suppose more dinner parties than I need have given, doctors here for myself and Fathma. I don't know . . . it went in every direction. But each thing separately is a drop in the bucket. It is just everything put together in the end. I suppose I've been bad, but not so bad. Please don't scold; I am miserable enough about the whole thing and would have pinched every penny as I am doing now, had I been less confident. Well, that is over the bridge and down the drain, like the money for Ceylon. But although Ceylon was wasted and I did not see the temples, or even Kandy, it has changed my life here to a degree that is scarcely believable. I very swiftly reduced expenses to a scale so much lower than anything C. has ever expected of me when I was here that she is at the moment back in the grain market. I think it is a healthy thing for C. to go to the market in any case, even if the funds were more adequate. Ramadan she will be going there a lot.

I am now exhausted. Ramadan would be an ideal time for me to escape to New York, I suppose, but I don't want to, until I know that I can come back here or that I can't, at least, not for a while—that is, if we are both too broke. I'll face that later too. If I go downhill again then I suppose I would go home. Finding it impossible to work again is the only thing I fear . . . the hell with Ramadan. I am rather grateful that C. does want to go to the market during that time. Because she can't come here in a straw hat, but must keep going back to the bottom of M'sallah to change into a veil and white gloves, it will be difficult for her to come regularly. And what with fasting, etc. She's been fasting now for two weeks. Hopscotch off and on, making up time. It's almost worse than real Ramadan. I am thinking of investing in a room I heard of, on the top floor of the Hotel Cuba. I will count it outside my budget, since it is not a permanent thing, but something I would like to try, just so I can get started working. Naturally when I first got back and realized about my taxes I was too accablée to do any work . . . too harassed, and still in that funny state. I think the room is a good idea, if it is still there. I have not seen it yet. But I will look at it. I can ask Mother to give it to me as a special present, or if it works out I shall simply keep it on as an outlet for as long as it does work out. Because that would mean I was working. As for C. and all that, I shouldn't even bother writing you about her since it is such a fluctuating uncertain quantity. At the same time I feel this terrible compulsion to write you about the geographical location of the grain market in relation to M'sallah and my house, and the awful amount of travelling she would have to do if she went often to the market during Ramadan, just to get in and out of her straw hat. I doubt that she will go often once the *Aïd* is over, but we'll see. I certainly do not wish to interfere with her work, ever (!). I have no right to, since my own position here is so precarious, and in any case I shouldn't. She has now expressed a desire to travel and to play tennis. Now I do have an upper hand that I never had when I spent more money. What is it? I suppose one must close one's fist, and allow them just the right amount of money to make it worthwhile and not shameful in the eyes of the neighbors. I understand many more of the family problems than I did. It was difficult before to find one's way in the maze. But for "the moment," I know that is over. Will explain when I see you, maybe, if I don't forget to. I'm sure you can't wait. I remember the glazed look you always got when I mentioned her before. I think however if that nonsense began again I would give up. If I could only work now I would feel quite peaceful.

Tangier looks worse. The Socco in the afternoon is mostly filled with old clothes. A veritable flea-market that I'm trying to preserve. I've been booming away at Phyllis about it, because she knows the new Administrator. I also asked her about my hair. She has me down on a list. It says: Janie, Grand Socco, hair. Which is just about it, isn't it? The same obsessions, over and over. When I am sure about my hair I will write. But I think the news is good. You will never know what that nightmare was like. I know you thought it was in my mind. I am going on with Bépanthène Roche. On the days I buy it I try to eat more cheaply, so that I can keep, as much as I can, within a budget. Phyllis gave me a blue bead for luck and to ward off the evil eye. Brion's restaurant is the only thing that does business in town. John Goodwin invited me to go to Spain any time during the Feria and Holy Week. He has an apartment for a month. But I'm not sure that the trip alone wouldn't come to a thousand pesetas or more. Also I never go anywhere, so why should I suddenly get to the Feria, since I didn't get to Madura. I would like to hear some Gypsies, but not with those tourists there. I do not think I will go. And certainly not if I'm working.

My terrace smells of male pipi. I suppose it will forever. Eric Gifford brought his male cat with him, Hassan, whom he never mentioned to me. Or else I wasn't paying attention. The worst of the bad weather is over, although the first two weeks at the Massilia were hell. Temsamany scared me so on the boat, about people being able to stay in one's house forever, that I offered them two weeks' grace in the house. I wrote you that I cheered up on the boat when I thought of Jorge Jantus, and sure enough having him as a neighbor has made a lot of difference to me. I rather like their little group, and they are so near I can pop in there. He is bringing me some kif today. I had a cigarette of kif last night before supper and rather liked the effect. I had some drinks too, so I don't suppose I can judge, but it changed the effect of the drink noticeably.

I had dinner with Fathma, who is staying on for three hundred a month instead of five hundred, full-time as before. They have both been cooperative about buying cheap food, and C. of course is in her element. But then, that was before she decided to go back to the market.

The baqals announced a three-day close-down in commemoration of the upset here two or three years ago, and they were closed one. *Plus ça change.* Now my left hand is tired. Please write, and especially about your book, and don't above all scold me or put me in a panic. We'll talk about it all when you come, if you ever do. I wonder if instead you'll go to England? Anyway, Bubble, I think the trip has done some good. Much love. I hope you are well and that it got really hot. Write everything.

Jane

Tangier, c. April/May 1955

60
To Libby Holman

Dearest Libby,

Yesterday I mailed you one of those horrible air letters, but I slipped it into something that looked like a fire plug, so I don't know whether or not it will ever reach you. Normally I mail letters from the B.P.O. As you may remember there are three post offices here, Spanish, American and French (substitute British for American, please), and all these post offices have their mailing boxes scattered about here and there. I stopped in front of one and hesitated trying to read what it said, and an Arab came up to me in rags and asked me what I wanted. I said I wanted a post box, and he said, "This is one." And I said, "Well I know that it is one but is it French, British, or Spanish? I want to mail a letter with a British stamp." "They are all alike," he said. "Put it in, they all go from here." I had to put it in because he stood there watching me and then he went off in his rags. Then the postman came along, a small boy with a pouch, and I said, "Does all mail leave from here?" He said, "Yes, yes, this is the Spanish post office box." I said "Well, I just mailed a letter from here with a British stamp." He shook his head and said, "This is for Spanish mail." I asked him what to do and he said I should wait until eight-thirty that night and then tell the postman to give me my letter when he came to collect the mail. I said, "I can't stand here, I will be too cold." It was then five-thirty. "At best," he said, "they will decide to mail it, but who knows?"

At best, perhaps they have, but if I don't write you immediately I will never know whether or not it has reached you and I shall worry. So please write me either way. I want to know how you are—I hope to God better, but I don't want to repeat myself because, at best, my other letter has arrived.

In the other letter I wrote a little about my play and in it I said that I hope that if I finished it, it would have a chance of running for a while because I needed to make a living and that I was afraid you might not like it and that it wasn't going to be very poetic. Actually I thought this over and decided that I could not really write very differently whether or not I needed money because I do not know how to write a commercial line, nor could I write *Waiting for Godot* if I was sitting with a million dollars in my pocket. I mention that because you like it so much. Paul thought it was very well written, in fact he said he was sure it was, but said he had never been so bored in his life by any script and couldn't finish it. Anyway, sometimes I am in despair about this play like today and sometimes I am not, like always.

ABOVE ALL please write me and tell me whether or not you received my other letter, and let me know how you are. Not that it was such an important letter but it was more important than this one because it had more things in it. The letter I wrote to my mother in Chicago, I sent care of Paul in Ceylon. I have trouble with letters, even when it comes to mailing them. But I will send this one from the B.P.O. direct. And if the one I sent didn't come, I'll try to remember the things that were in it and write it again. I hope you are well enough to write yourself but if you are not have Rose or whoever is with you write me immediately. I am worried. That was in the other letter.

Much love, Libby, as always

Jane

Tangier, January 16, 1957

61
To Paul Bowles

Dearest Paul,

I have been trying to write you for days but unsuccessfully. The fact is that I have been having the same trouble with my work that I had in Ceylon and before I left for Ceylon. I don't know whether to keep writing through the block or to get out of here now or in a month or two before I come to the end of my money. I know I can get passage back from somebody but there is always the question of leaving a little behind for Cherifa. I hope that I will come out of this all right. The fight against depression again is serious, since failure follows me into my dreams, and I have been awake for many nights, as I was in Ceylon. But there is no heat, thank God. If I left I would borrow from Libby and pay her back out of my month's checks there. I would give the money to Cherifa that I would be saving by living at Libby's. I don't really want to do this though it might be the nicest thing I can do. C. doesn't want me to either and she is very happy to have the house and says that I must not worry. She even said that with the rent she gets for the house she can live with her family and contribute her bag of flour a month and so you have done that much for my peace of mind, at least. Naturally she has gotten used to more than a bag of flour a month and I wonder if I shouldn't whip myself out of here no matter how much I dread doing it. The longer I wait the less I will have to give her, unless I asked Libby for an outright gift of a couple of hundred dollars. Actually, before I left Libby said to me that I shouldn't worry about money and that if I needed any to let her know. Then there are the little cats whom I adore, and C. herself, whom I can't bear to leave, and you too, who will be returning and I would not like to miss you though I am sure that you would probably not want to see me if I don't have a play done, and it would be a sad encounter to say the least. Actually I cannot picture any of this happening. I cannot picture leaving, nor can I picture your return and my having nothing to show you after all this time. Maybe none of this will happen. I hate to think of it and I get into a kind of terrible panic when I do. Still, if for *some reason* I did have to leave, I would naturally pay the rent here until

June or whenever the contract is up, and lock the door. But I would not leave the cats, naturally. They would have to come along. Ira read my fortune and said that someone's death was going to oblige me to travel across water, and that as a result of this death I would inherit a little money. I don't believe it, of course, but it did occur to me that I should tell you that in case of any emergency, or even if I suddenly became a lunatic and felt a compulsion to go just because I didn't want to, that I would put all of your things into the apartment here and lock the door leaving the key with Christopher or Ira. The person who was going to die was a woman, and I can't think of anyone but my mother who might leave me a few hundred dollars, but I do not really believe in cards.

I filled a notebook with my notes and suggestions for my play and even started writing the dialogue. And now today, for the first time in a week, I had a flash of an idea and so I will see if it does not help. It is impossible to write a play in the dark without having some idea of where one is going. I did get an idea but it was so definite that I couldn't go against it either. For nearly a week I have had dreams of not being able to go on with it and then my head got into such a bad knot that I took a lot of Equanil and knocked off work. Today my head feels better—less knotted. I wrote you a long beginning of a letter but it was so confusing I thought I would tear it up, and I did tear it up, but at least I had been writing *something*. And then after I had written you the first really sad page of the letter I tore up, I made some lentils and got an idea about cutting out one of the characters in my play. In fact two of them. One was a girl and the other a dead man. Like Gertrude's father in *Summer House*, who became such a bore to all of us. I think the girl was cut out because of a dream I had, about her and her girl friend. I dreamed they hated me and that they could never be in the play. I must write it. But am I fooling myself by insisting that I will? And by fooling myself, robbing C. of the last money that I can call my own? I am convinced that I should not think in these terms. Well, I will go on trying really hard for another month and see how I feel after that. I am sorry to bore you with this but I must at least mention my work or you will think that I am getting along beautifully and that makes me even more nervous. I will let you know if and when I get over this hump. I gather you are working as usual and I suppose Ahmed is too.

You never did answer my letters to Capetown. I rushed them off so that you could write on the boat and tell me at once how to treat your mail. I'm perfectly willing to send it *all* but do you want to spend all that money? There are many Xmas cards and other superfluous letters and I think *you* should decide what I am to do about them. As you know, air-mail to Ceylon is not cheap. In fact nothing is cheap. Meat prices have gone way up here, and other things have risen too. The Catalana is booming and none of us ever mention politics anymore. One does not feel any of that atmosphere in the streets, although the Socco Chico is still not a desirable place to go, according to Jorge. Not for political reasons especially but there are still a good many thugs around. They say there really is to be a casino here, and I suppose prices will rise even more. But it is so all over the world, and I think this is still the pleasantest place to be.

Dubz tips over all the little round tables, walks through gravy, stands ankle deep in sinks full of water, opens all doors with his fat paw, particularly the cupboard door where the food is kept and the bathroom door. The bathroom is his toilet, especially the tub. He eats everything in sight and even chews through loaves of bread wrapped in cellophane.

I loved hearing about June and Paula. I lost my heart to June too and often thought in my madder moments of spending the rest of my life in that house, and loving it. I still think of it with nostalgia. Is the rice still like wild animal rice in the corner of a cage? Ask Ahmed to tell me because I don't trust you to know. I don't see how the rest house food could be much worse than it was, nor how there could be much less food in the market. I enclose Rose Minor's letter about Libby. It is too grisly to dwell on and I feel terribly sorry for her. Do write her. I wrote twice. I hadn't heard in so long that I was worried, and then this came. I hope to God that she will be better now and that she tries to eat as much as she can. According to Christopher the operation permits one to eat just about anything but care must be taken not to eat too much at a time.

Please give my love to June and Ina and Quintus and Elsie.

Tell her that I have bought a bottle of pure silvikrin and that it has done my hair a lot of good. You don't say in your letter whether or not you are living at the hotel in Galle permanently. Are you? By the time you answer me I imagine most of the important mail you are expecting will have been headed off to Weligama directly. Meanwhile I will forward what I think I should forward, using my own judgement (which does not include Xmas cards). Please let me know whether or not you received my letter about the mandat and, as I said, don't let it lag too long or the money will be gone.

Do you feel that you do not want to return to Ceylon anymore? I would judge so by your letter. Two packages have arrived which I shall keep for you. One from the Fordyces, and the other from Conzett and Huber in Germany. The first, a book on African rites filled with pictures of little mud figurines (typical) and the second a calendar, framing a rather famous painting. Or perhaps it is not famous, but acts as if it were. A still life with a checkerboard in it from Conzett and Huber in Germany. *Who on earth is Harper?!* I met Edita Morris. The truth is that I hated her but liked her husband Ira. Please bury this letter if they should come down. I can just see it lying around on the alcove terrace—effect on one of the chairs painted silver.

Much love, as ever,
J.B.

P.S. Please write often—I love to hear about Ceylon.

Tangier, February 1, 1957

62
To Paul Bowles

Dear Paul: Tangier, Morocco

I have just had my fortieth birthday the day before yesterday, and that is always, however long one has prepared for it, a shock. The day was not as bad as the day after it, or the following day, which was even worse. Something coming is not at all like something which has come. It makes trying to work that much more difficult (or could it possibly be more difficult?), because the full horror of having no serious work behind me at this age (or successful work, in any sense) is now like an official fact rather than something in my imagination, something to be feared, but not yet realized. Well, I don't suppose you can understand this, since when you reached forty you had already quite enough stacked up behind you.

I realized about your birthday, but I don't think I mentioned it in my letters, or thought of it at the time I wrote you. Anyway, it is over. I did not tell anyone about mine except Cherifa, and I celebrated with her on the night of the twenty-first because on the twenty-second an old man from Xauen, an uncle or grandfather, was expected at her house. However, Christopher heard about it from George and called me on the twenty-second to ask if it were true, and then I did have a busy day. I sound like your mother about to say that Ulla came over and that they took a drive and later popped corn in the grate. In spite of hating it to be forty (Anne Harbach toasted me and said: "Life begins . . ." which was the last straw), I am still determined to write my play, and have no intention of going back to New York until my money runs out. I have somehow, thus far, staved off the terrible depression that was coming over me when I wrote you last—staved it off perhaps simply because I cannot ever again be the way I was in Ceylon. I mean that I will do everything in my power to pretend that I am not, even if I am. It was too horrible. And so I knocked off work entirely for a week and then went back to trying to write the play. My mind is not a total blank, which is more than I can say of the way it was before. Whether it will get beyond that, I don't know. I am sure you will come out all right because you always have.

Seth said his first word yesterday. "Dubz." He said it clearly three times, and again this morning. I daresay it is because Seth sits in the bathroom a lot and I am always lunging in after Dubz to stop him from using the tub, and of course calling out: "Dubz!" at the top of my lungs. I hope that he will keep saying it so you will hear him when you get back.

Mr. Rothschild has been here for three days and I like him. He is giving me a subscription to the Sunday Times for a year, and it will be delivered to me from New York by boat of course, so it will always be two weeks late. It is for Berred and Dubz, for their pans.

Radiant sunshine, balmy weather and scarcely any rain. The beaches are crowded. I had lunch with Mr. Mallan at the Catalana last week. The Mar Chica is booming again. Whether or not there are many Arabs in it I don't know. Apparently there is more drink than ever in their world, only not as openly. There seems to be not much fear about. Ramadan is in less than forty days, and I dread it as usual. Seth is so terribly noisy that I have to put him out on the terrace in order to do any work. I am furious that you are living in Colombo and have an oscillating standing fan. I would have loved that. If you like Weligama so much why don't you keep it . . . or aren't you prepared to live alone there? Actually I don't think you would like that for long. But maybe you won't be able to sell it. Your life in Colombo doesn't sound too expensive thank God so I imagine you'll stay there until you sell the house. Seth is driving me mad.

Dubz just fell into the toilet up to his waist and I had to help him to dry off. Mr. Mallan after beating around the bush for fifteen minutes finally asked me what color eyes Phyllis De la Faille has. He is utterly ridiculous. Please write me about him. Cherifa bought Seth a length of strong wire which she has fastened around his cup and the bars of his cage so that he can no longer dump his seeds on the floor. It is to be a great saving in money and I am glad. He just said "Dubz" again. I try to say it over and over again to him so that he won't forget.

Much love,

J.

February 24, 1957

63
To Libby Holman

Libby dear,

It was too much—the clipping they sent me. From Celebrity Service via a friend who works there. In fact the man who came over with me on the Andrea Doria, which has now sunk. If you get as little news as I do you are probably unaware of this. I know it through friends. I was so frantic I had to cable you and hear that night; that is why I gave Jay's address. The post closes early and I was not in my own "home," but up on the mountain taking care of a girl who had been through a complicated horrid abortion. The cable came early thank God but I was afraid to open it right off. Anyway I was so overwhelmed with joy to hear that he had not died. The clipping said critical and I was dreading the cable. This will not be a long letter because I don't know yet what the consequences of the accident are and am waiting anxiously for a letter from you or Rose. I can't be too gay until I know.

I hope the shock has not set you back. I was *so happy* about your letter from Jamaica. It was in a way the first real letter that I have had from you in many years and I have been missing that very much.

I did not answer right away for more than the usual reasons. Not really, but I had been working which was unusual and then it all collapsed—stopped—dried up—but this was only unusual because for the first time in years I thought I was going along well. It was a terrible block but I managed to work myself out of it with more effort than gift I suppose, but that doesn't matter. I was on the point of writing you a despairing letter about giving up, but then I did start again and was about to write more cheerfully when the letter came from the Andrea Doria man, with whom the Moroccan leather man (and scholar) is staying. (Charles Gallagher.) Because of this week which has been sheer hell (because of this girl's abortion), I have not done any work. I am terrified of getting back to it and finding that the spark has died. It was a fatal moment because I was functioning well for the first time in many a long year but I could not let her go to the hospital alone really and it turned out to be very painful and frightening. The doctor swore at her throughout the operation and scolded her for having an upside down womb and of course I might have had one myself with the baby in it for all I was able to detach myself from the girl whom I now *hate.*

She has been sheer hell for a solid week and I have stayed with her up on the mountain because there was no one else who would. Christopher Wanklyn and I stayed (he has a car), and we worried that she might hemmorage and be stuck without one. She was a bloody bore about getting up too soon and thus started something going which laid her back in bed for two days (and imprisoned us too), though I had begged her to lie still. We had fish and squashed spinach the whole time and once just spinach and potatoes, but when her clandestine lover came (who has no chin and trains horses), she gave him soufflé and chicken and gave us the afternoon off. I thought it was very ungracious. Also she scolded me and commanded me the entire week and was so cross the whole time with me and her poor servant that we both were frightened and Christopher was very disgusted, though not frightened. I was stuck however and could not answer her back because she would have ordered me out of the house (as she did once out of the hospital), and then she would have perhaps had a hemmorage. How does one spell that? I left Cherifa for a week and came back to find that she has taken up playing cards with two women both of whom, she says, look like Pekingese. I cannot believe they do—not both of them—and think she says this to please me. They are black and their husbands are dead white and work in movie houses. I believe it's really only one woman. How could they be so identical? She is either lying deliberately or her imagination is running wild. The poor thing has a dropped stomach and that is why she has been eating less and less and getting thinner all the time. I was going to write you about this, I was so worried. Now she has a strange truss-like corset with a rubber pump and feels much better. She ate a pound of bananas all at once last night like a monkey. It is Ramadan and I get up at two-thirty in the morning to prepare the three o'clock meal. At least I did last night when I returned from the mountain. We had a big fight and then made up. The fights are never serious. I do not yet make my own bread but I suppose I will. Dear Libby do you know of any shot that will put *weight* on people? Not for anemia or weakness, but something —the best thing for stimulating appetite and adding on fat. Apparently dropped stomachs need the support of fat, at least the "twenty-five cents a visit" doctor said so. Don't frighten me about the dropped stomach. I get hysterical about Cherifa the way one does about a child. But if you know of the best thing for putting on fat tell me. Perhaps you know because of Tim. Please let me hear the latest news fast. My love to darling

Rose and Betty, George, Alice and Gerry—also Skipper—and thank her for the Fat Boy's Book—and love to Ross and Monty—and to you always, J.

Tangier, April 10, 1957

64
To Paul Bowles

Dearest Bup,

I am forwarding this letter from Villiers. I thought it might be an invitation and so opened it, but no luck. It occurred to me that since you are spending the ridiculous extra money to go all the way to England, you might at least benefit by a visit somewhere to some capital. Ahmed certainly enjoys that even if you don't. How could you have messed up on his visa? Doesn't the Spanish Consulate exist in Ceylon? I suppose not. Boats are going through the Canal too, by the way, but maybe you didn't know that.

Berred has eczema. A famous mystery-story writer told me that it was probably from nerves. I think both cats are at a disadvantage together because neither one can get the attention he wants and demands. They are in a state all day worrying about their food and guarding their dishes against each other. At night poor Dubz gets shut in the outer room because Berred insists on sleeping with me. Sleeping is a bad word, since she has the habit now of making constant trips to the terrace and back to make sure that Dubz isn't lurking outside the window somewhere.

Seth almost broke his bars with rage because I went into the bathroom with a hat on, and he thought I was someone else. (Some man, since he seems to hate them most.) I don't think he should be with the green parrot until he learns to talk more, because it is obvious that when birds are together they don't learn anything. At least, they should not be in a small place where they can talk back and forth in their own language.

Ramadan is on, and Cherifa and I almost came to blows the other night. I insist that she joke at three in the morning if we are to get up then (and we do), but she refuses to treat the meal as a gay occasion. I have threatened to send her home for the month, and she in turn has threatened to stay there. I can't decide which is worse, to be alone or to go through it. I hate making appointments except with Christopher, and it gets lonely up on the ninth floor. Particularly since I am a virtual prisoner here because of the lift, and only go down with my maid, or else with the baqal boys when they deliver something from downstairs. I wrote you that there was a baqal in the building.

A boy has come here from New York, called Allen Ginsberg. He was given a letter to us through Leo Lerman. I have his book of poems, called *HOWL, and Other Poems*, with an introduction by William Carlos W. I suppose I must see him, but he is much more up your alley than mine. I will probably not be able to go on with my play if I do see him.

On the telephone he said: "Do you know Philip Lamantia?" I said: "No." He said: "He's this hep poet, been writing since he was thirteen, and he just had a vision in Mexico on *peyote*. (Peyoti, I gather.) I said: "Oy weh." Then he said: "Honest, it was a real vision, and now he's a Catholic." I said: "*Oy weh!*"

Then he named twenty-five men, none of whom I'd ever heard of, and I told him I'd been away a long time, and was too old anyway, and that I wasn't interested in peyote or visions. He said: "Do you know Charles Ford?" and I said: "Yes, because he's old." And he said: "Well, don't you take majoun day and night?" and I said: "I hate all that, and I'm sure you shouldn't see me." And he said: "Well, what about Zen?"

Anyway, he's here and he is a friend of Bill Burroughs, who appears constantly in his poems, together with references to TANGIERS (sic), and he is part of a group. The Zen Buddhist-Bebop-Jesus Christ-Peyote group. Carl Solomon is a Dadaist Bronx poet. The first *Howl* is dedicated to him. I think he is in Rockland State Hospital. Philip Lamantia, if that is his name, (I forget) used to write for *View*. Ginsberg asked me on the telephone whether or not I believed in God. I cannot decide whether or not he is up your alley. I am referring to Allen Ginsberg. With it all he sounds like a very sweet person. I imagine he shares Bill's habits.

I am not going to forward any more mail to Cape Town. None of it looks important, except a great thick ominous letter from Heger. But it is entirely too thick. Please write me when you get to England if you decide to go somewhere on the continent.

I have not worked on my play for a week because I've been on the Mountain. Patricia was ill and I had to take care of her. I'll tell you about that when you return. If I cannot get back to work I think I'll kill myself, for I have only a few months of grace left.

I am excited that you are getting nearer. I'll do my best with "My name is Seth." Give my love to Ahmed. The lemur sounded *adorable*. I'm *furious* not to have it. But I suppose it is best.

Much love, and congratulations on *Harper's Bazaar*.

Jane.

Tangier, Mid-April 1957

Toward the end of April 1957, one evening during the month of Ramadan, after a fight with Cherifa, Jane suffered a stroke. She was at the time forty years old.

Gordon Sager cabled Paul, who was en route from Ceylon, and wrote to Libby Holman about Jane's condition. In response Libby offered to help Jane financially and at Jane's request agreed to send her one hundred and seventy-five dollars a month.

It soon became apparent that Jane had suffered permanent damage from the stroke, including the impairment of the functioning of her hand, a residual aphasia, and a homonymous hemianopia of the right side (from either eye she could not see the right side of the visual field).

65
To Libby Holman

Dearest Libby

Twice I have tried to write this letter and each day I bog down on it. I can read a little better than I could before which makes it more difficult than it was the first day I wrote to you and now I a am filled with missgivings and depresion about the doctors. since Resneck wa not abole to understand very much of had happened. It may be a quesion of French and I am going to go to Doctor Spreit again and give him a tranlation of what Resneck wrote to see if it throws any light on it and thence to England or simultaneously. I am waiting for Paul to go and look up the name of the english doctor and which can probably be found at the english legation. I am writing this half automotically that is I can check back a little better than I could and make out what I have written if there is a clue to it. The french doctor sais that it will come back but it is slow. I am very low Libby and you know how hard it is to talk about these things and so I better not. I tried actually several days to write this not just two and there was so much to say and so many details and loosends and plans that I can't cope with, at least the writing about them is too difficult and so I've been swnowed under. Berreds wrist, or was it my own wrist, yes it was my own wrist, held me up for a week at least and is now already. It was really a question of weekness and having tried to hard to cut her meet and so I sprained the writs because I was weak. Meanwhile time past and and I was not clear and what I had written and explained to you and aparently according to Paul even my last letter, that is the wire about Polly, doesn't explain that I did receive the letter about the money.

now I have lost my place and I must go up to Pauls, to find it. But I see more and so I am hopeful but it is taking a long time. Libby I will simply go on as faras I can without checking with Paul and forgive me if I am repeating. I sent the wire to you without consulting Paul and he says that I still havn't answerd your question about the money you sent to me for the doctor. I thought I had when I wrote about hurting myself myself on Berreds wrist and then althogh I sealed that letter op I mean Paul seeded it He didn't read it but simply mailed it and in the interrum I might have tesecoped two letters into one, the one in my head and the one on the page. Anyway something was didn't exist since you didn't get my letter thanking you etc. (explaining I understood the arrangements and was so happy that it was taken care of). One explanation for

Dear Libby:

Jane has gotten into a state about writing this letter and has come up to me to ask me to finish it for her, because she is very eager to post it as soon as possible. I read what she had written aloud to her, and she thinks I should explain that she wants to translate Resnick's letter into French and give it to her doctor here, to find out if he thinks the consultation with a specialist is something which must be done soon—if "time is of the essence," as she keeps saying. Also, she wants me to say that she has not yet paid Spriet's bill because he has not presented it, and the reason for that is that last week when she visited him and asked for it, he told her that at the time she fell ill Phyllis De la Faille here in Tangier had asked that Janie's bill be sent to her, and that he had complied. This news brought on a virtual brainstorm in Jane, because she never sees Phyllis and feels rather ambivalent about her, and consequently horribly guilty about the idea of her having made such a gesture. She told the doctor to write Phyllis that she could not accept the gift, and she has also informed Phyllis herself indirectly, and the doctor is now sending her the bill, but it has not yet come. She wanted to be sure that you were informed of all these things. As soon as she gets the bill she will pay it, and that will be an end of it. I think that's about all. Jane says she will write you again in a few days. She does better than she did two or three weeks ago, and I think each time she tries to write she will find it easier. Of course, the difficult part is not being able to read over what she has typed. But I think there is a definite improvement in this letter over the others.

Dearest Libby I was not abble to finish this letter—and I must let Paul send this now. I am actually reading this which I can do in blotches. More about Berred later! I will write again as soon as possible.

Much love
J.

Tangier, Summer 1957

66
To Libby Holman

Dearest Libby

I am getting very nervous now naturally because everything seems endlessly complicated so much so that I seem not to be able to write down all the loose ends. I will write what I canand if I leave out half of it please forgive me but it is a gonza magella if there ever was one. Especially since I can't read it back which I am still unable to do though I would say and I pray that it is getting better slowly. I can read back snatuches if I have clues as you can see. In fact I have come a long way from just plain automatacic righting so I try to think of how bad it was and take courage. Ever since the letter from Dr. Resneck cam I have been very lost naturally because I hoped that what the doctor here was doing would turn out to be adequate and the right thing and that only time would be required to set things right. Now I have no idea what to hope for and so I have been despondent and am anxious to get going. I am very hapy—at least reassured that you are there and resnecc and that I will be I hope soon in the hands of someone competant. Paul is waiting for the answer to his letter to London which has not yet come though he wrote it as soon as he heard that he would have to go there and should not wait untill the fall when he has been envited to London in any case and would have his expenses payed except for the trip itself. He has written to this friend in Lonon who is called Pitt or Tip, and is hoping for an answer and permission to stay there while I am the dotors. It would be too much to hope for, an invetation for me as well but ut us impossible. If Paul has to pay for his own expenses a stay in London I suppose he won't be ablte to go be able go because he is very low and would have instead to wait untill the invitation is forthcoming. Meanwhile it might come any minute because these people, Pit or Tip, are not likely to stay very long away from london if they are out of london at the moment and not merely taking a little too long to answer the letter. They may in fact have another guest. Meanwhile I am frantic with all the uncertainties and it is very difficult for me to focus my thoughts and write them all down. In the beginning Dr. Sprite said that I should see a specialis and then later told me that it was not necessary but I remember he did say flying would not be advisable. Paul you know will not fly and I cannot ask him too unless it is a matter of life and death and I think I can get there either by train which is deadly between here and madrid but I think althoght exhausting would not kill me. At least I will ask the doctor. It is very bumpy and very hot but I don't imagine it woulld be dangerous only exausting. The best possibility which is by Japanese boat dirrectly from Tangier to London seens like the most possible solution but I cannot tell yet whether or not I can get on it (and Paul) untill the boat docks here. They drop pasangers off between Tokio and the Thanes and the is often room ror two passengers to London by the time. Libby I have lost my place again and it is difficult to find it. I can see passangers to London but the rest which is a simple word I can't make out. I was going to say before I left the the room it is possible to go to London from Tangier if the boat is not fully bucked. The man whom Paul spoke to at the steamsh ofice says there is a fifty fifty chance of getting on itor more. The other way is by land to through Spainwhich is to be avoided but I will find out from Spreit whether or not it would be actually dangerous for me. It is torrid until madried, with no water on the train but I guess cools off at night and I wouldn't die of it, just be tired. I don't know that my trouble has anything to do with being too hot or too cold, ; I can't go by myself because I can't see well enough or at least coordanate well enough yet to manage. Paul will or rather can pay his trip over and back. I am hoping that I won't have to stay there long naturally. I can pay the trip there maybe even back but I would rather have that in the till then count up my expenses when it is over and I have returned. I will leave money here because naturally my maid and Berred and my bills go on, but the trip over I can certainly manage with an eye to an eye to sending you the money for the trip back when I return. I am a little mixed up about what it has cos me to live a month since I am incapable of doing much and I had not been expecting to move at all. Please tell me what to do Libby and if Paul doesn't get his initation for his stay in london tell me what to do about that financialy. He can't even write about it he so counts on it because know what to do if he doesn't well, I've lost it again but I am simply incapable of writing this and Paul is much more so I'll have too. And this is why I havn't writen partly and partly because we have still no word from the doctor in London hasn't written yet.

I seem to be going into giberash because I cannot get help from anyone on this letter. Paul gets into a state and expects me to write it by myself. I am graterul that he will go with me and back naturally and pay his fair but I don't think can do much more than that—he is very low in funds though he can probably add another hundred dollars or so but as I said the whole things seems beyon him if he doesn't come up with the invetation. None the less I am playing to leave within two and one half weeks and if there is no japaneise boat I will take the train through spain if you are in occordance with this plan and tell me how to manage it finacialy. I will ad what is left of the money you gave me toward the expenses, 'n (NOT the monthley stipand) as I said toward expenses upintill the time I do leave here and the trip over. If there is money left I shall send it to you (I mean the five hundred) or kepp it if you want me too. Maybe it can pay the trip back as well, but I had better wait untill I see. I am sorry to have to write this letter at all but I may be leaving within two weeks or so, if I am lucky you had better send me some world. I am horribly deppressed because I don't seem to be seeing very much, and I worry about this more than anything naturally. But still it is more than I could see which was nothing and so I keep telling myself that. I know this is the worst letter you have had from me but it had to be written; Perhaps you will make sense out of it. I know that I must get to London. Please tell me what to do If Paul's friend doesn't turn up and if he does, you want me to about the money I'll need to start out with anyway. As I said I can manage the trip over and then I'll save how much more than that. I am too tired now to go on Libby unless you want to write me about the Villa Lobos gain which might sound like a welcome change to you after this. I wish that Gordon were here to write about these things. Maybe a letter of yours has crossed mine and clarifies everything. If anything is clarifie please send mine back so that use it again, for Villa Lobos next season. The spanish train is from eighten forty eitght.

I hope that this will be the last of these letters.

Love,
Jane

(Later) No letter yet from or Pauls friend—
P.s. Paul has just read this letter because I asked him too and he says that what I am trying to say because I told him what I was trying to see and it didn't seeme clear, was this;

I have enough money left out of the five hundred you sent me for trip up to London and even for the return jurney to Tangier or at least part of it.

For give this letter again. It must be as difficult for you as it is for me.

Love always,

J.

Tangier, Summer 1957

67
To Libby Holman

Dearest Libby

If you have lived through the last letter here is another one. I have been so disturbed since the letter from Resneck that I was incapable of writing you sooner than I did—and when I finally wrote the result was what you saw. It was terrible being, in a sense without a doctor, which is what I felt was my situation when Resneck wrote that he could not tell what had happened to me—at least not exactly by reading the report Spreite sent him via Paul's letter.

Yesterday I decided to make Paul translate the principle elements in Resnec's letter—that is whether it had been a thrombosis, or a hemmoradge and I took that part of the letter over to Spreit by myself. He was surprised because he thought he had explained that thoroughly and wrote out for me that it was definitely neither a thrombosis or a hemmoradge but stopped short of that thank God. He had been as I gather waiting to see whether it would be or not but there was no sine of it—me rely what he calls a confusion or some such word; I would judge that he is a good doctor though he has not claimed to be a neurologis naturally. He is all for a first rate nurologist taking those tests but I was very much releived that there was no danger of either the thrombosis or hemorrage having taken place and that Spreit after all seems perfectly aware of what happened and compotitnt. compotint. He vetoed the trip through spain although he would not say that I would die of it he said that a trip throught spain at this time of the year would have or could have serious consequences. A plain would be dangerous if it bit a oressurized plane and according to what I here not many of the planes in Tageir are pressurized and often they break down—that is the pressurizing aparatus does (if not the rest). That leaves the boat which we had written you about in the last letter—that is if you could make any sense out of that at all. At least the frightening element seems to have been grately dimineshed by Spreits clarification of the case, and I hope and am sure that you will feel some relief too. He said there was no element of worry incase I could not get passage right away but that a thorough teste was naturally the best assurance I could find for following the right treatment over a period of time.

I enclose Dr. Spreits letter in English and in French (which Paul will write for me presently) and he inturn woulld like a little message from Resneck saying whether or not he has received the newest resume of the case which he has just clarified for us. At least in so far as there has been no Thrambossis or Hemeroadge. The names I am using, all sound like englishman. Paul will write this out properly, but I must go upstairs. Give my love to everybody. I am sorry that you have to get into this Libby because I know your capacity for shouldering the responsibly and I know that it is not good for you. I actually have faith in Spreit and feel now that I have gone there and he has put the mistake straight that you should feel better too. In case there is no boat to London this month there will be later but there is a pretty good chance of their being passage according to the steamship office. Obviously there must have been some mistake in Paul's translation of Spreits message or Spreit himself did not explain enough to make it clear to Paul. Whatever, here is his latest message and Spreit would like an answer from Resnick when possible stating that he has received it. Meanwhile I am continuing to plan to go to London although there is yet no message from McMichael. Spreit thinks I am progressing slowly but surely and I suppose you can see that yourself. The last letter was particularly bad because there was too much in it and I couldn't tie up all those loosends and ifs and buts, which alas are still pending. We have not yet heard from Pit or Tip about Paul staying there or not staying there as a guest. We are hoping for that daily just as we are hoping for passage on the Japanese frater. Coming back from England to Tangier is even more difficult as you can imagine, since the fraiter doesn't come back this way but goes on its way through the Panama Canal and we will have to find some ship that is not solidly Booked to bring us back. That is why we are counting even more heavily on finding pit or tip so that at least Paul can stay there and stay free of charge untill we do arrange some way back.

I will let you know the second there is a rift in this—a rift in what?

I considere seriously that I am right to be less worried and I do have faith in Spreit. He is one of those who does not talk but he was interested and surprised that Paul or the language had not managed to convey what he had written to Resnick. Anyway here it is again. If there is anything new in plans because of this letter naturally wire me but I will take for granted that Resnick will still think I should get there as quickly as possible unless I hear to the contrary. Please try to get him to send a note to Spreitwho wants one at this point. Above all should I go to London anyway and try some other Specialis whom Resnick would recomand or not. Suppose Dr. McMichael is away for the summer. I don't want to throw this back at you but I don't want to take any steps without Resneck either. Meanwhile enough for now, or I shall start wrighting gibberish again, because I do get tired after awhile. I have a feeling that everything will somehow work out Libby so don't get in a worse stew than you must be in already. I still can't read very much without someone elses help but Spreit says it will come back slowly, and then I am hoping to get a letter from you that isn't at the mercy of whoever can read it to me.

Meanwhile love.

J.

Dear Libby: This seems to me to be by far the best letter Jane has written since she started. It is very encouraging, I think. I haven't seen them all, but of those I have seen, it is undoubtedly the most clearly conceived. This is Doctor Spriet's diagnosis, in French and English: "Spasme cerébral avec confusion et parésie intellectualle pendant quelques jours, mais aucun signe de hemorragie cerébral ni thrombose cerébrale." "Cerebral spasm with intellectual confusion and paresis during the space of a few days, but no sign of cerebral hemorrhage or of cerebral thrombosis." I think she is much better, myself, in every way, even her vision and concentration.

Love,
Paul

Tangier, Summer 1957

In August Jane was admitted to the Radcliffe Infirmary in Oxford and then moved to St. Mary's Hospital in London. She was suffering from very high blood pressure, a condition she had had for a number of years. At St. Mary's it was decided that her brain lesion was inoperable. On the way back to Tangier with Paul she began to experience epileptiform seizures. She returned to England in September and was sent from the Radcliffe Infirmary to St. Andrew's, a psychiatric hospital in Northampton, where she was treated with electric shock.

68
To Libby Holman

Dearest Libby,

This is a quick note that will be mailed from Naples, as we are leaving this ship now to land in Gibraltar. My typewriter sticks unmercifully, and I must have it cleaned, so that I can write you a longer letter. This is impossible.

I can't remember whether I told you that I received the money from Stamford almost at once. It was wonderful getting it all settled and I hope to God there is no more nonsense. I have a feeling I did write you this but such is the nature of shock treatment. I am much better Libby, almost jolly. I dreamed about you last night and you were not jolly. I am beginning to be able to read, with, effort, but I am very hopeful about it. Anyway more about that and everything, as soon as I fix my machine.

Thank you, Libby, always, and much love

Jane

Aboard the S.S. Orion, *November 1957*

In early 1958 Jane and Paul left Tangier for Portugal because of concern about the general situation in Tangier. There were wholesale arrests of certain European residents by the police. (Ahmed Yacoubi had also been arrested.) In Portugal Jane's condition once again deteriorated and in April she flew from Lisbon to New York, where Katharine Hamill and Natasha von Hoershelman had offered to have her stay with them.

69
To Paul Bowles

Dearest Paul

I am sorry to have waited so long and I was very happy to read your letter and to know that you for the moment at least were happy set and able to eat and therefore I presume to work—or you must be by now on your way to it. I dreamed of happines and felt it in my dream as solid as gold. It was this afternoon I dreamed of it and I had the doubtful satisfaction of knowing that at last there was someting in my life that was not facke or open to doubte in any way. I have never known such misery and so I shall perhaps servive. I hope to survive because I am natural, like that wretched woman in my story. There is nothing you can do except write me that there is some hope that we may go to mexico. I could fly because that I could then go to when the time came. I have not asked the doctor yet about altitudes—what affecrt they would have on me even if only temporarly. There I could find a maid or two at least and you would be there if I could get back to work. I think of these things when I feel hopefull but when I don't see any way out of here I am desperate. Berred and Cherifa I can't bear to think about and must tretend there dead as you did Ahmed. The most important is my eyes or that field of visian—whatever it was called—not the field of visian itself because that is gone but the ability to read—there was a special word for that but I can't remember what it was we used it all the time. That is surely the tragedy if there is one unless it is simply the fact that don't like to write anyway. Libby is drumming up money from sourse and another—some from Oliver—and some John Goodwin and some from Katherine and twenty five dollars from Natasha when she has her tooth work finished. She herself has contributed the sum you're already familiar with and will continue too for life. I think this is very sweet of her and the work she is doing with my pasport and calling up these people to ask for a small sum of money from each for as long as I need it is invaluable. I will have no place to live soon and the rent will have have to be payed but according to Libby there will be enought from the various soursces. Diane has has reappedred as if by a mirictle because I didn't know where to reach her and simply ran into her at least Natasha. She wants to take an apport with me and since there is no other place except an old lady's home or home for dissabled people scince for for various reasons nobody have me. Dionne is reatly improoved after two years of Inalisis and very warm. Mrs. Latouche is spending the nights with me and a nurse the dayse. It is simply because I cannot be alone I am too frigtened after the fit which took a long time coming on and I would no way to comunicate if it happened when I was alone here. Libby does not think I should be in fact she says it is out of the question and thinks there will be enough money for medisons and rent and a maid between the groupe. She is writing you all about it very soon, but she is terribly busy and I do not see her very much. It will be a good send to have Dionne because lauliness is my toupbist problemme ple the fear of being alonge because of these ghastly fits. I am staying leave on the hope that some day I will be able to write again—at least to be indepemdent. I started three days ago to have fit but I took a dillantine and it stoped it in the midle. Dyane saw it happening the palpatations and insanne pullse beating I called the doctor but the fact that it did not come to its conclusian but that I was able to stop it is hopefull. There is so much hopelessness in this situation that I did not write you. But I am not crazy and was never crazy and only fear will drive me crazy. The fit was very unpleasant and terrifying because I—I have lost my place and so cannot find it again. Surely you can make some sinse out of this letter and last enough read most of it. It is very difficult for me to write Bubby but I will certainly write again tomorow or even later tonight. Please do write my mother and sign it with an initial which I often have done to her when I did not happen to have a pen. I feel better and I take my pills three times aday it is a struggel now for survival. I don't think you should mention suiside as glibly as you have on occasion—but I don't think you would use that way out really. This may sound like a nonsequator but I am in a hurry and I reffer to a conversation we had in Portugal. You threatened suiside if you had no money or if you were trapped with me and I didn't cheer up or if you were trapped in America. Naturaly I have been in a bad state but I have to face it and not die of it. It will be wonderful if the pills really work but it will take a few monts two now won't it. It is awful writing this way not not rereading. I hope you are working and this letter reaches you wherever you are. I suppose Spaine is you nesxt stop if Portugal proves impossible for any longer. You ask me about money and I know you have any money very much but perhaps you could pay the doctor in London. The episode in Tangier has nearly broken my heart but not know I am getting cold and forget when I can. I am not actually but I preffer to pretend it is something that the didn't happen. Please for God's sake don't send me any masages saying that Cherifa is waiting for my return or expecting. I will only go back if you go back because the government has changed. Libby is still expecting to have a production in the near future so do not go too farway. I cannot write you too much because it brings the whole tangier horror back and I am utterly lost here in America and without you. Portugal was a ball compared to this, but people have been wonderful to me and Dian is coming to live with me a sublet apartment. I cannot live with Libby and she will explain that to you herself. She has been sweet and making great efforts collectin the Jane Bowles fund, which I started telling you about eartlier in in the letter. Please Paul wrok or you might as well be here in an offict which I never want you to be. Katherine has just arrived and she will mail this letter toninght so I must finish it before we sit down to dinner. She promises to explain what is happening because I am incabable of explaing it except that I will live in an aportment with Dyan for the nexet few month untill I say what will do next. Perhaps Mexico will be the answer but I must have somewhere to live now since Tenessee will be returning soon. I think that I I will make it somehow and above all for you do your work and don't go too Japan because you will be hearing from Liby soon. I hope you can read enough of this to understand and don't let it frighten you. There is no time for corections. It is like being naked and I hate it. I feel better then I did when I hit the "lows" as Libby calls them. My blood pressure was down today and I lost or rather gained five pouns. The readin is the saame. I hate to send you a letter like the is but it is better then a—nothing isn't it. But I was very sad and couldn't. Please wright me above all—and the less about Tangier the better unless the morrocon Government wants to make you president. I will write again and so will Katharine. Please pay money i owe in England. The rest is being taken care by friends—Katharine will explane.

Much Love—as ever—

J.

New York City, Early May 1958

70
To Paul Bowles

Dear Paul, New York City

I personaly—Jane Bowles I mean—cannot write you today. It is imposible. There is no point untill you do come over if and when you do and you are once more joined together with your clothes. It is a time for me when silence is the best for both. I am thinking of going to a place where they correct speach (therefore reading) a type of therapy that is new and has had good resolts supposedly. I consulted a nuroligist to see if there was anything I could do with this terrifying life of mine and he said speache therapy. (i.e. reading) They go together and it is better to work at something anyway even if it turns out to be of no avail. They don't us this in england I suppose because they are as usual far behing America in sience—at any rate. This doctor said that just reading and writing by myself of course could take a much longer time. He did not want to put a time limit on this anymore than the english did, but they are all quite aware of it here) . . what I have is called efasia. I cannot spell but that is what they say. I do not put much home in it but I must try anyway if I have the courage and if I think it will do me any good and if I can get the money. Naturally there is no limited time as usual but I suppose I could tell whether it was having any results or not. I will know more when I have been to the speeche center at Lenox Hill Hospital in a week and have consulted with the therapict there. I will know what it costs and if I can get any money for it which I am very worried about. I am not sure in fact I am pretty sure damned sure theat Libby doesn't want to spend any more on me—atleast that she can't afford two for the moment while she is gurding he loins for Yerma. It will take a pretty sumn and know of it tax deductuble. Aft about reading just by myself this doctor who is the head of lenox Hill said that I would need help. I am determined to get it if I feel it realy help me because I cannot go on this way—just sitting. I simply cannot. Please please don't think that I mean that you should pay for this I don't. I know you couldn't afford it. It won't be any fun I know but anything to hasten this waiting if it is at all possible. I am desperate because I am know fascing heavy time in a way that I didn't even when we were together in Portugal. It is not possible that it got worse. But it dead. My health is alright. I did not want to write you because I didn't want you to think me miserable but I am sure you are used to that. This seems to me the darkest time but perhaps something will break and I will be cleare cleare like I was in the air going to America. I love being in the sky and I did love being as close to the ground as possible. I loved Tangier very much. More than I knew even with all that talking but it is my sight my friedem that I want again.

It is terrible to have to be taken care of. I cannot get around her at all. But I did go out in Tangier. I went out to market and came back and spent nightss sleeping alone and not being afraid. Dione of course has to go out a lot and I have seen a few friends. John has diligently taken me out on the average of once a week. I have the same horror of stirring that I did have in Portugal, but I have to stir now and then to go to the doctors. Once night Sally and a friend of hers took me to a dyke night club, It was like going there after I died. A girl started talking to me and wanted only to talk about north africa. She was an econimest and believe in evolution as the for the trouble between arab and french, inevitable evolution, if I had met her in Morocco I would have decided that she was a communist but here it is differant. She hated your book more than any book she ever read, (Sheltering sky) so I felt very flatered and famous. Please don't feel gulilty which I know is your way about any present mess I was in before or am in now was entirey of my own making and not yours. I am heart broken about my life with c. but it is not that nearly so musch as the preasant which frightens me. I shall write you more about that but it is not important. I simply want to send her some word that I am not coming back so that she can plan accordingly. I cannot send her money either. [   ] but to keep going to the bank untill it is all used up. The only other suggestion I have is that you send her the equivalent of one thousand pesetas a month and that she keep goint to the bank to untill the end of her life. I don't ask you to do this because we have so little money and if you are going possible to live in Mexico and I too in the end it will mean a great deal of defferand to us. Yes one can still live in Mexico and there is a small town even not far from Mexico city, but lower down. a friend of ours told me that we could live for nearly nothing. I suddenly remember that I did not tell the doctor that I could nor read—he tested me on writing. Naybe they were right in england. I will see what they say in the speach centar. Please Paul forgive this letter I am doing the best I can and it is very deppressing not to know the words much better know than I did when I was in Tangier. I must stop now and I am hoping to see you above all. Please make up something for my mother, based on this . She is fine. Julian wants to go on eith the farse at least untill she is stronger then I'll probably have to see he. I don't know. Like yourself Julian says that one must not try to think more than a day ahead. I can't go on. I am suddenly so deppressed by the fact that I forget to mention to the doctor that I could write to a certain extant but not read that I am appaled. I can only hope the speach threapist who deals with all of those things will understand whether or not this has any bearing on the matter, or if is not more hopeless if one cannot read and less possible to cure.

I must stop this and enclose mothers letter. Despite the confusian. I know you hate not to hear at all. I am elive. Maybe in Mexico where people didn't read and write anyway—but that was only possible in Morroco. The Indian life is impossible for me and there would be no cherifas but it would be better than hear. I havn't much hope for this therapy but I must try it if it seems at all likely. I will know in a few days. Give my love to Maurice. much love, as ever

Jane.

Jane

Dear Paul, I just saw Libby who expects to come over here in a few weeks. It is very important and you will live at Libbys with Ross Evans and Libbys nephue. She said that she was all for the retraining in reading and writing and that Doctor Eran Belle who is the doctor I spoke to was recomended by Resnick as the best doctor in the country. (Unockn to me) Dyonnes friend actually recomented him but Dyone checked with Libby who check with Resnec. I hope there is really hope in this, because I cannot possibly go on this way forever or or for years. I don't know how you'll get over here or if there will be time before Mourice gets your stuff but it seems very important to Libby whom I know has a New york production in mind after she tries the play out and sees what she has in Denver firtst. She has just now got the theatre in Denver. I hope to God you havn't gone somewhere else. Meanwhile right one more letter to my mother and I will have to spill the beans too her when you are both in the same country. Please don't worry about that. It will be very hard but I will have to. Meanwhile just keep writing.

Love
Jane

Late May/Early June 1958

Jane was admitted to the psychiatric clinic of New York Hospital–Cornell Medical Center in White Plains on October 1, 1958. By mid-December her condition had improved sufficiently for her to return to Tangier with Paul. There she moved back into her apartment with Cherifa. She was also attended by a companion, Angèle, and a cook, Aicha.

71
To Libby Holman

Dearest Libby:

I am very sad not to have written you. It is too much of a task evaluating the whole situation and then writing what is important and what isn't. I can write down all my worries, and there are roughly about eleven major ones, including a very faint worry—not a worry actually, but an *awareness* that this is after all earthquake country, although we are not on the Agadir fault. That was such a nightmare. The reports on Agadir came here daily, and to top it off we had a tremor here. The people were so hysterical that they slept in the bullring all night. The Jews especially. I didn't know about it until the next morning. It is not fair to mention only the other worries since that one obsessed me for a good two months. Anyway, most of them will hold until I see you. But when will I see you? You write as if Paul and I were likely to go back to America together, or as if he would go back at all. He announced last night that he would have to see his parents eventually (I suppose within the next five years), which surprised me. So perhaps he will go back. I did not think that he would ever set foot in the United States unless it was to work. There don't seem to be any jobs for him any more now that he has so cut himself off from the market place in New York. He is more and more forgotten (even by Tennessee) unless it is simply that incidental music is too expensive and hardly worth importing someone to the States for, because of the fare. He would probably get more jobs if he lived in some accessible place, but naturally he wouldn't. And besides, his living expenses would be more, although they have trebled here in the last two and a half years. Many things are more expensive than they are in New York. Things have changed considerably, but I don't think there will be a revolution this year (according to my spies) and maybe not for many more years, depending on what happens in the rest of the world, naturally. I shall ask your permission not to mention politics. I don't like them any more.

The doctor does not want me to stay alone because of the danger that I might have a fit in the street or fall down and hit my head. I have a Spanish woman because she can keep accounts. My most solemn worry is about my work, and above all, do I really have any? Can I ever have any again? I will try to settle it this summer and next fall. (Within the next six or eight months.) For myself, anyway, because it has nothing to do with anyone else. Also there is nothing new except that I don't always know which is the stroke and which is the writer's block. I know some things have definitely to do with the stroke, and others I'm not sure of. The sheep festival is about to begin, in a month, and they are all buying their sheep now for the slaughter. I think that I will not be able to buy a sheep this year. They are too expensive for me, and Cherifa is having four teeth pulled, and later, a bridge made.

I have trouble with names, numbers, and above all the ability to add and subtract. I know perfectly well the general outlines. Two hundred dollars is less than three hundred dollars, and ten plus ten equals twenty, but the complicated divisions and subtractions and additions—! Adding more than two figures is impossible for me. That can be relearned, but I really need someone with me in this country, or they would all cheat me because I could not correct their own sums which are *always wrong*. So Angèle does that. I suppose that is the least of my worries, but I'm sure that none of this is psychosomatic, because I have no mental block about numbers, and they are worse than the rest. I don't think it would take more than six months to relearn the whole multiplication table. It is very funny but not bad, because I know what I need to know, and then can have someone else do the work. Some women are bad at computing even without strokes, and they are not as charming as I am. Don't ask Dr. Resnick anything. He might have discouraging news, and above all I must for once in my life keep my hopes up. Paul says that he spoke to the doctors and they said that nobody knew how much one could improve or how long it would take. The doctor in New York who sent me to that ghastly young man at Lenox Hill—I forget his name—said the hemianopsia was permanent, but not the aphasia, which has proved to be correct. I now know the meaning of all words. They register again on my brain, but I am slow because there is a tiny paralyzed spot in each eye which I apparently have to circumvent when I'm reading. One side is very bad, worse than the other, but on the whole I'm getting much more used to it. Don't say anything to Resnick because he can't possibly predict anything, and anyway he is apt to be frank, and maybe he would say something depressing. Undoubtedly. I have an awful feeling that I've written this whole thing before. I will send the blood pressure readings and ask if there are any new drugs besides serpasil. My own doctor is pleased with me.

Libby, there is so much talk about myself in this letter that I think I must stop. I have left half the things out that I wanted to tell you about. At least there are no politics in this one. I was fairly poetic in the old days. Much love,

J.

Tangier, 1960

72
To Libby Holman

Darling Libby,

I was just writing my third draft of a letter to you that has been in my mind for weeks. First of all there was my original draft which I did not quite approve of because in it I announced that I could no longer write because I simply had to see you and it made me sad to write because there were too many things we could say in a few minutes that could never be said on paper. I went on and on in this draft of a letter trying to explain everything and finally nothing satisfied me so I kept tearing up draft after draft of this letter which was supposed to be a thorough report on the progress of my rehabilitation, on my efforts to write again and on the state of Morrocco in general, and of Cherifas family in particular (nin children) above all I wanted to tell you about the struggles of trying to work again because it concerns me the most and unless I can give the true picture I feel that my letter to you is a false letter. I suppose I will be content when I again reach that state of despair due only to my "neurosis" (lack of talent I think) which is familiar to me. I am working hard to achieve that state, but it means writing every day however badly. (I write so that my brain will make knew tracks and compensate for whatever damage was made by the stroke.) Numbers I will have to relearn completely as I have written you and I should I'm sure go ahead and do it right away because it is a good exercise for the brain and so I May enter school again, next semester. I have gained waight too much but I am watching it. I am much calmer with this layer of fat but I am in despair about my looks; Paul is frightened of my being thin and thinks I am ugly when I am.

Libby I was just writing the third draft of the letter to you when yours came for Paul and naturaly I was very thrilled that you might be coming and I did stop trying to write you because it seemed so much simpler to wait. I am now prepared for you to come but terrified that you won't. However if you don't I shall have to go there anyway unless my mother should decide to come over here instead. I don't think she would unless I urge her too which I naturally would not do. Please Libby you do believe me that I write these terrible drafts all the time. They are mixtures of ameteur neuroligical reports—political predictions and attempts at little portraits of the eleven members of Cherifas immediate familly. For a while they were all living on a taxi number because the taxi had collapsed completely but the number was still intact so the familly was living on that. The brotherinlaw (cherifas sister's husband) had rented the taxi number to some other man for two years. Then came the government order forbiding all taxi numbers to be rented out—in other words each taxi number had to have a genuine flesh and blood taxi to go with it. This saga goes on for a long time and it used to get me down as much as the neurological birds I view that I felt obliged to give you with each new draft no matter how I tried to keep it out of the letter. I am reading much better Libby but I think I won't go on about this unless you are not coming over in which case I shall this year come over there. I hope to God you are coming because I can't wait and please let me know definnitely (can one ever be deffinite these days) if you are coming, Ahmed said he had a letter from you saying you were coming—a more recent one than Pauls.

I cut off the part of this letter because it got too messy and put it in the trash basket with other drafts for letters that I'd written you this month.

Libby thank you for the little owles. Was it my copy of Catcher in the Rey Rie? Rye?, or was it your copy and my owl picture. Do you remmember the long tale of the elf owles? Did you send it to me because you did remember or because you thought they were so adorable. I was so happy to see them again. I always talk about them and describe them to people and now I can show them to people which is much better than going on about them.

Wouldn't you like to have some? I hope that your husband

likes them. Have I ever met him? Congratualations. I am not going to correct this letter because it takes too long. Please write me again and let me know how your plans are proggressing for the trip here. Are you going to England or to Italy. Please forgive me for not answering your letter and I hope you understand. I have been very upset thinking about it this week—but when you read this one you will realize how difficult it is for me to express anything at all complicated without messing the paper up and making lots of drafts. I have made three for this one since yesterday and I am going to send it now. If you don't come I shall have to wait and see you in the spring or summer. Please give my love to Rose and forgive this awful mess of a letter. It is unintelligable with all these corrections. I will talk to you personally when I see you anyway. Maybe it is intelligable an unintressting which is worse but don't tell me about it.

I shall send this now because Old man Beden has just arrived. She lives in the apartment next door and wears little collars and ties. She is about seventy and has changed her friend for a new one, this year.

I shall reread only this last bit and then send this on no matter how bad it is.

all my love, always
Jane

Tangier, November 15, 1960

73
To Libby Holman

Dearest Libby,

This will be my last attempt at writing what I consider an impossible letter. It seems inordinately difficult to me and yet it shouldn't be.

Six months ago or even farther back Gordon Sager came through here on his way to Greece with a Merril Grant for three thousand dollars on which he was going to live for a while and write a book. He told me that John Meyers had suggested to him that I apply for the same kind of grant and he came here delighted with such news but I *wasn't.* It created a terrible promblem in my mind. I couldn't possibly apply for it and risk your hearing about it from the grape vine and I couldn't tell you I wanted more money without saying I needed more money which sounded awful. Things have doubled and trippled since our original estimate of what I needed and so we are always just on the edge of being short. Naturally Paul pays up the differance but I do think that insofar as I can help by getting this grant I *should* apply for it, and I wrote to them last week. I hope something will come of it. Because I got into one of my magillas over what in hell to write you, Paul who thought I was crazy said that maybe he would apply for it instead but Gordon thought he was too successful. Of course Paul *is* very well known without making much money or barely enough and so he gets the worst of both worlds. I suppose I get the best, as a kind of failure, and can therefore apply for a grant. The money can be used for anything as long as long as you are sincerely intending to work on something. Gordon describes it as a kind of "reward." He used his to visit his father in St. Louis, part of it in any case. But he did finish his book and he lived on it while he was finishing it. If I get it I shall add to the three hundred a little each month and maybe spread it out over a period of several years or months. I don't know what it would come to, in francs, or I might finance a trip to America for a physical check up and seeing my mother which I *must do.* Naturally I would see you too as I don't really think I could ever get you over here. Anyway I have decided to apply and probably I won't get it after all this in which case I shall go on as I am and thank God for what you give me because without that we couldn't make it at all. Naturally it is always nice to have more and I think Paul considers me crazy not to have applied for it before this; I know that it is right that I should pick up as much money as I can whenever I can to take some of the onus off of you and Paul. I am glad to have writen this letter because it seemed impossible to write and I hope the grant still exists I have taken so long to get around to asking for it.

I hope that I am able to write another play as I think a novel at this point would be impossible. My vocabulary is getting richer each day and I am remembering more and more words as I am able to read more but I think a novel would be a gargantuan task. Soon I should be back to my normal rate of one novel every eighteen month—but not for a while yet. Libby I know you won't get here somehow but Lilla Von Saher *will*! Do you remember her. The woman Tennessee called a big fat cow. She came to visit me in the nut house when I was there. By the way I hope I am not known as a "muschugana" now—*if I am* keep it away from me. I have become sensitive about it—like the others of course.

Mary Jane Ward made a fortune out of her experience (the snake pit, it was), but all I can remember about mine are the menues. Nothing has changed much. Like my play, but the food was differant. Potatoes instead of rice, and not enough cranbery sauce on Thanks Giving. I can joke about it now a little. I will be coming back but I am going to try and get something done first. John advised me to get something done or part of something at least before I returned and I aggree with him. I think it is going to be calm here—comparatively—at least it is expected to be a quit spell. Rumors and threats of revolution have been the atmosphere for too long now and I think it will be alright for a little while (famous last words)—but I am determined to ignore it if I can, even if there are more rumors. David is still here and Jay, but many people have left. Rose was telling me about Mexico and how cheap it was a few years ago (Cuerna Vaca). Is it? (In case we did eventually have to move somewhere else?) I have heard otherwise from some people who left here to live down there. I shall mail this before I get into another GonzaMagella. This one is called the "application for the Grant." I have about four more of them coming (letters like this but on other subjects). I shall also write a plain letter soon. I think of you and wonder about your friend in the glass house.

Much love,

Jane

Tangier, April 16, 1961

74
To Lilla Von Saher

Dearest Lilla

Just a note to tell you that your letters are here waiting for Paul and perhaps by the time you get this letter he will already be back writing you. He was coming back two days ago but then wired that he decided to stay on a little longer but surely not very long because neither he nor christopher have much money with them. Otherwise he would not be back for a long time—who knows. He has rented half a little house in Marrachesh—in the medina—just like a play house not a serious house—where they can go down and spend a few days or weeks paying less than if they always went to a hotel. Even though they go to very cheap hotels—or they did but now the only descent cheap one that they liked is closed or too noisy. Forget. Anyway your letters are here and he is sure to be back within a week or even less. I am afraid if I forward them they will get lost forever because he would be back here meanwhile or have gone somewhere else enroute before he came back. Be patient and you will here soon.

Much love, when will I see you
Jane

Tangier, 1961

75
To Libby Holman

Darling Libby,

I am sorry I have not written you and even sorrier that you did not come when I thought you were going to come. I was very dissappointed, naturally and so I did not even write to you.

I am coming over to see you—if you don't come here. My mother offered to come and see me if I did not feel up to coming over but I did say to her that I would make the trip if you didn't come here because I do want to see you and so I am coming but I don't know when. Paul is going to see his parents in Florida and so we will make the trip together coming and going.

I will have to spend half the time at least with my mother in New York but Paul will want to spend some time with his parents in Florida and also in New York or Wherever you are if you can put him up. We both want to do that—stay where you are most of all and so please write us when you will be *there* and when you would like us to come—between *now* and October. At least tell us if you are leaving for Europe at any point because we don't want to come then. Paul does not want to stay in a hotel at any point naturally because it is so expensive and even if you will lend him your apartment as you have done before we both want to come to America when you are there and free to see us. This should be a simple letter but I find it very difficult to write.

Since my operation I have a crooked stomach and I am thinking of having it made straight with an operation before I come. Do you think I should. I have a fat stomach on one side because my plastic plaque didn't come fare enough around, it was put on orriginally because of a hernia. I think it's the surgeon's fault and so I should be able to get it done for almost nothing, but who knows. I don't know what to do because a woman of depth should not think about her stomach after fourty-five. Do you agree with that. Please Libby darling tell us when to plan our trip unless it makes no defferance. At least write if there is any really *bad* time. Pasage is almost impossible both ways but we can't even start trying to get it untill we hear from you so do write a note quickly. We may have to come after the summer people have returned to america or before they start coming here. Much love as ever,

J.

Tangier, April 26, 1962

76
To Libby Holman

Darling Libby

I am almost too tired to write this letter but I must because I will not have time to hear from you if I don't.

I had a third operation three weeks ago and I have been too tired to write. Then I did a lot of shopping for a ball because I haven't done any in many years. I am too tired to give you the details. It was the Hernia again which he fixed up with a larger nylon plaque—and God knows whether or not it will come apart again this time. At any rate my stomach is a sight when I'm undressed so I am not going to undress. It really needs plastic surgery at this point but naturally I am not writing you about that but to make plans.

Paul wrote you but I don't think he was very explicit about our plans. I would have written but there was this operation which of course my mother *doesn't know about—again.*

Libby, as Paul probably told you, we are leaving around the six of September so I suppose we should be there around the twelfth. I can go straight to my mother's with Paul the first night if you like, and then go up to your house with Paul if you would like us to. I think Julian, my step-father, could take us to Greenwich or near Greenwich in his car if you are there and if it is a good time for you.

Paul would like to come to you as soon as possible after arriving in New York and then later go down to Florida to his mother's, at which point I would spend my time with my mother. We will have to find our own ways of getting back and forth at this period if you want us to visit you then. That can be worked out later. I don't know where you are and I realize it's much harder to commute from West Hampton where I imagine you are now than it would be from Greenwich. All this is pointless until I know whether you are anywhere at all where we can visit you, beginning I don't know what date—but the Independence leaves from Algeciras on the six which Rose can figure out for you herself.

If we can come straight to you, should we spend the night in my mother's hotel and then get out to where you are or not? Mother is agreeable to anything. Please write, she—or at least someone in the family—has a car as I understand—but we can manage anyway. Just let me know where you'll be and the telephone number and if you can have us.

Much love,

J.

Tangier, August 1962

77
To Libby Holman

Darling Libby

this should probably be a letter to Rose, a note rather because it is a businness letter. That is the sort of word I cannot spell since my stroke. And others of course that I am not aware of. I hope that you have *not* told Polly to hold my money in New York, untill I get home. I naturally will need it here to pay bills that can't be settled before I leave and which I will have to pay by post dated check before I get onto the boat. Your check does not get here until the fourth sometimes or even the fifth and I don't want a mess after I leave, on the 3rd or forth—for Gib.

So unless you have said anything to Polly which I doubt on your own huck (hook?) (another word which I know must be wrong) don't say anything at all or tell him to leave things as they are. I think you had better wire me if the money isn't going to come here for next month (September) but I hope you can fix it up if it isn't. I hate to leave debts behind me naturally—anyway enough of this.

Let Rose handle it and give her my love. I hope I hear from you in answer to my last letter. Judging from mothers last letter I don't think she does have a car but but I'm not absolutely sure.

Love, as ever
Jane

Tangier, August 13, 1962

78
To Libby Holman

Libby dear,

I am sending some presents back with Charles Gallagher the friend I love best in Tangier. Apparently you have met and so I don't have to introduce or explain. He is an expert on Morrocco but also laughs and jokes. He was an expert on Japan (oriental cultures) when you first met but this may have slipped your sieve-like mind, which is like my own. Everyday Charles tells me what he's doing here and I read all his resumes and articles but sometimes I forget anyway. Now he he is going to deliver a series of lectures at Universities all over the country and he will be in New York for a month before he begins. He is also going to some kind of convention held by college proffessors and "other experts." In any case I hope that you will find time to have a drink together, (his schedule is heavy too), so that he can deliver these gifts and give you news of myself and Paul. I have wondered about assigning the bags, and he suggests that I do. So the blue one (or peacock blue) is to go to Alice, the red to Jesse May and the brown to Betty. The little bright red wallet is for Rose Minor and the dark marroon wallet (man's size) is for George. If they are peeved with the colors I have assigned them tell them to settle it among themselves. I did not want to get them all alike naturally.

I am sorry to have taken so long about this. But I was not happy with the selection of gifts I found around the medina. They wanted bags and they wanted them to be Morrocan, naturally, they wanted shoulder straps—but alas there are none with shoulder straps except some truly hedious cow hide bags with desert scenes and sheeted women tooled into the leather. I don't think they would have liked those do you?

These bags may be useless, the straps are too short except for dwarfs and I am sad about that. But they could put spools into them. Just a lot of odd spools and hang them up in their rooms. I mean each person could hang his bag on a nail, and look at it. It is too bad about the shoulder straps. The old arab who sold them said these straps were the fashion today. I love you and miss you very much and will write a letter to you and to Rose. Meanwhile dear Libby I wish that you would send me just a note to tell me how you are and give them all a kiss for me. I was very happy with them there and want to come back. Thank Betty and Alice and Jesse and George for making my stay so pleasant and tell them I miss them and will come back.

always,
Jane

Tangier, c. November/December 1962

79
To Rena Bowles

Dear Mother B.

I wanted to get this letter to you by Xmas but now I suppose I'll be lucky if I reach you by the New Year. As you know I'm terribly lazy about writing and added to that I have this trouble with spelling since the stroke, which means that I have to get hold of someone if a word looks wrong to me. It is very annoying but need not stop me from writing a play or a book. That is simple laziness I suppose, though for several years I was unable even to read, all of which Paul must have written you about. I am so sorry about not being in the day you called me—or that I was going to call you or did I call you and get no answer? It is all so far away now that I can't remember what happened or even whether or not I haven't already written you on the same subject. If I have, forgive me. Paul had a spell of the Grippe and though he did not go to bed he was miserable and without any appetite, but now thank God he is well again. He's passed it on to me naturally which I did not mind because colds are not my particular weakness. I get over them quickly and they don't knock me out the way they do Paul. Arteries are my trouble, blood pressure etc. Two night ago we were up until one A.M. looking for the cat around the neighborhood of our apartment but she was nowhere and finally we started to bed very unhappily when we heard a far away meow . . . so we rushed onto the terrace where we had searched for her and called for her over and over again . . . and there she was hopping out of a huge arab pot inside of which she had been curled up the entire time. She finds all kinds of ways to torment us, and always has. She must be about sixteen years old and is kept alive by shots mostly because for years she has had bladder trouble. I wish you the best naturally for the New Year, and I'll try to write more often— Love to you Both—

Jane

Tangier, c. December 1962

80
To Ruth Fainlight

Dearest Ruth

This is just to let you know that I think of you all the time and wonder whether or not you will come back. I gave the letter to Fatima's husband, in fact I read it to him in Arabic and he was very pleased indeed. He was glad to have the picture she sent him and I told him she was sending more. You said this in your letter. I am glad to write about Fatima and her husband because I don't want to get onto myself. Things are going badly for me. My work has come to a standstill although I tried again this morning to start off on a new tack (spelling?). I did not scrap everything I had written but typed up the first eighteen pages of which I showed Paul ten. Paul was pleased and said that it sounded like myself and not someone else but he would have liked to see more. I would like to see more myself but I seem to have come to a dead end. I liked this letter best when I was writing about Fatima and her husband. Anyway I seem to get more and more discouraged and therefore it is difficult for me to write. I am afraid to have many mispellings which I think I warned you about in the past. In case you have forgotten, most of them are due to the odd affects the stroke had on my spelling but not all of them. There is no doubt that I spell better than I did before. (five years ago) It really is high time I got back to Fatima and her husband. This letter is going very badly.

About Fatima and her husband, I wish to tell you that Paul has forgotten how much money she gets a month but I haven't! She gets fifteen thousand francs a month and that is what I shall tell Paul to give Fatima's husband. As I remember He was to get fifteen thousand more at Sheep time but I am not as sure of this sum as I am of the other. Perhaps it was ten thousand! It is about time for the sheep money more or less so please write me what we're to give him.

Paul, whom I have just seen, told me that he was given money that was to be used each month for Fatima's husbands support but that no sheep had been mentioned. (He found a note on which everything was written out) Had you intended to send another check for that or is the sheep to come out of the check that Alan gave Paul for Fatima's husband. This is truly the kind of letter I love. The more I write it the better I love it. I hope you enjoy it as much as I do. Please study the wording of your reply so that I am sure to know exactly what to do about the sheep. The festival is still a month away but the longer Fatima's husband waits, the more expensive the sheep will get. He really should have bought it two years ago when it was a baby.

Ruth I miss you so very much I do not dare to think that you might possibly not return. By now Yvonne Gerofie has probably told you about Noel and I imagine you are seeing her and Mira. Terrible about Noel but I hope that at least the cancer has not had time to spread, yet.

How strange it must seem to you—having Yvonne and Mira there. I have only David occasionaly, (spelling), and Ira Cohn and Isabelle and every now and then as a great sexy treat—Mrs. McBey. I went to a fashion show at the Hotel Rif with Mrs. McBey and Veronica. One of the boys belonging to the cuban couple—Irving—loathes me. I have a feeling that I am going to be more and more hated as the years go by. I am thinking of leaving, but not yet. Please give my love to Tamara and Mira and Yvonne and of course Noel if you are allowed to see her. Is Sonia Orwell in London. Of course she is married to someone else now but I don't remember his name although I know him. Please write about the sheep. Tell me how you feel about London now, after your sad return because of your friend. Are you still going out a lot—is Alan gone?

Write me please—Love
Jane

Yvonne's address: Cumberland Hotel
Marble Arch, London W1.

Tangier, c. March/April 1963

81
To Ruth Fainlight

Dearest Ruth

I haven't written anything in so long, that I am afraid that I will forget how to use the typewrite, if this keeps up. I have not read anything either. I haven't the energy to read since it's always a bit difficult for me because of the hemynopia trouble resulting from the stroke which you know about and which, although it is a thousand times improved, slows down my reading so much that I fall asleep with the light on. I managed to stay awake for one week reading a book called, "Plain Girl", a book for children with large print. It was about a little Amish girl who wore a little apron to school, in fact a complete Amish costume—very quaint—you must have seen pictures of the

Amish in America. The Amish don't wear any buttons on their shoes nor do they ride in automobiles, nor do they use machinery of any kind. Their fields are plowed by hand. In rereading this I see that I say Buttons on their shoes. I seem to be more and more incapable of expressing anything. Anyway I managed to finish Plain GIRL after a week but after that I picked up a book called "Cybernetique et Société."! I bogged down after spending days on the preface which was purely tecnical and which required a working knowledge of physics. What is a working knowledge? On top of all this my bed seems to slant down instead of up which I would preffer and this too prevents me from reading anything because I am so exasperated all night. I wake up during the night and I realize that my bed is slanting down the very second I become conscious. I hope that some day this will all stop and that I will work a little because there is nothing else for me to do. I went to Sonia's yesterday and saw The Santscrit student who gave me news of the whole Lysergic acid set, headed of course by Sonia! I had not seen Sonia or anyone else (nor the Gerofies) for ten days because Libby Holman was here with her abstract Painter fisherman husband and she did not want to meet anyone nor go anywhere—so we stayed closeted for ten days. I did not write either letters or plays of course as you know. Her departure left me feeling sadder even than I had felt when she came and I am still trying to recover.

During the time that Libby was here I managed naturally to give Fatimas husband the money for the sheep and today he came for his monthly money which Paul gave him. He said he needed an extra five thousand francs which I gave him out of my own money although Paul refused to give him any because he wanted to follow Alan's instructions. Fatima's husband told me Fatima would give it back to me out of her salary. It is true that they always need more money for the children during the holidays and anyway he was very touching so I felt it was worth the risk though Paul thought you might dissaprove. I loved your letter. It was nice and fat and long and excuse me for writing you such a bad letter in return but it is better than no letter. I suppose that I shall go on excusing myself for my bad letters like a thirteen year old girl. There is to be a whole new invasion of beatnicks this summer coming to settle. Paul has taken a house in Arcila by the month—very expensive but worth it because he can no longer work at all in his studio. The woman above him hammers brass trays all night untill her croupier husband comes home from the casino at six, and the Yeshivabooka's who had moved into this building before you left, start cooking at seven in the morning. The kitchen's wall is against his bed so he never gets any peace at all. I have not yet written Frances. Please tell Fatima about her husband and write me *when* you return. Noël wrote that you had been busy every second since Alans' depparture—good. I wonder if you still want to return—or if you are only coming back because of Fatima! The GAZEBO has been rented and a bathroom added plus other improvements. Give my love to Noël and Mira if you see them and tell them I will write another note to them.

Much love Ruth—I still miss you terribly— Jane

P.S. Love to David of course and Alan if he's back. We received 2 postal cards from him—It sounds to me as if you might be going *there instead* of coming here. I hope not—give Alan my love and thank him for sending *two* cards instead of one joint card.

Tangier, c. May 1963

82
To Libby Holman

Darling Libby,

I have written and destroyed many letters since you left and now I cannot go on this way or you will think that I have forgotten you and that I was not happy with you and Louie. I was so happy with both of you that I have not yet recovered. I was so bereft after you left that it might have been better had Louie been a little mean while he was here. I was very happy with both of you, and give him my love. This letter is for him to. Jay raved about how you looked and he thought you had a new sweetness added to the way you looked which he attributes to Louie whom he loved. Louie is a favorite with Nancy and Sis as you know already but naturally you can see them in America if you want to. As for Alice I just refuse to mention her she gave me such pleasure. Please thank Rosie for her letter and tell her how happy I am that she liked the ashtray which troubled me so much, the decision troubled me in Tetuan.

I have bogged down really and not written you because so many complex and unintresting things have happened. They will bore you but I feel because of my german blood that I must give you a short but accurate account of what happened after you left. After you left the Tyznteshka Atlas mountains magilla complicated itself to such a degree that however much I try I don't think I *can* give you a german factual account of what happened. I don't know exactly at what point you left although I do think you were here when I would have had to add one hundred dollars to the rental of the car if they went by car, from here, at all. So then it was a question of going by train as far as Marrakesh and after that hiring a car. At that point I might have gone with Isabelle or not but suddenly Yvonne decided that she might leave with Isabelle and Isabelle's daughter herself which would have left no room for me in the car that was hired from Marrakesh onward. That meant that I would have to write Christopher Wynklin and propose that he drive his own car and me in a convey with the three women and a chauffeur, providing I payed for his gas and hotel rooms, food etc. As you know I think you do anyway, Paul by this time was out of the picture. This was complicated enough but Yvonne refused to decide whether or not she would go untill the last minute which need not have influenced me if I had wanted to write Christopher but it did because I knew I would feel worse if they *all* went and I didn't and I *might* have gone if Yvonne had gone because she is my favorite of the two. Yvonne did not want to decided anything untill the last minute, nor would she *sopple.* I think she was waiting for mail from Noel, actually, because she did not want to go across the Atlas with Isabelle if Noel wrote that she was going to sneak telephone calls to her from London, which Noel can't do while Isabelle is home because Isabelle refuses to have Noel's name mentioned in the house. Noel has her own room and could have sneaked calls to Yvonne when Mira, her friend, was asleep. I imagine all this was being decided by mail and meanwhile I was not writing Christopher, just soppling, without you or Louie to report to. Paul refused to discuss it at all. In fact he has gone away to Arcila which is another long letter. I got so weak, trying to decide about all this that I could barely drag around my room. I don't think I can really give you an accurate lifelize picture of all the differant elements in this Magilla. The proffesor who arrived suddenly and made it possible to further complicate things by offering to take Yvonne's place at the library whereas never before in thirty years has it ever been possible for Yvonne to leave on a trip with Isabelle. They have lived together for thirty years but actually Isabelle is really above Yvonne. I mean by this that she is her boss. No one else would employ Yvonne because although she keeps the books very well she is too gloomy and melancholic to wait on customers. There are many elements in this story and I must close now. The next letter will be another gonza Magella about Paul but I think this is enough about Isabelle and Yvonne. I wish you had seen them. I am so sad that you are gone.

Love darling always, and to Louie.

Jane

I have lost Gordon's address which you gave me.

Tangier, May 27, 1963

83
To Ruth Fainlight

Darling Ruth,

I am sad of course that you are not coming back but I can't say that I am in the least surprised. I expected it. By the time you had written me I knew anyway and dispite my dissapointment I think it is best for you. My life has turned into a veritable farce, schlepping between Arcila and Tangier as I do, and if I did not find it humorous I would weep.

Paul wrote Alan that he would be staying at Arcila and would therefore find it difficult to keep up his arrangment about the money from there, particularly as I myself go down all of the time and in fact plan to spend a solid block of time there at some future date. Naturally we come in here to get mail but to sincronyze (spelling?) all this with Fatima's husbands pay day might have become difficult since I would not trust anyone else to give him the money. Long ago I thought it a good idea to let the Librarie des Colonne handle it because Fatima's husband had ways of getting around me as you remember. You wrote me once that you thought he had a nerve asking for five thousand extra francs shortly after you had just given him the sheep money after I had given it too him because I am soft and I was sure the Gerofies would be more bisiness like. I took the five thousand out of the money Paul had for him, by the way, as soon as I received your letter. Now with Arcila it is better that you do arrange something more satisfactory for the man because in anycase I am not going to be here all of the time. In the spring I will go to America if not sooner. as I have just written so I would have to turn the man over to somebody else.

I have just had lunch with Yvonne and the two girls at their house except that nobody ate any lunch. Noel and I drank two litres of wine between us and even Yvonne had a little whisky. It seemed to me like some earlier time in my life, which was pleasant for a change. I turned up at Charles later with a lurching walk and slurred speach and he got rid of me as fast as he could.

But at any rate at this picnic where nobody had anything to eat at all either Noel or Yvonne told me that you had already arranged with the Gerofies to take over the money etc. I was surprised because there has been no answere from Alan to Paul's letter which he mailed him quite some time ago. I can't remember what Paul's letter said because the Arcila dance had already begun, and I never get anything straightened with Paul, nor do I remember anything that isn't written down. My mind is full of food that has to be taken to Arcilla because there is nothing there to eat at all except some tomatoes and some giant sized string beans and someimes fish is cought that Paul considers edible. Otherwise everything must be taken there in great baskets and burlap bags. You can imagine the lists that have to be made which is particularly difficult because Paul can never remember what there is left in the house when he comes here so that I am almost obliged to go there myself to see. It is easy enough to take the bus out there except that the seats have to be bought a day ahead (taxi or walk to the beach) so as to be sure to get on the bus (there are two good ones a day—early morning and five ocklock) but coming back of course is far worse because the bus starts at Larache and often comes through Arcila on its way to Tangier with no seats available at all. I such a case I just go back and spend another night in Arcila. It doesn't matter. There have been other events and complications and for that reason I have not written you but I still love you and will write you more next time. If you have arranged all with Yvonne all is well but please write me because we still have 10,000 francs of yours which we'll then turn over to her. Much love to Alan—and to you—

Jane

Tangier, Summer 1963

84
To Libby Holman

Darling Libby,

I wrote you an account of what had happened since you left, about the Atlas mountains trip and after that I did not write you.

You did not write me either. I am not complaining because it seems to me that I had promised to write a second letter all about the Arcila house and maybe you are still waiting.

Everything is so complicated here with Paul living there for the summer, but getting his food from here once a week that my life might better be shrouded in silence.

It exhausts me to explain how I managed this by mail almost as much as it does to live this way but I will give you a detailed account of the present routine as soon as I hear whether or not you are well or even alive. I have suddenly—well not so suddenly but bit by bit I am getting worried that all might not be well with you or the children or Loie. That is only because I have never been so long without hearing from you. Is it possible that you did not ever get my letter? Or are you still waiting for the second letter which I had intended to send. Any way Libby please write me and let me know if you did get my letter and if you and the children and Louie are allright.

I am likely to begin my ganza Magella about Arcila after that except that writing about it might make me cry. I'm supposed to laugh.

I had a letter from some young film producer who wanted the rights to my play. It would not be a Hollywood film naturally but one of those low budgeted New York films like—David and Liza. I don't know who the people are but Irma Herly does. She is a friend of theirs so if and when you go to New York try to find out something for me. But above all write me how you are immediately. Love to both,

Jane

Tangier, Summer 1963

85
To Isabelle Gerofi

Dearest Isabelle

I wanted to write you long before to tell you that Yvonne at least could count on me after eleven ocklock or eleven thirty if she wanted me to sleep with her. She said that she would call me if she felt she needed this but she never has yet.

Hélas I have sprained my finger and up intill now it has been too painfull to use.

Of course I have started this letter backward because at first I meant to ask you how you were and not tell you about something that is almost past now, since the whole point in mentioning my arragement at all with Yvonne was to stop your worrying in the Hospital.

I certainly hope that the opperation was not too painfull afterwards and I am waiting anxiously to hear all about it when you come.

Darling Isabelle my hand is still painfull and I cannot write a very long letter although I am going to have to write several necessary letters to other friends about my novel. Paul has gone away for awhile and so I have no one to help me.

I speak to Yvonne every day and she has been too busy to want anyone with her so far. At any rate my mother is leaving Monday. This is a kind of useless letter but I hope that Yvonne wrote you that she could have had me at night (!) if she wanted me that late. By some miracle Sherifa gave her kind permission.

I do hope that in spite of going to Belgium for an operation that you have had time for une petite détante. God knows. I think that Yvonne seems better when she works all the time, naturally. That is the system used in all sanatoriums where they treat nervous depressions.

Naturellement it cannot go too far. I am ready for a real lunatic asylem myself and tell Yvonne about it on the telephone every day.

I miss you and love you,

Jane

Tangier, September 1963

86
To Libby Holman

Darling Libby,

I imagine I wrote you about Paul's flight to Arcila shortly after you left. I think I told you that I was going to write you about all the complications in my next letter, in fact I know I did, and because they were so great I never wrote at all. Anyway I lived between both places all summer long running the food department from Tangier for both towns. Sometimes I would take the food out with me and sometimes the food would go back with Paul when he returned there on Friday's. He always came in once a week and if I did not go back with him bodily I would order his food for the week or however long he was going to be there. It was so complex that I shuddered everytime I started to write it to you. I know that you would have felt for me while Louie laughed but it was too much to even write, in the end. In fact I neither wrote you, nor a play nor did I write Katharine—nobody. I felt I had to explain all this, naturally, plus give you an account of how we managed without a car, and how even fitting my leg into the bus was difficult. I used to tell you all about it before I went to sleep at night and somehow I couldn't type it all. Now the summer is over and I feel that I can write you and not mention it (ossir). I am spending the week in Arcila but the whole thing will be over on the fifteenth of October or before if it starts to Rain.

However, someday I must tell you all of it. The Ice Box (fridge) which Paul bought that was dumped here at Arcila in its crate, and which turned out to be an Ice Box that would only work in Europe, and the chickens that went back and forth on busses with me or Paul all summer long because even chickens are inedible in Arcila unless they are killed when they are still in their mothers egg. As you know I like tough chickens and grissle better than sissy tended food but Paul as you remember doesn't.

Then started the Tsuris about my play. If in case of a production I did not know whether to stay put here or to go and spend the little money I might have earned on an off-broadway production, travelling back and forth on the shrimp cocktail boat, second class, which costs a fortune because it serves shrimp cocktails at most meals. Actually I was thinking of going third class. I would be usefull at the theater to my self only because I have the right of Veto *if I am present* (accepting the cast chosen by the director or not). I don't want a disgrace in New York whether the play makes money or not. Of course if Milly plays it I would love to see her once more before my death. I thought she was fantastic. All this was terribly difficult to decide from here and I sent my mother back from Tangier with a letter to Audrey explaining all my worries. My mother spent a month here and returned just about when Audrey herself came back to New York from her vacation. I was curious too about the director—Herbert Berghof, about whom I knew very little except bad things from someone who turned up here, called Alfred Chester, to whom Paul is not speaking any more because they had a fight. I don't know whether or not this Alfred Chester is qualified at all to talk about directors, but he must have had some grape-vine knowledge to say anything. Anyway I was having a fit and unnable to reach anybody because it was in the dead center of August. Alfred is a write—a critic—for the times and a novelist. His novel is wonderfull according to Paul (I mean short stories, because the novel is not finished) but that does not mean he knows much about directors. In fact later he told me I should not worry so much about his opinion. I went into a real kind of death rattle fandango over the whole thing bothering everyone in Arcila—where there was nobody except Paul and Cherifa and Alfred and then, in Tangier I would talk of nothing else.

At any rate that was the summer and since then Audrey has returned and my mother and Audrey and Oliver *and* Tennessee have all spoken together on the telephone. My mother reported all my fears plus posting the letter I sent to Audrey via her, from New York, so that now I am up to date more or less on my news. Audrey and Oliver say that Berghof is a wonderfull director but he is busy on another show at the moment, and so all that soppling about him was for nothing. Now of course I am soppling about not being able to have him. I should think that Mailand, the producer, would wait for him if he's that good.

He admires the play very much but I am not sure which version! Audrey and I went through that argument by mail months ago and I won't describe it to you. It was wourse than the buses and chickens. Libby, I saw Mike—we spoke of you a great deal and he was going to see you when he returned to New York. I was overjoyed naturally but know I have no word from you or him about how it worked out and if the meeting took place. As you remember you were seeing each other when I was there with you last fall. I am longing to see you again and I hope it will happen in the spring or in a year from now (next fall). Sis suggested that I go with her when she visits her child in November and I was sorely tempted. Naturally I don't even know what your xmas plans are and I doubt very much that I would come then anyway.

I don't *want* to go to Maryland now that Louisa is hooked by Tamara Geva. It's your fault because you didn't take me on turky day!

It would be good to know what your plans are though, from now on because I must see you in the spring or fall unless I do go for some reason sooner. I have a bladder complaint that might drive me home sooner.

Audrey does not advise my being there for the play if it's done. Please give all my love to Alice and Rose and give my love to Louie whom I hope is well and you to. Please write

as ever—

Jane

Acila, October 4, 1963

87
To Audrey Wood

Dear Audrey,

I have written pages on how I felt about this lightning production and how sad I was that I did not have even the opportunity to decide whether or not I would exercise my right to be present for casting and vetoing any choices I did not agree with. Yes, I would like to have been there although I do remember either writing you or asking you personally whether or not it would be necessary to be in New York if the play was done off Broadway.

I think you wrote that it wouldn't be; in fact I'm certain you did—and I obviously decided to put off my decision until I absolutely had to make it. I did the same about the two versions of the play—but when I came to a decision it was very firmly against the Ann Arbor version as you know. In this case I had decided in my mind that I would come to New York for my play and I would have had I known in time. I would have made another try with Libby to find the score with Gerald Cook—(a musician), and if that failed I would have found one of my many composer friends to choose some appropriate music, (in public domain.)

You don't mention any music in your letter and as far as I know the artistic director is in the West Indies. I know that he has done the sets—at least lent his name to them, but beyond that there seems to be no one in charge except Lyn, who is neither a set designer nor a musician.

Libby wrote me a brief letter enclosing the clipping about Summer House (accusing me of secrecy), and was so flabbergasted by Paul's answer, telling her of course that we knew nothing about the production, that she telephoned.

The last letter I received from you before the rehearsals started, was written on January 9. It said Berghof was still interested in directing and that you were very hopeful of getting a spring production. I heard nothing after that and would naturally like to know what on earth happened that made you either decide not to warn me or forget the matter completely (which I feel is very unlikely.)

Libby asked Paul if I wanted to stop the production and

Paul said: no—naturally. Unfortunately I was not home at the time.

I am now miserable and want only to know what happened, from you, and also what chances you think the play will have ever again if this production is a complete fiasco.

It is very important for me to know this if you, have anything encouraging to say to me. It is important to me for work on another play—the real reason why I never wanted some off-Broadway production to cope with at this moment.

It was Paul who persuaded me to sign the contract in the beginning but knowing myself, I never wanted to. I am particularly desperate about it's being done without Paul's music naturally, and am terrified that it's being done without any music.

I know that you must have done everything you could to make this production come about and that our interests are naturally the same but please write me what on earth happened and help me at a distance if you can, in case there is a fiasco. The play until now has had a good reputation: will it change that? Will a failure prevent its ever being tried again by a different group, with the music if we find it—or new music? The play was conceived with music and I would like to have written the director about this when the time came, or better still have seen him in New York—Anyway Audrey—I send you love as always—

Jane

Tangier, March 1964

88
To Libby Holman

Darling Libby,

I thank you a million times for everything you have done for me. You have acted as if you were right here, as much as it was possible, and that is a deep consolation to me for the slipshod way in which the others have acted so far.

What do you think it had to do with? Did Audrey misunderstand me? I think as I wrote you that I did ask her months ago if it was necessary for me to be there and she said no, absolutely not. I let it go at that, certain that she would in any case warn me in time, in case I did want to be there.

Obviously I would have come over if there was anything for me to do, but under the circumstances I would have been too late. It was already too late when I sent her the wire, although perhaps, if she had answered it, and I had known that the music wasn't necessarily lost, I could have come over with Paul's information in my teath like a dog and given it to you. She answered my wire by mail and by then it was too late.

On top of that a friend of mine seemed to be going off his rocker, and Paul and I were very occupied with that just during those terrible days when I was waiting for the answer from my wire to Audrey.

I wrote you a long letter first explaining why I had not written and then I wrote my mother and then I wrote Audrey. The letter to Audrey never seemed to end. I kept tearing it up and beginning again untill finally I wrote her a letter that was only two pages long, if that, and very much to the point. I had to reread these miserable letters and correct them so that in the end I strained my eyes which as you know are bad because of my limited field of vision. Of course I was under terrific tension and was writing more than I had in years. The result was eye strain and a stye which I have been treating with antibiotics. It is almost cleared up now but I haven't been able to write before this because I could not use my eyes at all.

Libby, stop worying about this. It seems a shame but "it was written." I never should have accepted the clause in my contract about Audrey supervising or any one else in the event of my absence. I remember Paul was all for my not going over, in case the play finally was produced. I never really did want to have it done off-Broadway—because I felt it was the kind of play that required a more than ordinarily good cast and I always wondred if the actors could be culled from the Actors Studio or any other acting school. It always seemed to me that there had to be at least one top rate actress in the cast and I am sure I am right. I daresay the younger people could be even better than they were on Broadway which wouldn't make them good! If you remember Lionel was played by a yenty.

I would have waited for Milly to be free if she had accepted to be in the play at all.

I was not sure of course when you wrote me about that some months ago what her actual position was going to be, nor were you. She was responsible for a little scene in my play which I can't imagine anyone else playing and I wanted to wait for her—it was written for her.

I am thoroughly depressed. They are forbidden to use any version except the Broadway version, as Audrey knows. We had enough correspondence about that last year.

I am glad you think that the play is in good hands. At this point it is up to the Gods. Thank you for sticking by me as always.

I love you,
Jane

Give my love to Louie.

Tangier, Spring 1964

89
To Libby Holman

Dearest Libby,

Please forgive me for not answering your letter at once. You knew how I felt and I wanted to write you sooner so that you wouldn't worry too much.

I have not got your letter near me and I am rushing off to Gibraltar at nine this morning. I hope Louies exhibition is successful and that he is pleased with the results. I had hoped to be there for it, but now I don't think I will be unless I take a flying leap.

Naturally I felt very badly about the play but it seemg to be a very great success with some bright people—such as you and the critic on the Village Voice and others (the Post) but I will not write a long letter about all this until tomorrow or the next day when I return from Gib.

I am just writing this now to tell you that Charles Gallaghar is leaving for New York, next Monday, and will call you up at Tree Tops where he will at least get Rose if not you and try to arrange some appointment with her. He wants very much to see you. He has messages for you from me and questions and also wants to see you and Louie if it is possible. I am sure you will want to see him so please warn Rose that he is calling. I will write more as I said in a day or two.

Thankyou for everything. I don't know how I would have gone through the play Gonzamagilla without you. Kiss Louie.

All my love to both of you
Jane

Tangier, June 18, 1964

90
To Libby Holman

Dearest Libby,

There is too much to tell. I have been harassed by one thing and another and so deppressed and worried and frightened that I simply have not written. Each day I worry about this and I think about you and Louis and Louie's exhibition. Don't think I have not thought about it. I wanted to write but I didn't. Naturally paintings are not like plays and so fortunately they can go on selling long after the show closes. Plays of course can be revived ten years later (I'm sure mine won't), nor would it be the same cast which I never saw, even if it were revived which it won't be. Darling Libby you were wonderful to me while the play was going on and I have not been very attentive, but I've been in a bad way. Now I feel better. Paul got a movie offer (to sell The Sheltering sky), I didn't think it was very good (thirty thousand dollars and no percentage in the gross) but Paul seemed very pleased. I think he would have been delighted with two hundred dollars! I know that Albie got five hundred thousand for Virginia Woolf, and I thought Paul should be more carefull about selling his most valuable property. As you know he has no income and makes money on selling articals to Holiday, mostly, which take him so long to write that he can't get out more than two a year and he is paid very badly. Any way I was very worried and at that moment Lee Shubert came to Tangier with Ira Shuberts secretary, a youngish man who is a friend and business manager as well and who also eats sanwiches with Ira, at three in the morning. I don't think he is even Jewish. Lee said he was a brilliant business man and so he told Paul to ask for fifty thousand, stretched out over a period of ten years, so that the taxes would be less. All this was very complex and Paul had to send many wires to his agent who had advised immediate acceptance of the original offer. Meanwhile Lawrence was drafting a letter and wire for Paul asking for more money on this ten year basis which for some reason was to make the taxes less for both Paul and the man who wanted to buy the Sheltering Sky, I understood none of this but Lawrence, who ate the sandwich with Ira, did understand it. Anyway it was not Lee Shubert but Ira and Lee *Gershwin*. It does not matter unless you know them. This seems to have nothing to do with my not writing you or anyone else but it does. Paul with Lawrence's help, after draftingthis very complex telegram which had in it something called a "built in contract," about how the money was to be spread out over a period of ten years and how Helen Strauss could nonetheless draw her agents fee at once if she wanted to, then waited for some answer. Lee Gershwin and Lawrence flew away to Paris and we waited. There was no answer from Helen Strauss for ten days and when a letter did come there was no mention at all of the film offer, only some refference to Larby's book and some other business matter—taxes, I think, but certainly nothing about the film. I felt that by being too zealous and advising Paul to ask Lee and Lawrence what to do I had possibly spoiled Paul's chances of getting even thirty thousand dollars or whatever it would have been after tax deduction. Paul tried to console me but he couldn't and everything got worse as time went by and still no answer came. Paul was very sweet but he did say that he would have accepted the original offer immediately and knowing him I'm sure he would have. He never worries about his old age at all, puts whatever money he gets in a checking account anyway and saves money by taking two or three hours a week comparing cooky prices and choosing the cheapest. He eats a lot of cookies and I think that for him they are the only reality.

I thought it was very lucky that Lee and this brilliant secretary had arrived here just when we were trying to answer Helen's wire so I naturally advised Paul to put the decision in his lap.

Finally a letter came saying that Paul's agent had put through the original deal—without a mention of whether she had even tried to get more or follow any of Paul's suggestions. Naturally I was glad not to have to go on soppling even though I did not understand any of Helen Strauss'es motives nor did Paul—nor did we know whether she had ever tried to follow Pauls advice. Paul had written her that he was being advised by Ira Gershwin's business manager who knew just how someone called Irving Paul Lazar drew up all of his contracts. He is the best agent in Hollywood and maybe Yenty Strauss was vexed and wouldn't follow any advice coming from those circles. I really felt awful during all this and so sorry that I had opened my mouth at all.

At the moment Paul is waiting for the "less good contracts" to arrive which he will sign unless there is some new hitch! (oy)

Now that I have explained all this nothing to you—I have neither time nor strength for anything interesting. Meanwhile give me news of Louies exhibition. If my agent had answered my wire in time or at all, I would have been there to see it. I have much more to write you and to ask you. Paul is not going to America as he thought he was—but nothing is certain. All that will have to come in my next letter.

Naturally he would not have written you about the film Gonza Magilla because he doesn't find it interesting and takes my soppling for granted. But I know he did write you about something. Love always and kiss Louie,

Jane

Give my love to Rose and Alice.

Tangier, June 23, 1964

91
To Libby Holman

Dearest Libby

I said this letter would be in sections—each one more boring than the other but I feel that I have to tell you all these boring details or I don't believe that I have written a real true letter. I don't think that I used to be this way but of course I do get worse with the years. David would say, "tiresome." This section will be about my mother and Paul's job in Florida which no longer exists. I don't know whether or not he wrote you about it and so I won't go into the matter like I did about "the built in clause", in his contract, because I just can't tell you everything over again if he has written it to you. He was going to America to lecture for three months at a very good salary but in the end the "Board" decided against him—although the University wanted him very badly and were very distressed when the board did not approve the choice unanimously. It was a state university and a southern one at that, and so I can think of many reasons why the answer was finally negative. I shan't go into them all and neither one of us knows the exact reason for the veto. It could have to do only with the kind of books he writes, which many southern Facists could easily not want their children to read. It could have to do with his long ago affiliations—who knows. I think he is greatly relieved not to have to lecture although it would have paid eight thousand dollars which he regrets naturally. He should see his mother anyway and his father and now I suppose he'll shell out the money anyway, but when? I was planning to come over with him in December, the three months of lecturing was to begin in January, and I would have gone in December to Florida when he was going to see his family. Obviously I was going to arrange to see you before or after—I didn't know, or at three differant times—in case you too came down to Florida, but now all my plans are nebulous. I *must* see you—and I'm sorry I didn't come this spring when Eugenia left on the Constitution. I preffered going with Paul because he was going to come back here with me whereas Eugenia was staying in the states for a long time. Perhaps when she comes again this summer I can catch her going over again toward Christmas and by then Paul would be ready to come too! (Osser) I am really worried about this because knowing Paul he will put off seeing his parents as long as he possibly can and I shall have to nag him. I suppose there is no hope of you're coming over—or are you thinking of it?

Did I write you that the Village Voice gave my play a wonderfull notice—a rather long review which I have lost. Then the other day, this same reviewer was written up in Time as the best one going. Except for the fact that it isn't running and that few people had the time to see it, I feel encouraged by the critical success of my play in that paper and the Post. I still think I should have been warned by Audrey that it was going on and that my *wire* should have been answered by a *wire* from Audrey and not by a letter a week later when it was obviously too late. Lyn blames the postponement of both the broadway show and my own for the fact that we got only second stringers (except for the Post), to review the play on opening night—and I do think she is right because I know that the Tribune at least, would have given me a respectable review if not a rave. That was all the fault of changing dates she said, since both plays were postponed and opened finally on the same night. But that in turn was their fault for deciding too late on the change in director. If I had been there I *might* have seen immediately that this original director was wrong for my play—and I might have never agreed to have him, and the opening dates might have thus been differant. Naturally it might have been worse if I had been ther but I don't think that Audrey should have kept me away. This Berghof always sounded wrong to me, for my play, and everyone I spoke to coming through here after it was too late to change anything told me he would be the kiss of death. Anyway I suppose it should be considered water under the dam but maybe it is my only play and I can't stop feeling sad about it.

Audrey has written me that some young man would like to take an option on the play for one thousand five hundred dollars and later when and if produced he would give me the finall payment (another fifteen hundred). In other words he offers three thousand or a percentage in the gross (or net?). I have no idea which. She herself says that in her opinion I should take the money (the fifteen hundred) and run! She goes on to say that she is sorry that he has so little experiance and that she had been waiting to see whether or not my play was a hit off broadway before telling me about him. In other words now that it was a flop, she advised me to take the money and run. I was so depressed by this that I never answered her either way and now I am about to but I wanted to write to you first before I wrote anybody. Libby the things that have been depressing me really can't go in a letter—some have to do with my personal life—others with Paul's which I can't of course write about or I suppose even talk about and some with the situation here which I certainly can't write about, either. The only thing that seems safe are contracts so I guess I'd better stick to them. My book is going to be published in England—maybe Paul wrote you about that. I really didn't want it to be and refused a year ago. The publisher at that time agreed with me—and wrote that it would be deppressing for me if it got bad reviews. Now he's written again having heard around London that it was some sort of modern classic and he had reread it since last year and *wants* to publish it. I can't imagine whom he's seen. Anyway I shall certainly *mind* when the reviews come out.

Much love,
Jane

P.S. I hope you will write soon and give me news of yourself and Louie and the whole family.

Tangier, June 30, 1964

92
To Libby Holman

Dearest Libby,

I promised you three dull letters and so far have sent you only two. Now I don't remember what this third letter was supposed to be about. Perhaps the fact that my book (old novel—since there is no new one) was to be published in England. I will go on about that in a minute. I have not heard from you at all since I wrote these letters nor has Paul and I am beginning to wonder if some mail has gone astray. Naturally I left you for a long time with out mail but that was because of my worry with contracts for Paul's novel—the movie contracts. It was of no interest this long letter but I really couldn't write anything else untill I told you about everything. Now I think there are new things but of course not knowing whether or not you received my old news I hesitate to write this third dull letter. No word about Louie or his show yet and so now I feel cut off as you must have felt when Larry—Ira Gershwins sandwich secretary was here and I did not write.

I have a feeling that at the end of my second letter I told you that my book was going to be published in England next year. I am filled with apprehension and have been warned by the publisher that I must not pay any attention to the critics. Last year he had been shown my book by Alan Sillitoe (The Lonelines of the Long Distance Runner) who read it here and liked it very much—and as a result of this Peter Owen asked Paul whether or not I wanted it published. He published one book of Paul's in England (Their Heads Are Green), but otherwise we did not know of him. His list however is distinguished and you would like him enough because he has had two nervous brakdowns and is not in the least a comercial type. I don't want to have my book published because again I shall be torn to bits by the press naturally and if it hadn't been for the publisher's insitance, and Paul's of course, I would not have concented to it. It is very odd, the fact that he is now so enthusiastic, because when he first read it he found it a very distinguished work I guess but he had not cared terribly when I refused to have it published. In fact he wrote Paul that he understood my feeling very well because there was nothing so deppressing for an author as a book that doesn't sell. Then almost a year later he wrote again that his wife and he had reread the book and he was even more enthusiastic about it than he had been the first time which he went on to say, had always been, for him at least, the final test of any work. He said too, that he had heard from various people around London that the book was a minor classic etc. and he did wish that I would allow it to be published. I don't understand his change of attitude but Paul says that I should have it done, and it is true that it would be nice to have copies of it again to give to a few friends. Maybe some people will like it those who are not enthusiasts of the "cut up" method.

Now I am so depressed about Gold Water and the whole negro civil rights scandal that I think to write of anything else is beside the point. Tennessee is here at the moment in his terrible hell because of Frankie and I see him although I don't feel it does much good. Libby, I will write you again.

Much love to all
Jane

P.S. I received Roses note—with you're change of telephone number. Otherwise I would think you were dead. I cut out the end of this letter because it was such a mess. I have now written three times and I really wonder how you are because there is no news.

If Polly calls you about my check—don't worry—it is now all straightened out at this end. For some reason it was sent to Casa. Is Louie all right? I feel something is wrong. I must close because I am in a rush. WRITE me.

Tangier, August 8, 1964

93
To Ruth Fainlight

Dearest Ruth,

Thank Alan for the quote he gave Peter Owen for the book jacket, and kiss the baby whose age I ignore. I go on missing you both too much. I have never really had it so good here in Tangier except much earlier when I was still in my thirties and I lived on the mountain and later in my own little house in the Casbah.

I am still brooding about a letter you sent me months ago in which you said you were looking around for a place to stay for awhile, (outside of England of course). I thought about this for a long time wondering whether or not you would try Tangier again, but the problems here were still fresh in my mind and I could not decide whether the problems were at that time worse or better or the same. I delayed writing for so long that I finally heard through Tamara that you had gone to Mallorca. I was very sad because I thought that maybe a letter from me might have influenced your decision.

As you probably remember, the stroke I had affected my my spelling rather badly though now it is much better than it was when you were here. I am still loath to write letters, partly because of that; half the time Paul is not available or I could just call out and ask him for the right spelling. He is spending this summer on the Mountain, (two doors away from the Gazabo) and very often I bring the food up there in a taxi. It is easier than last year when I used to take Chickens over to Arcila by bus or with friends who had cars.

Paul just came down with a letter from you (for him) in which you say that you look back on youre stay here with nostalgia. It is strange that the letter should have arrived just as I had written the above, about you and Mallorca. Would you consider coming to Tangier for awhile at any time—ever again? The problems *are* the same as I wrote a few minutes ago. It is of course getting more expensive all the time but I don't know how it compares with England. There is no point in my elaborating if you have no intention of coming ever again.

I am going to America in the spring—I suppose April. Last month David, who was driving up to London for Christmas, was trying to urge me to go with him and I was considering it because I wanted to see the oculist and Peter Owen if I could be of any help on my book, and you and Alan if you were there. I more or less decided against it because I could not picture myself staying anywhere (I know your set-up), and a hotel was not exactly a solution because I knew I could never get around by myself. Then David's cousin Caroline suggested her house as a solution for the whole three weeks which David plans to spend in London with his mother. She lives in North Wales.

She is very charming—mysterious, anti-social, melancholic and grave but responsive to wit. Having tried very hard to have a child she has adopted a son. If there is still enough reason for me to go to London I will go although now it would involve passage both ways on a boat, David having given up the idea of driving which would have been cheaper for me—I suppose. If I came I would certainly want to come to London to see you, to go to the oculist and to see Peter Owen if he thought it was important that I come to England. Paul just reminded me that he had suggested that I stay with him for the publication of my book but I should think that it would be more useful for me to go now (if useful at all.)

I don't expect to earn money on my book, but anything to forestall a bad reception, I mean one so bad that I will regret deciding to have it reprinted. I doubt that anything will help that except blurbs that will keep critics in check a little anyway. Thank God for Alan's.

I could go on forever about all this, the pros and cons of going or staying here but I fear that the letter will turn into a fifteen page ganze magilla of, "if's and but's" which I shall never send and then more months will go by and I will never write; but the letter could be used as a document for some doctor who specializes in states of anxiety.

The trip *will* be expensive for me in the end so please give me your opinion (you and Alan) if you have time on what good I could accomplish by coming to England in a couple of weeks.

I shall certainly write you again now that I've started but you may come to dread these tortured letters about tiny decisions. I am famous for them or I was when I was famous, with a few friends (most of whom are dead.)

I go to New York in April for a few months. That at least is decided and surely I could find an oculist there, don't you think?

Please write me, and tell me if there is any chance of your coming here in the near future.

Much love
Jane

Tangier, September 1964

94
To Libby Holman

Dearest Libby,

At least I have stopped writing those terrible letters to England and I can now write you. Perhaps you did not know about the "letters to England?" I shall tell you very briefly in case you have heard from me about them, but I very much doubt it because I tired my eyes so much writing them, that I did not have time to write you although, you have been, as always, very much on my mind. I did get your last letter to me answering my question, "Is Louis alright?" and since then I don't think I have answered any questions of your's or written at all. My "English trip" was such a gonza Magella that I couldn't even write you and I don't know why I call it my English trip when I didn't even make it. I could still take it maybe but I'm almost certain not to since I have given up my passage on the boat.

David was going to England for Christmas and suggested that I *drive* up with him. My god now I'm sure I wrote you all of this but I can't remember, exactly so I'll go on. Anyway I then started writing letters, asking for advice to my one literary friend in England (Ruth Sillitoe), to my publisher, to Sonia Orwell, to Mary Louise Aswell, to Cyril Connolly, asking them all whether or not I should go to England. My publisher had asked me last summer to try and be in London when the book came out, but I said I would hate that since I expected nothing but the worse from the critics and would rather hide out—here. He did not agree with that attitude and thought that my being on the scene might help. The matter was dropped and then David started with his "English trip." I had no place to stay of course nor anyone to stay with and so I was against it feeling that even if I managed the hotel by myself I would never manage getting around London. I had decided "No," but David who was adamant found a way. His Cousin Caroline invited me to stay with her at Veynal, a house she has in North Wales where I had already spent xmas once before when Paul and I motored with David to Paris and then to London. It was at the time of the "Sheltering Sky" (when it was first published I mean). All of this is neither here nor there but the decision was difficult to make, because I had always been terribly attracted to Caroline and was leery of making any decision on those grounds. I'll tell you why when I see you. Meanwhile the publisher was in New York so I could not ask him what he advised and so I wrote Ruth Sillitoe instead.

I told her that I could not make up my mind and asked her whether she thought it would be helpfull for me (as regarded the book) to go to London with David around xmas time instead of at the time of publication which was impossible for me or David. She answered that the publisher might give me a few parties which could *possibly* help the book along but that I would have to get that advice from him. I had given up my passage by then because although I had written her quite a while ago it took practically a month for her to answer without even considering the vageries of the post.

I then wrote Peter Owen directly feeling sure or almost sure that he must have come back from New York. That was another Gonza Magella letter asking for "Advice," even though my tiket had long since been given to someone else. I suppose I mean my *passage* on the Oriana not my ticket. The awful truth is that I am still wondering what to do and yesterday

David said to me, "Maybe you could *still* get passage if you wire immediately to the Orient Line." Isn't it horrible? I could not go "just for fun," and then hope that in some way it might be usefull to the book, because it is not *in me* to have *fun*, in such ways, now that I can't drink very much, although I do drink a little Vodka now which I didn't do before or did I? Vodka or Scotch, but never very much. Not enough to make a trip bearable—and certainly not delightfull. You know how I hate them. That is why I have to justify spending the money and going to England on a wild goose chase. Obviously if I were longing to go I would not really feel any need to justify myself. I don't want to go and therefore I must find a justification for going so that I can then force myself—I don't know. The symptons for the past two months—which is about when "the English trip" started, are the same old symptoms. Remember the Atlas trip that I didn't make with Yvonne and Isabelle Gerofie? I think even Louie was in on that one. It was the topic at the pool a few years ago. I don't even remember the details of that one—but there was a trip and a decision. I finally went over the Atlas mountains a year or two later.

Anyway since I began this letter (three days ago) I had an answer from Peter Owen who is in London now—just back from New York, as I thought he would be, and he says, "I gather from your letter that you hate the idea of coming to London, and in that case It would certainly not be worth the expense to come especially for the book as it it is certainly difficult to predict whether personal appearences on television (oy!!) etc. can be arranged. I thought perhaps you might be coming to London anyway and that it would suit you . . ." etc. I won't quote more but that was certainly enough for me. I decided immediately not to go to London and I felt very relieved. But then bit by bit I felt less sure particularly as Paul for some reason seemed to be all for it, even though I am coming over in the spring to see you, mostly and because Paul has decided that he must go and see his mother. Surely I have written you about all of this some time ago—at the time of the play and the Audrey Wood Crisis. Naturally if I went to England now I would certainly not go for any special reason but to prove that I could do what other people do so lightly. Paul said he would treat me to the trip which is not as I said, too expensive. Please don't write me that you think I should have gone because by that time it will be too late and you will only make me unhappy. This letter is written to explain my late silence. The next will be about my plans and yours. But I could not write any think untill I told you about the trip I did not *take* (unless I take it). Give my love to Louie and the family at Treetops.

Always—
Jane

(Sorry this letter is so long and messy.)

Tangier, November 26, 1964

95
To Libby Holman

Darling Libby,

I Think I should write this letter to you and Louie because I feel particularly bad about never having answered his telegramme. In the first place I went down to the post office twice and could not get anywhere near the wiket, there was such a mob, naturally; We can't telephone telegrammes from here but must go into town at certain hours. Then the "rains" came and it was impossible to move anyway. Then my fat friend Sonia died just when our relations were at their worse and I felt so bad about that I almost took to my bed. Her daughter was on her way to spend xmas with her so she came for the funeral instead. The telegramme made Paul and me laugh very much and I wanted to answer him immediately but it just wasn't possible. Between the bottle necks at the post office and the deluge and Sonia's death a few days later the time had Passed for my answer, which was of course something to make him laugh. I forget it now. But Louie I *didn't* go, but I soppled for a month and a half after xmas anyway—naturally; *I should have gone.*

I will tell you all about it when I see you but now I am wondering if I will see you ever this year. Libby, I was very upset by your plans for the spring but very happy for you that you are going on tour again, which is wonderful for you and everyone who loves to hear you sing.

After Sonia's death, Ramadan came, and I did not sleep

more than a few hours a night because I cannot sleep when others are up and about eating (cherifa and Eisha and the little girl). Of course in the day when Cherifa did sleep (always untill three thirty in the afternoon), Eisha and I were awake as usual. I never can sleep later than nine and I'm almost always awake by eight no matter when I go to bed as you know. During Ramadan I would not get to sleep untill six or seven in the morning. It was a wretched month and I did not have the strength to write to you and Louie and explain why I had not written. After those nerves then came my "book" (oy) which made me so nervous that I couldn't ask you all the questions I wanted to ask. Anyway I guess it hasn't done too badly (prestige at least). I will quote Peter Owen's letter in a minute and let you judge for yourself. I was afraid of an English "disgrace," but it was not like that at all. The Times I did not consider good at all except that he did not deny the value of the book he simply did not like it any more than he liked Ivy Compton Bernette, which is an excellent way to be put down. The blurb's were excellent and to quote Peter Owen, "The book is getting a big press here and is being treated as an important book as it deserves."

Actually he was very dubious about the press before he published it because he did not think many of the reviewers were up to it, so I guess he must be pleased. Now enough about the book. It is good that I now have more coppies of it. I don't see any point in sending you one via Peter Owen (the publisher) because it would certainly be much quicker for you to send for it yourself. Actually the service between here and England is not so bad but it would take longer than you're sending for it directly *if* you wanted it.

I am very preoccupied now by your departure. I worry that you will be gone before I arrive. Paul plans to go now in the beginning of April. When exactly do I have to arrive to catch you before you go. Or how long do I have to stay in America to catch you on you're return. Please answer this as fast as possible. If you're going to spend many months in Europe then of course I might not be able to wait. My mother has just had pneumonia. I did not hear from her for weeks and was getting more and more worried, in fact just about to wire when my uncle wrote that she had burned her hand cooking goulash. I did not believe it and so wired back asking for the truth. He wired that she was recovering from pneumonia and would write soon. I have wired her that I would come if necessary by plane; if not, by the next boat which leaves in March, and if not as I had planned with Paul in the beginning of April. I am worried that if she has no one but her nearly blind husband to help her she might exhaust herself. I naturally suggested she take some kind of maid or helper until she was well. I don't know anything. Not even whether she's in the hospital or home. If she wires me to come I will naturally go but it wouldn't help my seeing you much, would it, if I were down in Miami on my mother's couch. There are only two rooms, of course, and it is nowhere near town. God knows what I'll do. My step father is too blind to cook or drive and has gotten blinder in the last few months, so I daresay he can't help at all. I am waiting for a wire but meanwhile please write immediately telling me how much longer you'll be in America and when you are coming back. My plans were before at least if Paul agreed to go to New Mexico from Florida and then to go to TreeTops or vica versa. But at least it would give us more time in America—even time to see you after your European tour, if that's the only way it's going to work now. Is there any chance of getting you and Louie over here again? I don't feel that there is. Anyway please wire me or rather write me your dates—departure for Europe and return. This after the English trip is just too much. I am deeply sorry now that I did not go for Thanksgiving. I will send this now with a heavy heart.

Kiss all the family there—and love—

Jane

Tangier, Late January/Early February 1965

96
To Lawrence Stewart

Dear Lawrence:

We are planning to go to the U. S. in late March or early April, and there is a hope that we might go to New Mexico a little later, after we have visited our respective parents, who are all in Florida. We have friends in Santa Fe whom we want to see. One of these is Mary Lou Aswell, who published most of my stories in *Harper's Bazaar* many years ago when she was Literary Editor of that magazine. According to her, Truman is supposed to be arriving there in the Spring with most of Garden City. She and Truman are great friends, of course. I should love to see both of them, but who knows whether our dates will coincide. We won't be staying with Mary Lou, but with John Goodwin, another old friend. Tell Lee. Maybe she will come to Santa Fe while we are there.

We are both eager to have your opinion on Paul's new book. Are Lee and Ira going to be in California at any time in the spring, and do you think there would be any possibility of Paul's spending a few days with them and seeing the three of you? Probably you will be going around the world or something like that. Or maybe Lee will be in New York. In any case, please thank them for the Christmas telegram. I wanted to write them, but a friend of mine here in Tangier died just before Christmas, and I was so depressed I didn't get around to writing to anyone.

I really want you to see the new book, because I have a feeling it can be a great success, and I'd love to have your opinion and suggestions on how to handle it. Paul does not like to discuss it.

Please give my love to Lee and tell her the dress she gave me is David Herbert's favorite.

Love

Jane

Tangier, February 1965

97
To Libby Holman

Dearest Libby,

This time I shall try to stick to the point, although I preffer the ramblings off the main road, the alley ways, where Ugly Eisha eats her soup and bread at five in the morning, just before the cannon sounds, and the fast begins. Anyway those three or four weeks during which time I could not write because I had no energy left, have certainly ruined everything.

Had I known early enough which I would have, I suppose,

had I written you—I could have left in winter heavy seas or not. Now what shall I do? Mother wired last night, or rather, Julian, that she is better and out of the hospital and back home. I have written urging them to take a maid or helper because of his blindness, so that she does not have a relaps. The quickest boat that I can get to see *you* before you leave, sails from Casa Blanca on February twenty fifth landing the fourth of March in New York. Julian advises I come in April to see Mother with Paul. Paul does not want me arriving half cocked in New York with no one meeting me and with nothing arranged. Paul wants to see you as well naturally but of course it means something very special to me. What shall I do. After the English trip this is really too much for me.

Certainly you and Louie can see the problem. I am waiting for Paul to figure out a wire explaining all the facets but I don't think he will. I'll name them by mail now. To begin with I don't know that I can get a passage this late. I have to get to Casa of course and start wiring at once from here, but supposing that I *did* get it—a single—Then would I be with you for one day or three or not at all anyway. I have no idea when in March you leave as I explained in my last letter. Naturally Paul tries to travel with me because we can share a cabin and can see me through mobs at the boat in New York and I just hang on to him. Crowds confuse me and though I can see perfectly well straight in front of me I don't see on the sides and keep loosing sight of people at which Point I can get Panicky—still I have all my pills which I'd clutch and somehow I'm sure I'd get through. At any rate I'd preffer it to the claustrofobic nightmare of a plane. God knows that would be simpler (that is if you could meet me at the airport) but I suppose the best would be to see you after you came back from Europe if you weren't staying too long.

I think that I would have to stay after Paul went back to Tangier if you came back after June. I might have to get a first class cabin in order to be alone coming over now, at this late date—who knows. I suppose in *either* class I could try to arrange with the ships doctor to find someone to stay with me on the dock, untill I was met. I had intended staying with you at least ten days or two weeks to make it really count because much less would not be worth it do you think. I think since

Louie is so good at making my plans he can decide the whole thing for me. Paul and I are both devastated by the new turn in events although delighted that you are going on tour for youre sake as I wrote you. He says he knows you would never come *here* on a european tour, and there is no point in my thinging in those terms. I mentioned to you a possibility of our going to New Mexico which would seem to me even more possible if you are not anywhere in sight—we could wait in New Mexico ten days at Johnnie Goodwyn's "maybe." We were going there for several reasons—one of them (the most important), to see someone whom you don't know on the coast about Paul's book. I suggested he get advice from him and *if* it worked out at Johny's for a weekend I could see Mary Lou and Paul could go to Hollywood for a week end. I could never explain what all this is about and finish this letter as well. All this would be just a by product of our being in America in order to see my mother and spend some time with you and Louie. Now there remains only the duty of seeing my mother, Natacha and Katherine of course—and other by products. We cannot possibly change our plans to come untill the fall because our families are expecting us and would be very dissapointed if we didn't come. None of them are well anyway; Paul's father is in his eighties and bedridden. Obviously if I'm at my mothers which I *would* be in April I could wait there for awhile untill you came back from you're European trip which is when?

All of these things are difficult to wire but I might at least wire something. I had always thought that I would either go alone or come back alone (to Tangier), but I thought that it would be because I wanted more time in America to see you. Of course there are no possibiteas of my staying in New York at all unless at least Rose is there. There is of course Mother in Florida but God knows how long I could take that. I expected to stay there too or three weeks at the most, but I could stretch it a little if you were really coming home. Is there any place where Paul and I could stay, I mean, is there any room available at sixty first street for Paul. What with not knowing whether Rose is to be at Treetops or if she is to be on vacation I am really getting in a proper panic. I know too it is difficult to get back here during the high season, beginning in the middle of June or earlier, because people get passage so far in advance. If Paul is reduced to Hotels with neither you nor Ollie around he will surely go back as soon as possible, but in any case he always does anyway unless something else turns up like a job. The New Mexican situation is very nebulous.

Paul says (he is now awake at last) that he knows very well that unless I wire I will never be able to get to Casa so that I may wire at least so that I know when you are leaving Treetops and when you're coming back. Who knows the European trip might even be put off, but we must make our plans for even April almost at once.

According to what you say in you're wire I shall have to send you another wire if trying to catch the Casa boat seems plausable.

Much love to all,
Jane

Tangier, February 1965

98
To Libby Holman

Dearest Rose, Libby, Louie, Alice,

I don't know who is there and if Rose is not than I am really sunk. I think I shall write a note to Libby saying that she can open Roses letter in case Rose is not there.

Last night I had dinner with Mary I suddenly forget her name—(this happens since I had the stroke), but it will come back. Here it comes—BANK CROFT. I will not go into it untill I see you but during dinner she told me about you, Libby, and she said that she thought you're house would not be available to anyone because of the insurance complications which I was not surprised at. I said I felt that it would be difficult for you to put up *even* Paul in the top room that he used to occupy off and on, and I was practically sure that there would be no place for me in Shirley's room, so none of us were counting on anything, but Tree tops at some point. Now that we know more certainly about the Insurance I think I must begin making plans for our arrival in New York otherwise Paul will collapse. Mary Bankcroft suggested that we stay with her but Paul was not with me when I met them, and I doubt that either one of us would want to impose on someone we barely know. They said they had a big apt. with two extra bedrooms on Sutton place and that it would be no trouble at all to have us. I can't picture any of it or why she should be so generous but I certainly thanked her for the offer.

She said that we should simply call up from the dock and come over. Obviously even if I knew her better there would be no guarantee that she would be in when I called nor did I dare question her about it any more closely. I thought that when I came I would go at once to a hotel with Paul and from there make my arrangements for the next few days. I will certainly call her but only after I've spoken to you Libby or Rose or Louie but that too is full of complications, even if you should advise us to call her. It seems to me that one can't possibly stay with people one doesn't know however generous and sweet the offer is. I suppose for a night or two it wouldn't matter to them—if they have servants but I don't know how the house or apartment is run. Paul knows nothing of of this but in any case do thank her for me and tell her we'll call her when we come to New York naturally. The boat arrives on the second of April in New York which seems terribly soon. If we are lucky maybe Libby will be there as well and Louie and Rose and then I can at least find out something from somebody. I arrive on Sunday the second of April so that will be deppressing enough without not knowing exactly when I will see you. Naturally the concert dates are all important so I won't know whether you'll be there when I arrive in New York or not, naturally. I will write in time to tell you what to reserve for us in the way of rooms if possible, the very second I hear from Paul.

"Later"—I now have a letter giving the name of his hotel and the address so I can easily telephone Casa, in a day or two. After that I will write you exactly what accomodations we'd like if possible. I hope Libby that as soon as you are there you will invite us to TreeTops. I have writen mother that I would not know my plans untill I know yours. If this letter turns out to be to you Rose you'll give me the news. I doubt that I have you're telephone number but I can telephone my mother in Florida who will.

Anyway someone will know my number because I will be staying at the hotel you book us into. It is a shame the boat arrives on a Sunday because otherwise it might have coincided with one of you're days in New York Libby—and then maybe I could have driven out to the country with you.

I am tired now and I don't think I have made anything clearer by this letter. I should be leaving Tangier the twenty-fourth or third, of March, so you have time to write just a short note The Boat is the "Independance."

Love to all of you—
Jane

Tangier, February 1965

99
To Frances

Darling Frances

Thankyou for calling me. I wanted to call you but I had told you that I wouldn't unless you asked me to. It is an invasion of you're privacy I know and I thought it was best never to wake you up if the telephone was turned on and not to call and interrupt you in case you had friends. I wanted to call very much and finally when you didn't write me I decided that you were either against seeing me at all or ill. I worried terribly about you're being ill but still I never would have called. I am not going to New Mexico now that I have heard from you but I felt when you told me that I should go to Libby's that you might not want to see me again and I told you I was going to New Mesico. It came into my head because in the last weeks—or few days I had thought I would never see you again somehow and that New Mexico was best. Of course I could not do that anyway because there is not that much time left. Paul came in with Libby from East Hampton on Tuesday—having spent one night in Connecticut—and then wrote that he had several dates in New York, (one with Audrey), on wednesday and Thursday—whireas Libby decided to go back almost at once so he went to the Chelsea. Then John Goodwin called both of us from Sante Fe and Libby or Rose Transferred the call to the Chelsea. Paul left for Santa Fe—and I think he was wise. He has always thought, as I have, that it might be a place to settle when Tangier proved impossible. I will surely stay here and may have to take a room somewhere because it is much to difficult either fitting my shcedule to Libby's or inconveniancing all my friends. You are quite right I shall see Libby Tuesday night for drinks at least because I do not know what her plans are with Louie.

If she is going out which she might be I'll stay home alone or try to see Katharine or Dionne unless you are free. Anyway I'll get the luggage over to Libby after one ocklock unless for some reason she is not there. I have already written that I did not know whether or not I was [ ]

New York City, Early April 1965

100
To Frances

Darling Frances,

I seem to have bogged down in my depression and decided, at least that you were right, "that it was useless to send you a letter about a decision which was already made and certainly now to late to change." It is a hairraising document this letter, and the prose and cons of the decision to be made so minutely gone into that it really should be solde to a library for "Psychiatric research in extreme states of of anxiety."

I shall certainly hang on to the letter but it does seem dead now and I only wish that I hadn't told you that you shouldn't call. Actually some of you're discretion *had* come off on me for a moment but of course at the wrong moment when it was entirely unnecessary. That is inevitable when one tries to please without quite understanding what one has done wrong.

I guard David's secrets—when he tells me to and I would automatically anyway when I saw fit. I think he tells certain things to me and to Margaritte only because he knows we would never betray him. Anyway I do get the picture now, a little better, than I did before when I thought your secrecy and fear of being discovered had to do with Tangier though I must say that I suspected you would not seem more free in New York. Now that I know more or less that you should never be subjected to any panics that have to do with me, I am likely to exaggerate the other way, which I'm sure you would rather I do than the contrary. It's true that it would be difficult for me to telephone you again before thursday or friday because he would think me a "spend thrift," no matter who it was. Obviously if I called you every day as I long to he would think so even more and he would know how I felt about you. I don't care but my mother would mind his guessing anything and she knows me too well for me to hide much. She is quite remarkable in that way and wants me to be happy . . . however she would always hide that side my life [ ]

Florida, c. May 1965

101
To Libby Holman

Dearest Libby,

Paul has just written me that he has gone off to New Mexico. I was going to send him John Goodwin's letter and suggest that he do, just that—because John wrote me that he could not understand why Paul thought he had *not* invited him to Santa Fe which Paul had insisted on when I told him that he would be welcome there. We were still on the boat at the time. I had always thought of it as a possible place for us to settle when and if we leave Tangier and wanted him to judge for himself. I am afraid it costs more than *I* can afford but if Paul makes money here in there on the Coast then it would be a good plan. Even if I can't go I'm glad if he can. I was longing to go myself and Mary Lou Aswell and I had a long correspondence about it (from Tangier to Santa Fe). Not so long—one letter each. However I could not really see Mother and you and some friends in the East and still go there unless I flew now—or had come here in the beginning with Paul to Florida and then seen you at the end. God knows I think I have done very well so far having the train Trip or half of it behind me and still time to see you and other friends ahead of me. Here there are the largest sandwiches in the whole world and I can smell the dill pickles from mother's corner. I am very very sad and I hope that you and Louie are very happy. I am denying myself everything—Sandwiches—(corned beef and roast beef as well), plus cheesecake and motza Ball soup and Herring with sour cream. I don't think it's good to stuff with melancholia. There is a kind of sorrowfull compulsive eating that I might give way to but I think it brings on more despair than cheerful compulsive eating—so I go to the corner which is where they eat when they are not eating Chinease and I sit with them picking at a thin inferior fish while they stuff in the good things. There seems to be a pound of corned beef in every sandwich. The place is called "Pompernicks." It must seat about nine hundred people and is always crowded from four ocklock on. Not even beer is served. The lighting is so dazzling that I have to take a sedative because I am not normal. Anyway Libby I am so glad that at least Paul has gone to Sante Fe even though I couldn't. It is better that he should because it would do no good for me to go alone and like it if he didn't. I would even like New York or Connecticut. Don't frighten Louie—I mean somewhere anywhere not so far away as Tangier—because I have a feeling that I'm going to make more and more Trips because of my mother. I am terribly deppressed as I told you. I am coming back—arriving either monday or Tuesday, and I would like to get my things over to 61st street on Tuesday if the house is open as it usually is. Who Knows. Don't concern yourself with me. If you are eating in I shall probably have some drinks with you or a drink and if you are not there I will stay with Katharine or Frances. I wrote Frances a letter to which I have no answer and probably won't.

I shall probably hook up with Frances or Katharine for later so that you are free to go out if you have planned to and don't worry about me even if I've arranged nothing. I'm not much on eating at seven so don't concern yourself with any dinner plans untill I get there and make my plans with you, I can buy a sandwich anytime. I can certainly not go to a hotel the night I arrive whenever it is because they are a bit difficult I hear because of the world's fair. You must feel as free as you did when Paul was there because now having made the trip to Florida by myself I can certainly get back and forth to Tree-Tops when you are free and I am not busy in town. My travelling arrangements from now on are going to be very simple (osser). Please please look up Mildred Dunnoks address and telephone number, for me. I think you have it—at least the address or telephone number in Connecticut. She wrote me and the maid threw away the letter hers *and* Paul's. I am worried that it will take forever to get it from Audrey although I am writing her too.

I would call you but I am afraid that I would only be able to talk a few minutes—(three) calling from here but if you would like that I will. I would love to call you and stay on the phone longer but it is difficult—they are now being very carefull about money—We are almost always home except when we go to "Pompernicks" for dinner—back by 10 or 10:30—and anyway no one answers the phone here if we are not home. I may call you any way. I feel so sad here—but you'll understand if I don't talk long. I will write Rose. Love to Louie—

Jane

P.S. Don't sopple about the clean laundry I left in my room at 61st. I meant to have left it at Treetops. It is washed but not ironed—and it is not much—but it is a mistake. I will write Rose about telephoning me if you ever want the number and the hours, etc. I wish you would.

Write me when to call you.

Florida, May 3, 1965

102
To Libby Holman

Darling Libby,

It was wonderful to hear you talk because even though I always do like to hear you're voice I espacially needed to. I was very sad when you were not in on Monday and got so flustered that I must have confused Rose terribly. I understand now what happened I think. I meant to tell her that I was coming in on *Monday* and would go (if you were there and not somewhere else) to the "Flat" on Tuesday. but somewhere along the line Rose must have thought, or I must have said, I wanted to bring my luggage over on Monday at which point she would certain have said, "William isn't there on Monday." In fact she said it was William's day off on Monday, but as *I had understood it*, she said Tuesday. Later I pondered on this for many long hours because I knew that Tuesday *was* the day you always came in and so I couldn't understand it being Williams day off. Still I decided, if he was gone Tuesday I should not take my luggage over Tuesday. Than Frances called me, and I said I could not go over to you're house until Wednesday when William was back. I also invited her to dinner because I thought it was mean to leave her sitting there with my luggage —of course she was quite drunk on the telephone so she may not remember. who knows but if she does she will be upset if I change it, having asked her to keep me an extra night as a favor. I daresay she would like to have me there anyway, in fact she has always said so but it is so terribly difficult for both of us as you know. I cannot be with her unless I am entirely with her or at least from dinner time on because of the key situation. As you remember she was terrified to allow even the doorman or elevator boy to open the door for me nor did she want any one else to come back with me. Her fanatical secrecy about nothing at all is so irrational that I am frightened for her because of course I sniff a pschosis rather than a neurosis (sniff, indeed).

It would be nice to get the luggage to TreeTops if you leave with William before me but I have not decided where in the end my luggage should settle untill the final departure. I just don't know anything and I am more troubled than I have been in a long time. Meanwhile I had better not start trying to "explain" all the different possibilities for the luggage, which is now three different places—because this is the road straight back to White Plains, God forbid! As a matter of fact if F. and I both went there at least the luggage would be in one place, that is if I got the stuff from sixty-first and TreeTops.

Wonder if you read the Puppet Play and if so do you think they should do it, I do. Please Libby try to find Mildred's address or telephone number—she sent it to me and the cleaning woman got into my papers, and threw it away. Please also find out if David Jackson and Jimmie Merrill are still there. I don't see how we can see them any weekend except *this* weekend *if* you do want to go up there because the next weekend is Tony's weekend. Anyway I will talk about this when I see you on Tuesday

I thought David and Jimmie had shown the puppet play to the puppet boys but if they haven't why *don't* you. Tell Louie I'm sorry he didn't speak to me the night I called. I took for granted he was in town with you or at the studio, and then Rose told me he was on his "way out of the kitchen." Give him my love and kiss the cats for me.

I think I can only see F. by meeting her in a bar or restaurant because of the elevator situation. Oliver mentioned wanting to see us when he got back from the coast but God knows when that will be. Anyway please bring the puppet play *in with you* and find out about Jimmie and David and Milly if you can and it's not too much trouble. Perhaps I should not use the word psychosis in regard to F. but extreme neurosis—but I am no doctor. However I don't think White Plains would refuse either one of us. This letter is really ridiculous because yincha Alla I will see you on Tuesday—but at least you'll be prepared for the "discussion." Whatever I say I love F. very much because she is a tragic—fanatical—Electra kind of figure in a "tea pot."

New York City, May 14, 1965

103
To Cherifa

Querida Cherifa: 20 de mayo

Por fin ha llegado su carta y estoy muy contenta que Aicha está bien y que tu estás bien. Ayer llegué de Florida donde vive mi madre, y ya estoy otra vez en Nueva York. Hamed todavía no tiene teléfono, pero voy a mandar una carta a su dirección, para que venga a vernos en el hotel de Paul. Espero que todavía está aquí en America, y que no se ha ido a Alemania. Mil recuerdos otra vez a Aicha, la niña, tu hermana así que toda la familia.

No puedo escribir mucho porqué tengo muy poco tiempo ahora para acabar con mis cosas. Vamos a salir de aquí el día dos de junio y llegaremos, incha'Allah, a Casablanca más ó menos una semana después. Muchos recuerdos a Seth y al Berred si todavía está viva! Tengo muchas ganas de verte, y espero que estés contenta y de buena salud. Hasta muy pronto,

su amiga,
Jane Bowles

Translation

Dear Cherifa: May 20

Finally your letter has arrived and I'm very happy that Aicha is well and that you are well. Yesterday I arrived from Florida where my mother lives, and now I'm once again in New York. Hamed still doesn't have a telephone, but I'm going to send a letter to his address, so that he'll come to see us at Paul's hotel. I hope that he is still here in America and that he has not gone to Germany. A thousand remembrances again to Aicha, the little girl, your sister as well as the whole family.

I can't write much because I have very little time now to get things done. We're going to leave here the second of June and we will arive, God willing, at Casablanca a week later, more or less. Many remembrances to Seth and Berred, if she's still alive. I have a great desire to see you and I hope you are happy and in good health. Until very soon.

Your friend,
Jane Bowles

New York City, 1965

104
To Libby Holman

Darling Libby,

I wrote you as I remember a short and unsatisfactory not a little while ago and now I shall write you another short and equally unsatisfactory note again. I don't know what I said in the note which is going to make this note even worse than the last one? Did I tell you that I went to Casa Blanca because I didn't feel well or didn't I. Now I am back without any spectacular news from the doctor there. I am still suffering from slight dizzyness but not very much. I don't know how to spell that. Any way there is nothing new wrong with my brain so I guess it must have to do with my eyes or liver or my drugs (medicin). I never did have a thorough check up I guess I'm alright. Paul goes to Afghanastan, for Holiday Magazine at some point—I hope not too soon and certainly not if they haven't stamped out the recent Cholera epidemic, that stemmed from there, and had reached God knows where last I heard of it. Of course I don't know now whether the Cholera was heading east or west but in any case it was in Afghanastan when I heard about it. Ask Shirley. I am really in a black state and trying to keep it from Paul as much as possible—which means that I don't discuss myself and my life and my work too much (just a little). I miss you and I miss being near you and the friends I have left very badly. I am obviously as worried as I can be about what's going on in the U.S.A. and wonder about you're state of mind as I told you in my last note I think. Maybe you will write me about the boys in your next note. I am sorry Frances took up so much of my time (and my mother) when I was in America last but maybe I can come soon and arrange things differently (I can hear Louie growning).

I don't know when that will be this year or next but would like to come more frequently than I do. Obviously I am just talking in the air because I am depessed and feel isolated. Frances writes me but I don't think I could put myself through that again ever (famous last words)—but I really don't. Please write me some news and give my love to Lucia if I didn't send it last time and give me more news of Spivy. I should really be in East Hampton. I don't know what I'm doing here.

Libby Paul wrote the little new song to take the place of the old song that was lost (the one called the Frozen Horse). Did he or I write you about this? He has so much to do that I can never even keep track of that Frozen Horse which he was kind enough to write over again. He is never around when I write you so please if he hasn't written you, Tell the boys if you can that the new song is completed and ask them where Paul should send it. I suppose Paul might, have the address but I shall wait for you're instructions. Maybe Paul will write a more sensible letter. This letter is getting very involved so I'd better send it off.

Give Louie my love. If Rose is gone at the moment I suppose you won't write me.

Love to Alice if she's there and to Rosie if she is. I wish you'd get back into Tree Tops where you belong—so I can reach you more quickly—I suppose. How many more months are you going to be at the beach house any way? Have David and Jimmy gone away to Greece?

Much love
Jane

Please write—excuse this mess of a letter.

Tangier, August 26, 1965

105
To Libby Holman

Darling Libby, Tangier

It has been so long now that I do not even feel sure of how to spell you're name. I write less and less of anything because I run into so many spelling blocks that I give up and put the letter aside. I don't know that I am better or worse or rather whether my spelling is better or worse and why should it matter, but it does. I was so gratefull to get you're long letter that I was certain I was going to answer it at once but I didn't, now the letter is up on Paul's floor so I won't be able to answer it accurately. I don't remember the details of that letter but you did say that you wouldn't be responsible—or accountable for what you'd do if the boys were drawn into a war. I am not quoting you very accuratly but you're sentence went something like that. I have turned into a complete slob—I sit for hours and do nothing and at the same time I am nervous and erassable. This spelling is an example of why I don't write letters. "irasable" could be spelled in many different ways except this one, and since I don't know whether or not to look it up under "e" or "i" I am discouraged. Sometimes, in fact most often I don't send the letter at all. perhaps you understand—it looks so wrong to me and yet I cannot correct it unless I look up all the possible ways of spelling it, which is also difficult and half the time impossible. There is never any one near me with whom I can check except Paul and he is half the time not available. Naturally a secretary would be ideal. I am not suggesting that you send me one. Everyone is wild about Truman's book but I suppose I will never get through it, however I hope to be able to look at it eventually. Paul has written the "Little Players" because they never did ackowledge receiving my or rather his music for the little song Paul sent them a month or two ago. It is strange—I mailed it to them from Gib. registered so they must have received it. I told my friend Gordon Sager to ring you up He said he knew you and wanted very much to see you if you were free to see him. I'm sure you remember all about him and perhaps by now he has telephoned you. He wrote me and I never answered him but I hope to today. I have lost the letter with the concert date in it and as usual Paul has probably answered the letter and thrown it away. Gordon is staying in New York for awhile and so if he gave up trying to reach you or never did try I wish you'd call him and ask him for drink if you are not too busy. I would thus get direct news of you when he comes back or if he doesn't come back you could give me news of him. I am depressed and also very sleepy. I don't find letters satisfactory—they don't take the place of seeing the person at all and I am desperatly missing my close friends at the moment *more than ever* if possible which makes me less inclined to write less. I don't include Frances among my closest friends. She is something else of course (but I don't write her either). I suppose you saw Louisa for Thanks Giving etc. When I return I have no intention of staying with Frances though will have to stay in some hotel for a little bit of time I suppose in order to see the friends I want to see. With all you're boys and their girl friends looming in the future if not now, do you think there will ever be any room at Treetops again—for a two weak stay or whatever it was last time. I suppose this letter is premature but I might come and try to catch you before the East Hampton exodus begins and that means summer holidays—(no room for me anywhere), except in the very beginning as I remember. I don't know why I should bother you with all this now since I don't know really whether I'll come in the spring or the fall or the summer but obviously if you have any idea at this early date what you're plans are going to be I would like to know because my own always do depend on you're's to a large extent because I don't ever want to be there when and if you are certain to be away for a long spell. Please write to me and let me know at least whether you and Louie are well and whether the concert or concerts have or has take place and how everyone is in the house. I am sad to write you such a dull letter but perhaps the next one will be better.

All my love,
Jane

Tangier, December 1965

106
To Libby Holman and Louis Schanker

For Libby and Louie—

Won't you ever come back?

Please kiss all of my friends who are there and the children.

I have never sent a xmas card to anyone in my life but this is a very pretty one and is meant to lure you back—very sad not to be with you—

all love—
Jane

Tangier, December 1965

107
To Libby Holman

Dearest Libby

For days or perhaps months I have been looking for a letter you wrote me which made me feel very happy. I was in a bad state and I wish that Rose would look up somewhere the date of that letter.

I had all kinds of answeres ready for that letter in my head but each time I began thinking about answerering you I would get so excited that I would stand up and walk ghri right out of the room and even run about in circles and then out of the appartment entirely—instead of ansering answering you. It was a wonderfull letter and it came at the moment when I needed to be sure that you and TreeTops existed.

I am almost sure that Jay died after that very shortly but I'm not dead sure. I have been thinking that that was why I did not answer as quickly as I should have after all my excitement of running around the appartment. I will now spend an hour looking for a letter I found which was also of great comfort to me but I do not think this letter which I am now looking for was the one I reffer to. Just a minute.

Well I can't find even the letter I don't think it was nor the letter that I do think it was. Jay died on xmas morning—in his bar on the way to have his xmas lunch alone with Jessie Greene —who is eighty seven years old and who has been in love with him for many years. She had his preasants all wrapped up for him and the turquey—a gift from an Arab, was Stuffed and in the oven and waiting for him to arrive. He stopped off for a minute at the bar having just left her after they had gone to Church together as they always did. A couple of hours later While Jessie was waiting for him to come and eat his turque Lillie the bar woman called up and told Jessie that Jay couldn't come because he had died. It was a terrible shock to the whole town as he had been perfectly I was very unhappy Libby and spent many days with Jessie—because all of her close friends were in England for xmas and the few who were not were in Marrakesh.

Since than many things have happened and I have been looking around hoplessly for that particularly wonderull letter which maybe Rose has a record of. The one nearet to that date I found as I told you but but I don't think that is the one I mean. It was however written before Jay's death but I think too months before so I am eager to see it the one I found among my papers is the only letter or it indeed there was another one closer to the date of Jay's death but of course before and not after.

I want to get this letter off to you before the endless weekend begins. The murder of the sheep will take Place friday and their will be no mail coming or going untill next monday. Today it Thursday and I must reach the post now.

The deppression after Jay's death was bad and I did not start coming out of it for a month. For me it was the death of an eppoc—the spelling of that is driving me crazy but since Paul and I keep different hours and live on different floors I just can't correct anything. I know you wrote me that it did not matter. If I have not written I had reasons.

The confusion in my life has been fantastic and I think impossible to write about. I am not sick but I am not well or I am having change of life and the dissiness gets better and then worse. I wrote you about it a year ago—because I found an old letter about it last week. It was written nearly a year ago. Meanwhile Please write me again when you are going to go on tour—if you go Israel—I don't want to miss you and must know because I too am thinking of moving over to America for a couple of months at least so we must not cross. I don't want you to come here with Jay dead and Paul in the orient and me in Florida so please for God's sake write me again what you just wrote me about you're possibilities. Some times I get so disscouraged by my spelling that I don't ever want to write a letter again. I thought I would improve more than I have but it does not really matter does it.

I will write Katharine that you wrote me. I am glad that she is alive since I never put pen to Paper people give me up. It's quite naturall but writing letters drive me crazy because of the spelling. I could write a book more easilly maby mabey. The word maybe is a tippical word that I can't spell. Sometimes the word comes right in the end and sometimes not. Please please write me you're plans again just for the concert and for the possible trip. I would love to see the little Players. I have much more to write you and will try to go on tomorrow and sent it Monday. I will mail this without corrections because it's time you got a letter. I have much more to tell you. I know I wrote mostly about my spelling in my last letter and I know you wrote me that you would send me Rose maybe (on a longe chain?). Anyway tell Rosie to look up the dates of you're last two letters and mine. Give my love to the familly and thank you for the book and more in my next. I shall run to catch the post.

Tangier, April 1, 1966

108
To Libby Holman

Darling Libby,

My plans are at a virtual standstill. I don't know what to do. Martha who was, I thought, going to go over to America with me—and come back as well is now putting off her trip untill the fall. She says she will deffinitely go back with me in the fall because she needs to in order to keep up her residence in the U.S. She was going sooner because she wanted to take a stab at breaking her trust again, since the money she gets is less than ever before enough to make ends meet. However although her son and daughter finally agreed to sign certain documents necessary for the breaking of the trust, they think that she should not move until Mr. "Katz" of Cincinnati writes that there is reason for her to come over. I doubt that she will ever break her trust—that is succeed in doing so, but she swears she has to go over anyway once every two years to keep her residence, in the United States. If I go into that and who she is and why I even know her etc., I might as well ask you who is going to finish this biography after my death. Libby, my spelling worries me so much that I am afraid to come home and see what is wrong with me that wasn't wrong with me before. Maybe some premature deterioration due to the original stroke. I don't know. I don't know what is physical any longer and what is mental. I hoped always that I would get better but it does not look that way (the spelling), does it? I am frightfully depressed and I don't know how I can start off alone. Can I wait until the fall, untill Martha is sure to go? (osser) Anyway she "says" so. If there is anything wrong with me then I'm sure it's so bad that nothing will help it, and if there isn't, then I suppose it must be some reaction to all these years of drugs. I hope so. My book, *Two Serious Ladies*, I made no money at all or to be exact about four hundred dollars since publication including the advance. It is at the same time considered To be a literary success in certain circles which I never get into since I am not there, I am here. I don't know if I ever sent you the book or whether or not we decided that it was useless because you had read it. Perhaps we decided that you should have a copy in order to lend it to friends. I don't know. My memory is so bad because of my stroke and the premature senility that resulted that I keep forgetting everything. At the same time if you saw me you would notice that I am still charming and seem very very bright and even young. I am horribly worried about myself but on certain days I am less. Please ask Resnick if a neurologist is the best person to go to for possible beginings of Parkinson's Disease—after effects of a stroke, such as advanced hardening of the arteries, overdoses of drugs, but I think that poor Dr. Resnick will be unable to answer, so don't mention me. My doctor told me that she was sure I did not have Parkinson's Disease but she didn't *sound* sure. I might fly to England for two weeks where I can see my original stroke doctor if he is alive. Veronica Tennant is flying there and so perhaps Martha could join me from Paris and come back with me to Tangier. I cut all that part of the letter out because meanwhile Martha has decided to go to Italy and visit her dead daughter's tomb. (She has been dead for ten years but there is no room yet in the ground for her.) I don't think that I will go into this, either. Anyway, her live daughter is there and she *will* see her. I will go nowhere at the moment unless I am really in an awful state, that my woman doctor will recognize. Since I must come to America anyway and want to I shall do everything in one city that is country—although I suppose it is even more expensive than hopping across to London—and then later coming back here anyway which I must do. I just don't know. I'll think about it. Martha said she would go over with me if I needed a nurse (to London that is) in any emergency, but at my expense, of course, the way I paid that boy to go with me to Tangier several years ago. I gave him one hundred dollars to deliver me to Tangier and then he took the next boat on to Italy which had been always his final destination. I hope that I shan't have to do any of that, and can simply come alone and have someone meet me.

Several years ago I told Katharine that she must not hesitate to cut me off the list if she retired because she was worried about those twenty five dollars. I must write her and tell her not to worry because I'm sure she will be upset if I don't. Thank God for the money that you continue to send me which includes Oliver's share. Obviously I cannot write him about it but maybe when I see him this time I'll talk to him about it. The money means a lot to me. If someday it doesn't I will let you know at once so that it can be free for someone else—

I have Paul available today to correct the spelling of this letter and so I will wait until he gets down here. I have thought, as you know, about sending the letter without corrections but I think Paul would be horrified and ashamed for you to see so many mistakes, and you yourself could be depressed.

Louie's catalogue was a joy to both of us and I would love to be able to buy some of the sculptures, in fact all of them. If I could buy only one I would buy number eleven (bronze), I am crazy about it. Where is it? There is a lot more I could tell you—but I don't want to start in again. I hope to God that you have written though I deserve not to hear for awhile. I asked you questions about your present schedule and whether or not Israel was still on it. If there is any chance of your coming here I shan't stir. I don't think that I will right now anyway, but please let me know what you think you're going to do as I asked you in my last letter. I don't feel I have Parckinson's Disease today at all but I must have something. Martha's mother had it and that's where it all started. Those two ladies from the library were about to start over the yenti atlas again and I almost died thinking of Louie and you and me around the pool talking about my trip. Lee Gershwin was here and gave me a very modern tiny slip for skirts that are above the knees. Naturally I could not wear a skirt above the knee with my leg but I love the the baby slip. My slips are more like slips for a concert pianist. I was upset about the Leary scandal which Paul heard about from Susan Sontag, whom you've surely met or at least heard of. Much love to the whole family and please write me.

Jane

Tangier, May 10, 1966

109
To Hal Vursell

[ ] Paul and I decided to go on to Spain if those conditions didn't clear up by the time we arrived in Casa. It was alright but I would not have liked being on the boat alone with People possibly meeting me and possibly not because of the riots—or at least threatened riots. This happens in Casa but thus far has never happened in Tangier where I would get off anyway because it is my destination. I don't see why you should take the time to read all of this but it is perhaps to justify and clarify to myself as well as to you my own impotence to make a decision in this tiny little nightmare among other nightmares. I think therefore it is wise to stick to the plan of going quickly and thus avoiding anxiety all the way over because of Casa Blanca or Algeciras. I am going to have my typewriter fixed because it sticks. I am glad that I came to America now and not later when you would have been gone. Soon I will write Libby or telephone, perhaps both—certainly both becaus Libby has to know as soon as possible, about holding the weekend for me. Obviously there is *no way of my getting there*,

and back because of my peculiar incapacity—physical and psychic. Enough of that. I am getting into more and more trouble with my typewriter and must wind up quickly before it sticks forever—the train trip was fine and the duplex very livable. I don't know what I am being sent for the return but either a peculiar duplex or a bed room will do. I found out from the train conductor, (very charming), that the only thing I couldn't travel inside of was a "ROOmette". I'll see what that lady sends tomorrow or soon after. Nothing as yet. Thank Richard Holland for standing there in the station and not complaining. Actually it was one of the least depressing moments in my life and the station looked so nice. In spite of Casa and Algéciras if from your end things don't work out for my interviews unless I do stay here longer I will.

Give my love to Frank—naturally— devotedly

Jane

Miami, c. July/August 1966

110
To Gordon Sager

Darling Gordon

I have talked about you a great deal with Hal—that is on the night we dined. He is both a true friend and admirer of yours. It's a bore that my typewriter has been broken since I arrived because it is very difficult for me to write long hand. The stroke affected my right hand slightly—which is not important since there are typewriters. However I can only write a little at a time so I shall say little—only eessentials—before my hand buckles under—Another system is to lie down and dream for one hour untill one can go back to the writing table. This is about all I can take right now—Goodby I am going to dream.

I am back briefly—Gordon I am worried so please write me a line. I expect to come back either on a boat that leaves on the 22nd of August from here or on a boat that leaves the first of September. I shall let you know very shortly. I preffer the first date because that boat comes directly into Tangier and avoids Algecirras nerves. But I don't know if I can make it. If not I'll give you a choice of people to meet me—if *you* can't. I know you would if you aren't ill—I hope to God you're alright—much love—

Devotedly—

Jane—

Miami, c. July/August 1966

III

To Libby Holman

Dearest Libby—

It is very hard for me to write long hand since the stroke. Not very important but my hand buckles under after a very little time so I won't be able to sustain this for long.

Briefly—Frances can't drive me to Long Island. Boat leaves Monday noon August 22—and not Tuesday as Hal wrote me unless the American express people *here* are crazy. But then I doubt it because we checked twice. I would have to be in New York Sunday night even if its one in the morning and who in hell could drive me. Have late afternoon interviews Wednesday and Thursday. Naturally free after that but must be on time for boat Monday morning—I suppose around 10 or(?) 11 the latest —sailing at noon.

Looks very difficult fore you rather William or whoever would help.

Please telephone—tried tonight Tuesday—but no answer. Please telephone me any morning after ten or any evening from Friday the Fifth—onward. We stay up untill one. In the afternoon we go out.

Please call and we'll discuss it can't write any more—

Much Love

Jane

Miami, August 1966

112
To Paul Bowles

Dearest Paul,

I am delighted that you received my first letter that I wrote to the ships address. Today I had the letter written to me from "in the middle of Gatun Lake," on the fifth of August. I suppose I received it several days ago but it seemed to me like today because my typwriter has been on the blink and I had to eak out a few painfull letters by hand, one to David and one to Gordon and one to Mme. Roux—all of them to explain why I could not write which meant that I had to go into the weak condition of my hand a result of the stroke. I hope I'm not going to begin explaining this to you. I mention it because I have been so worried that the machine would not be back in time enough to write you. I certainly needed to send you more than a few lines. Now however my hand hurts because I did make all this effort to send word to friends and the position and now typing seems strange although a million times better than writing by hand. I am sending you Peter Owens account as I said I would. Julian says that if he gets thirty percent which is the final sum we settled on, as I remember, then his calculation would be about correct. I would earn about one thousand dollars according to Julian and I'm sure that you will agree with him. On publication of course I will get more.

I called up Dr. Dean, actually to have someone to hang on to while I was here because Naturally I was in a panic that I would somehow not be able to get out of here which panic still exists but I do have Dr. Dean to hang on to. He gave me any number of pills in a brown paper bag. I thought he had brought some groceries with him, (He came to see me. I did not have to go there.) untill he opened up the bag and showed me that it contained about fifty little celophane packets of pills each packet containing three tiny pills and these wrapped separatly although they are in unts of three in a packet each one isolated from the other. I fear this will turn into a "building the bridge", at "Camp Cataract". I know that you will be carefull not to hurt Peter Owens feelings about anything. The money has not yet arrived at my bank but that may be do to the Strike which continues as you know by you're ships radio—ships wireless I'm sure. As for my health I am bewildered by the sensations I have—the same symptoms as I have always had only much worse. I am going to the M.D. today and I will "Play it by ear". He is so busy that I could not get an appointment untill today which is the ninth. I arrived here on the twenty seventh. I think Dr. Dean is writing you a letter saying Mrs. Bowles is much better than she thinks she is. I can't get a cabin to myself on the boat and there are slim chances that any will turn up at the last minute. I am returning to New York City on the 15 of August, where Hal has arranged three interviews for me. Each one in a dark bar. I am terrified and wish that I had never accepted because they will want me to talk about Morocco, and books. I won't talk about the country I live in and can remember having red only a little of Susan S. Simone Weil, and you. The interviews are over by Thursday evening at which Point Hal will put me on a train to Stamford, arranging with Rose by telephone which train she's to meet. Then I spend the evening with Rose and she will drive me out to Libby's the next morning. Then back to New York on Sunday with Rose, who will leave me there in order to go back to her house in the country or town. Who knows.

Martha is thrilled because the cat has now eaten his first grass, while he was playing in the Garden. He was kept in by himself the first week and then gradually started eating pieces of fish with the others and Martha who gives half of her meat to the dogs and cats who are always grouped around her waiting.

I think I must stop now or this letter will not reach you. It was bad luck that I have had the use of the typwriter only one day.

I am happy that Libby wanted to see me badly enough to make all these arrangements. I am going to send this without corrections because I am afraid that if I reread it I'll miss the post.

I am delighted that you have liked your boat so far. It sounds wonderfull. I'll write to Bangkok, next. Martha has written me two of her usual sweet letters and even wired once because I told her how uncertain the mails were. I pray to God I'm on that boat by the twenty second. All my love

J.

Miami, August 9, 1966

113
To Gordon Sager

Dearest Gordon

Thank you for your letter. I have been worrying about you and also, I have been in a frenzy about the boats. I have decided that although I can use weeks here to track down Millie and Oliver (because I am sure Oliver will be sad not to have seen me) I have nonetheless decided that I will leave here in August and arrive at Tangier on the date I will give you as soon as I have seen mother who is in the next appartment. If I should decide otherwise I shall certainly send you a cable. I shan't send you any more explanations or I would get into one of those long painfull recitals that you know so well. I am trying to remain—precise, casual as well, as if the whole business didn't terrifie me. I am leaving the day after tomorrow for the Chelsea hotel. I am so deppressed that I can barely lift up my feet and drag into the next room. I shall not ask mother to correct this letter for me. If the boat whichever one it turns out to be arrives at some ungodly hour I don't know what I'll do. Hard to choose which Port would be the worst for *me*, Tangier or the other two but I have decided to try getting off at Tangier unless they suddenly change plans. I mean the boat. If that happens I shall sit in *Algecirras* and send millions of wires before they take me off to the nut house.

I'll go and get the sailing date from my mother since I really don't foresee getting off at Algecirras. My boat leaves on the 22 and arrives yincha allah, on the twenty ninth in Tangier. That means passing La semaine de Tangier in Tangier. After that who knows. I had news from Martha three times but now I don't hear. She is probably very very occupied, in fact she wrote me that she was. Please tell David I wrote him a letter naturally and tell the Gerofies that my typewriter has at last been Fixed but I won't have time now to write. Please give them all my love—and I miss you very very much,

Love,
Jane

Miami, August 1966

114
To Paul Bowles

Dearest Bup,

I did not think I could possibly send you the letter that I wrote you yesterday because it was too full of neurological meanderings opinions on my own, state of being, doubts about not having been to a Neurologist at all, finally, and mispelled words, etc.—that I destroyed it. I did get to Florida and back and finally here to Tangier. I came much too early as far as Martha is concerned because she is such a busy women still; It is hard for me to tell whether or not I shall ever see her as I did. She assured me that I would when she grew less busy but I see no end to it. I think she believes there is an end but I don't. There will be time when her friend Yvonne Silva leaves perhaps, unless her next visitor comes just as the present visitor leaves—which is very possible. I may go to England if things do go on this way but it is too early for me to tell. The voyage back to Tangier was a nightmare since they never knew really whether or not we could land in Tangier, untill the bitter end. It is always like that because of counter currents. Naturally I was worried all the way by the thought of having to land in Algecirras by myself and to keep my eye on seven pieces of luggage. You can image what I went through. Thank God I had Dr. Dean to call up in Miami because my terror there of landing forever in a "rest home" was grave. I got dizzier and dizzier so I fainally did call him. He said he knew a woman Neurologist but by the time I got arround to making the decision to see one, it was too late for me to see her and catch the train. I myself was of two minds about ever seeing one and I do believe that if I did, it should be a first rate one in England, if any. I think my symptoms may be neurotic but I think more likely that I am possibly suffering from the equivalent of the fits that I used to have and have no longer, at least have not had for nearly three years. I have missed Rabit but have left a message with Yvonne for next friday which is the day on which he comes. If by some miracle they take me with them to Marrakesh then I won't be here. However I will leave messages for him in anycase. He wants news of you which he has not received, so Mme. Jerofie said. Anyway I will keep my eye out for him and have him ring me up as soon as possible. Next Friday unless I have gone somewhere, but it will be soon. He comes every Friday to the book shop and is very polite. I intend to make an appointment with him or at least talk to him on the telephone. It does not look to me as if Martha would ever call me but perhaps she will again. The last two nights have been hell but you're cat is fine and very happy at Martha's. I think it was really Mario's girlfriend who did the work on him. But of course Martha would never admit that. He is happy and plays with imaginary mice in the garden. I know that he is better off here and is part of their family—much more than me. I'm sorry to tell you that Berred died.

You have a check at Yvonne Gerofies which she says has to be countre sighned, Which of course I can't do. I will go and take a look at it, from the outside and tell you who its from.

I think it's for deposit and I don't know why it has to be counter . . . signed? How would she know anyway since it is not open. Anyway I miss you terribly and I know that it was foolish of me to come this soon.

I could have stayed with Katharine. It doesn't matter. I am seeing Mrs. Dickson on Thursday, she wants my book or books and would like to write some friends to look you up in Thailand. Thank God for Dr. Dean in Florida. Otherwise I might never have gotten out of there—I was so frightened of loosing my mind and not being able to cope.

Much love naturally

J.

Tangier, September 1966

115
To Paul Bowles

Dearest Paul,

Carla Grissmann is typing out these few addresses for you, which I've guarded with my life and found very difficult to keep track of. Charles Gallagher says that you know these men anyway. There are: Bill Forbush, Kyoto. Also Bruce Rogers in some illegible place near Kyoto; Donald Richie, Tokyo.

Your letter was fascinating of course, but I have no news from here to give you. I'm worried about all kinds of things naturally but they don't bear writing about—and you are too far. I miss you very very much, but thank God you have landed somewhere, and I am now not Carla Grismann but myself continuing this letter. How I wish that I were with you now. I saw Bill for a few minutes, he called by to see me or I told Bryan to let him in—rather send him in. I don't quite remember. Bryan is here Charles is leaving in a couple of days and I am anxious to get this letter off so that it will reach you on time.

Charles felt that you would certainly be able to stay on in Bangkok but got these names in case. I can't tell what is going on because I am not seeing many people. I think Carla has fixed these margins so that they are too narrow. And so I have re done mine. I hope that you will write me even though I can't seem to answer your letters and stick even the slightest bit of fun into mine. I wanted to say morcel of fun into mine. Not a very good word and I can't spell it anyway. I suppose I was trying to write, "titbit" If that is the correct spelling.

. . . . Next day. This is Carla again (I did *not* fix the margins, they *were* like that, and I've just found out how to widen them—much better, non? Janie is on her way—)

Dear Paul, I just got your second letter today, from Bangkok, of the 22nd, and I wish more than ever that I'd gone with you. I seem to be very depressed, but don't worry. There's nothing you can do about it, and I hope that you do get out of that sticky climate. No, I don't think Martha would ever come out anywhere around there with me, her life seems very much booked up at the moment—her painter arriving soon and then Italy in the spring—I suppose you didn't ever really believe that I could come or that Martha would.

The little animal sounds delightful, but I don't think it should be moved around. I had heard that there were air-cooled flats in Bangkok, but you'd still have to wander around the steamy streets even if you did find one.

Yes, Mrabet is here but I can never get over to see him—I can send messages through Madame Gerofie—

Thank you for writing me such a long letter—nice long letter, and give my best to Oliver Evans.

It looks to me as if you'll be gone six months at least—Gordon would like to have rented your aprtment while you were away because he has decided to get out of York Castle. He realized the complications and he shall probably leave Tangier before long if he can't find another place. The children here started making little orchestras of tin cans—they begin their jam sessions early in the morning and go on til quite late in the evening—It is very terrifying—The place has become a real *slum* but what can I do.

Anyway, the little fur animal sounds adorable. The Blackcat seems very happy at Martha's so I think it would be mean to put him back in an apartment—

What is the name of the man who collects your *taxes*—if I had that to give Jack, he could arrange something with the English agent who represents Peter Owen. *May*be. Jack asked me for his name so that I could get out of English taxes on my *book* so I wrote him to get in touch with Jane Wilson, but I also wrote that we have joint taxes so I don't know whether he can do anything about the English tax. Anyway, I don't see what you can do about it—I haven't written Peter Owen at all. The whole thing is much too complicated. Howard Moorepark is the English agent in America on my book and he is the one who asks Clareman for the name of the man who collects my taxes. He seemed to think it was all easy to arrange but of course they did not know that I did not get taxed myself, just you. Much too complicated. Anyway, I hope you haven't gotten Peter's back up, which I'm sure you *haven't*. I would much rather write about the animal with the black fur face.

I suppose the names Charles gave for you aren't of much use but anyway I wanted to get them to you. Much love,

Tangier, September 28, 1966

116
To Hal Vursell

Tangier, Morocco
September 28, 1966

Dear Hal,

I know you're not back yet, but I wanted to let you know that I got here. Please send a copy of my book to

Dr. Henry L. Dean
150 East 22nd Street
Miami Beach, Florida.

I want one sent also to Libby Holman, Treetops, Merrie Brook Lane, Stamford, Connecticut.

I'm dictating this letter, because I don't have the courage to write it myself. Deep depression. I thought I'd get these two things done before I got any less capable. Dr. Dean helped while I was in Florida. I shall never forget how nice you were to me. I don't want to say any more right now because I don't feel this is an especially private letter. I hope to God you're alright and that everything is the way you would want it.

All my love,
Jane

117
To Paul Bowles

Dearest Paul,

Carla Grissmann paid the patente for me, I could never have done *any* of it by myself. I'm very frightened being here by myself and never realized how complicated it would be for me. Gordon is trying to help me, although he gets very fed up since I don't understand very much, indeed anything, about how to handle the money. I always have needed more than I get and now I'm terrified of leaving things up to the last minute. I should have gone with you no matter how hot or uncomfortable it might be. I could have stayed in the room. It particularly worries me that you don't have any idea of when you're coming back, although I can well under stand it. It terrifies me to live from month to month and so I have sent for extra money, via the bank, but even so until it comes I will be on tenterhooks, and *will* it come? I've had to drag Gordon to the bank manager because I can't express myself clearly. I still have money in the bank, though Gordon will find out how much, as I don't know where it's written. There's no point in writing about this as you can't do anything. What I want to be sure of is getting money out of my capital into my checking account, if necessary. I am not spending an extra *sous* but there always are a great many expenses beyond the $275. I naturally want to be well covered, particularly with you not here. What can I do if I suddenly have no money? You were always here to handle these things. The only friend I have here now at hand who can help me is Gordon if he will and doesn't get too irritated —he said he would on Monday. Paying your patente was an insane experience, ridiculous of course, as everything is here.

I think a stole would be best, because I never get around to having anything made. I have a red one, so pick something with greenish-blue in it?

I don't remember sending on any letter from the Swedish publisher except vaguely. It was about a photograph, and I think my mother has a good one, but it is all too complicated.

Sorry to bore you with my worries about the bank, but I decided it was best to have a reserve, and one to arrive here and not in Casablanca never to be *seen* again. Do you remember *that*? It still has not been found.

I worry about your being in so much *heat*. You don't say how long it will take you to get from Bangkok to Kyoto, so that I imagine you will be gone for years. Charles said it took a month to get from Bangkok to Japan. Would you then return the other way? Anyway I miss you very very much and please write me quickly. I really can't think of what color to have the stole in, and naturally if I were anyone else I would get a suit—too complicated. You will find a pretty color that will look nice on me. I didn't mean to tell you about my worries about the bank and money, etc., ways and means of doing these transactions, the bother I'm causing Gordon and worrying other friends but I can't free myself of this basic worry. We never did talk about money before you left, and there's nothing you can advise me about now. I'm very grateful for Carla writing this. Write me if you have any idea when on earth you'll be back. Martha is fine, but I wouldn't write her the nature of my worries if I were you.

The Siamese sound wonderful, I love those stubby tails.

Much love,

Tangier, c. September/October ? 1966

118
To Claire Fuhs

Dearest Mother, Tangier

I'm writing from Carla Grissmann's house where I'm spending the afternoon. She's an expert typist and I felt that I had to get a letter off to you first before I had tea. She suggested that I write this at her house as she types so much quicker than I do.

I'm *haunted* by the fact that I didn't stay with you long enough, and by the fact that I did not accept Julian's suggestion that he bring over the commentator so that I could listen to what he had to say. The whole thing seems to me a nightmare and I should have arranged things differently. Tell Julian I *realize* that and to forgive me. I could at least have encouraged him to bring the man up, and I'm very sorry.

I have no news to give you, except that Veronica is very very ill and they have sent for the family, as David doesn't want to take the responsibility. It makes her very happy to have her family there, although she is suffering a good deal.

I got your letter about the bank, I don't know whether there were any other checks after the last one you mentioned. I don't think so, as I certainly didn't make any out here. I'm very worried, because as they send the statements to you do you think I'll be able to get money here when I wire for it, or rather write? It is very difficult for me to figure out what to do, and I wonder if I shouldn't put them back to sending the statements directly to me. It's a mess. I've written the bank to honor any checks that might come in, including my own, but naturally I do worry now that I'm here alone. I can't really explain to you what I'm worried about 'cause it's too complicated, just that they might get mixed up. I'm so fed up that I'm almost ready to come back but with *whom*? I couldn't go through *that* again. All this will work out so don't *you* worry about it.

I'm well, and give Julian my very best love. And all my love to you,

September 30, 1966

119
To Paul Bowles

Dearest Paul,

. . . Dear Paul, this is Carla and with sending you my best greetings I wanted to write just a few words before Janie comes to you. I am here having a chat with her and since I type so much faster she said yes that I should write a few words: she has held up sending the last letter for fear it sounded too gloomy and didn't want you to fret, but since you might be leaving any moment she did want to send it off with this note added. A few "money" points have come up since she wrote, 1) the lost May check has been more or less traced, as having been paid into your account here on June 15th. Gordon will probably go down there to check.

I'm having Gordon do as much as he can as I can't cope with these money matters, as you know. As I've said I've sent for money because I want to keep ahead of the game here and it should be arriving somewhere between 2 and 4 weeks.

Martha has been very sweet to me and I've seen a lot of her but that will cease I imagine as soon as her house guests come, the young painter, Tony, and his wife. They're coming to stay with Martha who is at this moment alone and doesn't like that very much, any more than I do. However she is rapidly finishing her book and she works on it at least four hours a day, aside from making various trips with the car and her man Ahmed to some deserted beach, from where they bring back huge rocks I forget why. I had dinner there last night with George Greaves, and Cyril Hanson. I never said a word. Neither did they, until the very end. Martha entertained us all. Poor George is not feeling very well and is unable to drink anything. I wish I could get down to writing but I can't and you know all about that and what it does to me. I am longing for you to return but I know that it can't be done very soon. I'll send this quickly so that you'll have it before you leave. My mother told me that she had a beautiful picture of me in a magazine, I suppose from years ago—that because you mentioned the Swedish publisher. Jack Clareman thinks they can't get me out of British taxes because

I'm a resident of Morocco. Actually I'm *not* at the moment but I don't have the energy to go to that police place.

I have nothing but *complaints*, so I don't feel much like writing as you must know by now, but *please* don't let me down, and keep writing to *me*. This letter doesn't seem very much better than the *last* one, which I purposely withheld from you because I didn't want to upset you. I still don't. Isabelle is still attending to the money you left with her and as far as I know all goes well. I'm not awfully good at dictating letters because I've never done this before. Veronica has been desperately ill but seems to be getting a little better.

Write me more about fur animals and also when and *if* you plan to come back, if you know. I must have repeated this twenty times in my letter already. I am very *quiet* and don't find many amusing things to say or to write, that's why my mail is scarce, but I always remember that you said it's better to write a dull letter than no letter at all; so here is my dull letter, about as dull as a bank but not as useful.

Tangier, October 11, 1966

120
To Libby Holman

Dearest Libby,

My eyes are bad again—won't focus at all. I got much too nervous taking those trips and trying to fend for myself on the boat I imagine.

Anyway I am here but everything swimms before my eyes. It is a kind of "nervous breakdown," and I should never have gone. Or I should have stayed longer. It was folly to come back that quickly and I deeply regret it. I had no time to see anyone because of my obsessive terror that I would in the end not get back at all. I did not want to go on that trip with everyone to you're aunts for the weekend which you said you might invite me on if you could fit me in. I don't know whether or not you were serious about this or whether you knew I would balk at the idea of getting onto a plane. I don't know but I *would* have been better off getting on the plane than I am having come home.

Because of my eyes I can't read the zen book. It would be a great help right now. David Holman was very sweet. I wanted him to hide from You the state I was in—and it is not a state that is so noticable except that I am very quiet. I am writing these declarative sentences so that I can get through them before they turn into Gonza Magillas. At which point I would have to abandon them.

I told David Herbert who wanted very much to meet David—I told him that I was very much frightened that if you heard anything about a nervous breakdown You would cut me off I was half joking but it was a feer. David Herbert said I was crazy, but there is no limit to what I fear even so we went on with the conversation. Than David Herbert told the story to David Holman, which made everything terrible. Worse than that I told David Holman not to repeat it to you because it does sound crazy and he said he wouldn't dream of it so I'm repeating it to you and I'm sure David Holman will tell you that I'm not crazy. Just depressed and with reason. I'm trying to Pull out of it But I realize that this little deception I was trying to get away with was not going to cease bothering me. Untill I came straight to you with it.

It was a horrible fear that came over me when I was having lunch and so I came out with it to the other David, mine who then repeated it to you're David. Anyway please Don't cut me ough because you think I'm crazy or for any other reason. I manage the accounts with another friend very reliabe and count very much on you're gift to me—obviously.

I have no friend because no sooner was I back than began brooding [ ]

Tangier, October 1966

121
To Carson McCullers

Dearest Carson,

I was so happy to hear from you after all these years. I did not want to bother you, otherwise I would have given your name to my publisher and you might have written a short blurb. I can't write my letter, but am having it typed by a friend. Forgive me. [ ]

Tangier, October 31, 1966

122
To Libby Holman

Dearest Libby
I will be writing you— always
Jane

I hope to God you are well

Tangier, 1966

123
To Frances

Darling Frances Tangier
I am in such a depression that I can't answer any of your thoughtfully arranged questions. May I ask you one myself. Can you possibly go first to Paris (France) as you say or whatever other place you are going and then come on to me. The room upstairs is a mess but I could fix it up. I suppose you can not do it that way around or you would have suggested it to me. My life is one of great pain and torment now and I don't see my way out of this trap. If I go to America there would be only the state Hospital and in England the same because I don't have the money to pay for a getter place. My deppression has gotten worse and worse and I don't know what to answer you about coming right now. I would rather not say anything today but I'm writing you know not to leave England or France without leaving me an address. I don't know yet Whether I I would rather go or stay. That's why I can't write you. I suppose its too late now and you have gone to America. If you haven't then come here. You can tell by the way I write that I am in a bad way. Love
Jane

On the other hand come I should say if you don't have any other place you'd rather go first. I'm a little bit hard up

November 1966

124
To Paul Bowles

Dearest Bup,

I am afraid that by now it is too late to reach you for xmas and you're birthday. I feel quite sick about it and about not having written you. I have received all of you're letters and I don't think it was a good idea for me to stay here without you. The explanation of that will come later. They have been very kind about helping me but you always did that month by month more or less and now I don't seem to be able to accept any reasurance about whatever financial arrangements I make. It is hell. You're own letter sounded so sad that I had to write you although I have far less to say than you about my own my own confusion all of which Yvonne is trying to do her best to allay. I have no idea how to spell that word. Aisha to whom you sent the card is here and sends you love, or greatings as they do, and I did not tell Cherifa that the card was not for both of them, obviously. Mme. Roux may have written you by now or at least the letter may have written you about the possible opperation that I might have but I think I shan't have it and that I shall just stay as I am. Enormously fat in spots because my degestion is at a standstill. I long for you to come home but I can't really tell from you're letters how terribly long this is going to take. Naturally I was horrified by you're letter about my book but it is exactly what I expected. As you remember I did not really want it republished at all. But you say that books are written to be punlished. Tangier is humming with xmas activities and I am worried now that this letter will reach you too late for youre birthday or xmas. There have been no new terrors but theyre will be I suppose. O I am very worried about all kinds of things that I don't want to go into and can't. I did not write you for so long because I was in such a depression. Now it is something else. You're work seems very arduous and I'm sorry, almost in despair that you should be so lonely. Perhaps something will change. [ ]

Tangier, December 1966

125
To Libby Holman

Darling Libbie

I have been for six months in a nervous deppression—I will be well soon—

Love—
Jane

I think of you all the time—Love—Love—Love the interview that came out in the times was invented by the times man.

Tangier, February 1967

In mid-April 1967 Paul took Jane to Málaga, where she was admitted to a psychiatric hospital for women. There she again received shock treatment. The letters from here on are handwritten in a disordered script that is barely decipherable.

126
To Libby Holman

Dearest Libby—

I can write with out being ablle to sead ~~For Fat Fe~~ jet *y y y* yet. I hope that soon I can. I am very sad and also Bewildered—*you* seemed better I hope soon that you will right what happend or a little news—so that at least I will know whether or not your olcer is still alright. I cannot right you very much because I write the words with ~~the~~ being able to see them yet—so there isn't as much privacy ~~I have I as~~ as I could have if I needed no guidance. Readis is allmost out of the question but I am so much ~~beeter Beter~~ Better that ~~tope~~ I hope ~~I a~~ write ~~all~~ you to write you so y

Málaga, Spain, 1967

In May 1967 Paul brought Jane back to Tangier. Her condition worsened during the fall and in late December she moved out of her apartment, taking Cherifa with her, and went to stay at the Atlas, a small hotel near the Parade Bar. Sitting in the Atlas bar, she began to give away money, first cash and then checks. She gave away her clothing and all of her jewelry.

127
To Paul Bowles

Darling Paul—

It will be all explained—I mean, your financial dilemma—in one half hour. I mean, by me. It's true you should have a separate account. I have not spent as much money as you think. Please don't think it's your financial problem, *but mine*. We will talk it over and understand everything.

All my love
Jane

P.S. Alfred is the secretary.

Part of the love is for Alfred—

Tangier, January 11, 1968

Jane's condition deteriorated even further. She was in a very agitated state. Although she at first resisted returning to Málaga, she finally consented, and Paul took her back to the psychiatric hospital there.

128
To Paul Bowles

Dear Paul—

Please try to forgive me for the way I've behaved. I am longing to come back and start fresh again. I was not drinking when I went away and lived at the ~~Atlas~~ Atlas. I don't really know what I thought I was doing. I know that I have to fix my teath—I had ~~a~~ only a temporary arrangement on them which will have to be finished now. I've forgotten the name of the man [ ] Tangier (you use him too.) But naturally I would not be instend tha gng of Malaga. I would like to live in my ~~home~~ house—cook etc.

Please give my love to Noelle. Please Pall don't try to figure this out but believe me I want ~~I~~ to go back to Roux and get going with my ~~den~~ Dentist. I'll try to explain to you someday ~~abu~~ about the Atlas ~~bu~~ but I don't even understand most of it myself. It is very hard to write with no machine and I wish you would explain this to Libby & my mother.

Málaga, Spain, Spring 1968

129
To Paul Bowles

Dearest Paul—

thank you a million times for ~~ceep~~ ceeping in touch.

As you know its terribly hard for me to write—with out a ~~machin~~ machine and I don't even know kow w hiter I still can use one its been so long. I want very much to see you & get this [ ] way of life ~~over with~~ over with. I'm longing to come home and lead my li life. I don't feel like ~~wri~~ w riting because there is too much to dis cuss.

Actually there is nothing to discuss—except the fact that I am not home & & would like to be there ~~son~~ as soon as possible [ ] I chan't [ ] write about any thing but my dentist and ask how you are. The dentist should be in around a month if not know but it certainly must be soon. I sorry about having simply walked out and gone to the Atlas—I promise you I was not drinking. I want to go to dr I've suddenly

Málaga, Spain, Spring 1968

130
To Paul Bowles

Dearest Paul

~~W I you~~ Please call for me as soon as possible tomorrow afternoon. today is Monday I don't write a a long letter but I Is simplest ~~Is~~—I ~~a~~ leave it this way—so that it will be finished by monday—byme that's ~~temam~~ tomorrow.

I ~~supp e~~ suppose that will leave Noel in the awqward position of no bath room or me

Málaga, Spain, Spring 1968

In June 1968 Paul took Jane out of the hospital, where she had again received shock treatment. He had arranged for her to stay in a pension run by an American expatriate in Granada. At the end of ten days, he took her back to Málaga, where she was admitted to a casa de reposo, the Clínica de los Ángeles.

The last three letters are from the Clínica, where Jane stayed until her death in 1973.

131
To Paul Bowles

Dear Paul

I miss you very much and I miss not having hear from you for so long. Please come and see me and if possible to get me.

Could you come ~~right now?~~ here ~~you~~ quickly as possible ~~any way~~ and then we will see. [ ] Dr. says the [ ] orders you should take me. Please ~~write~~ come soon Much Love

Jane

Málaga, Spain, c. 1968/1969

132
To Paul Bowles

Darling Paul

~~I wonder if and I wonder if~~ I don't know what I was [ ] going to ask you but I but I certainly know that I miss you ~~desperdat you~~ very much and please come and get ~~me~~ here to see me and to get me if that is possible. I want so badly to go home

Málaga, Spain, c. 1968/1969

133
To Paul Bowles

Dearest Paul

Just right me another [ ] note and when you have written ask here ~~to a wom~~ talk to a woman called "Rgennia [ ]"—which is the way a mexican would spell her name but do it soon—

Lots of love

I'll finish this off [ ]. If I wanted to spend more time ~~*unclear*~~ *time* ~~if~~ I would let you kow—about any

Málaga, Spain, c. 1970

APPENDIX

Everything Is Nice

THE HIGHEST street in the blue Moslem town skirted the edge of a cliff. She walked over to the thick protecting wall and looked down. The tide was out, and the flat dirty rocks below were swarming with skinny boys. A Moslem woman came up to the blue wall and stood next to her, grazing her hip with the basket she was carrying. She pretended not to notice her, and kept her eyes fixed on a white dog that had just slipped down the side of a rock and plunged into a crater of sea water. The sound of its bark was earsplitting. Then the woman jabbed the basket firmly into her ribs, and she looked up.

"That one is a porcupine," said the woman, pointing a henna-stained finger into the basket.

This was true. A large dead porcupine lay there, with a pair of new yellow socks folded on top of it.

She looked again at the woman. She was dressed in a haik, and the white cloth covering the lower half of her face was loose, about to fall down.

"I am Zodelia," she announced in a high voice. "And you are Betsoul's friend." The loose cloth slipped below her chin and hung there like a bib. She did not pull it up.

"You sit in her house and you sleep in her house and you eat in her house," the woman went on, and she nodded in agreement. "Your name is Jeanie and you live in a hotel with other Nazarenes. How much does the hotel cost you?"

A loaf of bread shaped like a disc flopped on to the ground from inside the folds of the woman's haik, and she did not have to answer her question. With some difficulty the woman picked the loaf up and stuffed it in between the quills of the porcupine and the basket handle. Then she set the basket down on the top of the blue wall and turned to her with bright eyes.

"I am the people in the hotel," she said. "Watch me."

She was pleased because she knew that the woman who called herself Zodelia was about to present her with a little skit. It would be delightful to watch, since all the people of the town spoke and gesticulated as though they had studied at the *Comédie Française.*

"The people in the hotel," Zodelia announced, formally beginning her skit. "I am the people in the hotel."

"'Good-bye, Jeanie, good-bye. Where are you going?'

"'I am going to a Moslem house to visit my Moslem friends, Betsoul and her family. I will sit in a Moslem room and eat Moslem food and sleep on a Moslem bed.'

"'Jeanie, Jeanie, when will you come back to us in the hotel and sleep in your own room?'

"'I will come back to you in three days. I will come back and sit in a Nazarene room and eat Nazarene food and sleep on a Nazarene bed. I will spend half the week with Moslem friends and half with Nazarenes.'"

The woman's voice had a triumphant ring as she finished her sentence; then, without announcing the end of the sketch, she walked over to the wall and put one arm around her basket.

Down below, just at the edge of the cliff's shadow, a Moslem woman was seated on a rock, washing her legs in one of the holes filled with sea water. Her haik was piled on her lap and she was huddled over it, examining her feet.

"She is looking at the ocean," said Zodelia.

She was not looking at the ocean; with her head down and the mass of cloth in her lap she could not possibly have seen it; she would have had to straighten up and turn around.

"She is *not* looking at the ocean," she said.

"She is looking at the ocean," Zodelia repeated, as if she had not spoken.

She decided to change the subject. "Why do you have a porcupine with you?" she asked her, although she knew that some of the Moslems, particularly the country people, enjoyed eating them.

"It is a present for my aunt. Do you like it?"

"Yes," she said. "I like porcupines. I like big porcupines and little ones, too."

Zodelia seemed bewildered, and then bored, and she decided she had somehow ruined the conversation by mentioning small porcupines.

"Where is your mother?" Zodelia said at length.

"My mother is in her country in her own house," she said automatically; she had answered the question a hundred times.

"Why don't you write her a letter and tell her to come here? You can take her on a promenade and show her the ocean. After that she can go back to her own country and sit in her house." She picked up her basket and adjusted the strip of cloth over her mouth. "Would you like to go to a wedding?" she asked her.

She said she would love to go to a wedding, and they started off down the crooked blue street, heading into the wind. As they passed a small shop Zodelia stopped. "Stand here," she said. "I want to buy something."

After studying the display for a minute or two Zodelia poked her and pointed to some cakes inside a square box with glass sides. "Nice?" she asked her. "Or not nice?"

The cakes were dusty and coated with a thin, ugly-colored icing. They were called *Galletas Ortiz.*

"They are very nice," she replied, and bought her a dozen of them. Zodelia thanked her briefly and they walked on. Presently they turned off the street into a narrow alley and started downhill. Soon Zodelia stopped at a door on the right, and lifted the heavy brass knocker in the form of a fist.

"The wedding is here?" she said to her.

Zodelia shook her head and looked grave. "There is no wedding here," she said.

A child opened the door and quickly hid behind it, covering her face. She followed Zodelia across the black and white tile floor of the closed patio. The walls were washed in blue, and a cold light shone through the broken panes of glass far above their heads. There was a door on each side of the patio. Outside one of them, barring the threshold, was a row of pointed slippers. Zodelia stepped out of her own shoes and set them down near the others.

She stood behind Zodelia and began to take off her own shoes. It took her a long time because there was a knot in one of her laces. When she was ready, Zodelia took her hand and pulled her along with her into a dimly lit room, where she led her over to a mattress which lay against the wall.

"Sit," she told her, and she obeyed. Then, without further comment she walked off, heading for the far end of the room. Because her eyes had not grown used to the dimness, she had the impression of a figure disappearing down a long corridor. Then she began to see the brass bars of a bed, glowing weakly in the darkness.

Only a few feet away, in the middle of the carpet, sat an old lady in a dress made of green and purple curtain fabric. Through the many rents in the material she could see the printed cotton dress and the tan sweater underneath. Across the room several women sat along another mattress, and further along the mattress three babies were sleeping in a row, each one close against the wall with its head resting on a fancy cushion.

"Is it nice here?" It was Zodelia, who had returned without her haik. Her black crepe European dress hung unbelted down to her ankles, almost grazing her bare feet. The hem was lopsided. "Is it nice here?" she asked again, crouching on her haunches in front of her and pointing at the old woman. "That one is Tetum," she said. The old lady plunged both hands into a bowl of raw chopped meat and began shaping the stuff into little balls.

"Tetum," echoed the ladies on the mattress.

"This Nazarene," said Zodelia, gesturing in her direction, "spends half her time in a Moslem house with Moslem friends and the other half in a Nazarene hotel with other Nazarenes."

"That's nice," said the women opposite. "Half with Moslem friends and half with Nazarenes."

The old lady looked very stern. She noticed that her bony cheeks were tattooed with tiny blue crosses.

"Why?" asked the old lady abruptly in a deep voice. "*Why* does she spend half her time with Moslem friends and half with Nazarenes?" She fixed her eye on Zodelia, never ceasing to shape the meat with her swift fingers. Now she saw that her knuckles were also tattooed with blue crosses.

Zodelia stared back at her stupidly. "I don't know why," she said, shrugging one fat shoulder. It was clear that the picture she had been painting for them had suddenly lost all its charm for her.

"Is she crazy?" the old lady asked.

"No," Zodelia answered listlessly. "She is not crazy." There were shrieks of laughter from the mattress.

The old lady fastened her sharp eyes on the visitor, and she saw that they were heavily outlined in black. "Where is your husband?" she demanded.

"He's traveling in the desert."

"Selling things," Zodelia put in. This was the popular explanation for her husband's trips; she did not try to contradict it.

"Where is your mother?" the old lady asked.

"My mother is in our country in her own house."

"Why don't you go and sit with your mother in her own house?" she scolded. "The hotel costs a lot of money."

"In the city where I was born," she began, "there are many, many automobiles and many, many trucks."

The women on the mattress were smiling pleasantly. "Is that true?" remarked the one in the center in a tone of polite interest.

"I hate trucks," she told the woman with feeling.

The old lady lifted the bowl of meat off her lap and set it down on the carpet. "Trucks are nice," she said severely.

"That's true," the women agreed, after only a moment's hesitation. "Trucks are very nice."

"Do *you* like trucks?" she asked Zodelia, thinking that because of their relatively greater intimacy she might perhaps agree with her.

"Yes," she said. "They are nice. Trucks are very nice." She seemed lost in meditation, but only for an instant. "Everything is nice," she announced, with a look of triumph.

"It's the truth," the women said from their mattress. "Everything is nice."

They all looked happy, but the old lady was still frowning. "Aicha!" she yelled, twisting her neck so that her voice could be heard in the patio. "Bring the tea!"

Several little girls came into the room carrying the tea things and a low round table.

"Pass the cakes to the Nazarene," she told the smallest child, who was carrying a cut-glass dish piled with cakes. She saw that they were the ones she had bought for Zodelia; she did not want any of them. She wanted to go home.

"Eat!" the women called out from their mattress. "Eat the cakes."

The child pushed the glass dish forward.

"The dinner at the hotel is ready," she said, standing up.

"Drink tea," said the old woman scornfully. "Later you will sit with the other Nazarenes and eat their food."

"The Nazarenes will be angry if I'm late." She realized that she was lying stupidly, but she could not stop. "They will hit me!" She tried to look wild and frightened.

"Drink tea. They will not hit you," the old woman told her. "Sit down and drink tea."

The child was still offering her the glass dish as she backed away toward the door. Outside she sat down on the black and white tiles to lace her shoes. Only Zodelia followed her into the patio.

"Come back," the others were calling. "Come back into the room."

Then she noticed the porcupine basket standing nearby against the wall. "Is that old lady in the room your aunt? Is she the one you were bringing the porcupine to?" she asked her.

"No. She is not my aunt."

"Where *is* your aunt?"

"My aunt is in her own house."

"When will you take the porcupine to her?" She wanted to keep talking, so that Zodelia would be distracted and forget to fuss about her departure.

"The porcupine sits here," she said firmly. "In my own house."

She decided not to ask her again about the wedding.

When they reached the door Zodelia opened it just enough to let her through. "Good-bye," she said behind her. "I shall see you tomorrow, if Allah wills it."

"When?"

"Four o'clock." It was obvious that she had chosen the first figure that had come into her head. Before closing the door she reached out and pressed two of the dry Spanish cakes into her hand. "Eat them," she said graciously. "Eat them at the hotel with the other Nazarenes."

She started up the steep alley, headed once again for the walk along the cliff. The houses on either side of her were so close that she could smell the dampness of the walls and feel it on her cheeks like a thicker air.

When she reached the place where she had met Zodelia she went over to the wall and leaned on it. Although the sun had sunk behind the houses, the sky was still luminous and the blue of the wall had deepened. She rubbed her fingers along it: the wash was fresh and a little of the powdery stuff came off. And she remembered how once she had reached out to touch the face of a clown because it had awakened some longing. It had happened at a little circus, but not when she was a child.

CHRONOLOGY

NOTE ON THE TEXTS

NOTES

INDEX

Chronology

1917 Jane Stajer Auer is born February 22 in New York City. (Father, Sidney Auer, of German Jewish heritage, born in 1885 in Cincinnati, Ohio, and graduated from the University of Michigan. Mother, Claire Stajer Auer, of Hungarian Jewish heritage, was born in 1891 in New York City. Both parents are non-practicing. In 1912 when parents met, father was a resident of New York City and owned the Geisha Blouse Company and mother worked as a teacher. They married in August 1913.) At the time of Jane's birth, the Auers reside with Claire's mother, Mary Stajer, on West 88th Street in Manhattan. An only child, Jane is privately tutored by a French governess and then attends Madame Tisnee's, a French school in Manhattan.

1927–29 Father, now an insurance agent with an office in Manhattan, insists on leaving the city (mother had wanted to remain in Manhattan close to her mother and five sisters and to the fashionable Madame Tisnee's). Family moves to Woodmere, Long Island, where they rent a small house on 141 Elm Street. In Woodmere, attends public school, where she befriends Miriam Fligelman (later Levy). They will become lifelong friends. In 1929, writes in Miriam's autograph album:

> You asked me to write in your book
> I scarcely know how to begin
> For there's nothing original about me
> But a little original sin.

The question of sin becomes an important preoccupation in her fiction as well as in her life.

1930 July 2, father dies of a heart attack in his living room. Jane, away at summer camp at the time, is immediately sent home. Returns with mother to Manhattan, taking up residence in the Croydon Hotel at 12 East 86th Street, where one of mother's sisters lives with her family.

1931 After one semester at Julia Richman High School on East 67th Street, sent to Stoneleigh, an exclusive girls' school in Greenfield, Massachusetts. Before the end of the school year, falls from a horse and breaks her right leg. The leg is set but does not heal, and after a number of operations she develops tuberculosis of the bone.

1932 Mother takes her to a sanitarium in Leysin, Switzerland, for treatment. Spends much of the next two years in traction. In the sanitarium she is tutored by a Frenchman she greatly admires, though later she will say that he was "well versed in Greek mythology and venereal diseases." With him she studies Gide, Proust, Celine, Montherlant, and Louise de Vilmorin. Develops a series of phobias, including fears of mountains and elevators. While she is at Leysin, mother resides in Paris.

1934 Cured of tuberculosis but left with pain in her leg, returns to the U.S. with mother on the liner *Champlain.* On the boat reads Celine's *Voyage au Bout de la Nuit*, and is approached by another passenger, who turns out to be Celine himself. Believes this to be a sign. Upon their arrival in New York, tells her mother, "I am a writer and I want to write." To be near mother's relatives they move to the Hotel Meurice on West 58th Street. An unsuccessful operation is performed on Jane's leg, and a decision is made to stiffen the leg at the knee joint. Begins writing a novel in French, *Le Phaeton Hypocrite* (The Hypocrite Phaeton). Spends most of her time in Greenwich Village, exploring bars and the artistic and lesbian culture.

1936 Finishes her novel. Written in French in a mock naïve style, it is a burlesque of the Greek myth of Phaeton. All copies of the novel have been lost.

1937 Through the lyricist John Latouche, whom she met in a bar, attends the literary and musical salon at the home of Kirk and Constance Askew, where she meets, among others, Virgil Thomson, Maurice Grosser, Charles Henri Ford, and E. E. Cummings. Thomson later said, "People loved her but what she cared about no one knew." Latouche introduces her to Paul Bowles, telling Paul "there's this fantastic girl I want you to meet." Paul (born December 30, 1910) is a composer and a pupil of Aaron Copland. In late February, meets Paul, Latouche, and Erika Mann (daughter of Thomas) at the Plaza; they go to an apartment in Harlem where they sit on the floor, smoking marijuana. Barely responds when Paul tries to talk to her. Years later, she will write: "He wrote music and was mysterious and sinister. The first time I saw him, I said to a friend, 'He's my enemy.'" A few days later at a gathering in E. E. Cummings's apartment on Patchin Place in the Village, they meet again. Paul has come with Kristians Tonny, a Dutch painter, and Tonny's wife, Marie-Claire. The three of them discuss their plan to go on an extended trip to Mexico, and Jane announces that she will go with them. In mid-March boards a Greyhound bus with Paul and the Tonnys for New Orleans. On the bus sits with Paul; they talk constantly. Later, will tell Paul that it was on the bus that she fell in love with him. After several stops in the U.S. they cross the border. Is frightened of the older Mexican bus and the mountains and precipices; spends the rest of the journey refusing to leave the back of the bus with the native women. The night they arrive in Mexico City, hires a porter and leaves her three companions, who search for a cheap hotel. Lands in an expensive hotel where she becomes seriously ill with dysentery. After three days Paul and the Tonnys find her and arrange to meet her the next day, but she leaves Mexico City without a word the following morning. Travels to Arizona and California, where she has an affair with Genevieve Phillips, a woman she has been pursuing. In August, mother rents a house in Deal, New Jersey, and plans a weekend party. Although Jane has not spoken to Paul since leaving Mexico, she calls him and asks him to the party, mentioning that Virgil Thomson will be present. After that, sees Paul frequently, and, as Paul will put it, they "spin fantasies about getting married." Jane will receive a small inheritance when she marries and they plan to use that money to travel. Tells Paul she does not believe in having sex before marriage. They both say they believe in sexual freedom in marriage. He has had affairs with men and women, she only with women.

1938 February 21, marries Paul Bowles in a Dutch Reform church in Manhattan. They travel to Panama and Guatemala on their honeymoon. From Central America they travel to Paris, where they meet a number of artists, including the painter Max Ernst and the writer and painter Brion Gysin. Begins to work on the novel that will become *Two Serious Ladies.* Simultaneously, starts going out at night by herself to a lesbian bar. Paul, dismayed at being left alone, tries to persuade her to spend the evenings with him. When she refuses, Paul goes to Cannes. Once there, he asks her to join him. Refuses at first but shortly arrives. After an argument in which she accuses him of being a killjoy, he hits her. They reconcile and then rent a house for the summer in Èze-Village near Cannes. In September Orson Welles asks Paul to do the music for the farce "Too Much Johnson" and they return to the U.S., moving into the Chelsea Hotel. The production is delayed. Low on funds, they rent a cheap room without heat on the corner of Seventh Avenue and Eighteenth Street.

1939 Paul joins the American Communist Party, less out of ideology than "to get back at his parents." Jane also joins but complains that she does not understand a word of the reading material. Spends much of her time at Spivy's, her favorite bar, and with Latouche and Marianne Oswald, a nightclub singer. Early one morning comes home without her shoes. It is the middle of winter and Paul asks her where she has been. She says she has been wandering around the docks by herself. When he asks her why, she says, "Because that was the one place I didn't want to be. I'm terrified of it." With the money he makes writing the music for William Saroyan's play, *My Heart's in the Highlands*, Paul rents an old farmhouse on Woodrow Road in Staten Island. There he works on his opera "Denmark Vesey." (All copies of the work have been lost.) Jane works sporadically on her writing. On weekends many guests come to stay, including Leonard Bernstein and Judy Tuvim (Judy Holliday). During the week, she feels isolated and is often fearful of noises. Late that summer as the war in Europe is about to begin, Mary Oliver, an eccentric woman who helped Paul years earlier when he arrived in Paris penniless, comes to stay and becomes Jane's friend and drinking companion. Paul later writes that "the quantity of alcohol consumed at the farmhouse increased by the week." Unable to work, Paul leaves and moves to a room in Brooklyn Heights. He asks Jane to join him but she stays on with Mary Oliver.

1940 In March, moves with Paul into the Chelsea Hotel while he works on the score for Saroyan's play *Love's Old Sweet Song*. One night Paul comes back late to the Chelsea to find Jane hosting a loud party with much drinking. He tells her he has to work and she must get the guests to go home. She refuses. Once again he hits her. After that, she ends their sexual relationship. In late spring Paul agrees to do the score for a Department of Agriculture film. He proposes that they go to Albuquerque and Santa Fe for his research and then cross the border to Mexico. Uneasy about being alone with Paul, whom she calls "Gloom-pot," invites a drinking pal along, the writer Robert "Boo" Faulkner. In Mexico they spend the summer in a house in Acapulco, where they meet Tennessee Williams. Unable to write, Jane tires of Acapulco and goes with Tennessee to Taxco, where she rents a house. Paul follows. Begins an affair with a forty-five-year-old American expatriate and divorcee, Helvetia Perkins, an aspiring writer with a twenty-one-year-old daughter. In September, Paul returns to New York to write a theatrical score for the Theater Guild's production of *Twelfth Night*. Asked to stay on for work on another play, Paul asks Jane to join him. Arrives on Christmas Day and rents a separate room in the Chelsea Hotel, where she is joined a few weeks later by Perkins.

1941 Moves with Paul into a house on Middagh Street in Brooklyn, a residence for artists, among them the poet W. H. Auden and Benjamin Britten. Jane gets along well with Auden. Paul does not. In the summer, returns to Taxco with Paul, who has received a Guggenheim grant, and works on *Two Serious Ladies*. Relationship with Helvetia becomes more intense and more serious. In September, suffering from hepatitis, Paul enters a sanatorium in Cuernavaca. Jane brings him the manuscript of her novel. Its original title was *Three Serious Ladies* but Paul edits it, taking out the third serious lady. The excised sections will be published later as "A Guatemalan Idyll" and "A Day in the Open."

1942 In April, leaves Paul in Mexico City and goes with Helvetia to New York. With the help of John Latouche, submits her novel to Ivan van Auw, an agent with Harold Ober Associates. Stays with Helvetia at Holden Hall, an old house in Watkins Glen belonging to Paul's family. Relationship with Helvetia becomes increasingly difficult. One day late that spring Jane slits her wrists. Paul returns to the U.S. with the painter Antonio Álvarez.

1943 On April 19 *Two Serious Ladies* is published by Knopf. The reviews are mostly negative. Many critics find it incomprehensible. Visits Canada with Paul.

1944 Lives with Helvetia in New York and in Helvetia's house in Vermont. Continues to see Paul frequently. He keeps telling Jane that Helvetia is bad for her. Helvetia keeps telling Jane that she should leave Paul. "A Guatemalan Idyll" is published in *Cross Section.* Completes her puppet play "A Quarreling Pair," a dramatization of her quarrels with Helvetia.

1945 Early in the year, rents a house at 28 West Tenth Street in Manhattan with Paul, Helvetia, and Oliver Smith, a distant cousin of Paul's and a theatrical producer. Paul rents the fourth floor while Jane and Helvetia share the second. Smith is a great admirer of Jane's work and gives her money over a period of years to write a play. Starts work on *In the Summer House.* Continues to spend much time at bars and clubs and has many brief affairs with women. "A Day in the Open" is published in *Cross Section.* Influenced by the work he has done editing Jane's novel, Paul writes "The Scorpion," a dark mythical story. It is published in the magazine *View.* He travels to Central America during the summer with Oliver Smith.

1946 In February publishes "Plain Pleasures" in *Harper's Bazaar.* Paul publishes a second story, "A Distant Episode," in *Partisan Review* to great acclaim.

1947 Paul is offered a contract by Doubleday to write a novel. In July, with the money from the advance, he leaves for Morocco, a country he visited years earlier on the advice of Gertrude Stein. On the boat he writes "Pages from Cold Point," a story of a sexual relationship between a father and a son, a work that will be lauded by Norman Mailer as "letting in the world of hip." After Paul leaves, Jane moves out of the house on Tenth Street and goes to live in Connecticut at "Treetops," the estate of her friend Libby Holman, a famous torch singer. Writes a series of long letters to Paul about her work and her life and his success that she calls "agonizers." Goes to Vermont to see Helvetia and to New York to meet her mother. Begins an affair with Jody McLean, a middle-aged New England woman who owns a tea shop. Paul asks Jane to come to Morocco. Fearful of the journey, she keeps putting it off. Abandons her new novel. Paul buys a house in the Casbah of Tangier with Oliver Smith.

1948 In January, sails for Morocco with Jody. Finds Tangier to be exotic yet familiar, "as if she had dreamed it before she was born." Maintains extensive correspondence, including with Libby Holman, Natasha von Hoershelman, and Katharine Hamill. Visits Fez with Jody, Paul, and Edwin Denby. Has adverse reaction to *majoun*, a jam made from cannabis that Paul has begun taking, hallucinating and experiencing severe paranoia. Finishes story "Camp Cataract" in May at the Belvedere Hotel in Fez. Paul finishes his novel *The Sheltering Sky* in May. On reading it, is disturbed because Kit, the main female character, who bears some resemblance to Jane, ends up mad. Accuses Paul of predicting her doom. He denies it, insisting Kit is a fictional character. After Jody returns to the U.S., Paul introduces Jane to Cherifa, a young woman (born c. 1928) who has a stall in the grain market. Jane becomes obsessed with Cherifa. In July, Paul returns to New York to write the score for Tennessee Williams's *Summer and Smoke*. Stays in Tangier and continues her pursuit of Cherifa and Tetum, another Moroccan woman. *Harper's Bazaar* accepts "Camp Cataract." Paul returns to Tangier in December with Tennessee Williams, who expresses admiration for *In the Summer House*.

1949 Travels with Paul to the Sahara, where she writes "A Stick of Green Candy." It is the last story she will complete. *The Sheltering Sky* is published and becomes a best seller. In October, travels with Paul to England and then to Paris. Meets Alice B. Toklas. "Camp Cataract" is published in *Harper's Bazaar*. Paul leaves for Ceylon (now Sri Lanka) and begins his new novel, *Let It Come Down*. Stays in Paris for the winter with Jody. The relationship falls apart and Jody leaves. Begins to write a new novel, "Out in the World," and works on *In the Summer House*.

1950–51 Goes to New York, hoping for a production of her play, but it does not happen. Writes "East Side: North Africa," a nonfiction piece about her visits to the Moroccan women. It is published in *Mademoiselle* in April 1951. Paul's book of stories, *The Delicate Prey*, is published. In late June returns with Paul to Tangier. Paul has become deeply involved with Ahmed Yacoubi, a young Moroccan painter, whose career Paul encourages. Paul buys a new Jaguar convertible and hires Mohammed Temsamany as chauffeur. Continues to struggle with her work on the novel and her play, as well as jealousy of Yacoubi. *In the Summer House* is produced at the Hedgerow Theatre in Moylan, Pennsylvania, in August 1951. Paul leaves for India with Yacoubi in December.

1952 In January, returns to New York to try to arrange a New York production of *In the Summer House*. Stays with Libby Holman and with Oliver Smith. Paul's novel *Let It Come Down* is published in February. He buys the island of Taprobane off the coast of Ceylon.

1953 In March, Paul comes to New York with Yacoubi to write the music for *In the Summer House*. In May the play is performed at the University of Michigan in Ann Arbor. Rewrites the last act of the play under pressure from the director and others to make it more palatable to a Broadway audience. Tennessee Williams objects strongly to the changes. In December the play opens at the Playhouse Theater in New York. It is reviewed with some praise but with many reservations. Brooks Atkinson of *The New York Times* writes: "It is going to be difficult today to do full justice to Jane Bowles' *In The Summer House*. Perhaps it is going to be impossible. Scene by scene her play is original, exotic and adventuresome, but very little of it survives the final curtain. From the literary point of view it is distinguished: it introduces us to a perceptive writer who composes drama in a poetic style."

1954 *In the Summer House* closes on February 12 after a six-week run. Quoted in an interview in *Vogue* as saying, "There's no point in writing a play for your five hundred goony friends. You have to reach more people." Returns to Tangier and tries to start a new play. Blocked, persuades Cherifa to live with her part-time. William Burroughs visits Paul and Jane. Yacoubi, now living with Paul in a separate house outside the Casbah, insists Paul not visit Jane, as he fears Cherifa's "magic." Distressed by Yacoubi's influence on Paul and unable to write, suffers from depression. In late fall Paul asks her to go with him and Yacoubi to Taprobane. The island is tiny, only large enough for an octagonal house without doors and a small garden. Jane agrees to go but asks Mohammed Temsamany to accompany her.

1955 On Taprobane, struggles to work on her new play while Paul is writing *The Spider's House*, and drinks heavily. Taking a medication for high blood pressure that she has been warned must not be taken with alcohol, she becomes seriously depressed. In March, returns to Tangier, living again with Cherifa. In June Paul, having finished the novel, returns to Tangier with Yacoubi. Exasperated with Jane for not working, he tells her he won't see her unless she works (he later relents). In November Cherifa tells her that if Jane does not give her money, she will leave her. Offers to give Cherifa the house in the Casbah.

1956 The house is signed over to Cherifa. Travels to New York, Chicago, and L.A., then stays with Libby Holman at Treetops. Receives an advance to write a new play. Returns to Tangier and moves into an apartment next to Paul's. Persuades Cherifa to live with her full-time, ostensibly as a maid, but in reality Cherifa runs the household. The sexual side of their relationship ends. Paul travels to Ceylon with Yacoubi in December.

1957 In February "A Stick of Green Candy" is published in *Vogue*. Struggles to write her new play. Paul continues to publish travel pieces and short stories. Suffers a stroke on the night of April 4. It seriously affects her vision and her speech. Some in the Tangier community suspect Cherifa of having poisoned her, though Jane's drinking and disregard for the effects of her medication are medically deemed sufficient to have caused the stroke. Paul returns from his travels in May. After Jane has a series of epileptiform seizures, Paul takes her to England in August, first to the Radcliffe Infirmary in Oxford and then to St. Mary's Hospital in London. She is advised to learn to "cope" with her disability. Returns with Paul to Tangier, where her psychological state deteriorates. In September, returns to England, accompanied by a friend. She is seen at the Radcliffe Infirmary and is then transferred to Saint Andrew's, a psychiatric hospital in Northampton, where she is given a series of electric shock treatments. Yacoubi is arrested in Tangier for alleged indecent behavior with an adolescent German boy. In November, returns to Tangier. Yacoubi is again arrested and charged with "assault with intent to kill" the German boy. The case against him is later dismissed.

1958 Police interrogate Paul about Yacoubi and begin investigating Jane's relationship with Cherifa. Paul sells Taprobane. Travels with Paul to Funchal, Madeira, in Portugal; Mohammed Temsamany is repeatedly questioned about them. Paul starts to work on a new novel and persuades Jane to return to work on an earlier discarded novel, "Going to Massachusetts." Though her vision has improved somewhat, she says she has lost the ability to see and render her inner world. In April, returns alone to New York, where she stays in Tennessee Williams's apartment with a nurse paid for by friends Katharine Hamill and Natasha von Hoershelman. Katharine later remembered, "She'd have long spells of silence. She was very depressed. She understood what everyone said to her, but she would hardly speak. . . . We were frightened to leave her alone." Her doctor recommends that she see a speech therapist and gives her a series of writing assignments to treat her depression. For one assignment she writes, "I did not suffer a stroke at forty for nothing," suggesting she is still beset by an old preoccupation, an unnamable sin. In October, enters the psychiatric clinic of New York Hospital–Cornell Medical Center in White Plains, where she suffers two seizures, but by November her condition has improved. In December Paul takes her back to Tangier.

1959 Immerses herself in daily domestic life. On doctor's order she is not allowed to be alone and is accompanied everywhere by a Spanish maid.

1960 Jane and Paul move into separate apartments in the same building, the Immeuble Itesa in Tangier.

1961 Receives a grant of $3,000 from the Ingram Merrill Foundation to write a play. Begins play based on "Camp Cataract," but work proceeds only fitfully.

1962 Embarks on an affair with an English writer, Lady Frances (a pseudonym), the daughter of a countess. Frances leaves Tangier for New York in March. In September accompanies Paul to New York, where he will write the music for a new play by Tennessee Williams. Visits her mother briefly in Florida before returning to New York and spending her time with Frances, where she begins to drink. Paul persuades her to return to Tangier alone in November to work on her play.

1963 Begins an affair with the Princess Martha Ruspoli, the wealthy wife of an Italian prince. In March, there is an off-Broadway production in New York of *In the Summer House*. It closes after a short run. Paul works on a new novel, *Up Above the World*. In Jane's notebook, still trying to work on her play, she writes, "This is about people who build up an artificial destiny or life through which nothing can pierce. . . . The play has no ending, no solution."

1965 In January *Two Serious Ladies* is published in England and receives good reviews, but Jane regards the novel as the work of someone she once was but is no longer. In April, travels with Paul to New York. Goes to Florida to see her mother. She and Paul consider buying a house in Santa Fe. Returns with Paul to Tangier, where she begins to consume large quantities of alcohol and take large quantities of medication.

1966 A collection of her stories is published in England as *Plain Pleasures*. It is edited and prepared for publication by Paul, who turns "East Side: North Africa" into the story "Everything Is Nice." Farrar, Straus & Giroux publish *The Collected Works of Jane Bowles*. She regards the work as that of the "Dead Jane Bowles." Travels to New York in June with Paul after the death of both his parents and visits her mother in Florida. Paul leaves for Southeast Asia in July.

1967 Returns to Tangier alone and depression worsens. She is no longer able to eat or sleep. When Paul returns to Tangier in March, he takes Jane on the orders of her doctor to a psychiatric clinic for women in Málaga. Undergoes shock treatment. In August Paul brings Jane back to Tangier. She is afflicted by severe anxiety and depression. In late December, suddenly moves to the Atlas Hotel with Cherifa and spends her time drinking at the Parade Bar and conversing with the patrons. Gives away the money in the bank account she shares with Paul. He brings her back to her apartment. She becomes distraught and unmanageable.

1968 In January, Paul takes Jane back to the clinic in Málaga, where she is given medication and shock treatments. Begs Paul to take her back to Tangier. In June he takes her out of the clinic to stay at a private home in Granada. Her condition worsens. Paul moves her to a new institution, the Clínica de los Ángeles in Málaga. Paul accepts a teaching appointment in California.

1969 In February, in response to Jane's pleas, Paul brings her back to Tangier. Spends the days lying on the floor, predicting her doom; loses weight excessively. After four months Paul takes her back to the Clínica de los Ángeles.

1970 Suffers another stroke in May. Her condition deteriorates further and she loses her vision. Unable to move, barely able to speak, she converts to Catholicism.

1973 Dies on May 4 and is buried in an unmarked grave in a Catholic cemetery in Málaga, the Cementerio de San Miguel. In 1999, through the efforts of a young Spanish woman who is an admirer of Jane's writing, her body is moved to a new gravesite with a monument dedicated by the Málaga City Council.

Note on the Texts

This volume presents a selection from the writings of Jane Bowles (1917–1973). It contains the texts of two books, the novel *Two Serious Ladies* (1943) and the three-act play *In the Summer House* (1954), and, under the rubric "Stories and Other Writings," nine shorter works published from 1944 to 1966. It also contains, under the rubric "Scenes and Fragments," twelve items culled from Jane Bowles's notebooks—eight of them edited by Paul Bowles, the others by Millicent Dillon—and published in books and periodicals from 1970 to 1987. The concluding section prints texts of the 133 letters collected and edited by Millicent Dillon for her book *Out in the World: Selected Letters of Jane Bowles 1935–1970* (1985). An appendix prints the text of "Everything Is Nice," Paul Bowles's revision of Jane Bowles's autobiographical essay "East Side: North Africa" (1951), which was published, as a work of fiction, under Jane's name in 1966.

TWO SERIOUS LADIES

In the fall of 1938, the year in which she had married the composer Paul Bowles, Jane Auer Bowles began to write the novel that, five years later, was published as *Two Serious Ladies.* She was twenty-one, fresh from her honeymoon in Central America and in France, and had settled for the moment with her husband, then employed by the New Deal's Federal Music Program, in an unheated apartment in the Manhattan neighborhood of Chelsea. The writing of the first draft continued over the next three years, in temporary lodgings as various as an apartment in Greenwich Village, a farmhouse on Staten Island, rooms in the Hotel Chelsea, a commune for writers and artists in Brooklyn Heights, and several places in Mexico—in Jalapa, Acapulco, and, for two lengthy periods during 1940 and 1941, Taxco, a small town a hundred miles southwest of Mexico City. The first draft was completed, in Taxco, in November 1941.

This draft of the novel was titled "Three Serious Ladies." In addition to episodes concerning Miss Goering and Mrs. Copperfield, there were several episodes, set in Guatemala, concerning one Señorita Córdoba and other women of her acquaintance. Paul suggested to Jane that the work would be strengthened if she excised the Guatemalan material and sharpened the counterpoint of the two main stories. Jane followed his advice and revised the manuscript in early 1942. By arrangements made by a friend of the Bowleses, the lyricist

John Latouche, the revised manuscript was submitted to publishers by Ivan von Auw Jr., an associate of the Harold Ober literary agency, in New York.

Two Serious Ladies was published, in hardcover, by Alfred A. Knopf, Inc., New York, on April 19, 1943. A British edition, photographically reproduced from the Knopf printing, was published, in hardcover, by Peter Owen Ltd., London, in January 1965. The text of the Knopf printing is used here.

IN THE SUMMER HOUSE

Oliver Smith, a distant cousin of Paul Bowles and, in 1941, one of his and Jane's housemates in Brooklyn Heights, was a scenic designer for the stage and a sometime producer of plays. Deeply impressed with Jane's gifts for mimicry, improvised storytelling, and written dialogue, Smith told her repeatedly that one day he would commission a play from her. In 1943, with part of his earnings as producer of the musical *On the Town*, he gave her the first of several payments toward a script that, ten years later, he produced on Broadway as *In the Summer House*.

Jane began sketching out the play at the farmhouse of her then companion Helvetia Perkins, in East Montpelier, Vermont, shortly after the publication of *Two Serious Ladies*. The writing began in New York in early 1945, when Smith, who had secured the top three floors of a four-story townhouse at 28 West Tenth Street, leased the fourth floor to Paul Bowles and the second to Jane and Helvetia. By the end of 1946 Jane had completed a version of the first act, which she showed to her editorial acquaintance Mary Louise Aswell, the head of the fiction department at *Harper's Bazaar*. It appeared, as "In the Summer House," in *Harper's Bazaar* for April 1947.

The writing of the second and third acts was begun in Vermont and in France (in the company of Helvetia Perkins) and continued in Morocco (sometimes in the company of her husband, other times in rented rooms of her own). The first complete draft was finished in Tangier, in the spring of 1948, and was copyrighted on May 17 of that year as an unpublished work. In the spring of 1949 Tennessee Williams, then visiting Morocco, read and admired the play and recommended it to his dramatic agent, Audrey Wood, of the Liebling-Wood Agency. Jane rewrote the third act throughout the fall of 1949. In January 1950 Oliver Smith, working with Audrey Wood, secured an option to produce the play, and began the search for investors.

In the Summer House was given its world premiere on August 23, 1951, not by Smith but by the Hedgerow Theatre, a repertory company in Moylan, Pennsylvania, founded and led since 1923 by the actor-director Jasper Deeter. (Deeter, a friend of Jane's then companion Libby Holman, was granted non-exclusive rights to perform the play in repertory for two years, from August 1951 through July 1953.) Jane never saw the Deeter production, since she was living in Tangier during the entirety of its run. She returned to the United States in January 1952 in order to collaborate more easily with Oliver Smith on what she considered the "official" New York production. She continued rewriting the play's final act, working at Libby Holman's house in Connecticut or in Smith's house on Tenth Street. Smith produced a trial production at the Lydia Mendelsohn Theater, in Ann Arbor, Michigan, from May 19 to 23, 1953. He then found a coproducer, The Playwrights' Company, and began assembling the cast and crew for the Broadway production, which opened at the Playhouse Theater, on West Forty-eighth Street, in December 1953. Throughout the fall Jane continued to revise the play, responding to the needs of the producer, director, and cast during November rehearsals in New York and then during tryouts in Hartford, Boston, and Washington, D.C. The play, which opened on December 29, 1953, had fifty-five Broadway performances, closing on February 13, 1954.

In 1954, Louis Kronenberger, editor of the annual *Best American Plays* series, chose *In the Summer House* as one of the ten best plays of the 1953–54 season. A condensation of the play (presumably by Kronenberger) appeared in *The Best American Plays 1953–1954*, published by Dodd, Mead & Company, New York, in October 1954.

A book version of the play, *In the Summer House*, was published by Random House, New York, in November 1954. (The book included three publicity photographs of the original Broadway production by Eileen Darby, of Graphic House, Inc., which are not reproduced here.) The first Random House printing is used here.

STORIES AND OTHER WRITINGS

Collected under the rubric "Stories and Other Writings" are nine short works that Jane Bowles completed from 1941 to 1950 and that were published from 1944 to 1966. They are arranged in the order in which they were written. Six of these items were collected in *Plain Pleasures*, a collection of Jane's shorter works compiled by Paul Bowles and published by Peter Owen Ltd., London, in the spring of 1966. The British publisher copyedited the texts, without Jane's involvement, to make them conform to British orthography. The same six items also appeared in *The Collected Works of Jane Bowles*, an omnibus collecting *Two Serious Ladies*, *In the Summer House*, and *Plain Pleasures*, published by Farrar, Straus & Giroux, New York, in December 1966. In contrast to the Peter Owen edition of *Plain Pleasures*, Jane and Paul collaborated with Harold D. "Hal" Vursell, the editor and instigator of *The Collected Works*, on every aspect of this omnibus's publication.

"A Guatemalan Idyll" was written in Taxco, Mexico, circa 1940–41, as an episode of "Three Serious Ladies," the first draft of the novel published in 1943 as *Two Serious Ladies.* When, in early 1944, the editor Edwin Seaver asked Jane to contribute a story to a new literary annual that he was launching later that year, Paul Bowles suggested that she submit this narrative. (He also prepared the text for Seaver and suggested the story's title.) It first appeared in Edwin Seaver, ed., *Cross-Section: A Collection of New American Writing* (New York: L. B. Fischer, 1944), 368–96. It was reprinted in *Plain Pleasures* and *The Collected Works of Jane Bowles.* The text from *The Collected Works of Jane Bowles* is used here.

"A Day in the Open" was written in Taxco, Mexico, in 1940–41 as an episode of "Three Serious Ladies." It first appeared, again at Paul Bowles's instigation and with his editorial involvement, in Edwin Seaver, ed., *Cross-Section 1945: A Collection of New American Writing* (New York: L. B. Fischer, 1945), 52–63. It was reprinted in *Plain Pleasures* and *The Collected Works of Jane Bowles.* The text from *The Collected Works of Jane Bowles* is used here.

The words for the song "Song of an Old Woman" were written in Taxco, Mexico, during the winter of 1941–42. The music, for medium voice and piano, was composed by Paul Bowles, and the song was copyrighted by the songwriters in March 1942. "Song of an Old Woman" was published as sheet music by G. Schirmer, New York, in 1946. The Schirmer sheet music was reprinted, in facsimile, under the title "Farther from the Heart," in *Selected Songs,* by Paul Bowles (Santa Fe, NM: Soundings Press, 1984), the source of the text used here.

The words for the song "Two Skies" were written in Taxco, Mexico, during the winter of 1941–42. The music, for medium voice and piano, was composed by Paul Bowles, and the song was copyrighted by the songwriters in March 1942. According to Jeffrey Miller, in his book *Paul Bowles: A Descriptive Bibliography* (Santa Barbara, CA: Black Sparrow Press, 1986), sheet music of the song was privately printed in 1942 by Hargill Music Press, New York, but no copies of this printing are known to be extant. A copy of the song in the autograph of Paul Bowles is in the Jane Bowles Papers at the Harry Ransom Center, University of Texas, Austin. The lyrics as they appear in the Ransom manuscript were printed by Stacey D'Erasmo in "The Exiled Heart," a biographical article on Jane Bowles published in *Out* 7.11 (May 1999), 70–73, 118, 120. The text from *Out* is used here.

"A Quarreling Pair" was written in New York in 1944–45. It was commissioned by Charles Henri Ford, the publisher-editor of the arts quarterly *View*, as the second of two plays to be performed at a *View*-sponsored evening of puppet theater at Spivy's Roof, a nightclub at 139 East Fifty-seventh Street, New York, in early June 1945.

(The other play on the bill, "A Sentimental Playlet," was written by Ford and, like "A Quarreling Pair," featured incidental music by Paul Bowles.) The play first appeared, as "A Quarrelling Pair," in *Plain Pleasures*, 161–68. It also appeared, in a text slightly revised by Jane and Paul, in *The Collected Works of Jane Bowles*. (The stage directions were made more concise, and the name of the stronger puppet was changed from Mildred to Harriet.) Just before the omnibus's publication, the revised version was printed, as "A Quarreling Pair: A Puppet Play," in *Mademoiselle* 62 (December 1966), 114–16. The text from *The Collected Works of Jane Bowles* is used here.

The text of "A Quarreling Pair" incorporates the words for two songs written in New York in 1944–45. The music, for voice and piano, was composed by Paul Bowles, and both songs were copyrighted by the songwriters in the spring of 1945. The first song, "Bluebell Mountain," was published, as "My Sister's Hand in Mine," in *Selected Songs*, by Paul Bowles. The second song, "The Frozen Horse," remains unpublished.

"Plain Pleasures" was written in New York in 1945. It first appeared in *Harper's Bazaar* 80 (February 1946), 151, 212, 214, 216, 218–20, 222, 224, 226, 232. It was reprinted in *Plain Pleasures* and *The Collected Works of Jane Bowles*. The text from *The Collected Works of Jane Bowles* is used here.

"Camp Cataract" was begun in New York in 1943 and completed in Fez, Morocco, in 1948. It first appeared in *Harper's Bazaar* 83 (September 1949), 156, 231–39, 243, 245. It was reprinted in *Plain Pleasures* and *The Collected Works of Jane Bowles*. The text from *The Collected Works of Jane Bowles* is used here.

"A Stick of Green Candy" was written in Taghit, Algeria, in 1949. It first appeared in *Vogue* 129 (February 15, 1957), 64–65, 121, 123, 125–26. It was reprinted in *Plain Pleasures* and *The Collected Works of Jane Bowles*. The text from *The Collected Works of Jane Bowles* is used here.

"East Side: North Africa" was written in Tangier in 1950. It first appeared in *Mademoiselle* 32 (April 1951), 134, 159–64. The text from *Mademoiselle* is used here.

SCENES AND FRAGMENTS

Collected under the rubric "Scenes and Fragments" are twelve extended passages of fiction and drama culled from Jane Bowles's notebooks. These fragments, none of them dated by the author but all of them written in the 1940s and 1950s, were published in books and periodicals from 1970 to 1987. Eight of them were prepared for publication by Paul Bowles, Jane's literary executor and the custodian of her notebooks, after she was incapacitated by her final stroke. The rest ("Señorita Córdoba," "Looking for Lane," "Laura and Sally," and "The Children's Party") were prepared by her biographer Millicent

Dillon, with Paul Bowles's approval. The fragments are arranged here in their likely order of composition.

"Señorita Córdoba" was written in Taxco, Mexico, circa 1940–41, as an episode of "Three Serious Ladies," the first draft of the novel published in 1943 as *Two Serious Ladies.* It first appeared in *The Threepenny Review* 21 (Spring 1985), 18–21, the source of the text used here.

"Looking for Lane" was written in the late 1940s. It first appeared in *The Threepenny Review* 16 (Winter 1984), 24–29, the source of the text used here.

"Laura and Sally" was written in the late 1940s. It first appeared in *The Threepenny Review* 31 (Autumn 1987), 24–29, the source of the text used here.

"Going to Massachusetts," written in the early 1950s, is a fragment from an uncompleted novel of the same title. It first appeared, as "The Courtship of Janet Murphy," in *Antaeus* 5 (Spring 1972), 7–16. It was reprinted, under the present title, in *Feminine Wiles,* by Jane Bowles, a posthumous miscellany edited by Paul Bowles and published, in simultaneous hardcover and trade paperback editions, by Black Sparrow Press, Santa Barbara, California, in April 1976. The text from *Antaeus* is used here, under the title given the fragment in *Feminine Wiles.*

"The Children's Party," written in the early 1950s, is a fragment from the uncompleted novel "Out in the World." It first appeared, as an untitled excerpt from "Out in the World," in Dillon's book *Out in the World: Selected Letters of Jane Bowles 1935–1970* (Santa Barbara, CA: Black Sparrow Press, 1986), 307–9. Dillon gave it the title "The Children's Party" when she reprinted it in *The Portable Paul and Jane Bowles* (New York: Penguin Books, 1994). The text from *Out in the World* is used here, under the title given the fragment in *The Portable Paul and Jane Bowles.*

"Andrew," written in the early 1950s, is a fragment from the uncompleted novel "Out in the World." It first appeared in *Antaeus* 1 (Summer 1970), 38–42. It was reprinted in *Feminine Wiles.* The text from *Antaeus* is used here.

"Emmy Moore's Journal," written in the early 1950s, comprises two fragments from the uncompleted novel "Out in the World." The first fragment (which ends, on page 430 of the present volume, with the words "My husband likes it too") appeared in *Antaeus* 1 (Summer 1970), 34–37. "Emmy Moore's Journal" was reprinted, together with the second fragment (beginning after the section break on page 430), in *The Paris Review* 56 (Spring 1973), 12–18. The expanded "Emmy Moore's Journal" was reprinted in *Feminine Wiles.* The text from *The Paris Review* is used here.

"Friday," written in the early 1950s, is a fragment from the uncompleted novel "Out in the World." It first appeared, as the third item under the heading "Three Scenes," in *Antaeus* 27 (Autumn 1977), 43–45. The text from *Antaeus* is used here.

"'Curls and a quiet country face,'" which is perhaps more autobiographical essay than fiction, was written in the early 1950s. It first appeared in *Feminine Wiles*, 35–36, the source of the text used here.

"Lila and Frank" was written in the early 1950s. It first appeared, as the second item under the heading "Three Scenes," in *Antaeus* 27, 40–42. The text from *Antaeus* is used here.

"The Iron Table" was written in the early 1950s. It first appeared, as the first item under the heading "Three Scenes," in *Antaeus* 27, 37–39. The text from *Antaeus* is used here.

"At the Jumping Bean," the opening scene of an unfinished play of that title, was written in Ceylon (Sri Lanka) in 1955. It first appeared in *Feminine Wiles*, 37–47, the source of the text used here.

LETTERS

In the late 1970s, during the course of researching her biography *A Little Original Sin: The Life and Work of Jane Bowles* (New York: Holt, Rinehart & Winston, 1981; London: Virago Books, 1988), Millicent Dillon transcribed and photocopied scores of letters by Jane Bowles, some obtained from their recipients or private owners, others from institutional collections or published sources. Four years after completing her biography, Dillon collected 133 of these letters in *Out in the World: Selected Letters of Jane Bowles 1935–1970*, published, in simultaneous hardcover and trade paperback editions, by Black Sparrow Press in April 1985.

In her introduction, the editor wrote, in part:

> This volume contains 133 letters spanning the years 1935 to 1970. They begin with Jane Bowles's late teenage years in Greenwich Village, her marriage to the writer-composer Paul Bowles, and the writing of *Two Serious Ladies* in Mexico in the early Forties. Subsequent letters detail her decision to go to Morocco (where Paul Bowles had gone in 1947), her arrival in Tangier, and her beginning struggle with her writer's block, coincident with her passion for the Arab women she met. The letters continue from Paris and New York and once again from Tangier, through the onset of her terrible illness—she suffered a severe stroke at age forty—through her battle for recovery, to the words eked out before her final silence in a convent hospital in Málaga in 1973. [. . .]
>
> The sequence of the letters reflects accurately the change in her style of existence: from the early sense of certainty in her powers of wit and charm, to the puzzlement about what happened

to that certainty after her affair with Helvetia Perkins, to her wonderment as to her place and future course as a writer. The letters to Paul after her trip to Taprobane (Sri Lanka) with him and Ahmed Yacoubi divulge her terror and the sense of what is slipping away from her. The letters immediately after the stroke show her trying to discover and reveal what has happened to her.

(In a composition for a speech therapist in New York, not included in this book, she explained that she could not write: "If it is a failure of the will—then my will is sick—it is not lazyness . . . but there is such a thing as a failure of the will which is agony for the person who suffers from it. I did not suffer a stroke for nothing at my age—age—and I have gone far away down the path of no return . . .")

In her letters from Tangier from 1960 on, when she had recovered to a certain extent from her stroke, she tried not to reveal the fears of her own imminent decline. But from 1966 on, when the ultimate decline began, she had little else to speak of. The final letters, written in the convent hospital in Málaga, as she was losing all capacity to see and hear and speak, reveal her effort to write a single word, now the equivalent of what once was the effort to write an entire narrative.

Jane Bowles's letters written *before* her stroke have been corrected for inconsequential and erratic errors of spelling and punctuation. Written at top speed, often by hand, the letters prove what she said to Paul, that she didn't care about spelling or punctuation. The letters written after her stroke are printed here as they were written, since from then on her errors became a source of great concern to her.

It was Jane Bowles's custom never to date a letter, though occasionally she might begin with "Monday" or "the fourth," so the dating of all letters is an estimation based on the context of known events in her life. The exceptions to this uncertainty are the letters from the Holman collection, since the envelopes were retained and the posting date is in most instances legible.

The present volume prints Jane Bowles's letters as they appeared in *Out in the World*, together with Millicent Dillon's interstitial headnotes. The letters, however, are printed with a few alterations to Dillon's original editorial procedure. Bracketed editorial conjectural readings in the source texts, in cases where the original manuscript was damaged or difficult to read, are accepted without brackets in this volume when that reading seems to be the only possible one; but when it does not, or when the editor made no conjecture, the missing word or words are indicated by a bracketed two-em space, i.e.,

[ ]. In cases where the editor supplied in brackets punctuation, characters, numbers, or words that were omitted from the source text by an obvious slip of the pen or typewriter keyboard, this volume removes the brackets and accepts the editorial emendation. Bracketed editorial insertions used to expand abbreviations and contractions or clarify meaning have been deleted in this volume. Bracketed insertions that identify persons mentioned in the texts have been incorporated into the endnotes of this volume, as have the eighty-five footnotes that accompanied the letters in *Out in the World*.

Dillon originally used pseudonyms to preserve the anonymity of six women who had been Jane Bowles's lovers. Two of the women, "Nora" and "Cory," had previously been identified in letters published by Paul Bowles in *Feminine Wiles* as Natika Waterbury and Jody McLean. A third, "Marty," was identified as Marty Mann by a Paul Bowles biographer, Virginia Spencer Carr. Dillon's pseudonyms for these three women have not been preserved in this volume. However, Dillon did not preserve her notes identifying the final three, "Ellie," "Sally," and "Frances," and the women have not been identified elsewhere, therefore Dillon's pseudonyms have been used in this volume.

The following is a list of the letters included in this volume, in the order of their appearance, giving the source of each text as it was noted in *Out in the World*. Indications are made for those letters that included additions by Paul Bowles or were not in Jane Bowles's handwriting. Letters 115–19 and 121, written after Jane Bowles's stroke, were dictated to Carla Grissmann, a teacher at the American School in Tangier. For letters 126–33, written after Bowles received shock treatment in Málaga in April 1967, the transcriptions include not only vagaries of spelling and punctuation but also notations of crossed-out words. The following abbreviations are used to identify documents provided to Dillon by their original recipients or private owners and those that she found in institutional collections:

Baillou	Katherine Cowen de Baillou Papers, Hargrett Rare Book and Manuscript Library, University of Georgia, Athens
Bowles	Courtesy of Paul Bowles
Fainlight	Courtesy of Ruth Fainlight
Ford	Charles Henri Ford Papers, Harry Ransom Center, University of Texas, Austin
Hamill	Courtesy of Katharine Hamill
Hedgerow	Hedgerow Theatre Archives, Howard Gotlieb Archival Research Center, Boston University, Boston, MA
Holman	Courtesy of Jack Clareman and the Estate of Libby Holman

JBowles	Jane Bowles Collection, Harry Ransom Center, University of Texas, Austin
Levy	Courtesy of Miriam F. Levy
PBowles	Paul Bowles Collection, Harry Ransom Center, University of Texas, Austin
Thomson	Virgil Thomson Papers, Irving S. Gilmore Music Library, Yale University, New Haven, CT
VVechten	Carl Van Vechten Papers, Beinecke Rare Books and Manuscript Library, Yale University, New Haven, CT

Most of the documents provided to the editor by Paul Bowles have, since the publication of *Out in the World* in 1985, become part of the Paul Bowles Collection, Harry Ransom Center, University of Texas, Austin. Most of the documents provided to the editor by Jack Clareman and the Estate of Libby Holman are now part of the Libby Holman Collection in the Howard Gotlieb Archival Research Center, Boston University, Boston, MA.

1. To George McMillan, New York City, 1935. *Courtesy of George McMillan.*
2. To Miriam Fligelman Levy, New York City, 1936. *Levy.*
3. To "Spivy" LeVoe, Deal Beach, NJ, January 29, 1937. *Courtesy of the Estate of Bertha "Spivy" LeVoe.*
4. To Miriam Levy, New York City, February 1937. *Levy.*
5. To Miriam Levy, New York City, June 1937. *Levy.*
6. To Virgil Thomson, Asbury Park, NJ, August 31, 1937. *Thomson.*
7. To Virgil Thomson, San Jose, Costa Rica, March 23, 1938. *Thomson.* The first paragraph of this postcard is in the hand of Paul Bowles, the second in the hand of Jane Bowles.
8. To Virgil Thomson, Guatemala, April 21, 1938. Postcard. *Thomson.*
9. To Virgil Thomson, Èze-Village, France, 1938. *Thomson.*
10. To Mary Oliver, Staten Island, Summer 1939. *Baillou.*
11. To Charles Henri Ford, Staten Island, Fall 1939. *Ford.*
12. To Virgil Thomson, Taxco, Mexico, Late December 1941. *Thomson.*
13. To Virgil Thomson, Mexico City, January 1942. *Thomson.*
14. To Virgil Thomson, Taxco, Mexico, Early March 1942. *Thomson.*
15. To Virgil Thomson, Savannah, GA, April 1942. *Thomson.*
16. To Virgil Thomson, New York City, 1946. *Thomson.*
17. To Libby Holman, Florida, March 27, 1947. *Holman.*
18. To Paul Bowles, Stamford, CT, Early August 1947. *PBowles.*
19. To Paul Bowles, Stamford, CT, Late August 1947. *PBowles.*
20. To Paul Bowles, Stamford, CT, September 1947. *PBowles.*
21. To Paul Bowles, Stamford, CT, Late September 1947. *PBowles.*

22. To Paul Bowles, Stamford, CT, October 1947. *PBowles.*
23. To Paul Bowles, East Montpelier, VT, December 1947. *PBowles.*
24. To Libby Holman, Tangier, Morocco, March 24, 1948. *Holman.*
25. To Libby Holman, Tangier, Morocco, May 10, 1948. *Holman.*
26. To Paul Bowles, Tangier, Morocco, July 1948. *PBowles.*
27. To Paul Bowles, Tangier, Morocco, c. July/August 1948. *PBowles.*
28. To Paul Bowles, Tangier, Morocco, c. July/August 1948. *PBowles.*
29. To Natasha von Hoershelman, Tangier, Morocco, August 1948. *Hamill.*
30. To Paul Bowles, Tangier, Morocco, August 1948. *PBowles.*
31. To Katharine Hamill and Natasha von Hoershelman, Tangier, Morocco, August 1948. *Hamill.*
32. To Paul Bowles and Oliver Smith, Tangier, Morocco, September 1948. *PBowles.*
33. To Paul Bowles, Tangier, Morocco, October 1, 1948. *PBowles.*
34. To Libby Holman and Scotty, Tangier, Morocco, October 1948. *Holman.*
35. To Paul Bowles, Tangier, Morocco, October 1948. *Bowles.*
36. To Paul Bowles, Tangier, Morocco, October 1948. *Bowles.*
37. To Paul Bowles and Oliver Smith, Tangier, Morocco, October 1948. *Bowles.*
38. To Paul Bowles, Tangier, Morocco, November 1948. *Bowles.*
39. To Paul Bowles, Tangier, Morocco, November 1948. *Bowles.*
40. To Paul Bowles, Tangier, Morocco, December 1948. *Bowles.*
41. To Libby Holman, Tangier, Morocco, December 1948. *Holman.*
42. To Katharine Hamill and Natasha von Hoershelman, Taghit, Algeria, March 1949. *Hamill.* First appeared in *Feminine Wiles*, 63–64.
43. To Katharine Hamill, Tangier, Morocco, Late Spring 1949. *Hamill.*
44. To Libby Holman, Tangier, Morocco, August 29, 1949. *Holman.*
45. To Katharine Hamill, Tangier, Morocco, Late Summer 1949. *Hamill.*
46. To Libby Holman, North Wales, November 1949. *Holman.*
47. To Libby Holman, Paris, January 11, 1950. *Holman.*
48. To Paul Bowles, Paris, January 17, 1950. First appeared, as the first of three items under the heading "Letters to Paul Bowles," in *Antaeus* 13/14 (Spring/Summer 1974), 111–14. Reprinted in *Feminine Wiles.*
49. To Paul Bowles, Paris, Late January 1950. *PBowles.*
50. To Paul Bowles, Paris, February 13, 1950. *Bowles.*
51. To Paul Bowles, Paris, February 13, 1950. *Bowles.* First appeared, as the first item under the heading "Two Letters to Paul Bowles," in *Antaeus* 36 (Winter 1980), 131–33.

52. To Libby Holman, L'Étape, Pacy-sur-Eure, France, June 17, 1950. *Holman.*
53. To Libby Holman, L'Étape, Pacy-sur-Eure, France, June 26, 1950. *Holman.*
54. To Mike Kahn, New York City, January 1951. *Hedgerow.*
55a. To Carl Van Vechten, New York City, February 8, 1951. Postcard. *VVechten.*
55b. To Carl Van Vechten, New York City, February 12, 1951. Postcard. *VVechten.*
56. To Libby Holman, New York City, February 12, 1951. *Holman.*
57. To Libby Holman, New York City, February 18, 1951. *Holman.*
58. To Natasha von Hoershelman and Katharine Hamill, Tangier, Morocco, June 1954. First appeared in *Feminine Wiles.*
59. To Paul Bowles, Tangier, Morocco, c. April/May 1955. First appeared, as the second of three items under the heading "Letters to Paul Bowles," in *Antaeus* 13/14 (Spring/Summer 1974), 115–19. It was reprinted in *Feminine Wiles.*
60. To Libby Holman, Tangier, Morocco, January 16, 1957. *Holman.*
61. To Paul Bowles, Tangier, Morocco, February 1, 1957. *Bowles.*
62. To Paul Bowles, Tangier, Morocco, February 24, 1957. First appeared, as the last of three items under the heading "Letters to Paul Bowles," in *Antaeus* 13/14 (Spring/Summer 1974), 111–14. It was reprinted in *Feminine Wiles.*
63. To Libby Holman, Tangier, Morocco, April 10, 1957. *Holman.*
64. To Paul Bowles, Tangier, Morocco, Mid-April 1957. First appeared, as the second item under the heading "Two Letters to Paul Bowles," in *Antaeus* 36 (Winter 1980), 133–35.
65. To Libby Holman, Tangier, Morocco, Summer 1957. *Holman.* The opening part of this letter was typed by Jane Bowles. The part set as an extract (641.37–642.25) was written and typed by Paul. The closing is in the hand of Jane Bowles.
66. To Libby Holman, Tangier, Morocco, Summer 1957. *Holman.*
67. To Libby Holman, Tangier, Morocco, Summer 1957. *Holman.*
68. To Libby Holman, Aboard the *S.S. Orion*, November 1957. *Holman.*
69. To Paul Bowles, New York City, Early May 1958. *Bowles.*
70. To Paul Bowles, New York City, Late May/Early June 1958. *PBowles.*
71. To Libby Holman, Tangier, Morocco, 1960. First appeared in *Feminine Wiles.* A footnote to this letter in *Out in the World* reads: "This letter, written after Jane's stroke, is taken from published material, not from the original, and therefore does not show Jane's spelling errors or idiosyncratic punctuation."
72. Libby Holman, Tangier, Morocco, November 15, 1960. *Holman.*

73. To Libby Holman, Tangier, Morocco, April 16, 1961. *Holman.*
74. To Lilla Von Saher, Tangier, Morocco, 1961. *JBowles.*
75. To Libby Holman, Tangier, Morocco, April 26, 1962. *Holman.*
76. To Libby Holman, Tangier, Morocco, August 1962. *Holman.*
77. To Libby Holman, Tangier, Morocco, August 13, 1962. *Holman.*
78. To Libby Holman, Tangier, Morocco, c. November/December 1962. *Holman.*
79. To Rena Bowles, Tangier, Morocco, c. December 1962. *JBowles.*
80. To Ruth Fainlight, Tangier, Morocco, c. March/April 1963. *Fainlight.*
81. To Ruth Fainlight, Tangier, Morocco, c. May 1963. *Fainlight.*
82. To Libby Holman, Tangier, Morocco, May 27, 1963. *Holman.*
83. To Ruth Fainlight, Tangier, Morocco, Summer 1963. *Fainlight.*
84. To Libby Holman, Tangier, Morocco, Summer 1963. *Holman.*
85. To Isabelle Gerofi, Tangier, Morocco, September 1963. *Courtesy of Isabelle Gerofi.*
86. To Libby Holman, Arcila, Morocco, October 4, 1963. *Holman.*
87. To Audrey Wood, Tangier, Morocco, March 1964. *JBowles.*
88. To Libby Holman, Tangier, Morocco, Spring 1964. *Holman.*
89. To Libby Holman, Tangier, Morocco, June 18, 1964. *Holman.*
90. To Libby Holman, Tangier, Morocco, June 23, 1964. *Holman.*
91. To Libby Holman, Tangier, Morocco, June 30, 1964. *Holman.*
92. To Libby Holman, Tangier, Morocco, August 8, 1964. *Holman.*
93. To Ruth Fainlight, Tangier, Morocco, September 1964. *Fainlight.*
94. To Libby Holman, Tangier, Morocco, November 26, 1964. *Holman.*
95. To Libby Holman, Tangier, Morocco, Late January/Early February 1965. *Holman.*
96. To Lawrence Stewart, Tangier, Morocco, February 1965. *Courtesy of Lawrence Stewart.* A footnote to this letter in *Out in the World* reads: "This letter was not typed by Jane."
97. To Libby Holman, Tangier, Morocco, February 1965. *Holman.*
98. To Libby Holman, Tangier, Morocco, February 1965. *Holman.*
99. To Frances, New York City, Early April 1965. *Courtesy of "Frances."*
100. To Frances, Florida, c. May 1965. *Courtesy of "Frances."*
101. To Libby Holman, Florida, May 3, 1965. *Holman.*
102. To Libby Holman, New York City, May 14, 1965. *Holman.*
103. To Cherifa, New York City, May 20, 1965. *Bowles.* Paul Bowles provided the English translation.
104. To Libby Holman, Tangier, Morocco, August 26, 1965. *Holman.*
105. To Libby Holman, Tangier, Morocco, December 1965. *Holman.*
106. To Libby Holman and Louis Schanker, Tangier, Morocco, December 1965. *Holman.*

107. To Libby Holman, Tangier, Morocco, April 1, 1966. *Holman.*
108. To Libby Holman, Tangier, Morocco, May 10, 1966. *Holman.*
109. To Hal Vursell, Miami, FL, c. July/August 1966. *Bowles.*
110. To Gordon Sager, Miami, FL, c. July/August 1966. *Courtesy of Gordon Sager.*
111. To Libby Holman, Miami, FL, August 1966. *Holman.*
112. To Paul Bowles, Miami, FL, August 9, 1966. *PBowles.*
113. To Gordon Sager, Miami, FL, August 1966. *Courtesy of Gordon Sager.*
114. To Paul Bowles, Tangier, Morocco, September 1966. *PBowles.*
115. To Paul Bowles, Tangier, Morocco, September 28, 1966. *Bowles.*
116. To Hal Vursell, Tangier, Morocco, September 28, 1966. *Bowles.*
117. To Paul Bowles, Tangier, Morocco, c. September/October? 1966. *Bowles.*
118. To Claire Fuhs, Tangier, Morocco, September 30, 1966. *Bowles.*
119. To Paul Bowles, Tangier, Morocco, October 11, 1966. *Bowles.*
120. To Libby Holman, Tangier, Morocco, October 1966. *Holman.*
121. To Carson McCullers, Tangier, Morocco, October 31, 1966. *Bowles.*
122. To Libby Holman, Tangier, Morocco, 1966. *Holman.*
123. To Frances, Tangier, Morocco, November 1966. *Courtesy of "Frances."*
124. To Paul Bowles, Tangier, Morocco, December 1966. *Bowles.*
125. To Libby Holman, Tangier, Morocco, February 1967. *Holman.*
126. To Libby Holman, Málaga, Spain, 1967. *Holman.*
127. To Paul Bowles, Tangier, Morocco, January 11, 1968. *Bowles.* A headnote to this letter in *Out in the World* notes that, except for the second line of the postscript, it was written in the hand of Alfred Chester.
128. To Paul Bowles, Málaga, Spain, Spring 1968. *Bowles.*
129. To Paul Bowles, Málaga, Spain, Spring 1968. *Bowles.*
130. To Paul Bowles, Málaga, Spain, Spring 1968. *Bowles.*
131. To Paul Bowles, Málaga, Spain, c. 1968/1969. *Bowles.*
132. To Paul Bowles, Málaga, Spain, c. 1968/1969. *Bowles.*
133. To Paul Bowles, Málaga, Spain, c. 1970. *Bowles.*

APPENDIX

In 1965, shortly after he had successfully issued the first U.K. edition of *Two Serious Ladies*, the London publisher Peter Owen offered Paul and Jane Bowles the opportunity to bring out a collection of Jane's shorter fiction. Paul Bowles, who had kept a file of his wife's tearsheets and completed manuscripts, prepared a preliminary table of contents: "Plain Pleasures," "A Guatemalan Idyll," "Camp Cataract," "A Day in the Open," "A Quarreling Pair," and "A Stick of Green Candy." Then, upon rereading Jane's autobiographical essay "East Side: North Africa" (see pages 347–56 of the present volume), he revised the essay slightly, turning what she had written as a first-person memoir into a third-person work of fiction suitable for inclusion in the short-story collection. Jane acquiesced to Paul's organization of the book and to his revision of her essay.

"Everything Is Nice," Paul Bowles's variant version of "East Side: North Africa," first appeared as the second item in *Plain Pleasures*, 25–35. It was reprinted in *The Collected Works of Jane Bowles*. The text from *The Collected Works of Jane Bowles* is used here.

This volume presents the texts of the original printings chosen for inclusion but does not attempt to reproduce nontextual features of their typographical design. The texts are presented without change, except for the correction of typographical errors and the alterations in editorial practices noted above. Spelling, punctuation, and capitalization are often expressive features and are not altered, even when inconsistent or irregular. The following is a list of typographical errors corrected, cited by page and line number: 20.21, its; 23.15, no¶; 53.3, leanout; 63.29, friends. She; 72.1, "Its; 85.28, look; 87.24, Copperfield.; 114.23, penny.The; 126.32, streeet,; 127.28, "But; 148.2, morning.; 153.27, rearing; 154.23, parlour; 158.20, manner,; 169.27, This a; 183.37, *stops*; 185.33, Señora; 187.13, tráigame; 187.31, bread:; 189.19, si; 220.32, Goodbye.; 235.15, *head still*); 242.31, Conseulo,; 243.7, Senora; 245.5, acually; 247.25, Cathedral; 257.5, dauther's; 274.16, roughed; 290.28, nickles; 291.34, doutbful; 335.1, chair,; 345.26, unbelievalbe; 367.34, shame,"; 394.6, thought; 401.25, one; 411.14, her,; 421.30, Fall; 547.12, that; 560.32, nor not.; 562.10, you; 565.8, there; 590.27, should I give; 592.3, doessn't; 596.26, Dil.; 600.2, do so; 600.27, *musn't*; 605.6, responsibilty.; 616.5, Vogue; 619.15, for the playing; 638.13, missed; 705.6, over."; 718.3, arrive.l; 750.27, tattoed.

Notes

In the notes below, the reference numbers denote page and line of this volume (the line count includes headings). No note is given for material included in standard desk-reference books. Biblical quotations are keyed to the King James Version. For references to other studies and further information than is included in the Chronology, see Millicent Dillon, *A Little Original Sin: The Life and Work of Jane Bowles* (New York: Holt Rinehart & Winston, 1981).

TWO SERIOUS LADIES

31.32 Cristobal . . . Colon] Two cities on the north end of the Panama Canal named after Christopher Columbus (Cristóbal Colón in Spanish) founded in the 1850s by American workers of the Panama Railroad Company.

32.26–27 Hotel Washington] Famous Panama hotel built on the site of the Washington House, a residence for employees of the Panama Railroad Company. In 1910 the Washington House began to accept guests, and the same year, President William H. Taft authorized construction of a new hotel on the site. It opened in March 1913, when its first guest was businessman and philanthropist Vincent Astor.

57.1–2 *Over There*] Song composed in 1917 by George M. Cohan (1878–1942) upon the entry of the U.S. into World War I and popular with American soldiers.

62.9 "*Le bonheur*,"] French: Happiness.

64.6–12 "*Who cares if the sky . . . for me.*"] "Who Cares?" composed by George Gershwin with lyrics by Ira Gershwin for the musical *Of Thee I Sing* (1931).

71.16 Man O'War] Thoroughbred racehorse who won 20 of 21 races during his two-year career, including the 1920 Preakness and Belmont Stakes.

79.36–37 "*Te necesitan afuera*,"] Spanish: You're needed outside.

90.30 guacamayos] Spanish: Macaws.

94.23 "*Qué calor*!"] How hot it is!

94.31 *Qué barbaridad*!] How awful!

169.1 *tout de suite*] French: Right now.

IN THE SUMMER HOUSE

175.1 IN THE SUMMER HOUSE] *In the Summer House* was first performed at the Hedgerow Theatre in Moylan, Pennsylvania, directed by Jasper Deeter and Catherine Reiser, opening on August 23, 1951, and thereafter running in repertory. Oliver Smith, who had commissioned the play, then planned a second production of the play in New York. A trial production ran May 19–23, 1953, at the Lydia Mendelssohn Theater of the University of Michigan at Ann Arbor with a revised third act. It was directed by John Stix with Miriam Hopkins as Gertrude Eastman Cuevas, Mildred Dunnock as Mrs. Constable, and Anne Jackson as Vivian Constable. Tennessee Williams attended the opening, writing, "It is one of those very rare plays which are not tested by the theatre but by which the theatre is tested." Other reviews were generally poor.

For the Broadway premiere, Miriam Hopkins was replaced with Judith Anderson. Tryouts played in Hartford on November 26, 1953; in Boston on the 29th, where John Stix left and was replaced by José Quintero; and in Washington on December 14. Both in Boston and in Washington, Jane worked with Quintero and Judith Anderson on further revisions to the third act. It opened on Broadway at the Playhouse Theatre with new music by Paul Bowles on December 29, 1953, to favorable reviews, and closed after fifty-five performances on February 13, 1954. The Broadway production, produced by Oliver Smith and the Playwrights' Company, featured as cast:

Judith Anderson	Gertrude Eastman Cuevas
Mildred Dunnock	Mrs. Constable
Logan Ramsey	Lionel
Elizabeth Ross	Molly
Muriel Berkson	Vivian Constable
Paul Bertelsen	Figure Bearer
Miriam Colon	Frederica
Marjorie Eaton	Alta Gracia
Phoebe Mackay	Quintina
Don Mayo	Mr. Solares
Daniel Morales	Chauffeur
Isabel Morel	Esperanza
Marita Reid	Mrs. Lopez
George Spelvin	Another Figure Bearer
Jean Stapleton	Inez

176.2 *OLIVER SMITH*] Oliver Smith (1918–1994), a Broadway set designer, one of the founders of American Ballet Theater, and Paul's second cousin. Starting in 1945, Smith had given Jane money in order to write a play.

184.37–38 Acaba de decirte . . . oyes?] Spanish: She just said she's staying up there. Can't you hear?

185.33–34 Que me dejes . . . por favor.] Let me speak to Mrs. Eastman Cuevas please.

186.37–38 Fula! Esta . . . *Eastman Cuevas*!] Fula! This is the last time you're coming out with me. Now let me speak with Mrs. Eastman Cuevas.

187.13 Cállate, y tráigame el arroz con pollo.] Shut up, and bring me the chicken with rice.

188.27–28 Un rey y otros mas . . .] A king and others . . .

189.18 Una maravilla!] A wonder!

192.6 despiértense] Wake up.

193.29–30 A ver si tú y Esperanza nos cantan algo . . .] Why don't you and Esperanza sing us something . . .

193.31–32 Ay, mamá.] Oh, mother.

193.33–34 Esperanza, . . . y Frederica.] Esperanza, why don't you sing us something, you and Frederica.

194.3 Bueno—sí . . .] Very good—yes . . .

204.14–15 Acaba de decir . . . nunca?] She just said no thank you . . . don't you ever listen?

210.11–12 Frederica, ándele, tú también!] Frederica, come on, you too!

210.24 Despiértense!] Wake up!

210.34 Yes, querida. Música!] Yes, dear. Music!

210.40–211.1 Cuando sale . . . cantar.] When Mrs. Eastman Cuevas leaves the house, they'll start to sing.

213.6 *Russian Bank*] A solitaire game for two players.

232.10 ya llegamos . . .] We're here . . .

232.15 Guapa . . . que alegría . . .] Beautiful . . . Inez. Here we are . . . What happiness.

236.8–9 Ay dios . . . Qué pasa? Qué tiene?] Oh my God . . . What's happening? What's wrong with you?

STORIES AND OTHER WRITINGS

242.2 *Gracias a Dios*!] Spanish: Thank God!

258.16–17 Pastores, pastores, . . . también.] Shepherds, shepherds, we are going to Bethlehem / To see Mary and the child too.

259.24 the terrible earthquake] A 1773 earthquake in modern Antigua, Guatemala, known as the Santa Maria earthquake, destroyed much of the city and killed upwards of eleven hundred people, both immediately and as a result of starvation and disease.

259.27 the volcano named Fire.] The Volcán de Fuego, once believed by the locals to be the cause of the earthquakes.

260.15 *"Mi amante! Amante querido!"*] My lover! My darling lover!

272.9–10 *Good Night, Sweetheart*] "Goodnight, Sweetheart," popular 1931 song by British songwriters Ray Noble (1903–1978), Jimmy Campbell (1903–1967), and Reg Connelly (1895–1963). Its recording by bandleader Guy Lombardo (1902–1977) and his brother vocalist Carmen Lombardo (1903–1971) spent several weeks at the top of the U.S. charts.

272.28 *guaro*] A liquor distilled from sugarcane juices.

275.23 *Madame Butterfly*] Opera (1904) by Italian composer Giacomo Puccini (1848–1924).

350.32 Fatima's hand] Also called a Hamsa; believed to protect against the evil eye. Fatimah was the youngest daughter of the Islamic Prophet Muhammad.

SCENES AND FRAGMENTS

396.15 the Old Man and the Old Woman] New Hampshire rock faces.

LETTERS

453.17 *George McMillan*] Doorman, cashier, and bouncer for a club in the West Village, originally from Knoxville, Tennessee.

454.29 Pres. Holt] Hamilton Holt (1872–1951), president of Rollins College, in Winter Park, Florida, from 1925 to 1949.

455.1 Lupe] Lupe Levy, the daughter of an investment broker who lived in a penthouse apartment at the Hotel Carlyle.

455.10 *Miriam Fligelman Levy*] Human rights and peace activist (1916–1993) as well as coauthor of *Adam's World: San Francisco*, a children's book.

456.16 Miss Foulke] Jean Kane Foulke du Pont (1891–1985), suffragette, activist, and philanthropist, and Jane's former English teacher.

456.32 *"Spivy" LeVoe*] Bertha LeVoe (1906–1971), lesbian nightclub singer who entertained nightly as Madame Spivy in her nightclub, Spivy's Roof, located at 139 East 57th Street, from 1940 to 1951.

457.14 Morro Castle ghosts] The SS *Morro Castle* caught fire on September 8, 1934, killing 137 passengers and crew before it was beached near Asbury Park, New Jersey.

457.28 La Touche] John Latouche (1914–1956), who later wrote the lyrics for *Cabin in the Sky*, *Beggar's Holiday*, and *The Golden Apple*, as well as a number of other Broadway productions.

459.31 *Virgil Thomson*] Pulitzer Prize–winning composer and music critic (1896–1989) who collaborated with Gertrude Stein on two operas.

459.34–460.1 Il n'y a pas . . . ta musique.] French: There is no pen in my big house. I want to thank you a million times for inviting me to your preview. We love your music so much.

460.2–3 Il faisait chaud— . . . debout] It was hot—we had no money—the suitcase was heavy—Paul was asleep on his feet.

460.8 Maggie] Marian Chase Dunham (1915–1951), wife of film journalist Harry Dunham, a friend of Paul's.

460.10–11 c'est de la merde— . . . six heures.] This is crap—constant. I work every day five or six hours.

460.20 what Pavlik used to do to Gertrude] Russian surrealist painter Pavel Tchelitchew (1898–1957). According to Paul Bowles: "Gertrude Stein told me that Pavel Tchelitchew used to tell her, 'J'ai rêvé à vous cette nuit.' She thought it absurd."

460.21 J'ai rêvé à vous cette nuit.] I dreamed about you last night.

460.33 camelote] French: Junk.

461.15–16 C'est même pas bon . . . un peu.] It's not even good, for passing the time. Even a little.

461.17–20 J'aime ma maison . . . autour, ici.] I like my house and I'm learning to make cakes and puddings. I'm also from time to time searching for an idea. I assure you that there isn't a single one flying around, here.

461.31 *Mary Oliver*] Mary Crouch Oliver (c. 1907–?), a childhood friend of Paul's who had helped him in Paris in 1929. She had married department store heir Jock Oliver in 1929.

462.21 Harry Dunham] Film editor Harry Dunham (c. 1910–1943), a friend of Paul's who worked on several films for which Paul wrote music. He became involved in the Nazi youth movement and later joined the Communist Party.

463.17 Elsie Houston] Brazilian singer (1902–1943).

463.27 *Charles Henri Ford*] Charles Henri Ford (1908–2002), poet, artist, and filmmaker. In 1933 Paul had shared his house in Tangier with Ford and Djuna Barnes, and in the early 1940s Ford collaborated with Paul on the never-completed opera *Denmark Vesey*.

463.29 Pavlick] Pavel Tchelitchew, Ford's partner; see note 460.20.

464.9 Dilkousha] Princess Dilkusha de Rohan (1899–1961), born Alis Dilkusha Wrench, British couturiere who was the widow of Prince Carlos de Rohan (1895–1931).

464.9 Katousha] Dilkusha's partner, the Russian ballerina and later choreographer Catherine Devillier (d. c. 1959), born Ekaterina Deviliere, who had been prima ballerina of the Bolshoi Ballet during the Russian Revolution.

464.12 Juanita Hall] Juanita Long Hall (1901–1968), actor and singer with a background in choir directing who became the first African American to win a Tony Award for her role as Bloody Mary in *South Pacific* in 1950.

464.20–21 Parker Tyler] Parker Tyler (1904–1974), author and film critic who coauthored an experimental novel with Ford in 1933, *The Young and Evil.*

464.36 Mr. Saroyan] William Saroyan (1908–1981), American author and playwright who had refused the Pulitzer Prize in 1940 for his play *The Time of Your Life* because it was "no more great or good" than anything else he had written.

465.15–16 *The State of Music*] Thomson's 1939 book on the challenges confronting American composers.

465.18 "Mimi"?] Mimi Wallner (1920–2007), Thomson's copyist and secretary from 1940 to about 1945.

465.24 Maurice] Maurice Grosser (c. 1903–1986), American writer and painter and partner of Thomson's who produced several portraits of Jane. He wrote the scenario for both of Thomson's opera collaborations with Gertrude Stein, *Four Saints in Three Acts* (1934) and *The Mother of Us All* (1947).

466.18 Antonio] Antonio Álvarez, Mexican painter Paul and Jane had met in Taxco, Mexico, in late 1941.

467.8 I wrote two little . . .] Two songs, "Farther From the Heart" and "Song of the Old Woman," which Paul set to music.

468.11 Paul's off the paper] The *New York Herald Tribune,* for which Paul had been doing music reviews.

468.23 *Libby Holman*] Singer and actress (1904–1971) who gained notoriety in 1932 when she was charged with the murder of her husband of one year, Zachary Smith Reynolds of the Reynolds Tobacco family. The case was never brought to trial. Paul and Jane were introduced to Holman in 1945 by John Latouche.

468.25 Florence] Florence Codman, a writer and the publisher of Arrow Editions, which published work by Robert Fitzgerald and Ezra Pound, among others.

468.29 ossir] Ossir—a word used frequently in Jane's mother's family, possibly of Hungarian origin. It implies the denial of what's just been said.

468.31 Bubble] Nickname for Paul.

469.31 Topper] Christopher Reynolds, Libby's son (1933–1950).

469.32 Jody's] Jody McLean, Jane's lover.

471.10 "New Heroes" by Simone de Beauvoir] "New Heroes for Old" (1947), in which the French writer and philosopher Beauvoir (1908–1986) defends "metaphysical" novels.

471.37 souris] Tsuris. Yiddish for troubles.

473.22–23 Louisa Carpenter's] Louisa d'Andelot Carpenter (1907–1976), a DuPont heiress who was the first female master of the hounds in the United States and one of the first American women to become a licensed pilot.

473.23 Sister Bankhead's] "Sister" Eugenia Bankhead (1901–1979), sister of actress Tallulah Bankhead.

473.29–30 two *black Pekes*!!] Jane's Pekingese Donald had been killed by a car.

474.7–8 *what* to do about the apartment] Paul's apartment was on the top floor of the house at 28 West 10th Street in Manhattan. Helvetia Perkins and Jane had an apartment on one floor, and Oliver Smith on another.

474.12 Gordon] Gordon Sager (1915–1991), American novelist who met Jane and Paul in Mexico in 1940 and who later lived in Tangier in the mid-1950s. Two characters in his novel *Run, Sheep, Run* (1950) are based on Paul and Jane.

474.18–19 *Sons and Lovers*] *Sons and Lovers*, 1913 novel by English writer D. H. Lawrence (1885–1930).

475.28–29 Pearl Kazin] American journalist and literary critic (1922–2011) who worked as assistant literary editor of *Harper's Bazaar.*

475.29 Bazaar.] *Harper's Bazaar.*

475.31 Roditi] Édouard Roditi (1910–1992), American poet, critic, and translator of André Breton, as well as works from Spanish, German, and Turkish, who was a lifelong friend of Paul's.

475.38 Peggy Bate] Peggy Winsome Glanville-Hicks (1912–1990), Australian-born composer and music critic who wrote as Peggy Bate until her 1949 divorce from Stanley Bate.

476.3 The Fan] A present from Paul.

476.22 Grandma] Libby's mother.

476.28 I.B.'s] Iris Barry (1895–1969), English film critic who helped establish the London Film Society and the film department of the Museum of Modern Art in New York.

477.19 "inquiétant."] French: Disturbing.

477.20 Valéry] French poet and essayist Paul Valéry (1871–1945).

477.40 Aswell] Mary Louise White Aswell (1902–1984), journalist and editor for *Harper's Bazaar.*

478.26 the Cadiz explosion] On August 18, 1947, at a military storage depot in Cádiz, Spain, 1,737 mines, torpedoes, and depth charges accidentally exploded, killing 147 people and injuring 5,000 others.

478.28 Bobby Lewis] Robert Lewis (1909–1997), actor and director who was an original member of the Group Theater in the 1930s and cofounder of the Actors Studio in 1947.

479.4 Puppet] Helvetia Perkins's Pekingese.

479.10 *Sickness unto Death*] Book (1849) by Danish philosopher Søren Kierkegaard about his concept of despair, relating it to the Christian idea of original sin.

479.14 Teresa] Jane's name in a game she played with Paul about a parrot.

480.14 sequel of the Perrin story] Paul had written that he kept "running into the Perrins, mother and son, everywhere in Morocco and Spain."

480.33 Erika] Brand of portable typewriters.

481.19 D'abord] French: First.

484.3 Jean Stafford] Jean Stafford (1916–1979), American short story writer and novelist who won the Pulitzer Prize for Fiction in 1970.

484.19 my little *Cross-Section* stories] "A Guatemalan Idyll" and "A Day in the Open."

484.27 Arthur Weinstein] Arthur Gage, American Hollywood and theater manager and cousin of the artist Mark Rothko.

485.1 your "little novel"] *The Sheltering Sky.*

485.27 Dione] Dione Lewis, a friend Jane met in New York City in the 1930s.

487.21 tuyaux] French: Tips.

487.23 quién sabe] Spanish: Who knows.

488.3 Cannon Towel factory] Made by the Cannon Mills Company, founded in North Carolina in 1888. It continued to produce "Cannon," "Fieldcrest," and "Royal Velvet" towels until the company declared bankruptcy in 2003.

488.24 Gian-Carlo] Gian Carlo Menotti (1911–2007), Italian-born American composer and librettist whom Paul met in New York in the 1940s; his operas include *Amelia Goes to the Ball* (1935), *The Consul* (1950), and *The Saint of Bleecker Street* (1955).

488.25 Nick Ray] Nicholas Ray (1911–1979), American film director best known for *Rebel Without a Cause* (1955).

488.39 Nessler] Harry Nessler, the owner of the house at 28 West 10th Street.

491.15 George] George Davis (1906–1957), American novelist and editor at *Harper's Bazaar* and *Mademoiselle* of such writers as Truman Capote, Ray Bradbury, and W. H. Auden.

492.5 Viola Rubber] Violla Rubber (1907–1981), British-born theatrical producer and casting agent nominated for a Tony Award as associate producer of *The Night of the Iguana* in 1962.

492.6 Echols and Gould] Theatrical producers Randolph Echols and Will Gould.

492.6 *Folle*] French dramatist Jean Giraudoux's 1943 play *The Madwoman of Chaillot* (*La Folle de Chaillot*).

492.16–17 still looking for the perfect adaptation] Paul had previously been commissioned by Echols and Gould to do a translation of *La Folle de Chaillot*. It was finally produced in December 1948 in an adaptation by playwright Maurice Valency (1903–1996).

492.21 S. N. Behrman] Samuel Nathaniel Behrman (1893–1973), American playwright, screenwriter, biographer, and writer for *The New Yorker*.

493.28 Buzzy] Aaron Copland.

495.26 (C. Wilson)] John C. "Jack" Wilson (1899–1961), American theater director and producer who was also Noël Coward's business manager and lover.

495.38 Paul Godkin] Dancer with the American Ballet Theater (1914–1985) and choreographer; briefly involved romantically with Libby Holman.

496.7–8 *Bonanza Bound*] An unsuccessful 1947 musical by Adolph Green (1914–2002) and Betty Comden (1917–2006).

496.35–36 John Uihlein] Jane and Paul had spent the summer of 1946 in Uihlein's house in Southampton, New York.

496.37 Ruth Ellen] Ruth Ellen du Pont (1922–2014), later du Pont Lord, member of the prominent and wealthy Du Pont family.

497.34 the Marshall Plan] Officially the European Recovery Program, an American initiative to give economic support to rebuild Western European economies after the end of World War II. It was in operation for four years, beginning April 1948.

498.15 Helen Strauss] Helen M. Strauss (1904–1987), Paul's literary agent at the William Morris Agency from 1947 to the early 1970s.

498.17 your story] "A Distant Episode."

499.8–9 Arthur and Bobby's] Arthur Gold (1919–1990), duo-pianist with partner Robert Fizdale (1920–1995); their debut together in 1946 included music by Paul. Gold and Fizdale commissioned several pieces from Paul.

500.36 Bob Faulkner] Jane's friend who accompanied Jane and Paul to New Mexico in 1939. He worked on *The New Yorker* in the 1930s.

504.15–16 "*le néant*"] French: Nothingness.

504.19 the period of the "Villa"] Villa de France, hotel in Tangier.

505.2 Julian's] Julian Fuhs, Jane's stepfather, a German refugee and musician who married her mother in 1938.

505.10 the letter about the Clairvoyant] A letter from Paul had mentioned a warning, a prediction—of illness or death in connection with a journey—by a clairvoyant.

505.27 "que ce n'etait pas le moment encore."] French: It was not time yet.

507.25 *Ondine*] Play (1938) by French dramatist Jean Giraudoux, based on an 1811 novella about a knight who falls in love with a water sprite.

507.27 my long story] "Camp Cataract."

507.30 Leo Lerman] Leo Lerman (1914–1994), American writer and editor and friend of both Paul's and Jane's. Formerly editor of *Vogue* and *Vanity Fair*, in the 1940s he was contributing editor to *Mademoiselle*.

508.28 your story] "How Many Midnights."

508.36 the one about Prue and the other two women] "The Echo."

508.37 *sumamente*] Spanish: Extremely.

512.33 The dog] A present from Libby.

513.36 Treetops] Libby Holman's estate in Stamford, Connecticut.

514.30 Chez Roig] A restaurant in Varadero, Cuba.

515.15 Scotty] The housekeeper at Treetops.

517.7 Palais Jamai?] A hotel in Fez.

517.19 Lupe Velez] María Guadalupe Villalobos Vélez (1906–1944), Mexican and American stage and film performer, who portrayed the "Mexican Spitfire" in a series of films in the early 1940s.

518.37 The Mountain] Vieille Montagne, or Old Mountain, a fashionable neighborhood in Tangier.

519.8 hanootz] Stall.

519.9 Lantzmann] French journalist and writer Jacques Lanzmann (1927–2006), who lived briefly with Jane and Paul in Tangier.

519.20 Quinza] With whom Cherifa lived.

519.23 Dean] Joseph Dean (c. 1885–1963), born Don Kimfull; Anglo-Egyptian ex-cocaine dealer who had been implicated in the death of English musical comedy actress Billie Carleton in 1918; he changed his name and became proprietor of Dean's bar, where the English of Tangier went.

520.24 that Rif section] The Rif is a mountainous region east of Tangier.

520.27 garçonnière] French: Bachelor flat.

521.7 people like Jay, Bill Chase] American expatriates Jay Haselwood (d. 1965) and Bill Chase owned the Parade Bar in Tangier.

521.10 royalties on *The Glass Menagerie*] Paul wrote the incidental music for Tennessee Williams's 1945 play.

521.15 the *Bazaar*] *Harper's.*

522.39 I reworked it] "Camp Cataract."

523.3 Frances McFadden] Managing editor of *Harper's Bazaar* (1902–1987).

524.6 Margaret McKean] Margarett Sargent McKean (1892–1978), modernist painter and sculptor, who had formerly been Jane's lover.

524.24 Klim] Instant powdered milk.

525.39 Débrouilles toi—enfin!] You can figure it out—finally!

526.15 Aid Es Seghir] Or Eid al-Fitr, a Moroccan feast day to break the Ramadan fast.

527.10 The Herrera soup] Harira, a tomato, lentil, and chickpea soup often served to break the fast after Ramadan.

529.2 *Natasha von Hoershelman*] Natasha von Hoershelman (1909–1985), a writer for *Fortune* magazine and a close friend of Jane's; they met in New York City in the late 1940s.

529.12 Katharine] Katharine Hamill, a writer for *Fortune* and a friend of Jane's.

530.9 Sylvia] Sylvia Marlowe (1908–1981), a harpsichordist Jane met in New York City in the late 1930s.

530.20 Lola] Natasha's sister.

532.19 H.B.] *Harper's Bazaar.*

532.25 Ivan Von Auw] Jane's literary agent (1903–1991), who worked for Harold Ober Associates from 1938 until 1978. He also represented Pearl Buck, James M. Cain, Agatha Christie, Langston Hughes, Ross Macdonald, Muriel Spark, and Dylan Thomas, among others.

533.4 Carl Van V.] Carl Van Vechten (1880–1964), American writer and photographer who was a patron of writers and artists of the Harlem Renaissance and the American avant-garde.

533.28 the war's coming any minute] The 1948 Palestine War, during which the country of Israel was established. In June 1948, there were anti-Jewish riots in Oujda and Djerada, Morocco.

534.2 Carson] Carson McCullers.

534.21 *Katharine Hamill*] See note 529.12.

534.26 *Fortune*] Where Katharine and Natasha worked.

535.11–12 perhaps on the street to avoid elevators.] Jane was terrified of elevators.

537.20 séjour] French: Stay.

538.11 éclairage] Lighting.

543.22 (the Ayd El Kebir)] The Eid al-Kebir or Eid al-Adha, Muslim holiday honoring Abraham's willingness to sacrifice his son Isaac at God's command.

544.24 Polly] Benet Polikoff (1898–1970), Libby's lawyer.

545.23 at Libby's] At Libby's New York townhouse.

547.12 Ahmed's] Ahmed ben Driss el-Yacoubi (1928–1985), Moroccan painter and friend of Paul's.

547.38 the Berlin crisis] From June 1948 to May 1949, the Soviet Union blockaded rail, road, and canal access to the city of Berlin and the Western Allies organized an airlift to provide the city with food and fuel.

548.6–7 *au lieu de cent*] Instead of one hundred.

548.11 Franquistos] Fascists, or supporters of Spanish dictator Francisco Franco (1892–1975).

551.26 *ça reviendrai au même*] It will amount to the same.

553.27 hélas] Alas.

555.23 qadi] Arabic: Magistrate.

555.24 adoul] Notary.

555.27 *Through the Looking Glass*] Sequel (1871) to the novel *Alice's Adventures in Wonderland* by English writer Lewis Carroll (1832–1898).

555.34 *louche*] French: Devious.

556.35 *introuvable*] Unobtainable.

558.4 Moulay Yacoub] A province of the Fèz-Meknès region of Morocco known for its thermal waters.

558.6 Dewey] Thomas E. Dewey (1902–1971), governor of New York from 1943 to 1955, was the Republican presidential candidate in 1944 and again in 1948, losing to Franklin D. Roosevelt and to Harry S. Truman, respectively.

558.10 *pénible*] Annoying.

559.37 Gore] Gore Vidal (1925–2012), American writer and intellectual.

561.27–28 The Madrileños] I.e., from Madrid.

562.7–8 *On verra, . . . autrement.*] We'll see, all that's needed is to start over differently.

563.1 Gibraltar problem] In 1948 an "Aliens Order" made entry into Gibraltar more difficult for foreign visitors.

563.12 *Kif-kif*] Kif-kif—Maghrebi for six of one and a half-dozen of the other.

570.31 the Lorca plans] Paul wrote an opera, *Yerma*, for Holman based on a play by Spanish poet Federico García Lorca (1898–1936).

571.18 the Mouloud] Or Mawlid, the celebration of the birthday of Muhammad.

578.21 Themistocles Hoetis] Nom de plume of George Paul Solomos (1925–2010), American publisher, poet, filmmaker, and novelist.

581.34 "soupe hôtel" in Paris] The Hôtel de l'Université, where Jane could cook when she stayed in Paris.

581.36 David Herbert and Michael Duff] The Honorable David Herbert (1908–1995), younger son of the 15th Earl of Pembroke and longtime Tangier resident. Sir Michael Duff, 3rd Baronet (1907–1980), British statesman and socialite.

581.39 this house] The Duff family estate, Vaynol, in North Wales.

582.3–4 Jack Wilson's] John C. Wilson (1899–1961), American theater director. He directed the Broadway production of *Gentlemen Prefer Blondes* for which Oliver Smith did the production design.

582.18–19 Parties were given for him every second in London] Paul's *The Sheltering Sky* had just been published.

582.25–26 Audrey Wood] Audrey Wood (1905–1985), Jane's agent, whose clients also included Tennessee Williams and Carson McCullers.

584.29 Peggy Reille] Rosamond Reille Bernier (1916–), American journalist, editor, art lecturer, and socialite who lived in Mexico with her first husband, Lewis Riley Jr. They invited the Bowles to stay with them on their first trip to Mexico.

585.8–9 the Boeuf] Le Boeuf sur le Toit, a Paris nightclub.

586.9 Frank Price] Manager of the Paris branch of Doubleday Publishing.

587.13 Alice Toklas] Alice Babette Toklas (1877–1967), American member of Parisian avant-garde and life partner of Gertrude Stein.

588.1 Natika Waterbury] Natica Waterbury (d. 1978), American photographer, pilot, editor, and patron of the abstract art movement.

588.2 Sonia Sekula] Sonia Sekula (1918–1963), Swiss surrealist and abstract expressionist artist who was active in the New York City art scene throughout the 1940s and 1950s.

588.3 Mary Reynolds] Mary Louise Reynolds (1891–1950), American surrealist artist and bookbinder who resided in Paris and was the companion of Marcel Duchamp.

588.3–4 Lionel Abel and Pegeen] Lionel Abel (1910–2001), an American playwright and essayist most famous for his play *Absalom*. Pegeen Vail Guggenheim (1925–1967), painter and daughter of the art collector Peggy Guggenheim and the Swiss painter Laurence Vail.

588.4–5 her husband Hélion] French painter Jean Hélion (1925–1967), who married Guggenheim in 1946. They divorced in 1956.

588.6 Sidéry] Sherban Sidéry, French author and translator.

588.23 Connolly] Cyril Connolly (1903–1974), English critic and novelist who founded the British literary magazine *Horizon*.

588.30 Esterhazy] Tommy Esterhazy, a Hungarian nobleman in Tangier as a refugee; he was to oversee work on the Bowleses' house.

588.39 *Blondes*] *Gentlemen Prefer Blondes*, 1949 musical based on the 1925 novel of the same name by Anita Loos (1889–1981). Oliver Smith was one of the producers.

589.29 Grand Socco] Large market square in the middle of Tangier.

590.37–38 the Monocle] Le Monocle, one of the first and most famous of Paris's lesbian nightclubs.

591.1–2 after you had left for the South] In 1938, on their honeymoon trip.

591.2–4 "Elle n'est plus . . . châteaux."] French: She is no longer in the profession. She got married and she owns two huge castles.

591.27–28 "matimshishi temma—Fluz besef—hamsa miat francs."] Arabic: "Don't go there. It's very expensive. Five hundred francs."

592.34 Ivan] Ivan Bernkoff, Oliver Smith's stepfather.

593.28 Sybille Bedford] Sybille Bedford (1911–2006), German-born English novelist, essayist, and journalist; her books include *The Sudden View: A Mexican Journey* (1953), *A Legacy* (1956), and *Jigsaw* (1989).

595.14 mandat-carte] French: Postal order.

595.16–17 infroissable] Wrinkle-free.

596.1 paysages] Scenery.

596.30 Marie-Laure de Noailles] Marie-Laure de Noailles (1902–1970), French socialite and supporter of the arts, famous for her support of the surrealist movement.

597.18 Brion] Brion Gysin (1916–1986), English painter, writer, recording artist, and restaurateur; author of *The Exterminator* (1960, with William Burroughs) and *The Process* (1969).

598.14–15 what Paul has written you] Paul was in Tangier.

598.22–23 in case the Westport production never comes off] There was no Westport production of *In the Summer House*.

598.36 Garson Kanin] Garson Kanin (1912–1999), American playwright, director, and musician.

599.25 Bud] Bud Williams, Libby's manager.

606.4 *Mike Kahn*] Libby Holman's nephew who was then working at the Hedgerow Theatre.

606.13–14 Jasper Deeter . . . businesslike way] Jasper Deeter was director at the Hedgerow Theatre, where *In the Summer House* was produced in 1951.

606.23 *Carl Van Vechten*] See note 533.4.

607.3 Fania Marinoff and Saul Mauriber] Fania Marinoff (1890–1971), Russian-born American actress married to Carl Van Vechten. Saul Mauriber (1915–2003), Van Vechten's assistant and lover.

607.16–17 easier for me to send the letter . . . explain the whole thing] Jane's mother and stepfather owned a jewelry store in Dayton, Ohio, and apparently they were having financial difficulties.

607.27 Marty] Marty Mann (1904–1980), a new lover. She had been an early female member of Alcoholics Anonymous and campaigned to have alcoholism recognized as a disease.

608.12 Priscilla] Priscilla Peck, Marty Mann's longtime partner, who was an art director for *Vogue* magazine.

608.20 Heber] Robert Heber-Percy (1911–1987), English eccentric who inherited the Faringdon House in Oxfordshire, an estate frequented by many artists and writers.

608.36 The director of *Come Back Little Sheba*] Daniel Mann (1912–1991) directed the 1950 play *Come Back, Little Sheba* by William Inge (1913–1973) as well as its 1952 film version.

609.8 Tennessee's *Rose Tattoo*] Play (1951) by Tennessee Williams, directed on both Broadway and in its 1955 film adaptation by Daniel Mann.

609.17 Alice Bouverie] Ava Alice Muriel Astor Pleydell-Bouverie (1902–1956), wealthy American socialite and supporter of the arts.

610.6 Maureen Stapleton] Maureen Stapleton (1925–2006), American film and Broadway actress.

610.17 Peter] Peter Lindamood (1914–1972), an aspiring writer from Columbus, Mississippi, who knew Tennessee Williams.

614.31 Frankie] Frank Phillip Merlo (1921–1963), Sicilian American actor and Tennessee Williams's partner, who traveled with Paul and Williams from New York to Tangier and then Morocco in 1948. Before Williams, Merlo had been in a relationship with John Latouche.

614.37–38 the ex-Marchioness of Bath . . . Mister Fielding] Daphne Winifred Louise Fielding (1904–1997), British socialite and author and one of the so-called Bright Young Things of the 1920s. In 1927 she married Henry Thynne, 6th Marquess of Bath. They divorced in 1953 and later that year she married Major Alexander Wallace Fielding (1918–1991).

615.12–13 Indo-China Oppenheimer period] In April and May 1954, the Viet Minh won a decisive victory against the French, and the Geneva Conference resulted in an agreement between North Vietnam and France in which Indochina was granted independence from France. At the same time the controversial Oppenheimer security hearing of the actions of J. Robert Oppenheimer, the former head of the Los Alamos Laboratory, which had produced the atomic bomb during World War II, resulted in the revocation of his security clearance.

615.14 George Broadfield] Lloyd George W. Broadfield III, American writer and friend of the poet Edward Field.

615.22–24 *Vogue* . . . goony friends] Jane had told a *Vogue* interviewer, "There's no point in writing a play for your five hundred goony friends. You have to reach more people."

615.29 Walter Kerr in the Trib] Walter Kerr referred to the quote in an article for the *New York Herald Tribune*, "Writing Plays for Goons": "The hack may say what he means and say it flatly. The talented man may say what he means and say it richly. But the talented man who insists upon his right not to say it at all, to hug his meaning like a secret close to his breast, to serve his goony friends rather than the gaping audience, is better off out of the theater. All hail to Jane Bowles for her happy pronouncement."

618.38 Haymaker shirts] Ladies' sportswear clothing label known for its polo shirts.

623.26 the temple of Madura] Meenakshi Amman Temple in Madurai, Tamil Nadu, India, a historic Hindu temple dedicated to Parvati, goddess of fertility also known as Meenakshi, and the god Shiva.

624.34 *magillahs*] Megillah. Yiddish: a long and involved story.

624.35 Mrs. Trimmer] Mother of an Anglican clergyman whom Paul met in Colombo, Ceylon, in 1951. The Trimmers owned a tea plantation.

624.36 *tajine*] A stew. "Tagine" is a Moroccan word that refers to both the conical cooking vessel and the food made in it.

625.1 Berman painting] Russian Neo-romantic painter Eugène Berman (1899–1972), who was a friend of the Bowleses'.

626.20 accablée] French: Overwhelmed.

627.11 Phyllis] Countess Phyllis della Faille de Leverghem, an American who married a Belgian nobleman.

627.18 Bépanthène Roche] A hair loss treatment.

627.22 John Goodwin] John Goodwin Lyman (1886–1967), Canadian artist and critic, founder of the Contemporary Arts Society in Montreal.

627.36 Jorge Jantus] Spanish film writer and director.

627.39 kif] Kief, the trichome or hair part of the cannabis plant, which is more potent than the plant itself.

629.20 *Waiting for Godot*] Samuel Beckett's 1953 play.

629.35 Rose] Rose Minor, Libby Holman's secretary.

631.10 Christopher or Ira] Christopher Wanklyn (1926–1998), Canadian painter and journalist who lived in Morocco. Ira Victor Morris (1903–1972), American journalist and author.

631.22 Equanil] A mild sedative.

632.11 The Catalana] A restaurant in the Medina.

632.19 Dubz] One of Jane's cats.

633.1 silvikrin] A hair growth product.

633.13–14 the Fordyces . . . Conzett and Huber] Michael Fordyce, a resident of Tangier in the 1950s with his wife and two children. Conzett and Huber was a German publisher that printed Paul's travel book *Yallah* (1956).

633.19–20 Edita Morris . . . husband Ira] Edita Morris (1902–1988), Swedish American author and humanitarian, known for the novel *The Flowers of Hiroshima* (1959).

634.14 Ulla] Paul's aunt, Ulla Winnewisser Danser (1889–1972).

634.16 Anne Harbach] Longtime resident of Tangier, ex-daughter-in-law of American lyricist and librettist Otto Harbach.

634.30 Seth] The parrot.

634.39 Berred] Another cat.

635.32 It was too much—the clipping they sent me] Of the news of film actor Montgomery Clift's (1920–1966) car accident on May 12, 1956, when he fell asleep at the wheel and hit a telephone pole.

637.39 Tim] Holman's adopted son Timothy Holman Reynolds (1945–2010).

638.3 Monty] American actor Montgomery Clift.

638.8 Villiers] David Villiers, English poet and friend of Paul's, who wrote a musical setting for Villiers's poem "The Heart Grows Old."

639.9 Allen Ginsberg] American poet (1926–1997), best known for his poem *Howl* (1956).

639.15 Philip Lamantia?] American surrealist poet (1927–2005).

639.24 majoun] A Moroccan pastry ball of honey, fruit, and nuts, often made as a cannabis edible.

639.27 Bill Burroughs] William S. Burroughs (1914–1997), American Beat author most famous for his novel *Naked Lunch.*

639.30 Carl Solomon] Carl Solomon (1928–1993), American writer and friend of Allen Ginsberg.

639.32 Rockland State Hospital] Psychiatric facility in New York.

640.9 "My name is Seth."] A phrase Paul had suggested Jane teach the parrot. "[It] sounds," he wrote, "like an autobiographical novel's title . . . something awful by Robert Graves on Biblical times."

640.12 congratulations on *Harper's Bazaar.*] Paul had sold a short story, "The Frozen Fields," to *Harper's Bazaar.*

640.35 Resneck] Dr. William Resnick, Libby's doctor.

641.4 the english doctor] Dr. Resnick had suggested that Jane go to England to consult with a British neurologist, Dr. John McMichael.

651.3 Diane] Dione Lewis (see note 485.27).

651.9–10 Mrs. Latouche] John's mother.

651.22 dillantine] Phenytoin, sold under the name Dilantin, an antiseizure medicine.

655.21 She is fine] Jane's mother was recovering from a cancer operation.

656.4–5 Doctor Eran Belle] Dr. Aaron Bell, a neurologist connected with Lenox Hill, Bellevue, and Beth Israel Hospitals in New York City.

657.1–2 the Agadir fault] On February 29, 1960, a major earthquake hit the city of Agadir, in western Morocco, almost completely destroying it.

658.37 serpasil] High blood pressure medication also prescribed for psychotic symptoms.

660.39 your husband] Louis Schanker (1903–1981), an abstract painter, was Holman's third husband.

661.32 Merril Grant] Merrill Grant (1932–2015), American television producer.

661.34 John Meyers] John Bernard Myers (1920–1987), American writer, art dealer, and gallery owner who promoted many artists and writers of the New York School.

663.2 Lilla Von Saher] A Hungarian ex-movie starlet and author (1902–1969) who was friends with Tennessee Williams.

663.5 "muschugana"] Meshuggener. Yiddish for crazy.

663.8 Mary Jane Ward] Mary Jane Ward (1905–1981), American author best known for her semi-autobiographical book *The Snake Pit*, an account of her stay in a mental hospital.

667.8 Gib] Gibraltar.

668.32 *Rena Bowles*] Rena Winnewisser Bowles (1884–1966), Paul Bowles's mother.

669.30 *Ruth Fainlight*] American poet and translator (b. 1931) who had been living in Tangier with her husband, English novelist Alan Sillitoe (1928–2010), and their baby, David.

669.34 Fatima's] Fatima was an Arab woman who had gone to London with the Sillitoes to work for them.

670.40 Yvonne Gerofie] With her sister-in-law Isabelle, Yvonne Gerofi ran a Gallimard bookstore in Tangier, the Librairie des Colonnes, from the early 1950s through the 1970s. Before moving to Tangier they had run a successful bookshop and art gallery in Brussels.

671.5 Ira Cohn] Ira Cohen (1935–2011), American poet, editor, and photographer. While living in Tangier he published a literary magazine, *GNAOUA*, which introduced the work of Brion Gysin, William S. Burroughs, and others.

671.6–7 Mrs. McBey] Marguerite McBey (1905–1999), American photographer and painter and longtime resident of Tangier.

671.11 Tamara] Tamara Geva (1907–1997), born Tamara Gevergeyev, Russian-born American actress, ballerina, and choreographer.

671.13 Sonia Orwell] Second wife (1918–1981) of George Orwell.

671.16–17 your friend] Sylvia Plath, who had committed suicide on February 11, 1963.

671.33 "Plain Girl"] *Plain Girl* (1955), children's novel by Virginia Sorensen (1912–1991).

672.7 "Cybernetique et Société."] French edition of *Cybernetics: Or the Control and Communication in the Animal and the Machine* (1948, revised 1961) by American mathematician Norbert Wiener (1894–1964); it popularized the use of the term "cybernetics."

672.16 Sonia's] Sonia Kamalakar, an aristocratic Georgian Russian who moved to Morocco with her husband, Narayan, on a scientific expedition.

674.8 Tyznteshka] Tizi n'Tichka, the highest pass in Morocco over the Grand Atlas Mountains.

675.6–7 the library] Gallimard Agency in Tangier.

678.7 David and Liza] *David and Lisa* (1962), film about a mentally ill young man, directed by Frank Perry.

678.7–8 Irma Herly] Irma Hurley (1929–2009), American stage and screen actress.

678.14 *Isabelle Gerofi*] See note 670.40.

679.4 une petite détante] French: A little relaxation.

680.21 Milly] Mildred Dunnock (1901–1991), American stage and screen actress who originated the role of Big Mama in Tennessee Williams's *Cat on a Hot Tin Roof* and the role of Linda in Arthur Miller's *Death of a Salesman*.

680.27 Herbert Berghof] Austrian actor and director (1909–1990) and founder of the HB Studio for acting in New York City.

680.29 Alfred Chester] American writer and literary critic (1928–1971), author of *Here Be Dragons* (1955), *Jamie Is My Heart's Desire* (1956), *The Exquisite Corpse* (1967), and others.

682.2 *Audrey Wood*] See note 582.25–26.

682.14–15 the two versions of the play] See note 175.1.

682.19–20 Gerald Cook] Gerald Cook, American pianist and accompanist for the jazz artist Alberta Hunter (1895–1984).

686.20–21 Paul got a movie offer] *The Sheltering Sky* was not made into a movie until 1990, directed by Bernardo Bertolucci and starring Debra Winger and John Malkovich.

686.24–25 Albie . . . Virginia Woolf] Edward Albee's 1962 play *Who's Afraid of Virginia Woolf?* was made into a movie in 1966, directed by Mike Nichols and starring Elizabeth Taylor and Richard Burton.

686.31 Ira Shuberts secretary] Lawrence Delbert Stewart (1926–2013), Ira Gershwin's archivist and later biographer.

687.18–19 Larby's book] *A Life Full of Holes* (1964), a collection of stories by Larbi Layachi (1937–1986), a Moroccan storyteller, that had been recorded and translated by Paul.

688.5 Irving Paul Lazar] American literary and talent agent and producer (1907–1993). He represented Lauren Bacall, Truman Capote, Ira Gershwin, Cary Grant, Moss Hart, Ernest Hemingway, Gene Kelly, Vladimir Nabokov, Cole Porter, and Tennessee Williams, among others.

689.14 his long ago affiliations] Paul had been a member of the Communist Party for a short period in the 1930s.

692.2–3 (The Loneliness of the Long Distance Runner)] Short story collection (1959) by English writer Alan Sillitoe (1928–2010). The title story was adapted into a film in 1962, with Sillitoe writing the screenplay.

692.4 Peter Owen] Peter Owen (1927–2016), founder of English publishing house Peter Owen, Ltd. He published both Paul's and Jane's works.

692.28–29 the "cut up" method] Technique popularized in the 1950s and '60s by William S. Burroughs in which a source text is cut up and reordered to create a new work.

692.30 Gold Water] Senator Barry Goldwater (1909–1998) won the 1964 Republican presidential nomination on a platform supporting rollback or forcible change of regime, rather than containment, of the Soviet Union, which his opponents feared would spark nuclear war.

694.16 David's cousin Caroline] Caroline, Lady Duff (1913–1973), the second wife of Sir Michael Duff, 3rd Baronet (see also note 581.36). Jane and Paul stayed at their estate, Vaynol, in Wales, when Paul's novel *The Sheltering Sky* was published.

699.2 Eisha] Aicha, who worked for Jane.

700.32 *Lawrence Stewart*] See note 686.31.

701.10 Paul's new book] *Up Above the World.*

706.12 *"Frances"*] Pseudonym. An English writer, the daughter of a countess, with whom Bowles began an affair in 1962. See also Chronology for 1962 and Note on the Texts, page 777.

708.2–3 he would think me a "spend-thrift,"] Julian Fuhs, Jane's stepfather.

711.29 the Puppet Play] The puppet play, "A Quarreling Pair," was originally performed at Spivy's nightclub under the auspices of *View* magazine, in 1946.

711.33 David Jackson and Jimmie Merrill] David Noyes Jackson (1922–2001), American writer and artist, and the partner of James Merrill (1926–1995), American poet.

711.35–36 Tony's] Libby's adopted son Anthony Holman Reynolds (b. 1947).

711.39 the puppet boys] Francis J. Peschka and W. Gordon Murdock, who created the Little Players in 1952, a troupe that produced puppet plays for adults.

712.12 yincha Alla] Insha'Allah, or Inshallah. Arabic: "God willing."

712.17 103] Formal letter written by Paul for Jane, to be read to Cherifa in Arabic by a member of Cherifa's family.

713.3 Hamed] Cherifa's nephew.

714.15 Lucia] Lucia Cristofanetti Wilcox (1902–1974), Lebanese American painter who organized an artists' colony on Long Island that included Jackson Pollock, Max Ernst, and others.

714.18–19 the old song] From the puppet play "A Quarreling Pair"; see pages 284–87 in this volume.

715.28–29 Truman's book] *In Cold Blood.*

718.7 Lillie the bar woman] Lily Wickman, the new owner of the Parade Bar.

719.28 Martha] Princess Martha Ruspoli de Chambrun (1899–1984), a resident of Tangier, whom Jane met in 1963, and who subsequently became her lover. A descendant of the Marquis de Lafayette, she was estranged from her Italian nobleman husband.

720.38 Veronica Tennant] Veronica Duff Tennant (1904–1967), sister of Sir Michael Duff (see note 581.36).

722.8 Lee Gershwin] Leonore Strunsky Gershwin (1900–1991), wife of Ira Gershwin.

722.12 the Leary scandal] Timothy Leary (1920–1996), a psychologist who had been fired from his post as a Harvard lecturer in 1963, where he had conducted experiments on the therapeutic potential of LSD. The Bowleses had met Leary in 1961 when he made the first of several trips to Tangier. He was arrested in 1965 and again in 1966 for possession of marijuana, and Diane di Prima and Allen Ginsberg created an informal Timothy Leary Defense Fund that sent letters arguing that Leary was being targeted for his ideas rather than for his marijuana possession. Paul had received one of these letters.

722.13 Susan Sontag] American writer, critic, and activist (1933–2004).

722.18 *Hal Vursell*] Harold D. Vursell, Jane's editor at Farrar, Straus & Giroux, which was about to publish Jane's *Collected Works.*

723.19 *Gordon Sager*] See note 474.12.

725.20 if he gets thirty percent] From the American publication of *The Collected Works of Jane Bowles.*

725.39 the Strike] The 1966 Airline Strike, in which 35,000 airline workers of five airlines went on strike from July 8 to August 19, affecting 60 percent of the U.S. airline industry.

727.28 La semaine de Tangier] Tangier Week. A weeklong public festival usually held in May but for a few years in the 1960s, in September.

728.34 Rabit] Mohammed Mrabet (b. 1936), Moroccan storyteller whose stories were translated by Paul.

729.21 Mrs. Dickson] Frances Leftwich McKee Dixon (1920–1992), wife of the consul general, Benjamin Franklin Dixon III.

729.32 Carla Grissmann] A teacher at the American School in Tangier (1928–2011).

729.35–36 Bruce Rogers . . . Donald Richie] Bruce Rogers (1870–1957), American typeface and book designer, famous for his classical designs. Donald Richie (1924–2013), American author, Japanese historian, and film critic.

730.6 Bryan] Brion Gysin (see note 597.18).

730.38 Oliver Evans] American poet, translator, and biographer (1915–1981).

731.15 Jane Wilson] American abstract expressionist and landscape artist (1924–2015).

731.19–20 Howard Moorepark] Howard Moore-Park, a literary agent.

731.21 Clareman] Jack Clareman (1916–2011), Libby Holman's lawyer.

733.12–13 the Swedish publisher] Of *Two Serious Ladies.*

737.2 David Holman] Libby's nephew, son of her brother Alfred.

737.33 *Carson McCullers*] American Writer (1917–1967) who had written a letter of admiration to Jane on the publication of *Plain Pleasures.*

739.22–23 the possible opperation] Dr. Roux had suggested that Jane might need an operation for intestinal adhesions.

741.17 Alfred is the secretary.] All but last line handwritten by Alfred Chester; see note 680.29.

Index

Abel, Lionel, 588
Abelle, Billie, 576–77, 580
Acapulco, Mexico, 466
Actors Studio, 684
Afghanistan, 713
Agadir, Morocco, 657
Ahmed (Moroccan man), 735
Aicha (Moroccan woman), 656, 699, 701, 712–13, 739
Alabama, 496
Albee, Edward: *Who's Afraid of Virginia Woolf?* 686
Algeciras, Spain, 592, 666, 722–23, 727–28
Algeria, 562, 573, 576, 591, 593
Algiers, Algeria, 591
Algonquin Hotel (New York City), 609
Álvarez, Antonio, 466
Andrea Doria disaster, 635–36
Ann Arbor, Mich., 611, 682
Antwerp, Belgium, 583
Arabic language, 501, 516, 519, 523, 528, 531, 535, 541–42, 557, 565, 591, 669
Arizona, 459
Asbury Park, N.J., 459
Asilah (Arcila), Morocco, 673, 675–80, 693
Aswell, Mary Louise, 477, 491, 515, 522, 530, 532–34, 543, 547, 587, 696, 701, 703, 708
Atlas Mountains, 494, 515, 674, 677, 697
Auer, Claire Stajer (Claire Fuhs) (Jane's mother), 453–54, 456–57, 473, 476, 481, 484, 487, 490–91, 505–8, 521–22, 528, 535, 557, 566, 607, 626, 655–56, 662, 664, 666–67, 680–81, 684, 688, 699–700, 702–3, 705, 708–10, 714, 727, 733, 735, 742; letter to, 734
Auer, Sidney (Jane's father), 453
Authors League Fund, 575

Bagnold, Enid, 615
Bangkok, Thailand, 726, 729–30, 733
Bankcroft, Mary, 704–5
Bankhead, Eugenia, 473, 480, 496, 673, 681, 689
Barry, Iris, 476, 530, 580
Bate, Peggy, 475, 516, 525
Beatniks, 672
Beaton, Cecil, 579–80, 596
Beauvoir, Simone de: "New Heroes," 471
Beckett, Samuel: *Waiting for Godot*, 629
Beden (Moroccan woman), 661
Bedford, Sybille, 593–94
Behrman, S. N., 492
Belgium, 679
Bell, Aaron, 654, 656, 658
Bellin, Ira, 571, 588, 592, 604, 631
Beni Abbes, Algeria, 573–76, 593
Berghof, Herbert, 680–82, 690
Bergner, Elizabeth, 486
Berlin, Germany, 547
Bernkoff, Ivan, 592
Bonanza Bound (musical), 496
Boussif (Algerian man), 519, 528, 531, 542–43, 550, 555
Bouverie, Alice Astor, 609
Bowles, Claude (Paul's father), 664, 669, 689, 700, 703
Bowles, Jane Auer: living in New York City, 453–59; explores Greenwich Village, 453–54; sexuality of, 454, 473, 480, 516, 519, 523, 530–31, 551, 591, 613; writing difficulties of, 455–56, 460, 465, 470–73, 477, 484–85, 490–91, 498, 543, 585–86; at Deal Beach, 456–57; reading of, 456, 465–66, 471, 477, 479, 485, 737; in Mexico with Paul Bowles, 459; marries Paul, 460; in France, 460–61; with Paul in Staten Island, 461–64; second trip to Mexico with Paul, 464–67; in Cuba, 468–69, 472–73; with Helvetia Perkins in Florida and Vermont, 468–70, 504–12; with Libby Holman in Connecticut, 470–503; health of, 478, 515, 517, 566, 569, 623, 640–48, 659, 665–66, 671,

702, 725–26, 728–29, 736–38, 740–41, 743; relationship with mother, 481, 491, 505–6, 557, 607, 655, 662, 664, 666, 688, 708, 734; on Arab culture, 494, 501, 527–29, 536–37, 565, 572, 635; and houses, 501–2, 520–21, 536–39, 547, 549–56, 577–78; alcohol and drug use by, 501, 548, 590; critiques story by Paul, 508–9; joins Paul in Morocco, 512; in Fez with Paul, 513, 515–17, 525; relationship with Cherifa, 516, 519, 523, 529–30, 548, 551, 565, 571–72, 612, 620–22, 626, 630, 650, 712–13, 741; studies Arabic language, 516, 519, 523, 528, 531, 535, 541–42, 557, 565, 591, 669; on marriage to Paul, 516–18, 585; writings promoted by Paul, 521, 532–34, 542–43, 547; on Muslim holidays, 526, 528–29, 540–41, 543, 546, 555, 591, 614, 616, 626, 635, 638, 640, 698–99; Paul's miscalculation of money for, 540–46, 549; relationship with Tennessee Williams, 559–61, 563, 566, 575, 614–15, 621, 692; in Beni Abbas with Paul, 573–76; in Wales, 581–82; in Paris, 581–98; and cats, 592, 634, 638, 650, 733; in Pacy-sur-Eure, 598–606; returns to America for production of *In the Summer House*, 606–11; in Ceylon with Paul, 623–25, 627; visit from Allen Ginsberg, 639; suffers stroke, 640–48; goes to England for medical treatment, 649; leaves Tangier due to political unrest, 649–50; goes to New York City for medical treatment, 653–58; returns to Tangier, 656; *Two Serious Ladies* published in England, 691–94, 696, 699; visits mother in Florida, 708–10, 714, 734; gets medical treatment in Florida, 725–26, 728–29; goes to Málaga for medical and psychiatric treatment, 740–44

WORKS: "Camp Cataract," 502, 513, 515, 532–34, 547, 575, 579, 587, 725; *Cross-Section* stories, 484; *In the Summer House*, 468, 484, 488, 507, 582, 584, 588–89, 606, 608–9, 611, 631, 680–85, 689–90, 697; "Out in the World," 470–74, 477, 481, 484–85, 490–91, 516, 532–35, 543, 555; *Le Phaéton Hypocrite*, 453; "Plain Pleasures," 468, 484; [second play], 623, 629, 631, 634, 636, 639–40, 663; *Two Serious Ladies*, 461, 463–65, 468, 471, 478, 503, 691–94, 696, 699, 720, 731

Bowles, Paul: in Mexico with Jane Auer, 459; marries Jane, 460; in France, 460–61; works on music for Mercury Theater, 461; with Jane in Staten Island, 461–64; second trip to Mexico with Jane, 464–67; travels to Morocco, 470, 474–76, 478, 504–7, 509–11; in Spain, 470, 476, 478, 480, 486; joined in Morocco by Jane, 512; returns to New York City, 512, 515, 524–25, 529, 533, 535; in Fez with Jane, 513, 515–17, 525; travels in Atlas Mountains, 515; and Jane's health, 517; promotes Jane's writing, 521, 532–34, 542–43, 547; miscalculates money for Jane, 540–46, 549; develops friendship with Gore Vidal and Tennessee Williams, 559–61, 563, 566, 589, 596, 614; in Beni Abbas with Jane, 573–76; travels to Ceylon, 581, 583, 585, 598; literary success in England, 582–83; returns to Tangier, 598; bout with typhoid, 614; with Jane returns to Ceylon, 623–25, 629–30, 633, 635; Allen Ginsberg comes to Tangier to see, 639; and Jane's stroke, 640–48; accompanies Jane to England for medical treatment, 649; in Tangier when Jane returns from New York City, 659, 662; plans to visit parents in Florida, 664, 666, 689, 700, 703; rents house in Asilah, 673, 675–80; writes articles for *Holiday* magazine, 686, 713; travels to New Mexico, 700–701, 703–4, 706, 708–9; travels to Thailand, 729–30, 733; accompanies Jane to Málaga for medical treatment, 740–44

JANE'S LETTERS TO: 470–512, 516–28, 535–44, 546–67, 585–98, 623–28, 630–35, 638–40, 650–56, 725–26, 728–33, 735–36, 739–44

WORKS: *Denmark Vesey* (opera), 461, 463–64; "The Echo," 508; "How Many Midnights," 498, 508–9; music for *The Glass Menagerie*, 521; music for *In the Summer House*, 683; music for *Summer and Smoke*, 512, 515, 529; *The Sheltering Sky*, 470, 485, 502, 507, 513, 515, 533, 549, 551, 582, 654, 686–88, 691, 696; *The Spider's House*, 623; *Their Heads Are Green*, 692; *Yerma* (opera), 570, 582–83, 598–604, 608, 654
Bowles, Rena (Paul's mother), 634, 664, 666, 689, 700, 703; letter to, 668–69
British Post Office (Tangier), 510, 519, 555, 575–76, 592, 628–29
Broadfield, George, 615–16
Burroughs, William, 639, 730

Cádiz, Spain, 478, 486
California, 459, 498, 622, 701
Canada, 487–88
Cape Town, South Africa, 632, 639
Capote, Truman, 580, 588–89, 596, 701
Carpenter, Louisa, 473, 480, 496, 513, 571, 681, 716
Carroll, Lewis: *Through the Looking Glass*, 555
Casablanca, Morocco, 539, 616, 693, 702, 704–5, 712–13, 722–23, 733
Casbah (Tangier), 516, 520, 532, 543, 550, 557, 565, 613–14, 620, 623, 693
Catalana café (Tangier), 632, 635
Central Park Zoo, 476
Ceylon (Sri Lanka), 581, 583, 585, 589, 596, 598, 623, 625, 629–30, 632–35, 638, 640
Chaplin, Charles, 609
Chase, Bill, 521, 531, 571
Chelsea Hotel (New York City), 465, 467, 509, 511, 706
Cherifa, 516, 519, 523, 526–31, 535, 541–43, 546–48, 551, 558, 561, 565, 571–72, 574, 577, 591–92, 595, 612–13, 616, 618–22, 624–26, 628, 630–31, 634–35, 637–38, 640, 652, 654–56, 658–60, 679, 681, 699, 739, 741; letter to, 712–13
Chester, Alfred, 680–81, 741
Chicago, Ill., 606, 609, 629
Christianity, 529, 618, 624
Clareman, Jack, 731, 735
Cleveland, Ohio, 535
Clifford, Henry, 594
Clift, Montgomery, 636, 638
Clínica de los Ángeles (Málaga), 743
Codman, Florence, 468, 475, 477–79, 482, 489, 575–76
Cohen, Ira, 671
Colomb-Béchar, Algeria, 562, 576, 591
Colombo, Ceylon, 635
Compton-Burnett, Ivy, 699
Connecticut, 470–503, 581, 599, 601, 706, 709
Connolly, Cyril, 588, 696
Conzett & Huber (publisher), 633
Cook, Gerald, 682
Copland, Aaron, 466, 493
Costa Rica, 460
Cramer, Jacqueline, 562
Cuba, 457, 468–69, 472–73, 514, 605
Cuernavaca, Mexico, 663

Dakar, French West Africa, 533
David and Lisa (film), 678
Davis, George, 491, 525, 532, 543, 554, 562
Dayton, Ohio, 521, 528, 535
Deal Beach, N.J., 456–57
Dean, Henry L., 725–26, 728–29, 732
Dean, Joseph, 519, 523
Deeter, Jasper, 606
Delaware, 574–75
Delkas Music Company, 475
Della Faille de Leverghem, Phyllis, 627, 635, 642
Denby, Edwin, 484, 512, 516, 521
Denver, Colo., 656
De Rohan, Dilkusha, 464, 597
Devillier, Catherine (Katousha), 464
Dewey, Thomas E., 558
Dixon, Frances, 729
Dostoevsky, Feodor, 485
Doubleday (publisher), 470, 549
Duff, Caroline, 694, 696
Duff, Michael, 581, 589
Dunham, Harry, 462–63
Dunham, Marion, 460, 487, 497, 502, 507

Dunnock, Mildred, 680, 684, 709–12, 727
Du Pont, Ruth Ellen, 496

East Hampton, N.Y., 666, 706, 714, 716, 724
East Montpelier, Vt., 468, 504–12, 554
Echols, Randolph, 492–93
Eggers, Constance Stajer, 453–54
Egypt, 502, 507, 538, 557
Eid el Kebir, 543, 546, 555, 591
Eid es Seghir, 526, 528
England, 581–83, 593–95, 628, 638, 640–41, 643–49, 652–53, 661, 691–97, 699–700, 702, 718, 720–21, 728, 731, 735, 738
Erika (typewriter brand), 480
Esterhazy, Tommy, 588, 592, 595–98
Evans, Oliver, 730
Evans, Ross, 638, 656
Èze-Village, France, 461

Fainlight, Ruth (Ruth Sillitoe), 696; letters to, 669–73, 675–77, 693–95
Fatima (Moroccan woman) and husband, 588, 612–13, 621, 624–25, 628, 669–73, 675–76
Faulkner, Robert, 464, 500–501
Fez, Morocco, 476, 494, 509, 511–13, 515–17, 524–25, 532, 549–50, 558–59, 561, 574, 578
Fielding, Daphne Winifred Louise and Major Alexander Wallace, 614–15
Fire Island, 529–30, 574, 608
Fizdale, Robert, 499
Flanner, Janet, 574–76
Florida, 468–70, 664, 666, 688–89, 700, 703, 705, 707–13, 719, 722–29, 732
Forbush, Bill, 729
Ford, Charles Henri, 493, 639; letter to, 463–64
Fordyce, Michael, 633
Fortune, 534, 611
Foulke, Miss (teacher), 456
France, 460–61, 479, 501–2, 568–70, 581–607, 610, 738
Frances (pseudonym), 673, 709, 711–12, 714, 716, 724; letters to, 706–8, 738–39
Franco, Francisco, 548
Fuhs, Claire. *See* Auer, Claire Stajer
Fuhs, Julian (Jane's stepfather), 505–6, 508, 655, 666, 700, 702–3, 725, 734
Fuller, Donald, 490

Gallagher, Charles, 636, 667, 676, 685, 729–31, 733
García Lorca, Federico, 571; *Yerma*, 570, 583, 603, 608, 654
Germany, 547, 633, 712–13
Gerofi, Isabelle, 671–72, 674–76, 697, 727–28, 730; letter to, 678–79
Gerofi, Yvonne, 670–72, 674–79, 697, 727, 729, 739
Gershwin, Ira, 686–88, 691, 701
Gershwin, Leonore, 686–87, 701, 722
Geva, Tamara, 671, 681, 693
Gibraltar, 507, 512, 516, 558, 561, 563–64, 594, 597, 605, 649, 667, 685, 715
Gifford, Eric, 627
Ginsberg, Allen, 639; *Howl*, 639
Giraudoux, Jean, 492–93; *Ondine*, 507
Glenora, N.Y., 462
Gloucester, Mass., 486–87, 489
Godkin, Paul, 495, 499–500, 512
Gold, Arthur, 499, 512
Goldwater, Barry, 692
Goodwin, John, 627, 650, 701, 703, 706, 708
Gould, Will, 492–93
Granada, Spain, 743
Great Barrington, Mass., 478, 487
Greaves, George, 735
Greece, 661, 714
Greene, Jessie, 717–18
Greenwich, Conn., 666
Greenwich Village, 453–54
Grissmann, Carla, 729–30, 732–35
Grosser, Maurice, 465–66, 477, 488, 655–56
Groton, Conn., 487
Guatemala, 460
Guggenheim, Pegeen Vail, 588
Guggenheim, Peggy, 593, 596–97
Guinness, Kay, 535, 574
Gysin, Brion, 473, 597, 627, 730

Haiti, 506
Hall, Juanita, 464
Hamed (Moroccan man), 712–13

Hamill, Katharine, 529–30, 611, 650, 652–53, 679, 703, 707, 709, 719, 721, 729; letters to, 534–35, 573–80, 611–23
Hanson, Cyril, 735
Harbach, Anne, 634
Harper's Bazaar, 475, 521, 523, 532–34, 640, 701
Haselwood, Jay, 521, 523, 531, 543, 546, 550, 553, 571, 592, 635, 663, 673, 717–19
Hassan, Salvador, 542, 544–46
Havana, Cuba, 457
Heber-Percy, Robert, 608
Hedgerow Theatre, 606, 609
Hélion, Jean, 588
Herbert, David, 581, 594, 614–15, 663, 688, 694–97, 701, 707, 725, 727, 734, 737
Hoetis, Themistocles, 578
Holiday (magazine), 686, 713
Holland, Richard, 723
Holman, Anthony (Tony), 711, 735
Holman, Christopher (Topper), 469, 476, 513–15, 517, 594
Holman, David, 737
Holman, Elizabeth (Libby), 470–71, 478–80, 483, 488, 491–93, 495–96, 510, 517, 521, 524–26, 546, 548, 550–51, 553, 560–61, 563, 566, 590, 594, 596, 630, 632, 640, 650–52, 654, 656, 672, 682, 706–7, 722, 726, 732, 742; letters to, 468–70, 512–16, 544–46, 567–72, 579, 581–85, 598–611, 628–29, 635–38, 640–50, 656–68, 673–75, 677–81, 683–93, 695–706, 708–22, 724, 736–38, 740–41
Holman, Timothy (Tim), 637
Holt, Hamilton, 454
Honolulu, Hawaii, 506, 508
Hotel Atlas (Tangier), 741–42
Hotel Belvedere (Fez), 513, 517
Hotel Carlton (Mexico City), 465
Hotel Cuba (Tangier), 626
Hotel De Soto (Savannah), 467
Hotel el Farhar (Tangier), 512, 516, 541, 543, 546
Hotel Meurice (New York City), 458–59
Hotel Rembrandt (Tangier), 614, 625
Hotel Rif (Tangier), 671
Hotel Villa de France (Tangier), 515, 518, 527, 540, 554, 558
Houston, Elsie, 463
Hurley, Irma, 678
Hyde Park Hotel (New York City), 453

India, 623–24, 627
Indochina, 615–16
Inge, William: *Come Back, Little Sheba*, 608
Ireland, 596
Irving Trust Company, 544–46
Israel, 718, 721

Jackson, David, 711–12, 714
Jamaica, 460, 506, 636
James, Henry: *The Portrait of a Lady*, 466
Jantus, Jorge, 627, 632
Japan, 652, 667, 729, 733
Jones, Margo, 512–13
Journal of Commerce, 508
Jung, Carl G.: *Psychological Types*, 466

Kafka, Franz, 555, 597
Kahn, Mike, 609, 681; letter to, 606
Kamalakar, Sonia, 698, 701
Kandy, Ceylon, 625
Kanin, Garson, 598, 601
Kansas, 467
Kazin, Pearl, 475, 521, 523, 532–34
Kerr, Walter, 615–16, 622–23
Kierkegaard, Søren: *Sickness unto Death*, 474, 479
Knopf, Alfred, 533
Knopf (publisher), 478, 484, 498, 532–34, 542, 547
Ktiri, Abdessalem, 547
Kyoto, Japan, 729, 733

La Línea, Spain, 597
Lamantia, Philip, 639
Lanzmann, Jacques, 519, 548
Larache, Morocco, 677
Latouche, John, 457, 459, 465, 483–85, 489–90, 493, 496–97, 568, 579, 582, 609
Latouche, Mrs. (John's mother), 651
Lawrence, D. H.: *Sons and Lovers*, 474
Layachi, Larbi, 687
Lazar, Irving Paul, 671, 688

Leary, Timothy, 722
Lenox Hill Hospital (New York City), 653–54, 658
Lerman, Leo, 507, 639
LeVoe, Spivy, 524, 714; letter to, 456–57
Levy, Irving, 455–56
Levy, Lupe, 455
Levy, Miriam Fligelman: letters to, 455–56, 458–59
Lewis, Bobby, 478
Lewis, Dione, 485–87, 489, 575, 651–52, 654, 656, 707
Leysin, Switzerland, 453
Lindamood, Peter, 610
Lindbergh, Charles, 579
Lisbon, Portugal, 650
Lloyd, George, 585
London, England, 558, 581–83, 594, 643–49, 652–53, 671, 674, 691–92, 694, 696–97, 721
Los Angeles, Calif., 488, 496, 503

Madrid, Spain, 548, 561, 564, 569, 571, 604
Madura temple (India), 623–24, 627
Maine, 486, 488–89
Málaga, Spain, 740–44
Mallorca, 693–94
Mann, Daniel, 608–9
Marillier-Roux, Yvonne, 720, 725, 739, 742
Marinoff, Fania, 607
Marlowe, Sylvia, 530, 597
Marrakech, Morocco, 516, 549, 559, 562, 564, 571, 616, 664, 674, 718, 728
Marseille, France, 573
Marshall Plan, 497
Martinique, 591
Marty (pseudonym), 607–8, 610, 622
Maryland, 496, 502, 681
Massachusetts, 460
Massilia café (Tangier), 625, 627
Matisse, Henri, 547
Mauriber, Saul, 607
McBey, Marguerite, 671, 707
McBride, Mary Frances, 575–76
McCullers, Carson, 471, 534, 562; letter to, 737–38
McFadden, Frances, 523, 580
McKean, Margarett, 524, 580, 609–10
McLean, Jody, 469, 480, 505–6, 515, 549, 551, 556, 559–64, 566–74, 580–81, 583–86, 588, 591, 593–97
McMichael, John, 641, 647–48
McMicking, Hubert, 558
McMillan, George: letter to, 453–55
Mendoubia (Tangier), 527, 555–56
Menotti, Gian Carlo, 488, 493
Mercury Theater, 461
Merlo, Frank, 614, 692
Merrill, James, 711–12, 714
Mexico, 459, 464–67, 479, 488, 497, 639, 652, 655, 663
Mexico City, Mexico, 466, 655
Meyers, John B., 661
Miami, Fla., 700, 708–11, 722–29, 732
Minor, Rose, 629, 632, 636, 638, 661, 663, 666–68, 674, 681, 685, 688, 692, 703–6, 710, 712, 714, 717–19, 726
Mitchell, Noëlle, 671, 673–74, 676, 742–43
Mohammed (Moroccan man), 528
Monocle bar (Paris), 590–91
Moorepark, Howard, 731
Morocco, 470, 474–76, 478–81, 486–88, 490, 493–96, 500–581, 583–85, 587–92, 594–97, 602–5, 608, 610–50, 652–723, 726–42
Morris, Edita, 633
Morris, Ira, 633
Morris Agency, 519
Morro Castle disaster, 457
Moulay Yacoub, Morocco, 558
Mrabet, Mohammed, 728, 730
M'sallah, Morocco, 526–28, 536–38, 549–50, 553–54, 557, 562, 565, 567, 611, 626

Naples, Italy, 594, 649
Nation, 466
Nessler, Harry, 488
Netherlands, 521
New Canaan, Conn., 478, 489, 495
New Directions (publisher), 551
New Jersey, 457
New Mexico, 558, 573, 700–701, 703–4, 706, 708–9
New York City, 453–59, 461–68, 472–73, 476–77, 481, 484–85, 487–90,

492, 495–96, 500, 503, 505, 507–9, 512, 515, 524–25, 529, 533, 535, 537, 541–42, 544–45, 549, 551, 556, 560, 563, 568–69, 574–76, 578–79, 583–84, 588–89, 594, 600, 604, 606–11, 615–16, 625–26, 634, 639, 650–58, 664, 666–67, 678, 680–85, 689, 695–97, 701–7, 709–13, 716, 724, 726–27
New York Herald Tribune, 468, 615–16, 690
New York Hospital–Cornell Medical Center (White Plains), 656
New York Post, 685, 689–90
New York Times, 634
Noailles, Marie-Laure de, 596–97
Northampton, England, 649
Norwalk, Conn., 464
Nyack, N.Y., 496, 512

Ober, Harold, 532, 535
O. Henry Award, 498
Oliver, Mary, 463–64, 558–60, 562, 566–68, 571, 597; letter to, 461–63
Olivier, Laurence, 588
Oppenheimer, J. Robert, 615
Orwell, Sonia, 671–72, 696
Ouezzani, Mohammed, 543, 549
Owen, Peter, 692–94, 696–97, 699, 725, 731
Oxford, England, 649

Pacy-sur-Eure, France, 598–606
Palais Jamai (Fez), 517, 524
Palestine, 575–76
Parade Bar (Tangier), 548, 571, 741
Paris, France, 461, 468, 478–79, 549, 568, 573, 575, 577–78, 580–97, 599, 601–2, 604–7, 615–16, 623, 687, 696, 720, 738
Partisan Review, 470, 484
Peck, Priscilla, 608–9
Perkins, Edgar, 472
Perkins, Helvetia, 464–66, 468–72, 474–75, 477–78, 481–82, 484–90, 494, 497–500, 503–4, 510–11, 515, 520–22, 524–26, 529, 551, 553–55, 558, 560, 563, 565–66, 569–72, 577, 579–80
Phillips, Genevieve, 456–57
Pittsfield, Mass., 477
Plath, Sylvia, 671
Polikoff, Bennet, 544–45, 641, 667, 693
Polo, Marco, 514
Porter, Katherine Anne, 480; "Pale Horse, Pale Rider," 477
Portugal, 470, 649–52, 654
Price, Frank, 586, 590
Putney, Vt., 469

Quinza (Moroccan woman), 519, 547, 561, 565, 574, 577

Racine, Jean: *Phèdre*, 589
Radcliffe Infirmary (Oxford), 649
Ramadan, 529, 540–41, 614, 616, 626, 635, 638, 640, 698–99
Ray, Nick, 488
Reille, Peggy, 584, 588
Resnick, Dr. William, 640–43, 646–48, 656–58, 720
Reynolds, Christopher, 470, 476
Reynolds, Mary, 588
Richie, Donald, 729
Rif Mountains, 520
Robeson, Paul, 464
Roditi, Édouard, 475
Rogers, Bruce, 729
Rollins College, 454
Rome, Italy, 602, 605, 616
Ronda, Spain, 480
Rubber, Violla, 492
Ruspoli de Chambrun, Martha, 719–22, 726–31, 733, 735

Sager, Gordon, 474–76, 489, 502, 560, 586, 596, 640, 645, 661–62, 675, 715–16, 725, 730–33, 735; letters to, 723–24, 727
Sahara Desert, 573–74, 581
Saïd, Kouche, 549–50, 592, 595
St. Andrew's Hospital (Northampton), 649
St. Mary's Hospital (London), 649
Salinger, J. D.: *The Catcher in the Rye*, 660
Salisbury, England, 583
Salisbury Inn (Great Barrington), 478, 487–88
Saltzer, Carl, 453
Saltzer, Florence Stajer, 453–54

San José, Costa Rica, 460
Santa Fe, N.M., 700–701, 706, 708–9
Saroyan, William, 464–65
Sartre, Jean-Paul, 471, 485; *The Age of Reason*, 475–76
Saturday Review of Literature, 488
Savannah, Ga., 467, 469
Schanker, Louis, 660, 672–75, 677, 679, 681, 685–86, 688, 691, 693, 695, 697–700, 702–5, 707–8, 711–12, 714, 716, 721–22; letter to, 717
Scotty (housekeeper at Treetops), 515, 524, 526, 542, 569, 579, 603; letter to, 544–46
Sekula, Sonia, 588
Shour, Birdie Stajer, 517
Sidéry, Sherban, 588
Sidi Menari, Morocco, 616–18
Sillitoe, Alan, 670–73, 675–77, 693–95; *The Loneliness of the Long Distance Runner*, 692
Sillitoe, David, 671, 673
Silva, Yvonne, 728
Smith, Oliver, 474, 477–83, 485–91, 494–98, 500–505, 507, 511, 515–16, 518, 521–22, 542, 544–45, 548, 551, 558, 563, 565–66, 570, 575, 577–79, 581–82, 584, 587–88, 590, 592, 594, 598–606, 610, 622, 624, 650, 681, 704, 721, 727; letters to, 535–39, 552–54
Solomon, Carl, 639
Sontag, Susan, 722, 726
South Africa, 496
Southampton, N.Y., 496
Spain, 470, 476, 478–80, 486–87, 512, 522, 548, 559, 561–62, 564, 568–70, 578–79, 581, 583–84, 590, 594, 598–605, 627, 644–45, 652, 722–23, 740–44
Spriet, Dr. R., 641, 643–44, 646–48
Stafford, Jean, 484
Stamford, Conn., 470–503, 513–14, 524–25, 583, 598–602, 649, 685, 700, 703–5, 709–11, 714, 716–17, 726, 732
Stapleton, Maureen, 610
Staten Island, 461–64
Stein, Gertrude, 460
Stewart, Lawrence, 687, 691; letter to, 700–701
Stowe, Shirley, 470, 606, 704, 711
Strauss, Helen, 498, 597, 687–88
Swanson, Gloria, 579
Sweden, 733, 735
Switzerland, 453, 607, 610

Tangier, Morocco, 476, 479, 487, 494, 501, 504–7, 513–81, 583–85, 587–88, 591–92, 594–97, 602, 604–5, 610–50, 652–723, 727–42
Taprobane, Ceylon, 623, 633, 635
Taroudant, Morocco, 516
Taxco, Mexico, 464–67
Tchelitchew, Pavel, 460, 464
Tehuantepec, Mexico, 466
Temsamany (Moroccan man), 616–19, 623, 625, 627
Tennant, Veronica, 720, 734, 736
Tetuan, Morocco, 674
Tetum (Moroccan woman), 523, 527, 530–32, 535, 541–43, 546–48, 550–51, 557–58, 565, 571–72, 574, 577, 591, 616–19
Thailand, 726, 729–30, 733
Thomson, Virgil, 478, 484; letters to, 459–61, 464–68; *The State of Music*, 465
Timbuktu, French West Africa, 559, 563, 568, 573
Time, 689
Times (London), 699
Toklas, Alice B., 587–89, 592
Tokyo, Japan, 729
Tonny, Kristians, 459
Tonny, Marie-Claire, 459
Town and Country, 471, 474
Treetops estate. *See* Stamford, Conn.
Trinidad, 460
Truman, Harry, 558
Tunis, Tunisia, 560–61
Tyler, Parker, 464

Uihlein, John, 496

Valéry, Paul, 477
Van Gogh, Vincent, 585
Van Vechten, Carl, 533; letters to, 606–7
Varadero, Cuba, 469
Velez, Lupe, 517
Venice, Italy, 596
Veracruz, Mexico, 466

Vermont, 468–69, 496–500, 503–12, 530, 534, 544, 554
Vidal, Gore, 559–61, 563–64, 583, 589, 596
View (magazine), 639
Viking (publisher), 507
Village Voice, 685, 689
Virginia, 609
Vogue, 615–16
Von Auw, Ivan, 532–35, 542–43, 547
Von Hoershelman, Lola, 530, 535, 573, 575–76, 578
Von Hoershelman, Natasha, 577–78, 580, 611, 650–51, 703; letters to, 529–30, 534–35, 573–76, 611–23
Von Saher, Lilla, 663; letter to, 663–64
Vursell, Hall, 723–24, 726; letters to, 722–23, 731–32

Wales, 581–82, 694, 696
Wanklyn, Christopher, 631–32, 634, 636–37, 639, 674
Ward, Mary Jane, 663
Waterbury, Natika, 587–91, 596
Weil, Simone, 726
Weinstein, Arthur, 484
Welty, Eudora, 587
Westport, Conn., 598–604
White Plains, N.Y., 656, 711–12
Wickman, Lily, 718
Wilcox, Lucia Cristofanetti, 714
Williams, Bud, 599–600, 602
Williams, Tennessee, 559–61, 563–64, 566, 570, 575, 579, 582, 614–15, 621, 652, 657, 663, 692; *The Glass Menagerie*, 521; *The Rose Tattoo*, 609; *Summer and Smoke*, 512, 515, 529
Williams, William Carlos, 639
Willis, John, 567
Wilson, Jane, 731
Wilson, John C., 495, 582, 601, 603
Winchell, Walter, 456
Wood, Audrey, 582, 584, 588, 597, 606, 609, 624, 680–81, 683–85, 690, 697; letter to, 682–83, 706, 710
Woodmere, N.Y., 455
Works Projects Administration, 462
World War II, 465–67, 514, 578

Xauen, Morocco, 613, 634

Yacoubi, Ahmed, 547, 613–14, 623, 632, 638, 640, 649–50, 660

Zen Buddhism, 639, 737
Zero (magazine), 578
Zodelia (Moroccan woman), 542, 546, 574
Zohra (Algerian woman), 591, 612, 616

This book is set in 10 point ITC Galliard, a face designed for digital composition by Matthew Carter and based on the sixteenth-century face Granjon. The paper is acid-free lightweight opaque that will not turn yellow or brittle with age. The binding is sewn, which allows the book to open easily and lie flat. The binding board is covered in Brillianta, a woven rayon cloth made by Van Heek–Scholco Textielfabrieken, Holland. Composition by Dedicated Book Services. Printing and binding by Edwards Brothers Malloy, Ann Arbor. Designed by Bruce Campbell.

THE LIBRARY OF AMERICA SERIES

The Library of America fosters appreciation of America's literary heritage by publishing, and keeping permanently in print, authoritative editions of America's best and most significant writing. An independent nonprofit organization, it was founded in 1979 with seed funding from the National Endowment for the Humanities and the Ford Foundation.

1. Herman Melville: Typee, Omoo, Mardi
2. Nathaniel Hawthorne: Tales & Sketches
3. Walt Whitman: Poetry & Prose
4. Harriet Beecher Stowe: Three Novels
5. Mark Twain: Mississippi Writings
6. Jack London: Novels & Stories
7. Jack London: Novels & Social Writings
8. William Dean Howells: Novels 1875–1886
9. Herman Melville: Redburn, White-Jacket, Moby-Dick
10. Nathaniel Hawthorne: Collected Novels

11 & 12. Francis Parkman: France and England in North America

13. Henry James: Novels 1871–1880
14. Henry Adams: Novels, Mont Saint Michel, The Education
15. Ralph Waldo Emerson: Essays & Lectures
16. Washington Irving: History, Tales & Sketches
17. Thomas Jefferson: Writings
18. Stephen Crane: Prose & Poetry
19. Edgar Allan Poe: Poetry & Tales
20. Edgar Allan Poe: Essays & Reviews
21. Mark Twain: The Innocents Abroad, Roughing It

22 & 23. Henry James: Literary Criticism

24. Herman Melville: Pierre, Israel Potter, The Confidence-Man, Tales & Billy Budd
25. William Faulkner: Novels 1930–1935

26 & 27. James Fenimore Cooper: The Leatherstocking Tales

28. Henry David Thoreau: A Week, Walden, The Maine Woods, Cape Cod
29. Henry James: Novels 1881–1886
30. Edith Wharton: Novels

31 & 32. Henry Adams: History of the U.S. during the Administrations of Jefferson & Madison

33. Frank Norris: Novels & Essays
34. W.E.B. Du Bois: Writings
35. Willa Cather: Early Novels & Stories
36. Theodore Dreiser: Sister Carrie, Jennie Gerhardt, Twelve Men
37. Benjamin Franklin: Writings (2 vols.)
38. William James: Writings 1902–1910
39. Flannery O'Connor: Collected Works

40, 41, & 42. Eugene O'Neill: Complete Plays

43. Henry James: Novels 1886–1890
44. William Dean Howells: Novels 1886–1888

45 & 46. Abraham Lincoln: Speeches & Writings

47. Edith Wharton: Novellas & Other Writings
48. William Faulkner: Novels 1936–1940
49. Willa Cather: Later Novels
50. Ulysses S. Grant: Memoirs & Selected Letters
51. William Tecumseh Sherman: Memoirs
52. Washington Irving: Bracebridge Hall, Tales of a Traveller, The Alhambra
53. Francis Parkman: The Oregon Trail, The Conspiracy of Pontiac
54. James Fenimore Cooper: Sea Tales

55 & 56. Richard Wright: Works

57. Willa Cather: Stories, Poems, & Other Writings
58. William James: Writings 1878–1899
59. Sinclair Lewis: Main Street & Babbitt

60 & 61. Mark Twain: Collected Tales, Sketches, Speeches, & Essays

62 & 63. The Debate on the Constitution

64 & 65. Henry James: Collected Travel Writings

66 & 67. American Poetry: The Nineteenth Century

68. Frederick Douglass: Autobiographies
69. Sarah Orne Jewett: Novels & Stories
70. Ralph Waldo Emerson: Collected Poems & Translations
71. Mark Twain: Historical Romances
72. John Steinbeck: Novels & Stories 1932–1937
73. William Faulkner: Novels 1942–1954

74 & 75. Zora Neale Hurston: Novels, Stories, & Other Writings

76. Thomas Paine: Collected Writings

77 & 78. Reporting World War II: American Journalism

79 & 80. Raymond Chandler: Novels, Stories, & Other Writings

81. Robert Frost: Collected Poems, Prose, & Plays
82 & 83. Henry James: Complete Stories 1892–1910
84. William Bartram: Travels & Other Writings
85. John Dos Passos: U.S.A.
86. John Steinbeck: The Grapes of Wrath & Other Writings 1936–1941
87, 88, & 89. Vladimir Nabokov: Novels & Other Writings
90. James Thurber: Writings & Drawings
91. George Washington: Writings
92. John Muir: Nature Writings
93. Nathanael West: Novels & Other Writings
94 & 95. Crime Novels: American Noir of the 1930s, 40s, & 50s
96. Wallace Stevens: Collected Poetry & Prose
97. James Baldwin: Early Novels & Stories
98. James Baldwin: Collected Essays
99 & 100. Gertrude Stein: Writings
101 & 102. Eudora Welty: Novels, Stories, & Other Writings
103. Charles Brockden Brown: Three Gothic Novels
104 & 105. Reporting Vietnam: American Journalism
106 & 107. Henry James: Complete Stories 1874–1891
108. American Sermons
109. James Madison: Writings
110. Dashiell Hammett: Complete Novels
111. Henry James: Complete Stories 1864–1874
112. William Faulkner: Novels 1957–1962
113. John James Audubon: Writings & Drawings
114. Slave Narratives
115 & 116. American Poetry: The Twentieth Century
117. F. Scott Fitzgerald: Novels & Stories 1920–1922
118. Henry Wadsworth Longfellow: Poems & Other Writings
119 & 120. Tennessee Williams: Collected Plays
121 & 122. Edith Wharton: Collected Stories
123. The American Revolution: Writings from the War of Independence
124. Henry David Thoreau: Collected Essays & Poems
125. Dashiell Hammett: Crime Stories & Other Writings
126 & 127. Dawn Powell: Novels
128. Carson McCullers: Complete Novels
129. Alexander Hamilton: Writings
130. Mark Twain: The Gilded Age & Later Novels
131. Charles W. Chesnutt: Stories, Novels, & Essays
132. John Steinbeck: Novels 1942–1952
133. Sinclair Lewis: Arrowsmith, Elmer Gantry, Dodsworth
134 & 135. Paul Bowles: Novels, Stories, & Other Writings
136. Kate Chopin: Complete Novels & Stories
137 & 138. Reporting Civil Rights: American Journalism
139. Henry James: Novels 1896–1899
140. Theodore Dreiser: An American Tragedy
141. Saul Bellow: Novels 1944–1953
142. John Dos Passos: Novels 1920–1925
143. John Dos Passos: Travel Books & Other Writings
144. Ezra Pound: Poems & Translations
145. James Weldon Johnson: Writings
146. Washington Irving: Three Western Narratives
147. Alexis de Tocqueville: Democracy in America
148. James T. Farrell: Studs Lonigan Trilogy
149, 150, & 151. Isaac Bashevis Singer: Collected Stories
152. Kaufman & Co.: Broadway Comedies
153. Theodore Roosevelt: Rough Riders, An Autobiography
154. Theodore Roosevelt: Letters & Speeches
155. H. P. Lovecraft: Tales
156. Louisa May Alcott: Little Women, Little Men, Jo's Boys
157. Philip Roth: Novels & Stories 1959–1962
158. Philip Roth: Novels 1967–1972
159. James Agee: Let Us Now Praise Famous Men, A Death in the Family, Shorter Fiction
160. James Agee: Film Writing & Selected Journalism
161. Richard Henry Dana Jr.: Two Years Before the Mast & Other Voyages
162. Henry James: Novels 1901–1902
163. Arthur Miller: Plays 1944–1961
164. William Faulkner: Novels 1926–1929
165. Philip Roth: Novels 1973–1977

166 & 167. American Speeches: Political Oratory
168. Hart Crane: Complete Poems & Selected Letters
169. Saul Bellow: Novels 1956–1964
170. John Steinbeck: Travels with Charley & Later Novels
171. Capt. John Smith: Writings with Other Narratives
172. Thornton Wilder: Collected Plays & Writings on Theater
173. Philip K. Dick: Four Novels of the 1960s
174. Jack Kerouac: Road Novels 1957–1960
175. Philip Roth: Zuckerman Bound
176 & 177. Edmund Wilson: Literary Essays & Reviews
178. American Poetry: The 17th & 18th Centuries
179. William Maxwell: Early Novels & Stories
180. Elizabeth Bishop: Poems, Prose, & Letters
181. A. J. Liebling: World War II Writings
182. American Earth: Environmental Writing Since Thoreau
183. Philip K. Dick: Five Novels of the 1960s & 70s
184. William Maxwell: Later Novels & Stories
185. Philip Roth: Novels & Other Narratives 1986–1991
186. Katherine Anne Porter: Collected Stories & Other Writings
187. John Ashbery: Collected Poems 1956–1987
188 & 189. John Cheever: Complete Novels & Collected Stories
190. Lafcadio Hearn: American Writings
191. A. J. Liebling: The Sweet Science & Other Writings
192. The Lincoln Anthology
193. Philip K. Dick: VALIS & Later Novels
194. Thornton Wilder: The Bridge of San Luis Rey & Other Novels 1926–1948
195. Raymond Carver: Collected Stories
196 & 197. American Fantastic Tales
198. John Marshall: Writings
199. The Mark Twain Anthology
200. Mark Twain: A Tramp Abroad, Following the Equator, Other Travels
201 & 202. Ralph Waldo Emerson: Selected Journals
203. The American Stage: Writing on Theater
204. Shirley Jackson: Novels & Stories
205. Philip Roth: Novels 1993–1995
206 & 207. H. L. Mencken: Prejudices
208. John Kenneth Galbraith: The Affluent Society & Other Writings 1952–1967
209. Saul Bellow: Novels 1970–1982
210 & 211. Lynd Ward: Six Novels in Woodcuts
212. The Civil War: The First Year
213 & 214. John Adams: Revolutionary Writings
215. Henry James: Novels 1903–1911
216. Kurt Vonnegut: Novels & Stories 1963–1973
217 & 218. Harlem Renaissance Novels
219. Ambrose Bierce: The Devil's Dictionary, Tales, & Memoirs
220. Philip Roth: The American Trilogy 1997–2000
221. The Civil War: The Second Year
222. Barbara W. Tuchman: The Guns of August, The Proud Tower
223. Arthur Miller: Plays 1964–1982
224. Thornton Wilder: The Eighth Day, Theophilus North, Autobiographical Writings
225. David Goodis: Five Noir Novels of the 1940s & 50s
226. Kurt Vonnegut: Novels & Stories 1950–1962
227 & 228. American Science Fiction: Nine Novels of the 1950s
229 & 230. Laura Ingalls Wilder: The Little House Books
231. Jack Kerouac: Collected Poems
232. The War of 1812
233. American Antislavery Writings
234. The Civil War: The Third Year
235. Sherwood Anderson: Collected Stories
236. Philip Roth: Novels 2001–2007
237. Philip Roth: Nemeses
238. Aldo Leopold: A Sand County Almanac & Other Writings
239. May Swenson: Collected Poems
240 & 241. W. S. Merwin: Collected Poems
242 & 243. John Updike: Collected Stories
244. Ring Lardner: Stories & Other Writings
245. Jonathan Edwards: Writings from the Great Awakening
246. Susan Sontag: Essays of the 1960s & 70s

247. William Wells Brown: Clotel & Other Writings
248 & 249. Bernard Malamud: Novels & Stories of the 1940s, 50s, & 60s
250. The Civil War: The Final Year
251. Shakespeare in America
252. Kurt Vonnegut: Novels 1976–1985
253 & 254. American Musicals 1927–1969
255. Elmore Leonard: Four Novels of the 1970s
256. Louisa May Alcott: Work, Eight Cousins, Rose in Bloom, Stories & Other Writings
257. H. L. Mencken: The Days Trilogy
258. Virgil Thomson: Music Chronicles 1940–1954
259. Art in America 1945–1970
260. Saul Bellow: Novels 1984–2000
261. Arthur Miller: Plays 1987–2004
262. Jack Kerouac: Visions of Cody, Visions of Gerard, Big Sur
263. Reinhold Niebuhr: Major Works on Religion & Politics
264. Ross Macdonald: Four Novels of the 1950s
265 & 266. The American Revolution: Writings from the Pamphlet Debate
267. Elmore Leonard: Four Novels of the 1980s
268 & 269. Women Crime Writers: Suspense Novels of the 1940s & 50s
270. Frederick Law Olmsted: Writings on Landscape, Culture, & Society
271. Edith Wharton: Four Novels of the 1920s
272. James Baldwin: Later Novels
273. Kurt Vonnegut: Novels 1987–1997
274. Henry James: Autobiographies
275. Abigail Adams: Letters
276. John Adams: Writings from the New Nation 1784–1826
277. Virgil Thomson: The State of Music & Other Writings
278. War No More: American Antiwar & Peace Writing
279. Ross Macdonald: Three Novels of the Early 1960s
280. Elmore Leonard: Four Later Novels
281. Ursula K. Le Guin: The Complete Orsinia
282. John O'Hara: Stories
283. The Unknown Kerouac: Rare, Unpublished & Newly Translated Writings
284. Albert Murray: Collected Essays & Memoirs
285 & 286. Loren Eiseley: Collected Writings on Evolution, Nature, & the Cosmos